JUNKWRAITH

ELLINOR RICHEY

JUNKWRAITH © 2021 ELLINOR RICHEY

PUBLISHED BY TOP SHELF PRODUCTIONS, AN IMPRINT OF IDW PUBLISHING, A DIVISION OF IDEA AND DESIGN WORKS, LLC. OFFICES: TOP SHELF PRODUCTIONS, C/O IDEA & DESIGN WORKS, LLC, 2765 TRUXTUN ROAD, SAN DIEGO, CA 92106. TOP SHELF PRODUCTIONS®, THE TOP SHELF LOGO, IDEA AND DESIGN WORKS®, AND THE IDW LOGO ARE REGISTERED TRADEMARKS OF IDEA AND DESIGN WORKS, LLC. ALL RIGHTS RESERVED. WITH THE EXCEPTION OF SMALL EXCERPTS OF ARTWORK USED FOR REVIEW PURPOSES, NONE OF THE CONTENTS OF THIS PUBLICATION MAY BE REPRINTED WITHOUT THE PERMISSION OF IDW PUBLISHING.

IDW PUBLISHING DOES NOT READ OR ACCEPT UNSOLICITED SUBMISSIONS OF IDEAS, STORIES, OR ARTWORK.

EDITOR-IN-CHIEF: CHRIS STAROS

ISBN: 978-1-60309-500-6   24 23 22 21   4 3 2 1

VISIT OUR ONLINE CATALOG AT TOPSHELFCOMIX.COM.

PRINTED IN KOREA.

PROLOGUE - PERSISTENT BELONGINGS

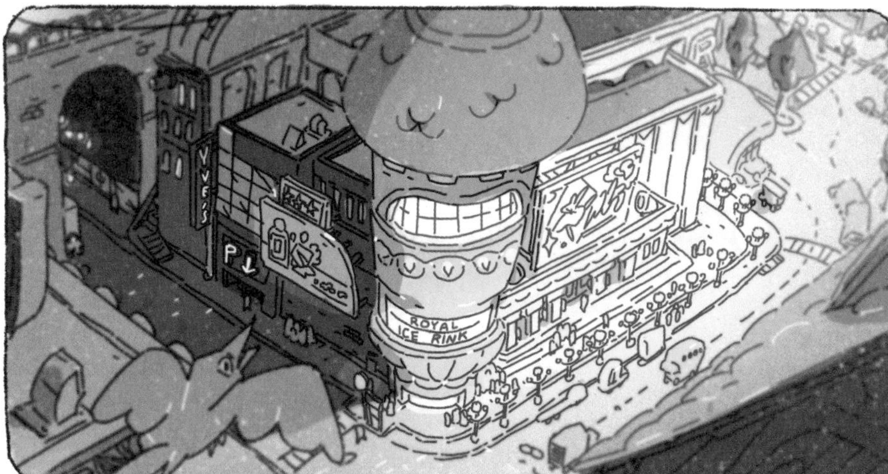
VVESS
P
ROYAL
ICE RINK

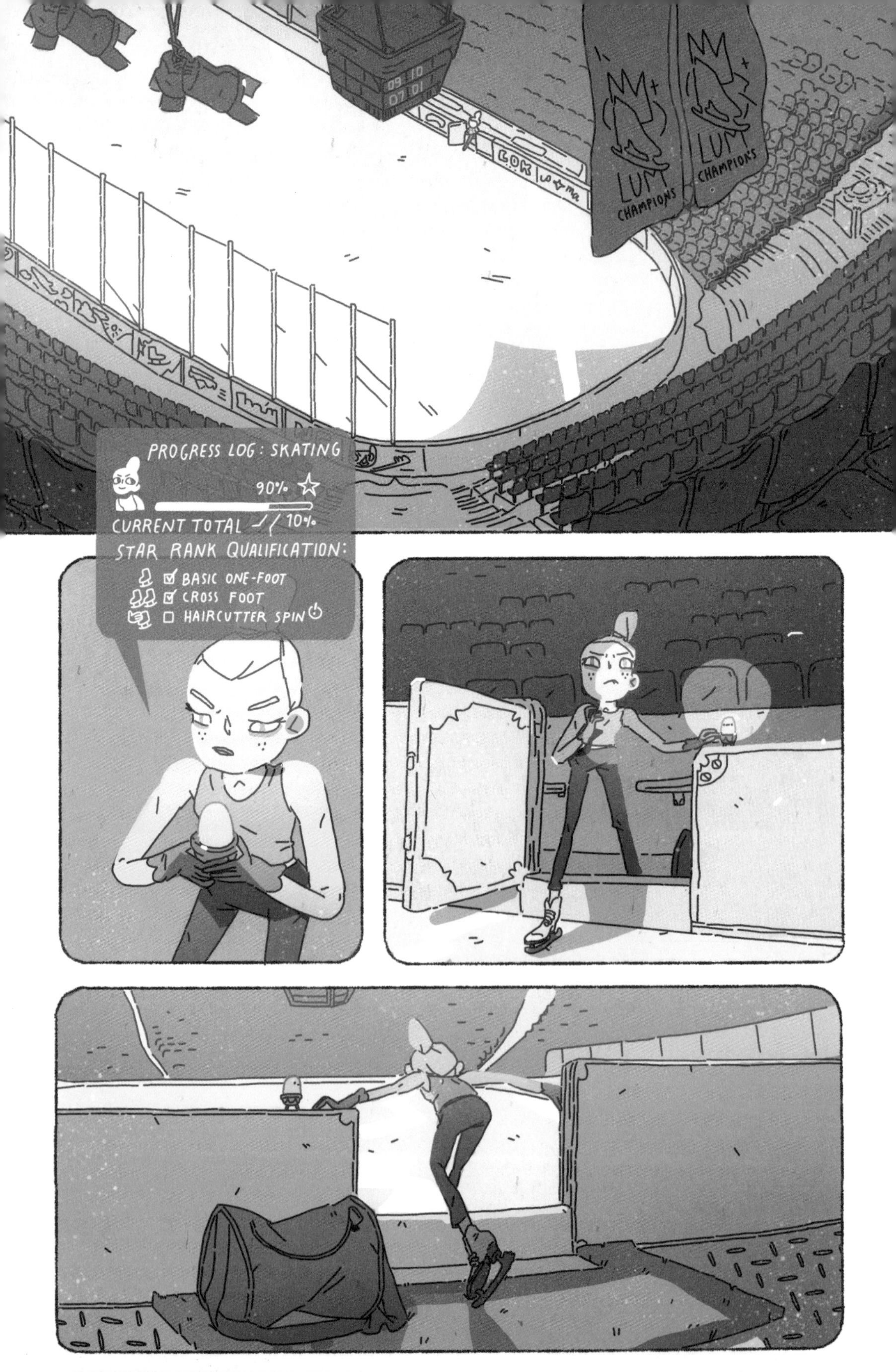
09 10
07 01
BOK
LUM CHAMPIONS
LUM CHAMPIONS
PROGRESS LOG: SKATING
90% ☆
CURRENT TOTAL // 10%
STAR RANK QUALIFICATION:
☑ BASIC ONE-FOOT
☑ CROSS FOOT
☐ HAIRCUTTER SPIN

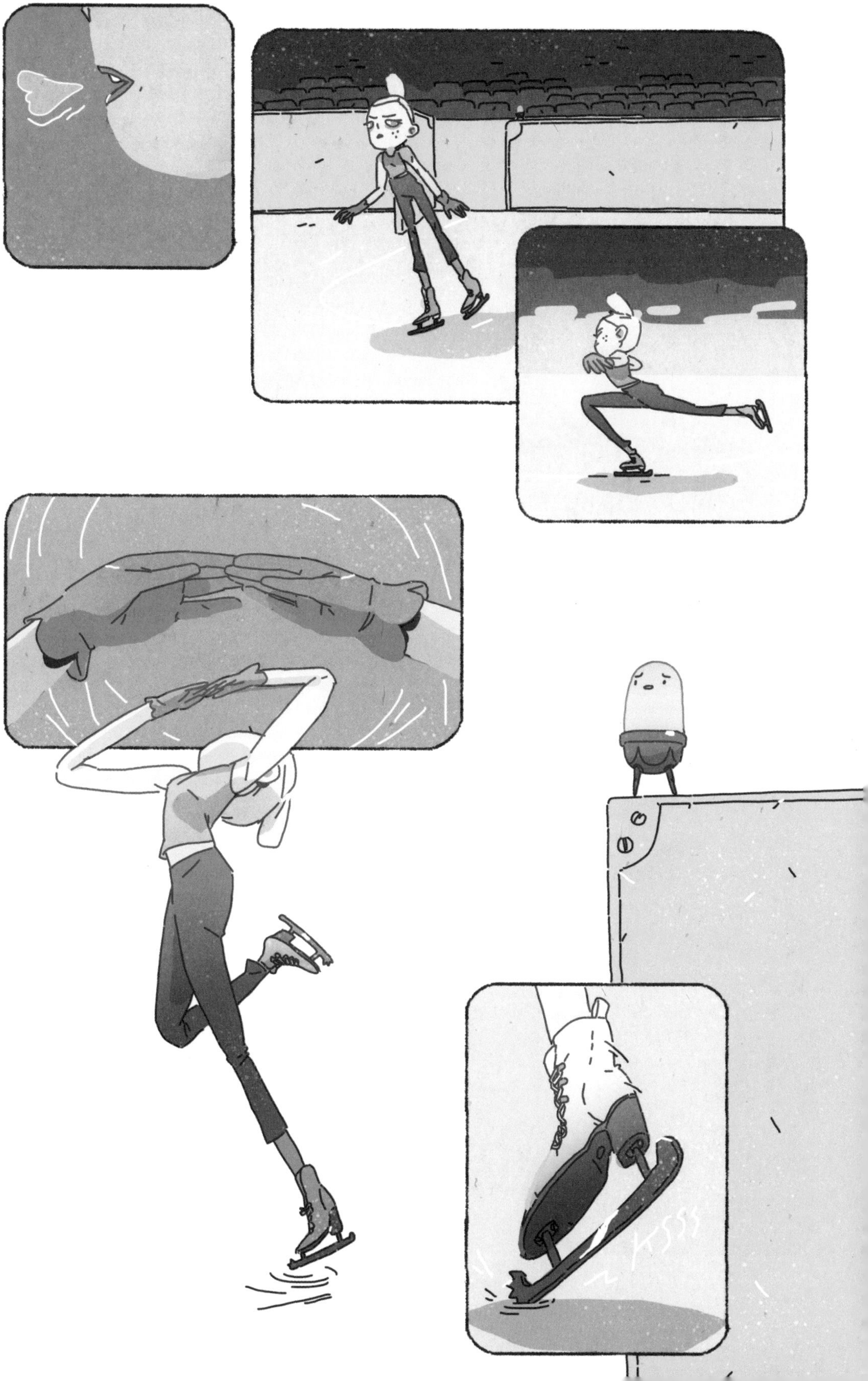
KSSS

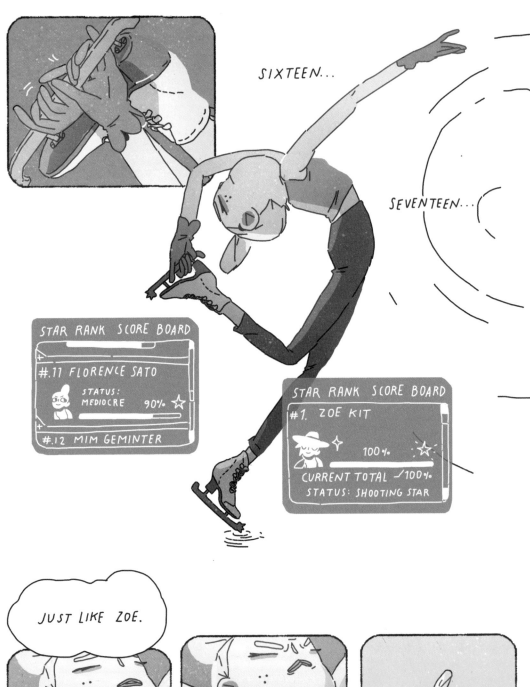

SIXTEEN...

SEVENTEEN...

STAR RANK SCORE BOARD

#.11 FLORENCE SATO

STATUS:
MEDIOCRE   90% ☆

#.12 MIM GEMINTER

STAR RANK SCORE BOARD

#1. ZOE KIT

100%

CURRENT TOTAL 100%
STATUS: SHOOTING STAR

JUST LIKE ZOE.

JUST ONE MORE —

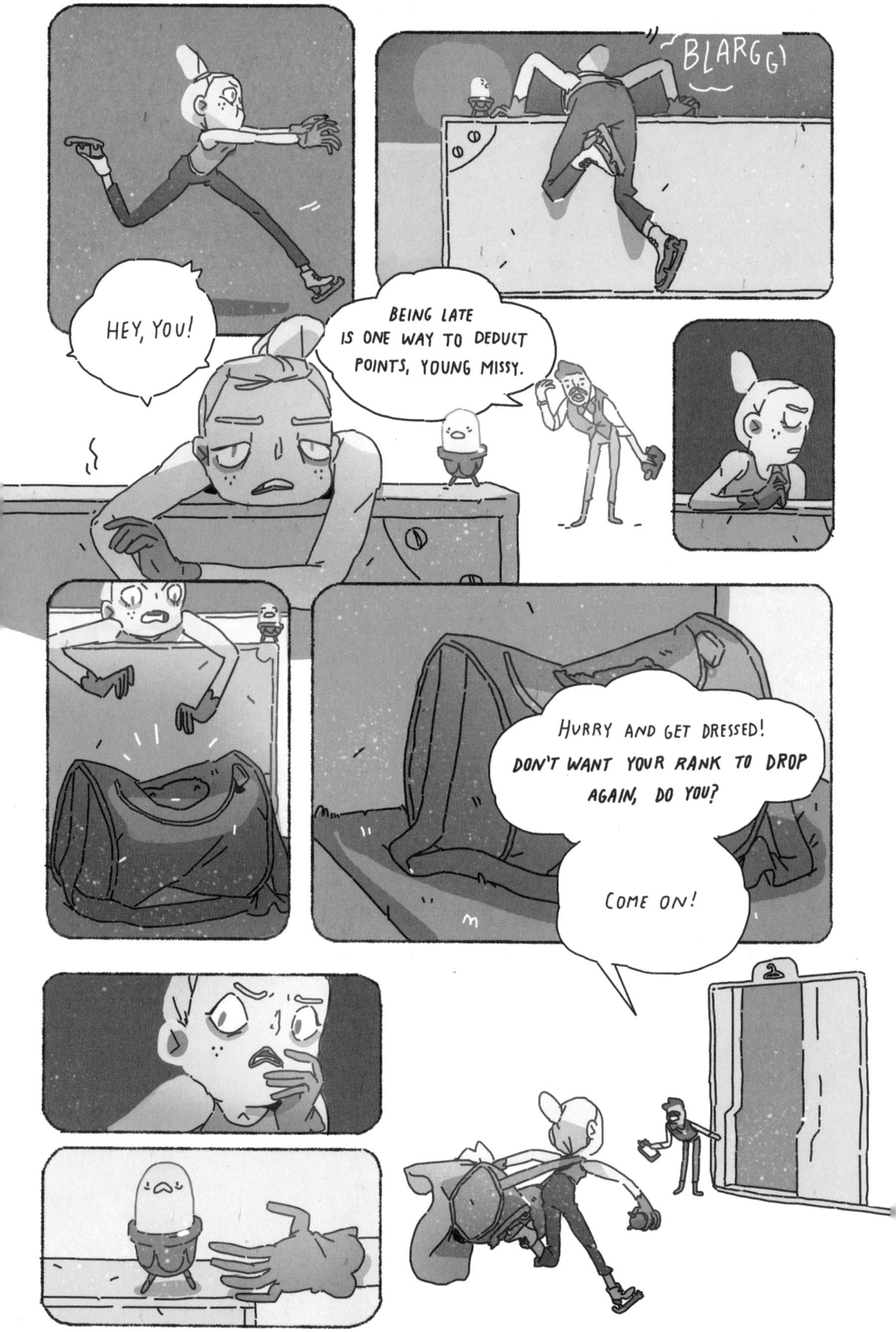
BLARGG!
HEY, YOU!
BEING LATE IS ONE WAY TO DEDUCT POINTS, YOUNG MISSY.
HURRY AND GET DRESSED! DON'T WANT YOUR RANK TO DROP AGAIN, DO YOU?
COME ON!

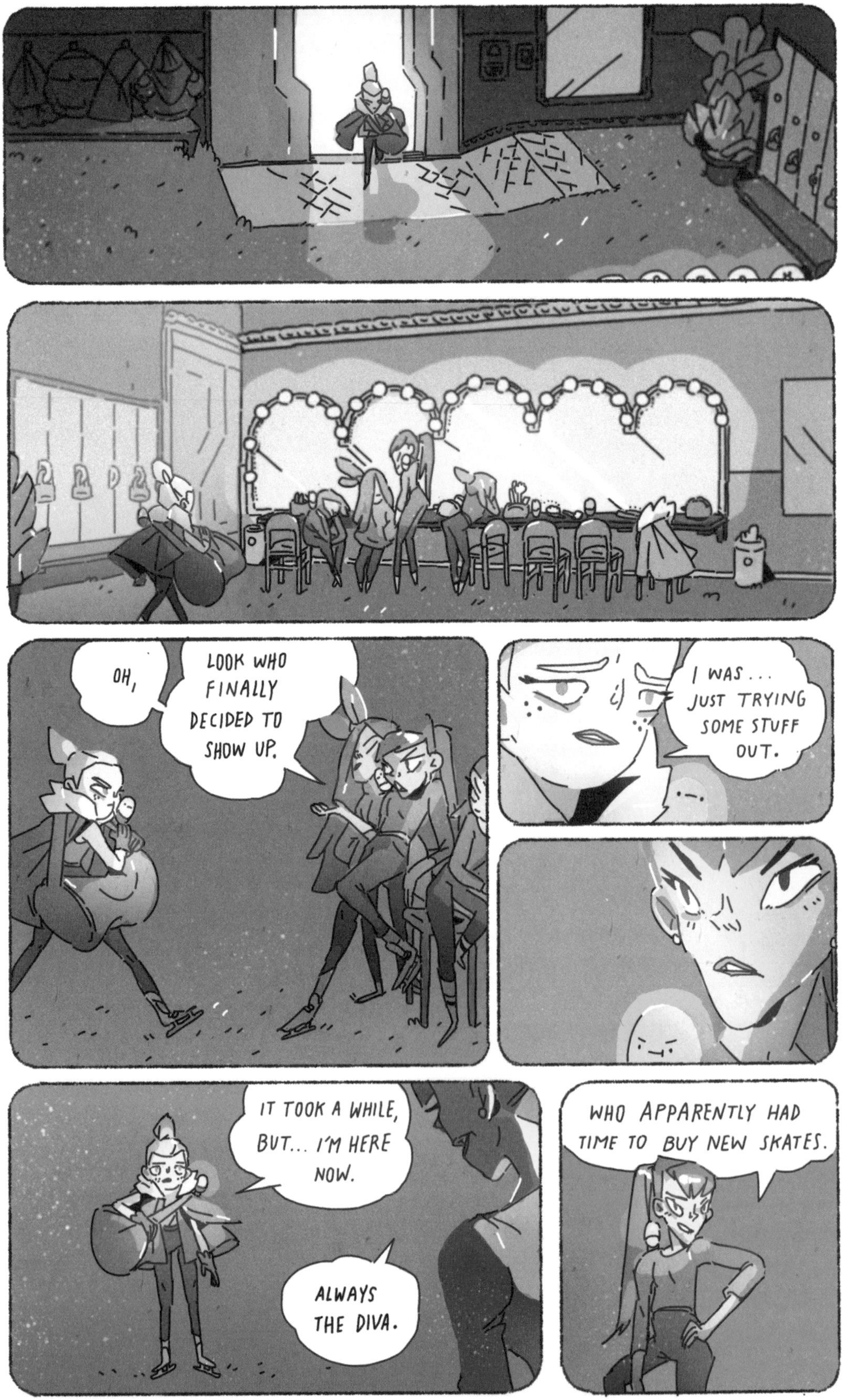
OH,
LOOK WHO FINALLY DECIDED TO SHOW UP.
I WAS... JUST TRYING SOME STUFF OUT.
IT TOOK A WHILE, BUT... I'M HERE NOW.
ALWAYS THE DIVA.
WHO APPARENTLY HAD TIME TO BUY NEW SKATES.

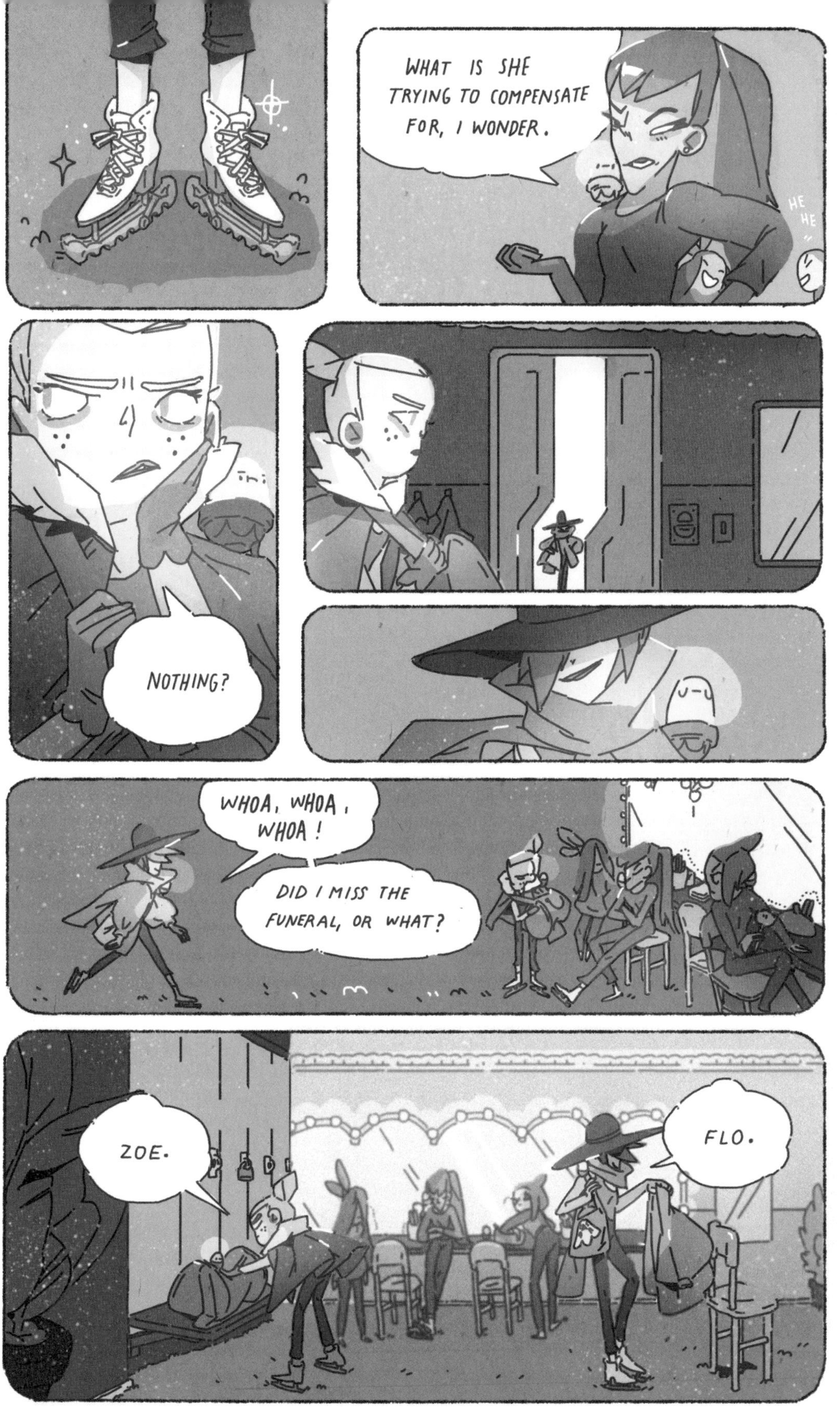
WHAT IS SHE TRYING TO COMPENSATE FOR, I WONDER.
HE HE
NOTHING?
WHOA, WHOA, WHOA!
DID I MISS THE FUNERAL, OR WHAT?
ZOE.
FLO.

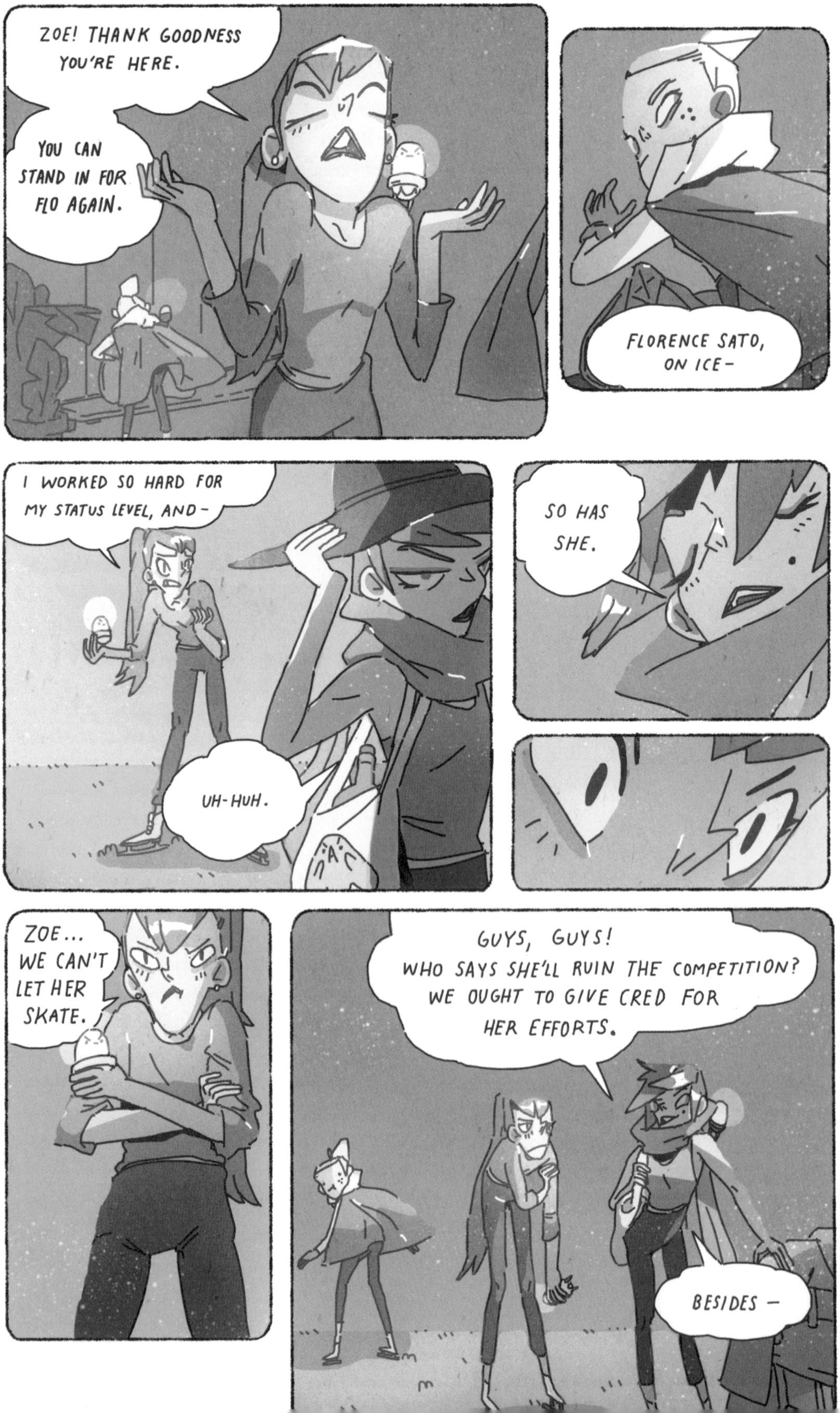
ZOE! THANK GOODNESS YOU'RE HERE.
YOU CAN STAND IN FOR FLO AGAIN.
FLORENCE SATO, ON ICE-
I WORKED SO HARD FOR MY STATUS LEVEL, AND-
UH-HUH.
SO HAS SHE.
ZOE... WE CAN'T LET HER SKATE.
GUYS, GUYS! WHO SAYS SHE'LL RUIN THE COMPETITION? WE OUGHT TO GIVE CRED FOR HER EFFORTS.
BESIDES -

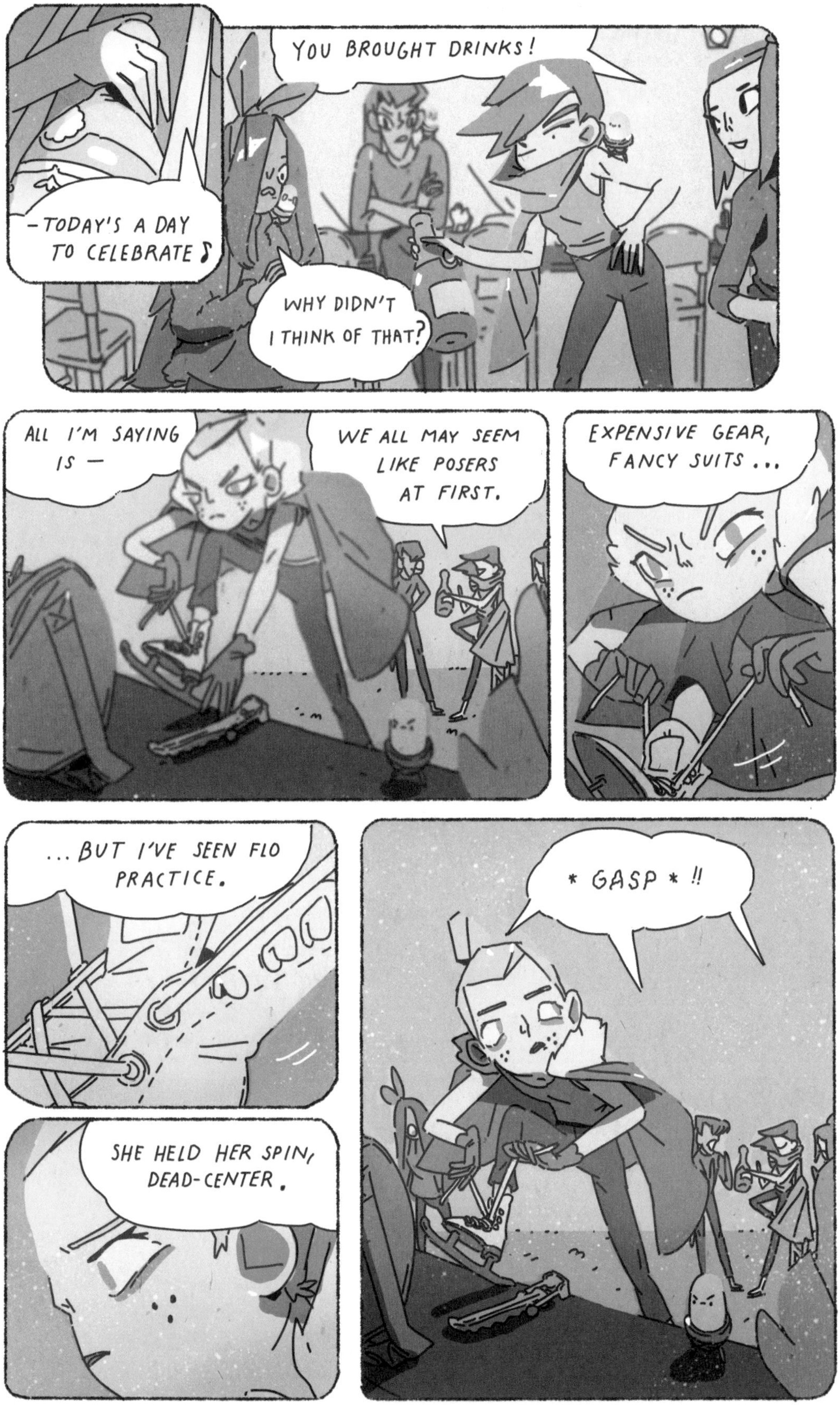

YOU BROUGHT DRINKS!
–TODAY'S A DAY TO CELEBRATE♪
WHY DIDN'T I THINK OF THAT?
ALL I'M SAYING IS —
WE ALL MAY SEEM LIKE POSERS AT FIRST.
EXPENSIVE GEAR, FANCY SUITS...
...BUT I'VE SEEN FLO PRACTICE.
SHE HELD HER SPIN, DEAD-CENTER.
* GASP * !!

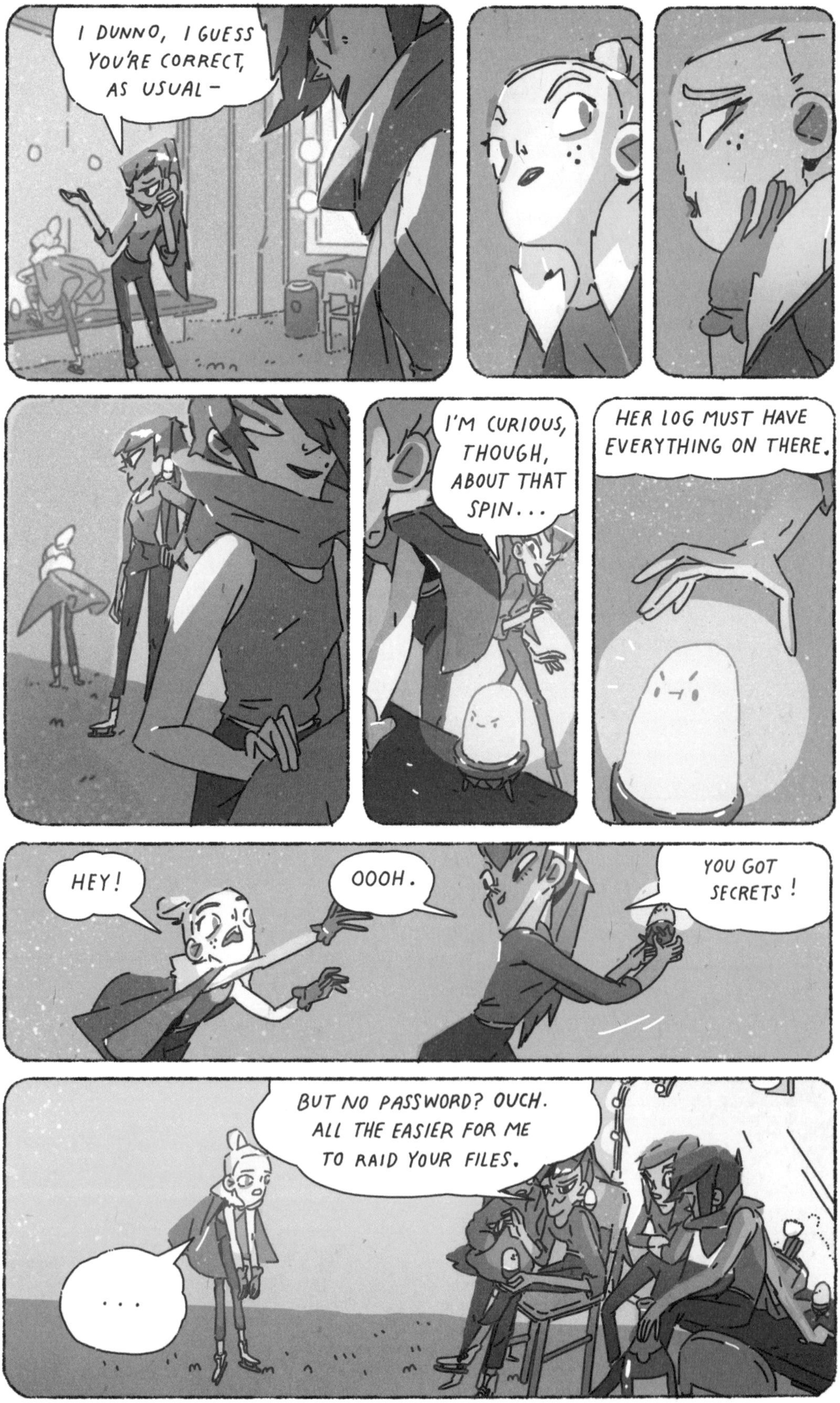
I DUNNO, I GUESS YOU'RE CORRECT, AS USUAL—
I'M CURIOUS, THOUGH, ABOUT THAT SPIN...
HER LOG MUST HAVE EVERYTHING ON THERE.
HEY!
OOOH.
YOU GOT SECRETS!
BUT NO PASSWORD? OUCH. ALL THE EASIER FOR ME TO RAID YOUR FILES.
...

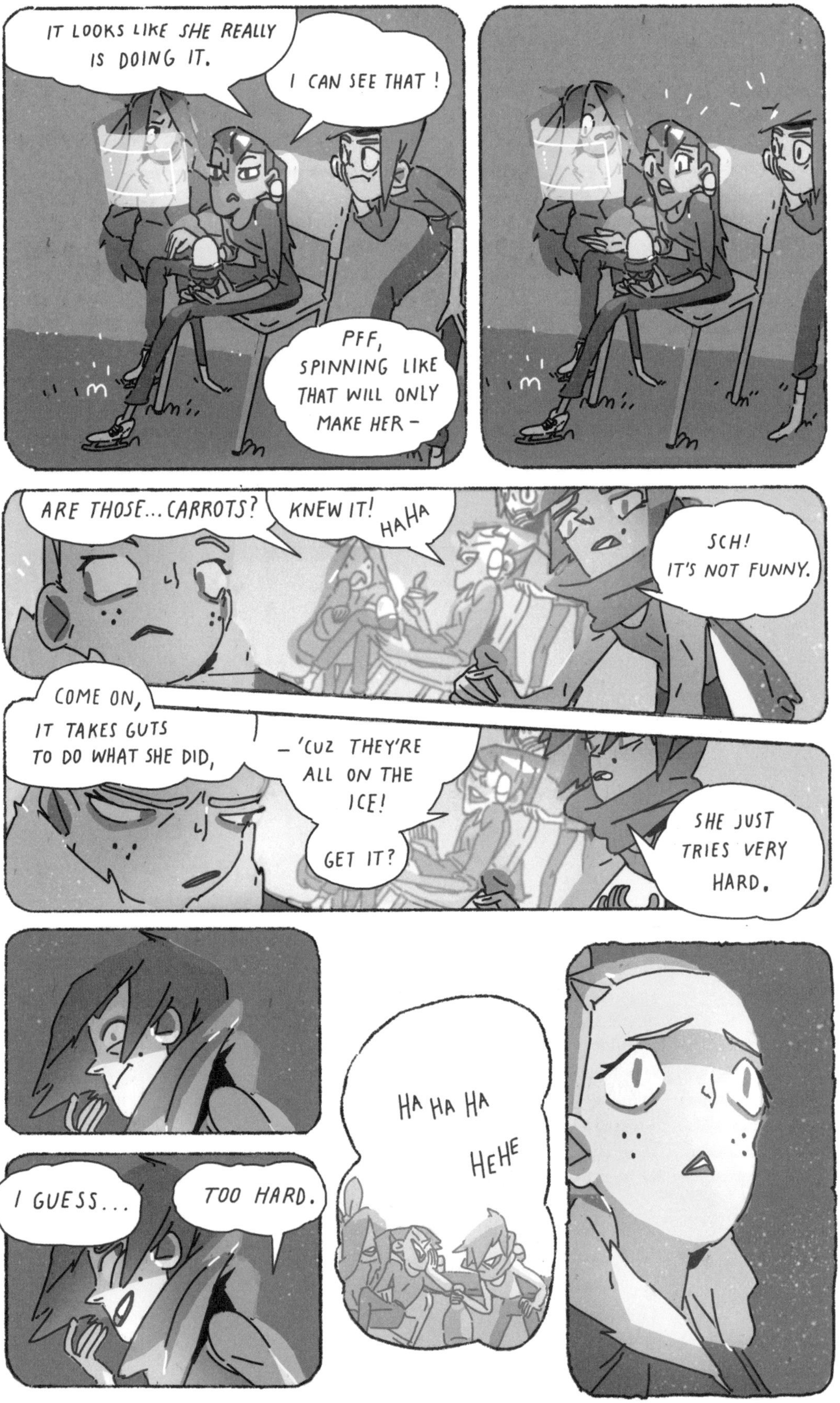
IT LOOKS LIKE SHE REALLY IS DOING IT.
I CAN SEE THAT!
PFF, SPINNING LIKE THAT WILL ONLY MAKE HER–
ARE THOSE... CARROTS?
KNEW IT! HAHA
SCH! IT'S NOT FUNNY.
COME ON, IT TAKES GUTS TO DO WHAT SHE DID,
–'CUZ THEY'RE ALL ON THE ICE!
GET IT?
SHE JUST TRIES VERY HARD.
I GUESS...
TOO HARD.
HA HA HA
HEHE

EPISODE 1 - PERSISTENT BELONGINGS

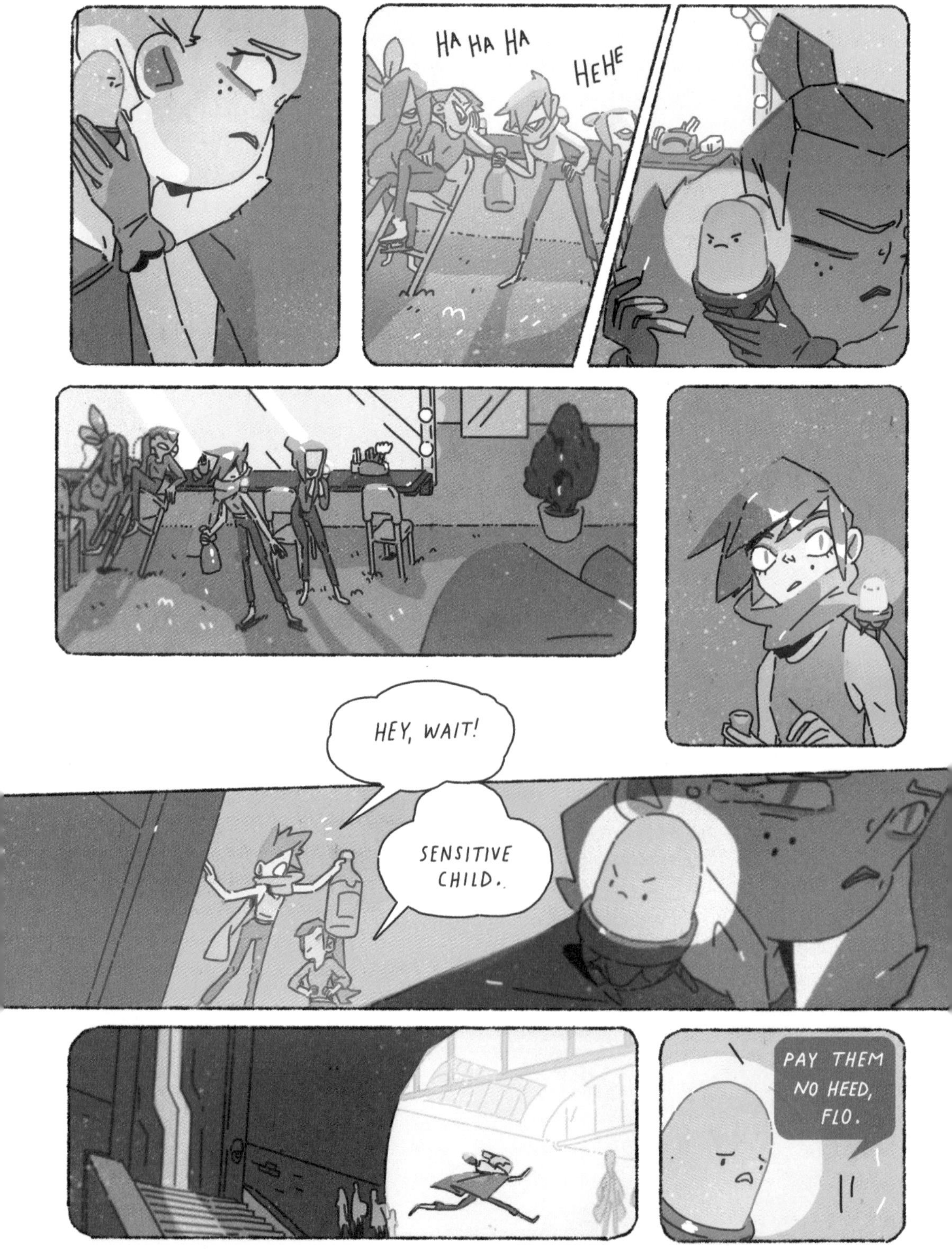

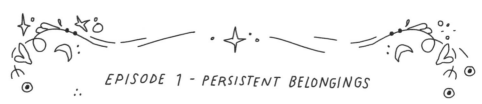

HA HA HA
HEHE
HEY, WAIT!
SENSITIVE CHILD.
PAY THEM NO HEED, FLO.

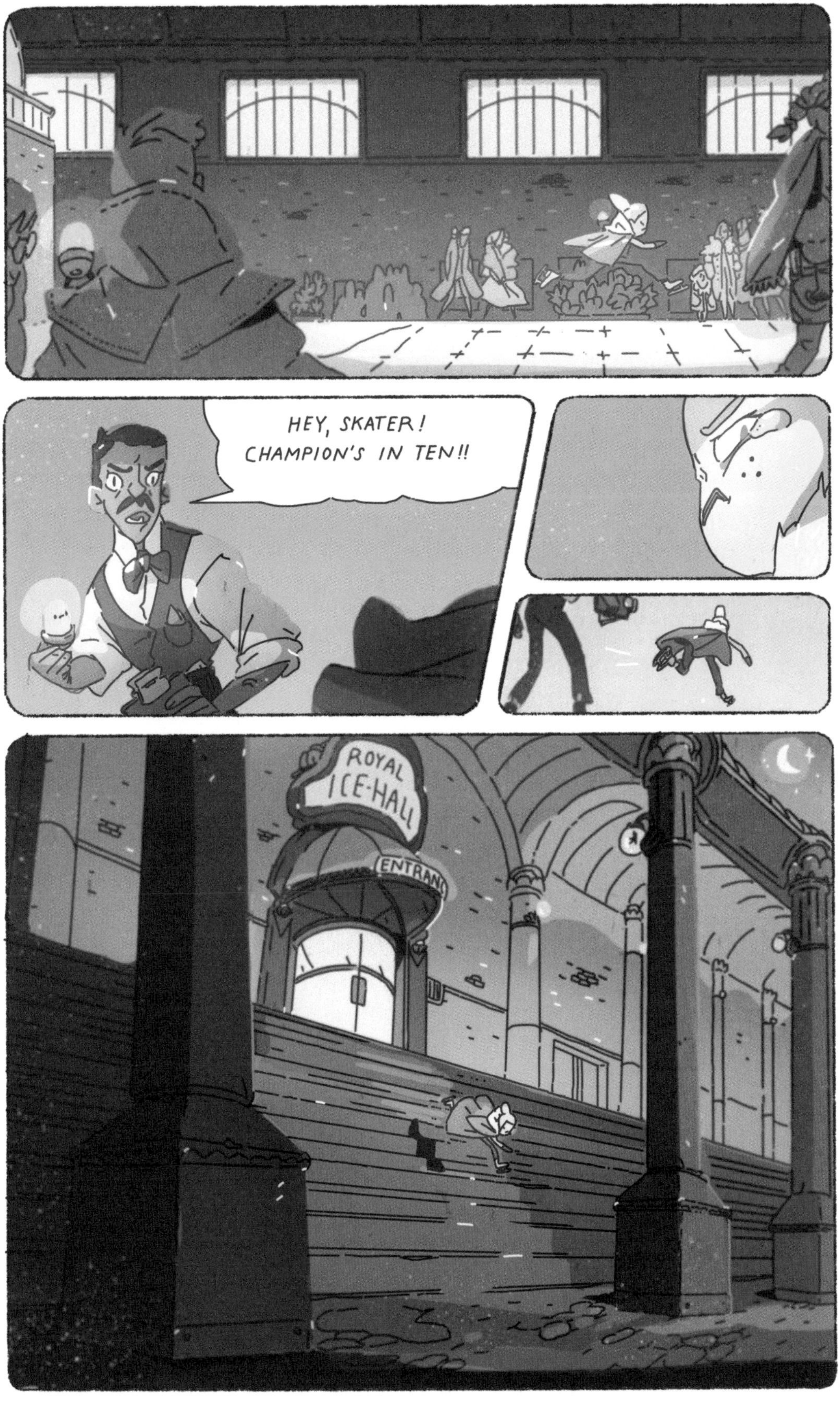
HEY, SKATER! CHAMPION'S IN TEN!!
ROYAL ICE-HALL

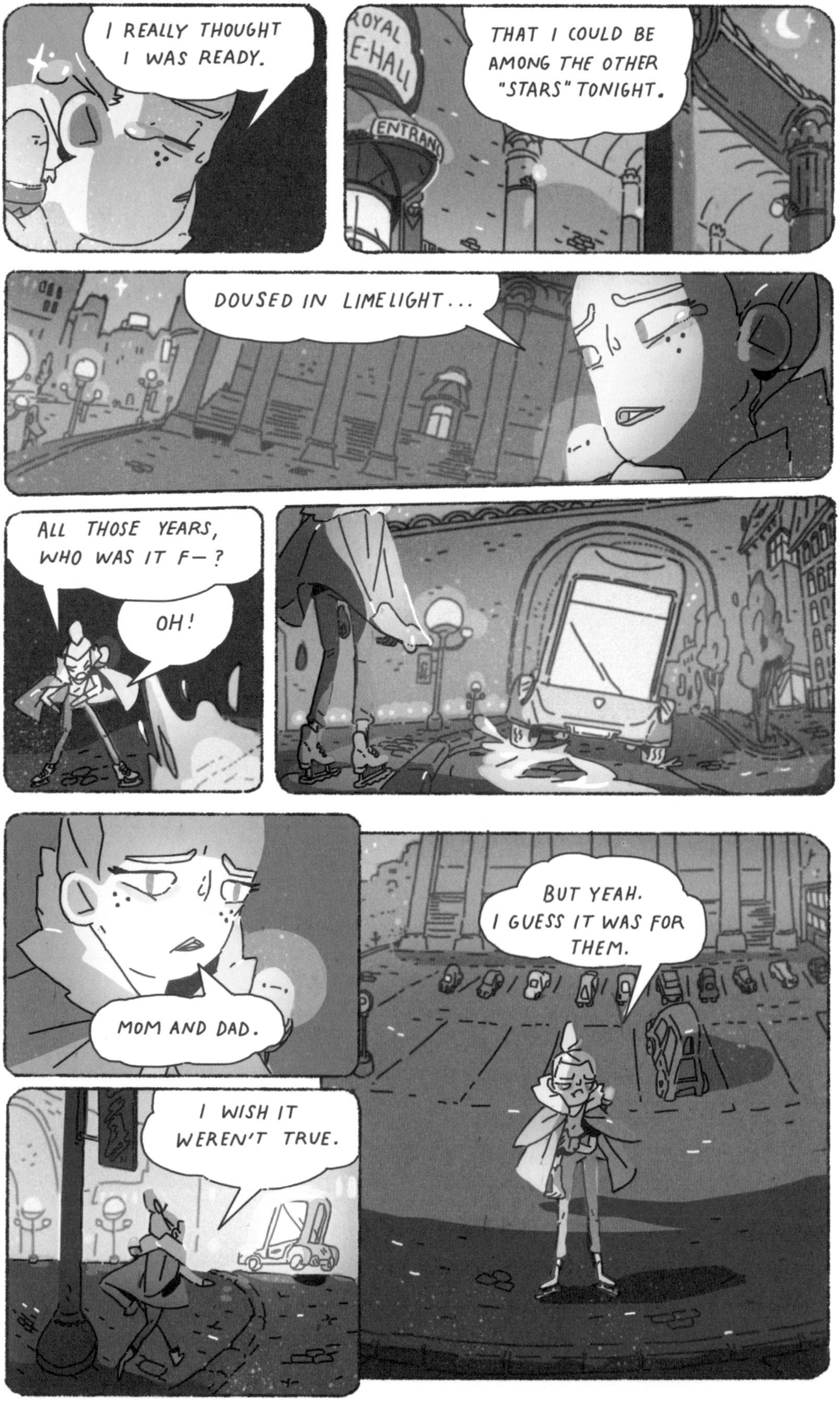
I REALLY THOUGHT I WAS READY.
ROYAL
E-HALL
ENTRAN
THAT I COULD BE AMONG THE OTHER "STARS" TONIGHT.
DOUSED IN LIMELIGHT...
ALL THOSE YEARS, WHO WAS IT F—?
OH!
MOM AND DAD.
BUT YEAH. I GUESS IT WAS FOR THEM.
I WISH IT WEREN'T TRUE.

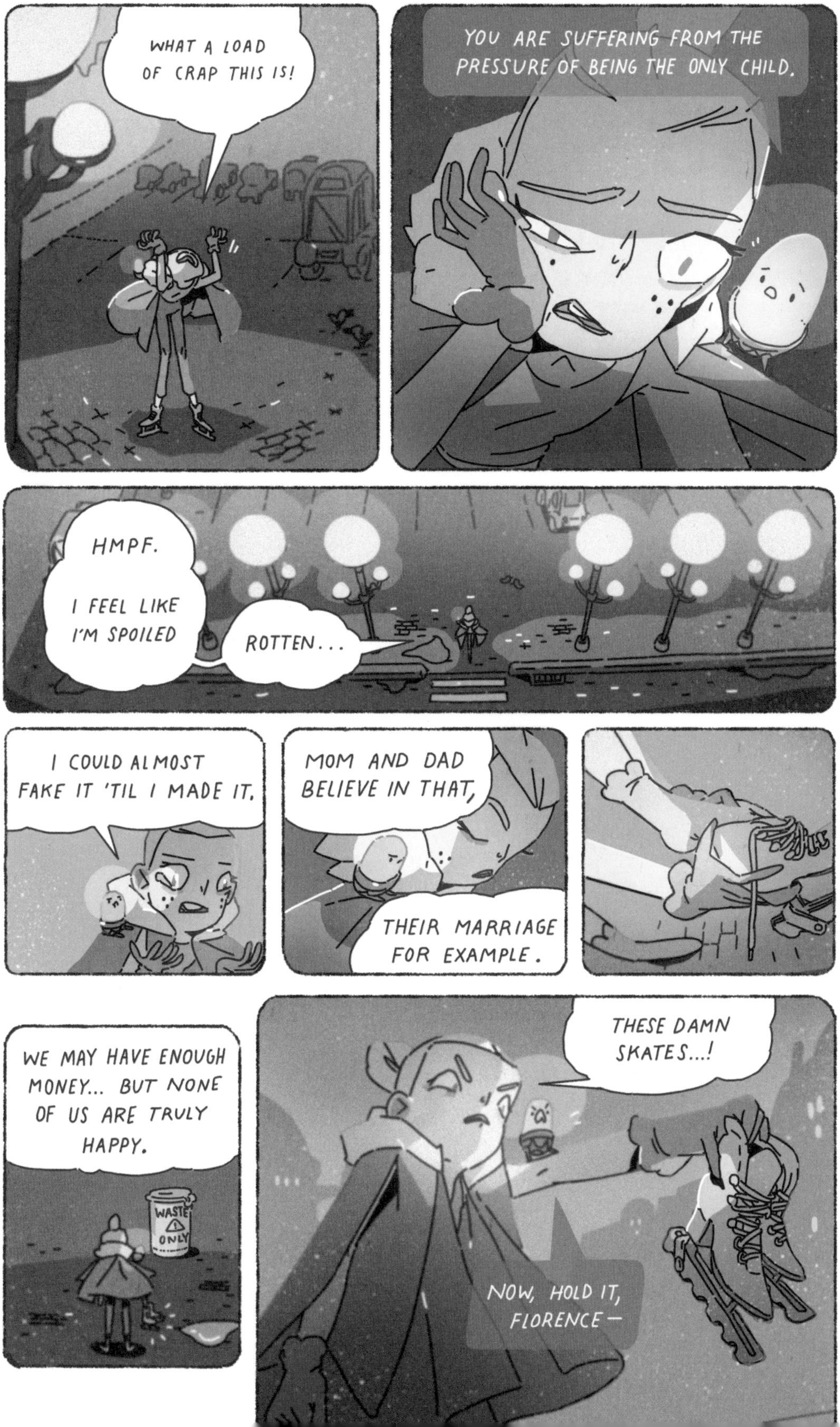
WHAT A LOAD OF CRAP THIS IS!
YOU ARE SUFFERING FROM THE PRESSURE OF BEING THE ONLY CHILD.
HMPF.
I FEEL LIKE I'M SPOILED
ROTTEN...
I COULD ALMOST FAKE IT 'TIL I MADE IT.
MOM AND DAD BELIEVE IN THAT,
THEIR MARRIAGE FOR EXAMPLE.
WE MAY HAVE ENOUGH MONEY... BUT NONE OF US ARE TRULY HAPPY.
WASTE ONLY
THESE DAMN SKATES...!
NOW, HOLD IT, FLORENCE—

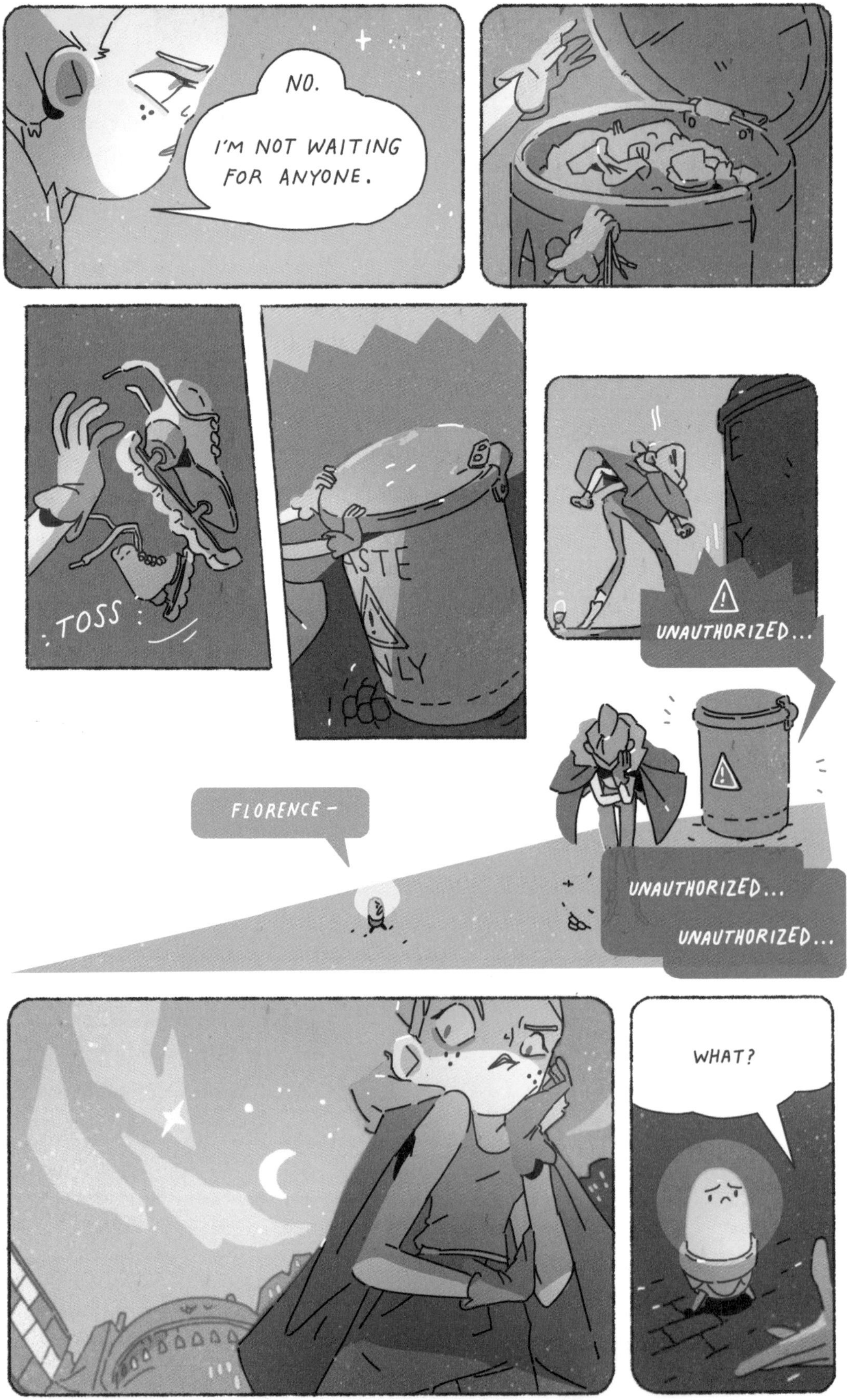
NO.
I'M NOT WAITING FOR ANYONE.
TOSS
UNAUTHORIZED...
FLORENCE-
UNAUTHORIZED...
UNAUTHORIZED...
WHAT?

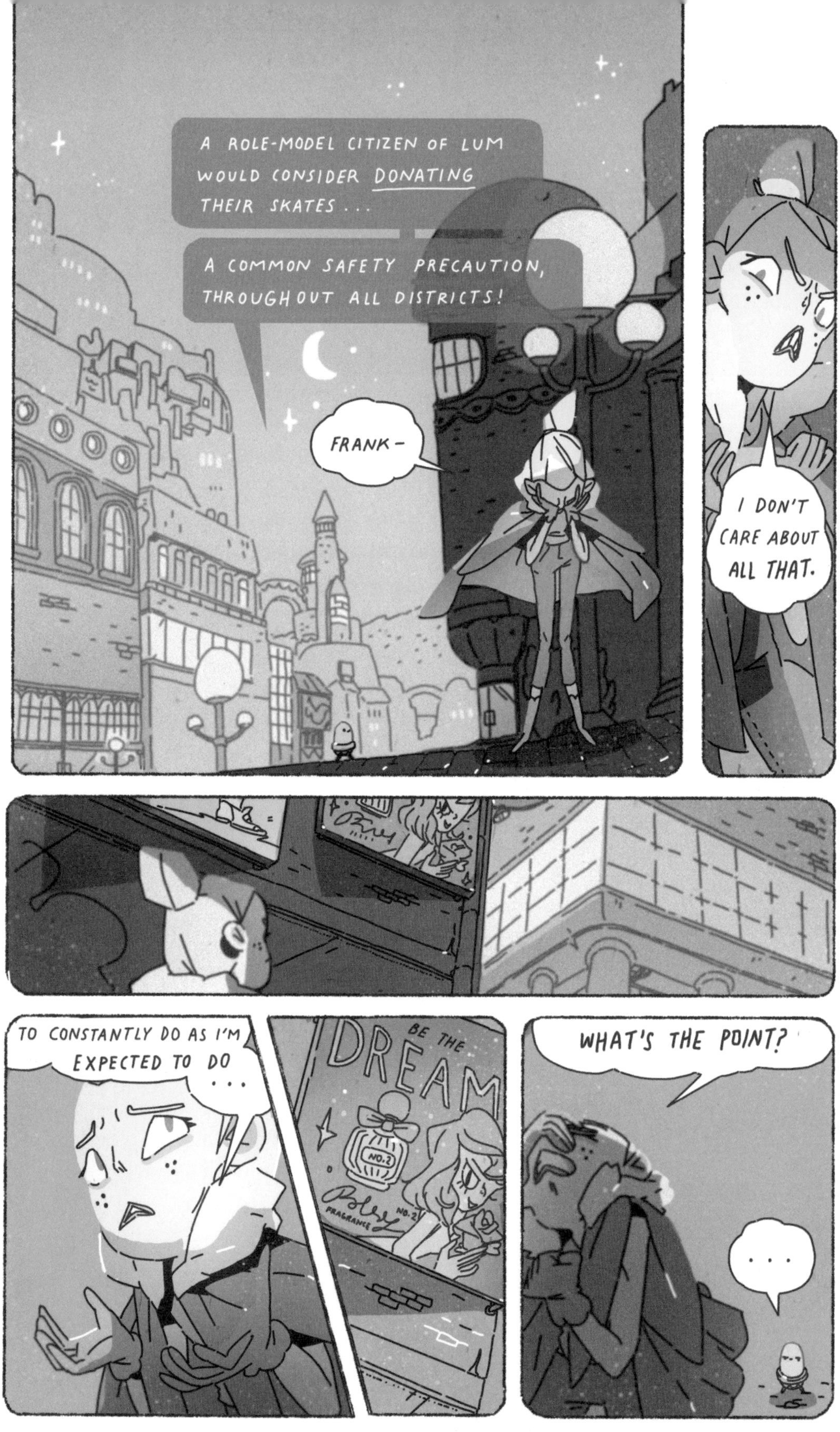
A ROLE-MODEL CITIZEN OF LUM WOULD CONSIDER DONATING THEIR SKATES...
A COMMON SAFETY PRECAUTION, THROUGHOUT ALL DISTRICTS!
FRANK-
I DON'T CARE ABOUT ALL THAT.
TO CONSTANTLY DO AS I'M EXPECTED TO DO ...
BE THE DREAM
NO.2
FRAGRANCE
WHAT'S THE POINT?
...

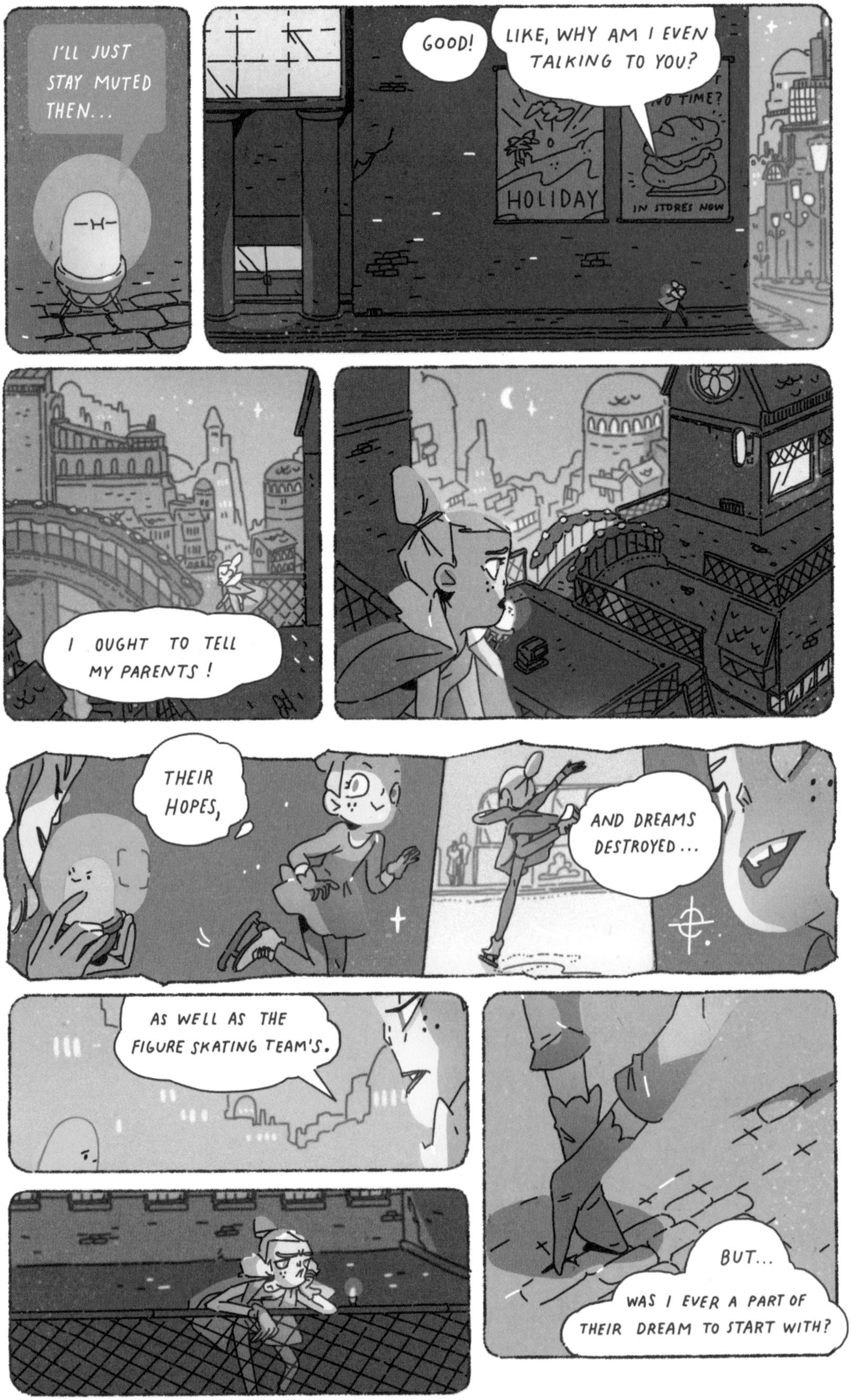
I'LL JUST STAY MUTED THEN...
GOOD!
LIKE, WHY AM I EVEN TALKING TO YOU?
HOLIDAY
IN STORES NOW
I OUGHT TO TELL MY PARENTS!
THEIR HOPES,
AND DREAMS DESTROYED...
AS WELL AS THE FIGURE SKATING TEAM'S.
BUT...
WAS I EVER A PART OF THEIR DREAM TO START WITH?

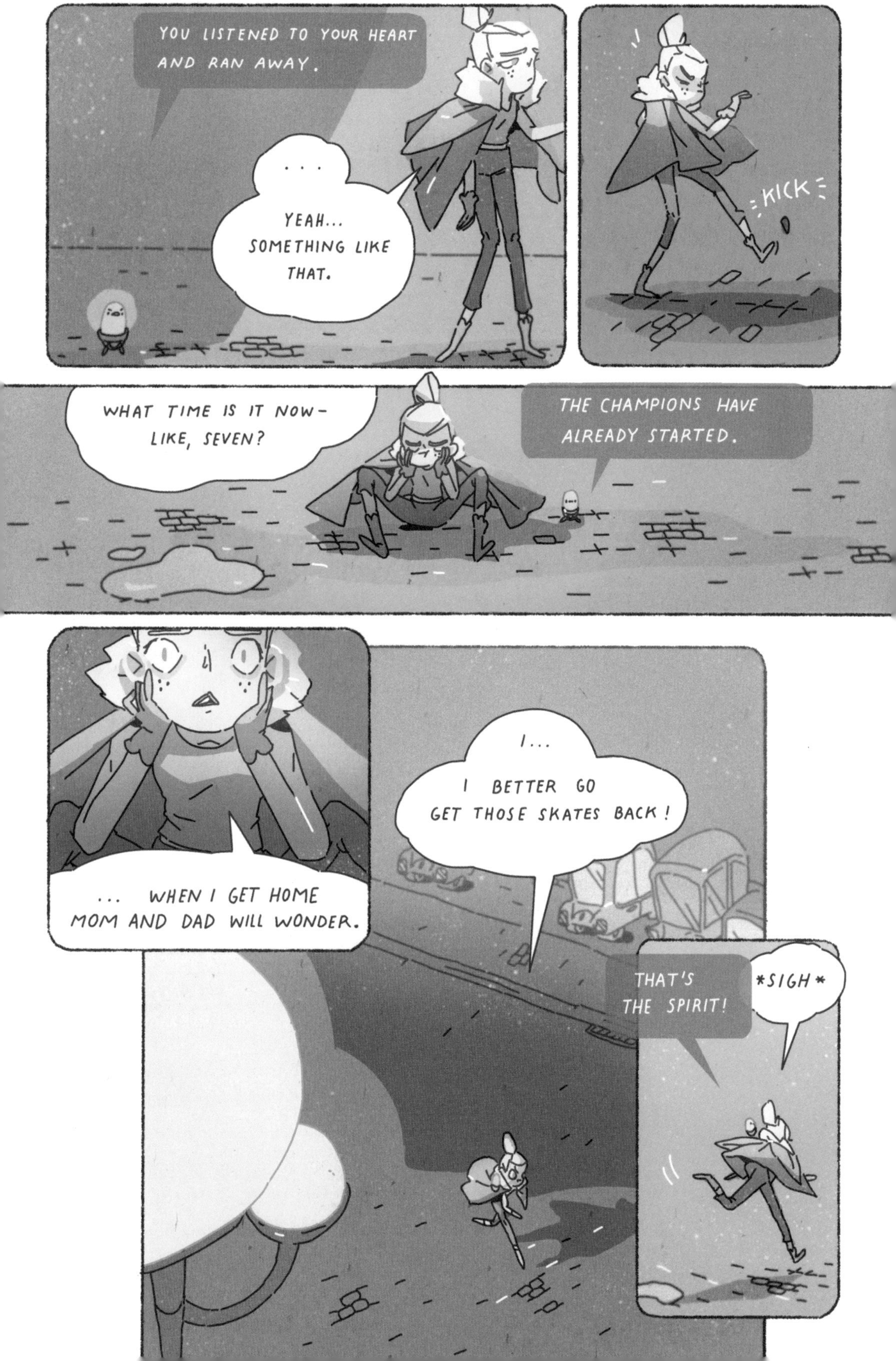

YOU LISTENED TO YOUR HEART AND RAN AWAY.
. . .
YEAH... SOMETHING LIKE THAT.
KICK
WHAT TIME IS IT NOW- LIKE, SEVEN?
THE CHAMPIONS HAVE ALREADY STARTED.
... WHEN I GET HOME MOM AND DAD WILL WONDER.
I...
I BETTER GO GET THOSE SKATES BACK!
THAT'S THE SPIRIT!
SIGH

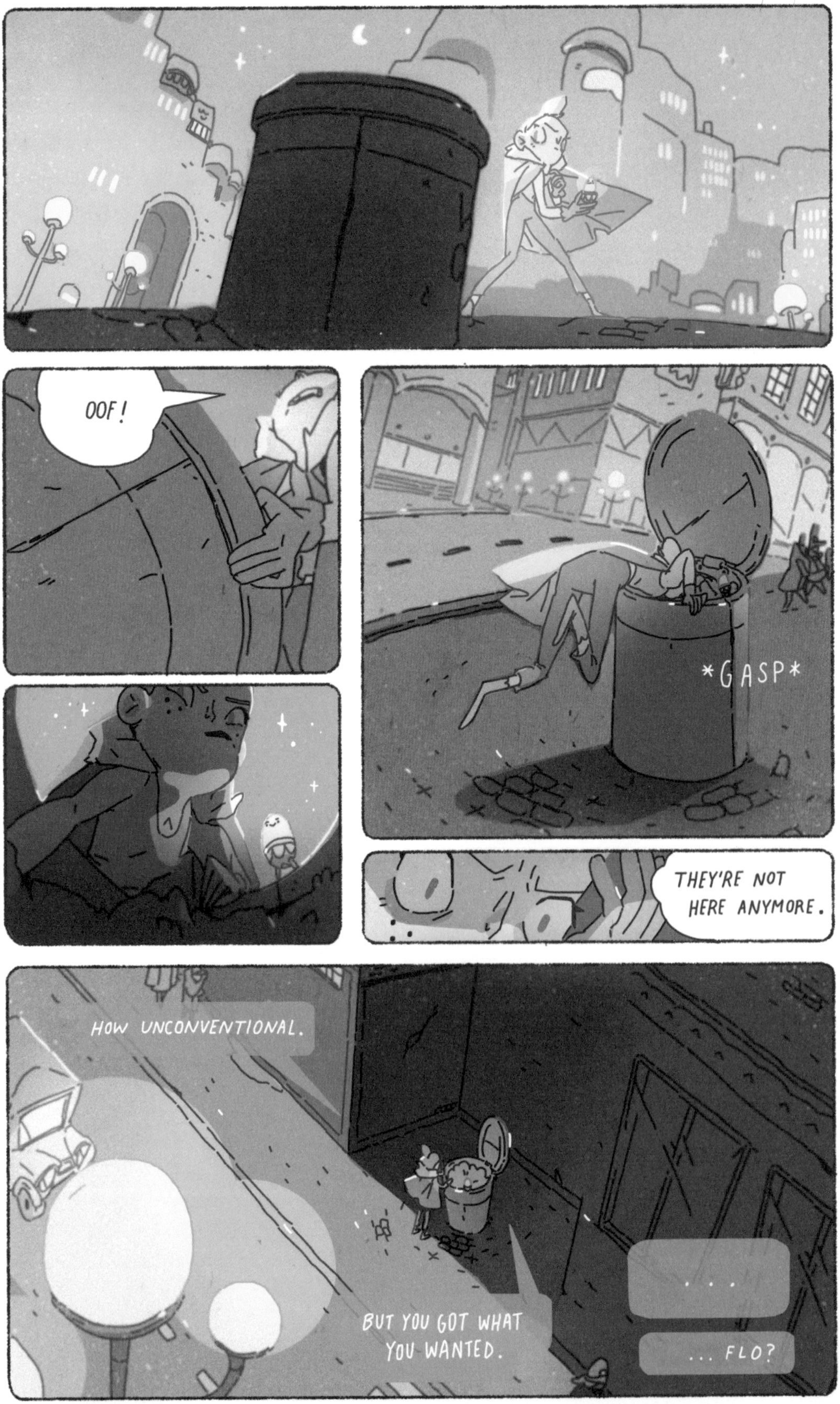
OOF!
GASP
THEY'RE NOT HERE ANYMORE.
HOW UNCONVENTIONAL.
BUT YOU GOT WHAT YOU WANTED.
. . .
... FLO?

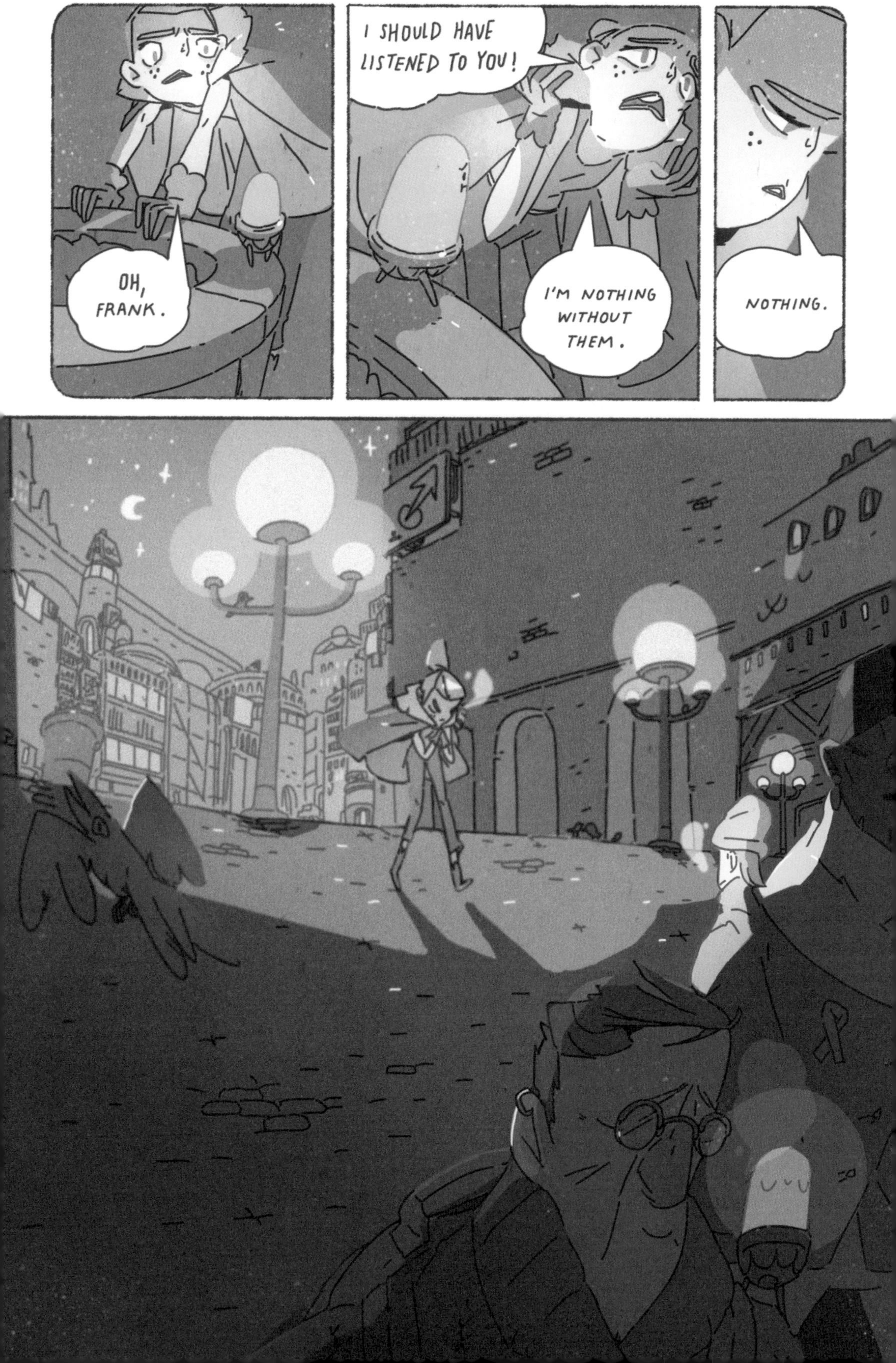
OH, FRANK.
I SHOULD HAVE LISTENED TO YOU!
I'M NOTHING WITHOUT THEM.
NOTHING.

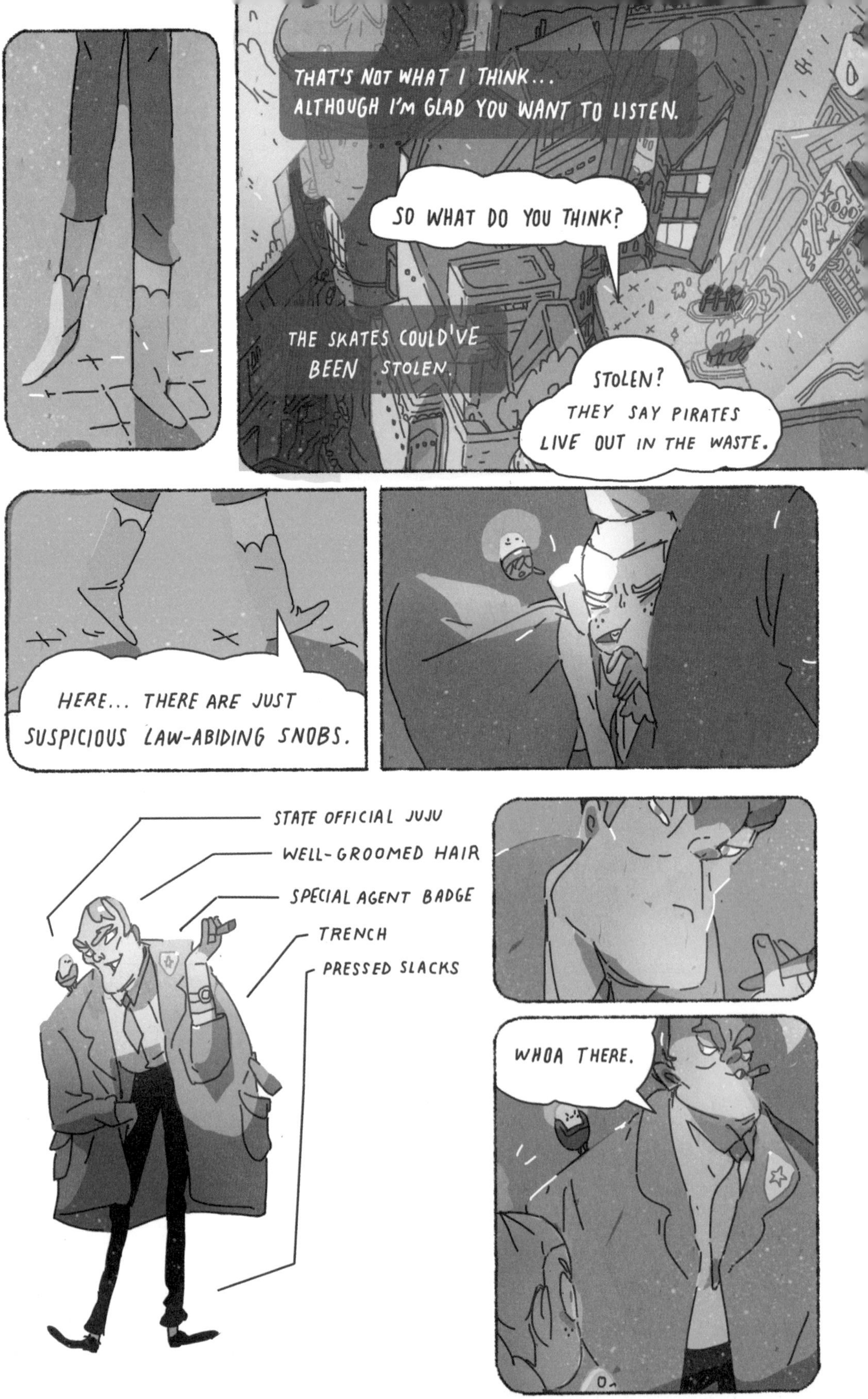

THAT'S NOT WHAT I THINK...
ALTHOUGH I'M GLAD YOU WANT TO LISTEN.
SO WHAT DO YOU THINK?
THE SKATES COULD'VE BEEN STOLEN.
STOLEN? THEY SAY PIRATES LIVE OUT IN THE WASTE.
HERE... THERE ARE JUST SUSPICIOUS LAW-ABIDING SNOBS.
STATE OFFICIAL JUJU
WELL-GROOMED HAIR
SPECIAL AGENT BADGE
TRENCH
PRESSED SLACKS
WHOA THERE.

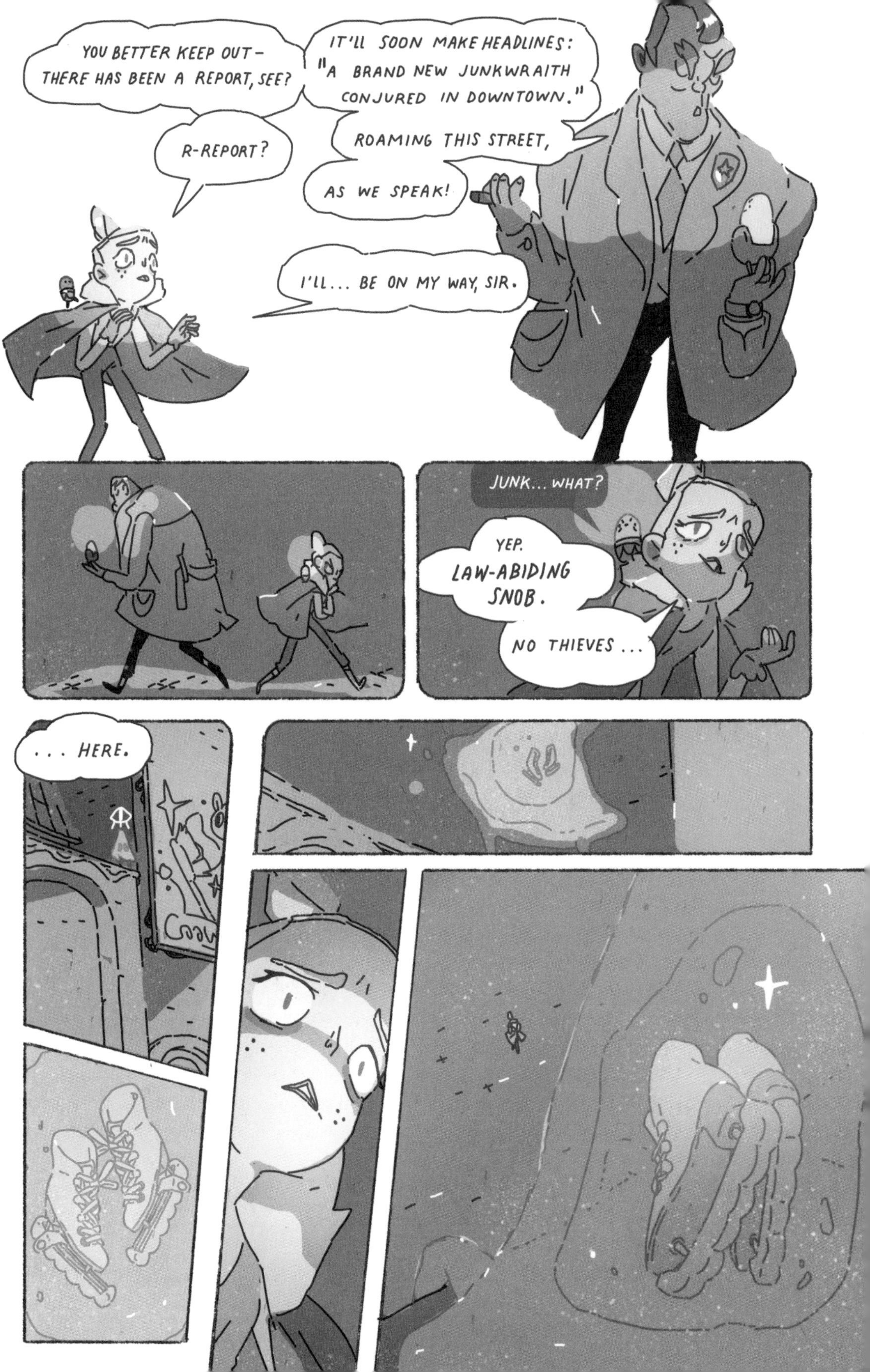
YOU BETTER KEEP OUT- THERE HAS BEEN A REPORT, SEE?
IT'LL SOON MAKE HEADLINES: "A BRAND NEW JUNKWRAITH CONJURED IN DOWNTOWN."
R-REPORT?
ROAMING THIS STREET,
AS WE SPEAK!
I'LL... BE ON MY WAY, SIR.
JUNK... WHAT?
YEP. LAW-ABIDING SNOB.
NO THIEVES ...
. . . HERE.

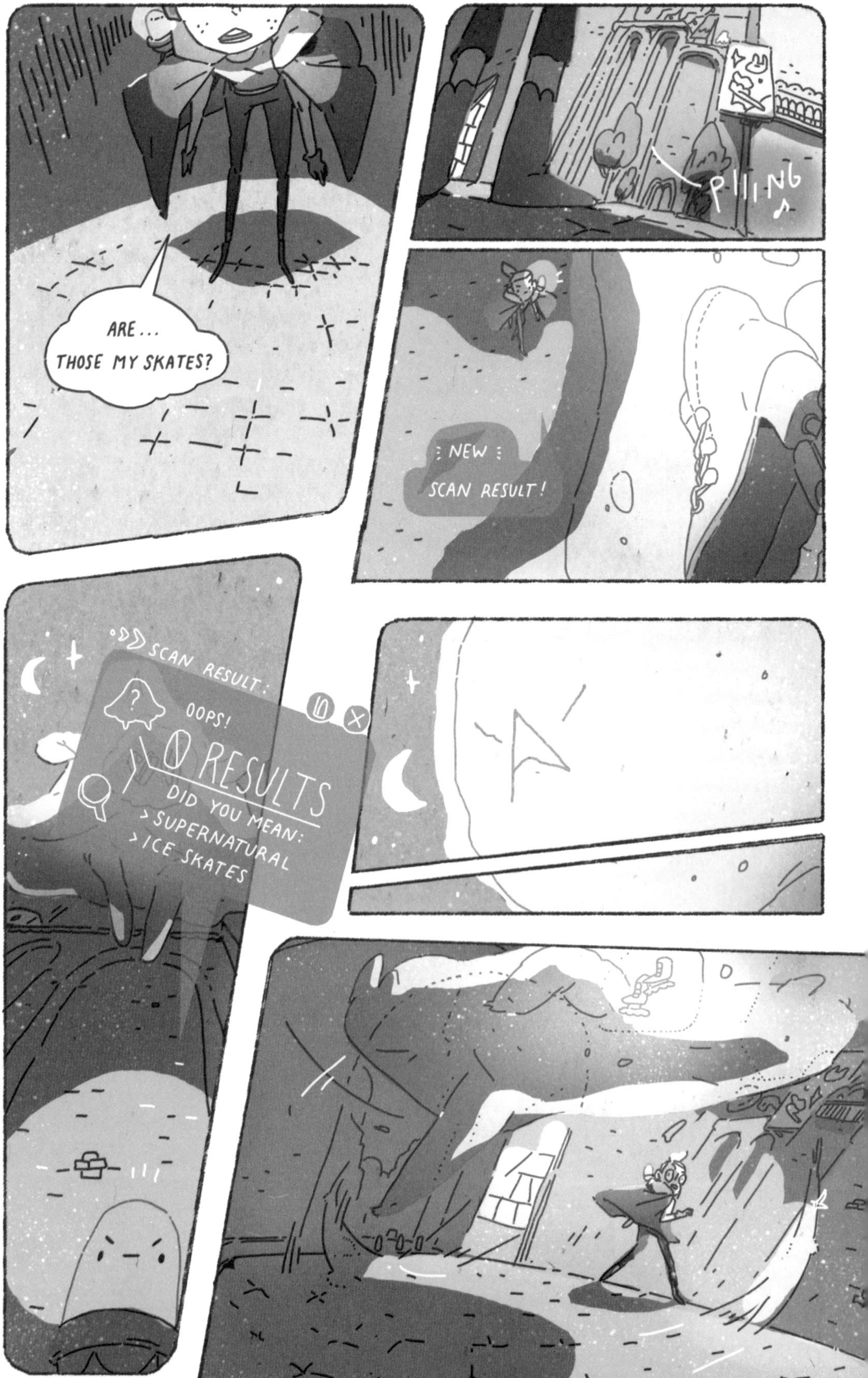

ARE... THOSE MY SKATES?
PIIING
NEW SCAN RESULT!
SCAN RESULT:
OOPS!
0 RESULTS
DID YOU MEAN:
>SUPERNATURAL
>ICE SKATES

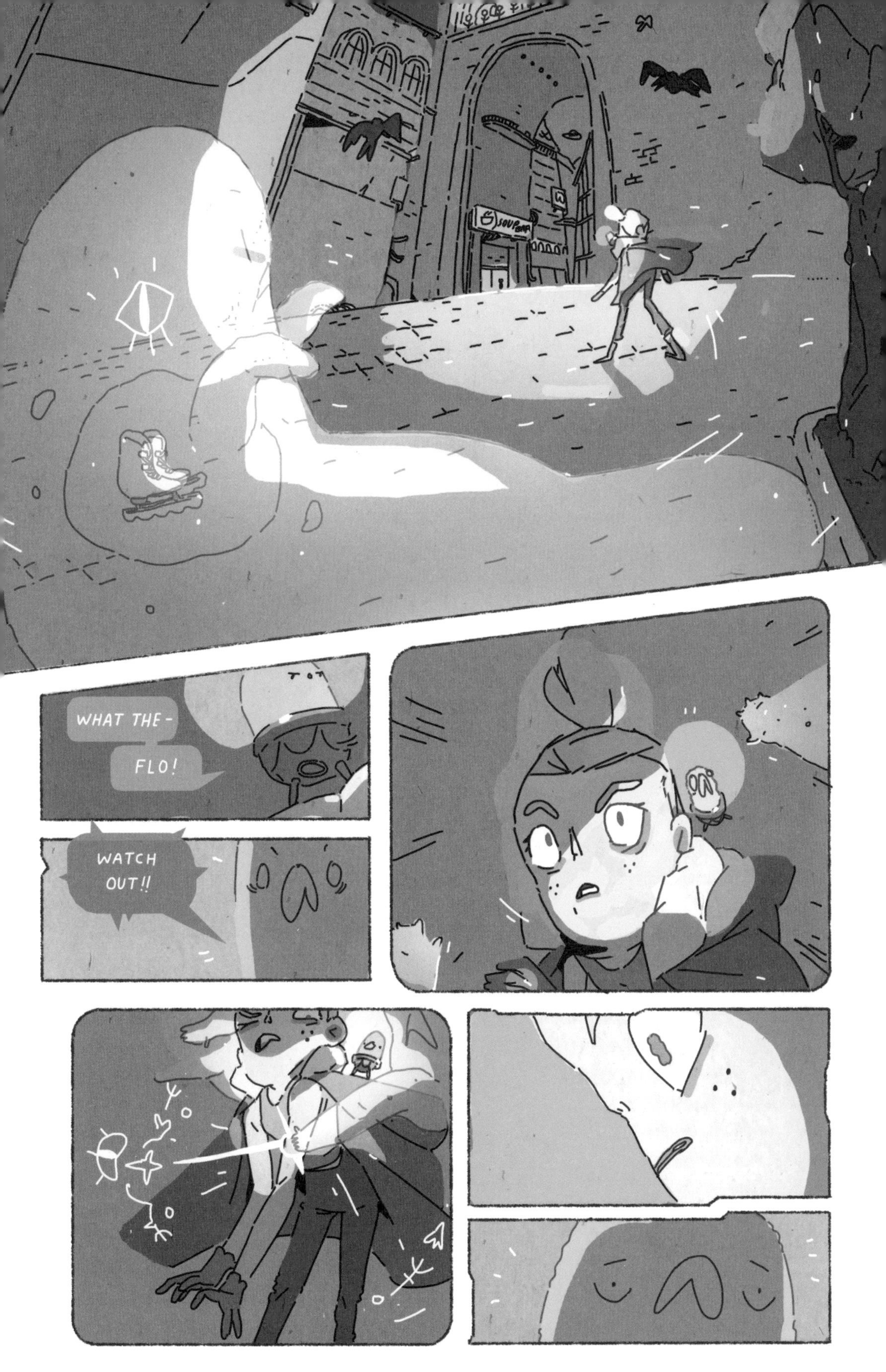
SOUP
WHAT THE-
FLO!
WATCH OUT!!

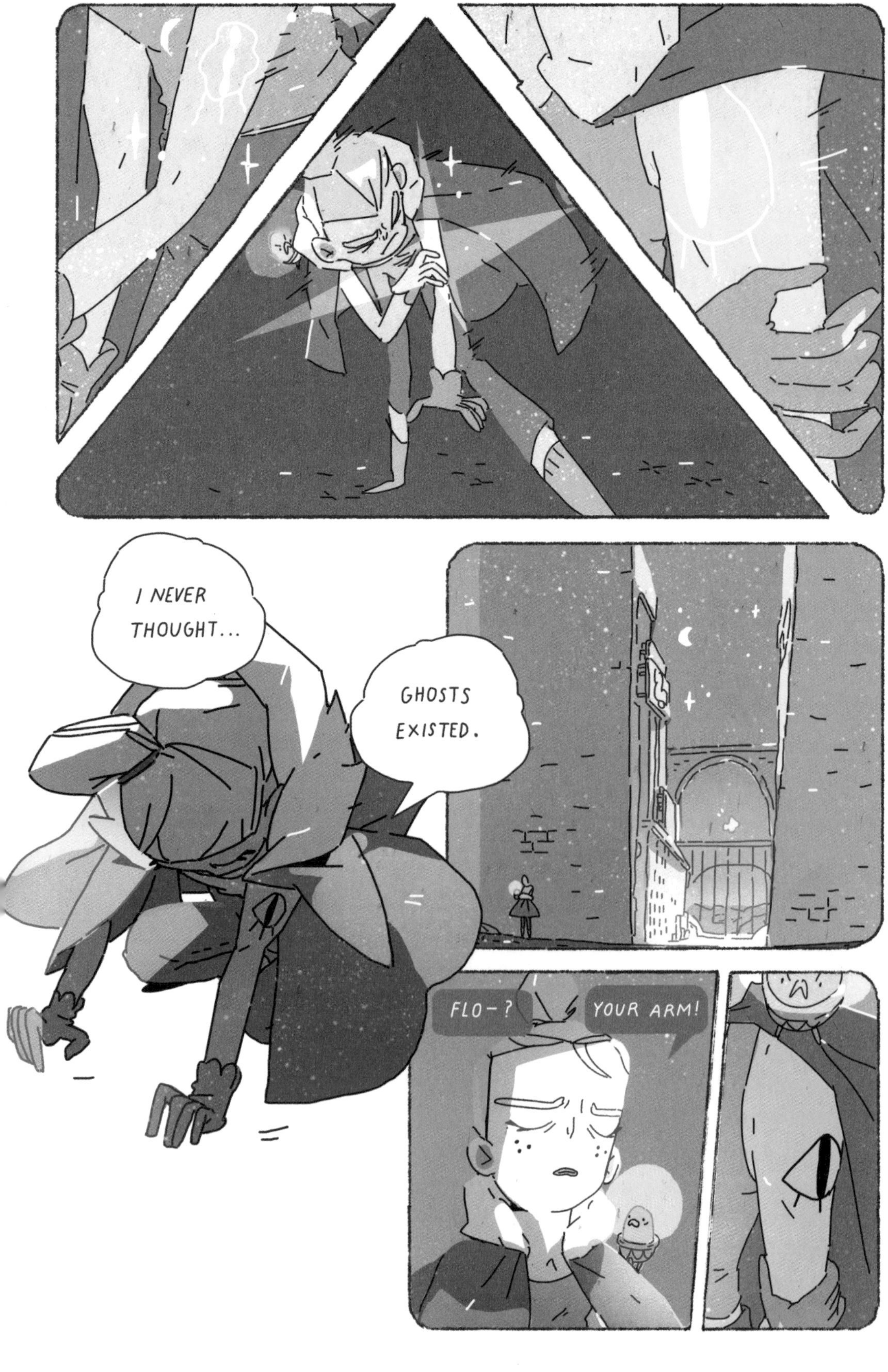
I NEVER THOUGHT...
GHOSTS EXISTED.
FLO-?
YOUR ARM!

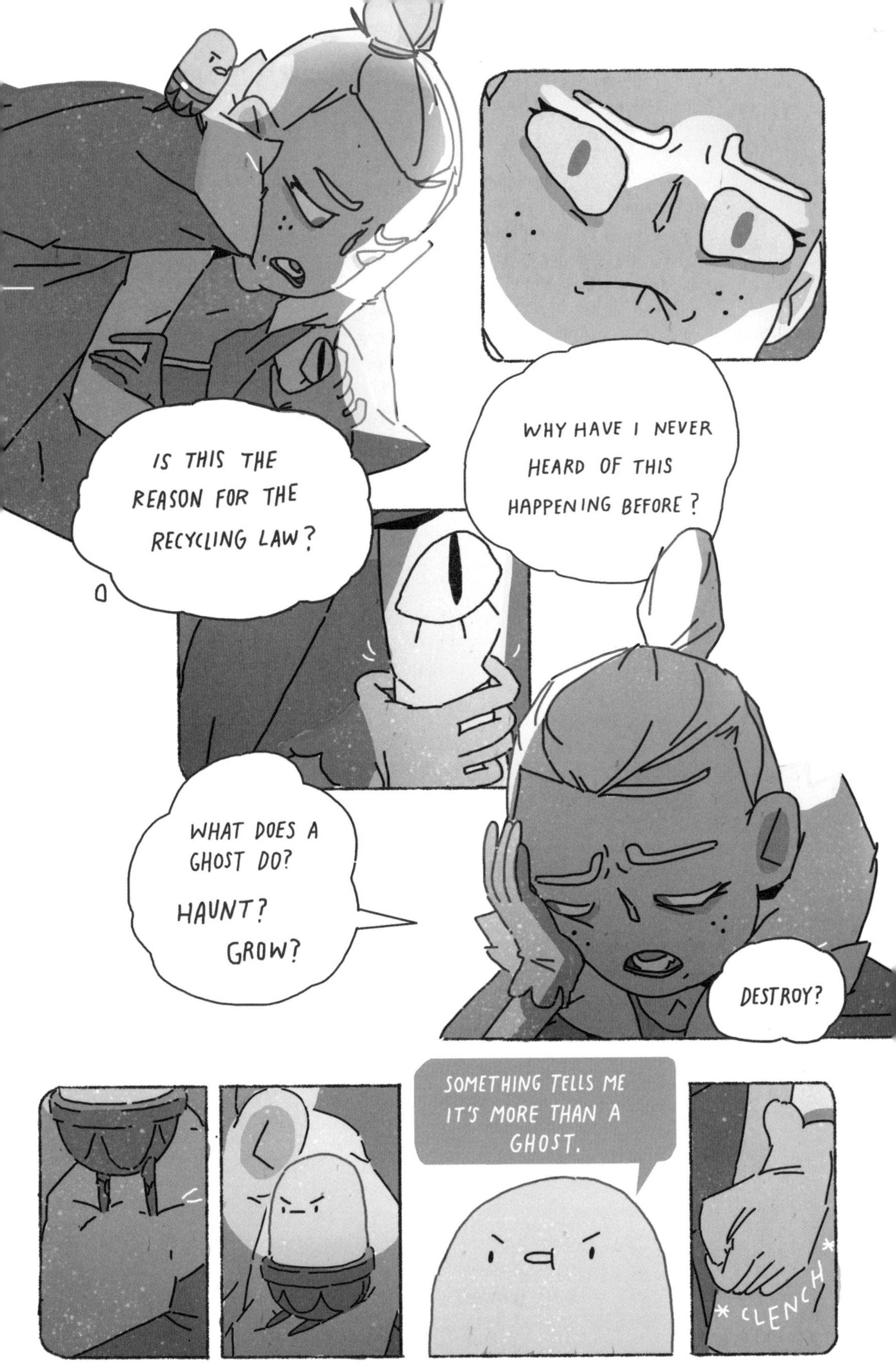
IS THIS THE REASON FOR THE RECYCLING LAW?
WHY HAVE I NEVER HEARD OF THIS HAPPENING BEFORE?
WHAT DOES A GHOST DO?
HAUNT?
GROW?
DESTROY?
SOMETHING TELLS ME IT'S MORE THAN A GHOST.
CLENCH

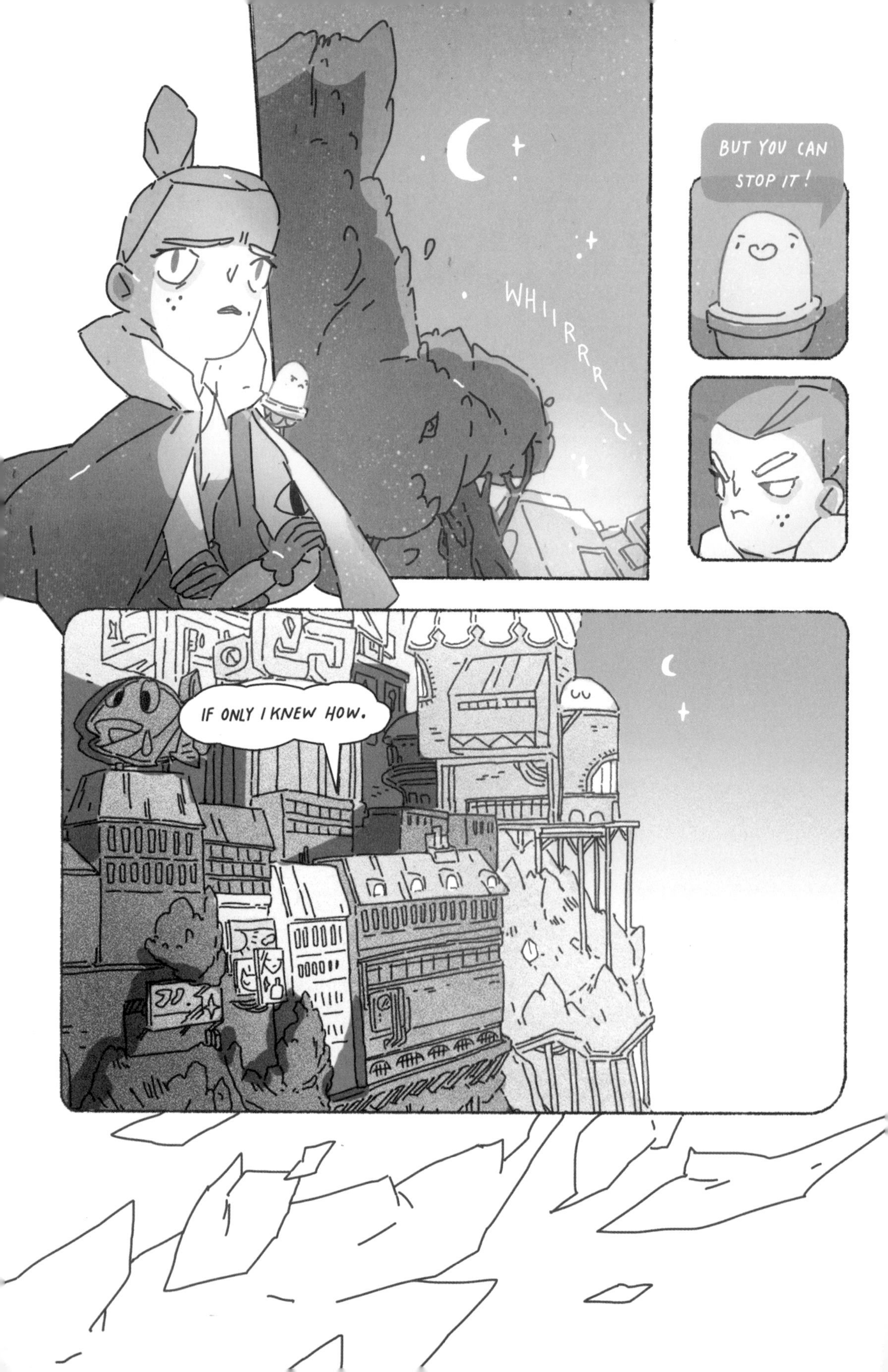
WHIIRRRR
BUT YOU CAN STOP IT!
IF ONLY I KNEW HOW.

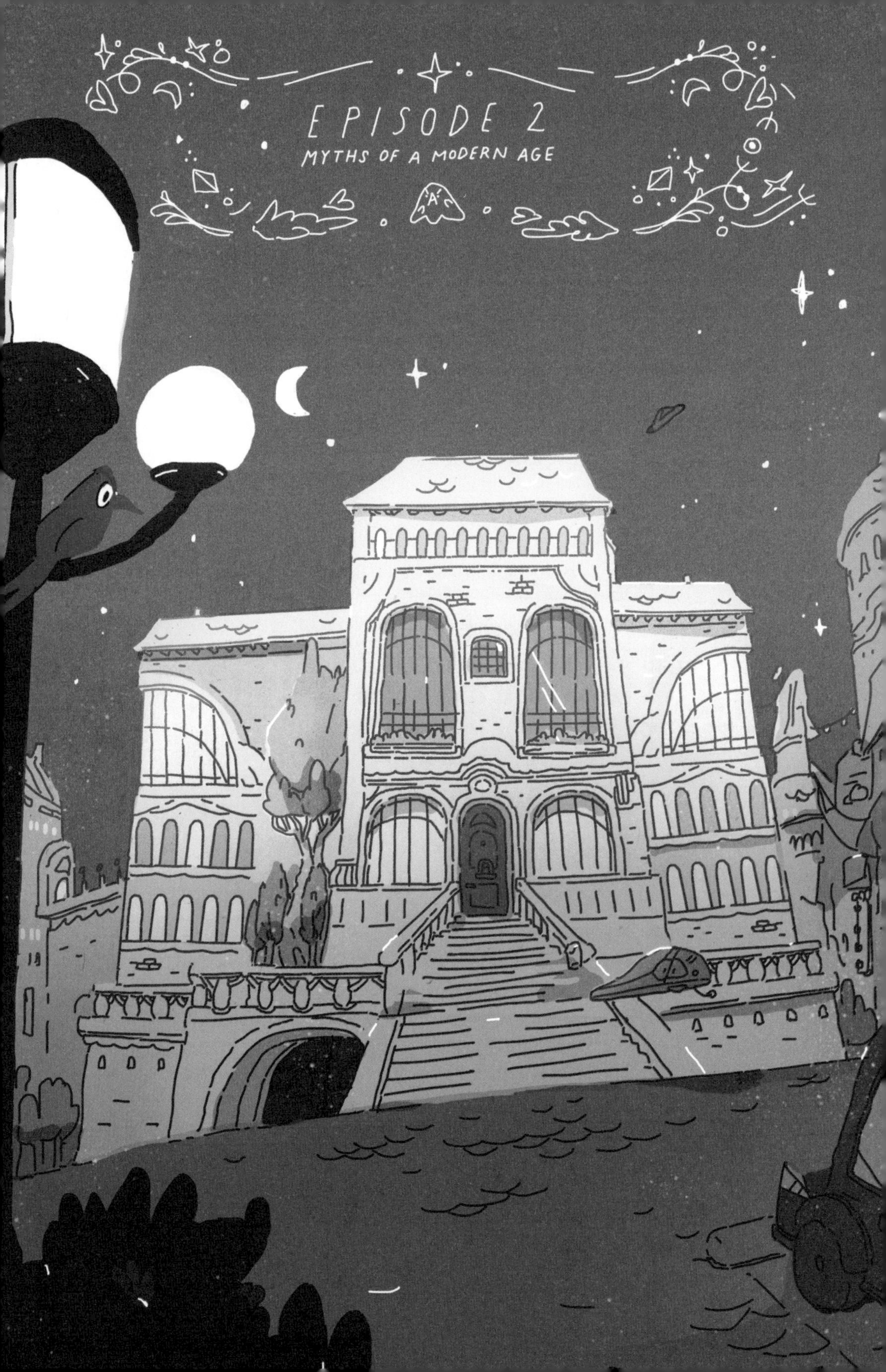
EPISODE 2
MYTHS OF A MODERN AGE

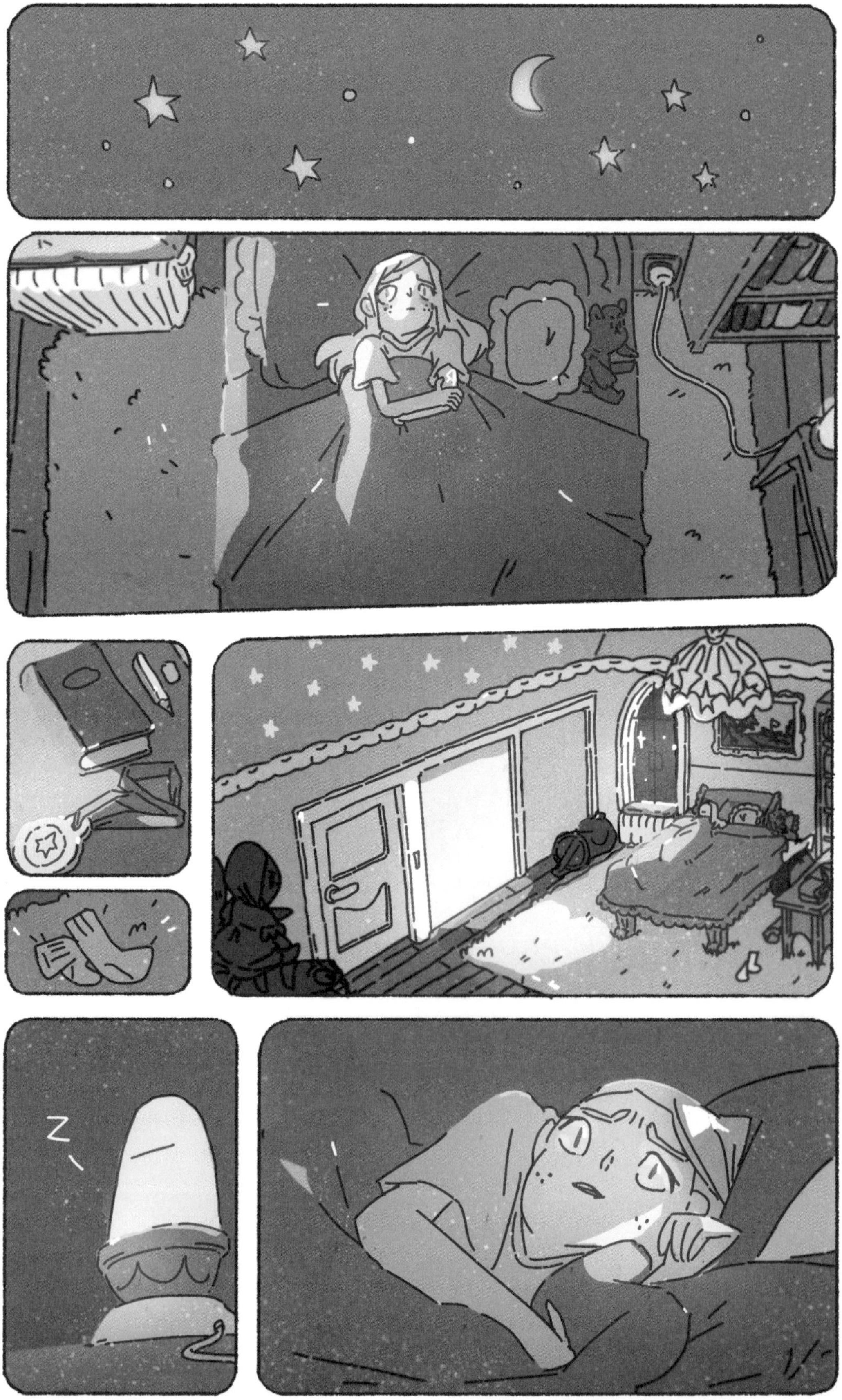
Z

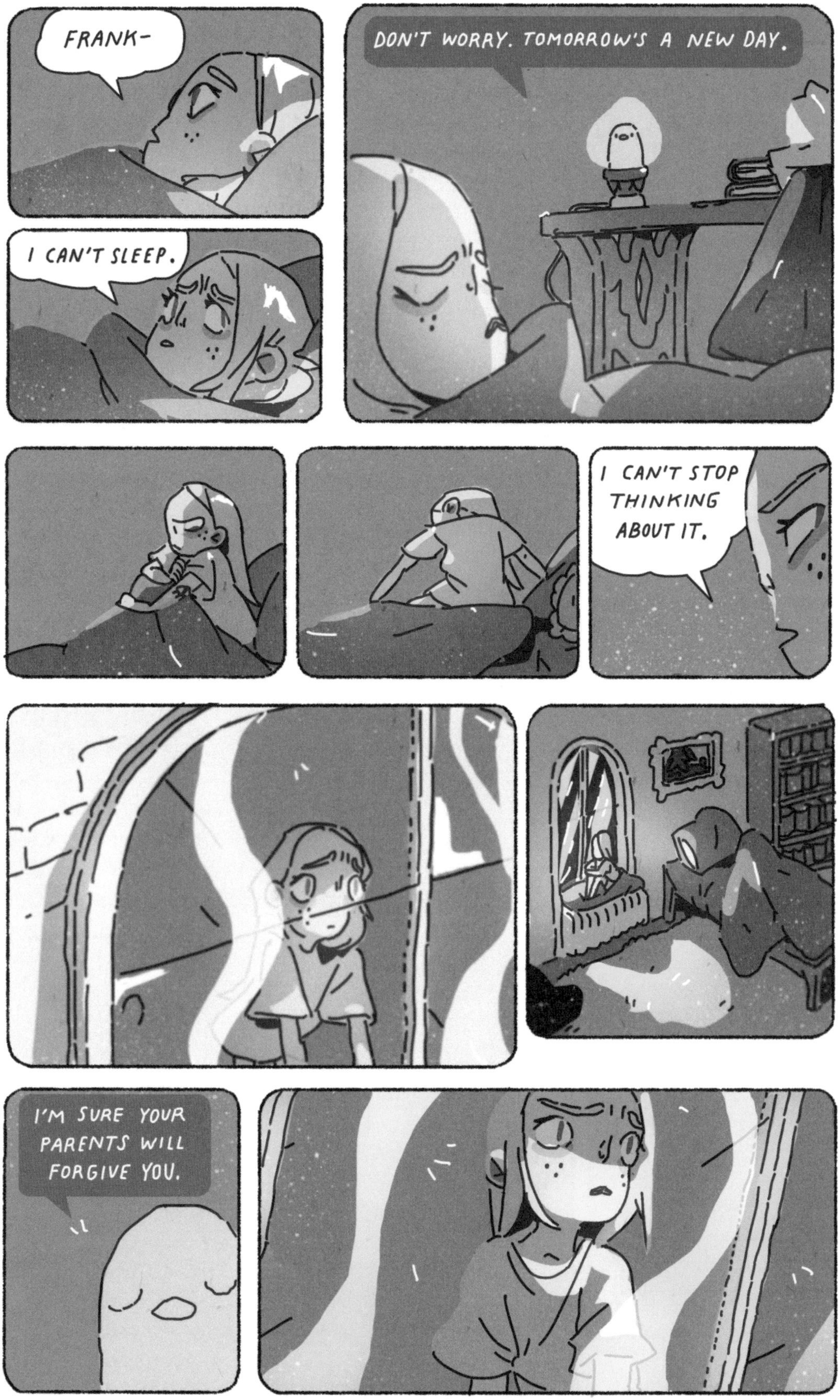
FRANK-
I CAN'T SLEEP.
DON'T WORRY. TOMORROW'S A NEW DAY.
I CAN'T STOP THINKING ABOUT IT.
I'M SURE YOUR PARENTS WILL FORGIVE YOU.

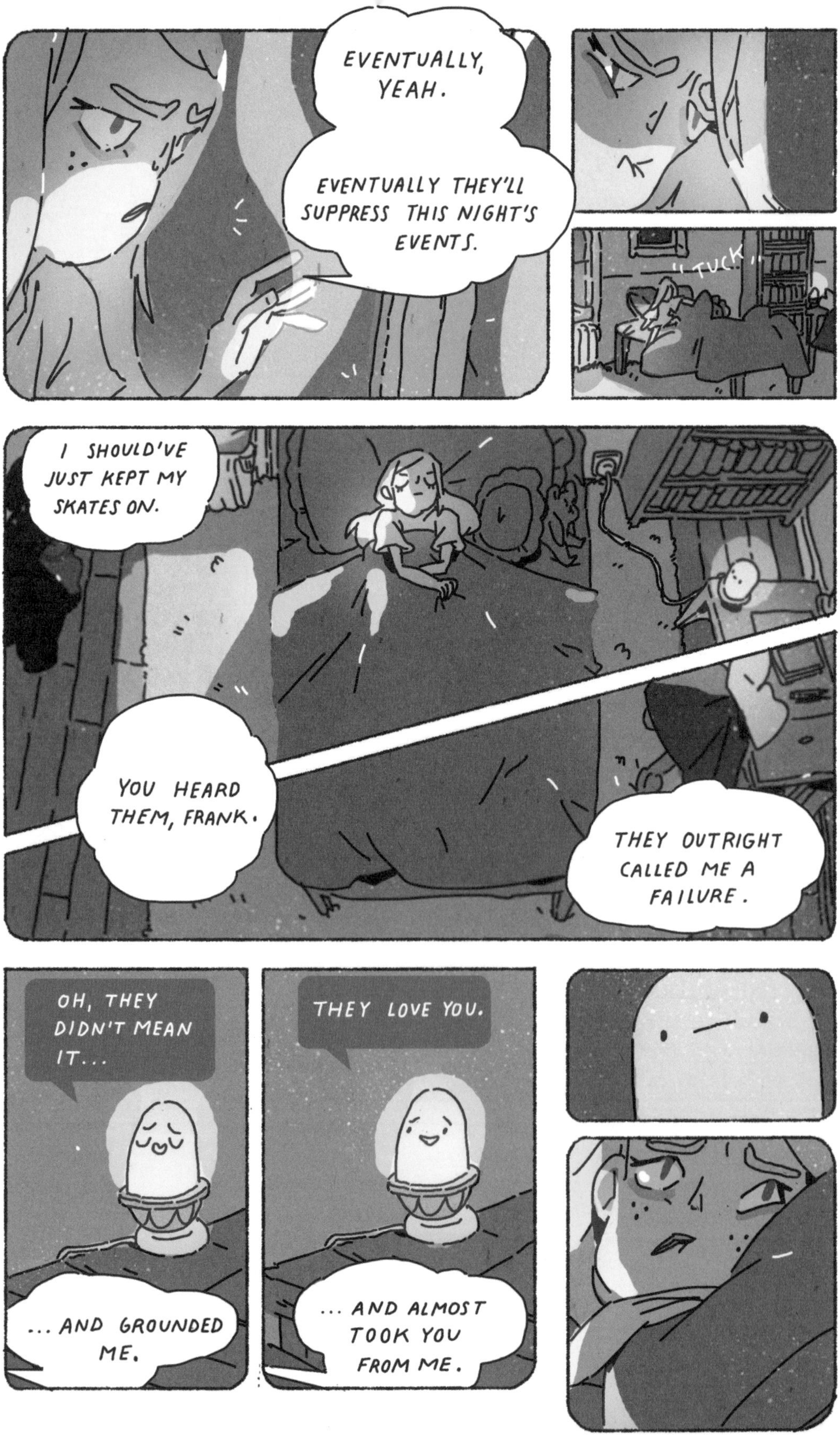

EVENTUALLY, YEAH.
EVENTUALLY THEY'LL SUPPRESS THIS NIGHT'S EVENTS.
"TUCK"
I SHOULD'VE JUST KEPT MY SKATES ON.
YOU HEARD THEM, FRANK.
THEY OUTRIGHT CALLED ME A FAILURE.
OH, THEY DIDN'T MEAN IT...
...AND GROUNDED ME.
THEY LOVE YOU.
...AND ALMOST TOOK YOU FROM ME.

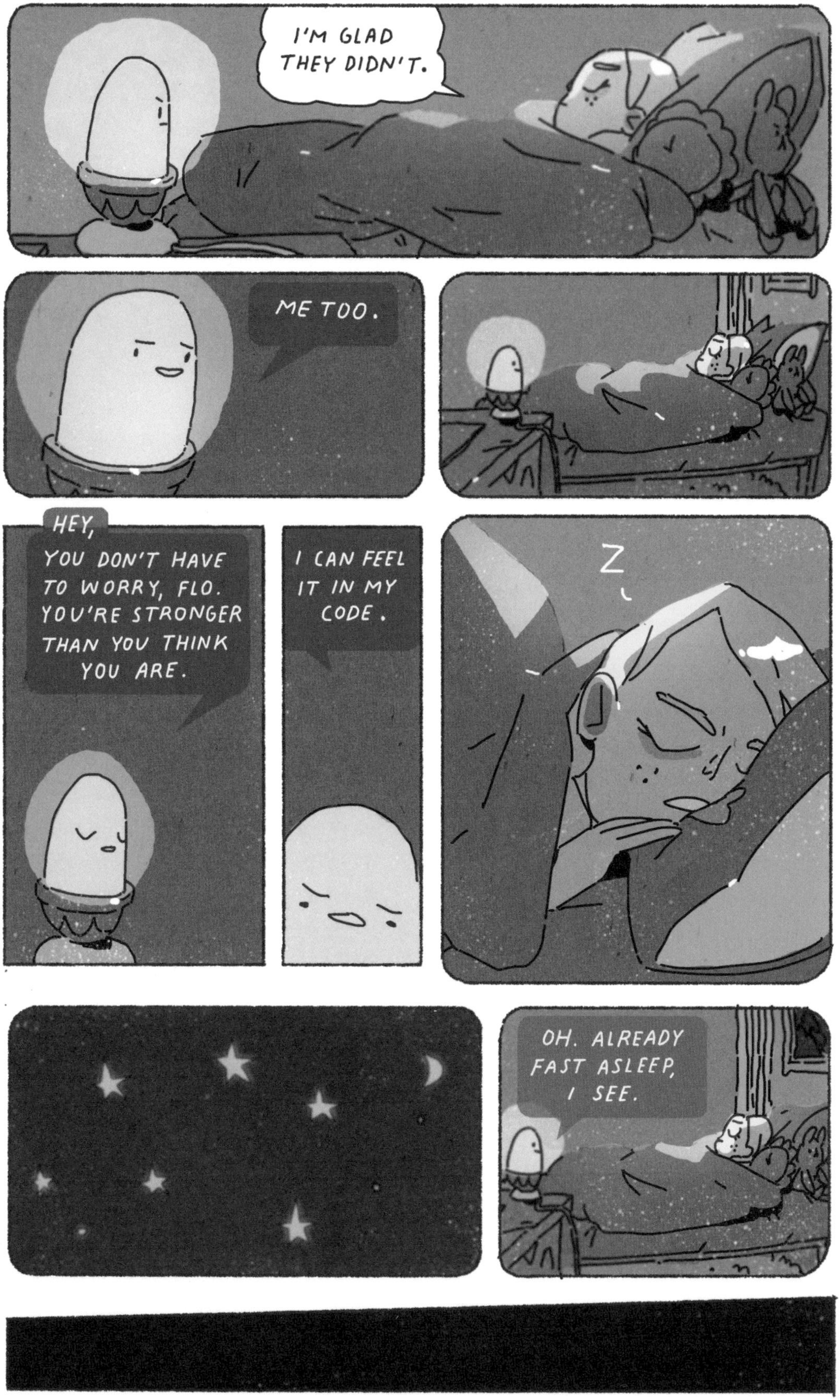
I'M GLAD THEY DIDN'T.
ME TOO.
HEY,
YOU DON'T HAVE TO WORRY, FLO. YOU'RE STRONGER THAN YOU THINK YOU ARE.
I CAN FEEL IT IN MY CODE.
Z
OH. ALREADY FAST ASLEEP, I SEE.

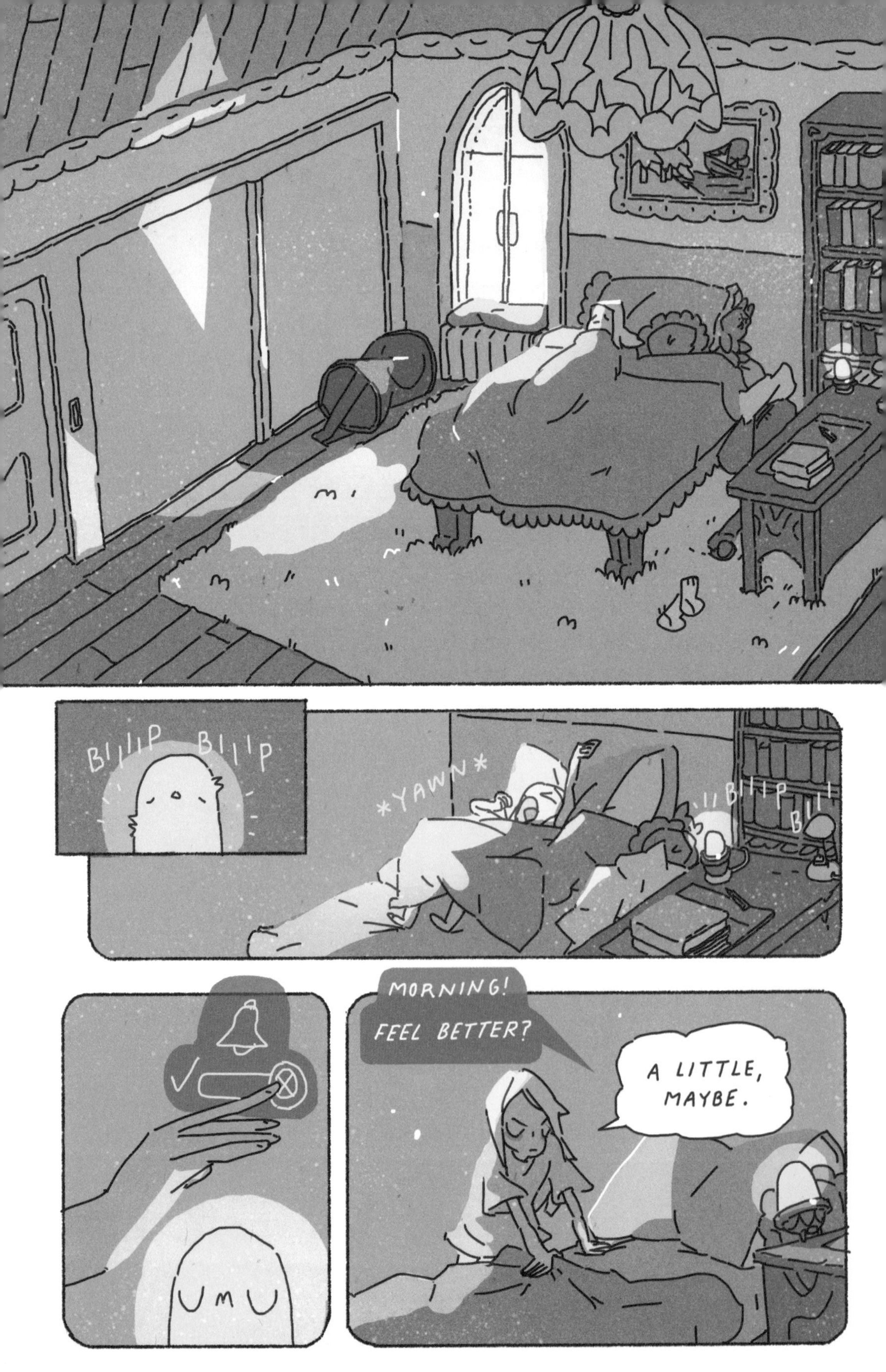
BIIIP BIIIP
YAWN
BIIIP BIII
MORNING!
FEEL BETTER?
A LITTLE, MAYBE.

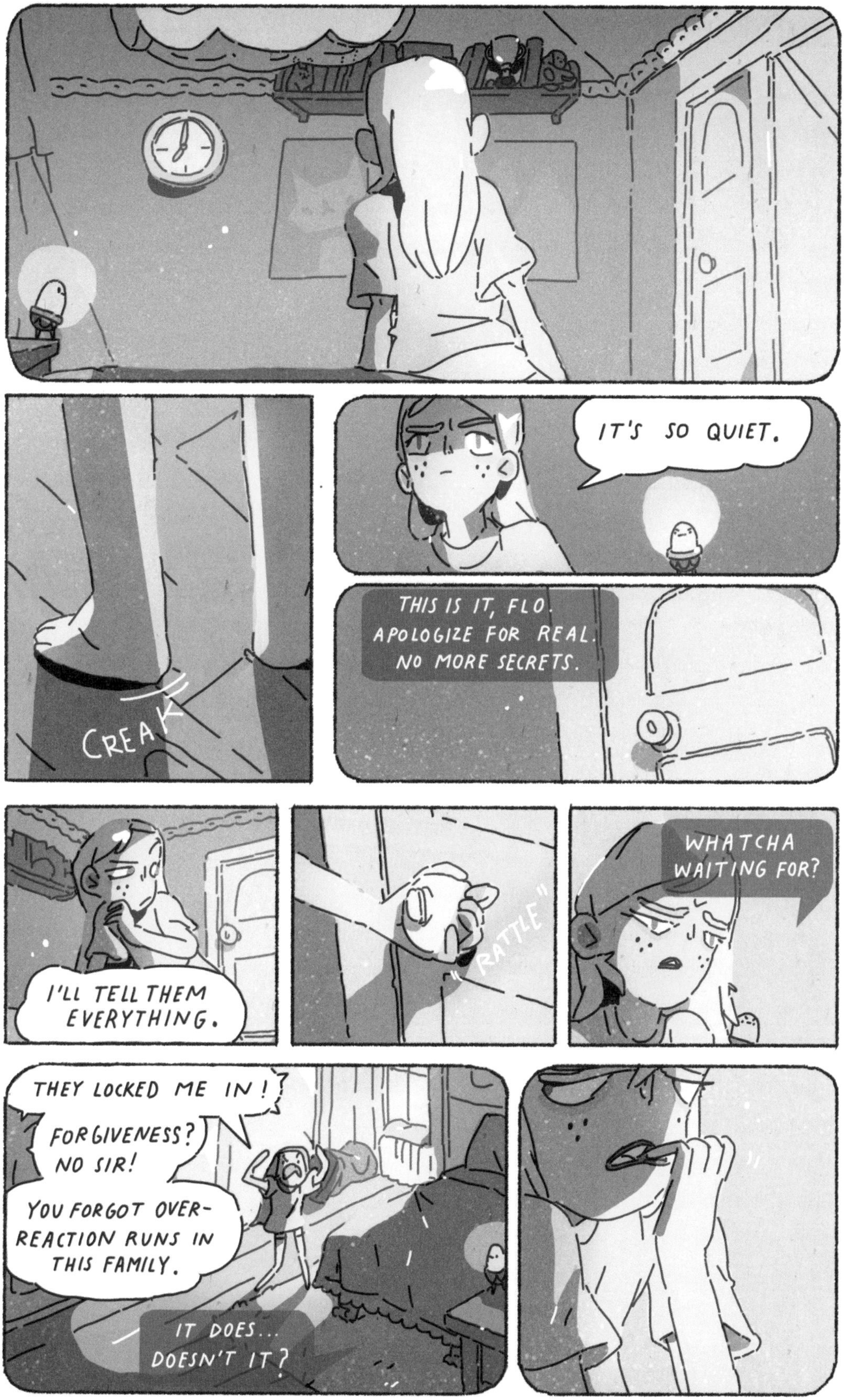
IT'S SO QUIET.
CREAK
THIS IS IT, FLO. APOLOGIZE FOR REAL. NO MORE SECRETS.
I'LL TELL THEM EVERYTHING.
"RATTLE"
WHATCHA WAITING FOR?
THEY LOCKED ME IN!
FORGIVENESS? NO SIR!
YOU FORGOT OVER-REACTION RUNS IN THIS FAMILY.
IT DOES... DOESN'T IT?

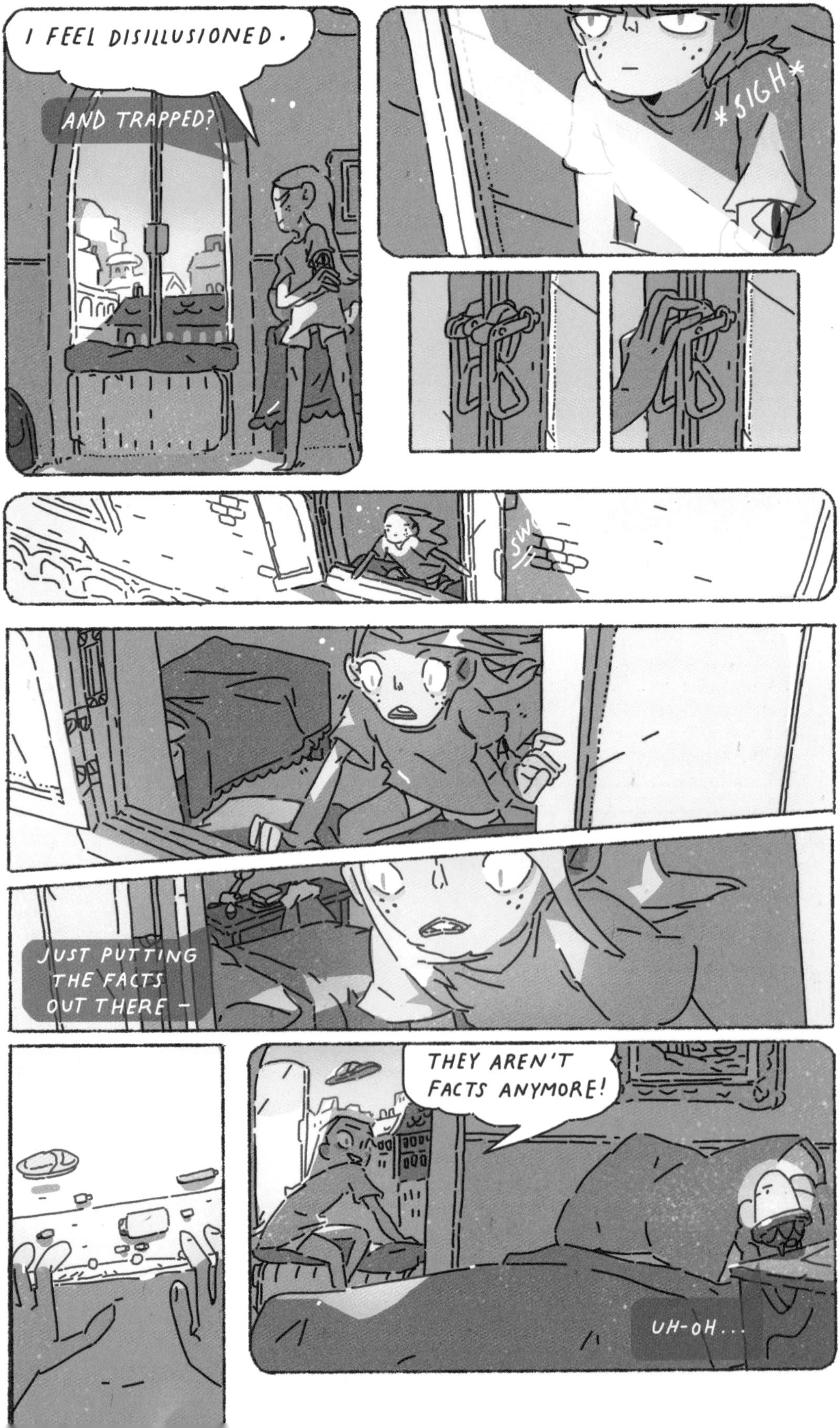
I FEEL DISILLUSIONED.
AND TRAPPED?
SIGH
JUST PUTTING THE FACTS OUT THERE –
THEY AREN'T FACTS ANYMORE!
UH-OH...

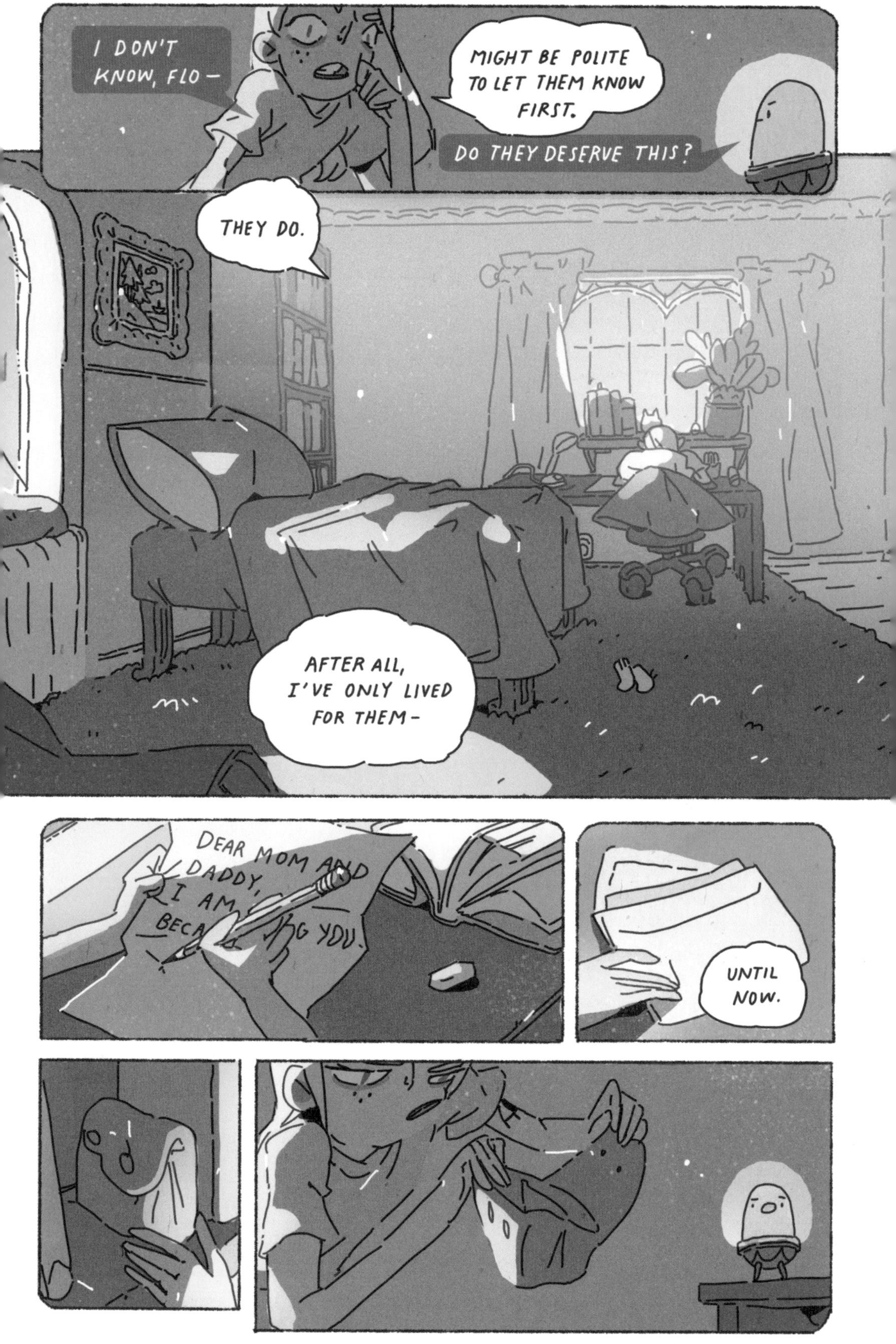

I DON'T KNOW, FLO—
MIGHT BE POLITE TO LET THEM KNOW FIRST.
DO THEY DESERVE THIS?
THEY DO.
AFTER ALL, I'VE ONLY LIVED FOR THEM—
DEAR MOM AND DADDY, I AM
UNTIL NOW.

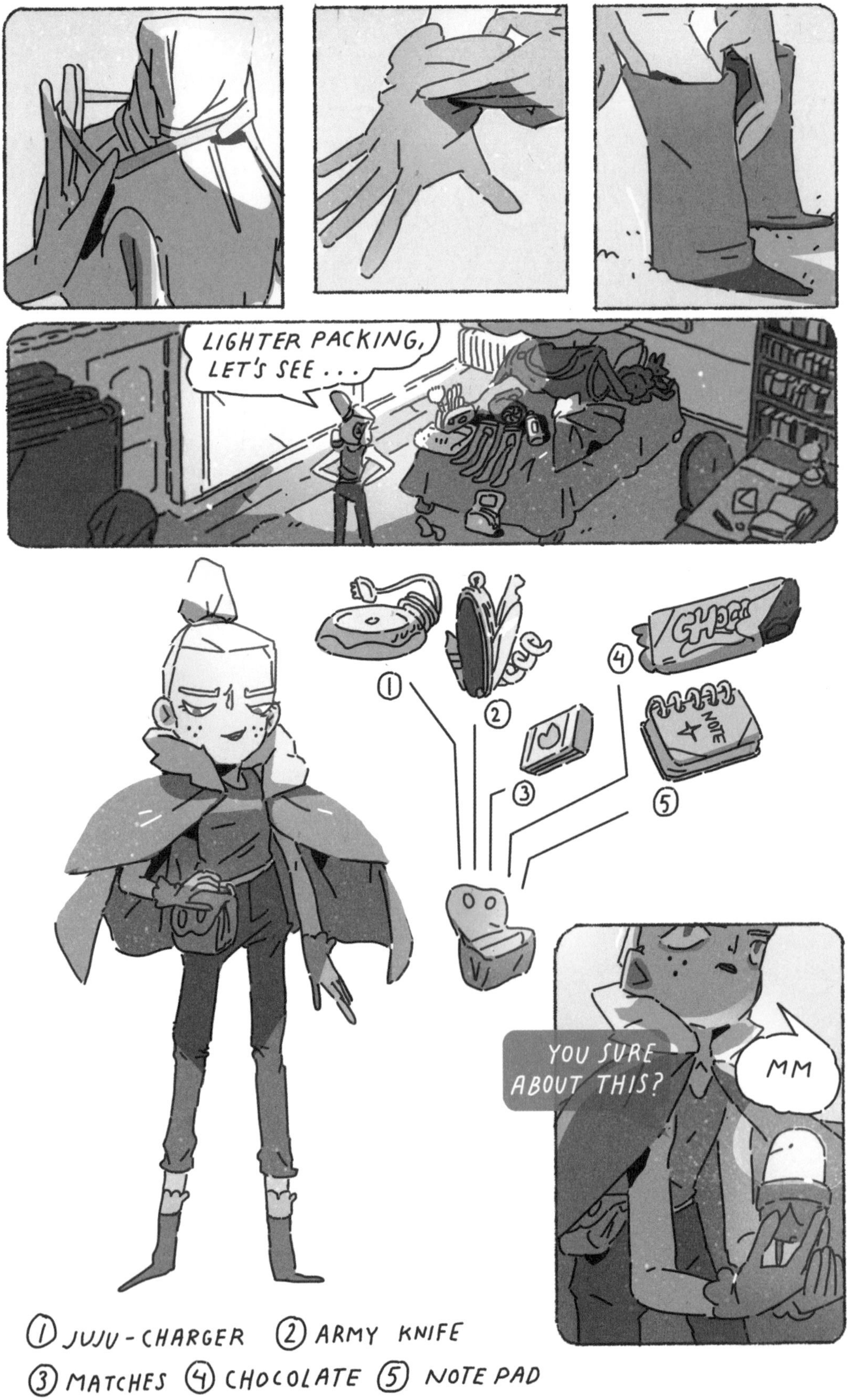

LIGHTER PACKING, LET'S SEE . . .
1
2
3
4
5
YOU SURE ABOUT THIS?
MM
① JUJU-CHARGER ② ARMY KNIFE
③ MATCHES ④ CHOCOLATE ⑤ NOTE PAD

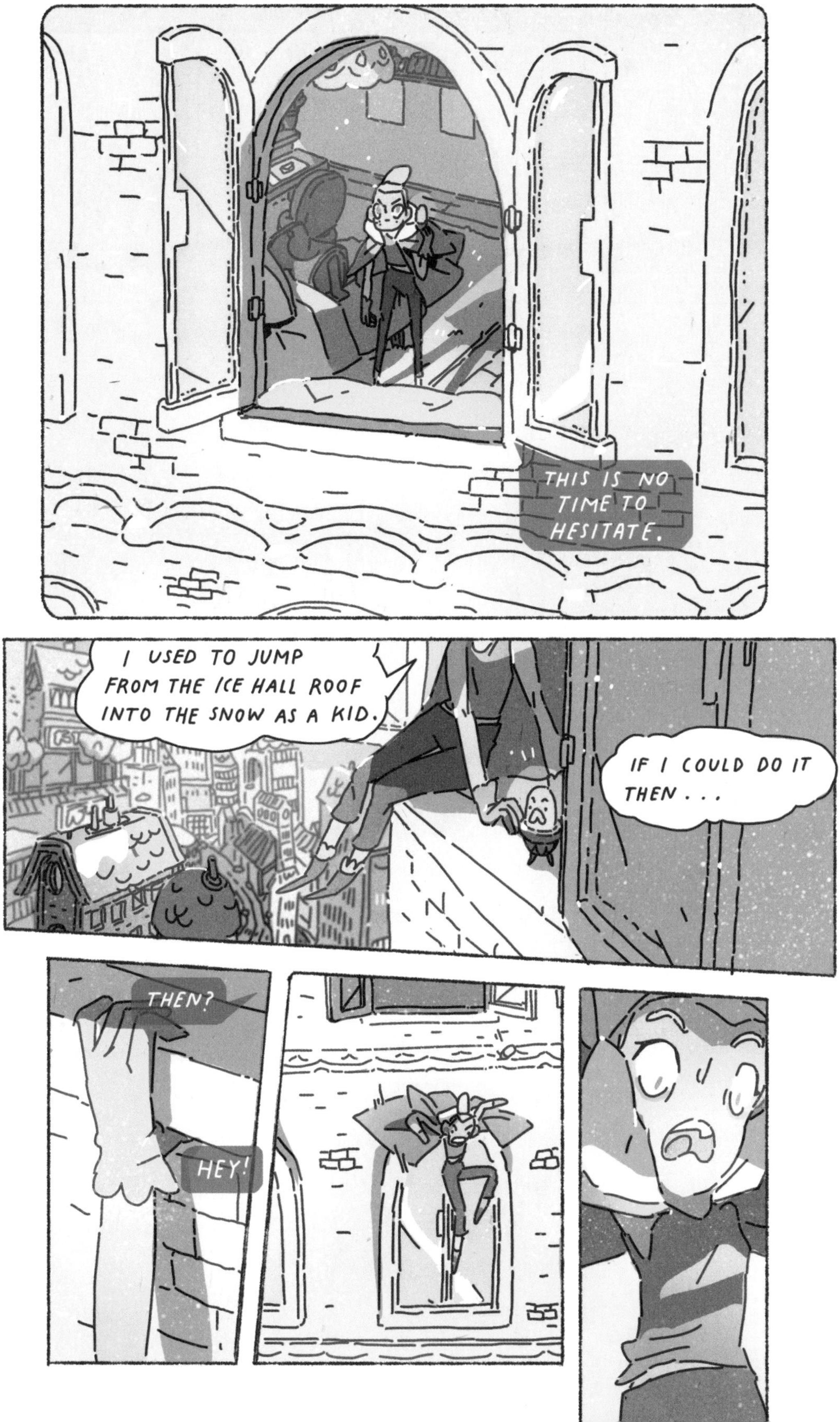
THIS IS NO TIME TO HESITATE.
I USED TO JUMP FROM THE ICE HALL ROOF INTO THE SNOW AS A KID.
IF I COULD DO IT THEN . . .
THEN?
HEY!

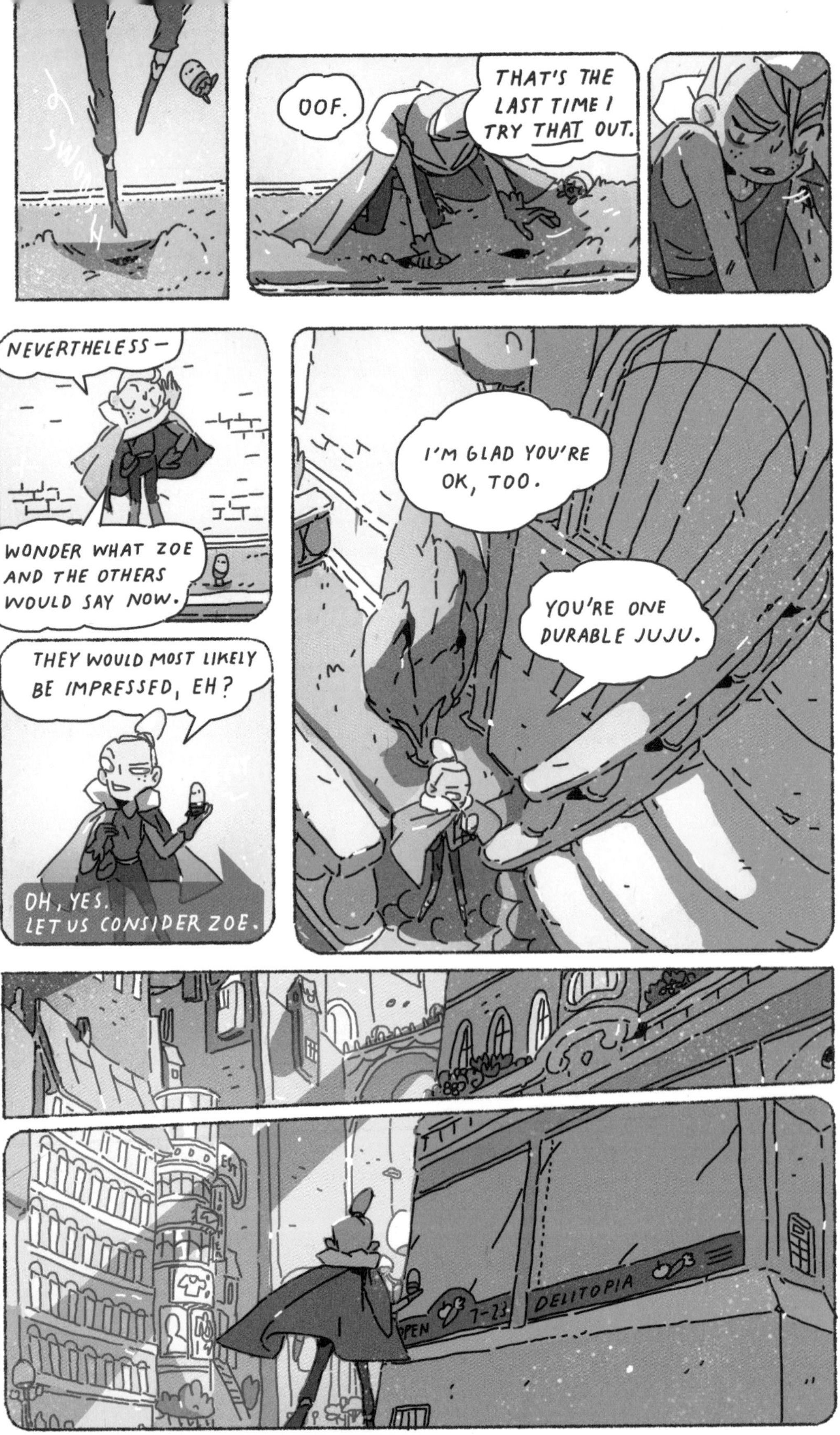
SWOOSH
OOF.
THAT'S THE LAST TIME I TRY THAT OUT.
NEVERTHELESS—
WONDER WHAT ZOE AND THE OTHERS WOULD SAY NOW.
THEY WOULD MOST LIKELY BE IMPRESSED, EH?
OH, YES. LET US CONSIDER ZOE.
I'M GLAD YOU'RE OK, TOO.
YOU'RE ONE DURABLE JUJU.
OPEN 7-23
DELITOPIA

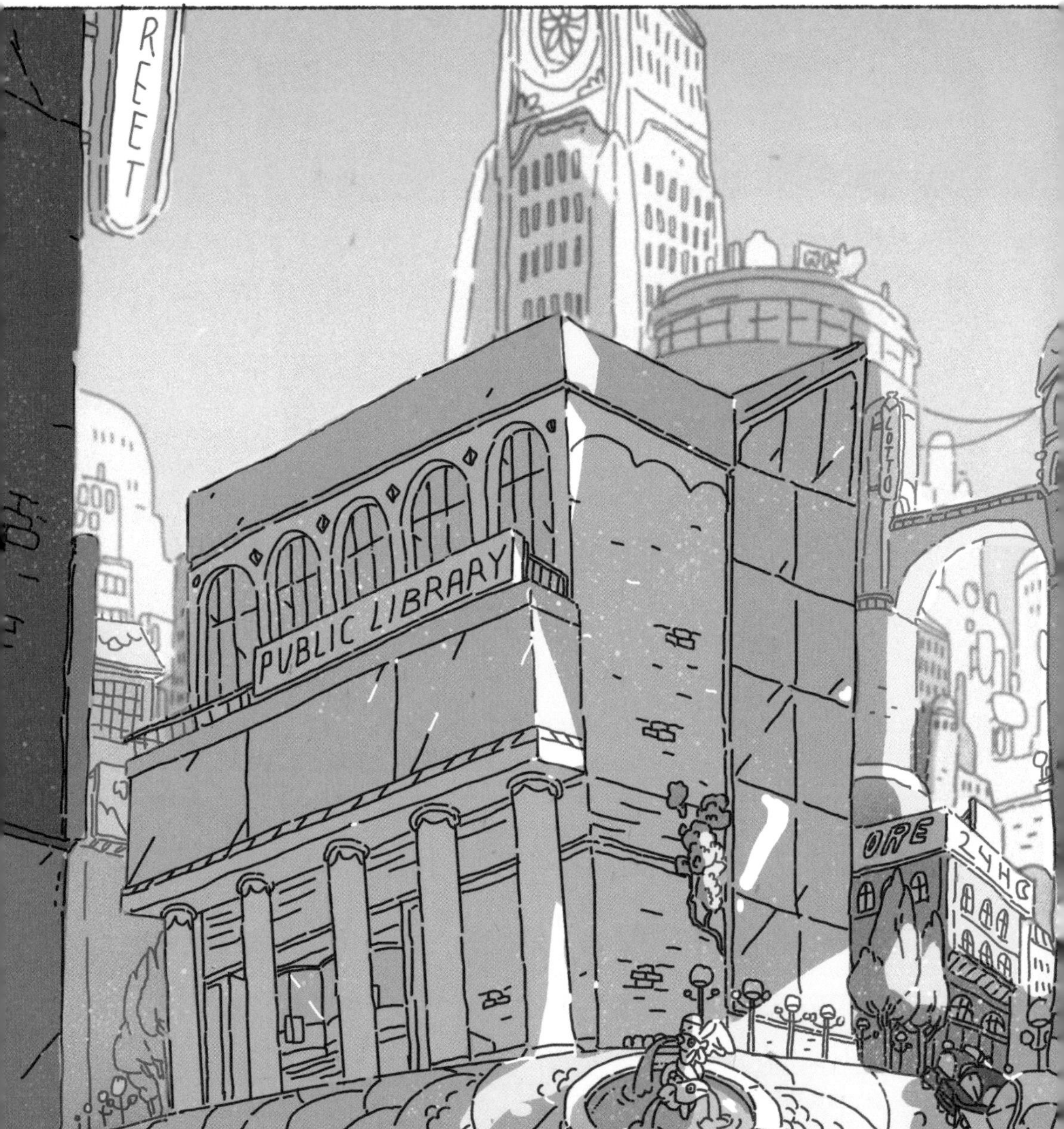
REET
PUBLIC LIBRARY
LOTTO
ORE
24HO

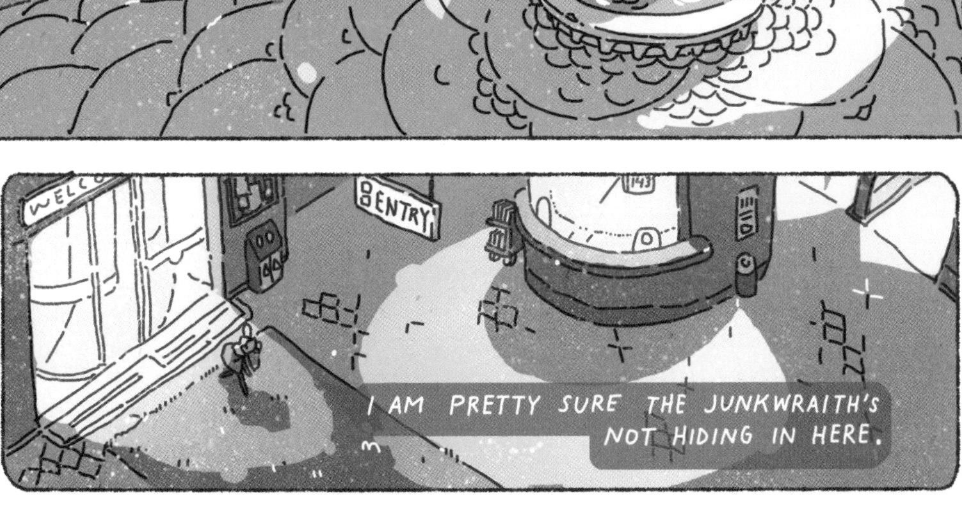
ENTRY
I AM PRETTY SURE THE JUNKWRAITH'S NOT HIDING IN HERE.

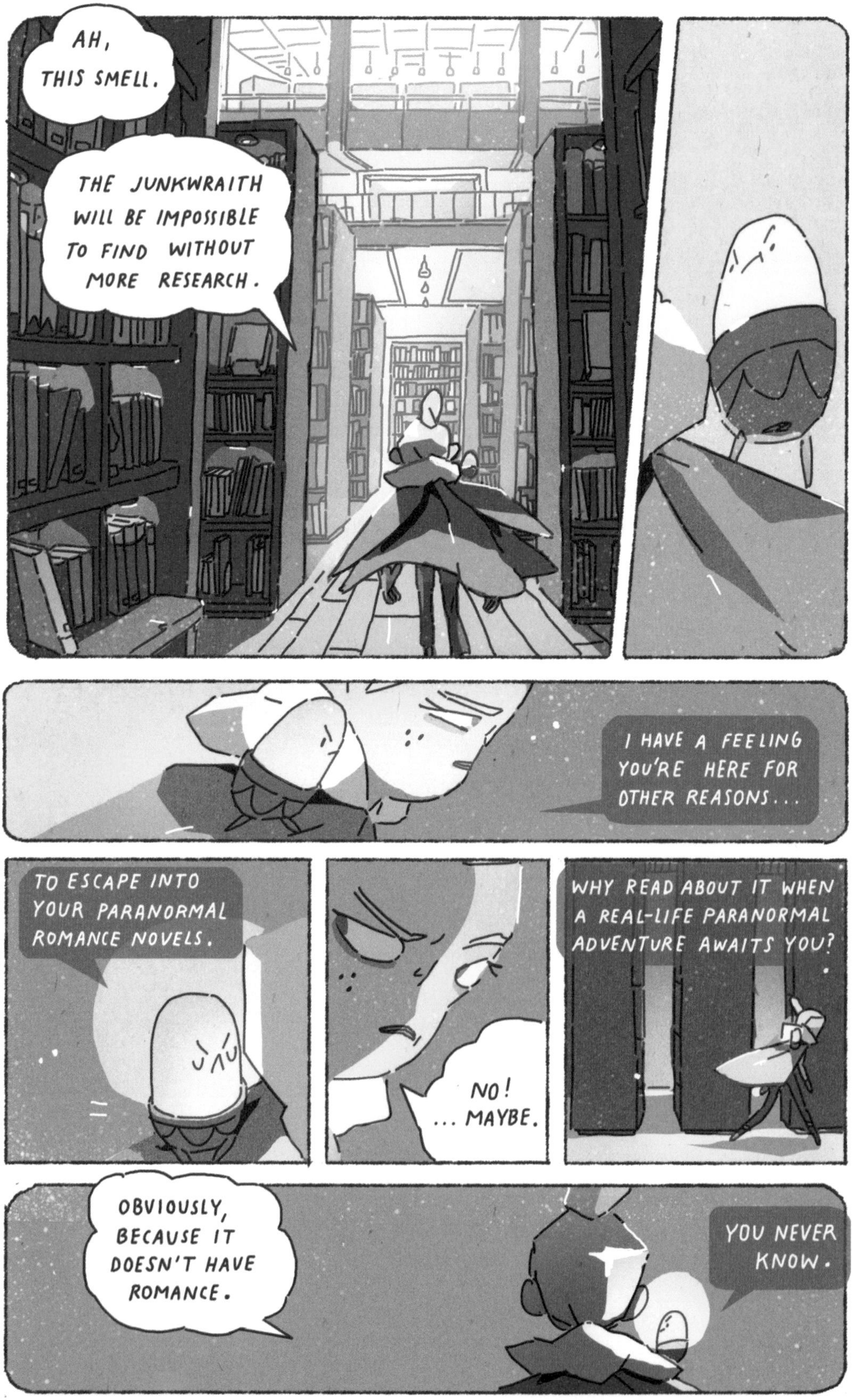
AH, THIS SMELL.
THE JUNKWRAITH WILL BE IMPOSSIBLE TO FIND WITHOUT MORE RESEARCH.
I HAVE A FEELING YOU'RE HERE FOR OTHER REASONS...
TO ESCAPE INTO YOUR PARANORMAL ROMANCE NOVELS.
NO! ... MAYBE.
WHY READ ABOUT IT WHEN A REAL-LIFE PARANORMAL ADVENTURE AWAITS YOU?
OBVIOUSLY, BECAUSE IT DOESN'T HAVE ROMANCE.
YOU NEVER KNOW.

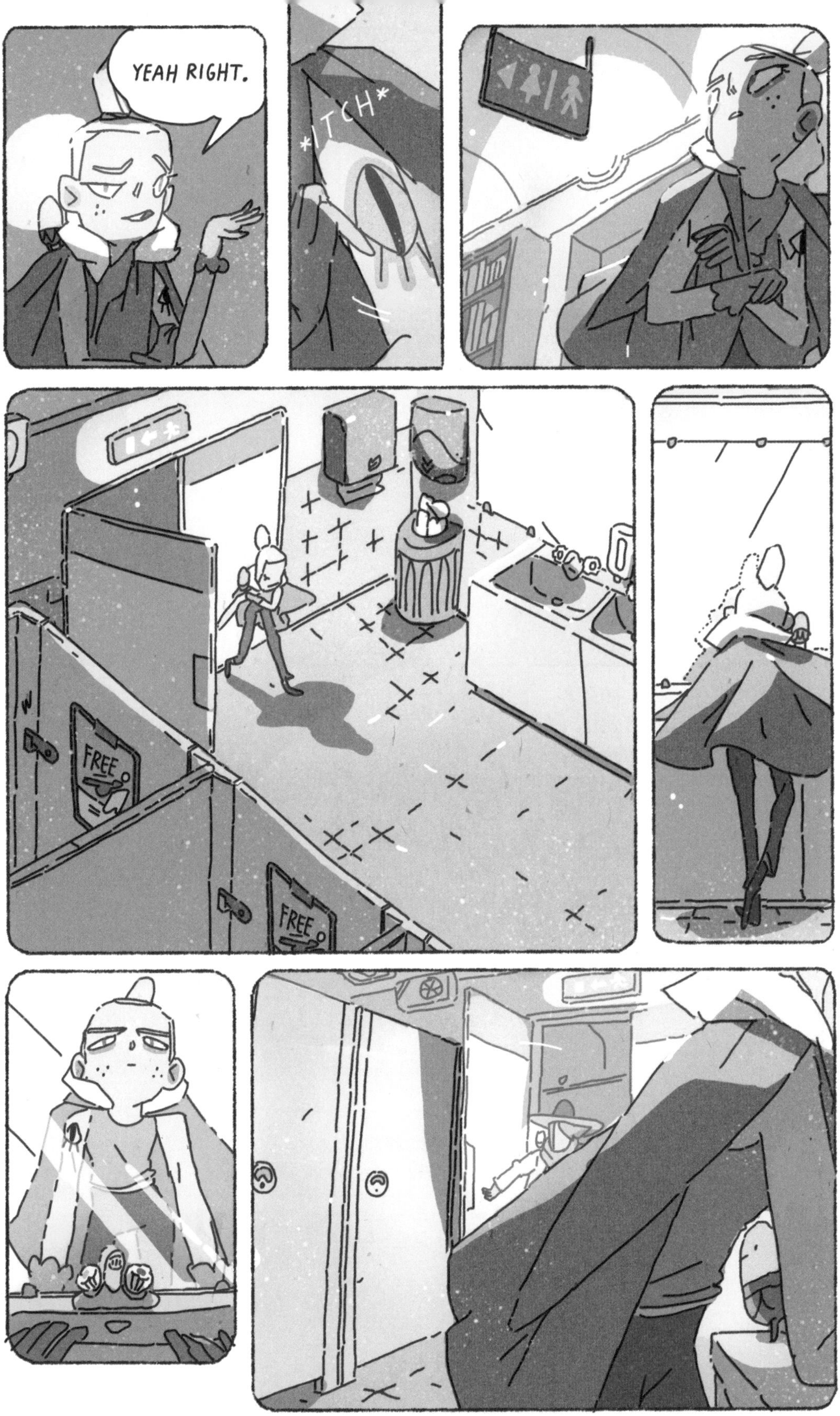
YEAH RIGHT.
ITCH
FREE
FREE

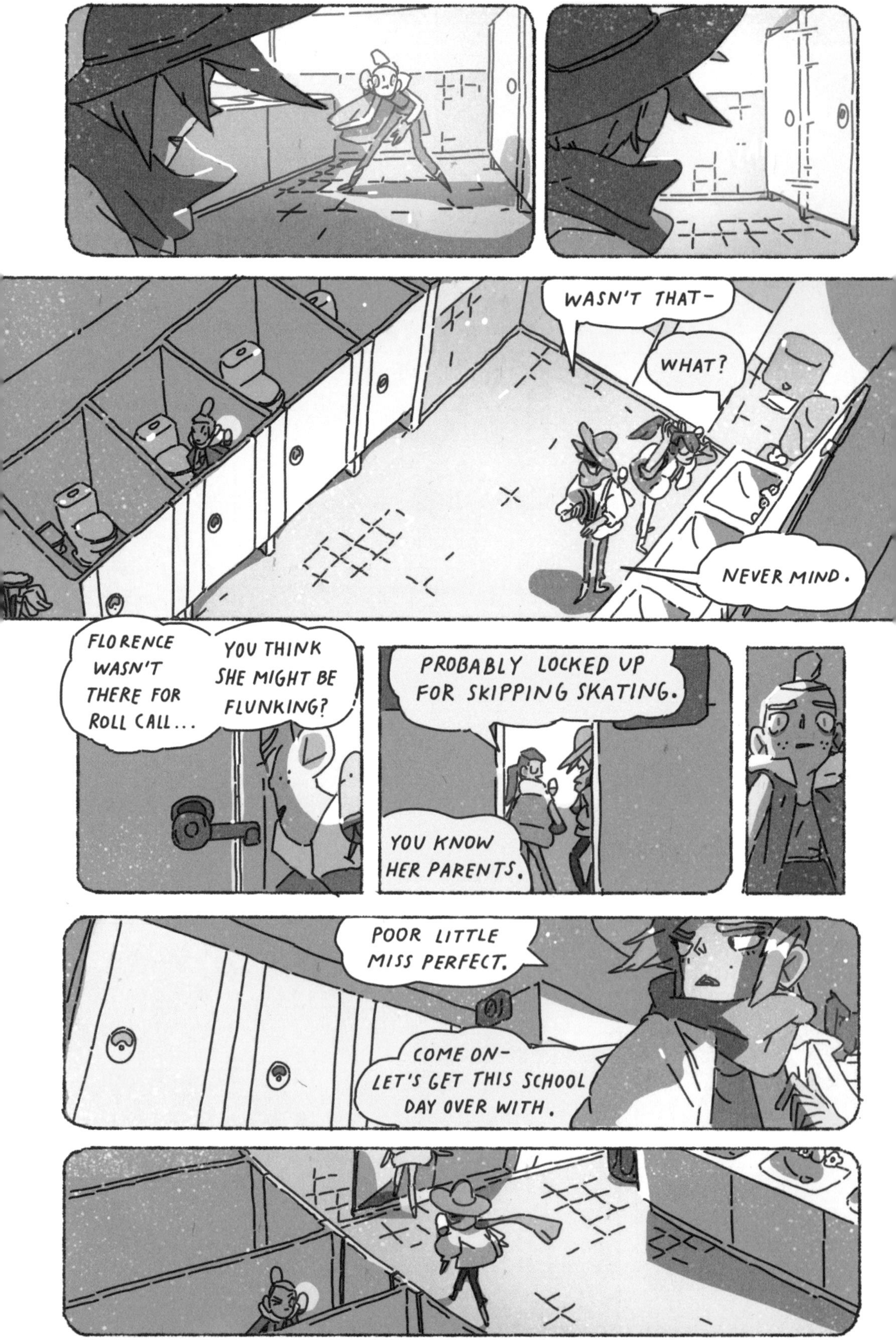
WASN'T THAT-
WHAT?
NEVER MIND.
FLORENCE WASN'T THERE FOR ROLL CALL...
YOU THINK SHE MIGHT BE FLUNKING?
PROBABLY LOCKED UP FOR SKIPPING SKATING.
YOU KNOW HER PARENTS.
POOR LITTLE MISS PERFECT.
COME ON- LET'S GET THIS SCHOOL DAY OVER WITH.

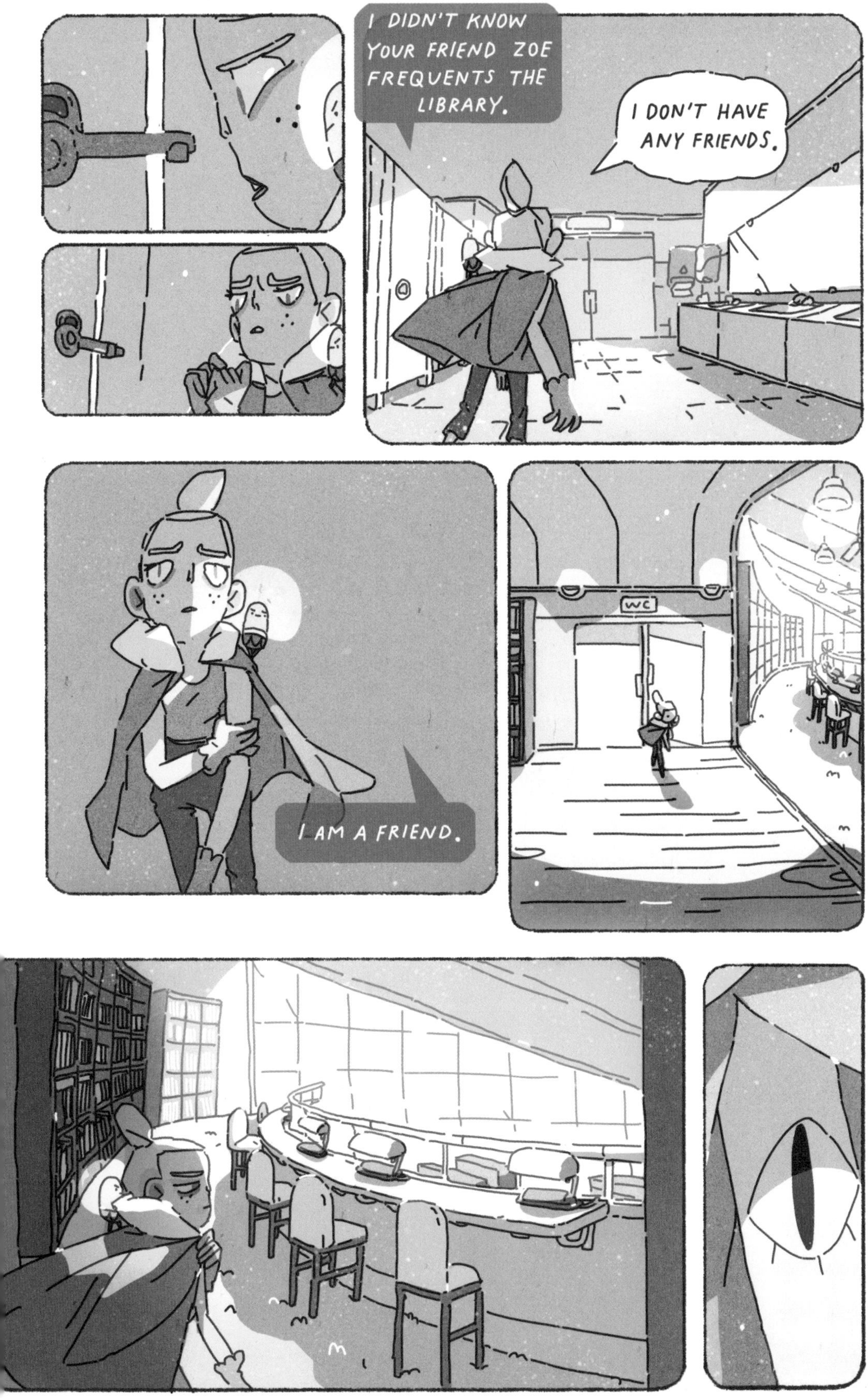
I DIDN'T KNOW YOUR FRIEND ZOE FREQUENTS THE LIBRARY.
I DON'T HAVE ANY FRIENDS.
I AM A FRIEND.
WC

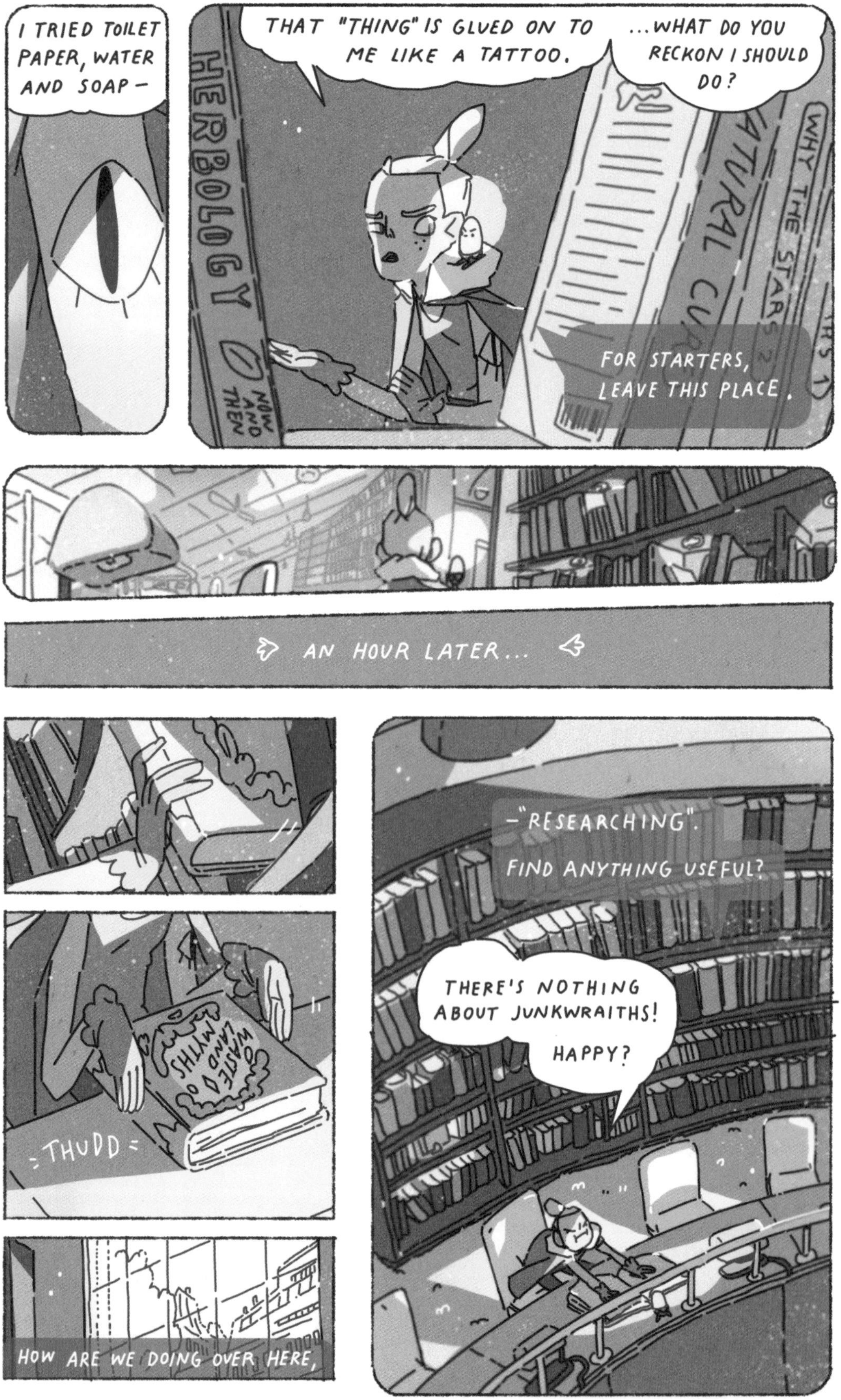
I TRIED TOILET PAPER, WATER AND SOAP—
THAT "THING" IS GLUED ON TO ME LIKE A TATTOO.
...WHAT DO YOU RECKON I SHOULD DO?
HERBOLOGY
NOW AND THEN
WHY THE STARS
FOR STARTERS, LEAVE THIS PLACE.
AN HOUR LATER...
WASTE LAND MYTHS
THUDD
HOW ARE WE DOING OVER HERE,
—"RESEARCHING".
FIND ANYTHING USEFUL?
THERE'S NOTHING ABOUT JUNKWRAITHS!
HAPPY?

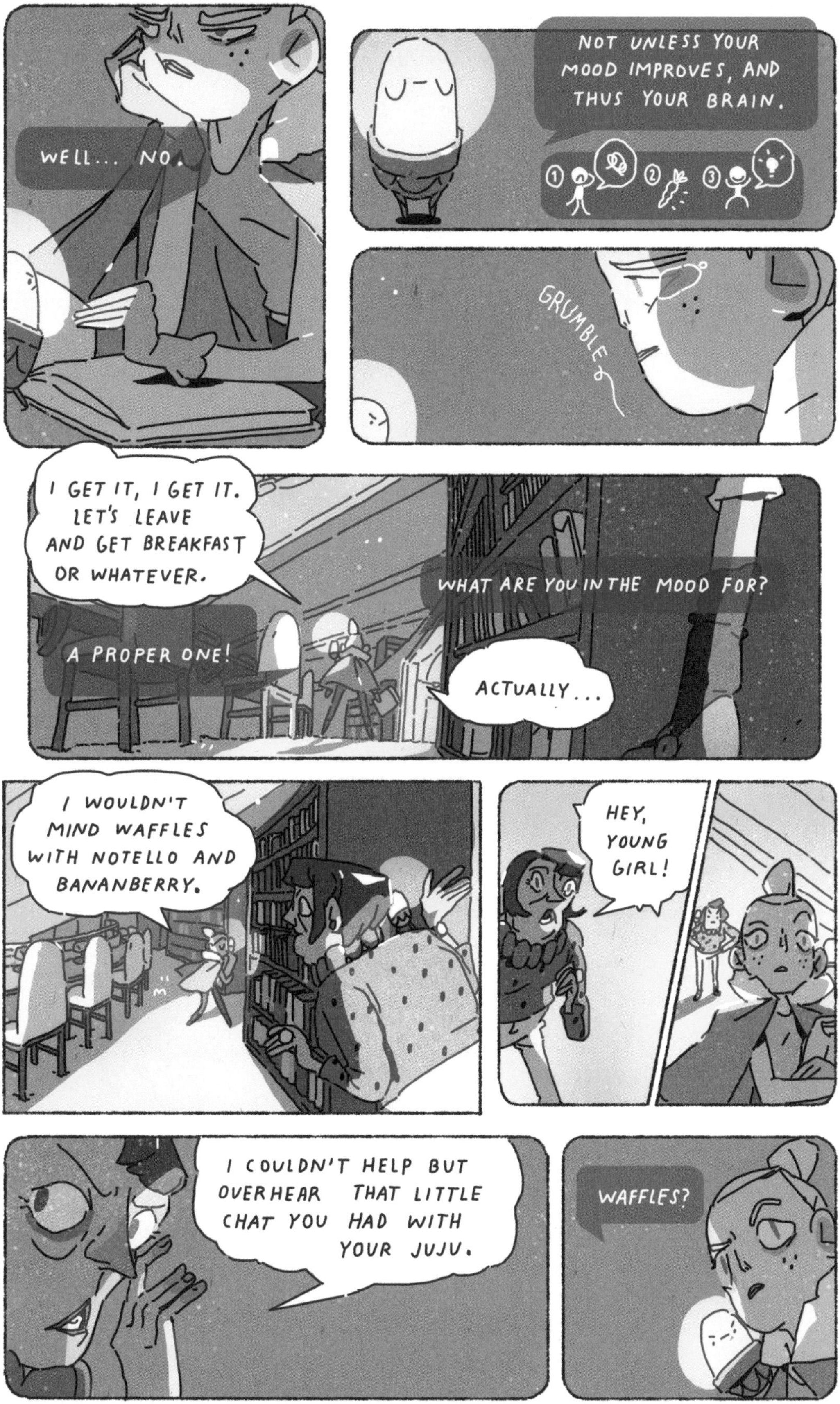
WELL... NO.
NOT UNLESS YOUR MOOD IMPROVES, AND THUS YOUR BRAIN.
1
2
3
GRUMBLE
I GET IT, I GET IT. LET'S LEAVE AND GET BREAKFAST OR WHATEVER.
A PROPER ONE!
WHAT ARE YOU IN THE MOOD FOR?
ACTUALLY...
I WOULDN'T MIND WAFFLES WITH NOTELLO AND BANANBERRY.
HEY, YOUNG GIRL!
I COULDN'T HELP BUT OVERHEAR THAT LITTLE CHAT YOU HAD WITH YOUR JUJU.
WAFFLES?

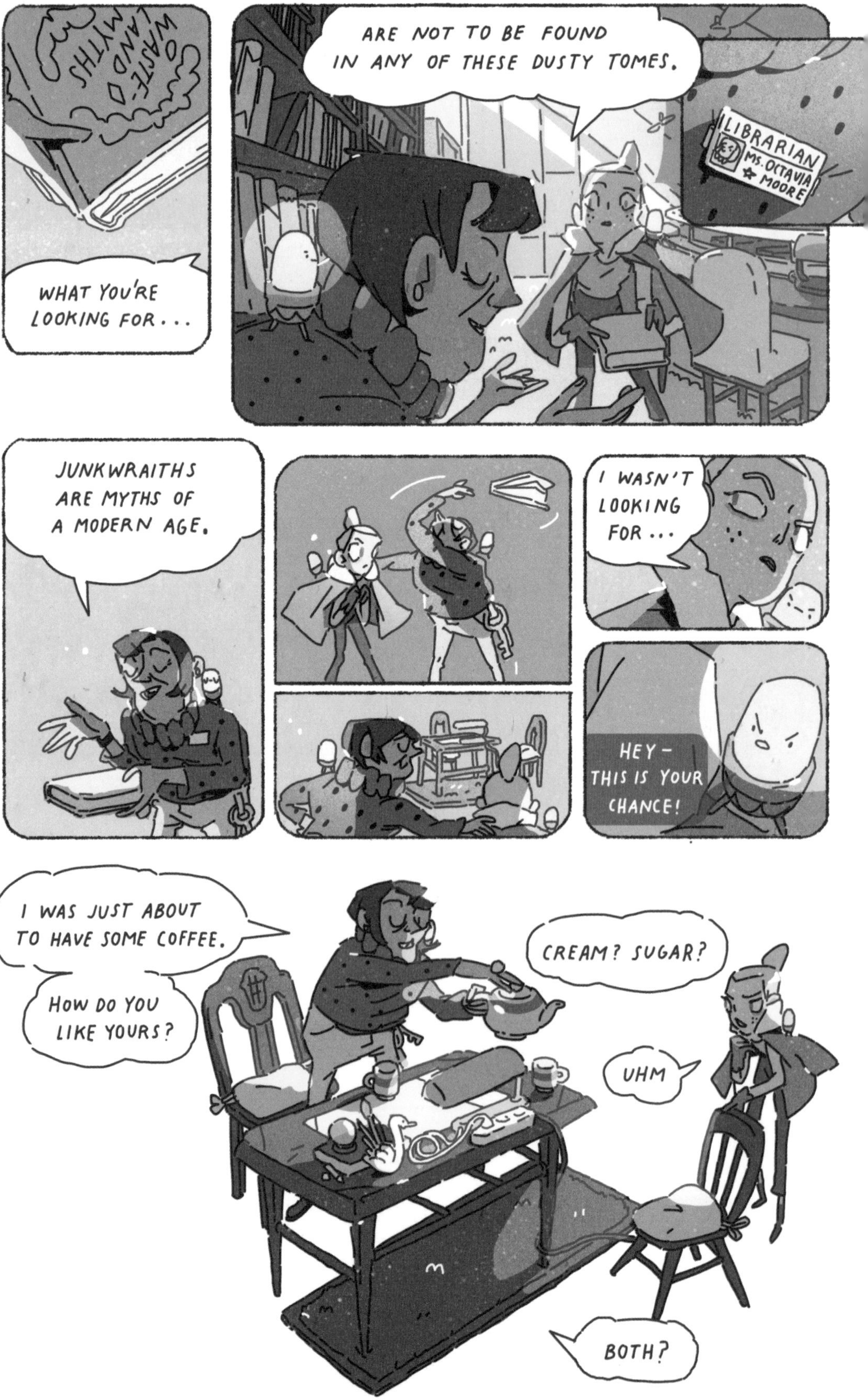

WASTE-LAND MYTHS
WHAT YOU'RE LOOKING FOR...
ARE NOT TO BE FOUND IN ANY OF THESE DUSTY TOMES.
LIBRARIAN MS. OCTAVIA MOORE
JUNKWRAITHS ARE MYTHS OF A MODERN AGE.
I WASN'T LOOKING FOR...
HEY - THIS IS YOUR CHANCE!
I WAS JUST ABOUT TO HAVE SOME COFFEE.
HOW DO YOU LIKE YOURS?
CREAM? SUGAR?
UHM
BOTH?

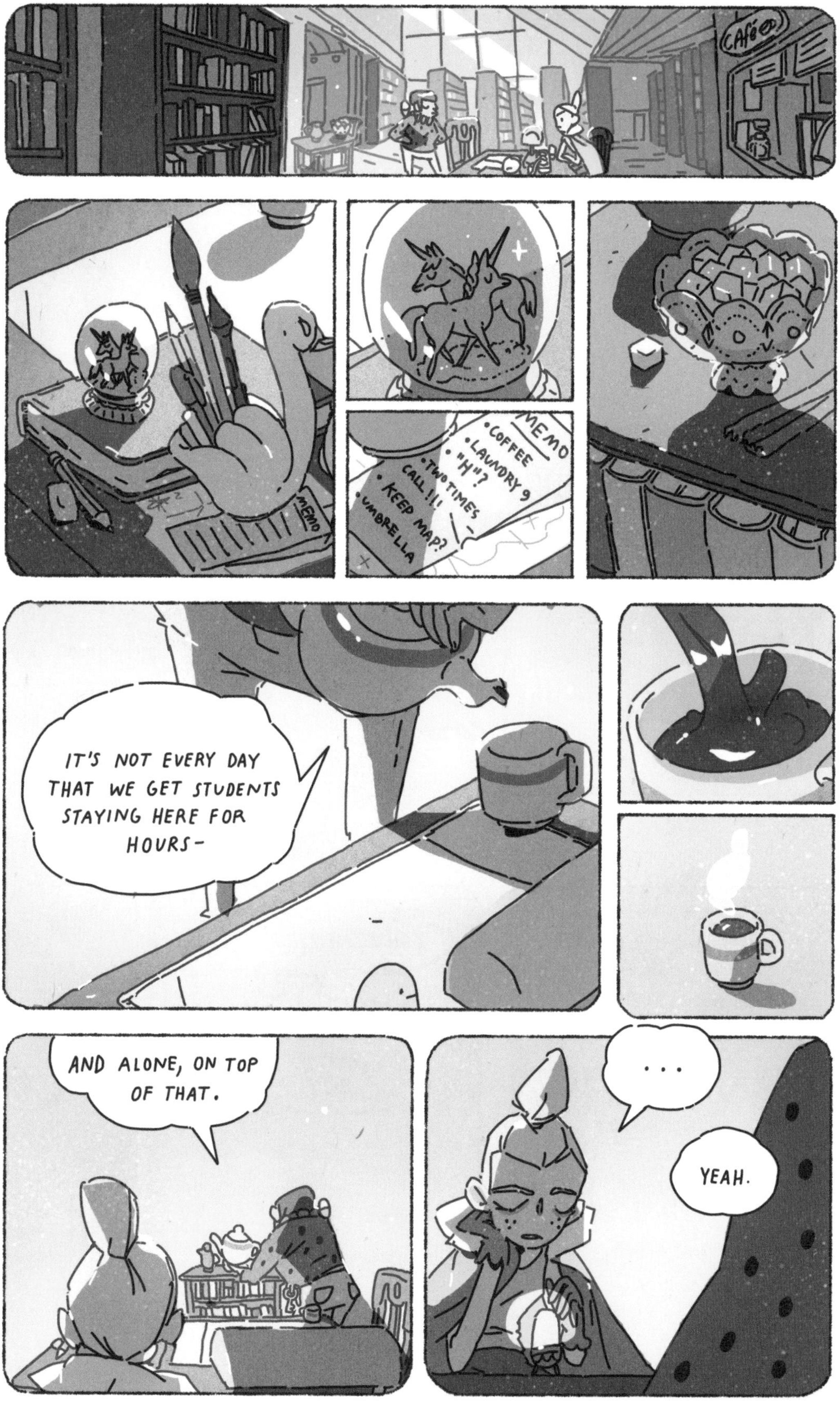
CAFé
MEMO
MEMO
• COFFEE
• LAUNDRY 9
• "H"?
• TWO TIMES
CALL !!!
• KEEP MAP?
• UMBRELLA
IT'S NOT EVERY DAY THAT WE GET STUDENTS STAYING HERE FOR HOURS-
AND ALONE, ON TOP OF THAT.
...
YEAH.

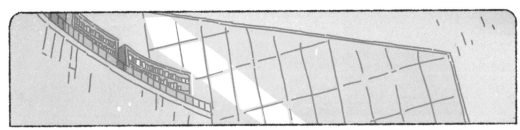

HERE.

A CHARGER! THANKS

2%

DON'T MENTION IT.

YOU BETTER TAKE CARE OF THAT JUJU.

3%

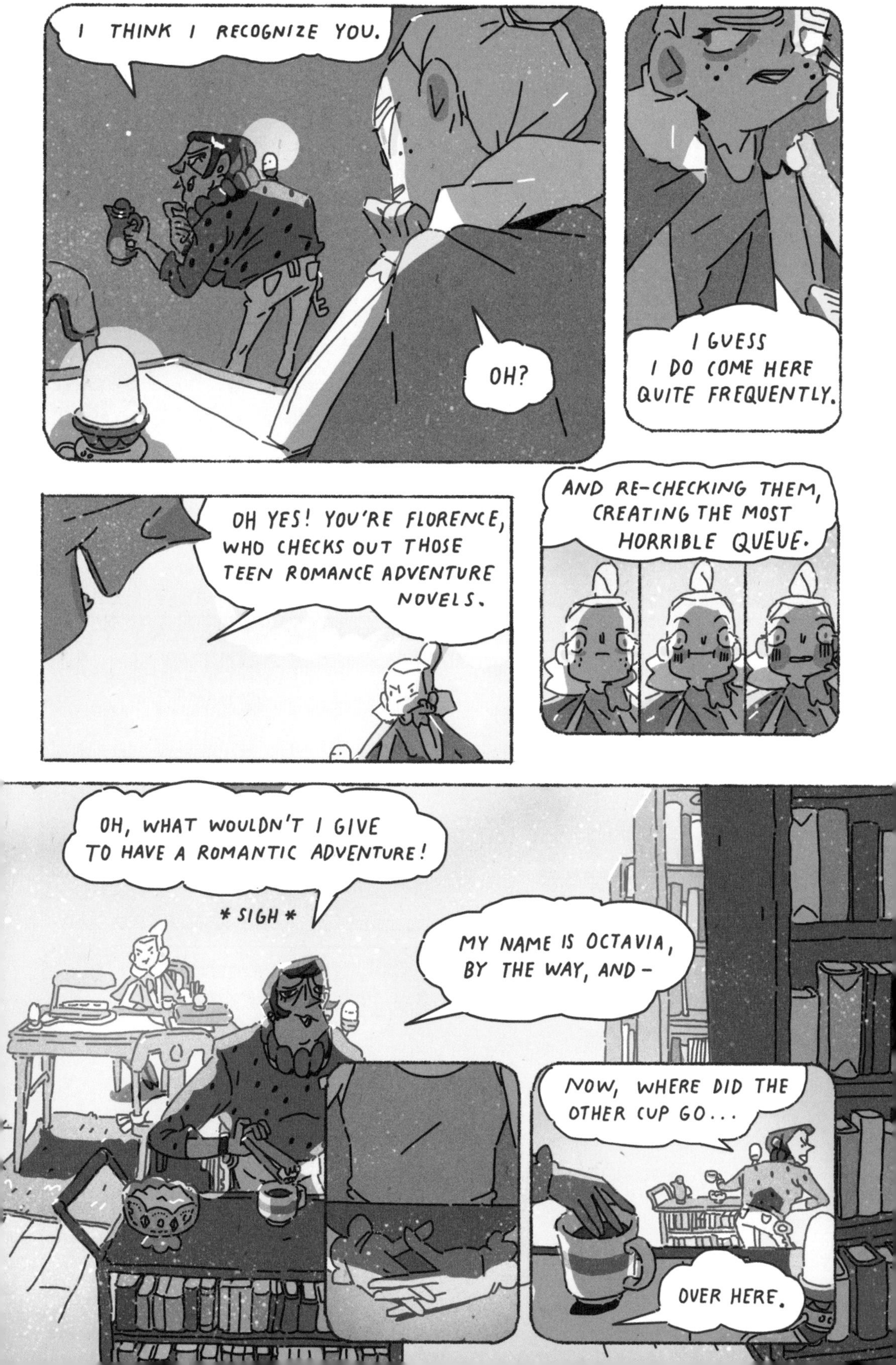
I THINK I RECOGNIZE YOU.
OH?
I GUESS I DO COME HERE QUITE FREQUENTLY.
OH YES! YOU'RE FLORENCE, WHO CHECKS OUT THOSE TEEN ROMANCE ADVENTURE NOVELS.
AND RE-CHECKING THEM, CREATING THE MOST HORRIBLE QUEUE.
OH, WHAT WOULDN'T I GIVE TO HAVE A ROMANTIC ADVENTURE!
SIGH
MY NAME IS OCTAVIA, BY THE WAY, AND–
NOW, WHERE DID THE OTHER CUP GO...
OVER HERE.

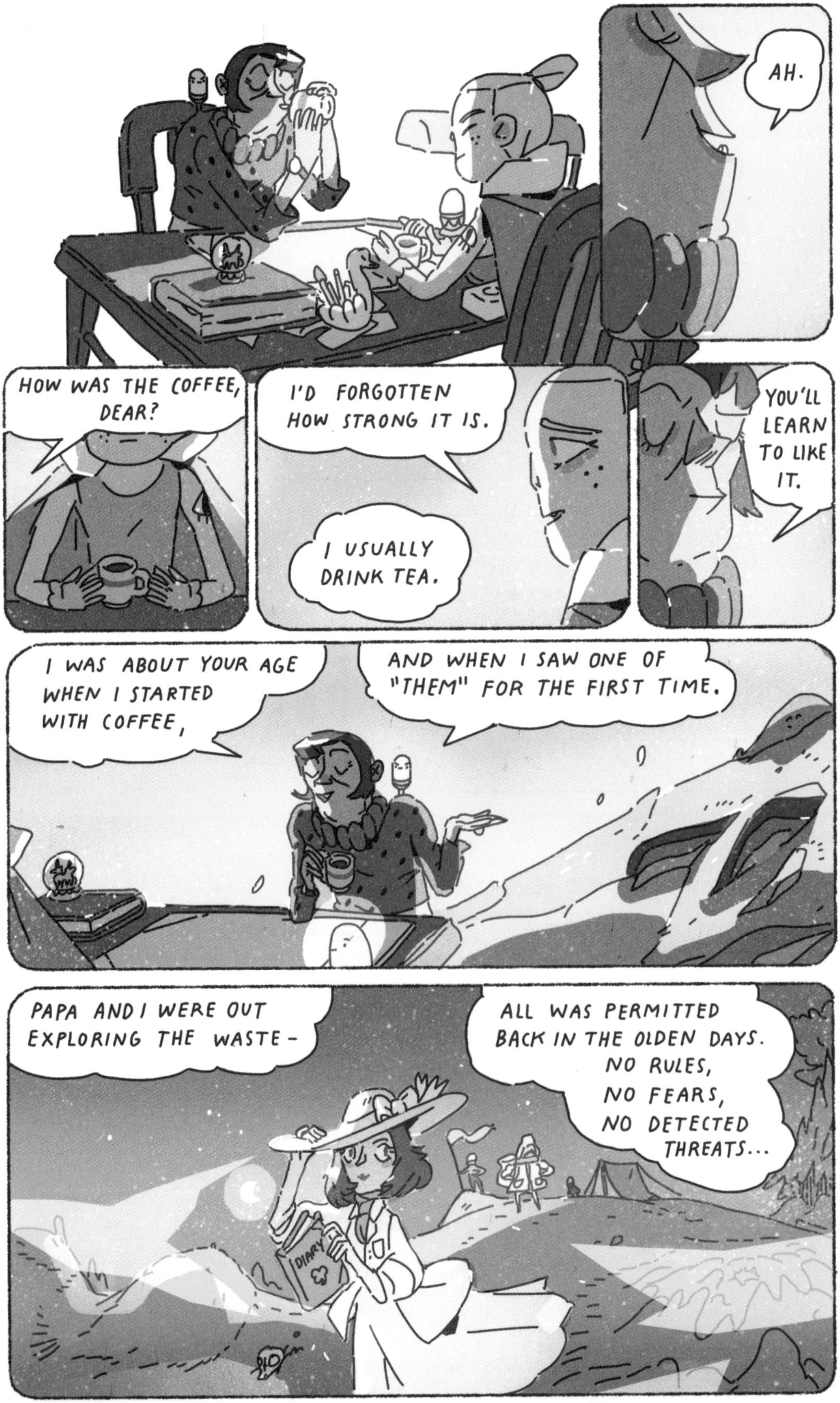
AH.
HOW WAS THE COFFEE, DEAR?
I'D FORGOTTEN HOW STRONG IT IS.
I USUALLY DRINK TEA.
YOU'LL LEARN TO LIKE IT.
I WAS ABOUT YOUR AGE WHEN I STARTED WITH COFFEE,
AND WHEN I SAW ONE OF "THEM" FOR THE FIRST TIME.
PAPA AND I WERE OUT EXPLORING THE WASTE-
ALL WAS PERMITTED BACK IN THE OLDEN DAYS.
NO RULES,
NO FEARS,
NO DETECTED THREATS...
DIARY

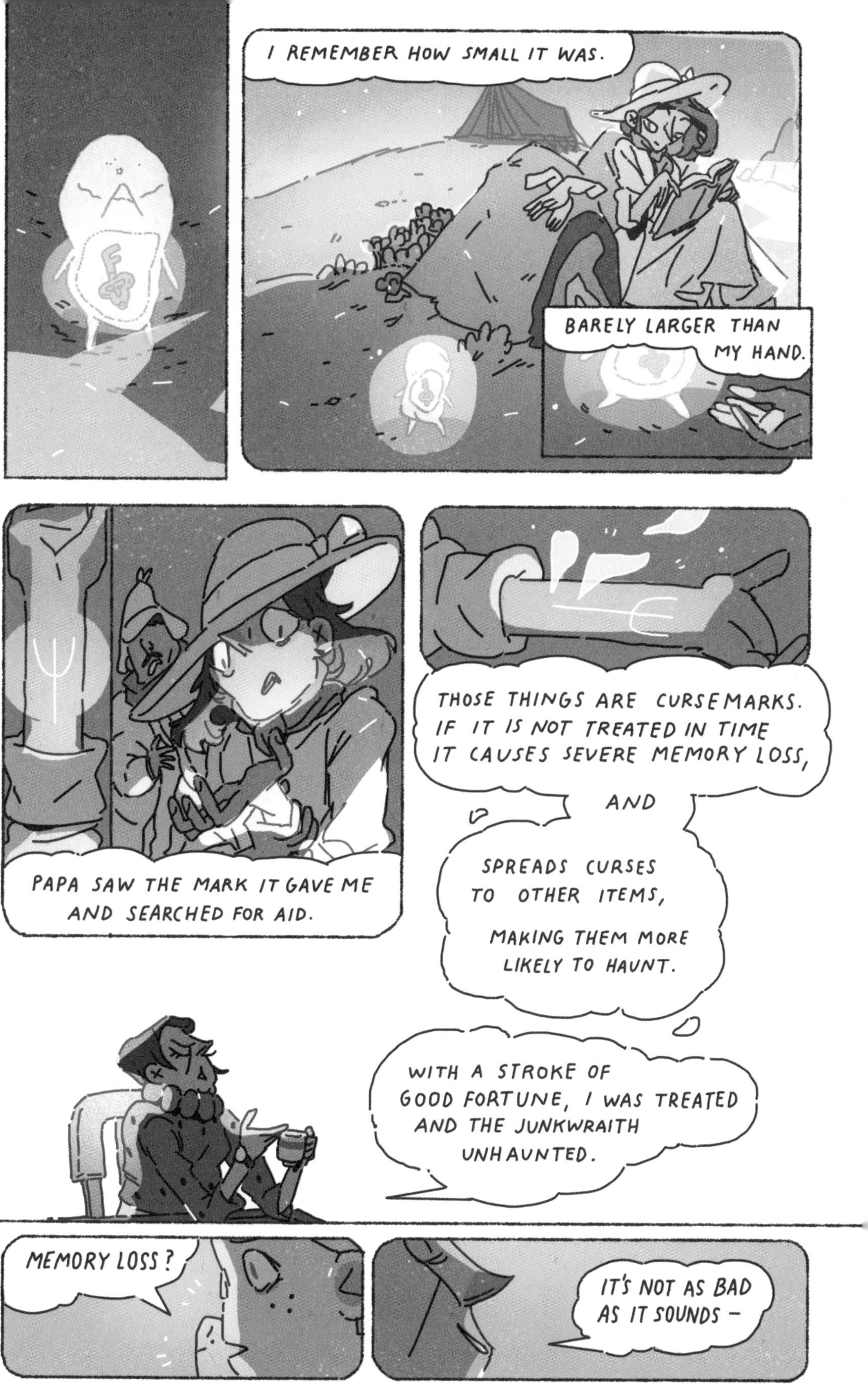
I REMEMBER HOW SMALL IT WAS.
BARELY LARGER THAN MY HAND.
PAPA SAW THE MARK IT GAVE ME AND SEARCHED FOR AID.
THOSE THINGS ARE CURSEMARKS. IF IT IS NOT TREATED IN TIME IT CAUSES SEVERE MEMORY LOSS,
AND
SPREADS CURSES TO OTHER ITEMS,
MAKING THEM MORE LIKELY TO HAUNT.
WITH A STROKE OF GOOD FORTUNE, I WAS TREATED AND THE JUNKWRAITH UNHAUNTED.
MEMORY LOSS?
IT'S NOT AS BAD AS IT SOUNDS –

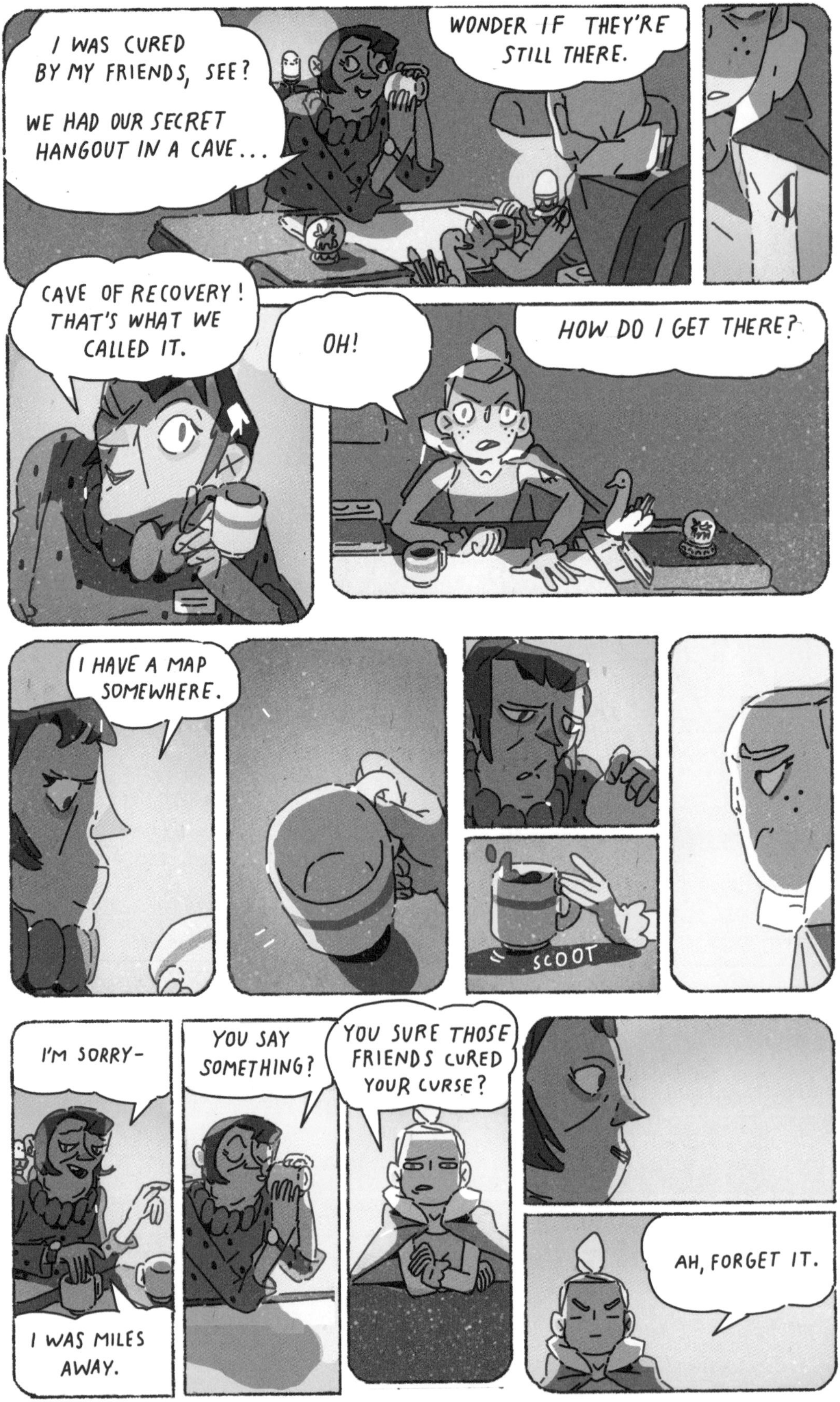
I WAS CURED BY MY FRIENDS, SEE?
WE HAD OUR SECRET HANGOUT IN A CAVE...
WONDER IF THEY'RE STILL THERE.
CAVE OF RECOVERY! THAT'S WHAT WE CALLED IT.
OH!
HOW DO I GET THERE?
I HAVE A MAP SOMEWHERE.
SCOOT
I'M SORRY-
I WAS MILES AWAY.
YOU SAY SOMETHING?
YOU SURE THOSE FRIENDS CURED YOUR CURSE?
AH, FORGET IT.

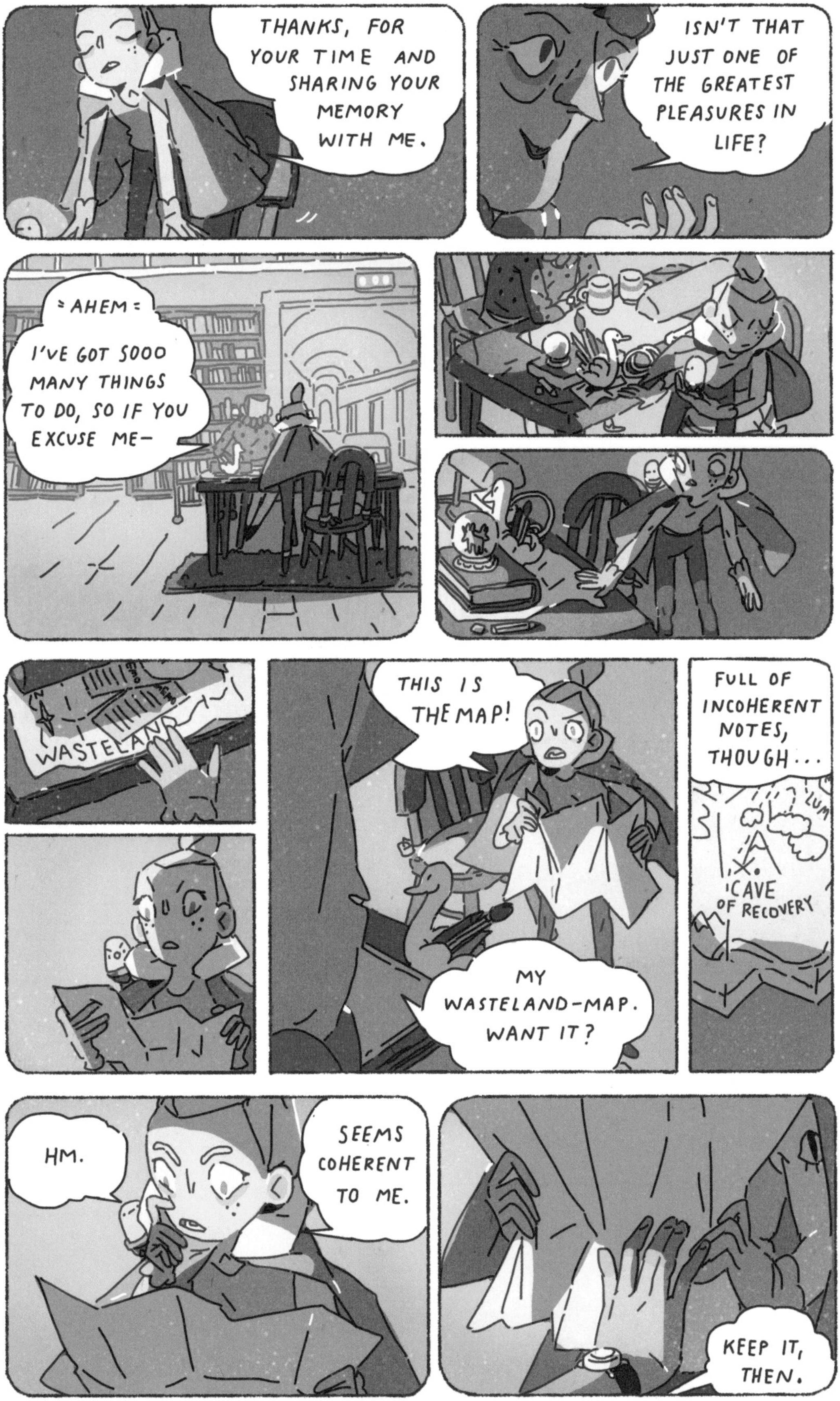
THANKS, FOR YOUR TIME AND SHARING YOUR MEMORY WITH ME.
ISN'T THAT JUST ONE OF THE GREATEST PLEASURES IN LIFE?
=AHEM=
I'VE GOT SOOO MANY THINGS TO DO, SO IF YOU EXCUSE ME—
WASTELAND
THIS IS THE MAP!
MY WASTELAND-MAP. WANT IT?
FULL OF INCOHERENT NOTES, THOUGH...
CAVE OF RECOVERY
HM.
SEEMS COHERENT TO ME.
KEEP IT, THEN.

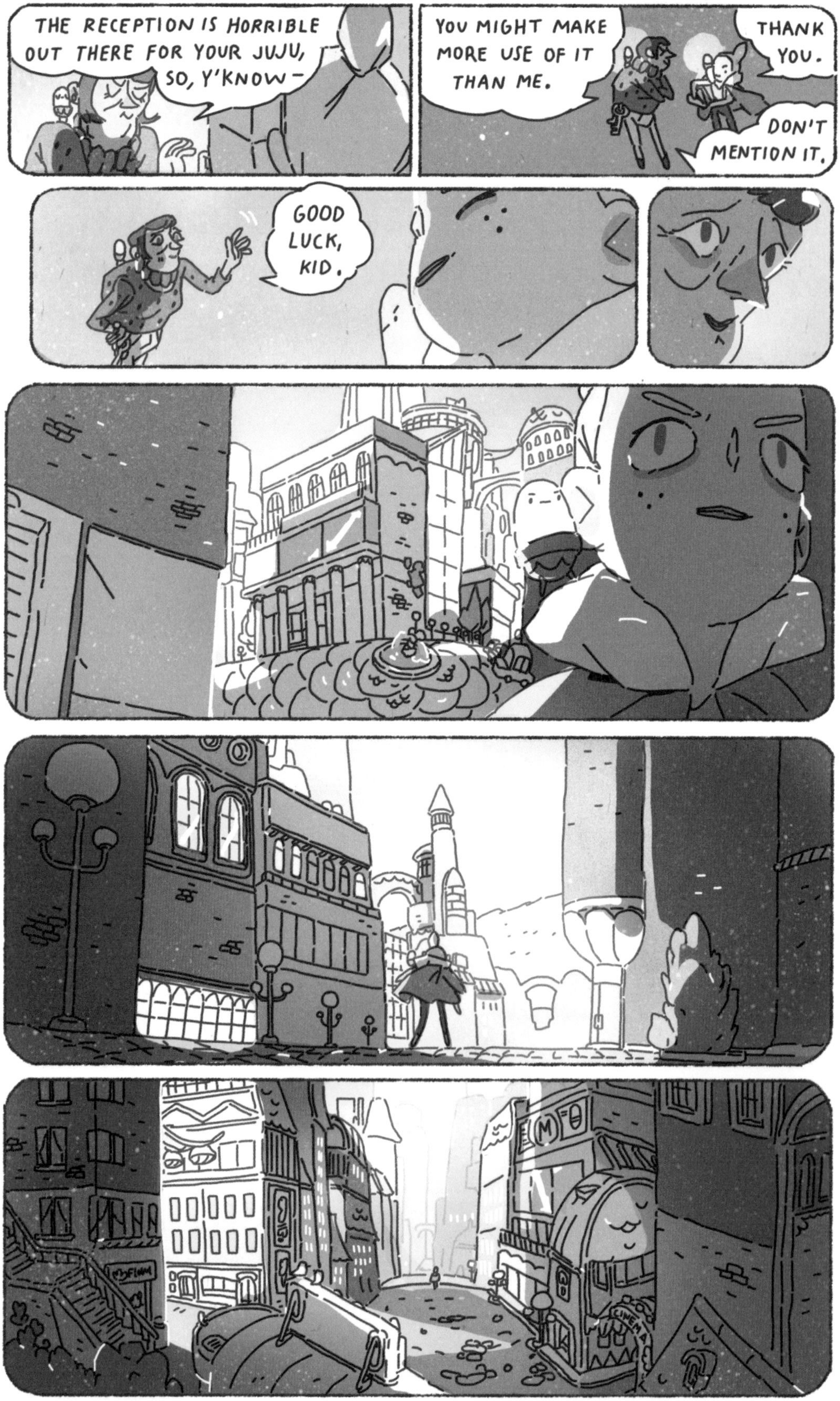
THE RECEPTION IS HORRIBLE OUT THERE FOR YOUR JUJU, SO, Y'KNOW—
YOU MIGHT MAKE MORE USE OF IT THAN ME.
THANK YOU.
DON'T MENTION IT.
GOOD LUCK, KID.
CINEMA

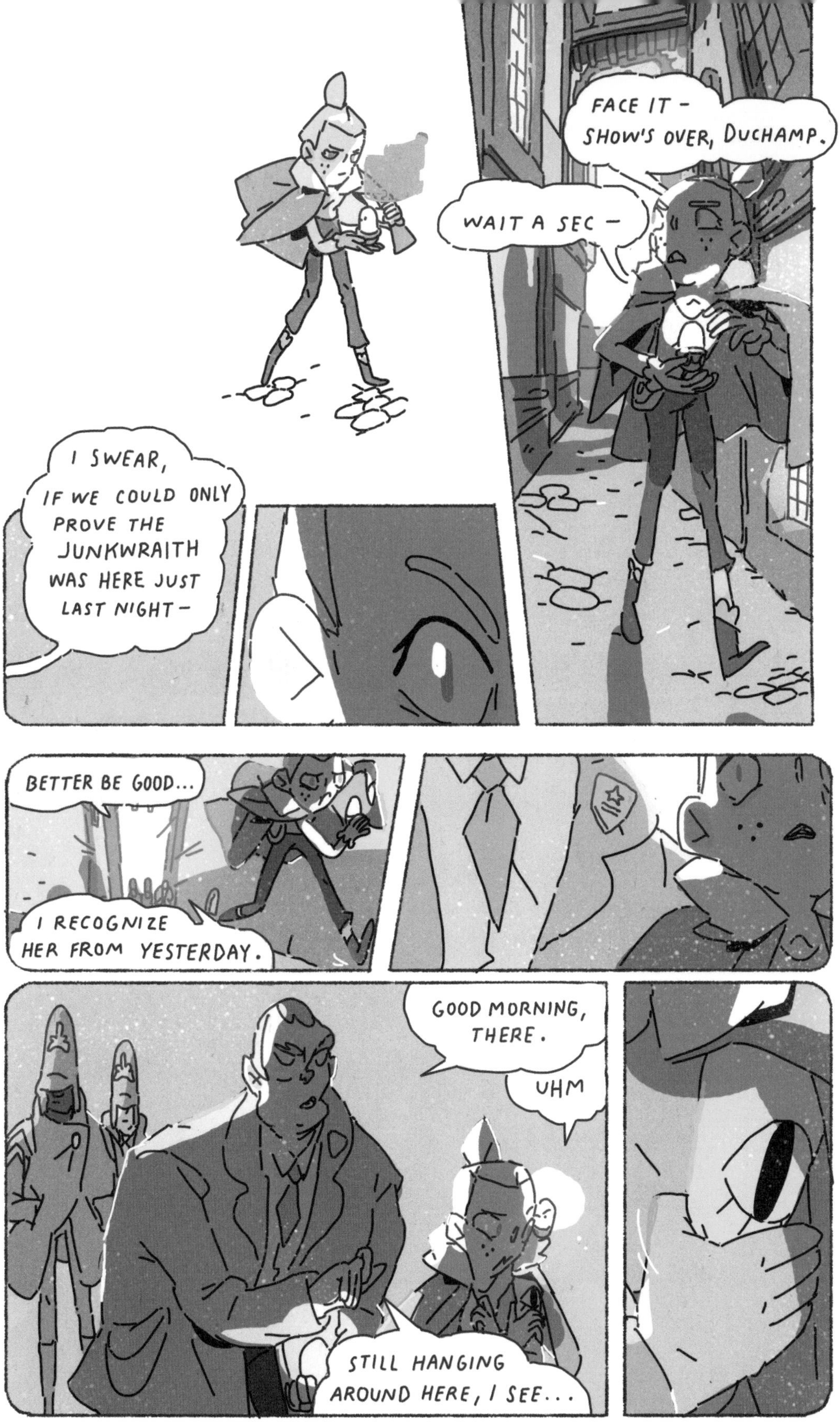

FACE IT - SHOW'S OVER, DUCHAMP.
WAIT A SEC -
I SWEAR, IF WE COULD ONLY PROVE THE JUNKWRAITH WAS HERE JUST LAST NIGHT -
BETTER BE GOOD...
I RECOGNIZE HER FROM YESTERDAY.
GOOD MORNING, THERE.
UHM
STILL HANGING AROUND HERE, I SEE...

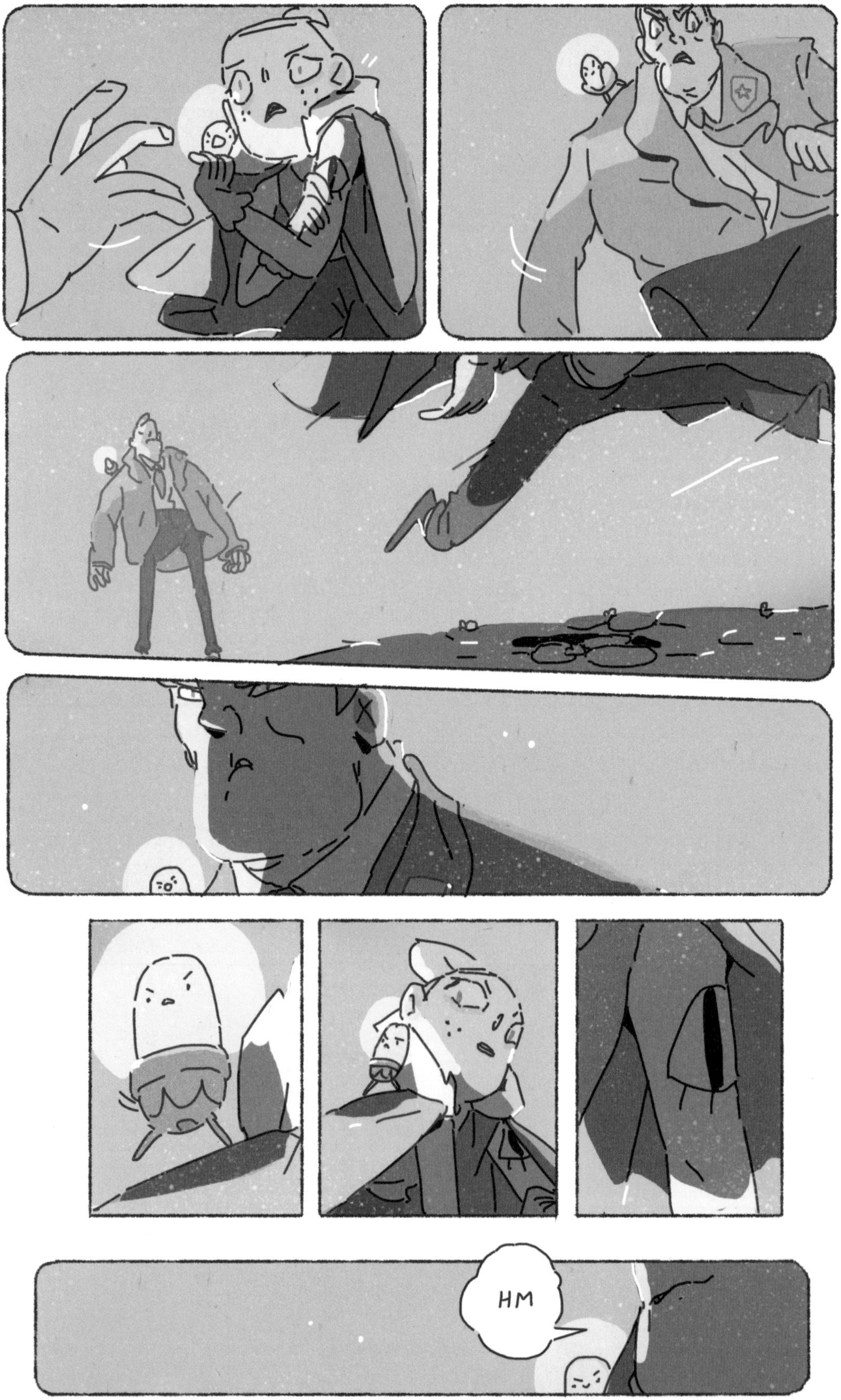
HM

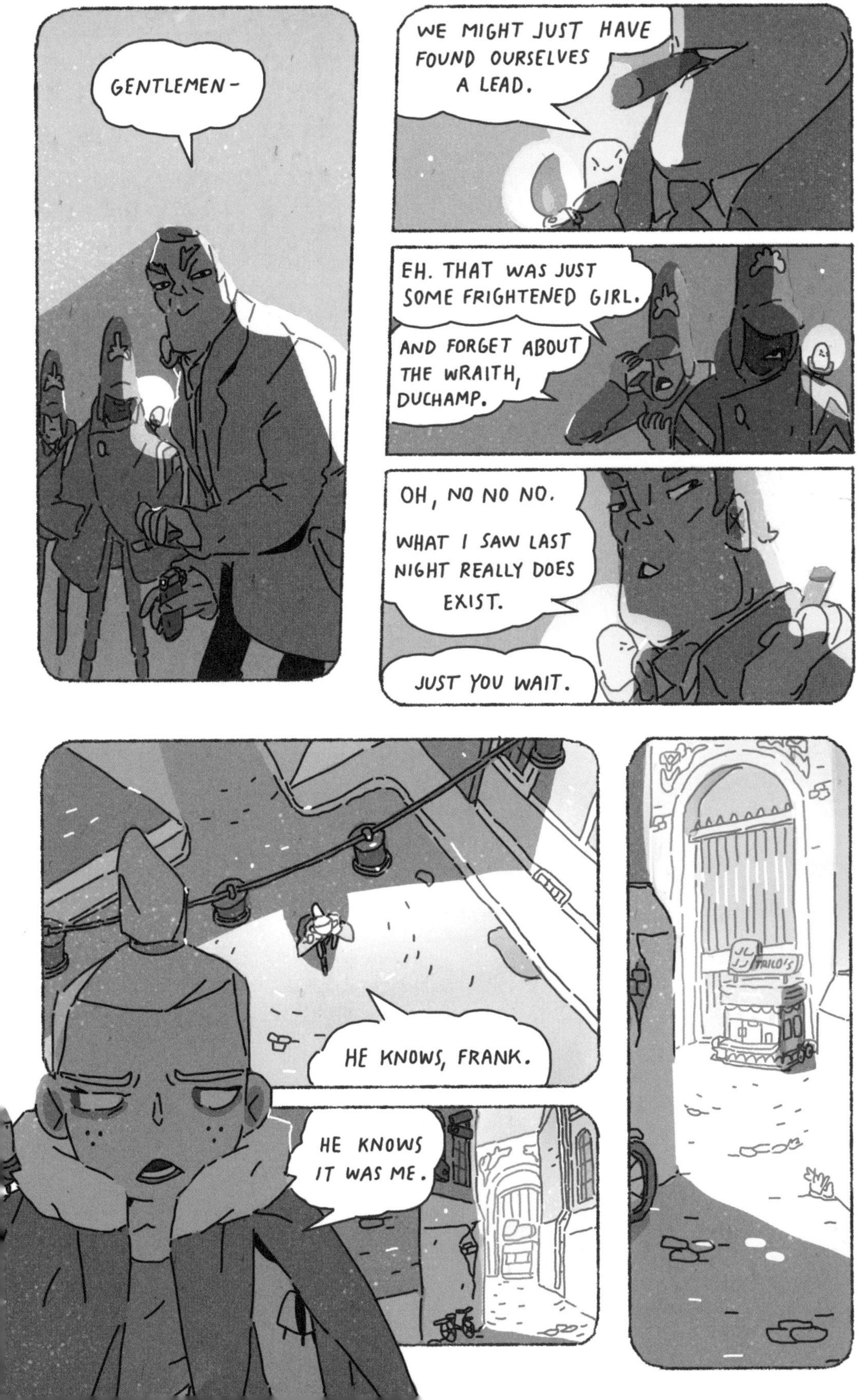
GENTLEMEN-
WE MIGHT JUST HAVE FOUND OURSELVES A LEAD.
EH. THAT WAS JUST SOME FRIGHTENED GIRL.
AND FORGET ABOUT THE WRAITH, DUCHAMP.
OH, NO NO NO.
WHAT I SAW LAST NIGHT REALLY DOES EXIST.
JUST YOU WAIT.
HE KNOWS, FRANK.
HE KNOWS IT WAS ME.

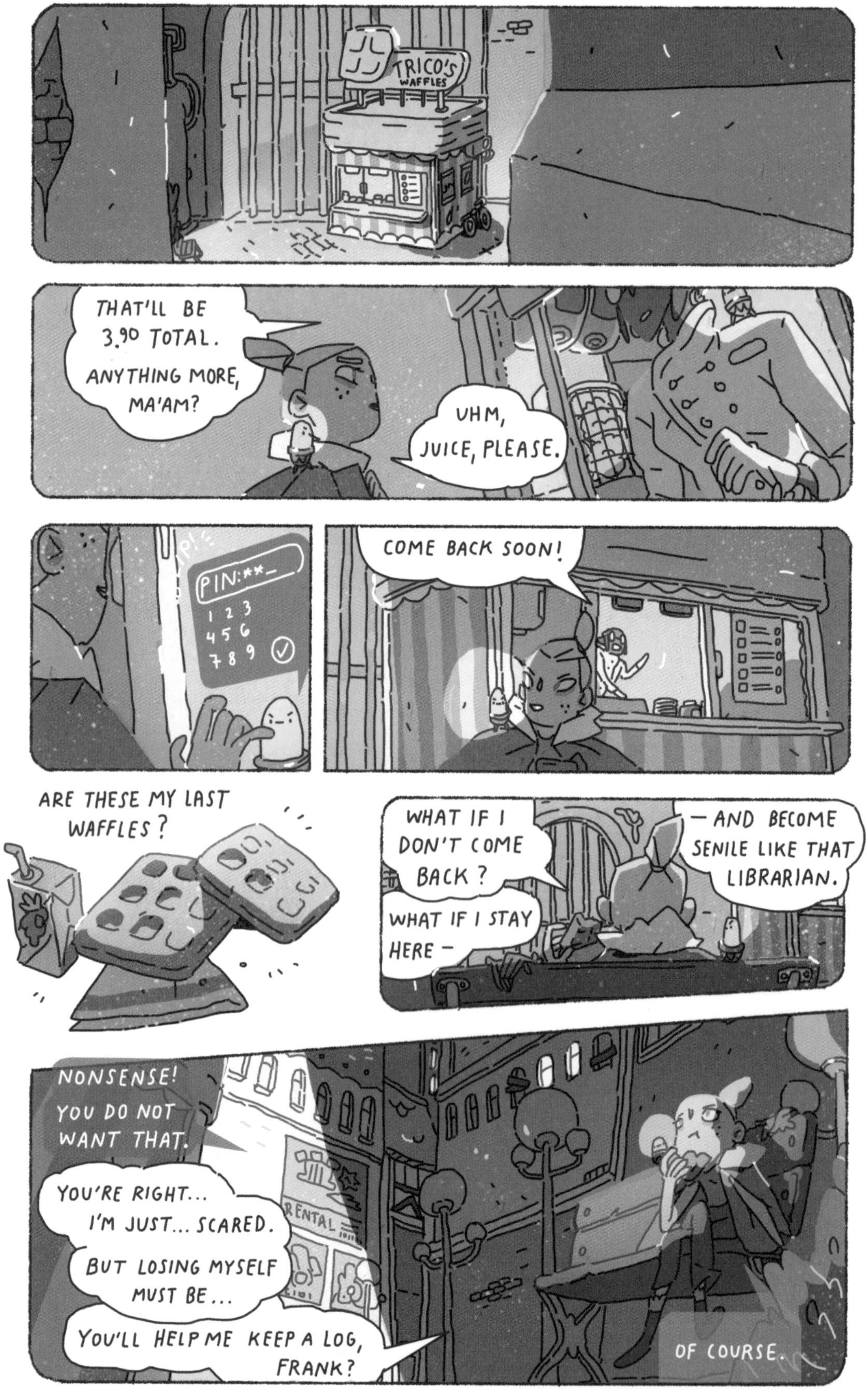
TRICO'S WAFFLES
THAT'LL BE 3.90 TOTAL.
ANYTHING MORE, MA'AM?
UHM, JUICE, PLEASE.
PIN:**_
1 2 3
4 5 6
7 8 9
COME BACK SOON!
ARE THESE MY LAST WAFFLES?
WHAT IF I DON'T COME BACK?
WHAT IF I STAY HERE –
– AND BECOME SENILE LIKE THAT LIBRARIAN.
NONSENSE! YOU DO NOT WANT THAT.
YOU'RE RIGHT... I'M JUST... SCARED.
BUT LOSING MYSELF MUST BE...
YOU'LL HELP ME KEEP A LOG, FRANK?
OF COURSE.
RENTAL

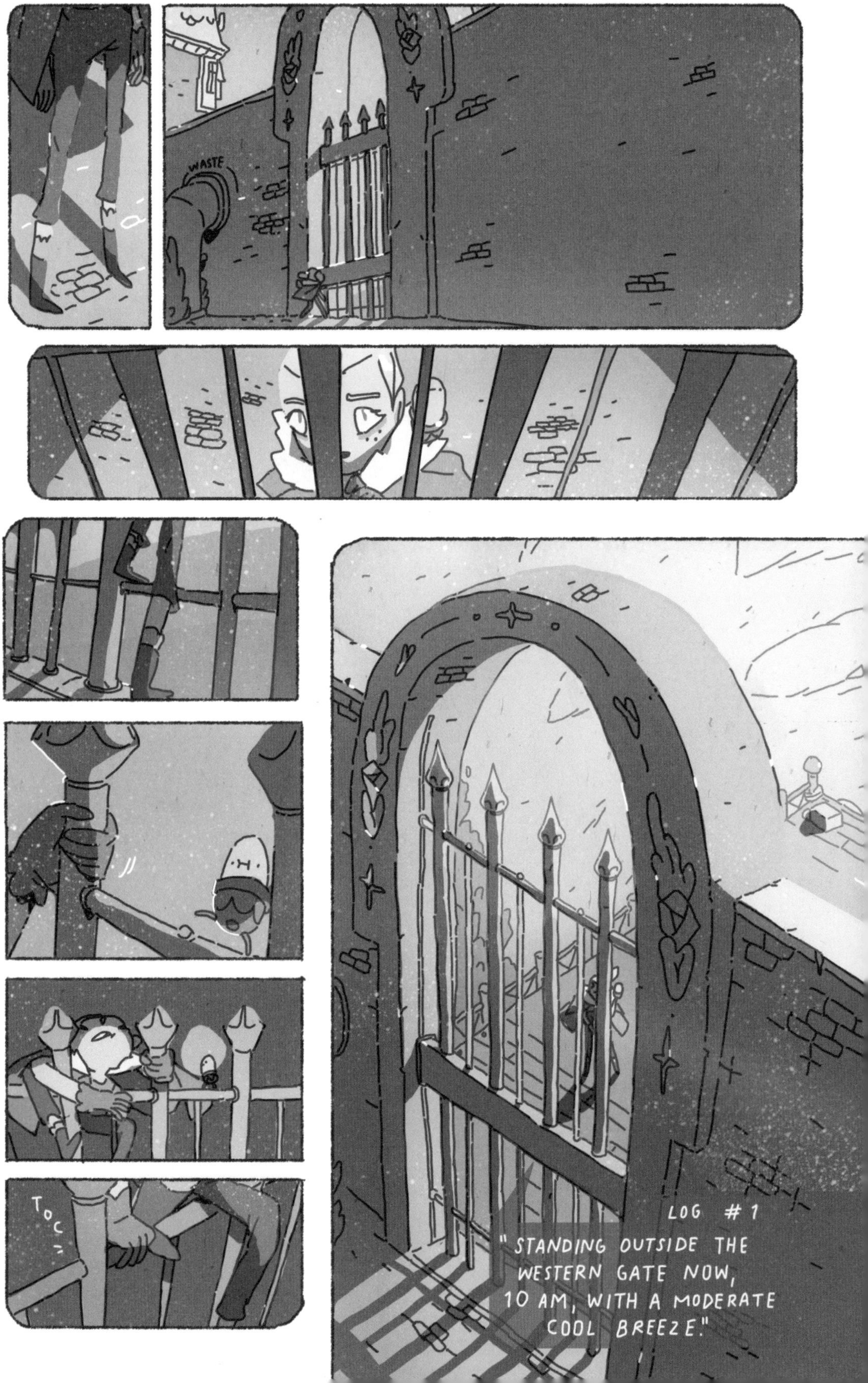
WASTE
TOC
LOG #1
"STANDING OUTSIDE THE WESTERN GATE NOW, 10 AM, WITH A MODERATE COOL BREEZE."

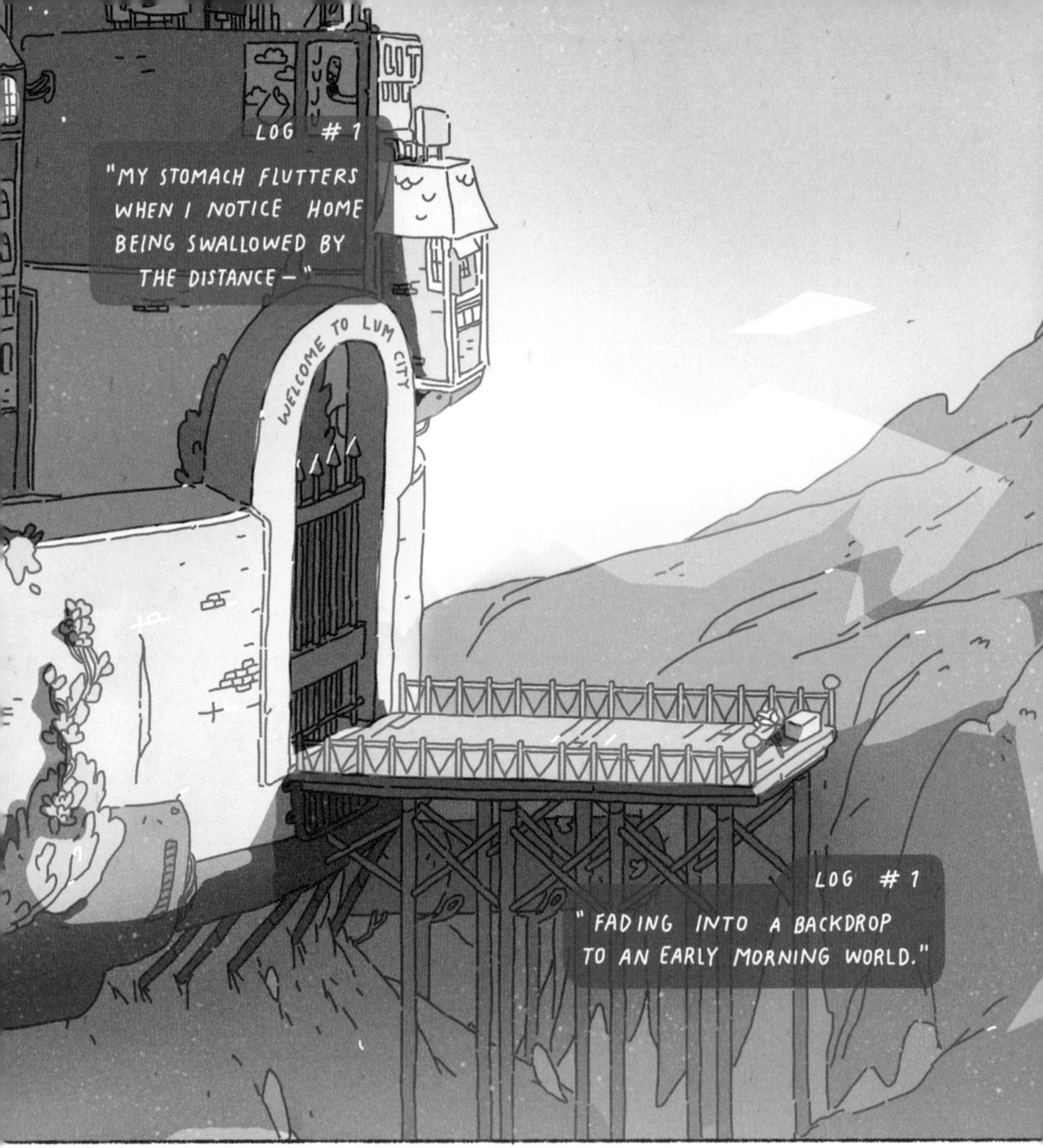
JUJU
LIT
LOG #1
"MY STOMACH FLUTTERS WHEN I NOTICE HOME BEING SWALLOWED BY THE DISTANCE—"
WELCOME TO LUM CITY
LOG #1
"FADING INTO A BACKDROP TO AN EARLY MORNING WORLD."

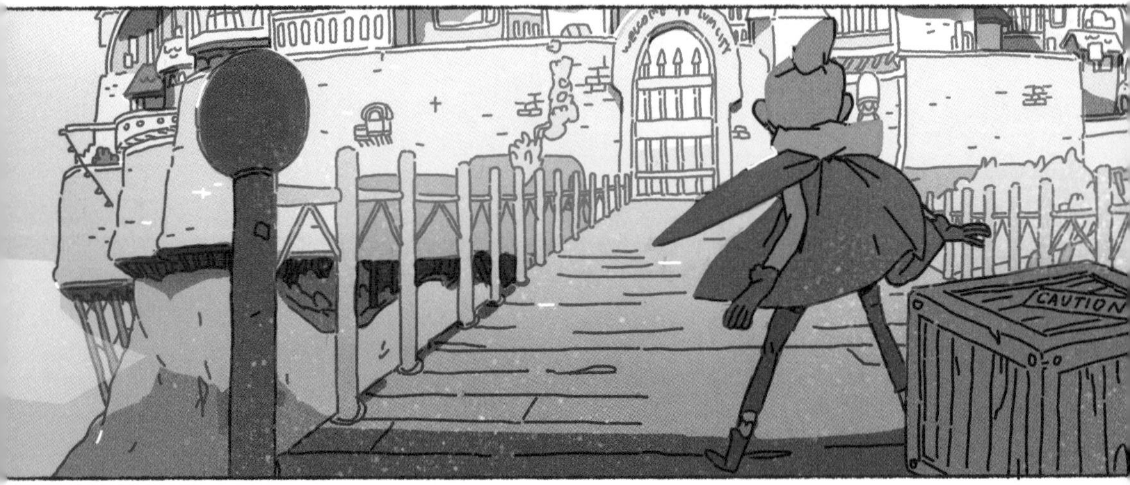
WELCOME TO LUM CITY
CAUTION

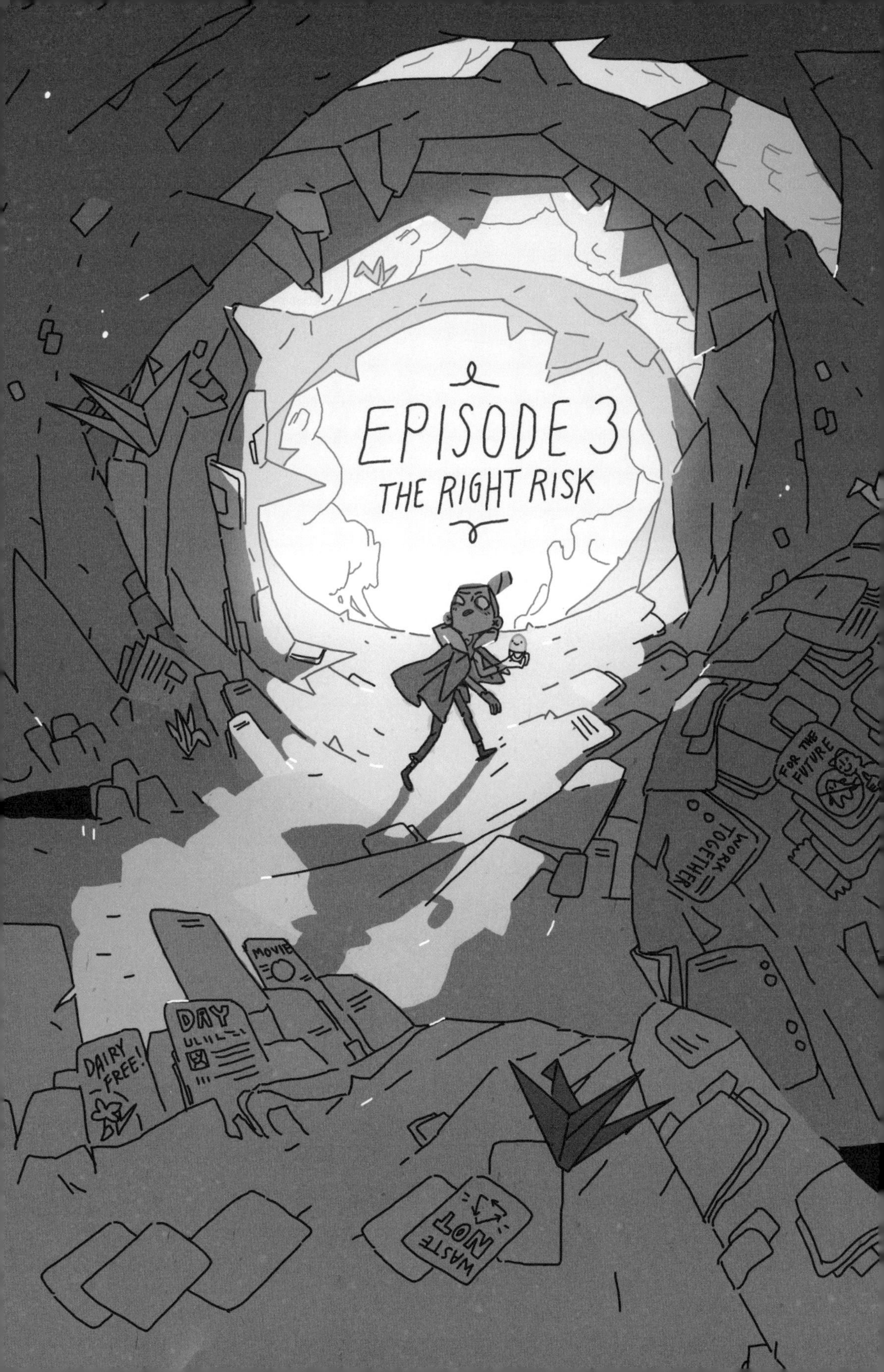
EPISODE 3
THE RIGHT RISK
FOR THE FUTURE
WORK TOGETHER
MOVIE
DAY
DAIRY FREE!
WASTE NOT

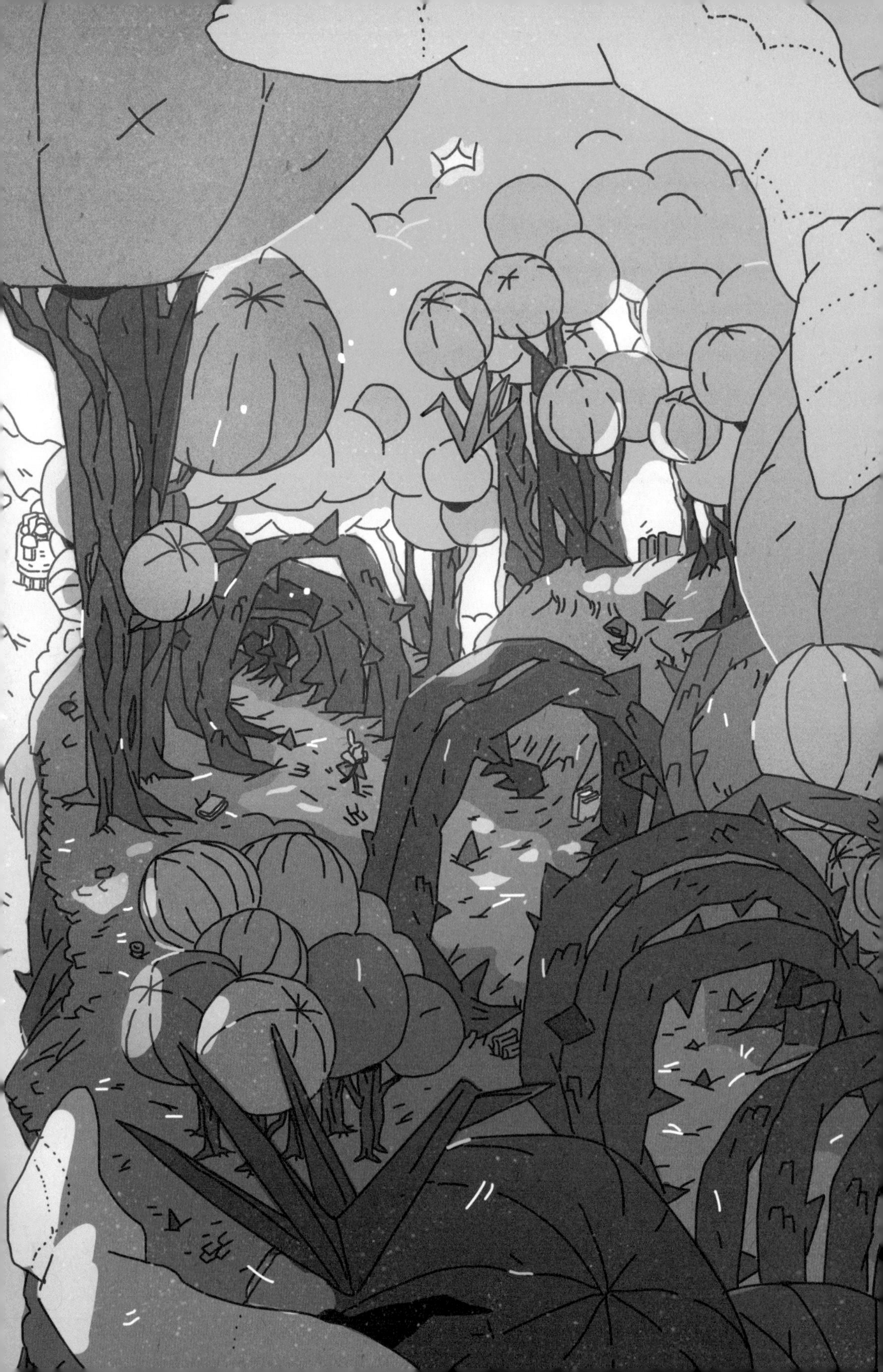

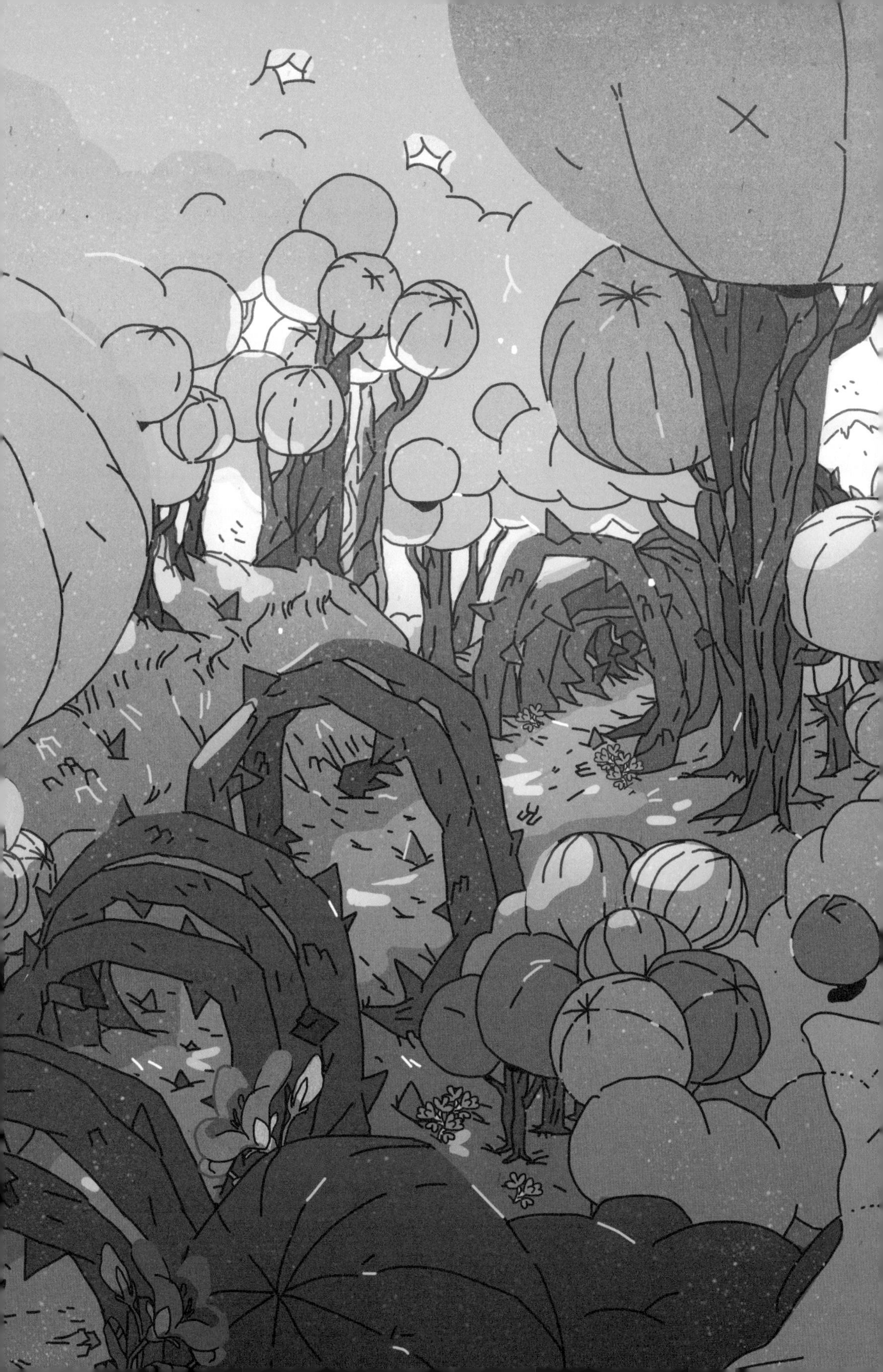

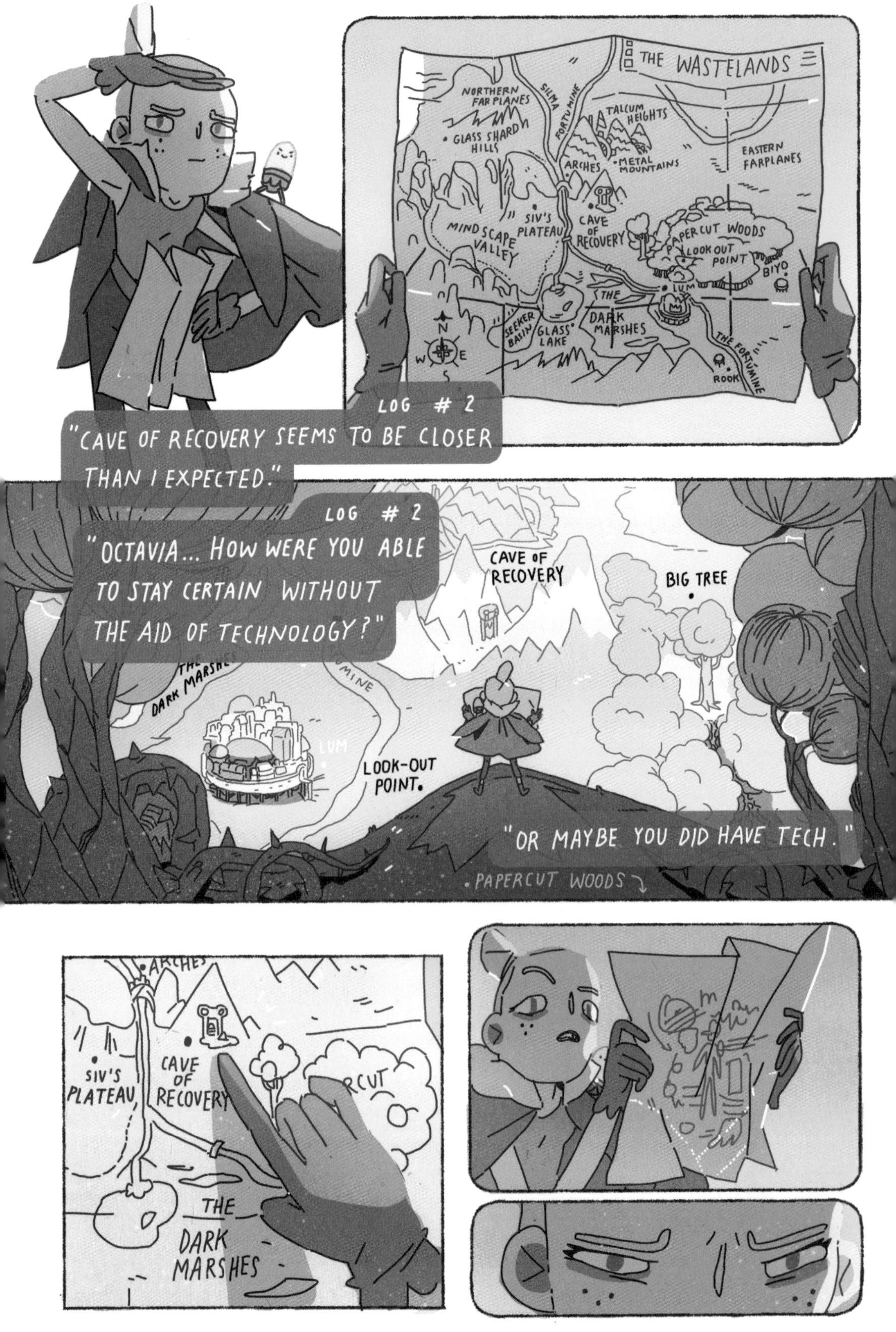
THE WASTELANDS
NORTHERN FARPLANES
SILMA
FORTUMINE
TALCUM HEIGHTS
GLASS SHARD HILLS
ARCHES
METAL MOUNTAINS
EASTERN FARPLANES
SIV'S PLATEAU
CAVE OF RECOVERY
MINDSCAPE VALLEY
PAPERCUT WOODS
LOOK OUT POINT
BIYO
LUM
THE DARK MARSHES
SEEKER BASIN
GLASS LAKE
THE FORTUMINE
ROOK
N
W
E
S
LOG # 2
"CAVE OF RECOVERY SEEMS TO BE CLOSER THAN I EXPECTED."
LOG # 2
"OCTAVIA... HOW WERE YOU ABLE TO STAY CERTAIN WITHOUT THE AID OF TECHNOLOGY?"
CAVE OF RECOVERY
BIG TREE
THE DARK MARSHES
MINE
LUM
LOOK-OUT POINT
"OR MAYBE YOU DID HAVE TECH."
PAPERCUT WOODS
ARCHES
SIV'S PLATEAU
CAVE OF RECOVERY
RCUT
THE DARK MARSHES

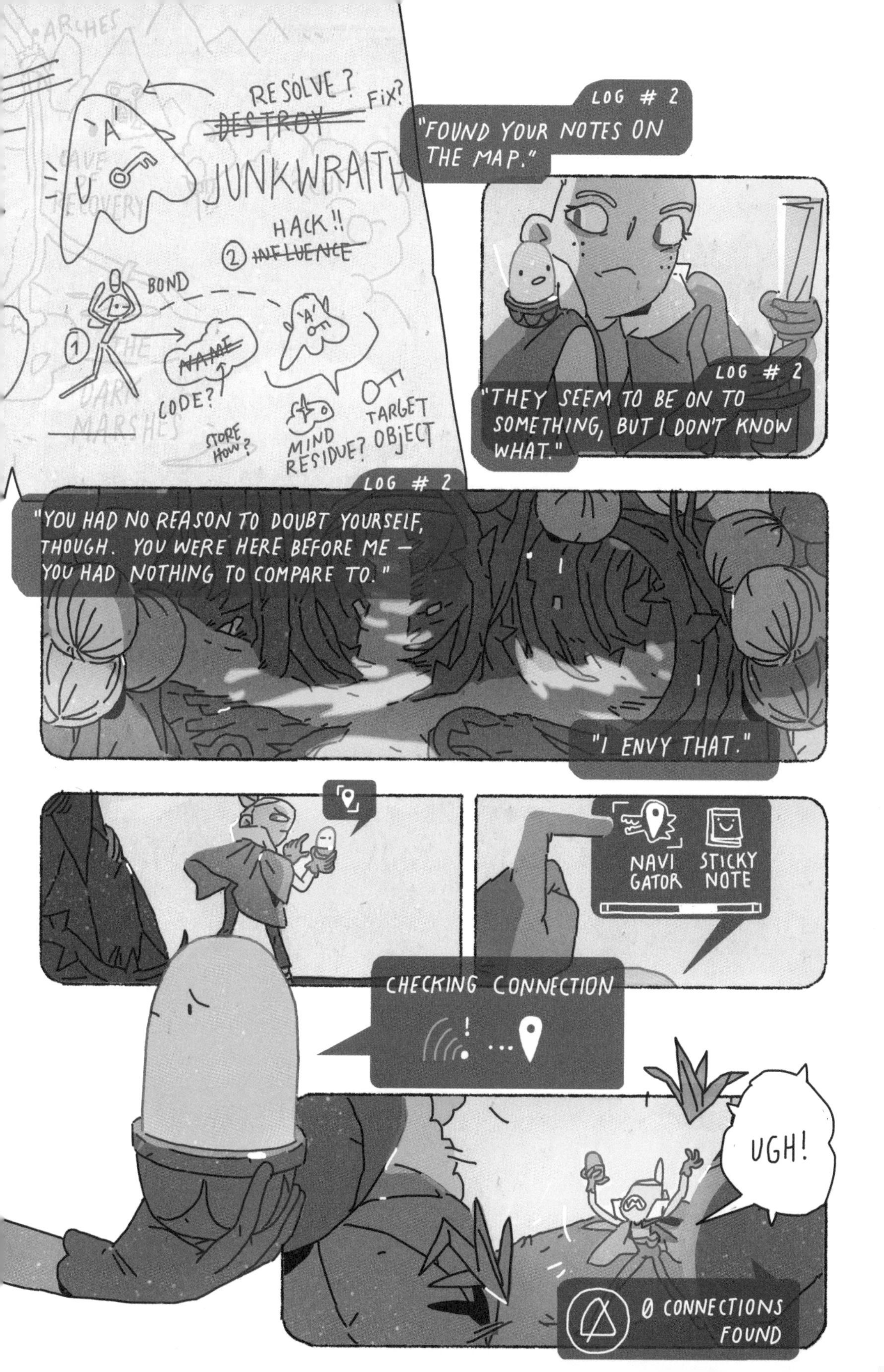
ARCHES
RESOLVE ?
DESTROY
FIX?
JUNKWRAITH
HACK !!
② INFLUENCE
BOND
①
NAME
CODE?
STORE HOW ?
MIND RESIDUE?
TARGET OBJECT
LOG # 2
"FOUND YOUR NOTES ON THE MAP."
LOG # 2
"THEY SEEM TO BE ON TO SOMETHING, BUT I DON'T KNOW WHAT."
LOG # 2
"YOU HAD NO REASON TO DOUBT YOURSELF, THOUGH. YOU WERE HERE BEFORE ME — YOU HAD NOTHING TO COMPARE TO."
"I ENVY THAT."
NAVI GATOR
STICKY NOTE
CHECKING CONNECTION
UGH!
0 CONNECTIONS FOUND

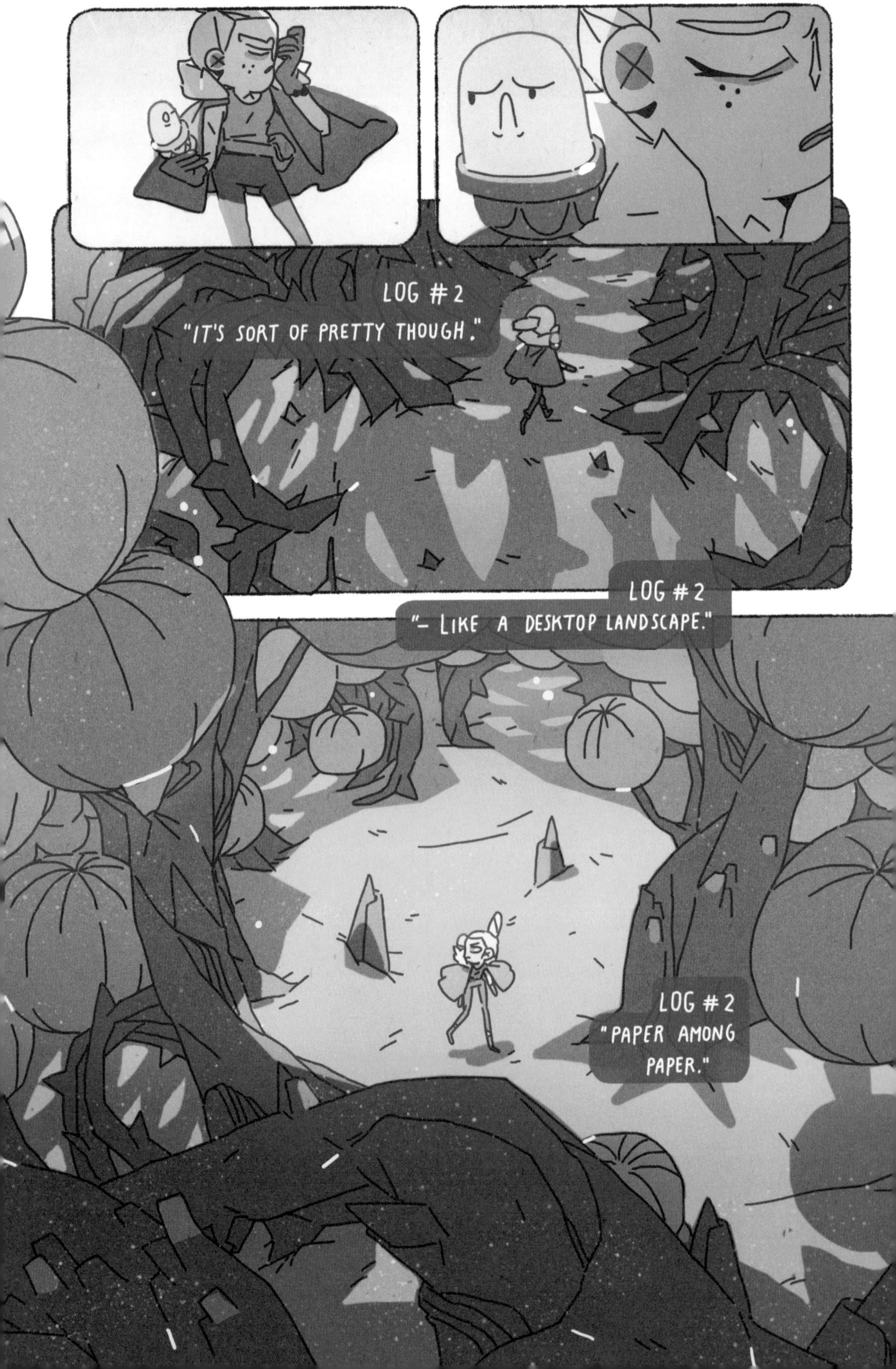
LOG #2
"IT'S SORT OF PRETTY THOUGH."
LOG #2
"– LIKE A DESKTOP LANDSCAPE."
LOG #2
"PAPER AMONG PAPER."

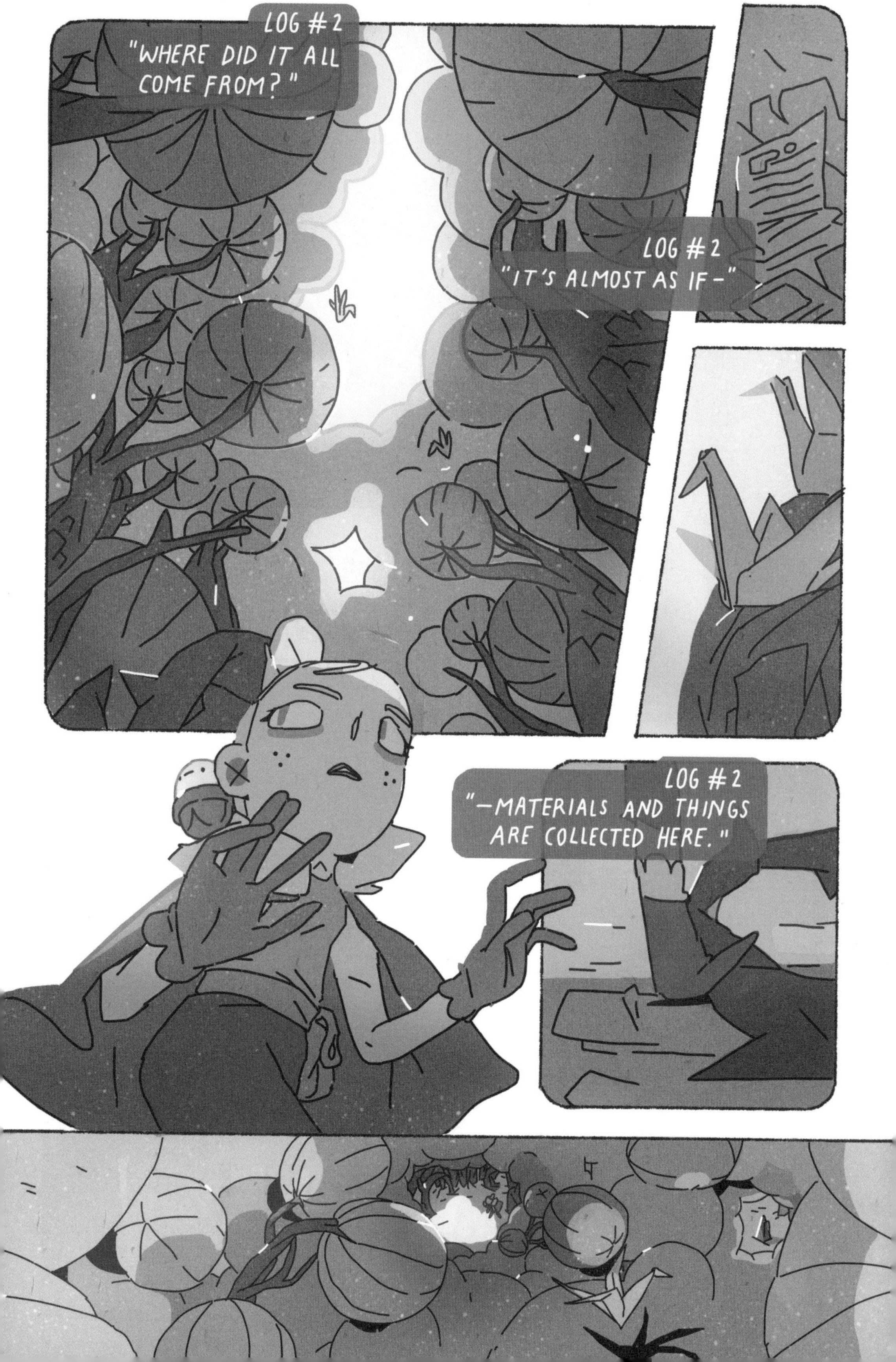
LOG #2
"WHERE DID IT ALL COME FROM?"
LOG #2
"IT'S ALMOST AS IF–"
LOG #2
"–MATERIALS AND THINGS ARE COLLECTED HERE."

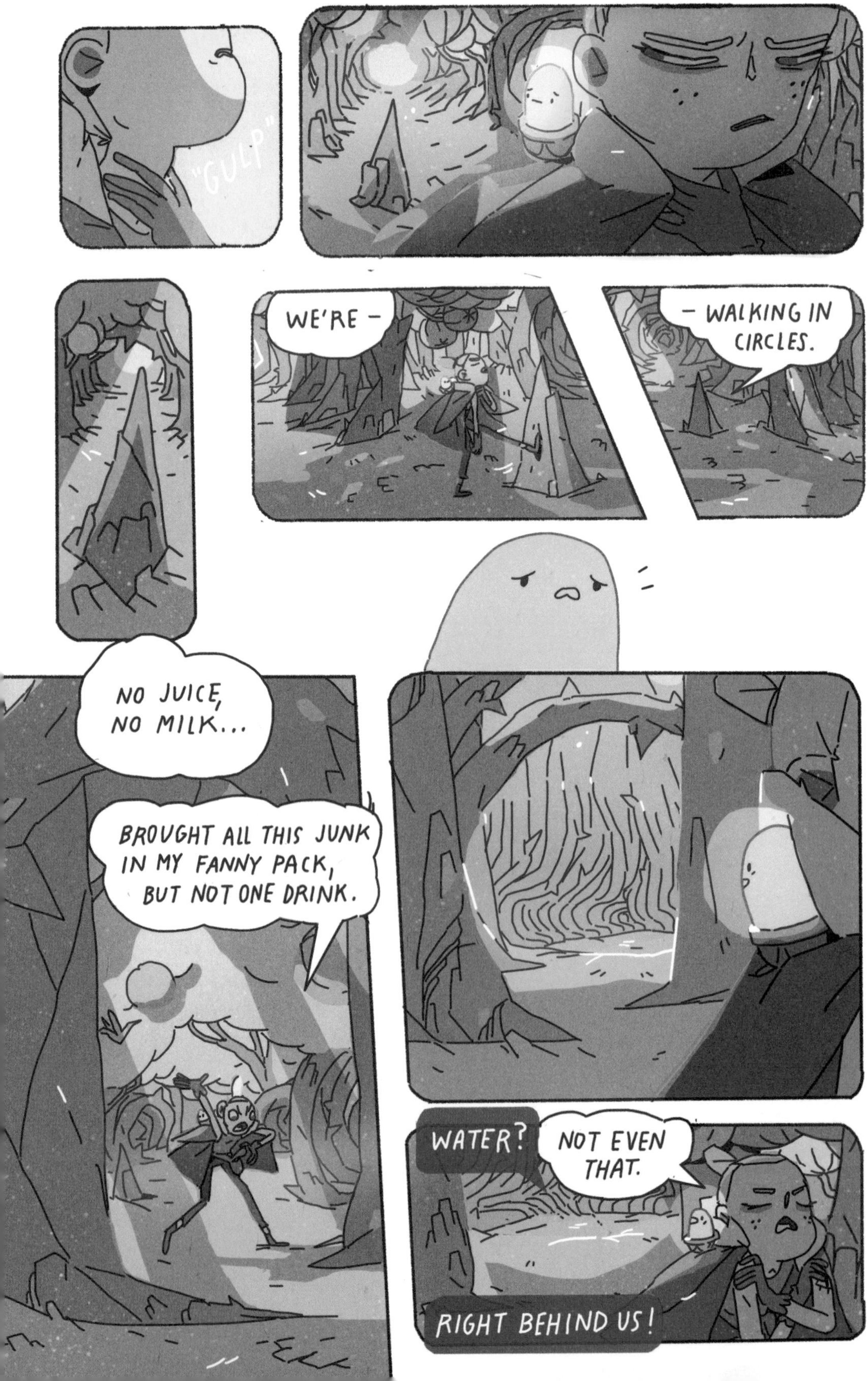
"GULP"
WE'RE -
- WALKING IN CIRCLES.
NO JUICE, NO MILK...
BROUGHT ALL THIS JUNK IN MY FANNY PACK, BUT NOT ONE DRINK.
WATER?
NOT EVEN THAT.
RIGHT BEHIND US!

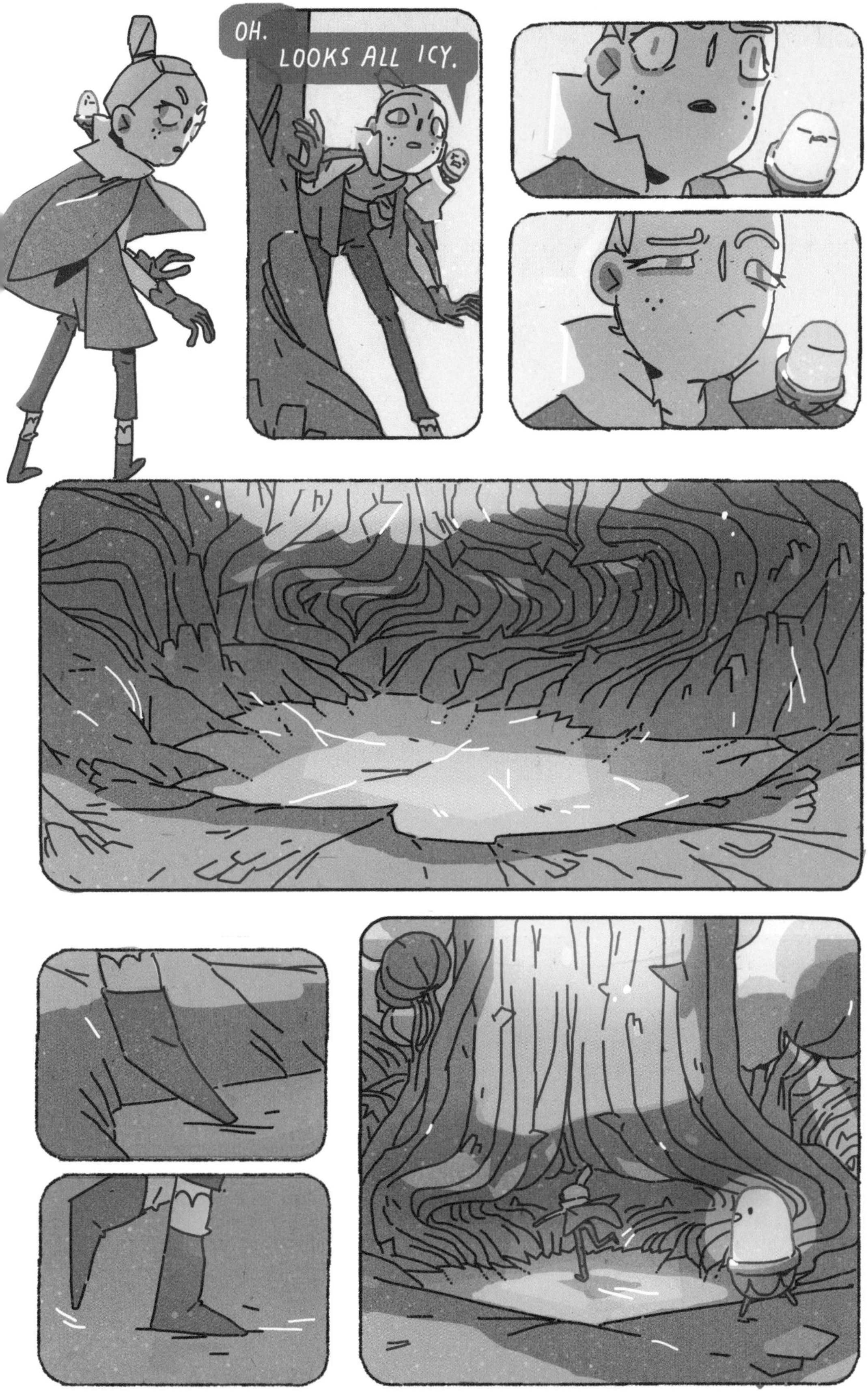
OH.
LOOKS ALL ICY.

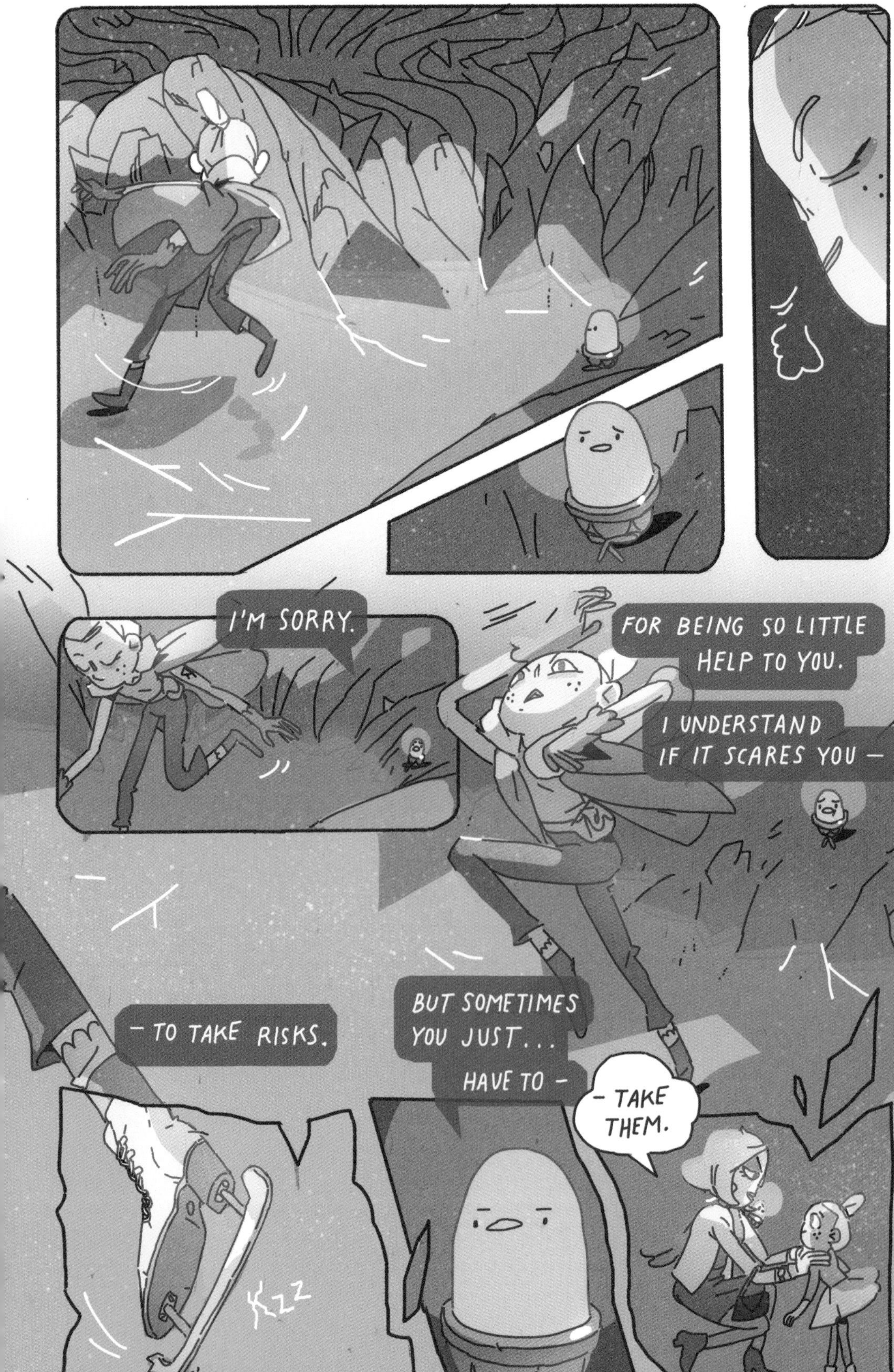
I'M SORRY.
FOR BEING SO LITTLE HELP TO YOU.
I UNDERSTAND IF IT SCARES YOU –
– TO TAKE RISKS.
BUT SOMETIMES YOU JUST...
HAVE TO –
KZZ
– TAKE THEM.

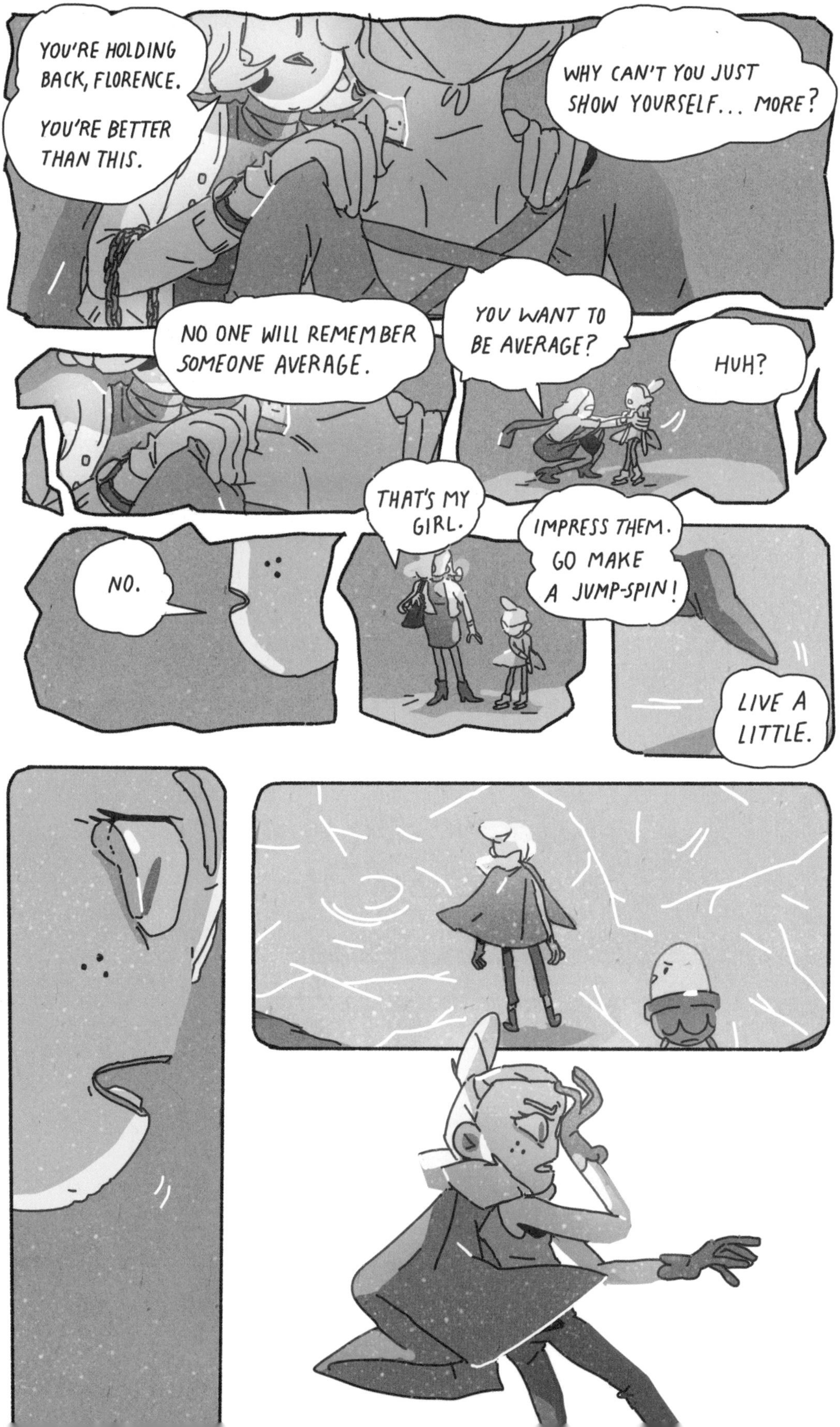
YOU'RE HOLDING BACK, FLORENCE.
YOU'RE BETTER THAN THIS.
WHY CAN'T YOU JUST SHOW YOURSELF... MORE?
NO ONE WILL REMEMBER SOMEONE AVERAGE.
YOU WANT TO BE AVERAGE?
HUH?
NO.
THAT'S MY GIRL.
IMPRESS THEM. GO MAKE A JUMP-SPIN!
LIVE A LITTLE.

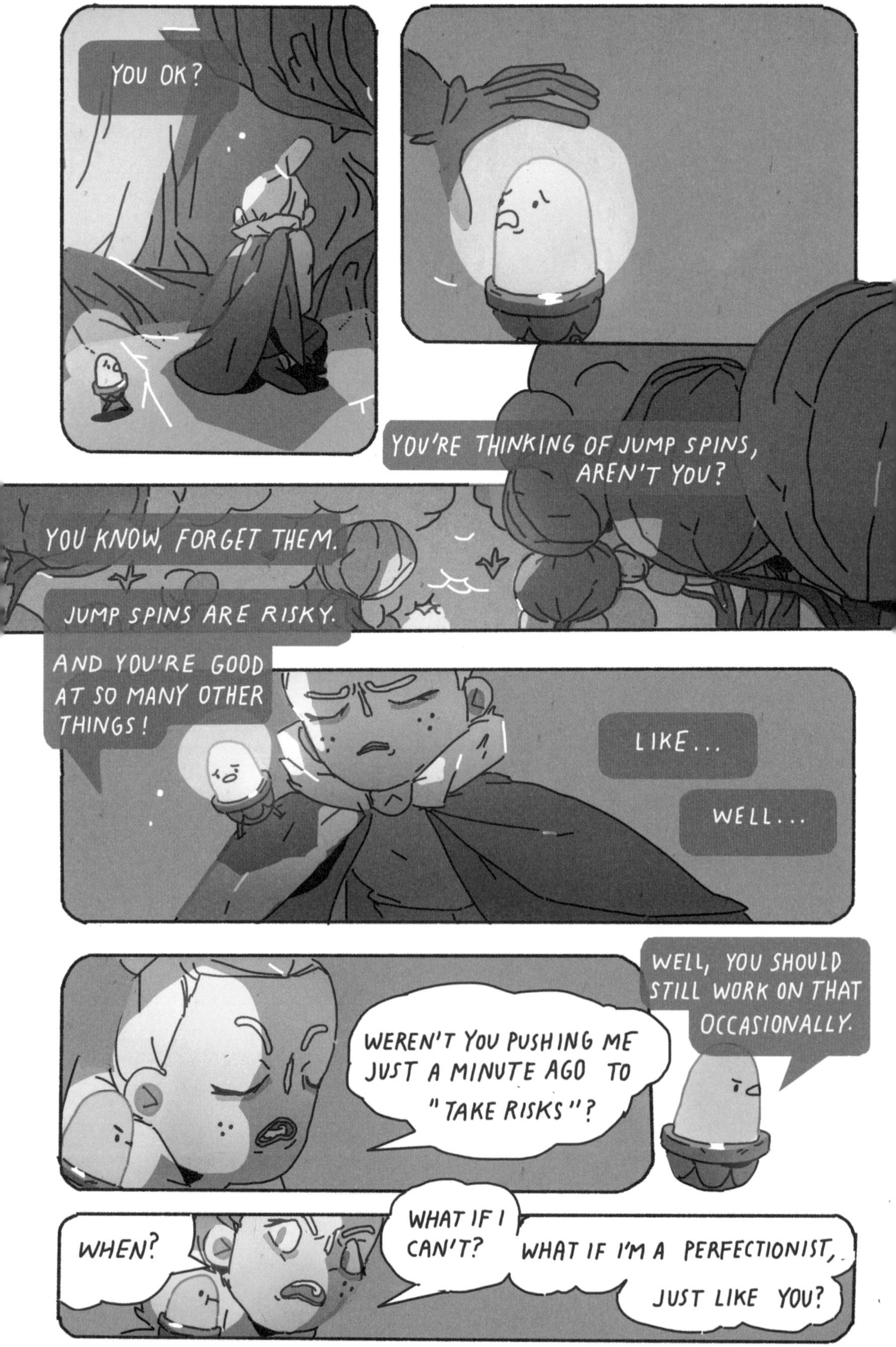
YOU OK?
YOU'RE THINKING OF JUMP SPINS, AREN'T YOU?
YOU KNOW, FORGET THEM.
JUMP SPINS ARE RISKY.
AND YOU'RE GOOD AT SO MANY OTHER THINGS!
LIKE...
WELL...
WELL, YOU SHOULD STILL WORK ON THAT OCCASIONALLY.
WEREN'T YOU PUSHING ME JUST A MINUTE AGO TO "TAKE RISKS"?
WHEN?
WHAT IF I CAN'T?
WHAT IF I'M A PERFECTIONIST, JUST LIKE YOU?

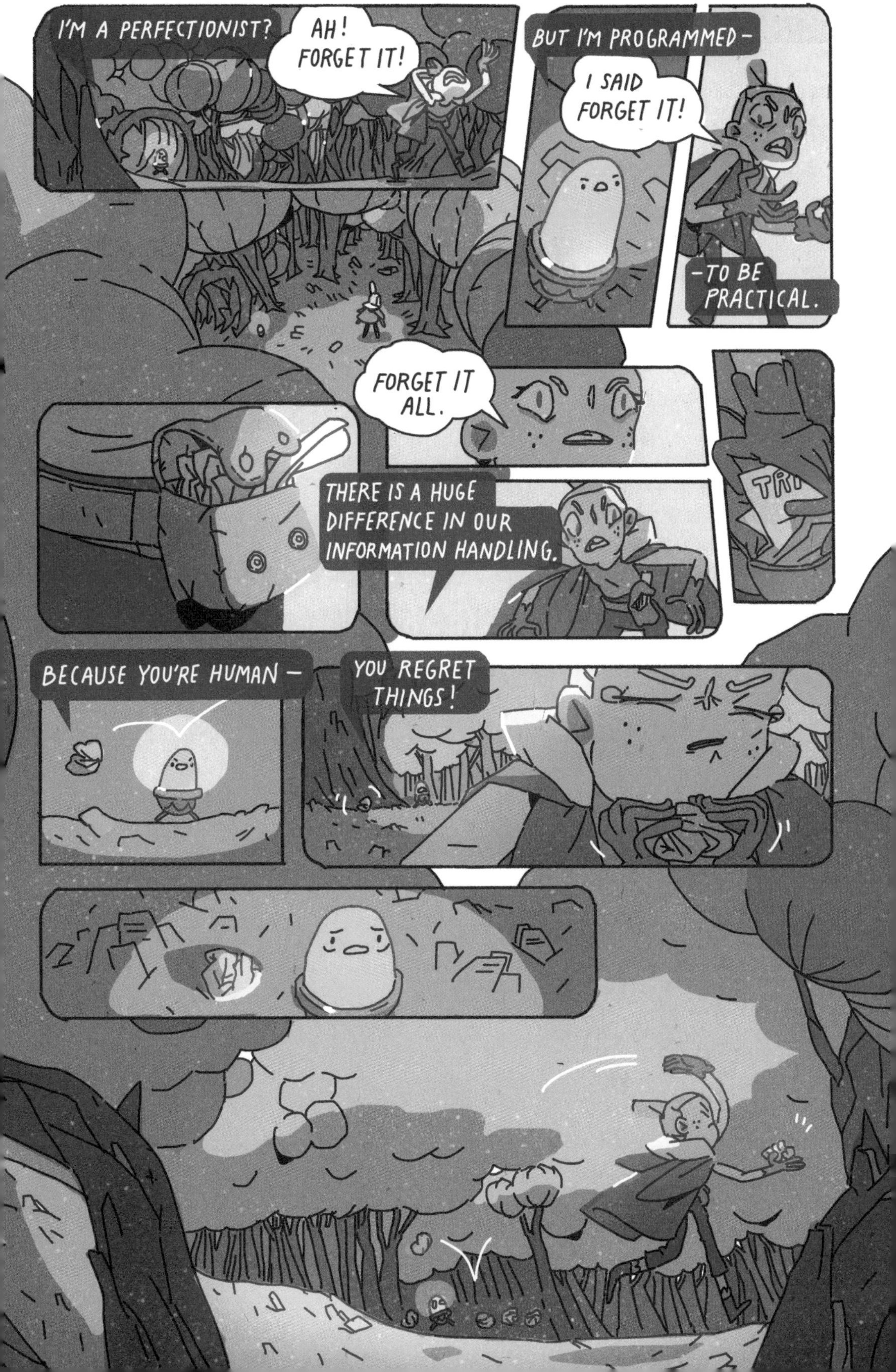
I'M A PERFECTIONIST?
AH! FORGET IT!
BUT I'M PROGRAMMED-
I SAID FORGET IT!
-TO BE PRACTICAL.
FORGET IT ALL.
THERE IS A HUGE DIFFERENCE IN OUR INFORMATION HANDLING.
BECAUSE YOU'RE HUMAN-
YOU REGRET THINGS!

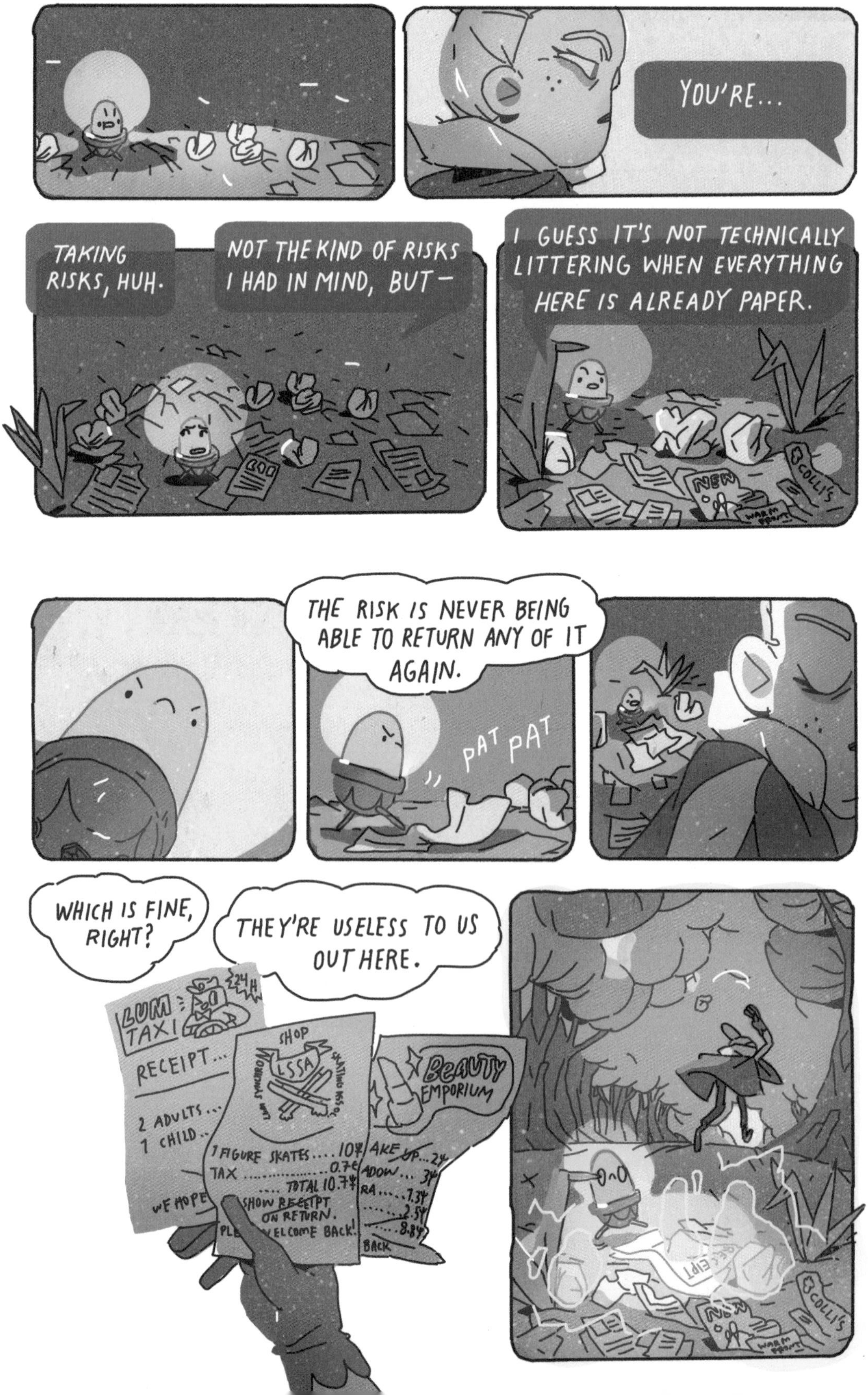

YOU'RE...
TAKING RISKS, HUH.
NOT THE KIND OF RISKS I HAD IN MIND, BUT—
I GUESS IT'S NOT TECHNICALLY LITTERING WHEN EVERYTHING HERE IS ALREADY PAPER.
NEW
COLLI'S
THE RISK IS NEVER BEING ABLE TO RETURN ANY OF IT AGAIN.
PAT PAT
WHICH IS FINE, RIGHT?
THEY'RE USELESS TO US OUT HERE.
LUM TAXI
24H
RECEIPT...
2 ADULTS...
1 CHILD...
WE HOPE
SHOP
LSSA
1 FIGURE SKATES.....10¥
TAX ....0.7¢
.... TOTAL 10.7¥
SHOW RECEIPT ON RETURN.
PLE WELCOME BACK!
BEAUTY EMPORIUM
BACK
RECEIPT
COLLI'S

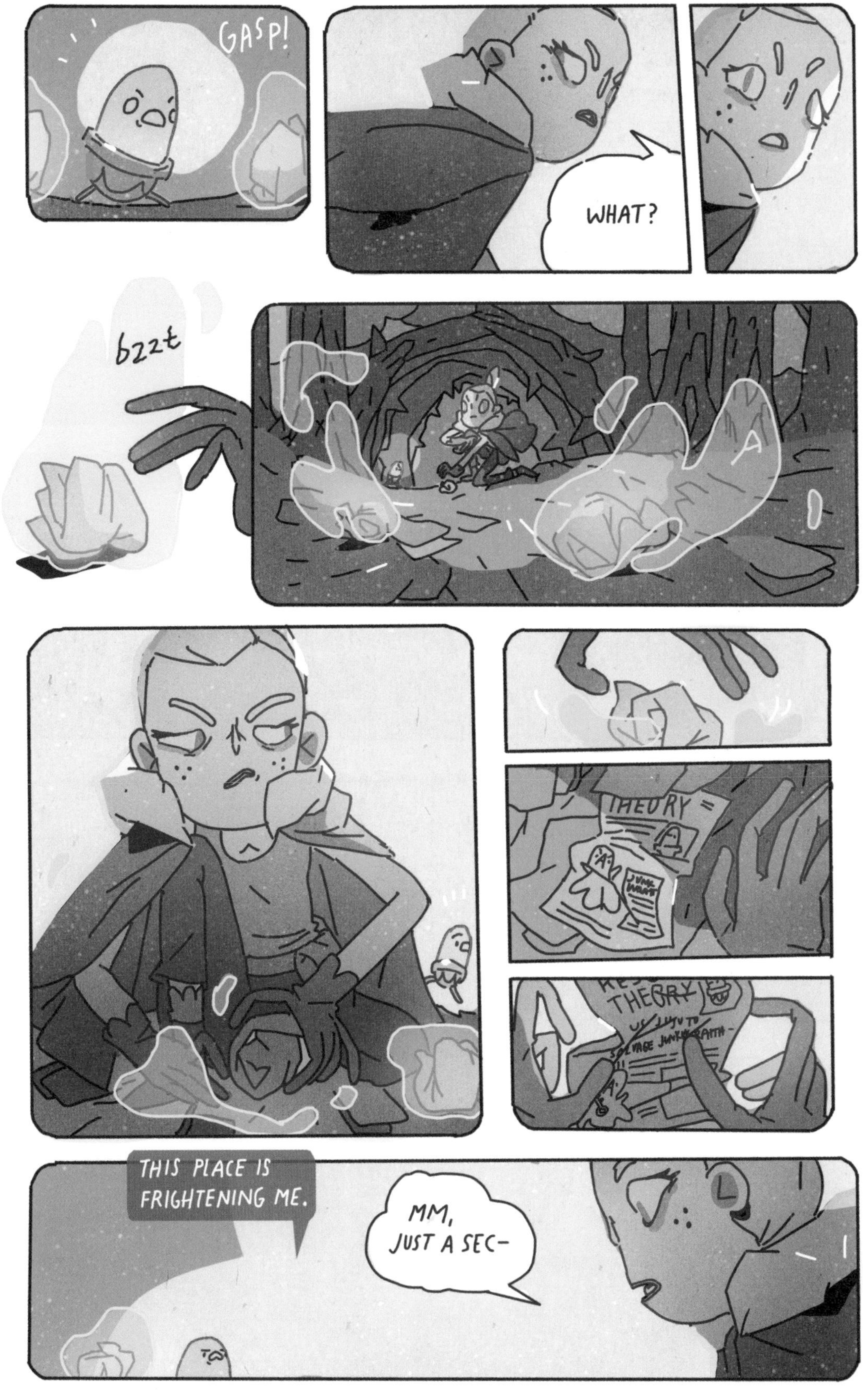
GASP!
WHAT?
bzzt
THEORY
THIS PLACE IS FRIGHTENING ME.
MM, JUST A SEC-

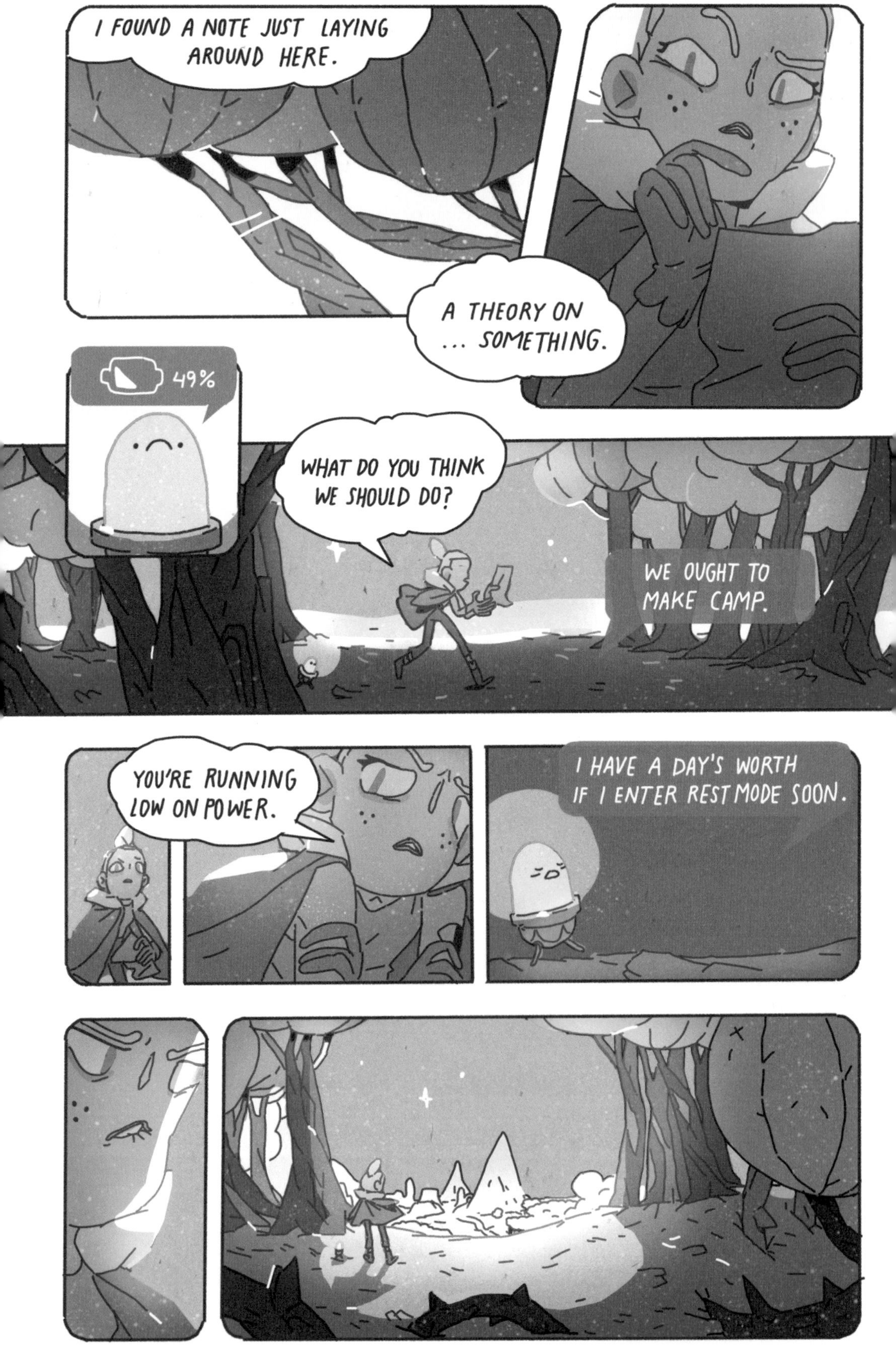
I FOUND A NOTE JUST LAYING AROUND HERE.
A THEORY ON ... SOMETHING.
49%
WHAT DO YOU THINK WE SHOULD DO?
WE OUGHT TO MAKE CAMP.
YOU'RE RUNNING LOW ON POWER.
I HAVE A DAY'S WORTH IF I ENTER REST MODE SOON.

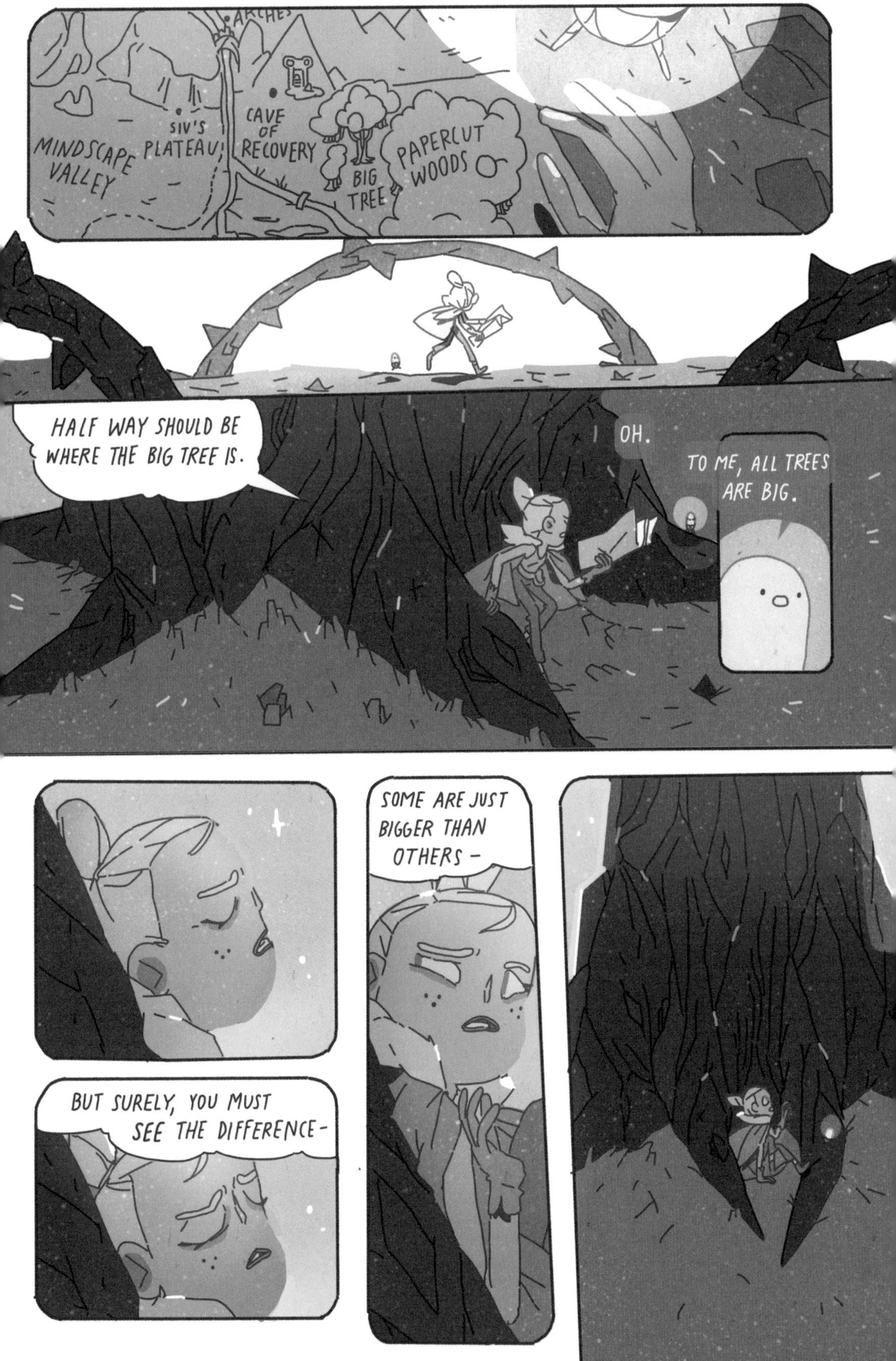
ARCHES
SIV'S PLATEAU
CAVE OF RECOVERY
MINDSCAPE VALLEY
BIG TREE
PAPERCUT WOODS
HALF WAY SHOULD BE WHERE THE BIG TREE IS.
OH.
TO ME, ALL TREES ARE BIG.
SOME ARE JUST BIGGER THAN OTHERS -
BUT SURELY, YOU MUST SEE THE DIFFERENCE-

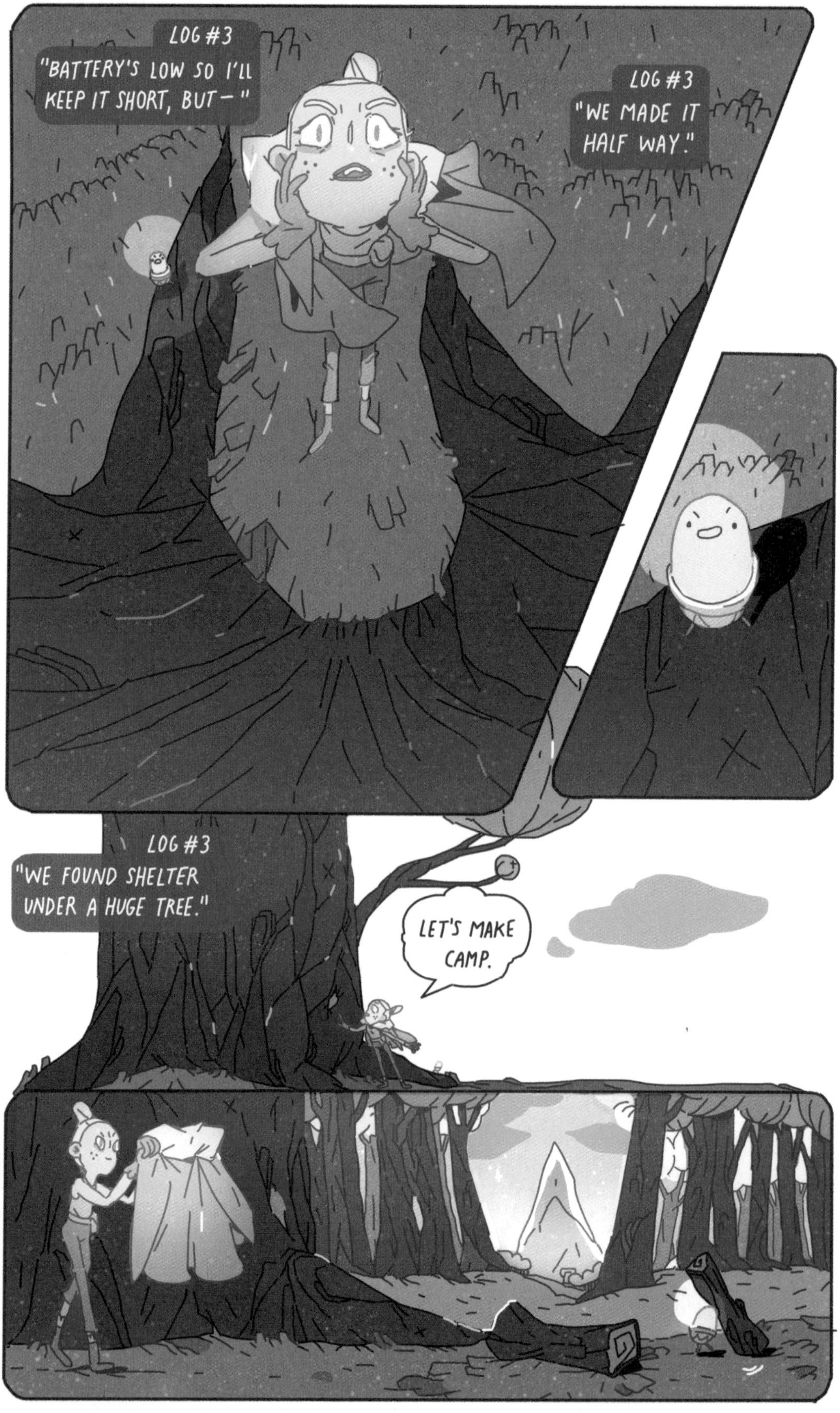
LOG #3
"BATTERY'S LOW SO I'LL KEEP IT SHORT, BUT–"
LOG #3
"WE MADE IT HALF WAY."
LOG #3
"WE FOUND SHELTER UNDER A HUGE TREE."
LET'S MAKE CAMP.

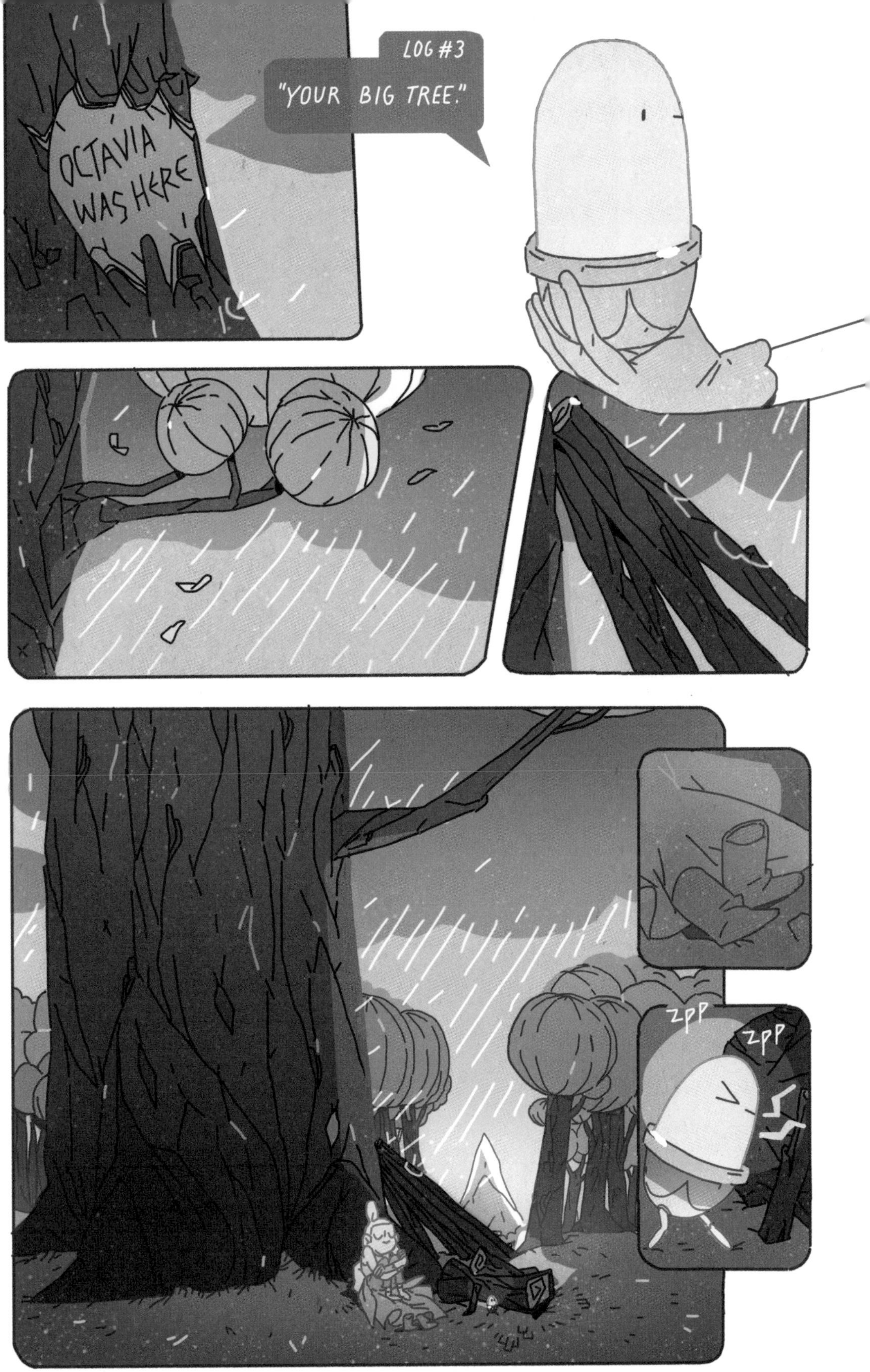
OCTAVIA WAS HERE
LOG #3
"YOUR BIG TREE."
ZPP
ZPP

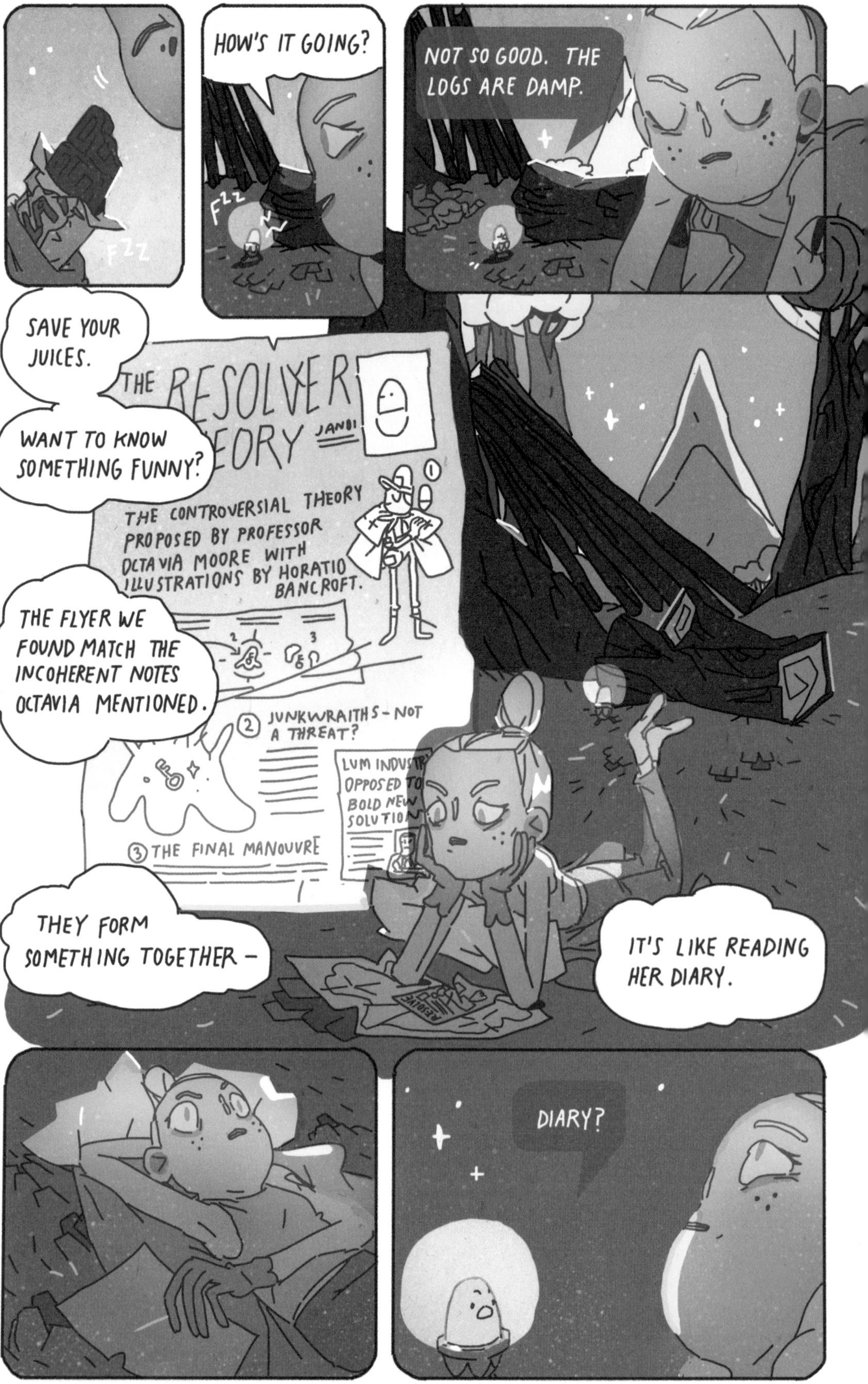

F ZZ
HOW'S IT GOING?
FZZ
NOT SO GOOD. THE LOGS ARE DAMP.
SAVE YOUR JUICES.
WANT TO KNOW SOMETHING FUNNY?
THE RESOLVER THEORY
THE CONTROVERSIAL THEORY PROPOSED BY PROFESSOR OCTAVIA MOORE WITH ILLUSTRATIONS BY HORATIO BANCROFT.
THE FLYER WE FOUND MATCH THE INCOHERENT NOTES OCTAVIA MENTIONED.
② JUNKWRAITHS - NOT A THREAT?
LUM INDUSTR OPPOSED TO BOLD NEW SOLUTION
③ THE FINAL MANOUVRE
THEY FORM SOMETHING TOGETHER -
IT'S LIKE READING HER DIARY.
DIARY?

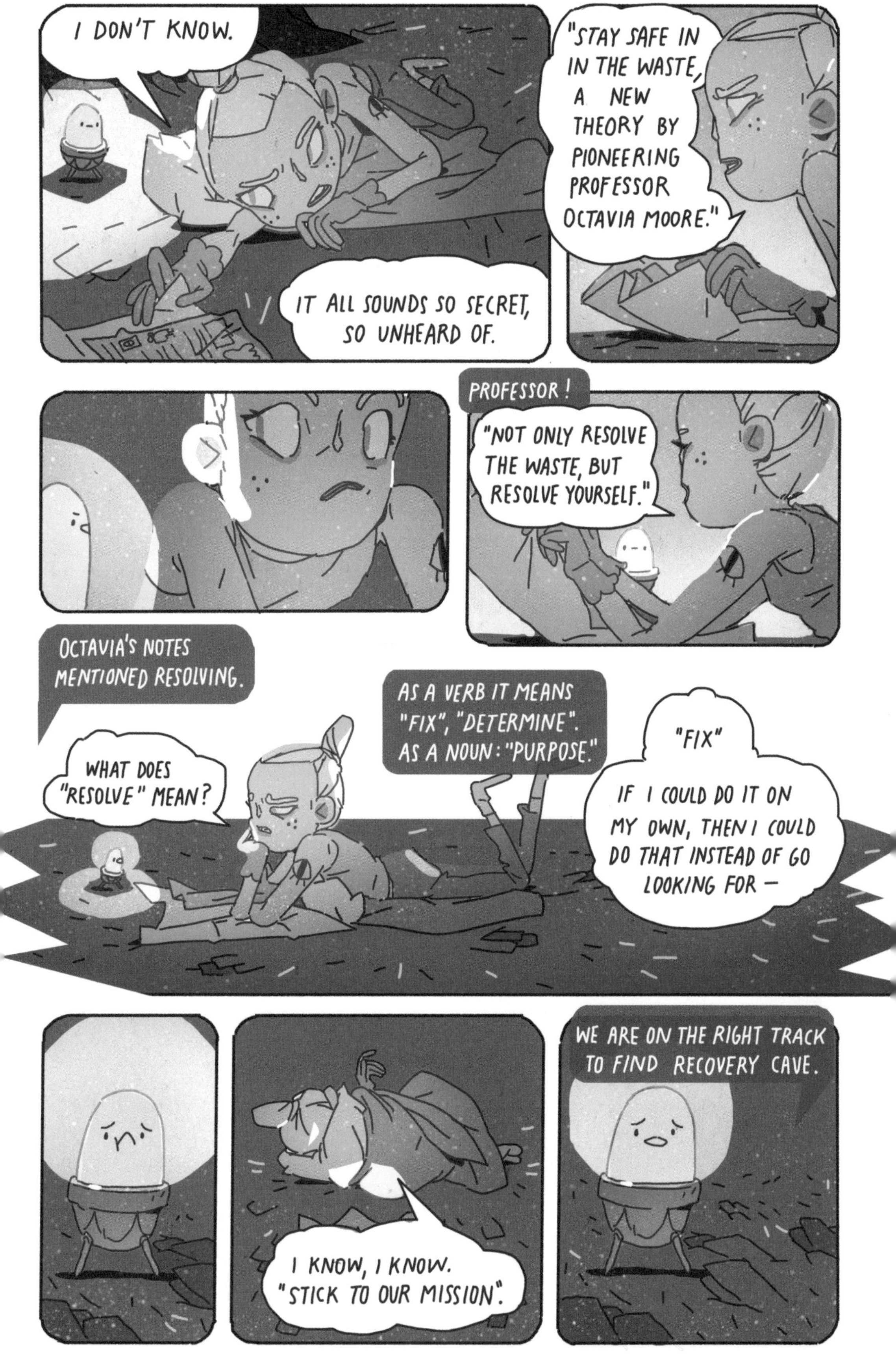
I DON'T KNOW.
IT ALL SOUNDS SO SECRET, SO UNHEARD OF.
"STAY SAFE IN IN THE WASTE, A NEW THEORY BY PIONEERING PROFESSOR OCTAVIA MOORE."
PROFESSOR!
"NOT ONLY RESOLVE THE WASTE, BUT RESOLVE YOURSELF."
OCTAVIA'S NOTES MENTIONED RESOLVING.
WHAT DOES "RESOLVE" MEAN?
AS A VERB IT MEANS "FIX", "DETERMINE". AS A NOUN: "PURPOSE."
"FIX"
IF I COULD DO IT ON MY OWN, THEN I COULD DO THAT INSTEAD OF GO LOOKING FOR —
I KNOW, I KNOW. "STICK TO OUR MISSION".
WE ARE ON THE RIGHT TRACK TO FIND RECOVERY CAVE.

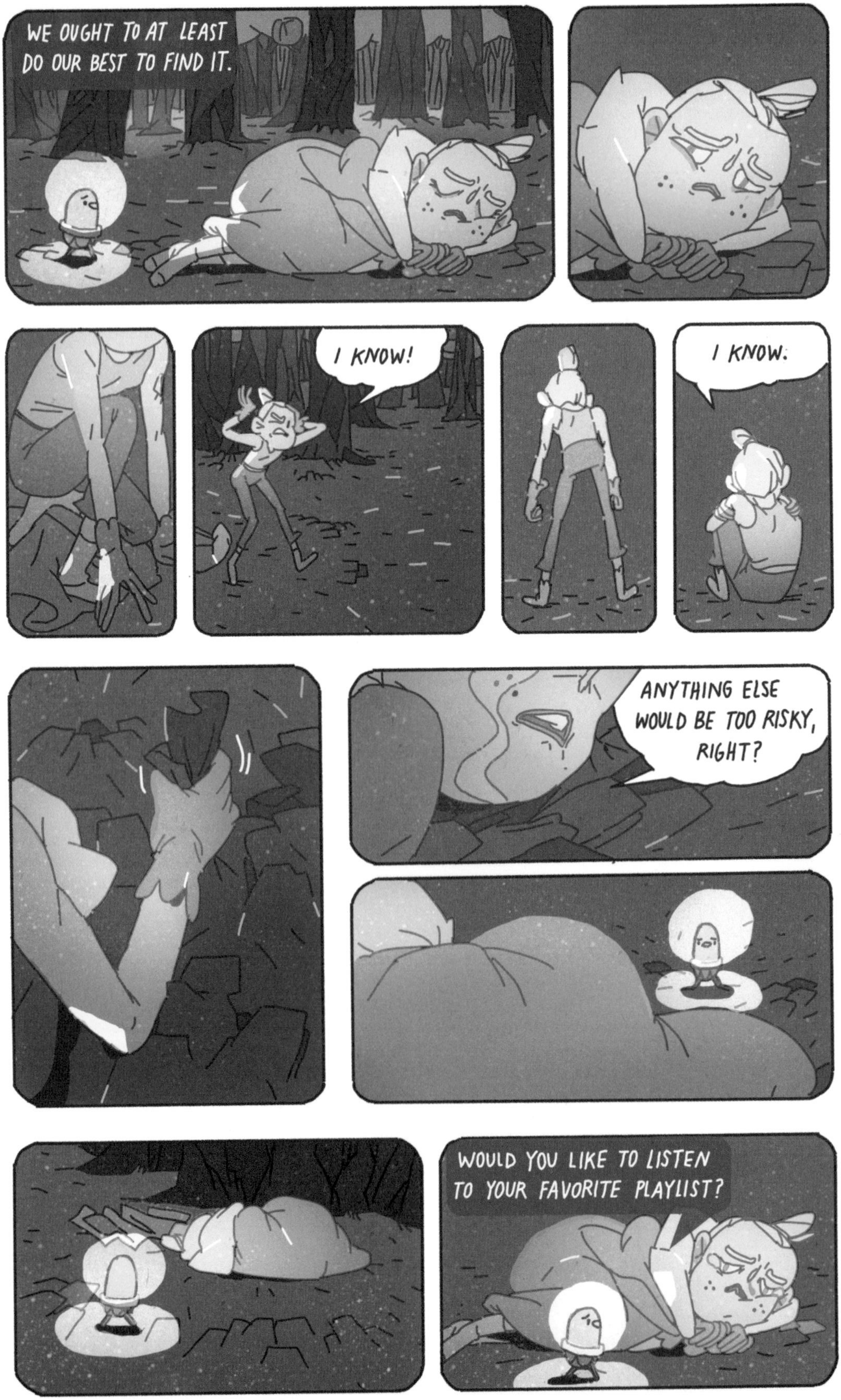
WE OUGHT TO AT LEAST DO OUR BEST TO FIND IT.
I KNOW!
I KNOW.
ANYTHING ELSE WOULD BE TOO RISKY, RIGHT?
WOULD YOU LIKE TO LISTEN TO YOUR FAVORITE PLAYLIST?

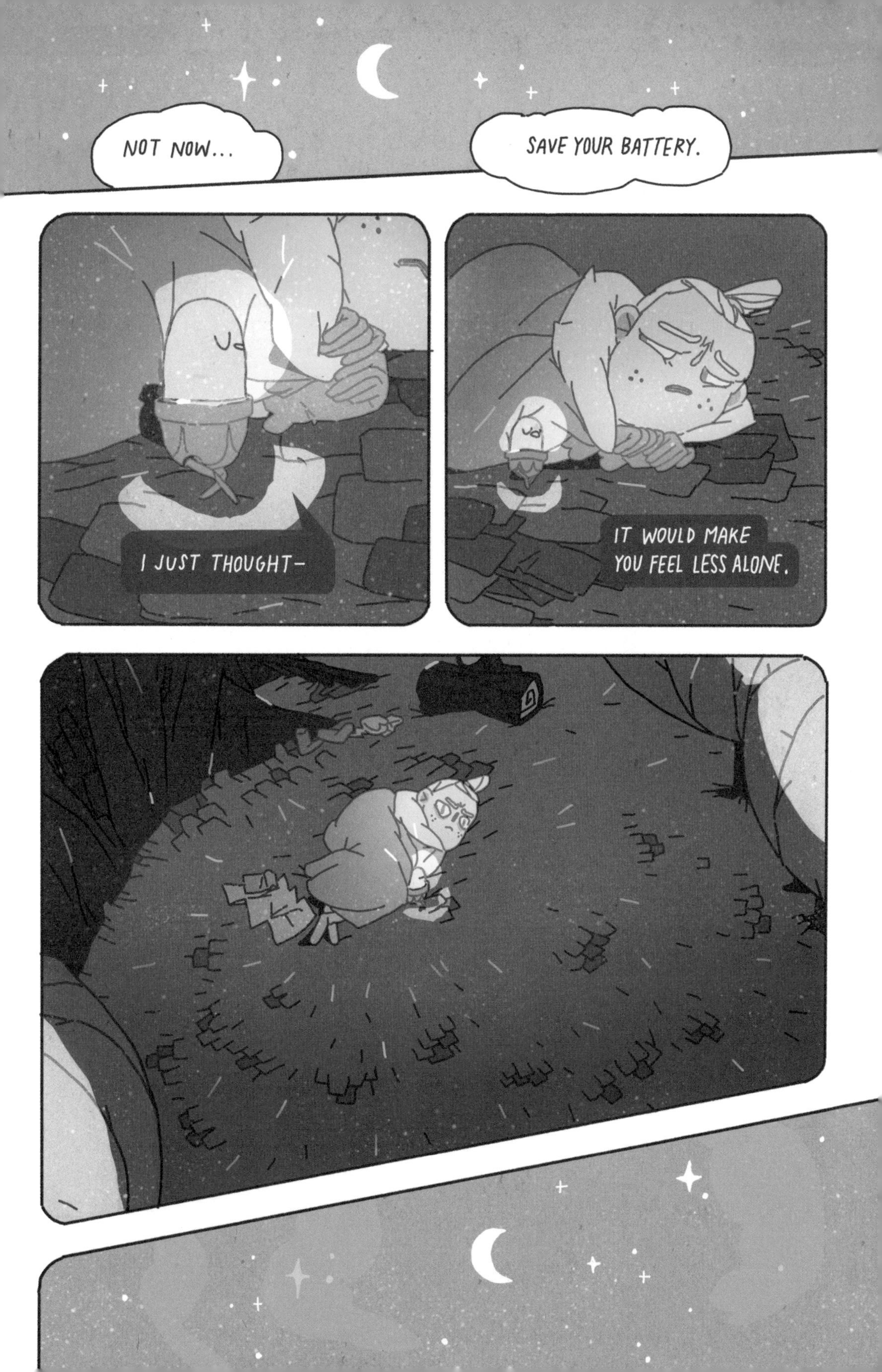
NOT NOW...
SAVE YOUR BATTERY.
I JUST THOUGHT-
IT WOULD MAKE YOU FEEL LESS ALONE.

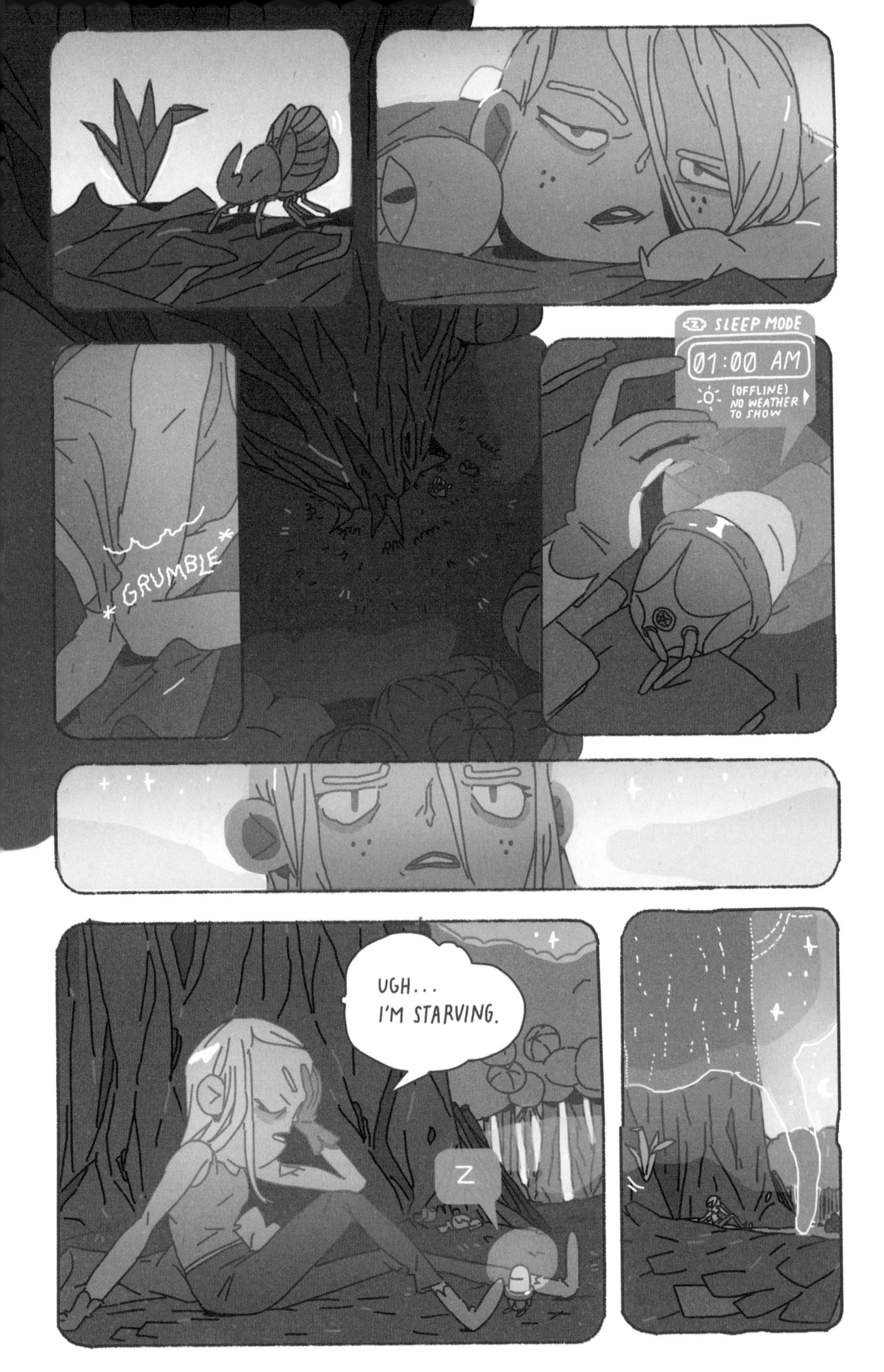
SLEEP MODE
01:00 AM
(OFFLINE) NO WEATHER TO SHOW
GRUMBLE
UGH... I'M STARVING.
Z

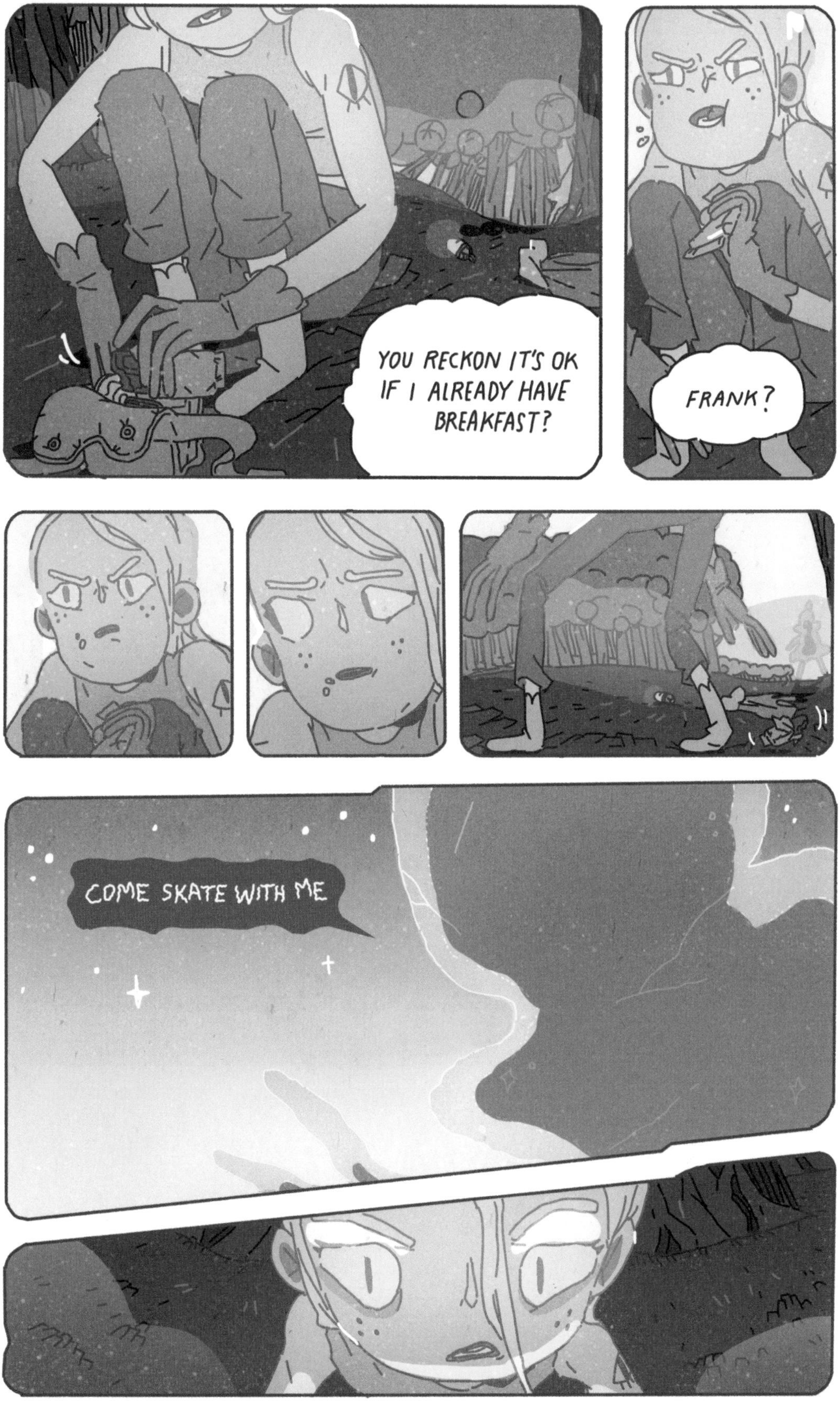
YOU RECKON IT'S OK IF I ALREADY HAVE BREAKFAST?
FRANK?
COME SKATE WITH ME

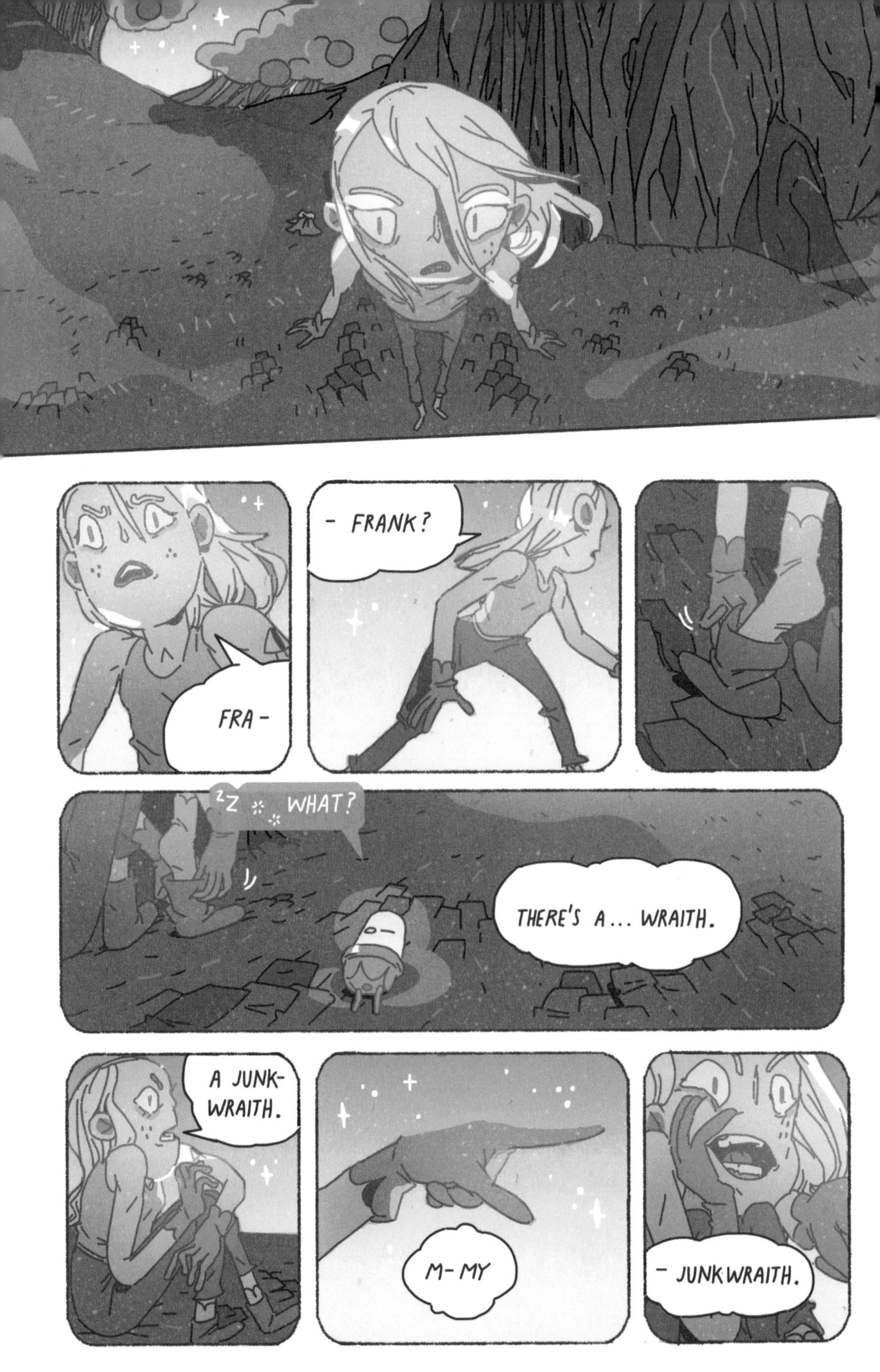
FRA-
- FRANK?
zZ WHAT?
THERE'S A... WRAITH.
A JUNK-
WRAITH.
M-MY
- JUNKWRAITH.

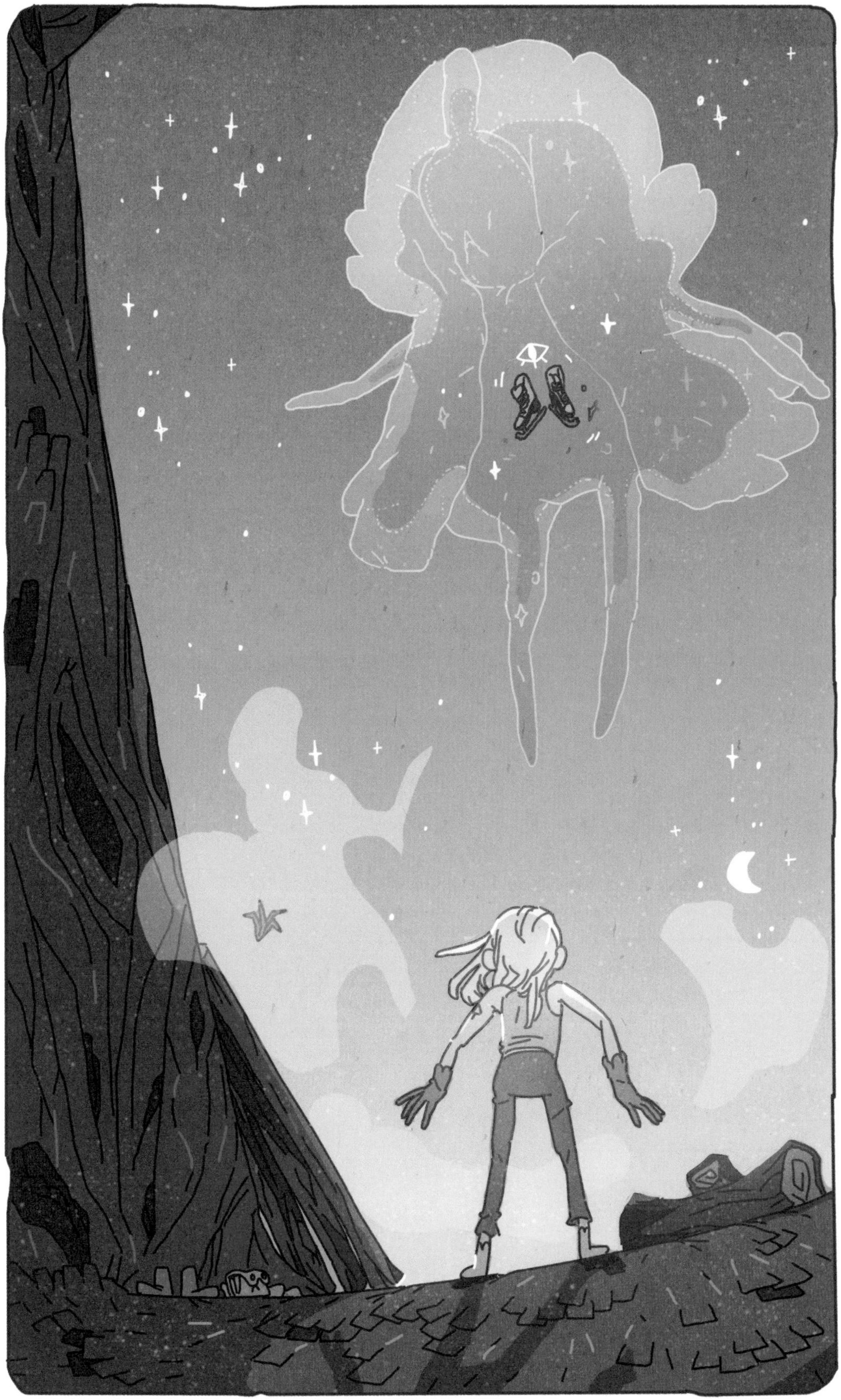

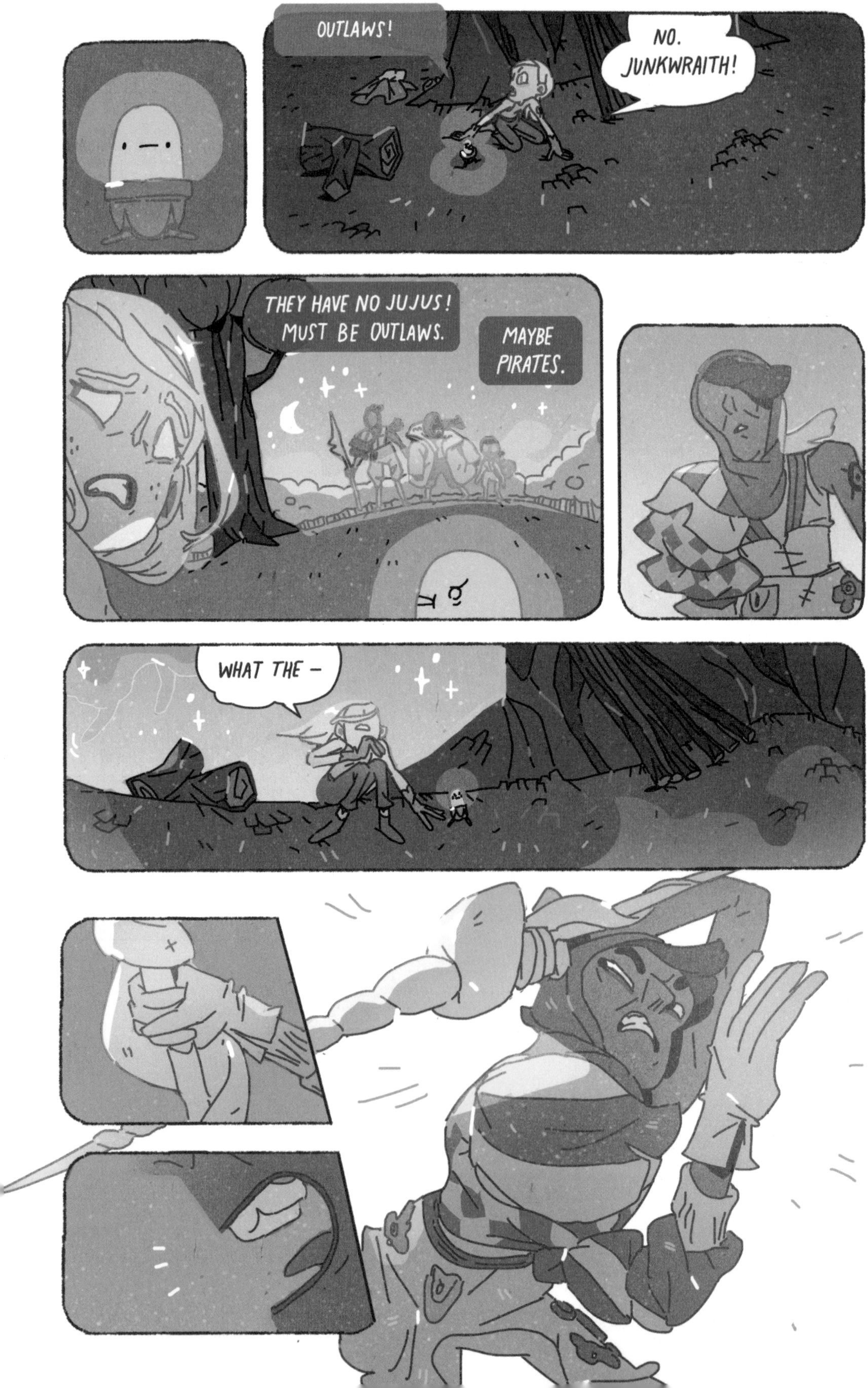
OUTLAWS!
NO. JUNKWRAITH!
THEY HAVE NO JUJUS! MUST BE OUTLAWS.
MAYBE PIRATES.
WHAT THE -

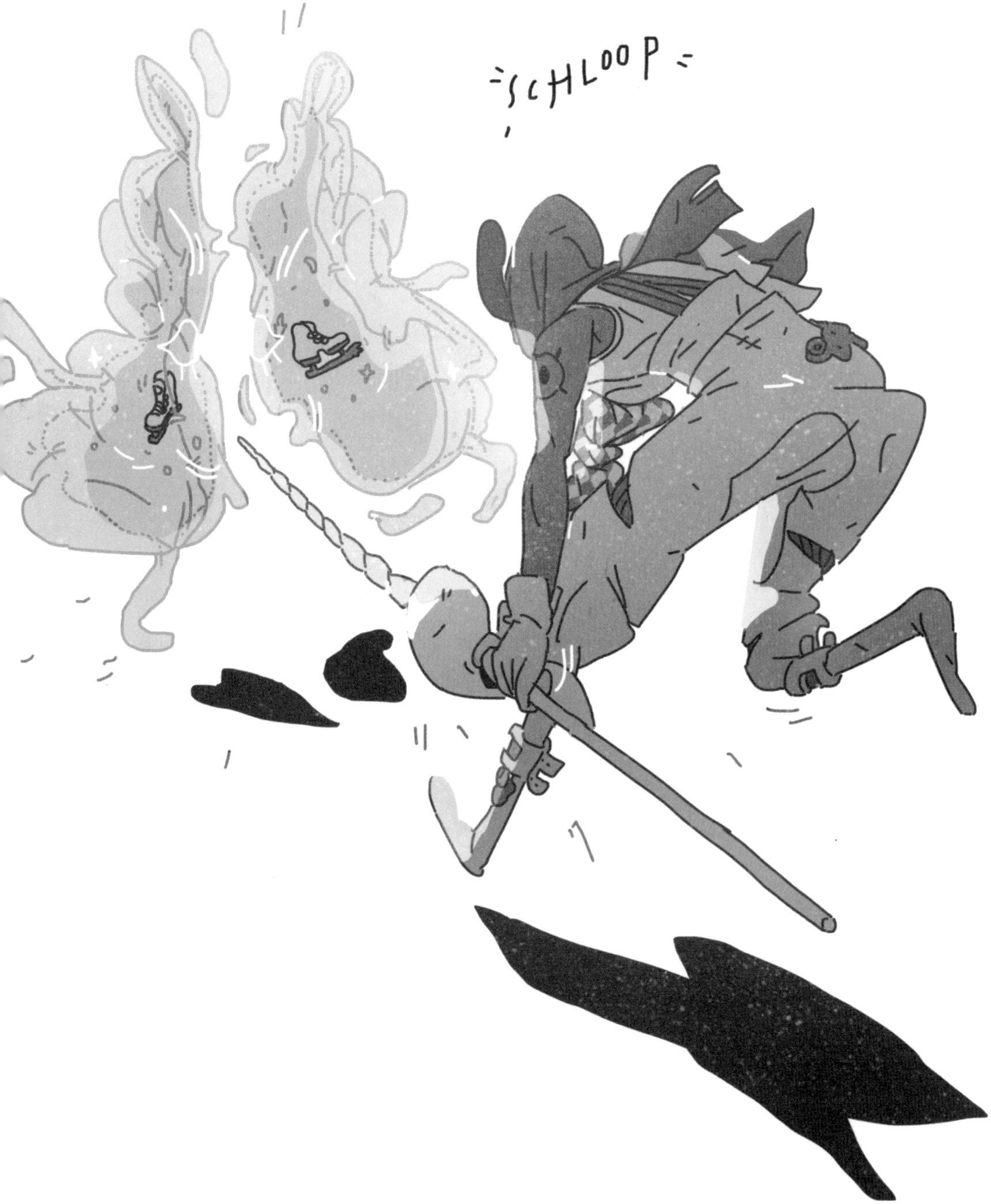
SCHLOOP

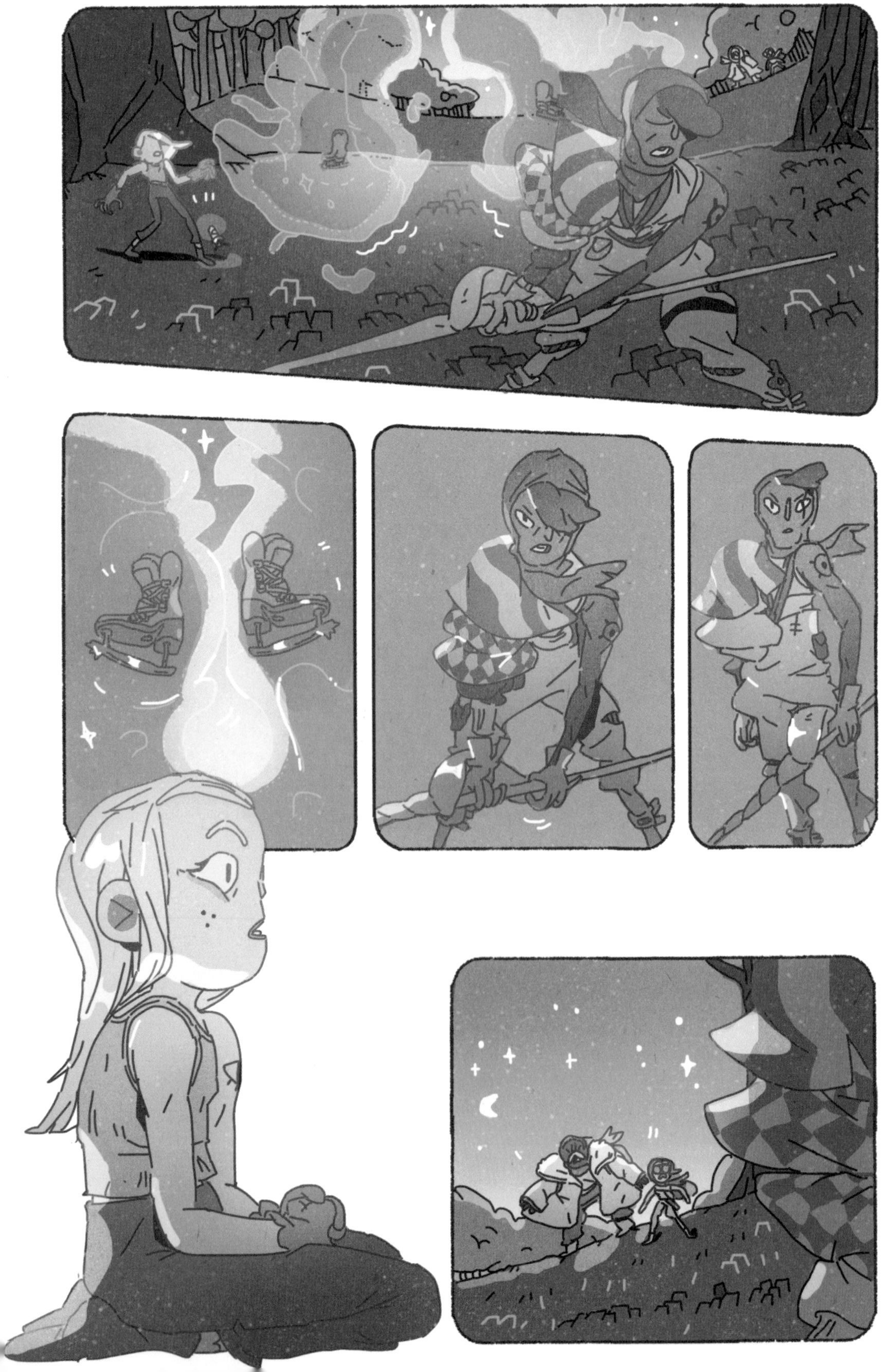

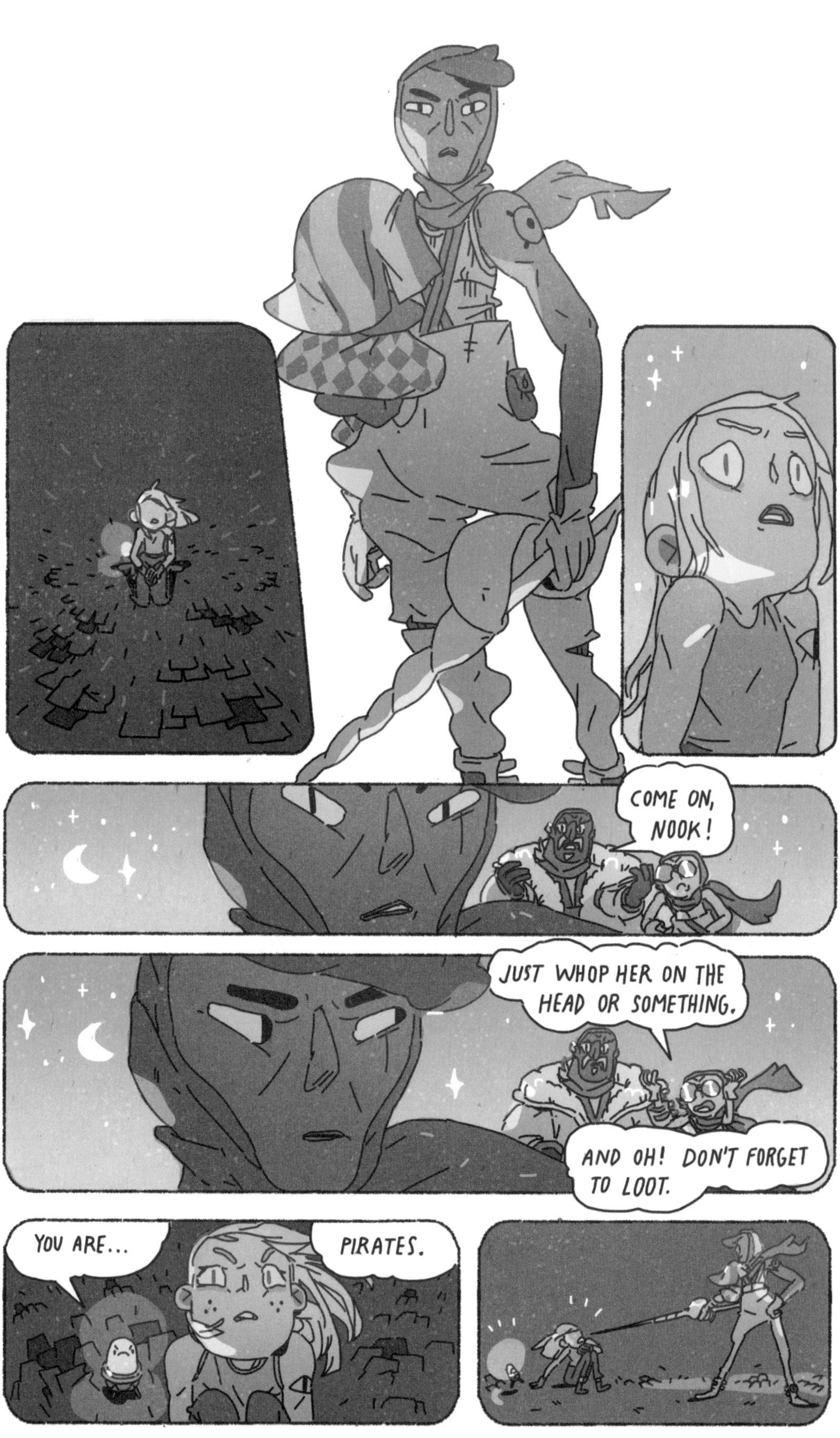
COME ON, NOOK!
JUST WHOP HER ON THE HEAD OR SOMETHING.
AND OH! DON'T FORGET TO LOOT.
YOU ARE...
PIRATES.

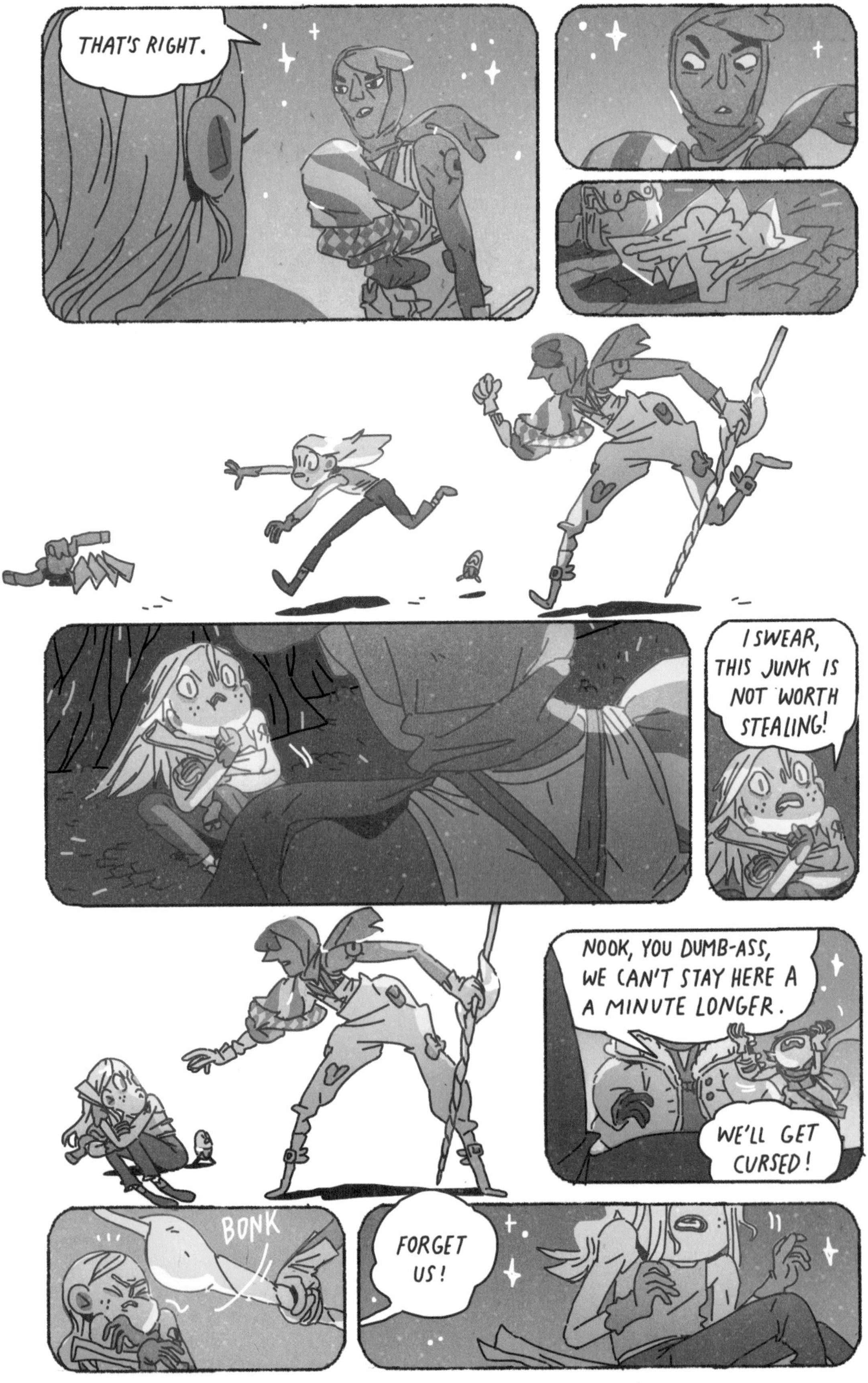
THAT'S RIGHT.
I SWEAR, THIS JUNK IS NOT WORTH STEALING!
NOOK, YOU DUMB-ASS, WE CAN'T STAY HERE A A MINUTE LONGER.
WE'LL GET CURSED!
BONK
FORGET US!

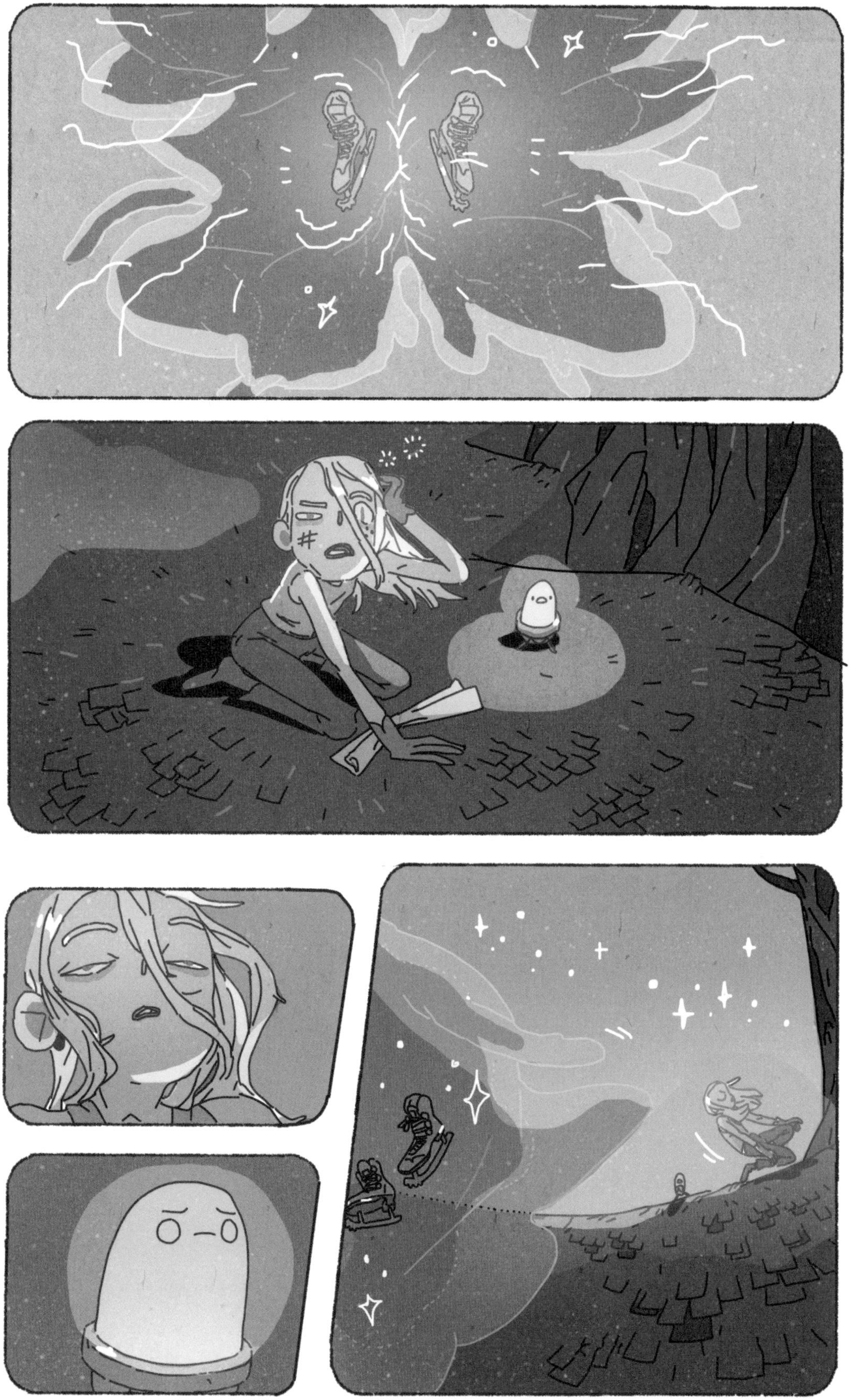

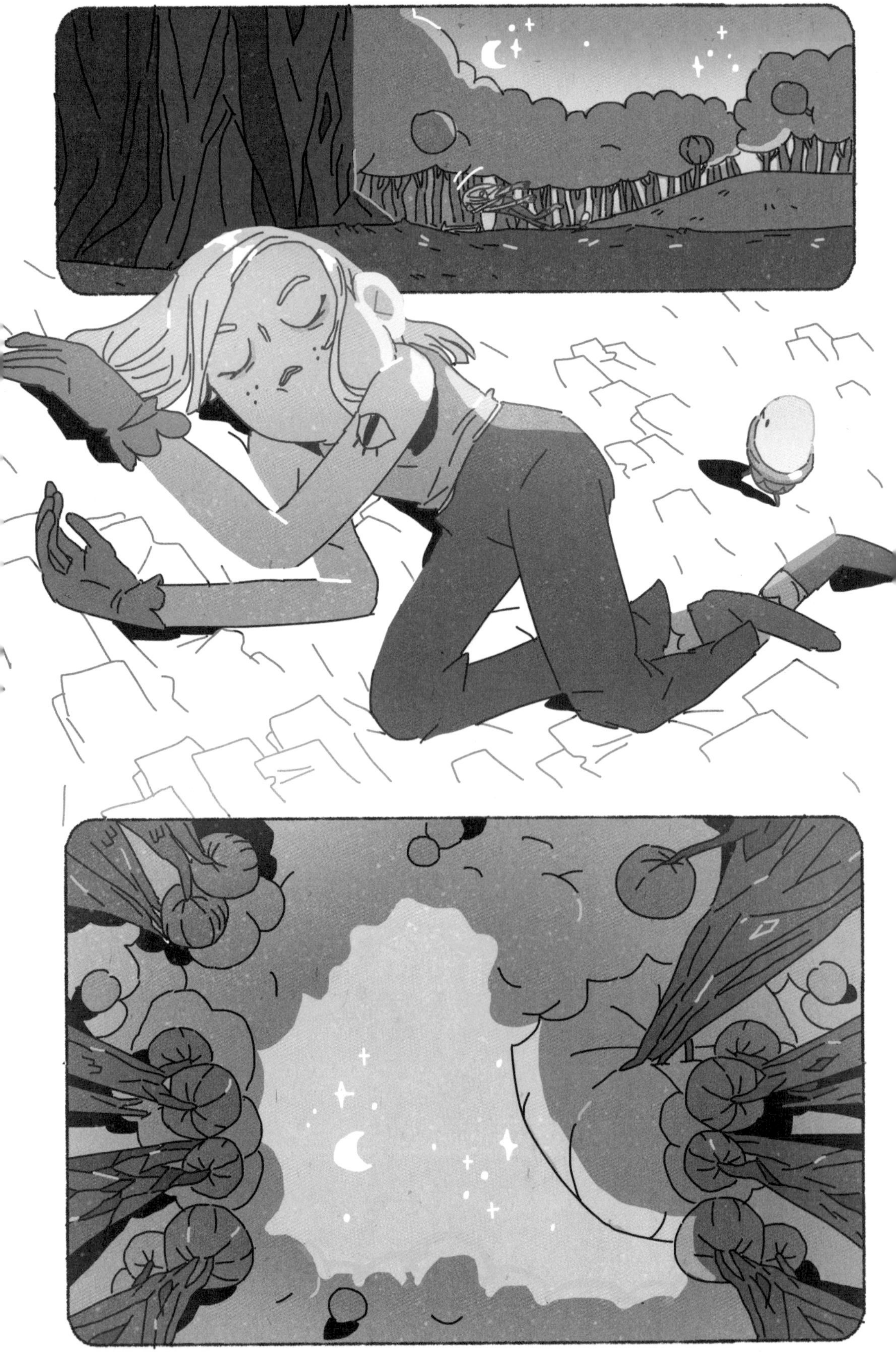

EPISODE 4
THE CAVE OF RECOVERY

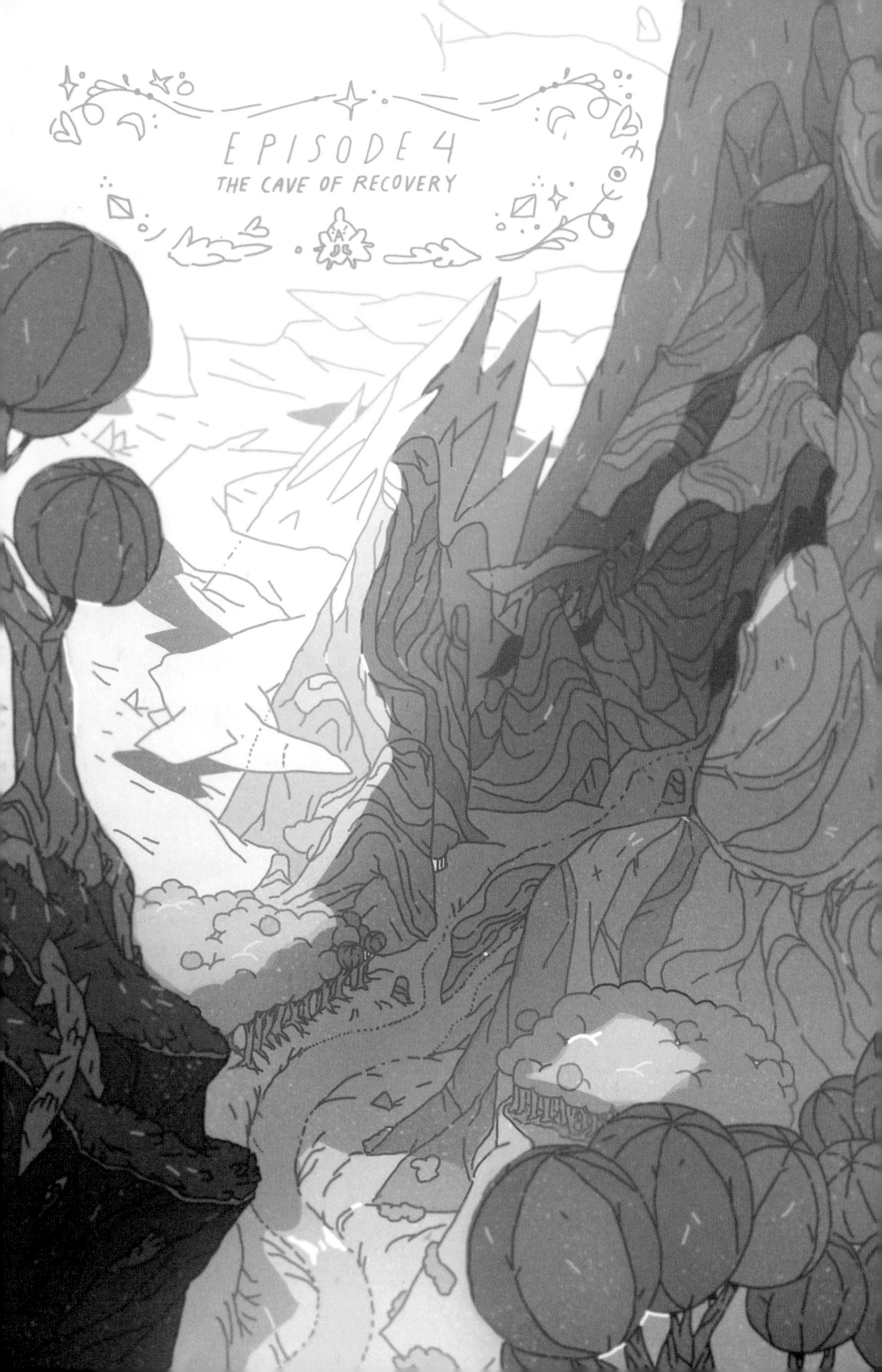

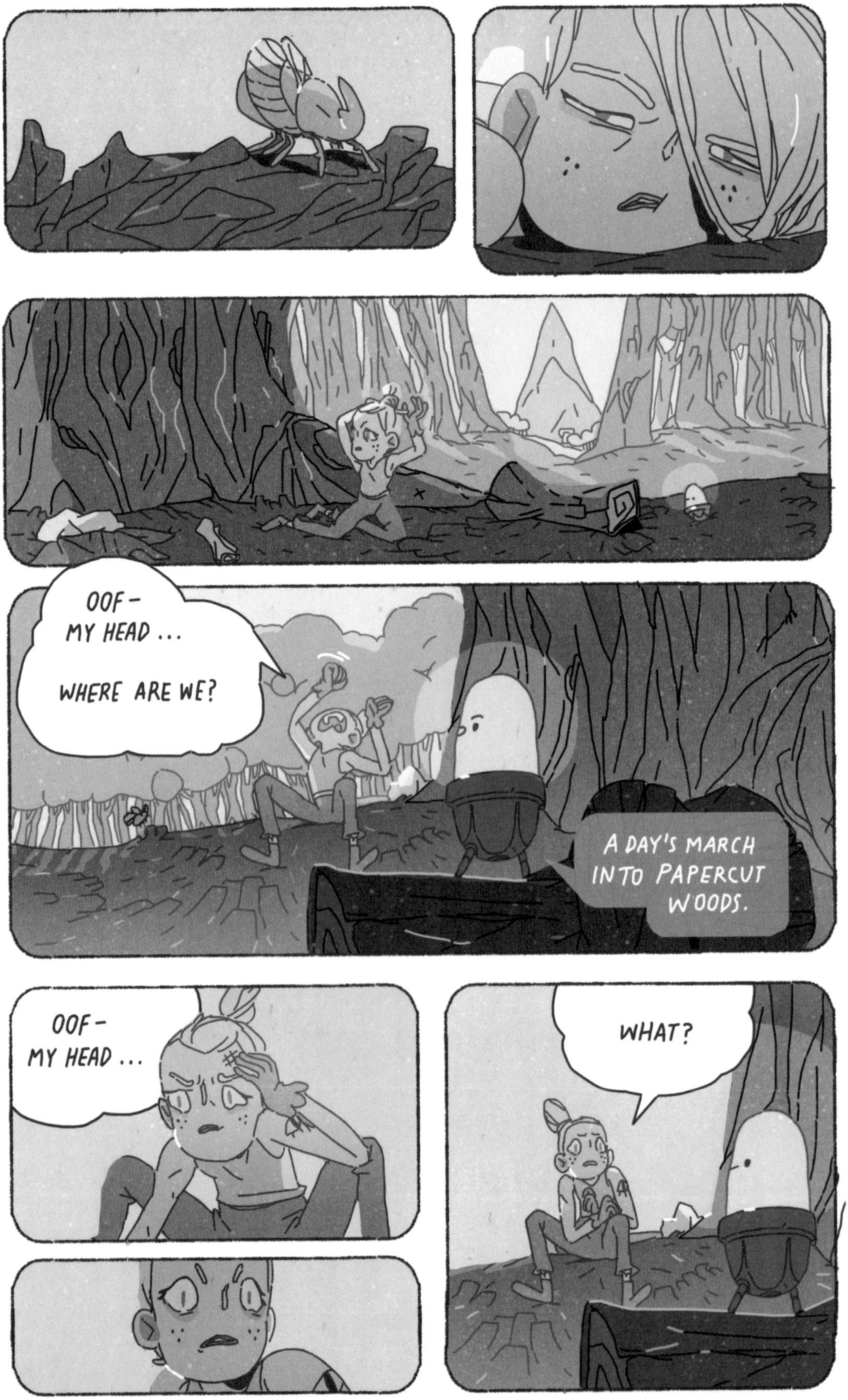
OOF- MY HEAD ... WHERE ARE WE?
A DAY'S MARCH INTO PAPERCUT WOODS.
OOF- MY HEAD ...
WHAT?

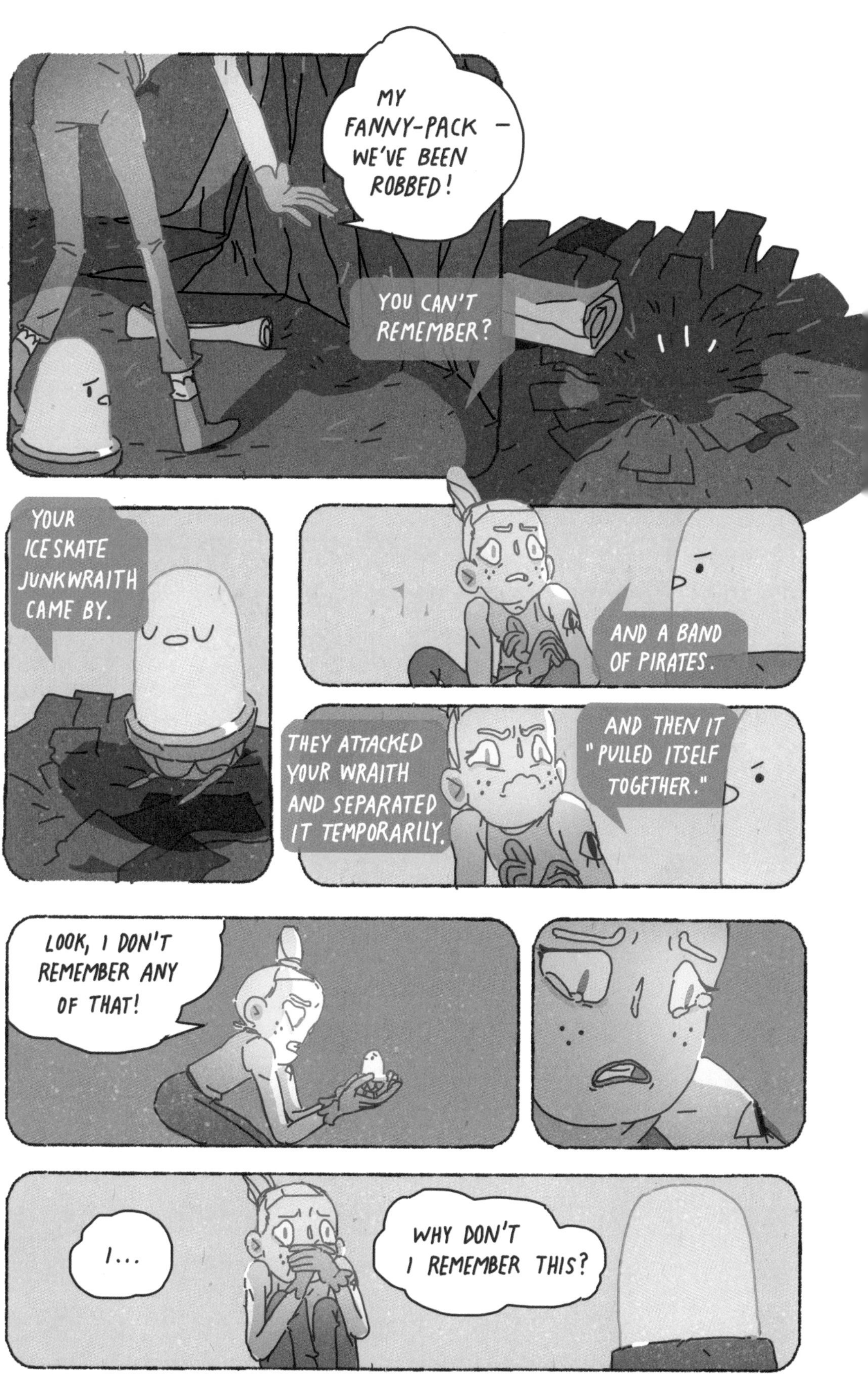
MY FANNY-PACK — WE'VE BEEN ROBBED!
YOU CAN'T REMEMBER?
YOUR ICE SKATE JUNKWRAITH CAME BY.
AND A BAND OF PIRATES.
THEY ATTACKED YOUR WRAITH AND SEPARATED IT TEMPORARILY.
AND THEN IT "PULLED ITSELF TOGETHER."
LOOK, I DON'T REMEMBER ANY OF THAT!
I...
WHY DON'T I REMEMBER THIS?

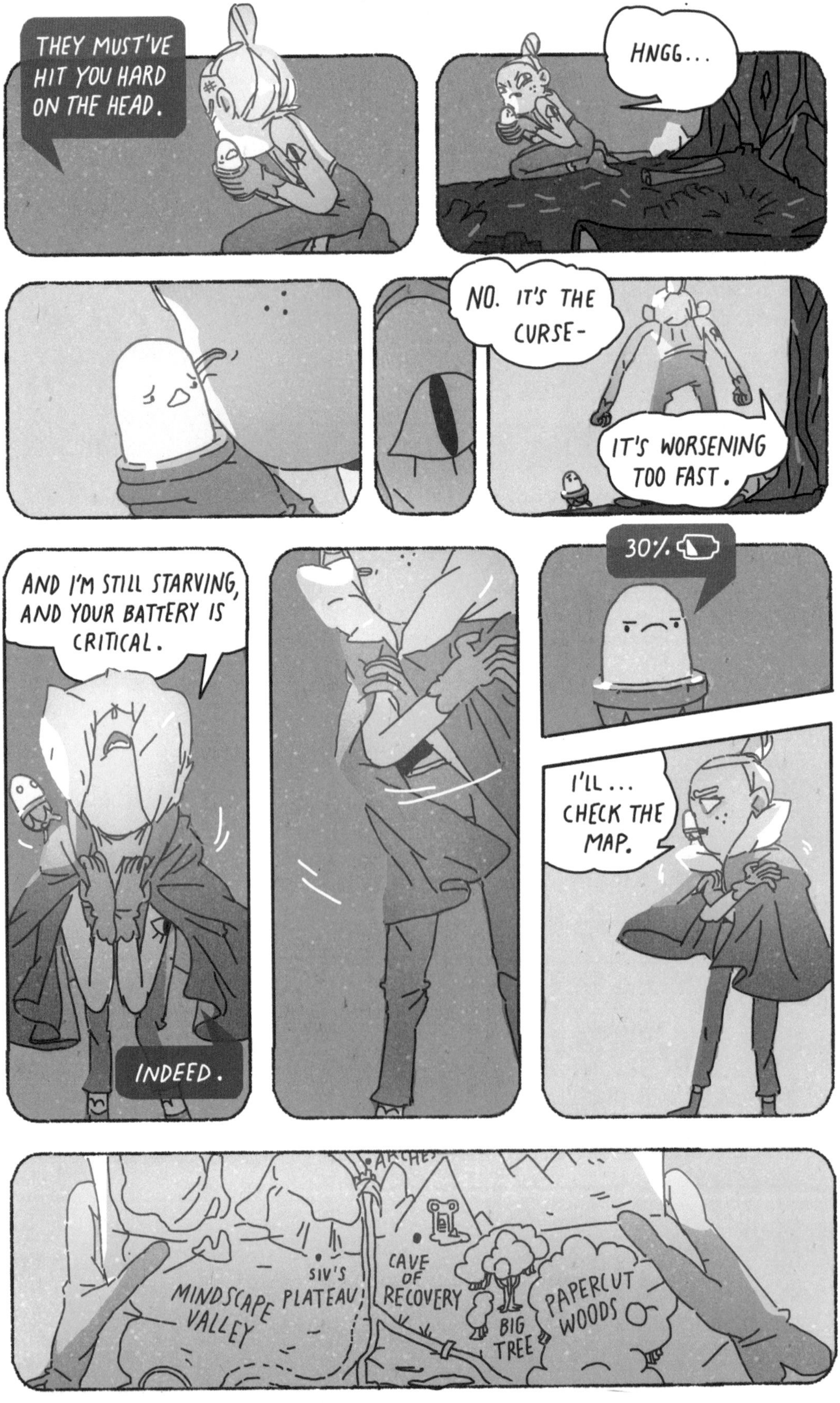
THEY MUST'VE HIT YOU HARD ON THE HEAD.
HNGG...
NO. IT'S THE CURSE-
IT'S WORSENING TOO FAST.
AND I'M STILL STARVING, AND YOUR BATTERY IS CRITICAL.
INDEED.
30%.
I'LL... CHECK THE MAP.
MINDSCAPE VALLEY
SIV'S PLATEAU
CAVE OF RECOVERY
BIG TREE
PAPERCUT WOODS

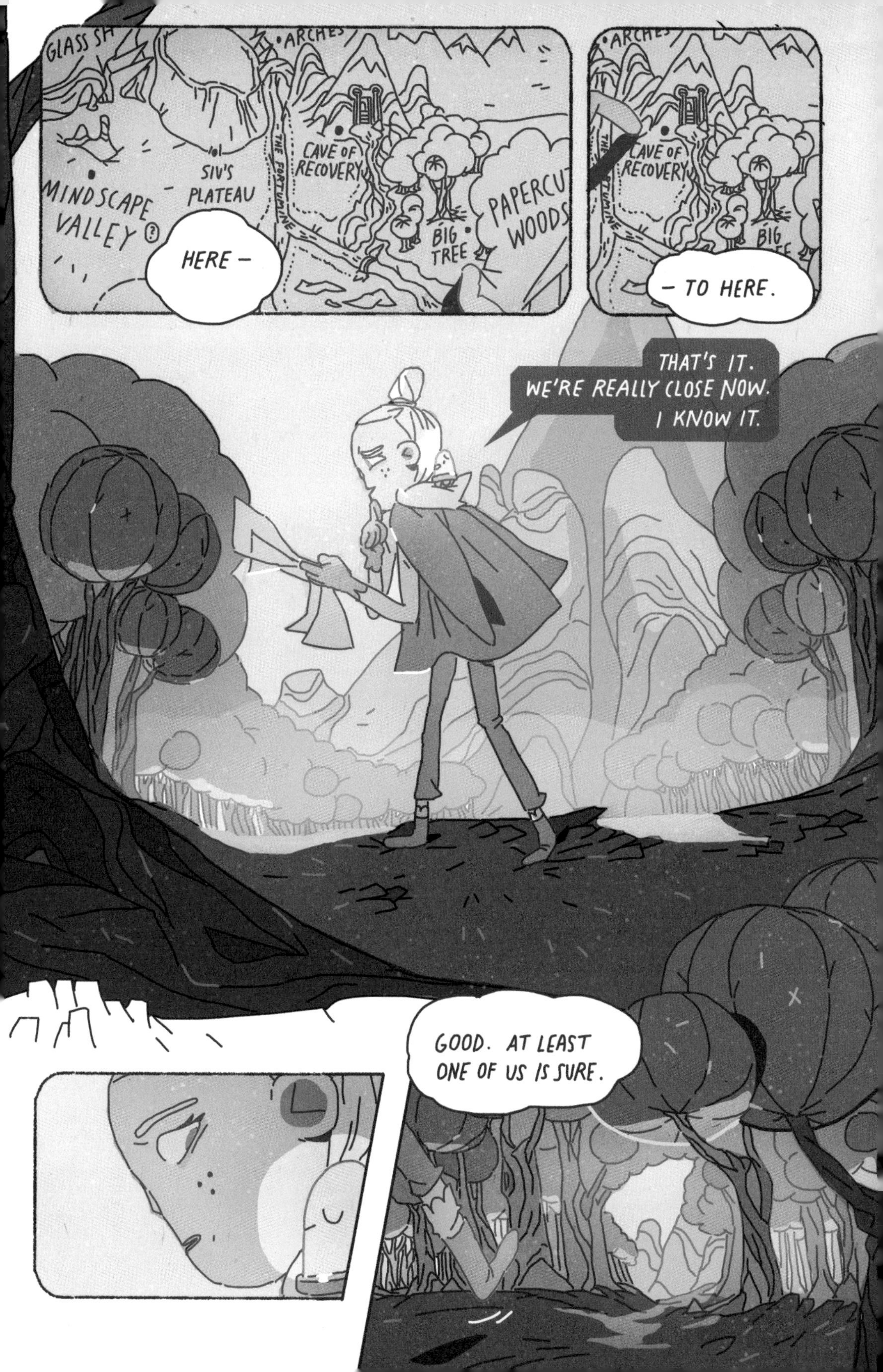
GLASS SH
ARCHES
MINDSCAPE VALLEY
SIV'S PLATEAU
THE FORTUMINE
CAVE OF RECOVERY
BIG TREE
PAPERCUT WOODS
HERE –
– TO HERE.
THAT'S IT. WE'RE REALLY CLOSE NOW. I KNOW IT.
GOOD. AT LEAST ONE OF US IS SURE.

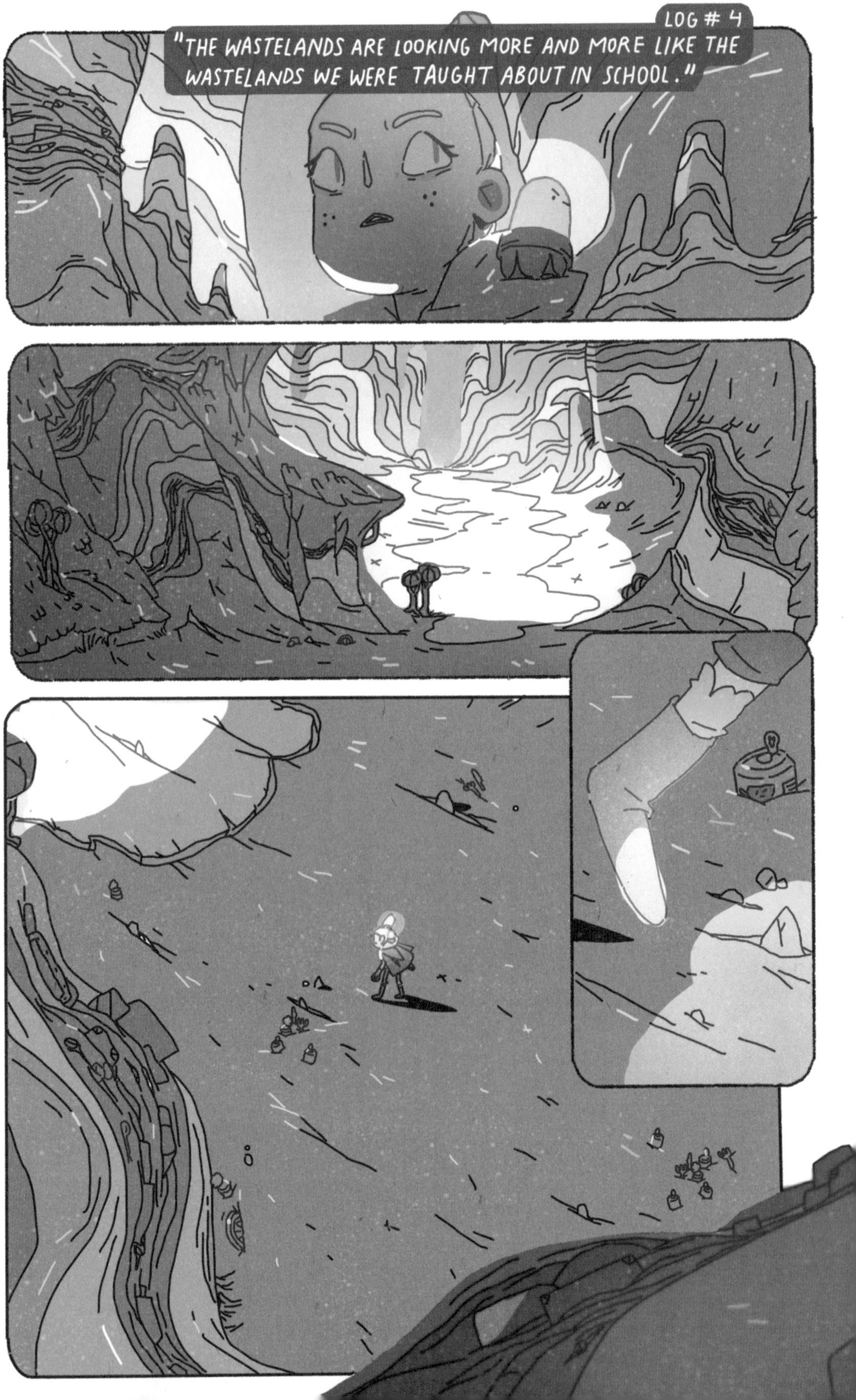
LOG # 4
"THE WASTELANDS ARE LOOKING MORE AND MORE LIKE THE WASTELANDS WE WERE TAUGHT ABOUT IN SCHOOL."

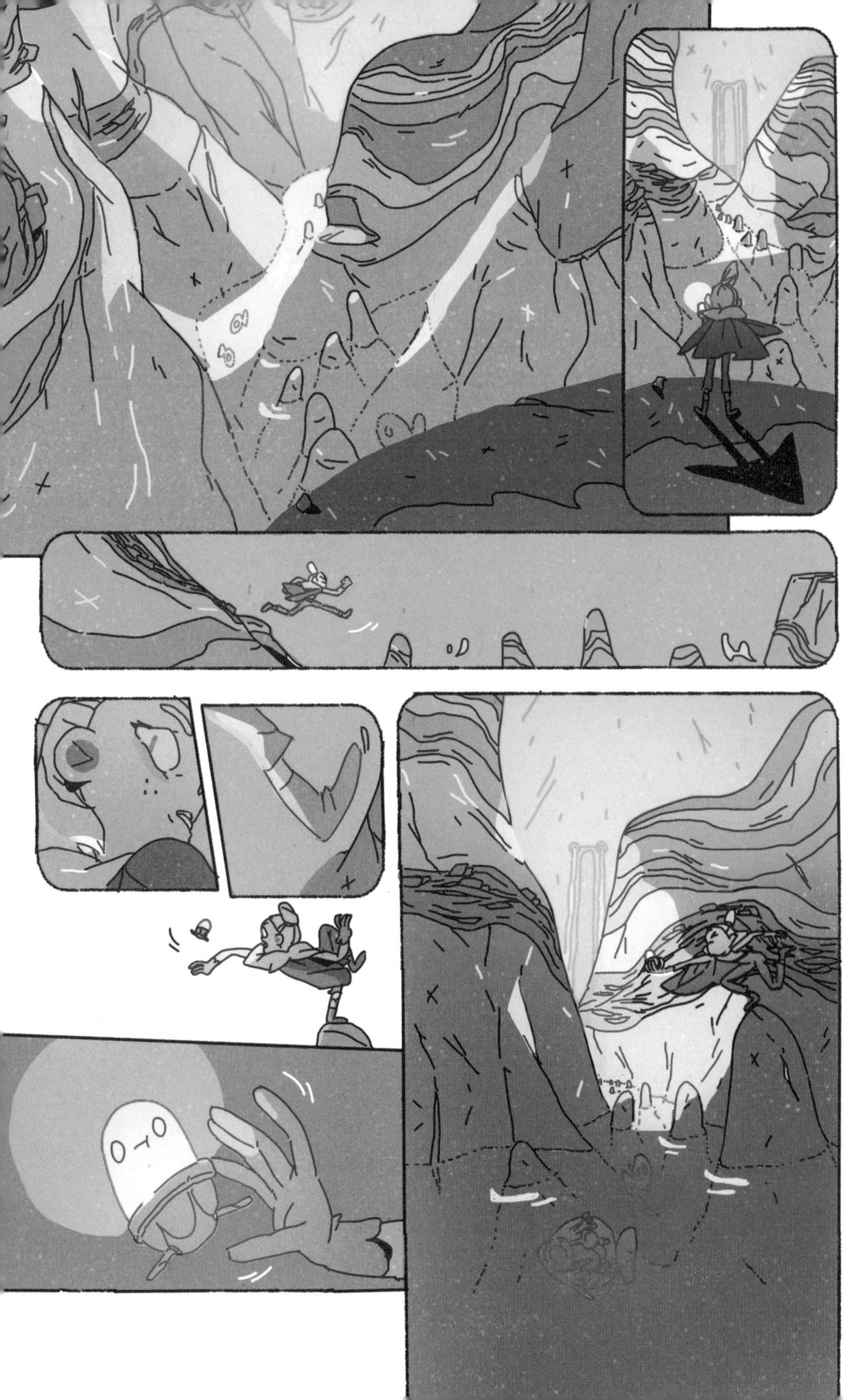

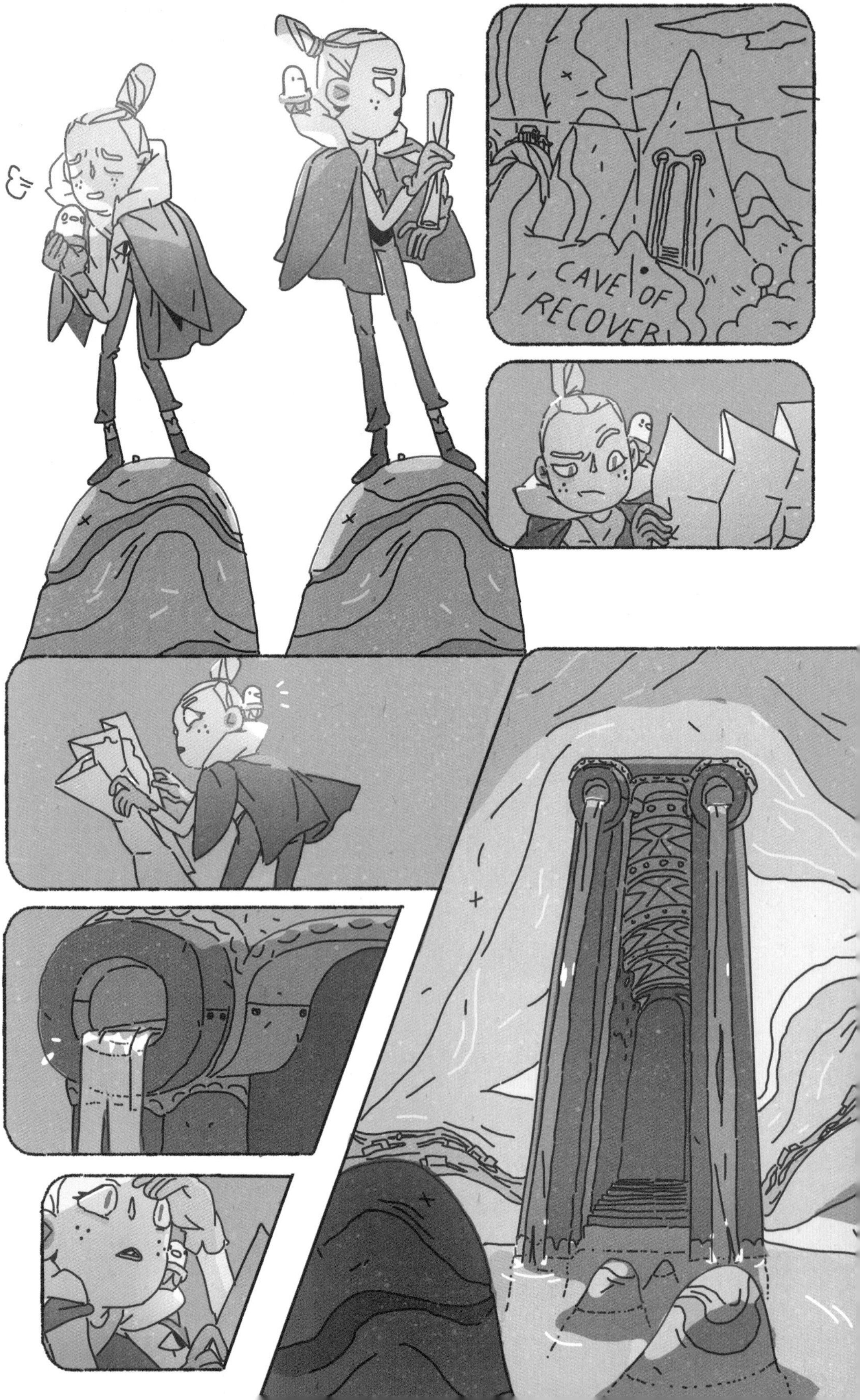
CAVE OF
RECOVER

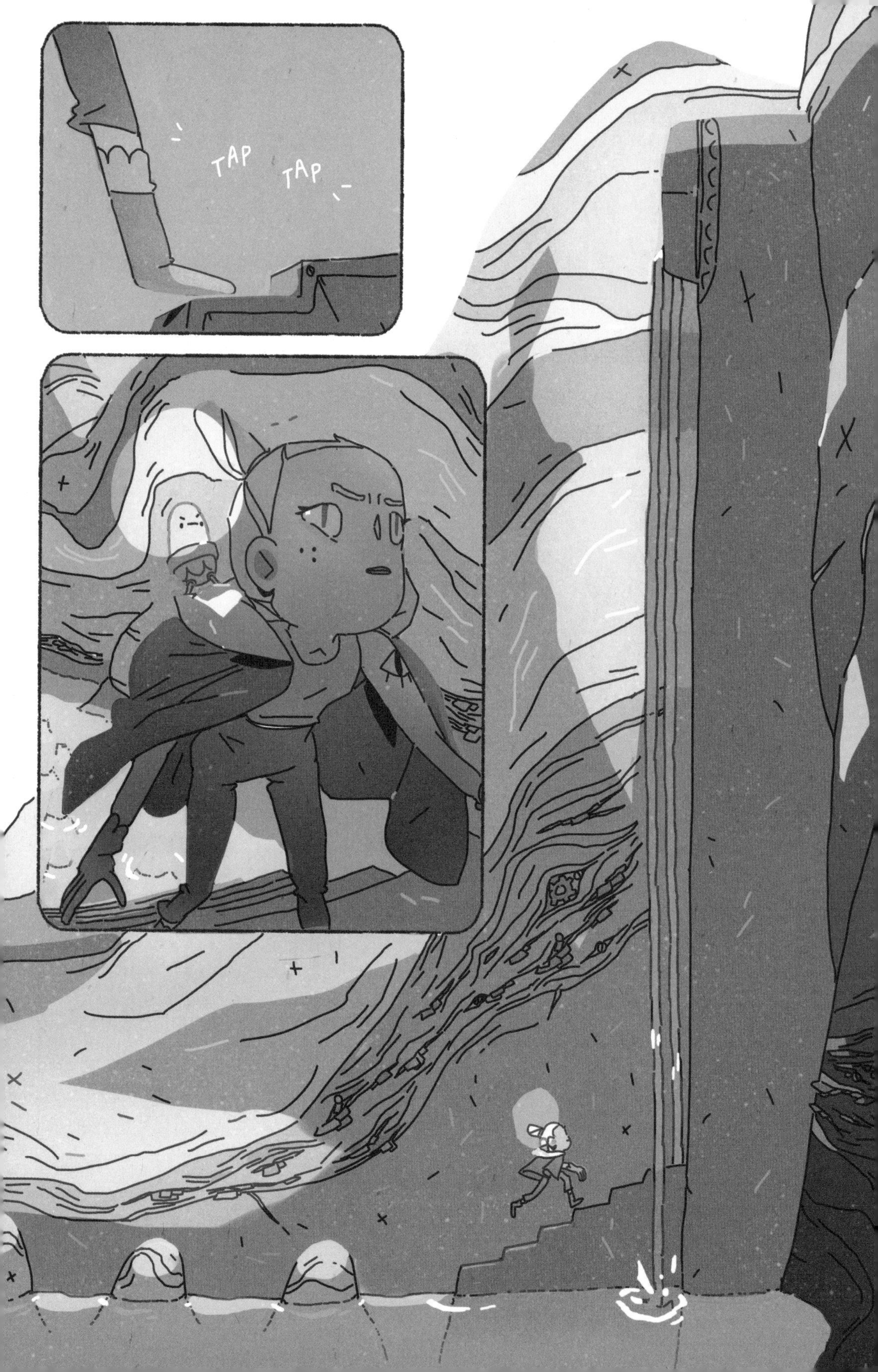
TAP
TAP

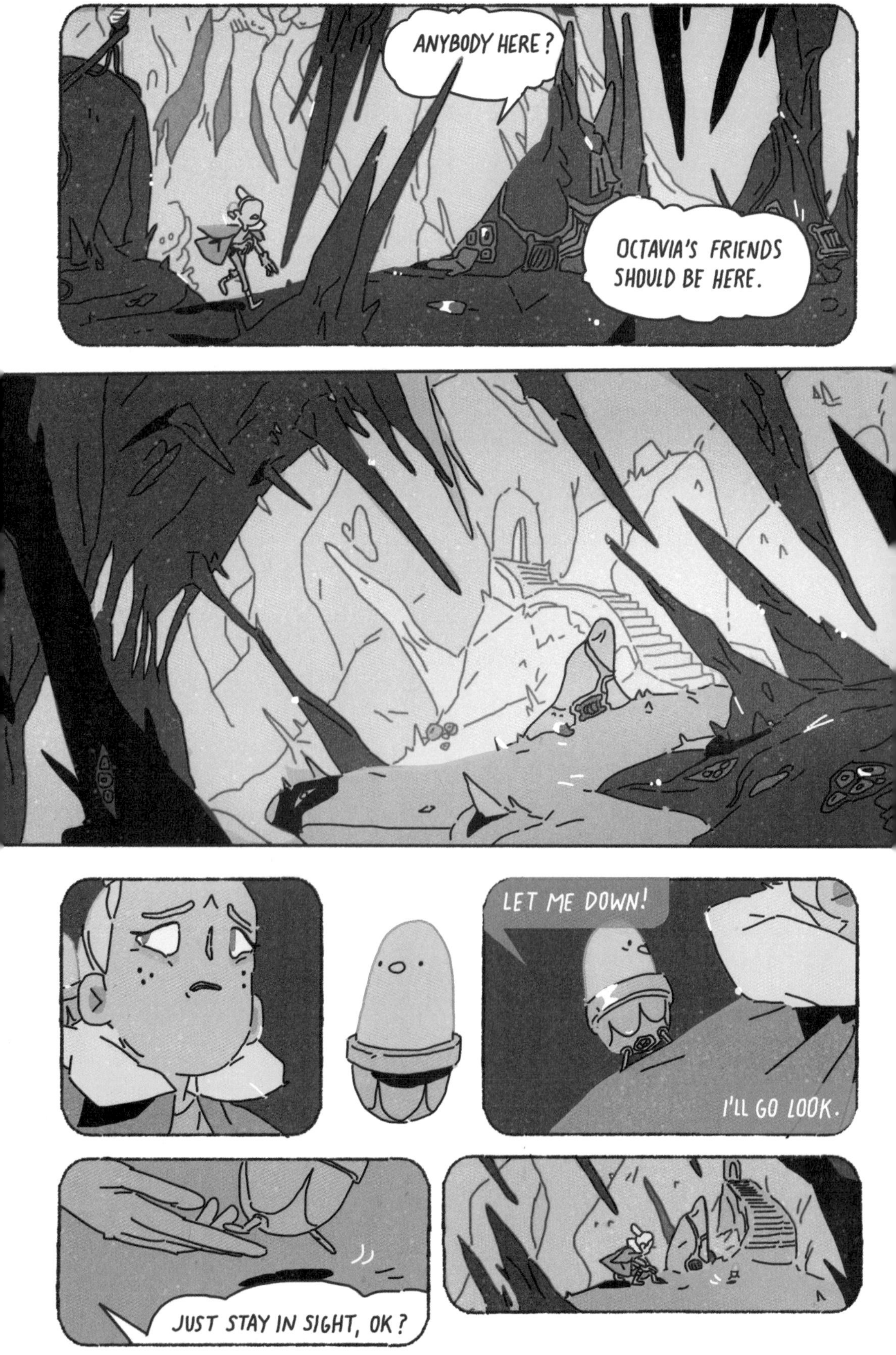
ANYBODY HERE?
OCTAVIA'S FRIENDS SHOULD BE HERE.
LET ME DOWN!
I'LL GO LOOK.
JUST STAY IN SIGHT, OK?

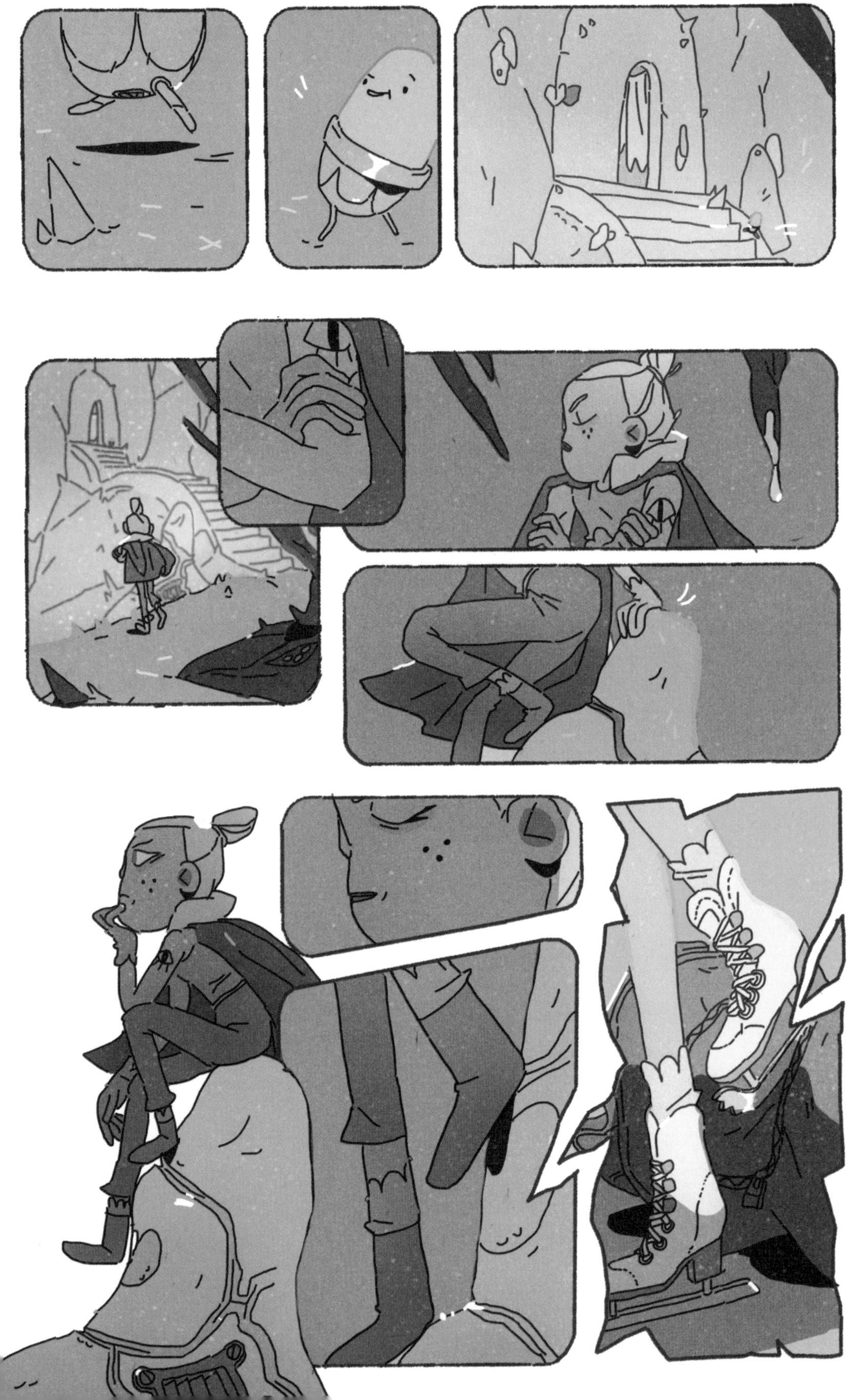

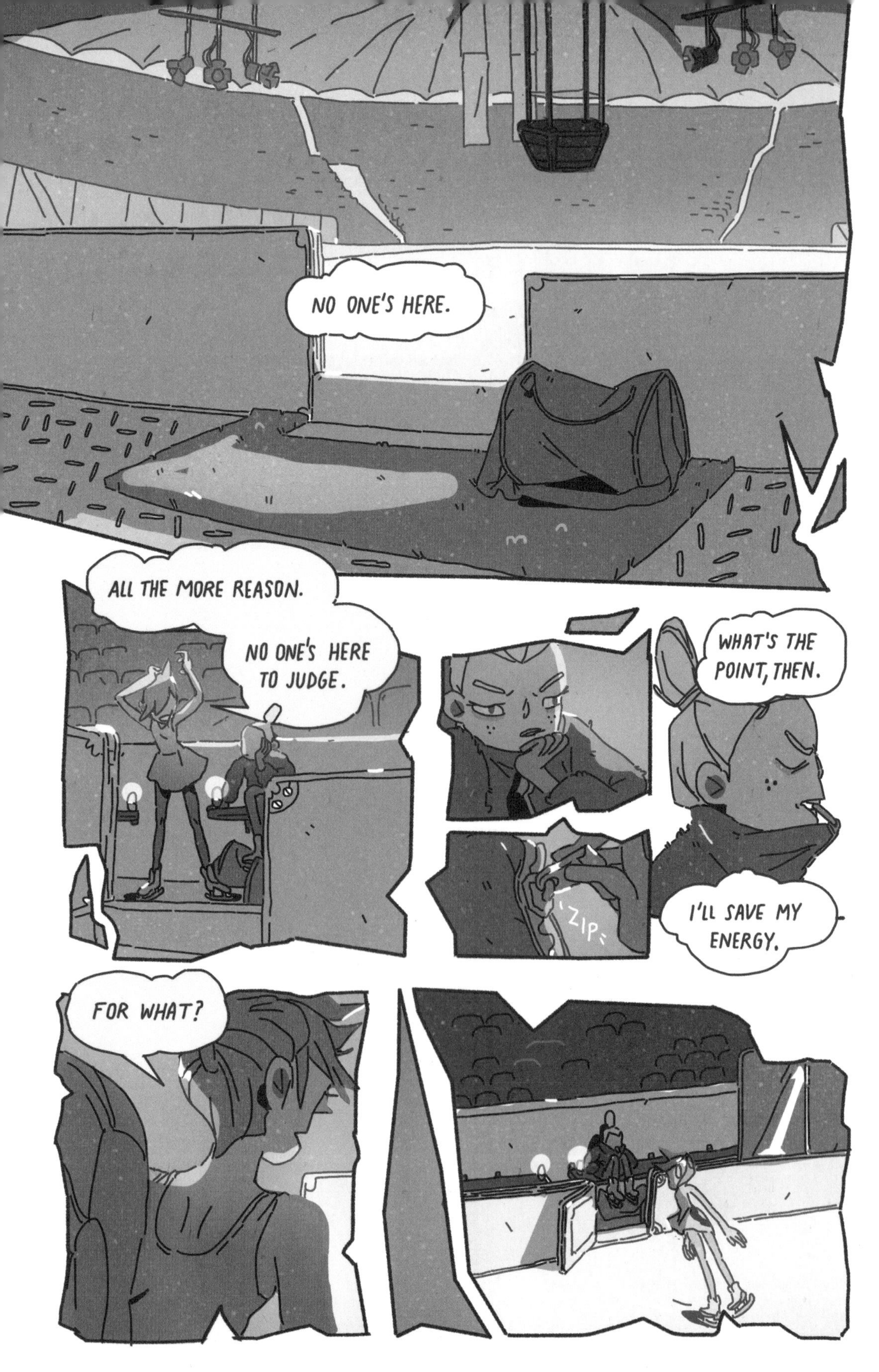
NO ONE'S HERE.
ALL THE MORE REASON.
NO ONE'S HERE TO JUDGE.
WHAT'S THE POINT, THEN.
ZIP
I'LL SAVE MY ENERGY.
FOR WHAT?

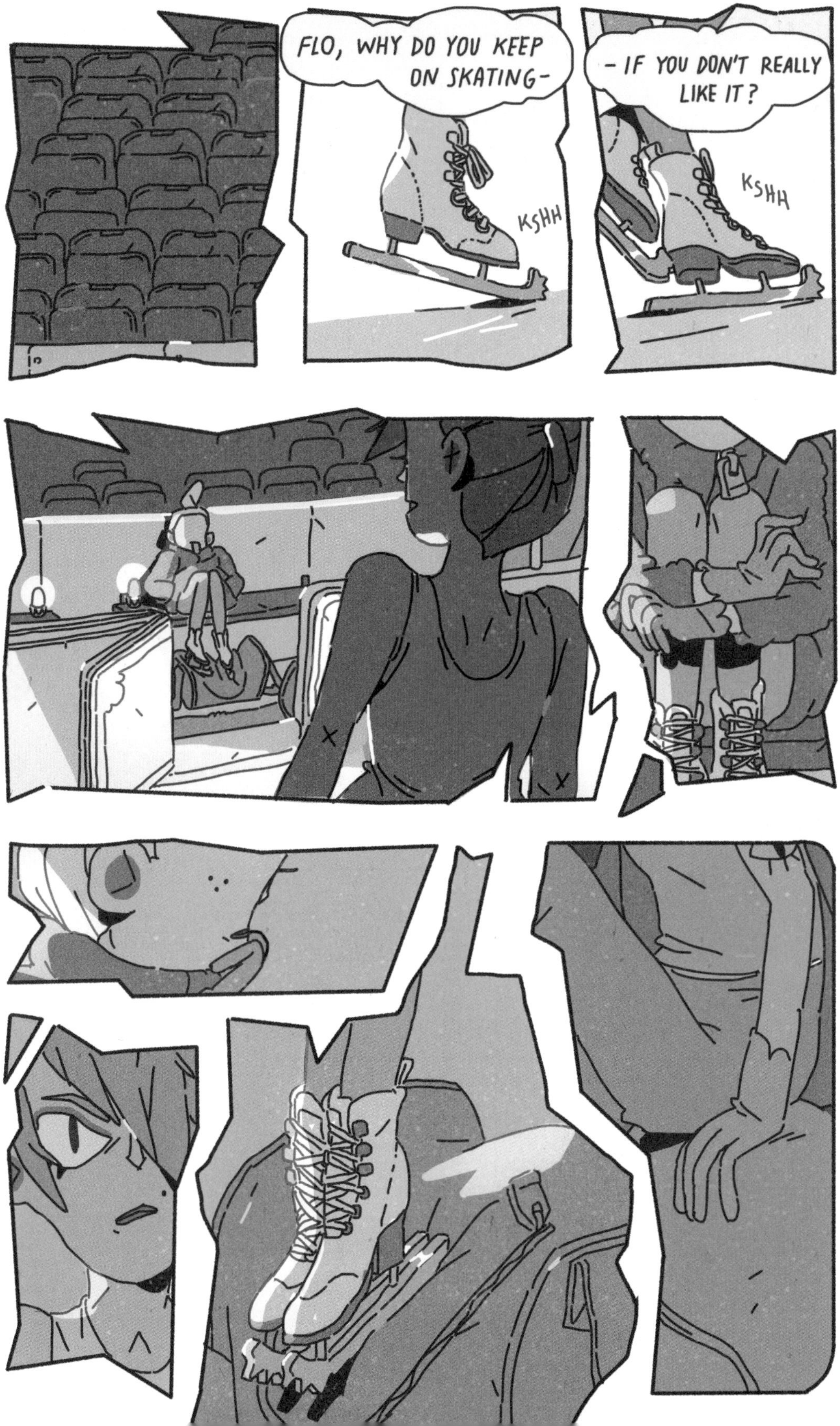

FLO, WHY DO YOU KEEP ON SKATING-
KSHH
- IF YOU DON'T REALLY LIKE IT?
KSHH

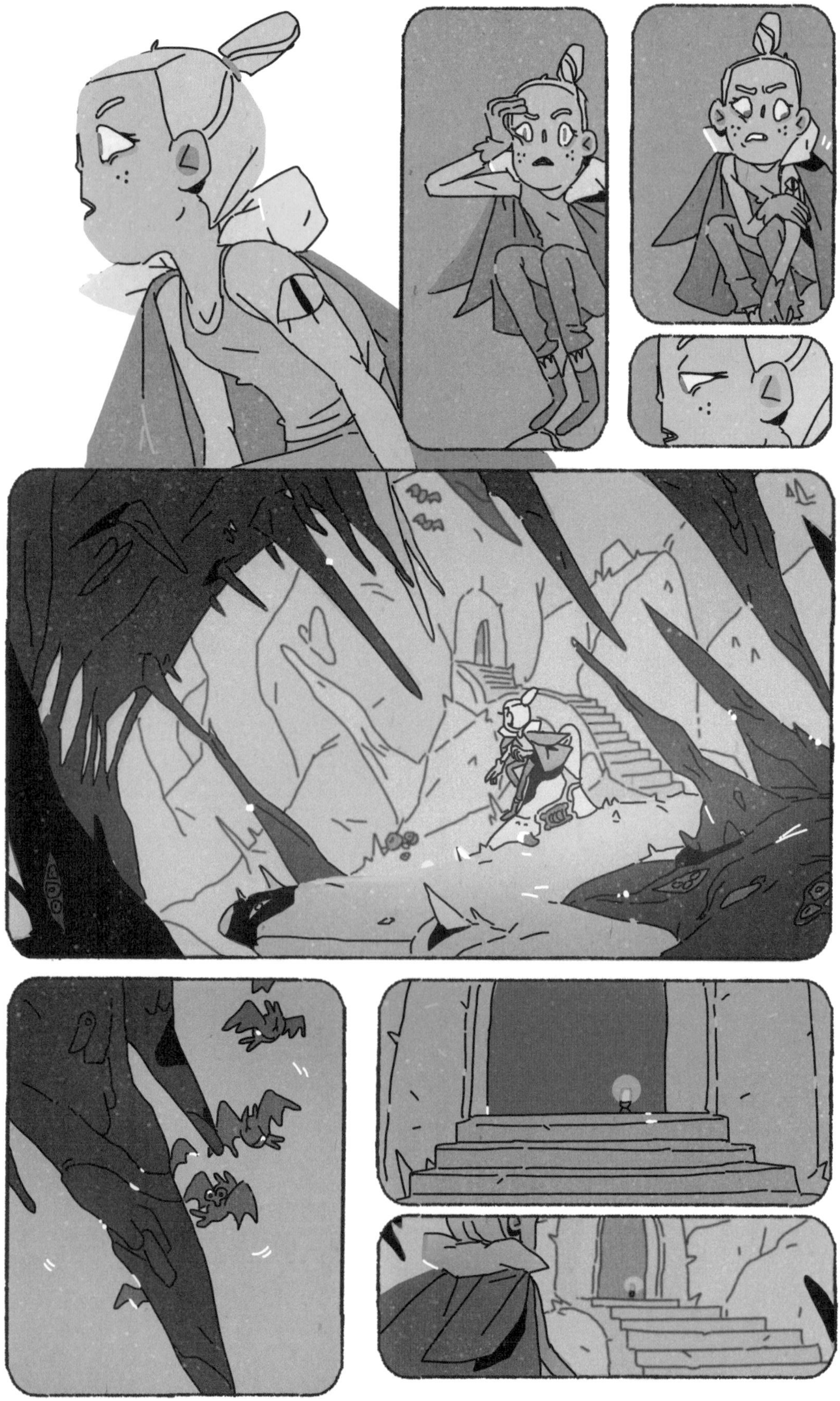

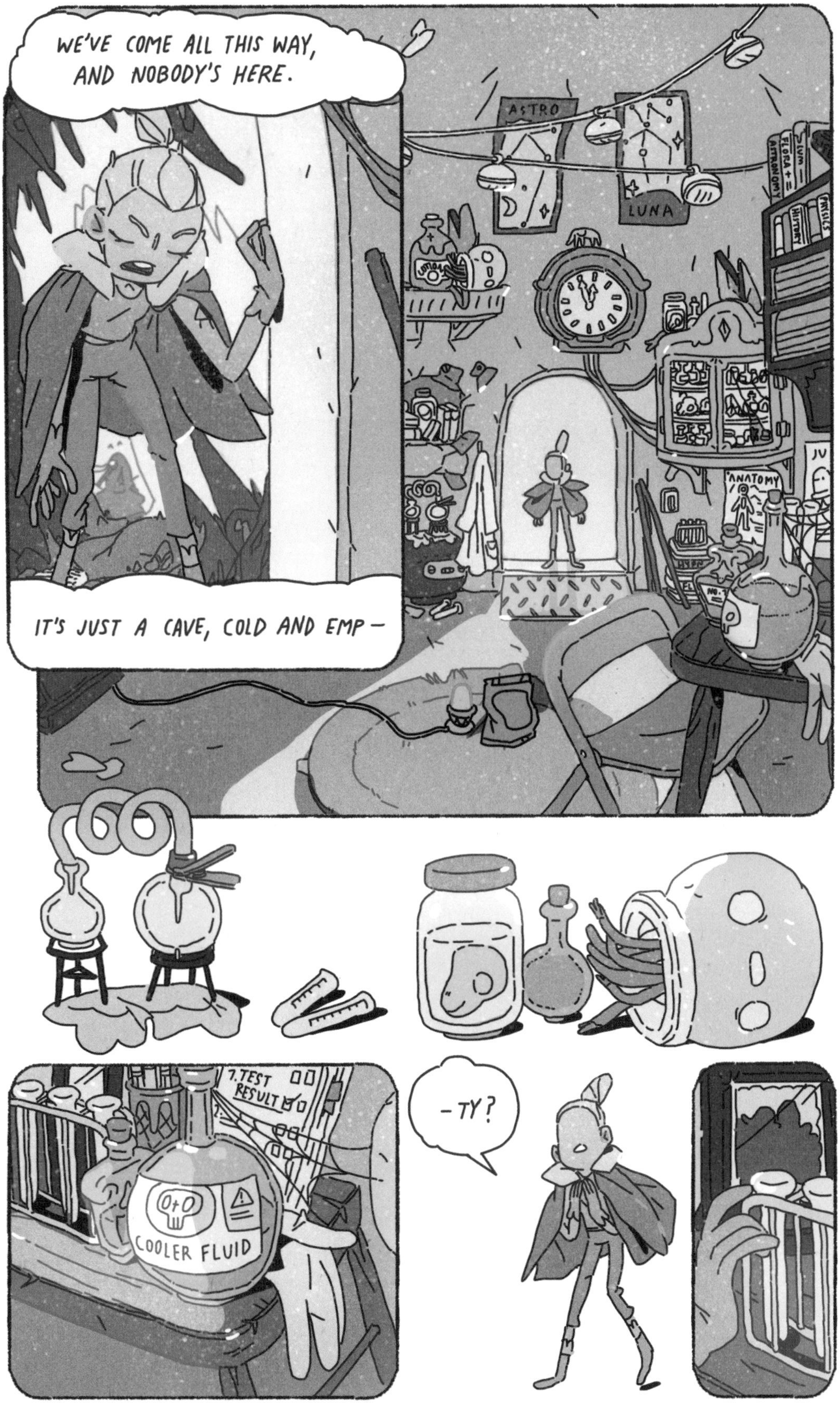
WE'VE COME ALL THIS WAY, AND NOBODY'S HERE.
IT'S JUST A CAVE, COLD AND EMP—
ASTRO
LUNA
LOTION
FLORA + FAUNA
ASTRONOMY
PHYSICS
HISTORY
ANATOMY
7. TEST RESULT
COOLER FLUID
—TY?

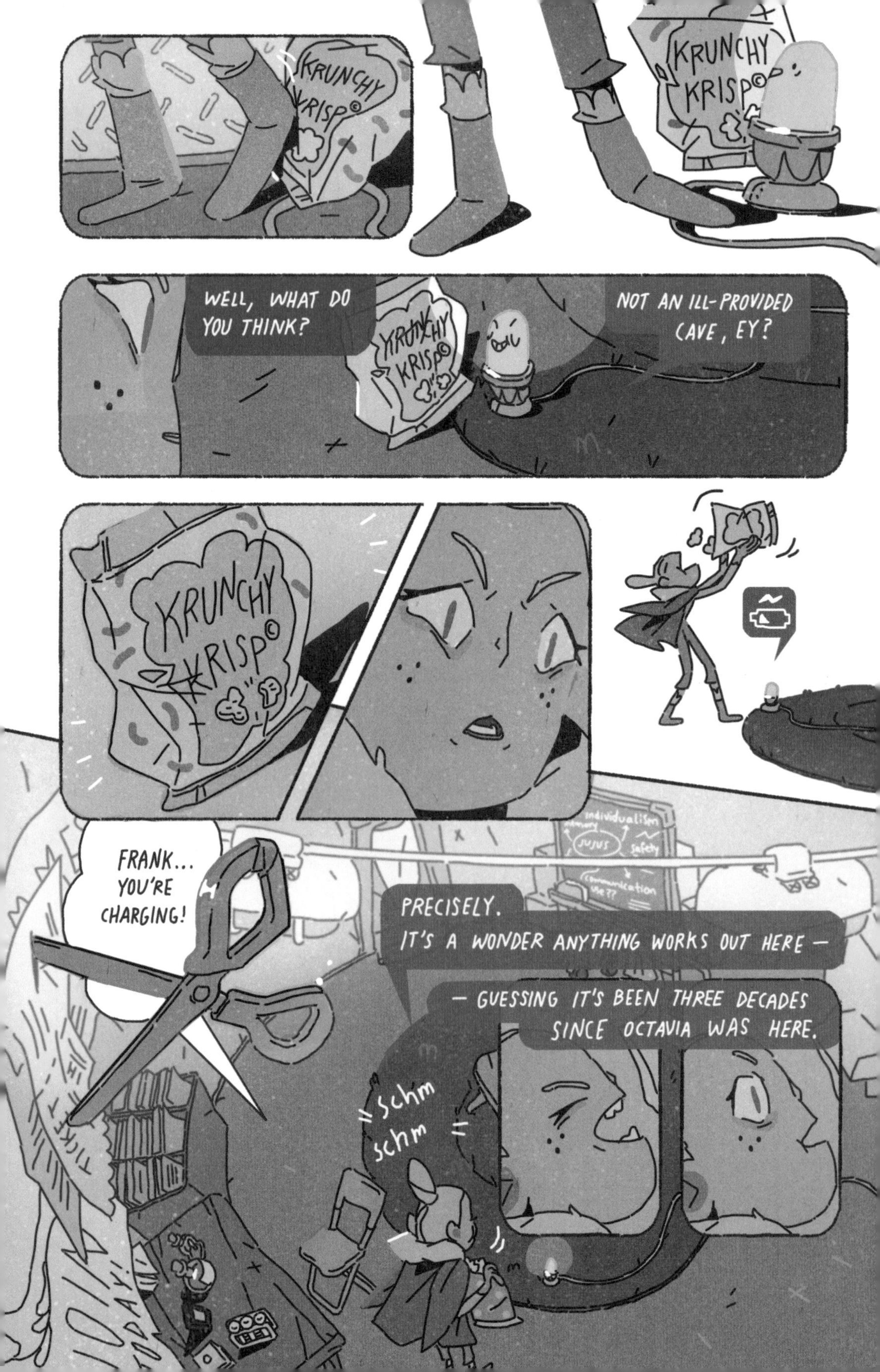
KRUNCHY KRISP©
WELL, WHAT DO YOU THINK?
NOT AN ILL-PROVIDED CAVE, EY?
KRUNCHY KRISP©
FRANK... YOU'RE CHARGING!
PRECISELY.
IT'S A WONDER ANYTHING WORKS OUT HERE —
— GUESSING IT'S BEEN THREE DECADES SINCE OCTAVIA WAS HERE.
schm schm

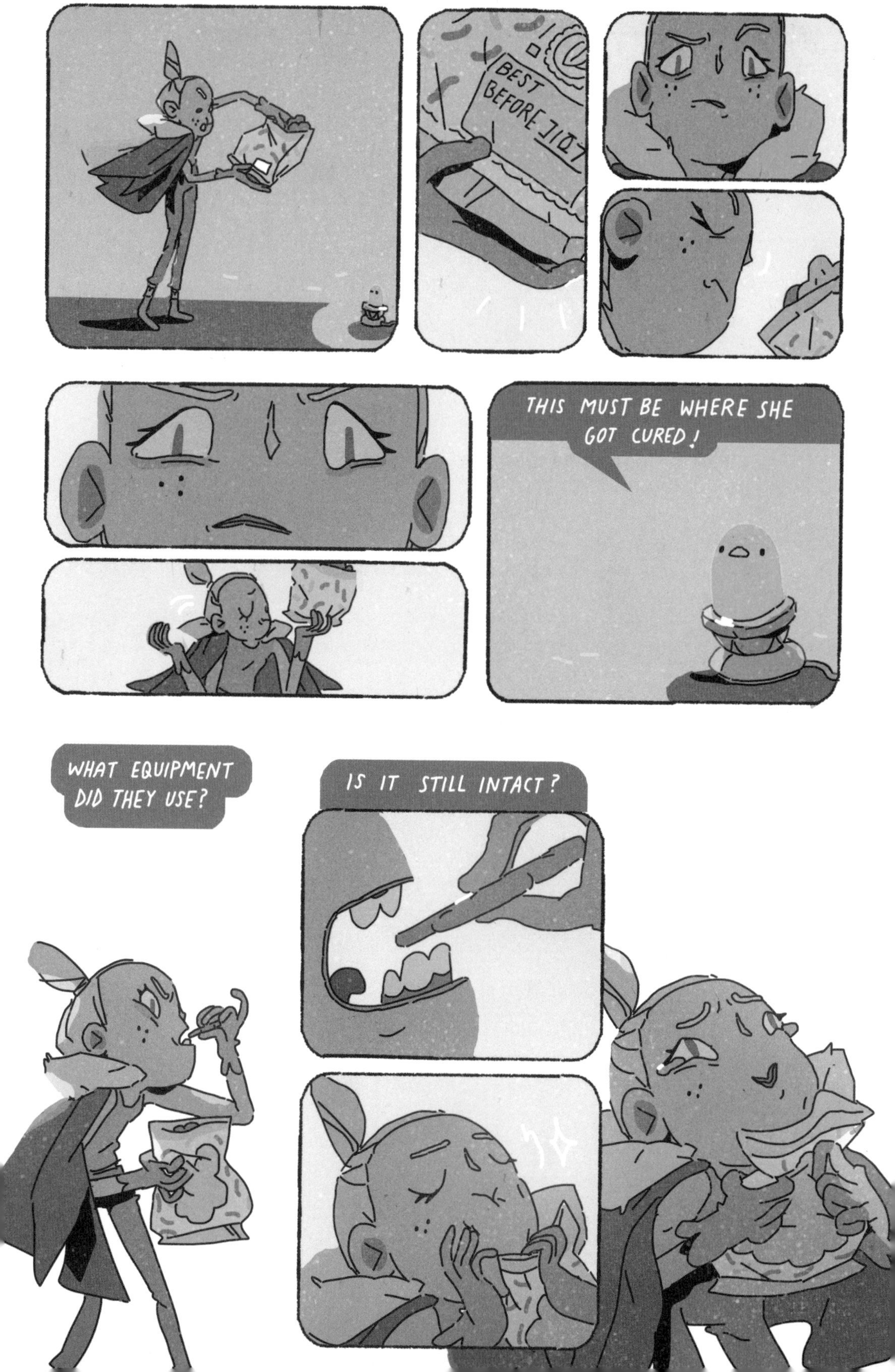
BEST BEFORE
THIS MUST BE WHERE SHE GOT CURED!
WHAT EQUIPMENT DID THEY USE?
IS IT STILL INTACT?

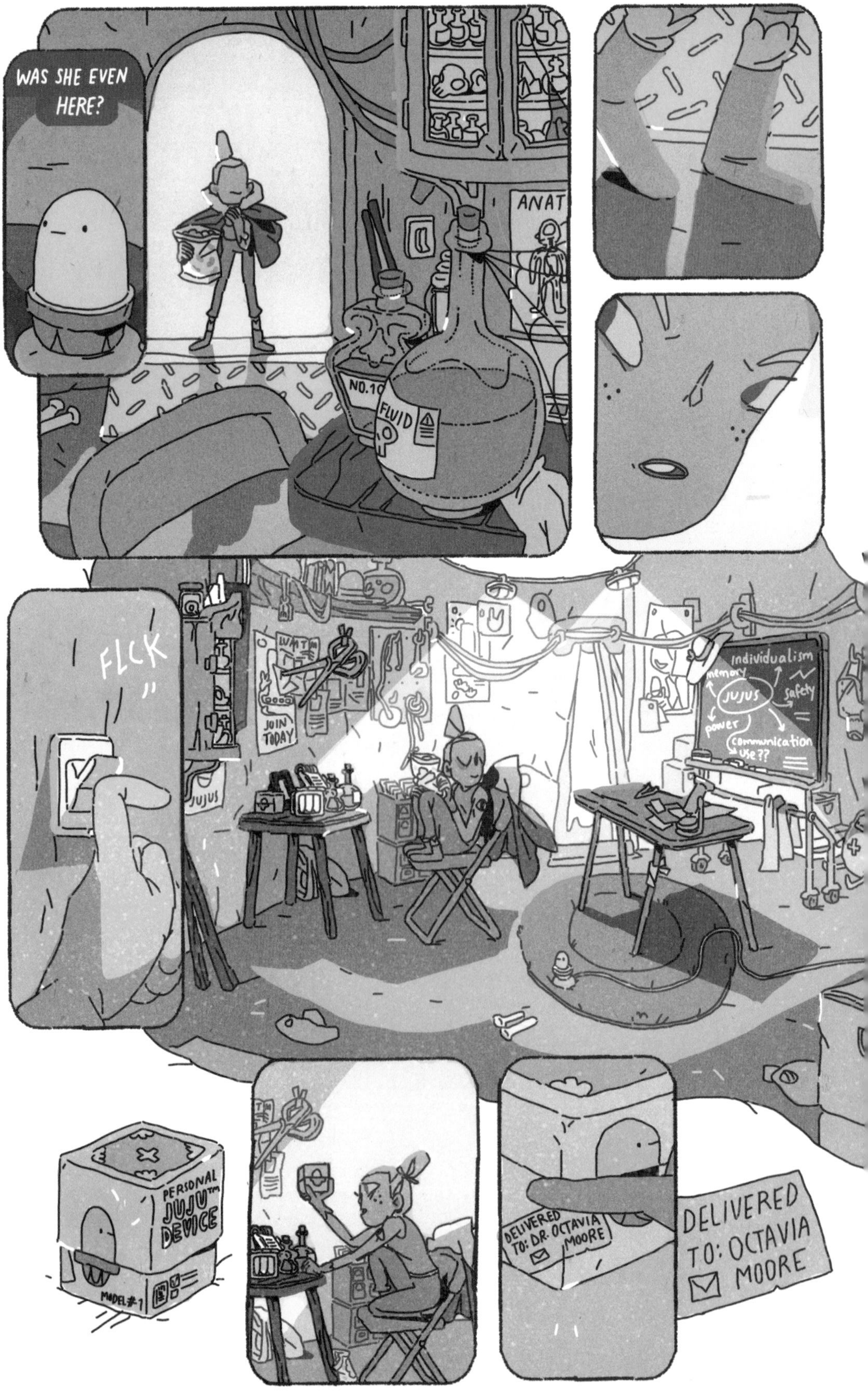

WAS SHE EVEN HERE?
NO.10
FLUID
ANAT
FLCK
JOIN TODAY
JUJUS
individualism
memory
JUJUS
safety
power
communication
use??
PERSONAL JUJU™ DEVICE
MODEL #1
DELIVERED TO: DR. OCTAVIA MOORE
DELIVERED TO: OCTAVIA MOORE

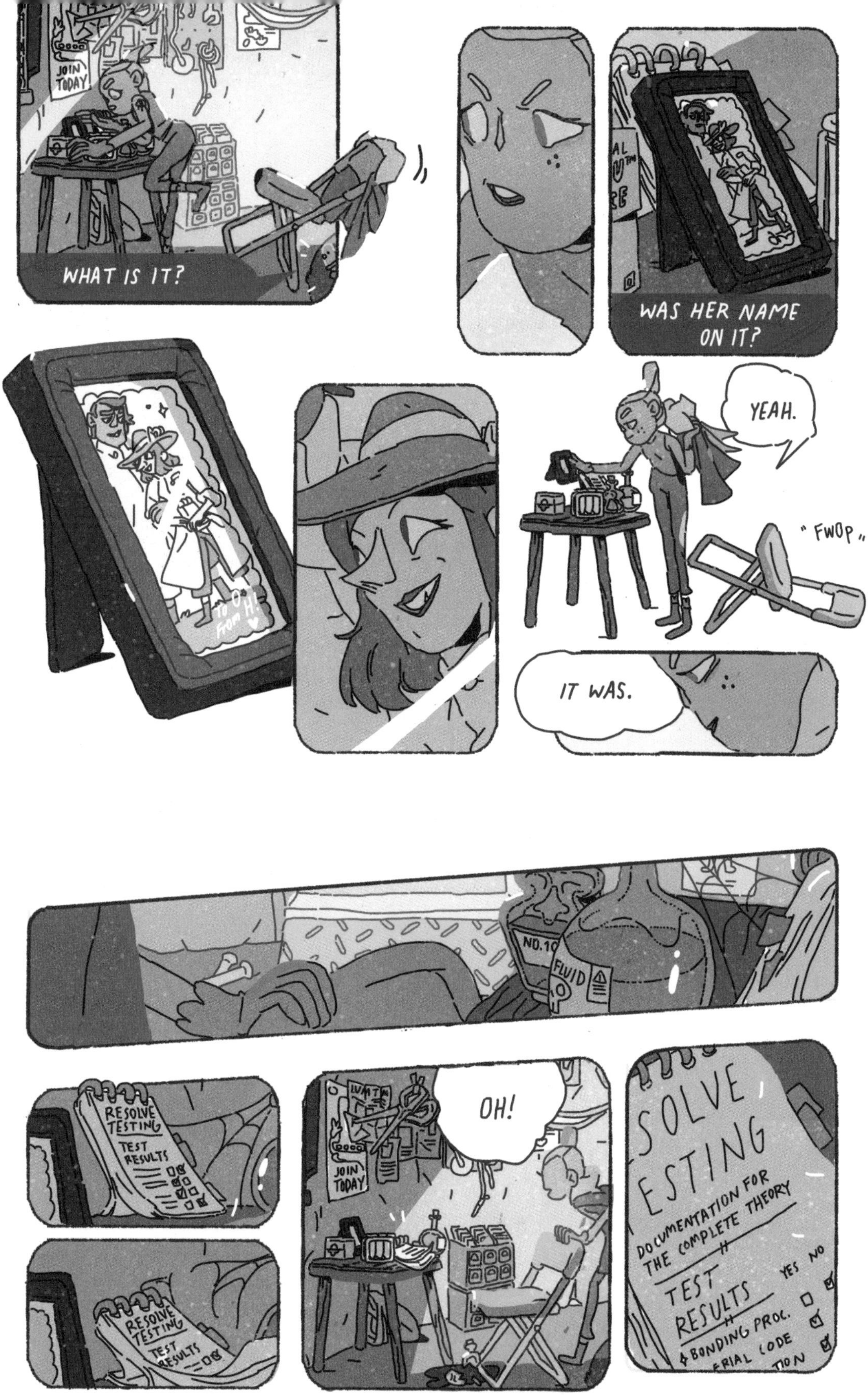
JOIN TODAY
WHAT IS IT?
WAS HER NAME ON IT?
To O From H!
YEAH.
"FWOP"
IT WAS.
NO.10
FLUID
RESOLVE TESTING
TEST RESULTS
RESOLVE TESTING
TEST RESULTS
OH!
JOIN TODAY
SOLVE
ESTING
DOCUMENTATION FOR THE COMPLETE THEORY
TEST RESULTS
YES NO
BONDING PROC.
ERIAL CODE
TION

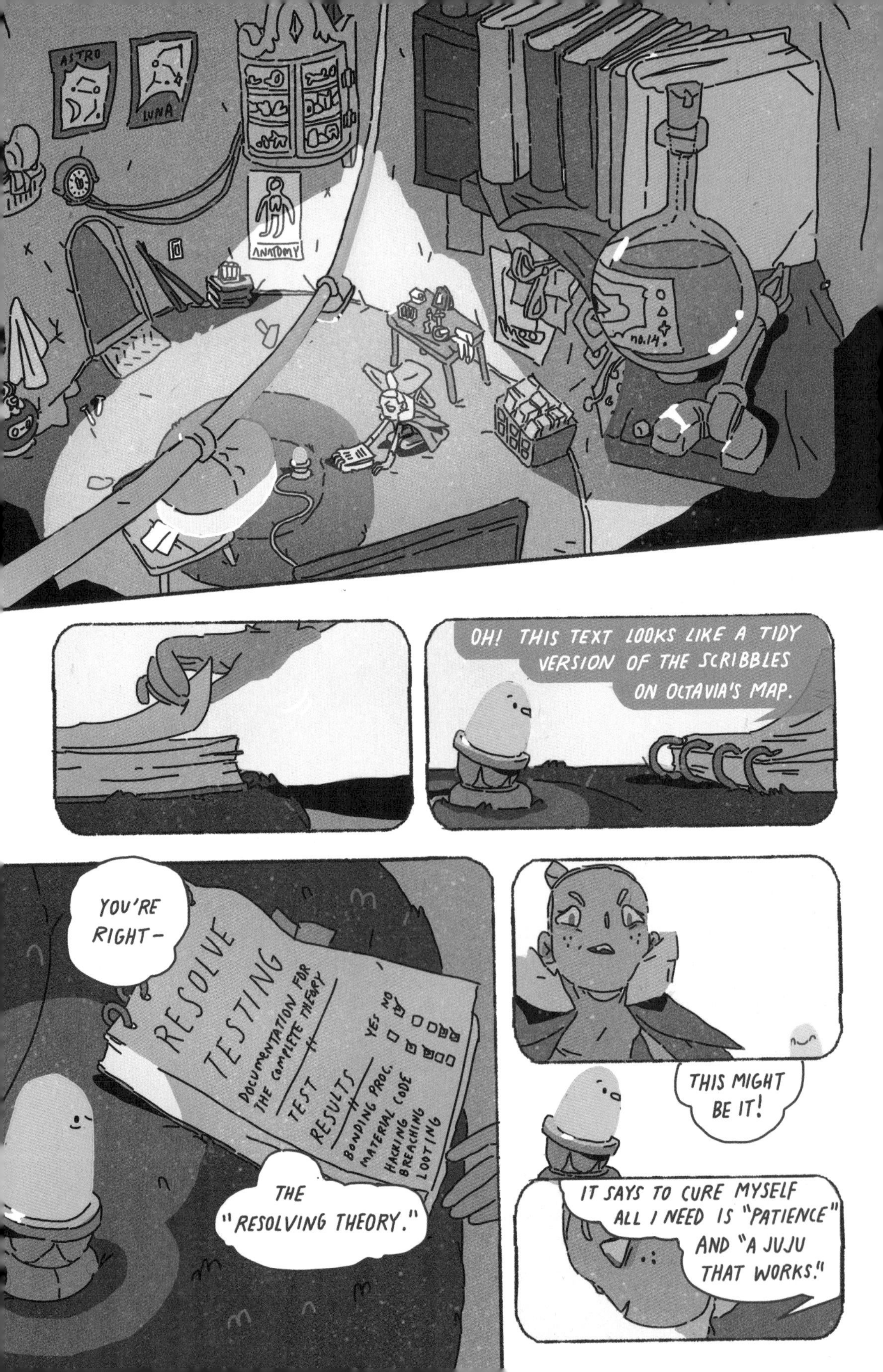
ASTRO
LUNA
ANATOMY
OH! THIS TEXT LOOKS LIKE A TIDY VERSION OF THE SCRIBBLES ON OCTAVIA'S MAP.
YOU'RE RIGHT—
RESOLVE TESTING
DOCUMENTATION FOR THE COMPLETE THEORY
TEST #
RESULTS
YES NO
BONDING PROC.
MATERIAL CODE
HACKING
BREACHING
LOOTING
THE "RESOLVING THEORY."
THIS MIGHT BE IT!
IT SAYS TO CURE MYSELF ALL I NEED IS "PATIENCE" AND "A JUJU THAT WORKS."

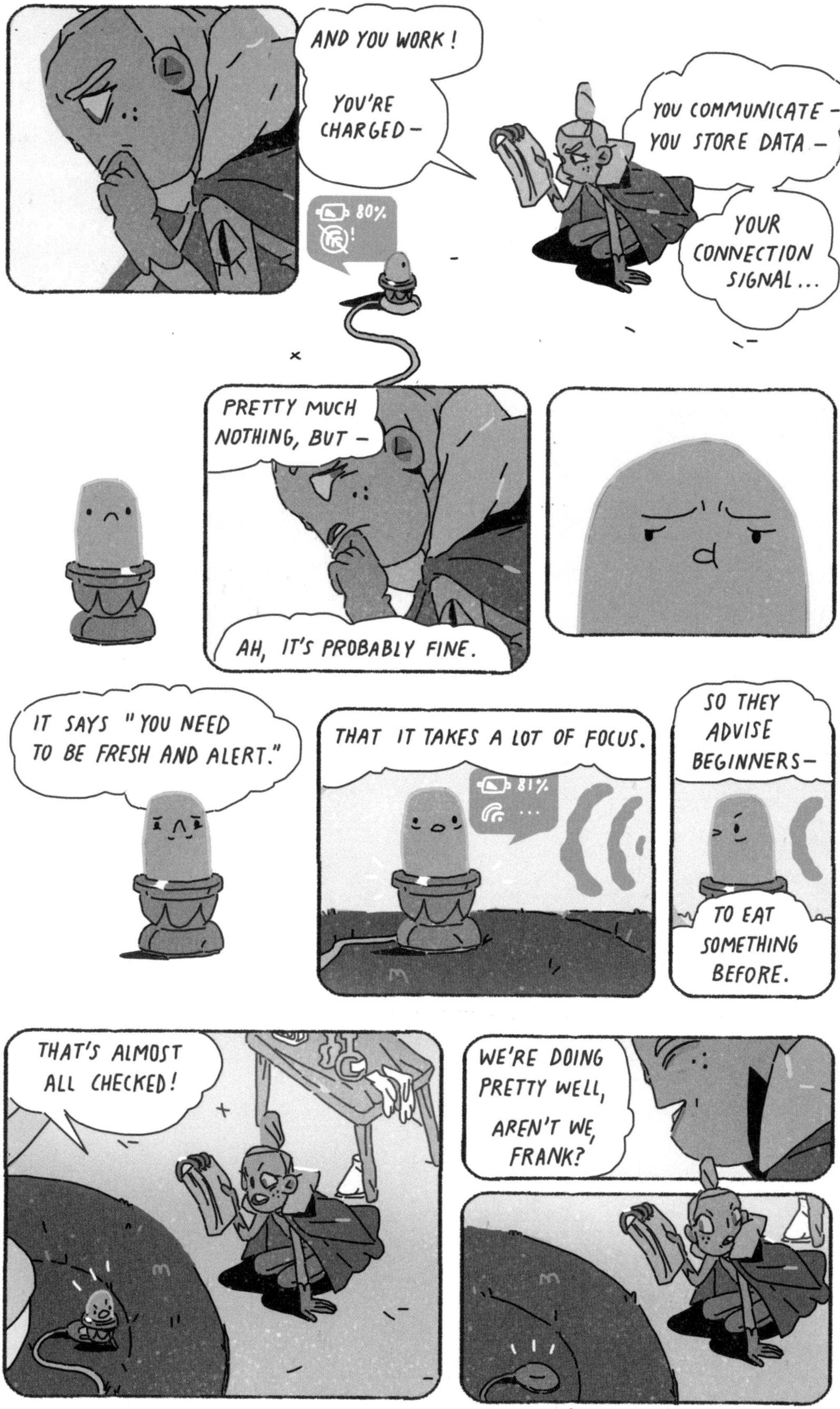
AND YOU WORK!
YOU'RE CHARGED—
YOU COMMUNICATE— YOU STORE DATA—
YOUR CONNECTION SIGNAL...
80%
!
PRETTY MUCH NOTHING, BUT—
AH, IT'S PROBABLY FINE.
IT SAYS "YOU NEED TO BE FRESH AND ALERT."
THAT IT TAKES A LOT OF FOCUS.
81%
...
SO THEY ADVISE BEGINNERS—
TO EAT SOMETHING BEFORE.
THAT'S ALMOST ALL CHECKED!
WE'RE DOING PRETTY WELL,
AREN'T WE, FRANK?

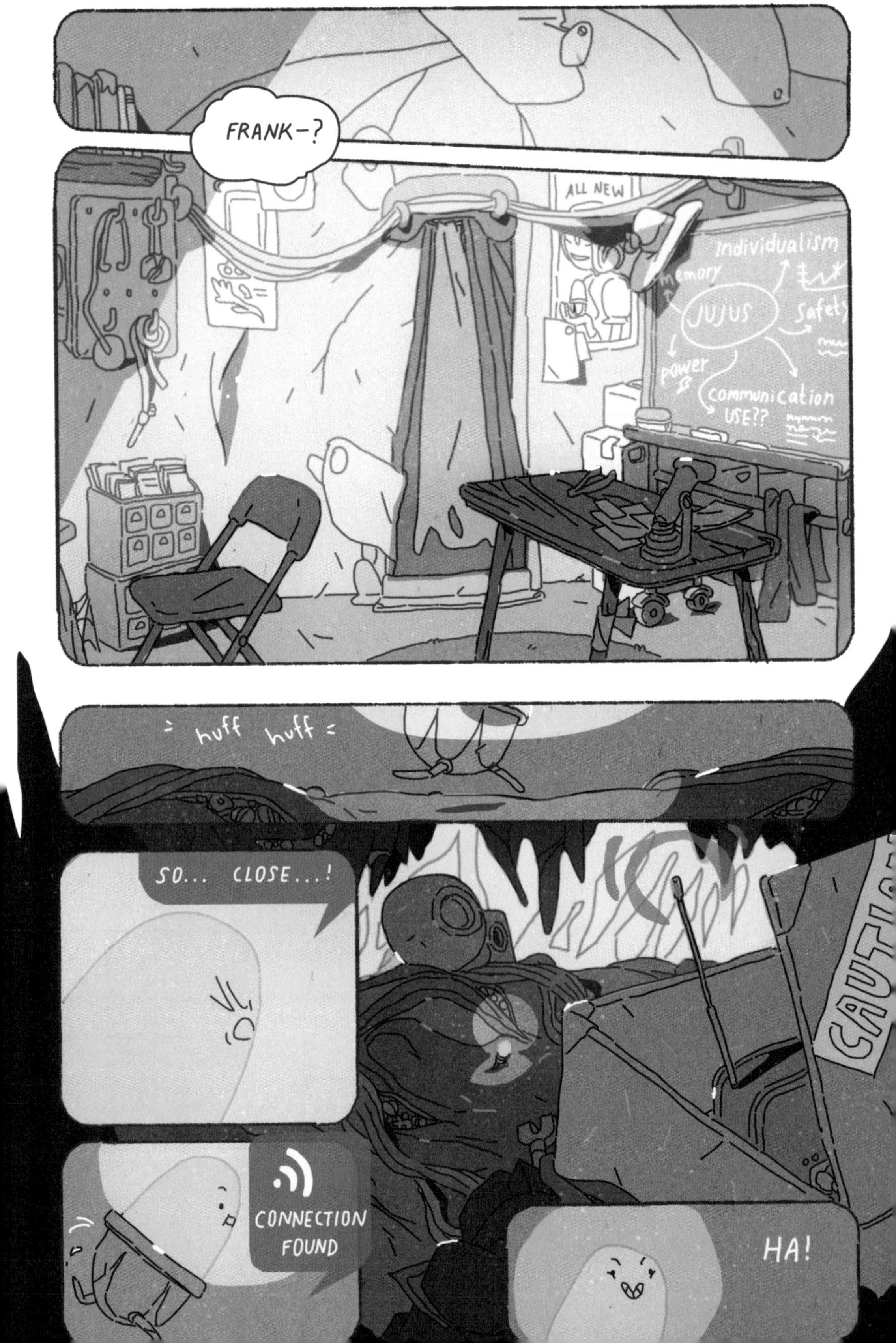
FRANK-?
ALL NEW
individualism
memory
JUJUS
safety
power
communication
USE??
huff huff
SO... CLOSE...!
CONNECTION
FOUND
HA!

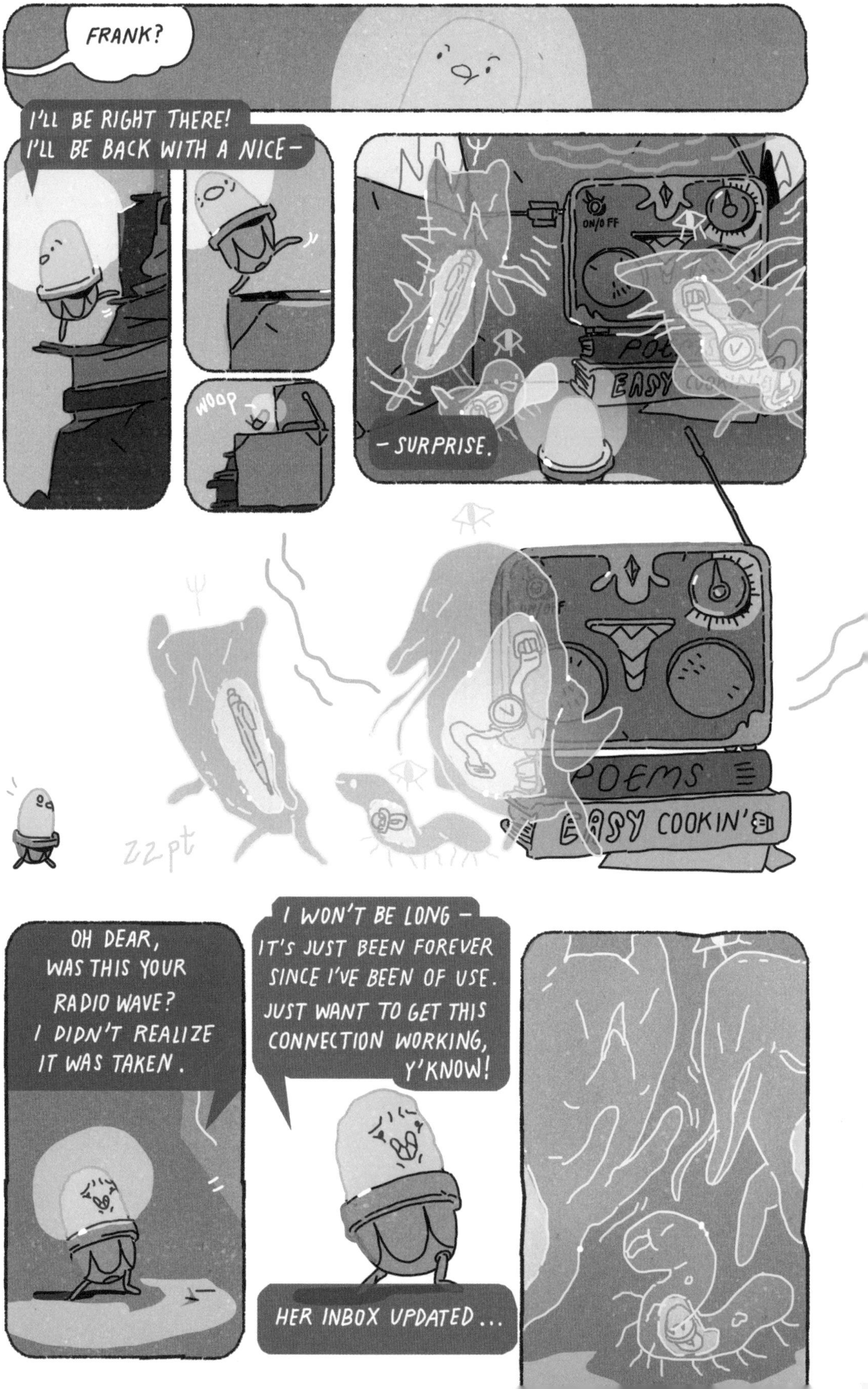
FRANK?
I'LL BE RIGHT THERE! I'LL BE BACK WITH A NICE—
WOOP
—SURPRISE.
ON/OFF
POEMS
EASY COOKIN'
ZZPT
OH DEAR, WAS THIS YOUR RADIO WAVE? I DIDN'T REALIZE IT WAS TAKEN.
I WON'T BE LONG— IT'S JUST BEEN FOREVER SINCE I'VE BEEN OF USE. JUST WANT TO GET THIS CONNECTION WORKING, Y'KNOW!
HER INBOX UPDATED...

OH!
++
15
UNREAD
RESOLVE
TESTING
DOCUMENTATION FOR THE COMPLETE THEORY*
TEST
* NOTE!! IN THE WASTE, ALL COMMUNICATION DEVICES MUST REMAIN OFFLINE.

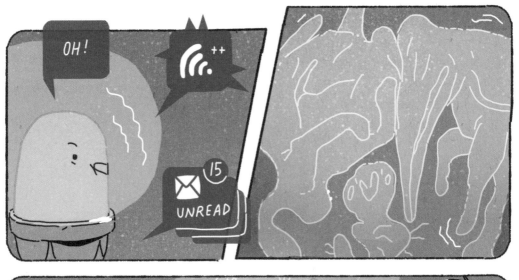

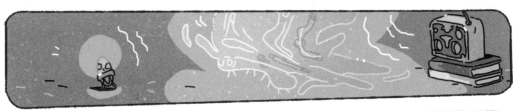

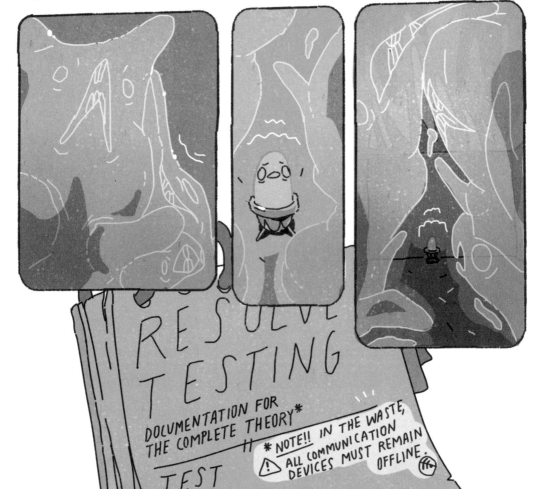

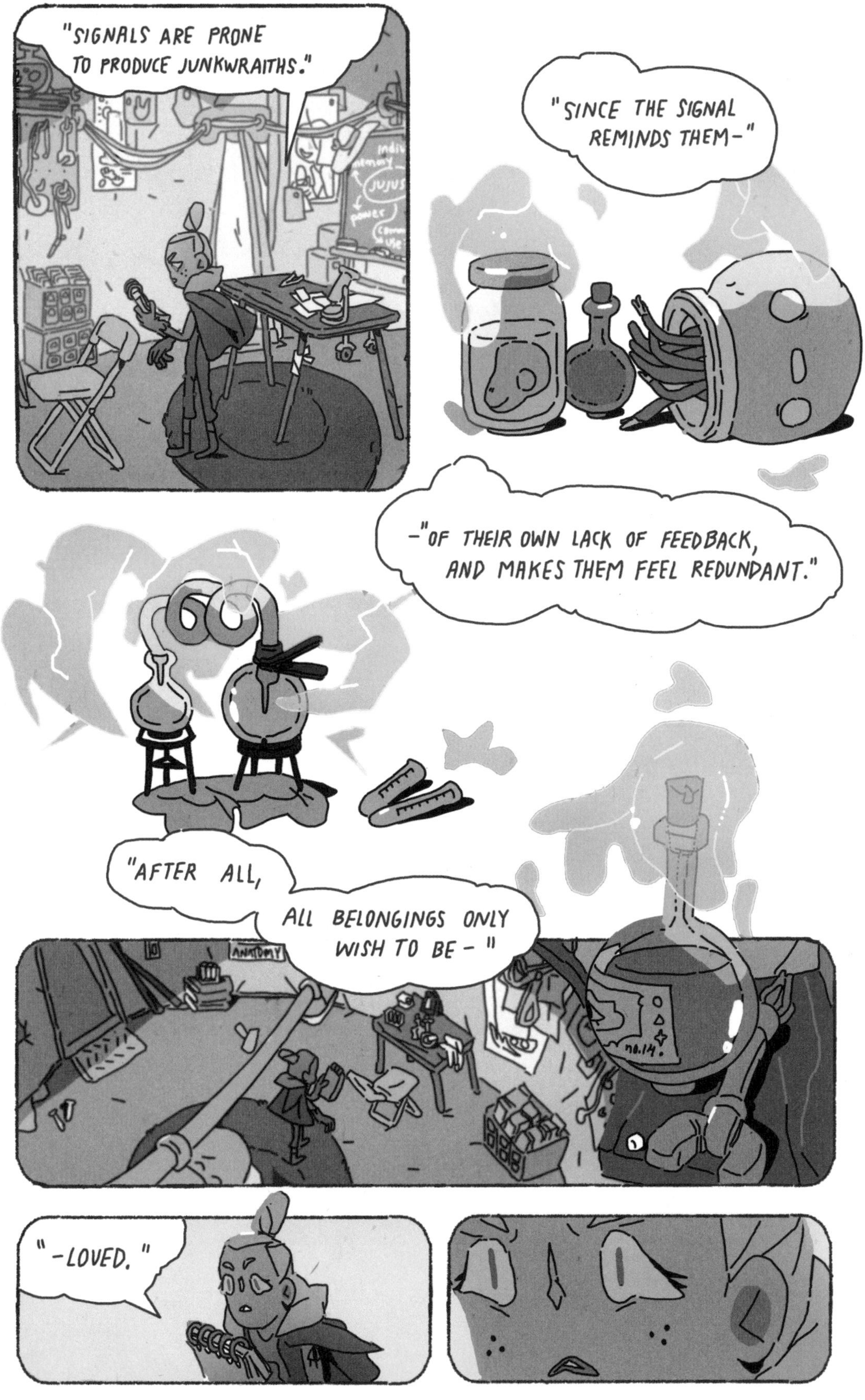
"SIGNALS ARE PRONE TO PRODUCE JUNKWRAITHS."
"SINCE THE SIGNAL REMINDS THEM-"
-"OF THEIR OWN LACK OF FEEDBACK, AND MAKES THEM FEEL REDUNDANT."
"AFTER ALL,
ALL BELONGINGS ONLY WISH TO BE- "
ANATOMY
no.14.
"-LOVED."

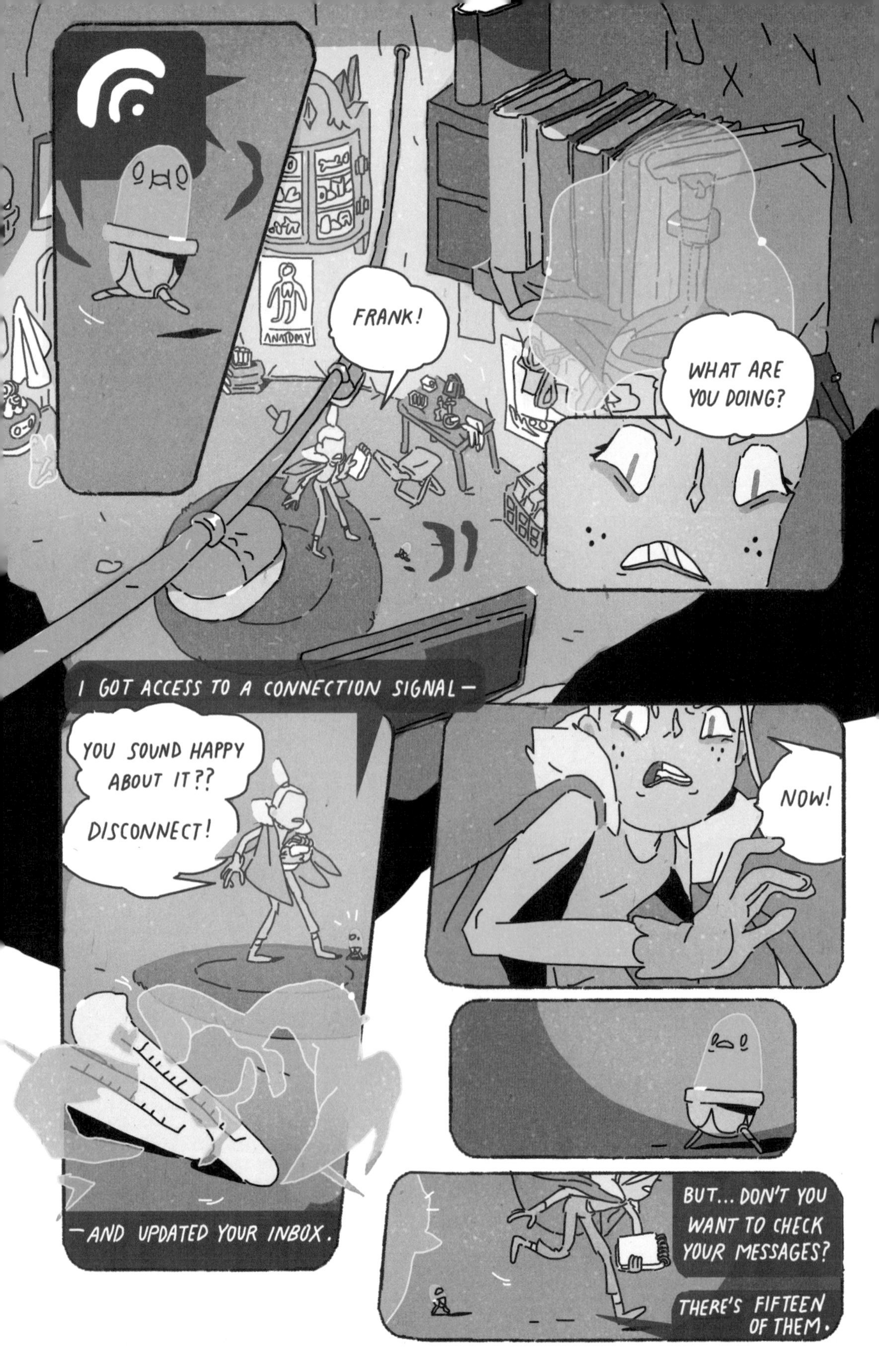
FRANK!
WHAT ARE YOU DOING?
I GOT ACCESS TO A CONNECTION SIGNAL—
YOU SOUND HAPPY ABOUT IT??
DISCONNECT!
NOW!
—AND UPDATED YOUR INBOX.
BUT... DON'T YOU WANT TO CHECK YOUR MESSAGES?
THERE'S FIFTEEN OF THEM.

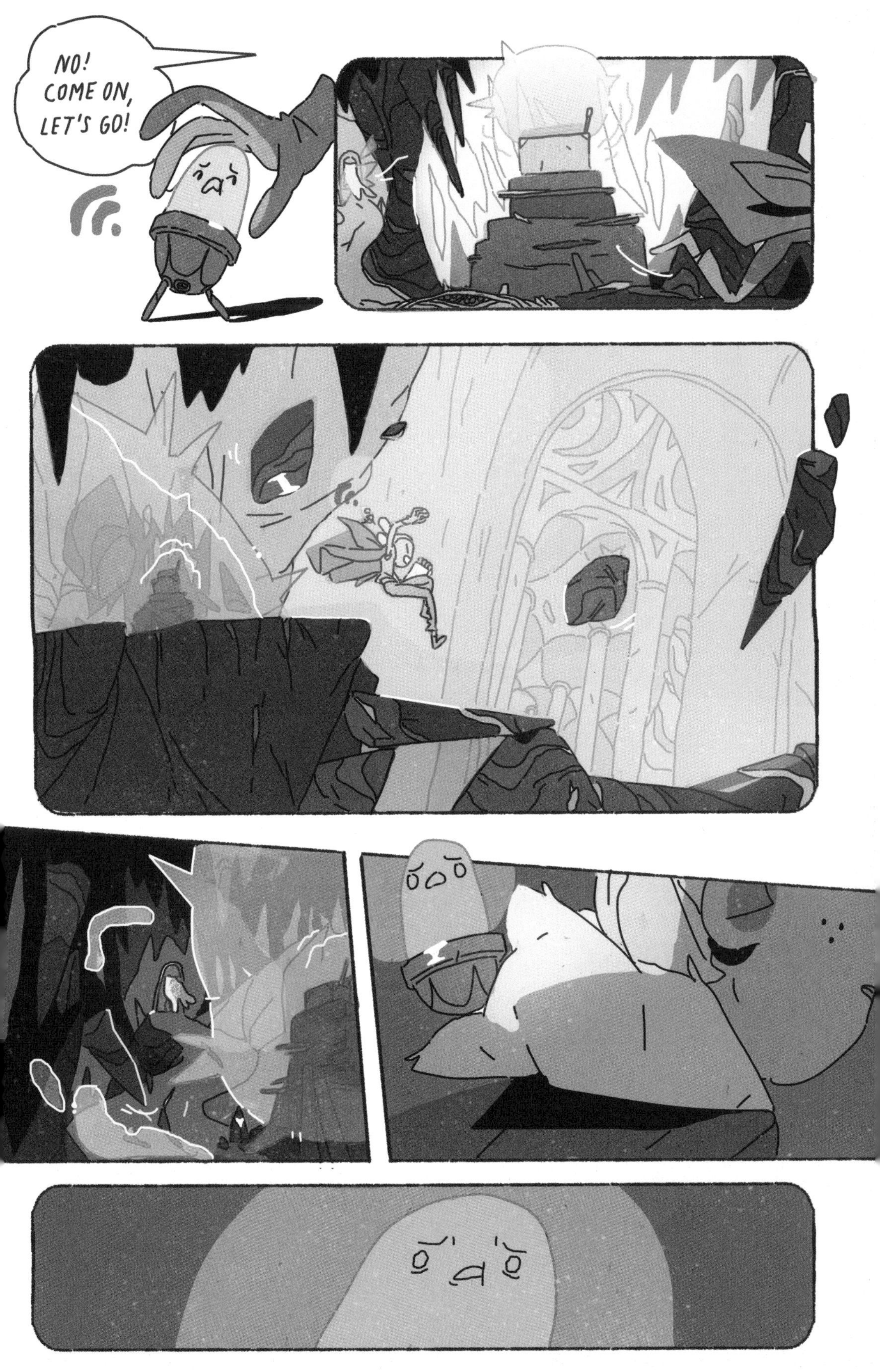
NO! COME ON, LET'S GO!

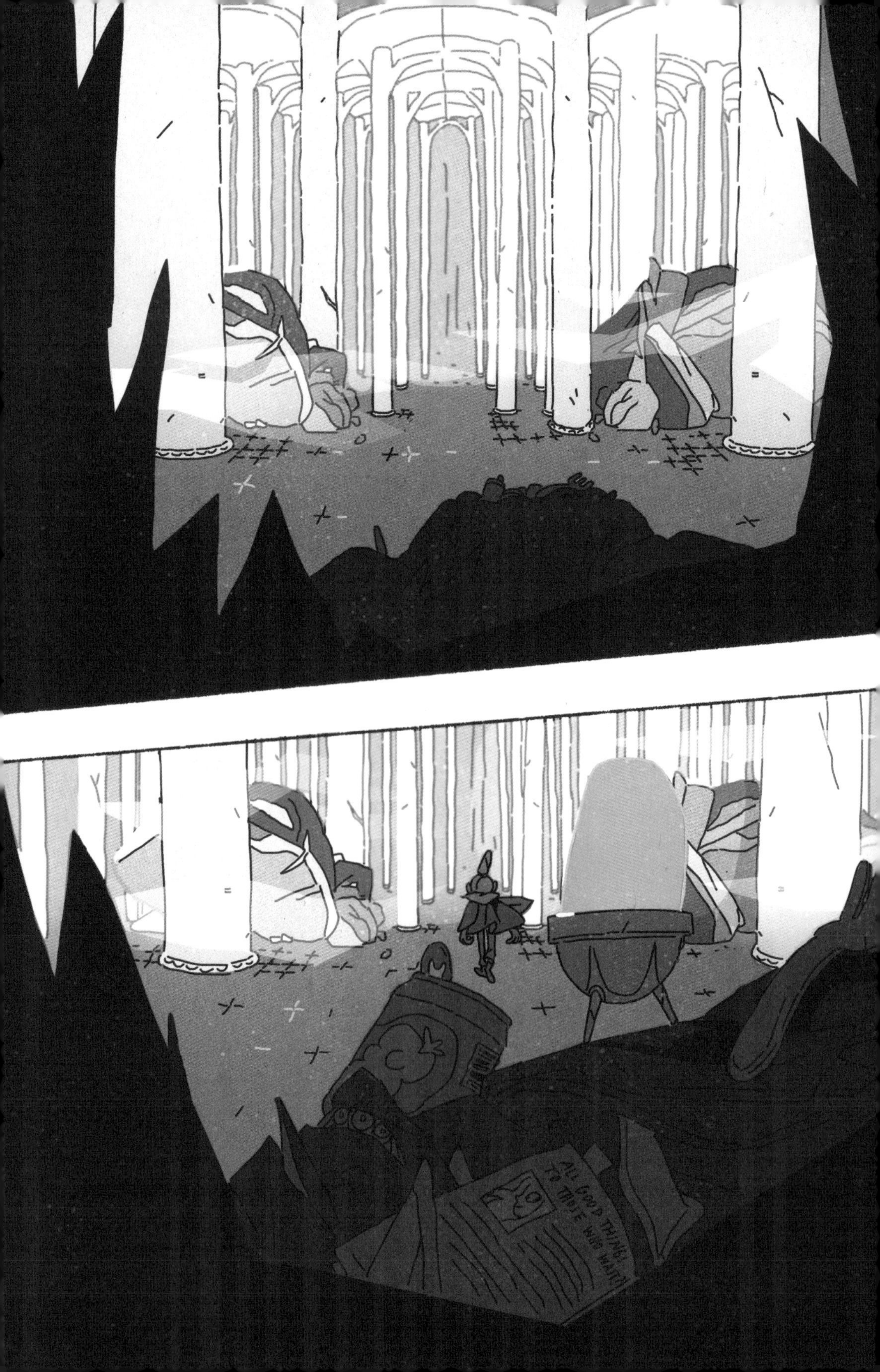
ALL GOOD THINGS
TO THOSE WHO WAIT

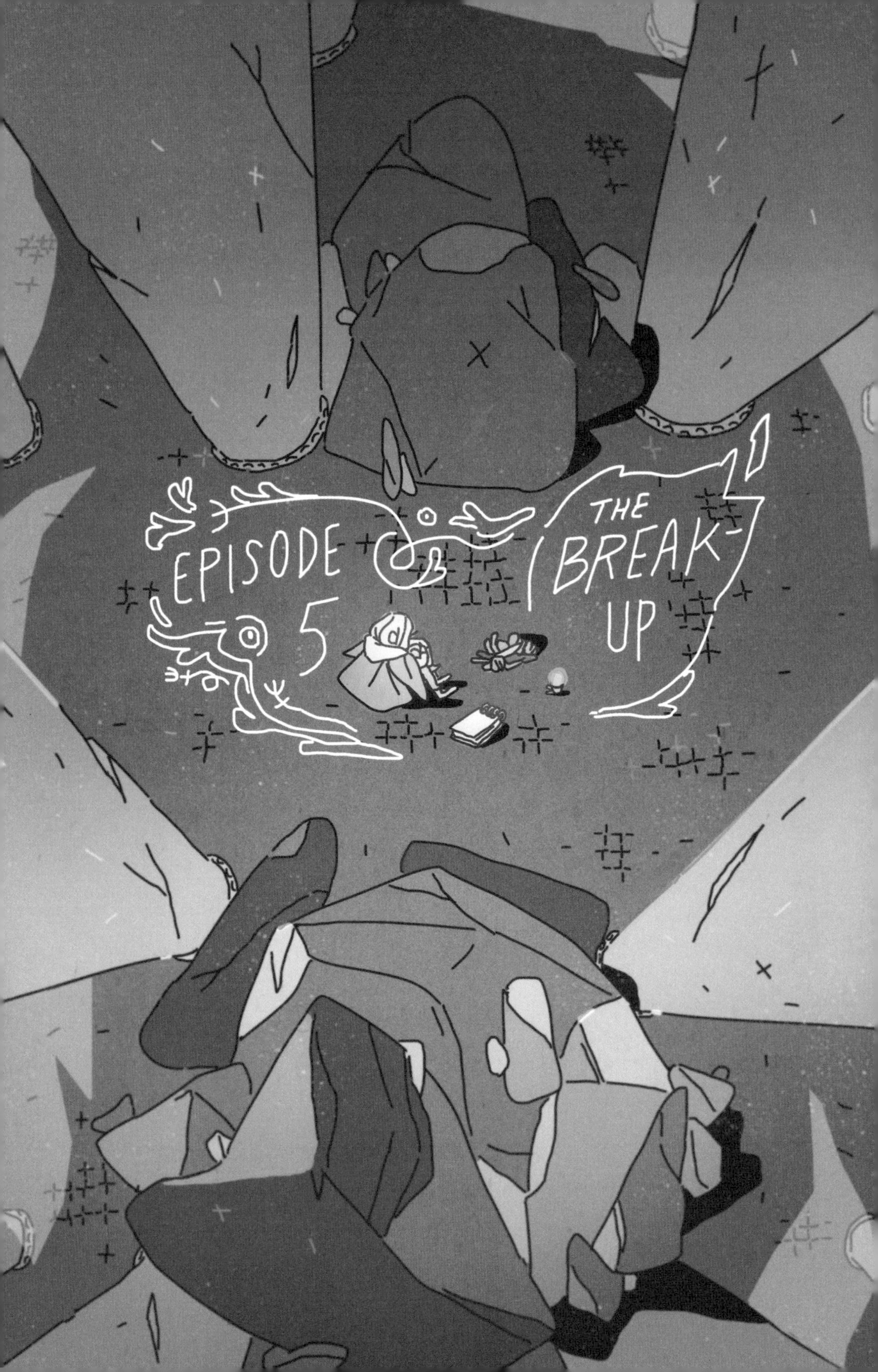
EPISODE 5
THE BREAK-UP

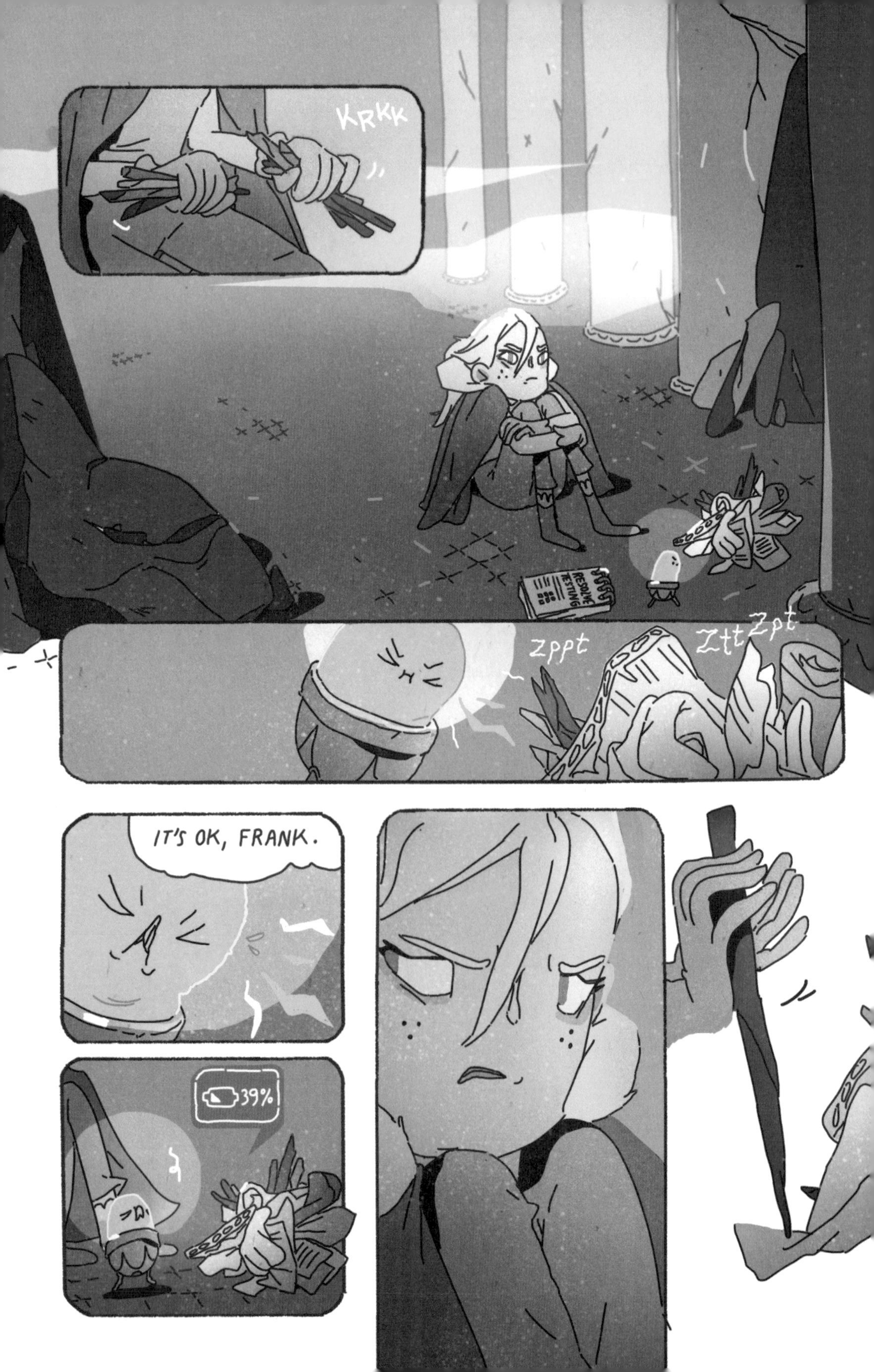
KRKK
RESPONSE TESTING
ZPPT
ZTT
ZPT
IT'S OK, FRANK.
39%

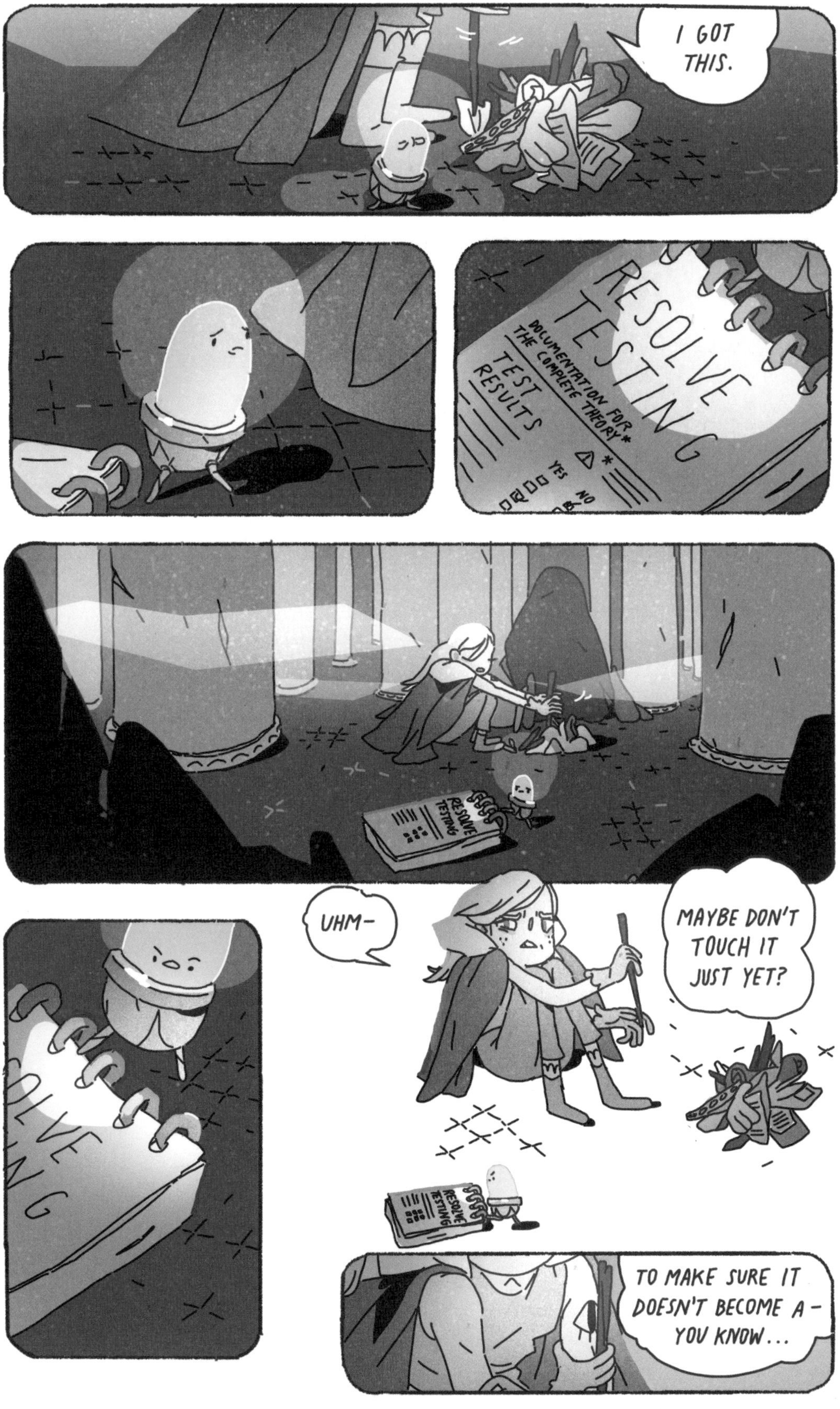
I GOT THIS.
RESOLVE TESTING
DOCUMENTATION FOR THE COMPLETE THEORY*
TEST RESULTS
YES
NO
RESOLVE TESTING
UHM-
MAYBE DON'T TOUCH IT JUST YET?
RESOLVE TESTING
TO MAKE SURE IT DOESN'T BECOME A- YOU KNOW...

OH.

SNP

COME ON, STUPID FIRE!

RESOLVE TESTING

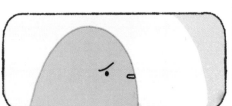

I'VE GOT JUUUST THE TICKET!

SOME MUSIC TO BRIGHTEN THE MOOD.

CONNECTING...

NO!

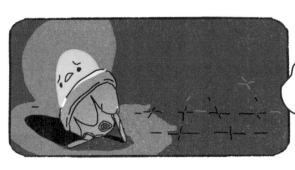

I'M SORRY —

I JUST—

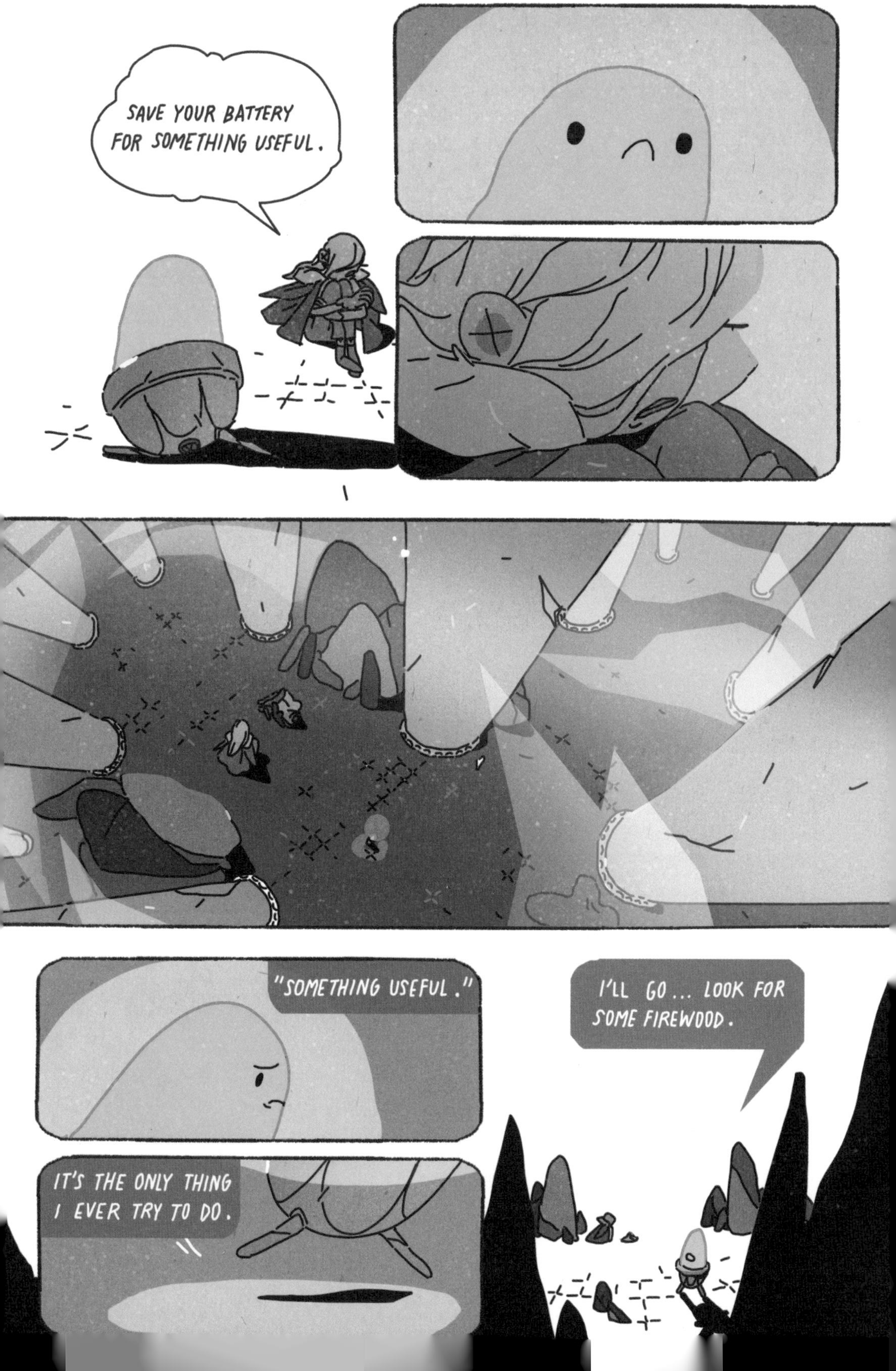
SAVE YOUR BATTERY FOR SOMETHING USEFUL.
"SOMETHING USEFUL."
IT'S THE ONLY THING I EVER TRY TO DO.
I'LL GO... LOOK FOR SOME FIREWOOD.

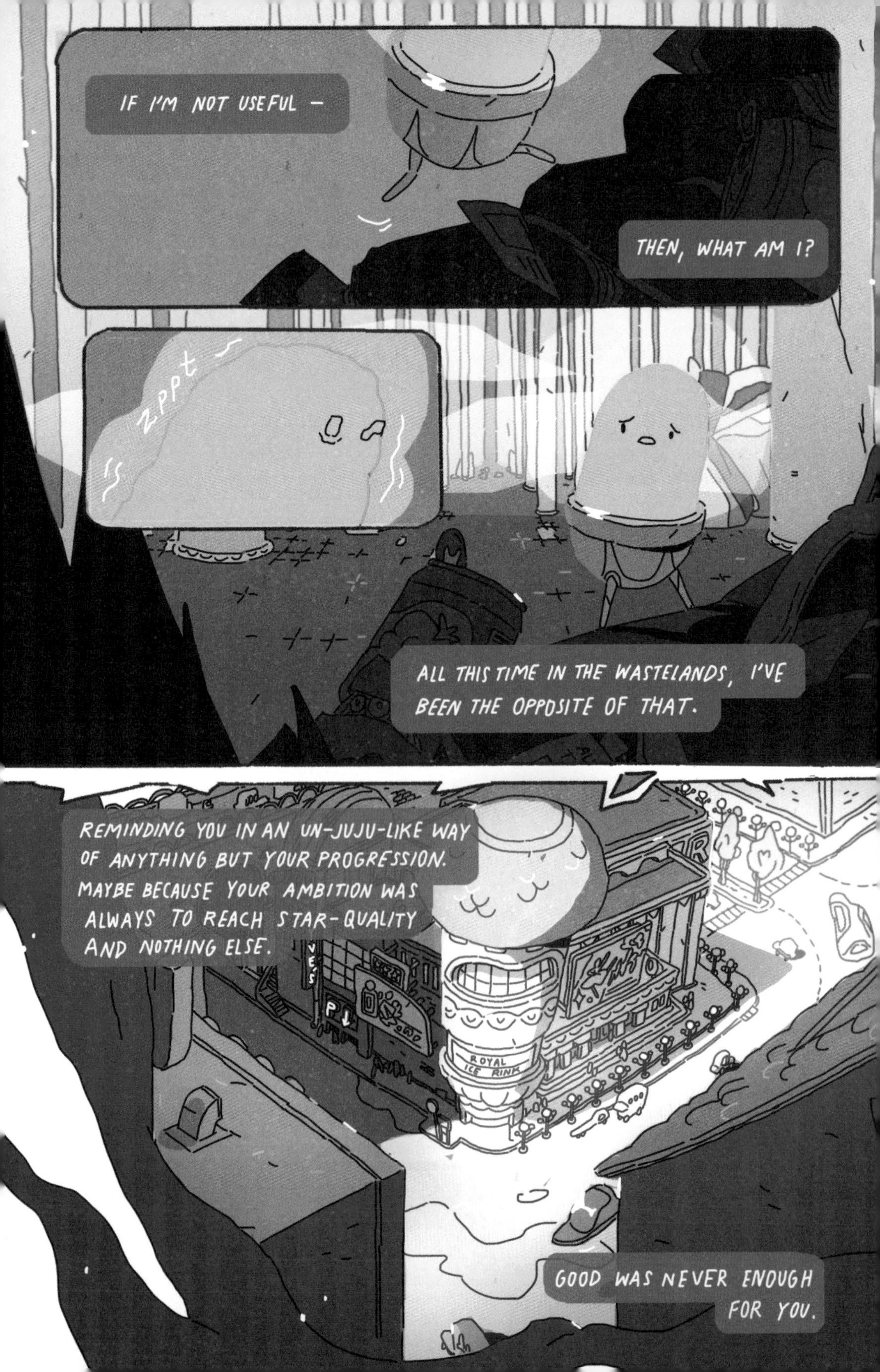
IF I'M NOT USEFUL –
THEN, WHAT AM I?
ZPPT
ALL THIS TIME IN THE WASTELANDS, I'VE BEEN THE OPPOSITE OF THAT.
REMINDING YOU IN AN UN-JUJU-LIKE WAY OF ANYTHING BUT YOUR PROGRESSION.
MAYBE BECAUSE YOUR AMBITION WAS ALWAYS TO REACH STAR-QUALITY AND NOTHING ELSE.
ROYAL ICE RINK
GOOD WAS NEVER ENOUGH FOR YOU.

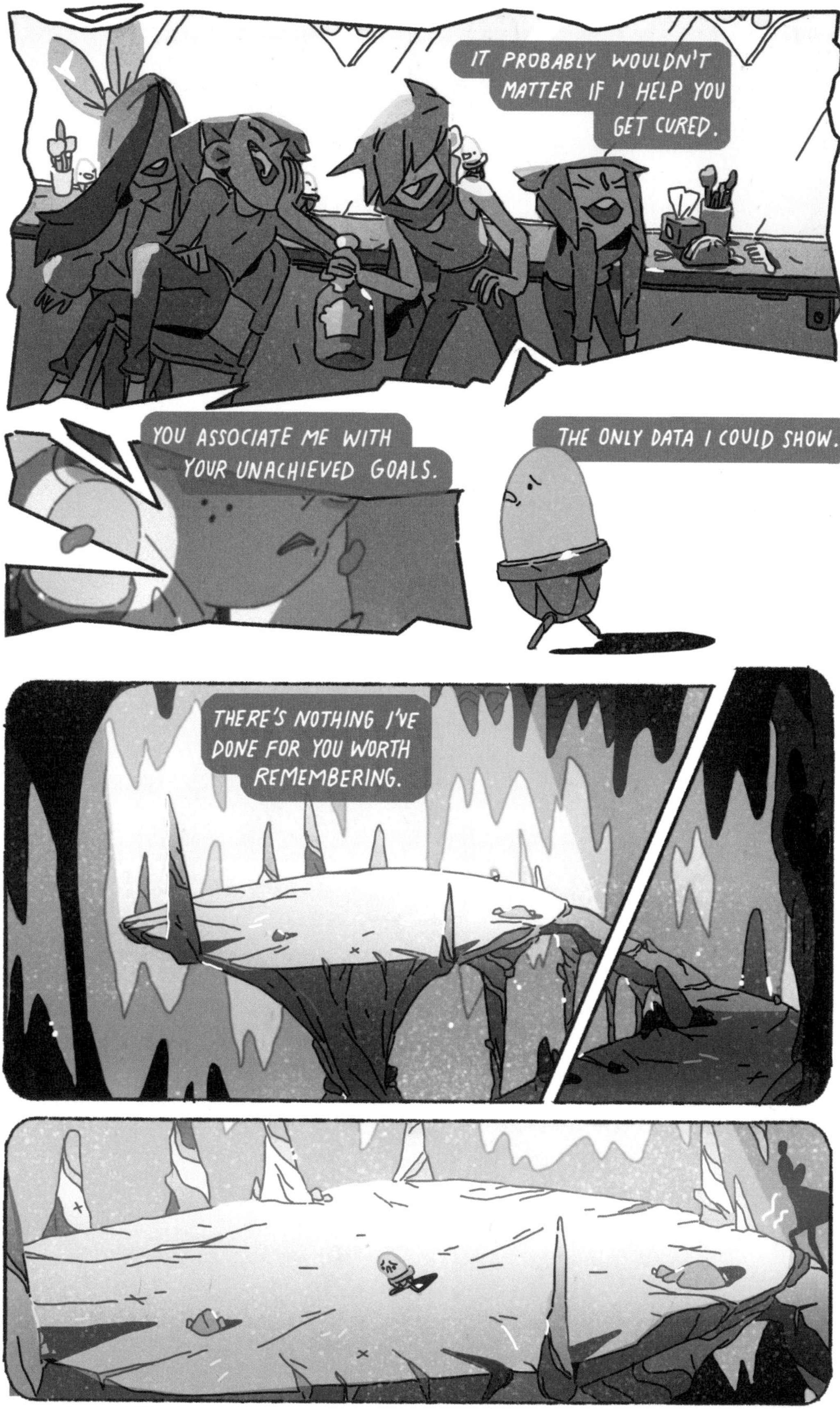
IT PROBABLY WOULDN'T MATTER IF I HELP YOU GET CURED.
YOU ASSOCIATE ME WITH YOUR UNACHIEVED GOALS.
THE ONLY DATA I COULD SHOW.
THERE'S NOTHING I'VE DONE FOR YOU WORTH REMEMBERING.

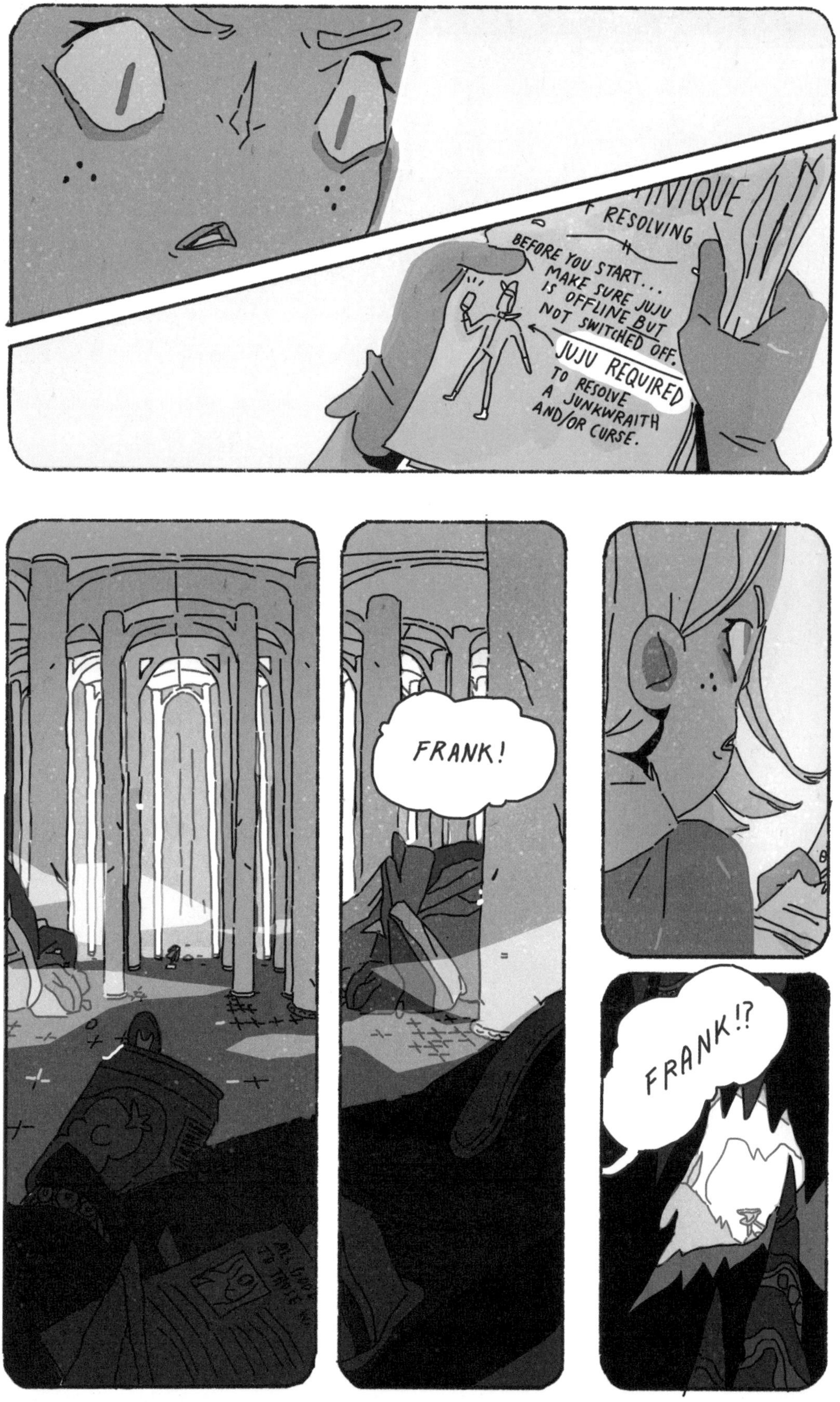
RESOLVING
BEFORE YOU START... MAKE SURE JUJU IS OFFLINE BUT NOT SWITCHED OFF.
JUJU REQUIRED TO RESOLVE A JUNKWRAITH AND/OR CURSE.
FRANK!
FRANK!?

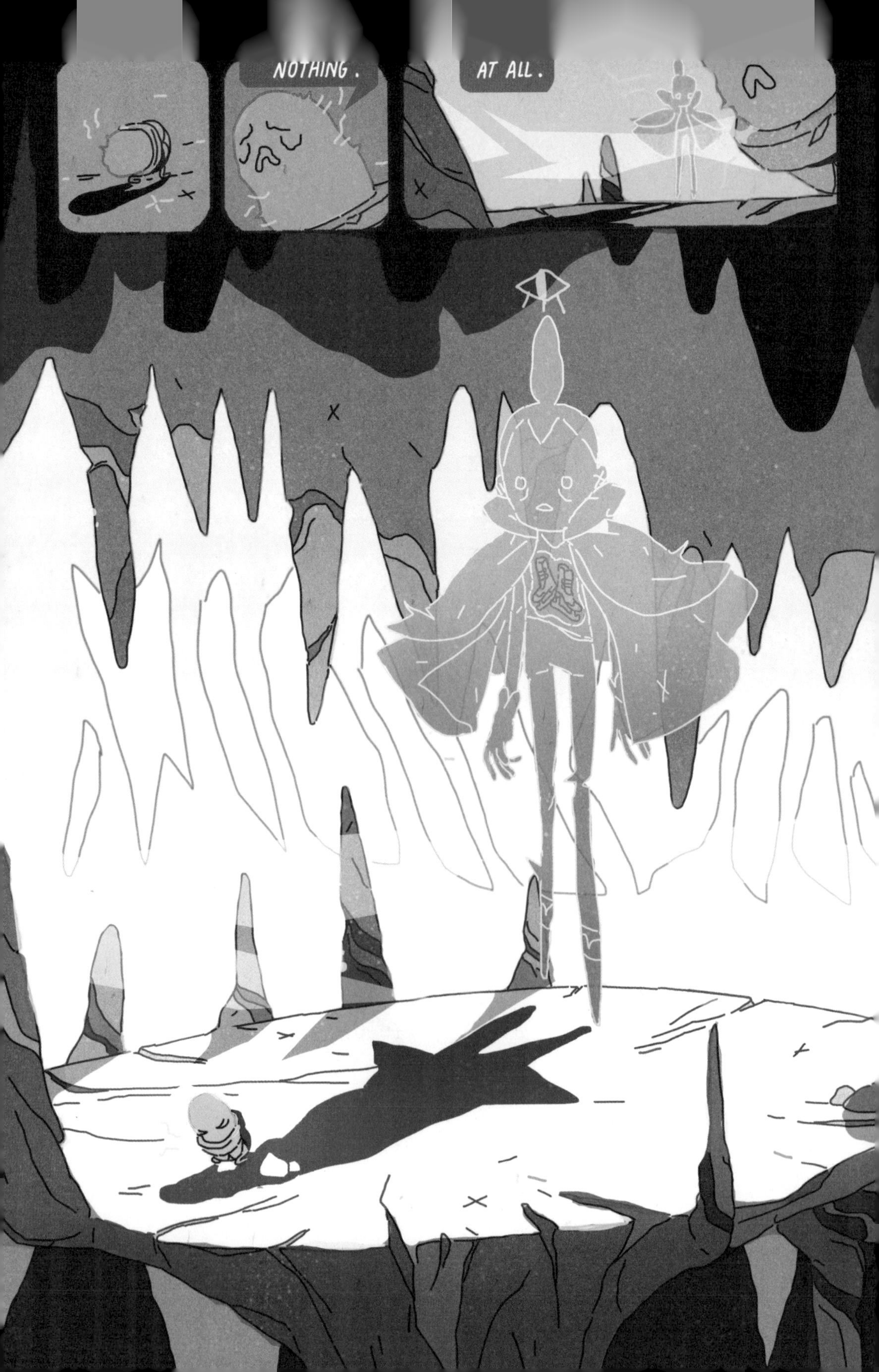
NOTHING.
AT ALL.

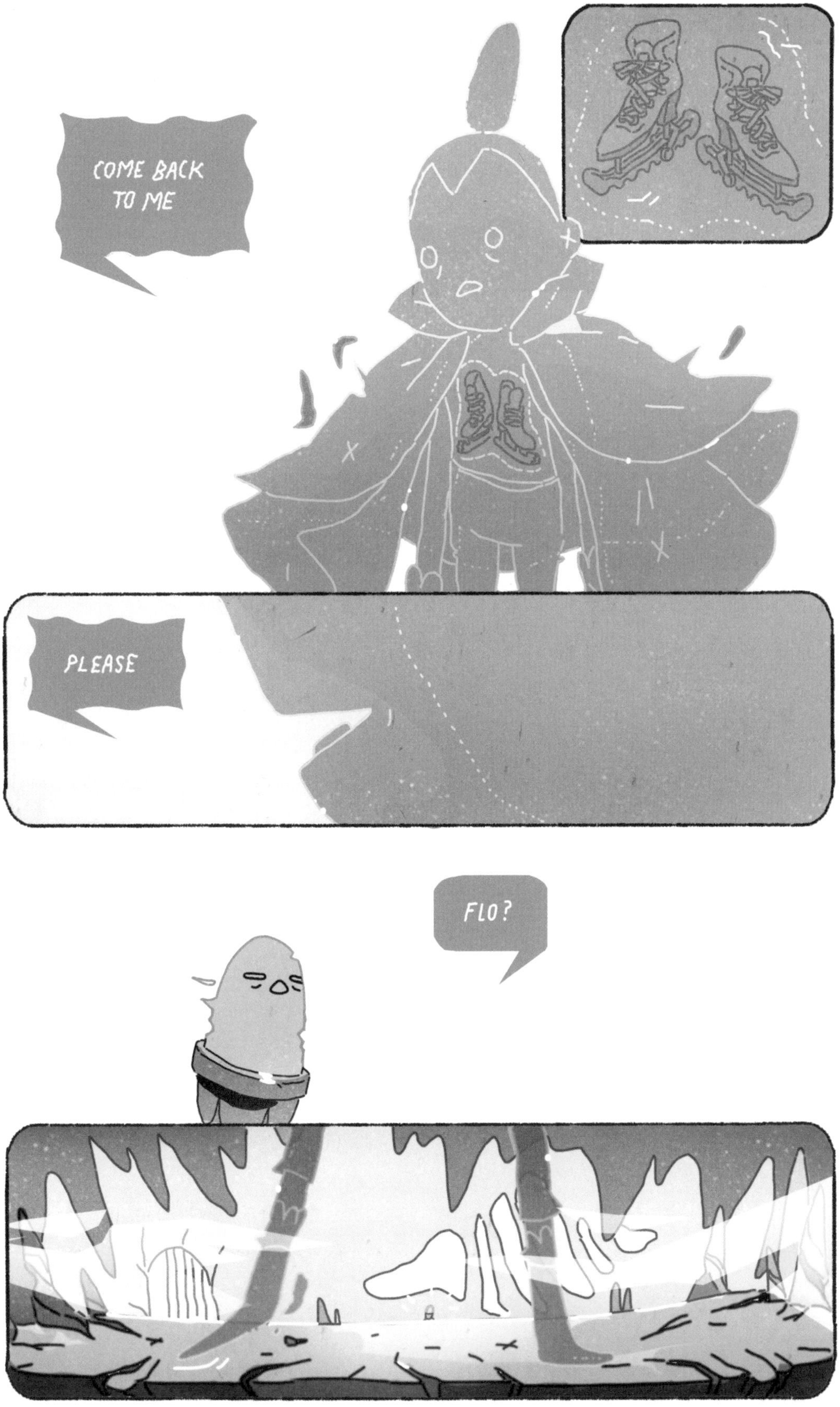
COME BACK TO ME
PLEASE
FLO?

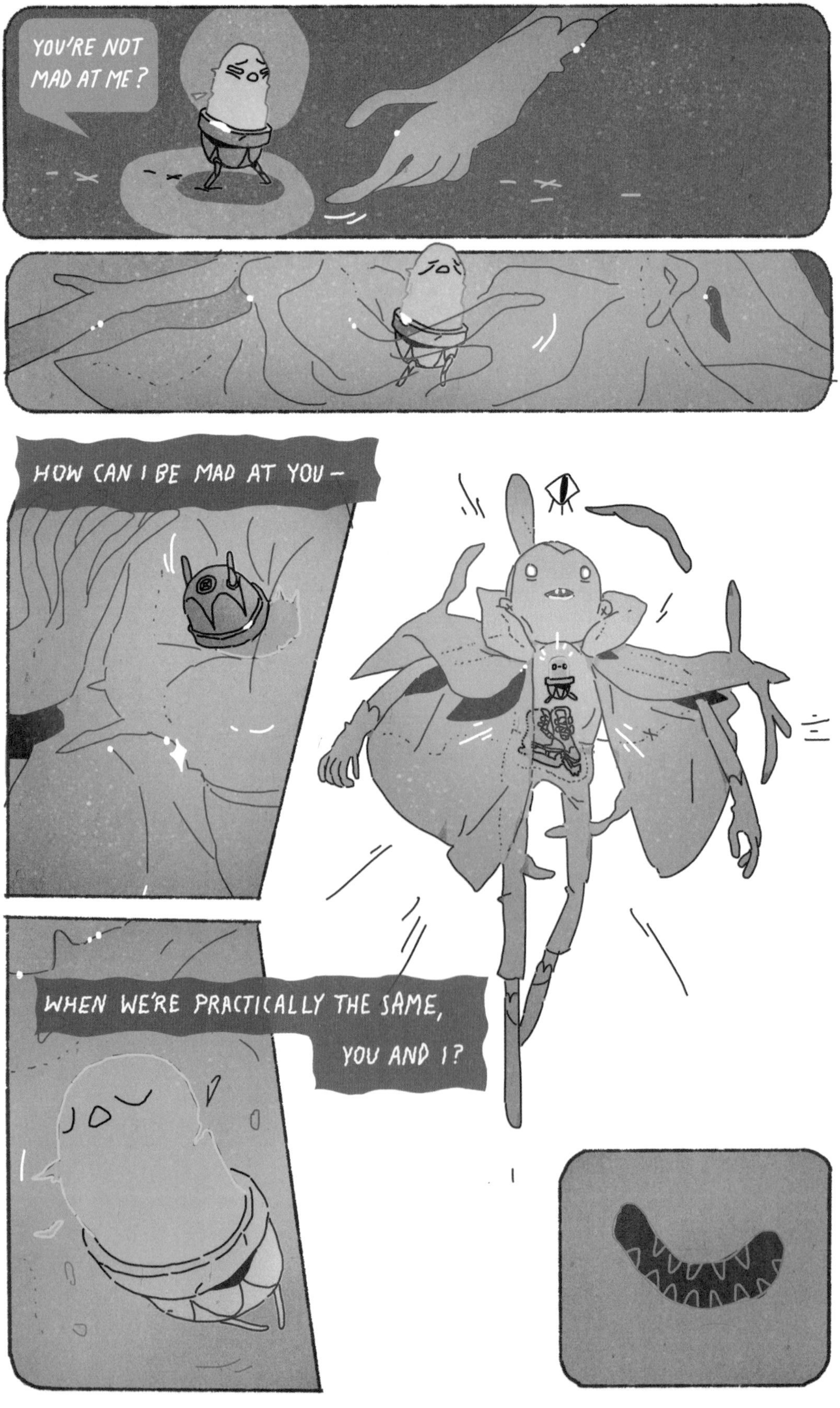
YOU'RE NOT MAD AT ME?
HOW CAN I BE MAD AT YOU—
WHEN WE'RE PRACTICALLY THE SAME,
YOU AND I?

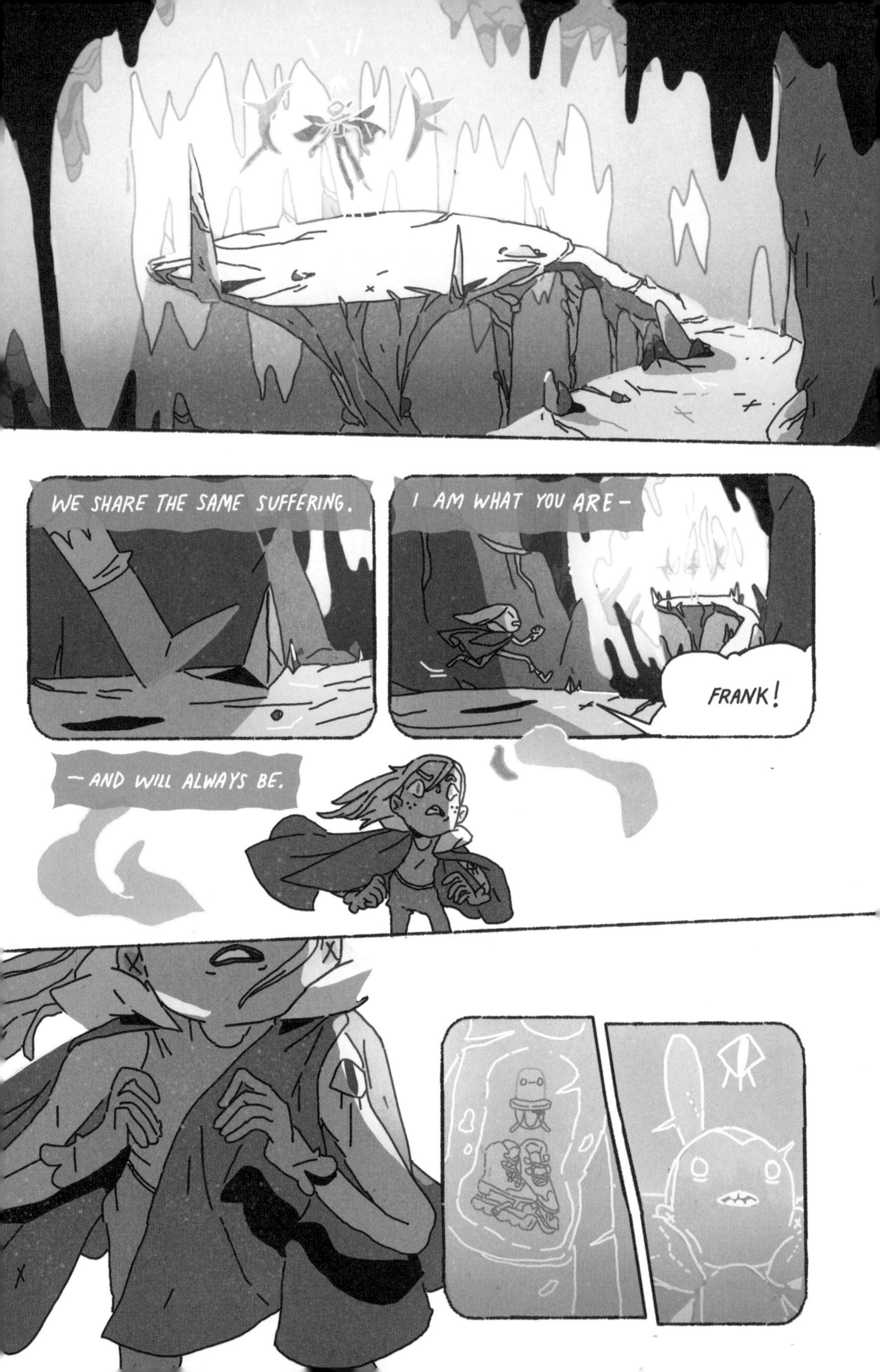
WE SHARE THE SAME SUFFERING.
I AM WHAT YOU ARE—
FRANK!
—AND WILL ALWAYS BE.

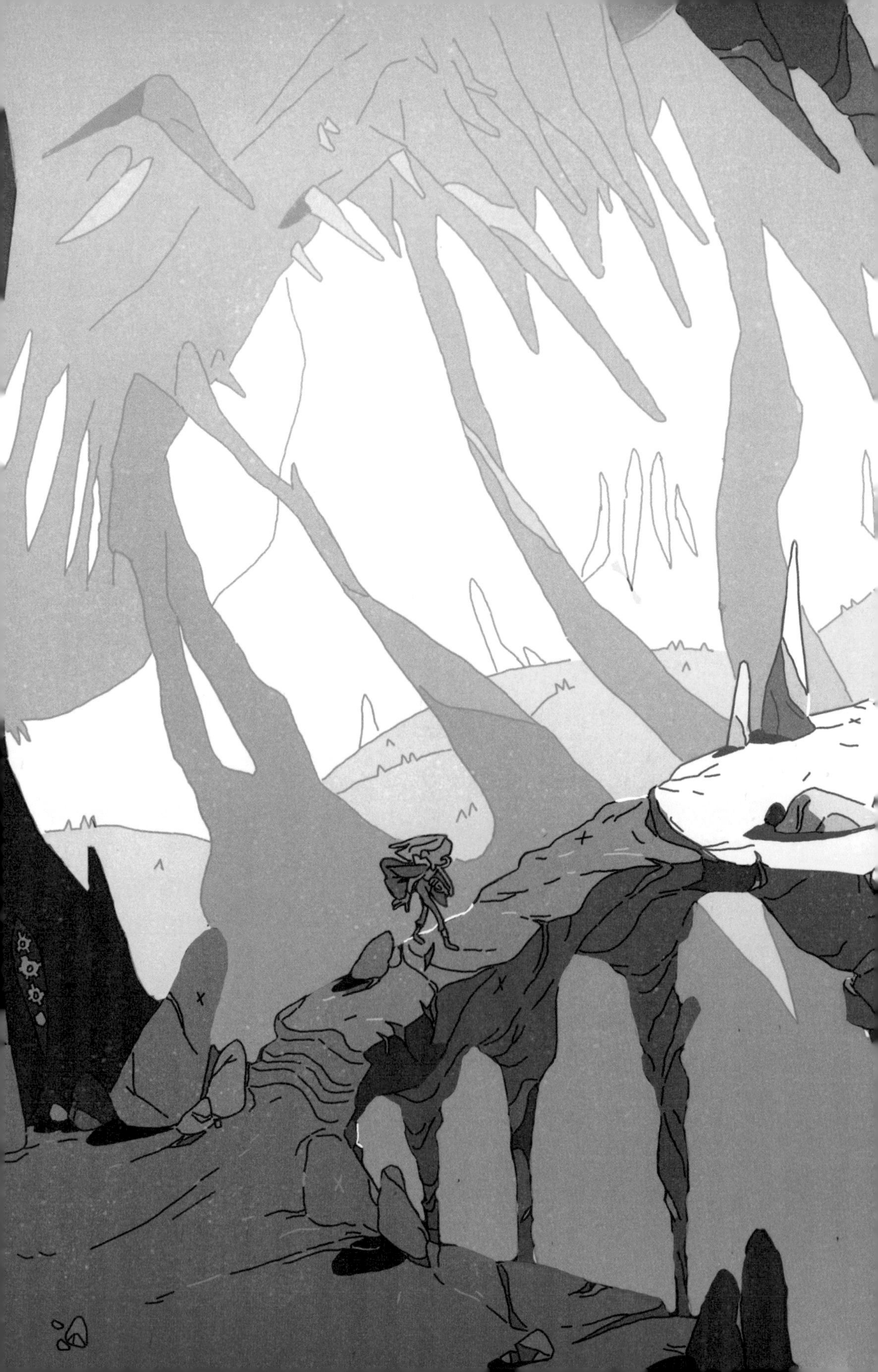

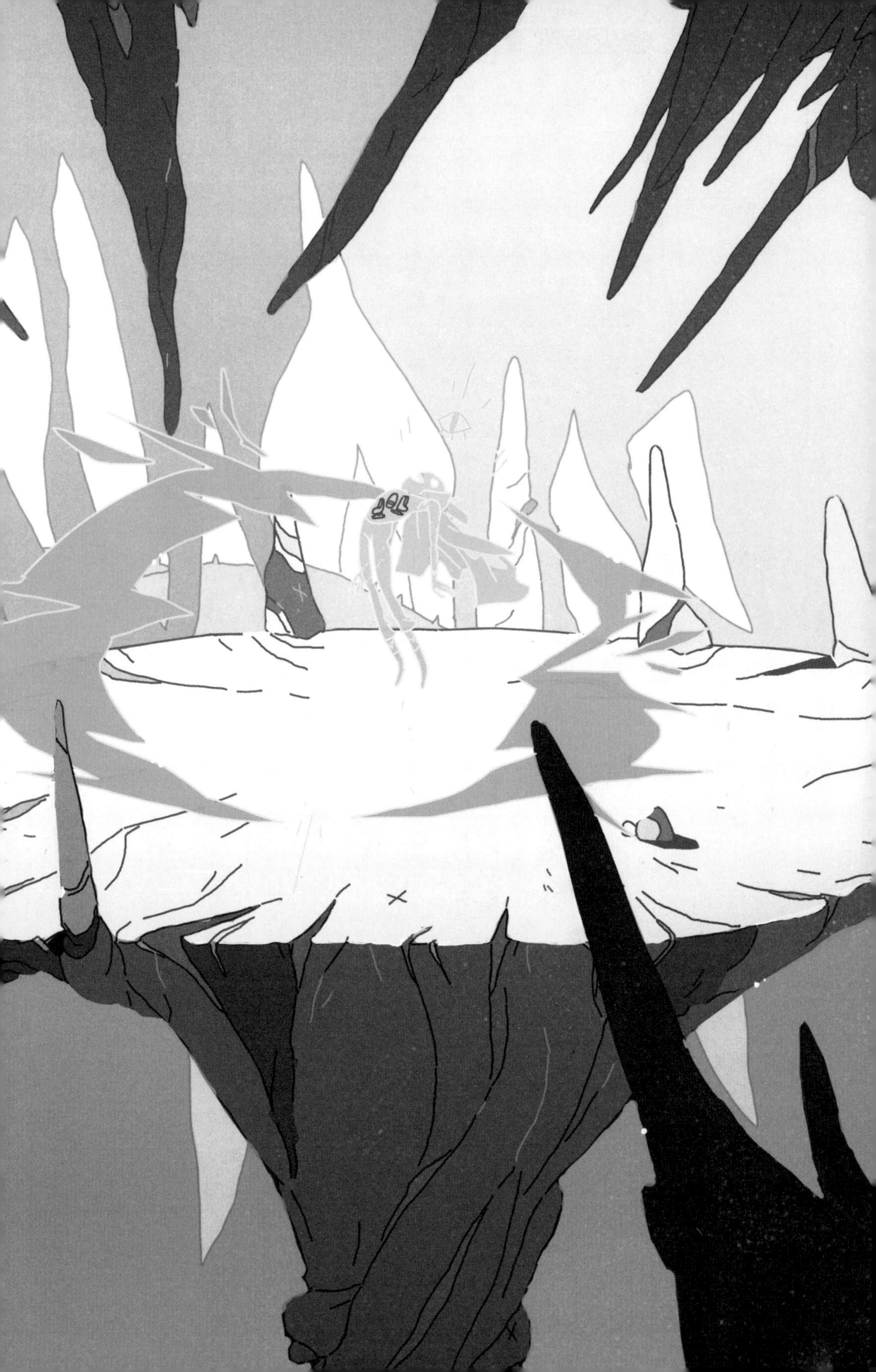

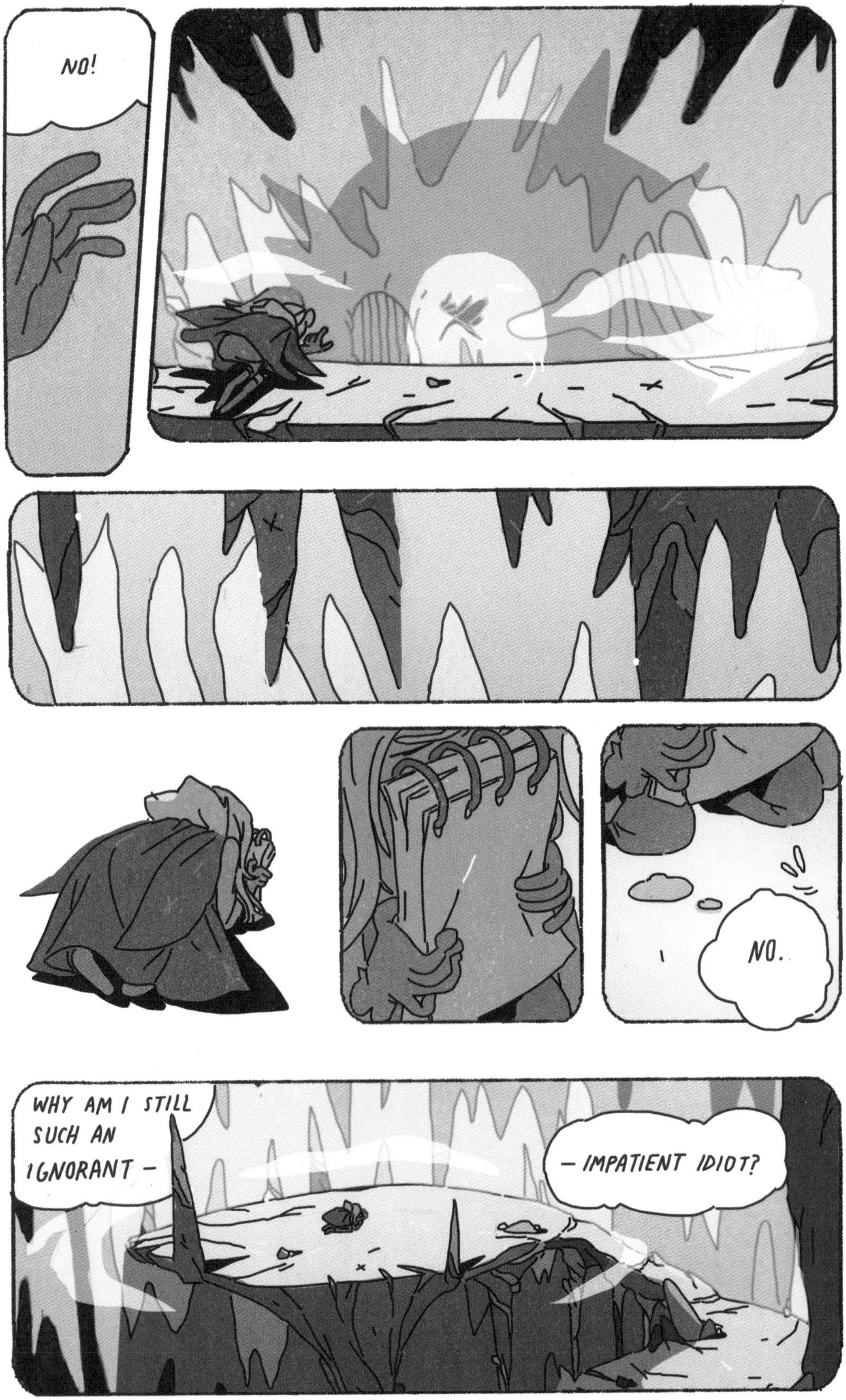
NO!
NO.
WHY AM I STILL SUCH AN IGNORANT —
— IMPATIENT IDIOT?

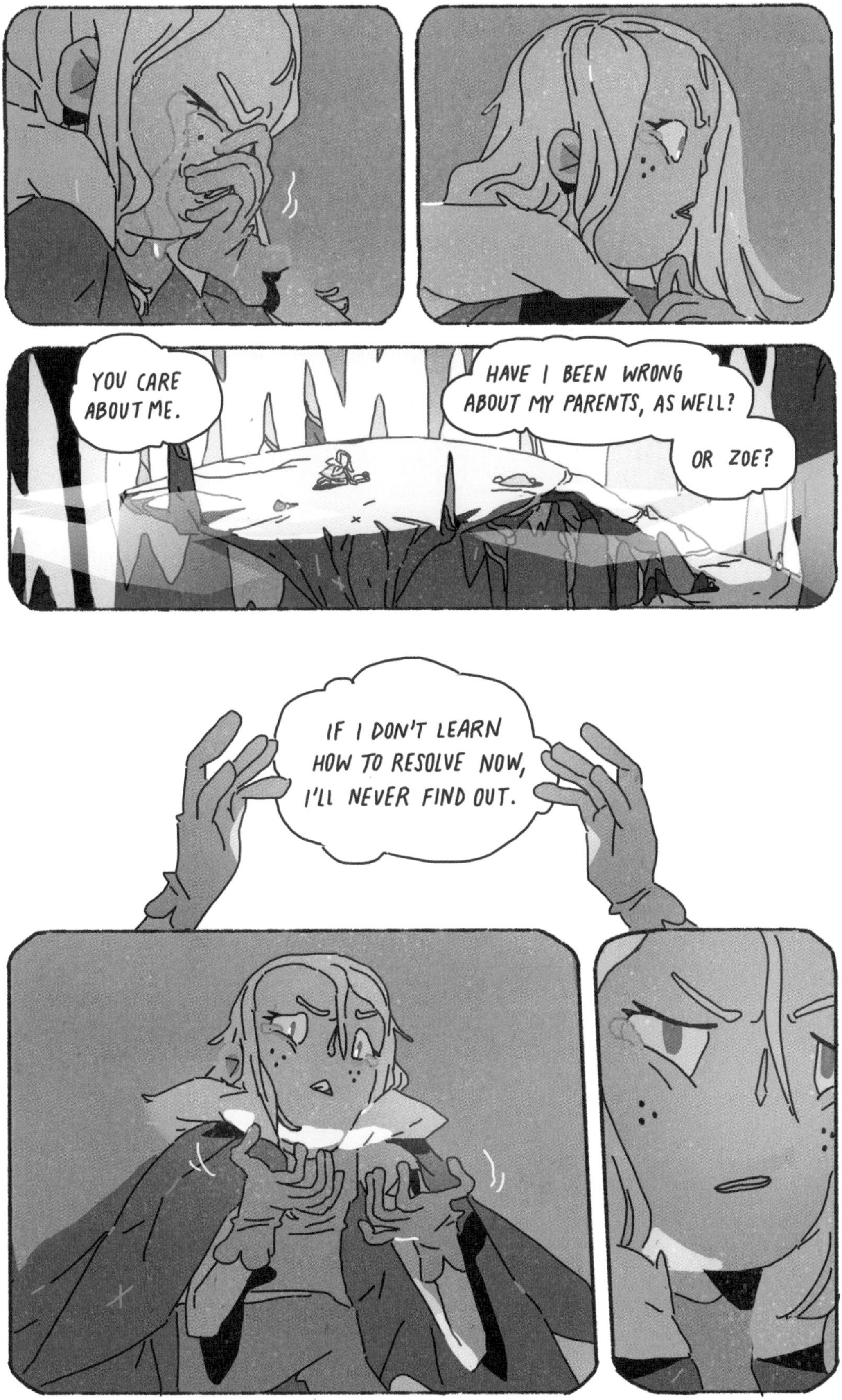
YOU CARE ABOUT ME.
HAVE I BEEN WRONG ABOUT MY PARENTS, AS WELL?
OR ZOE?
IF I DON'T LEARN HOW TO RESOLVE NOW, I'LL NEVER FIND OUT.

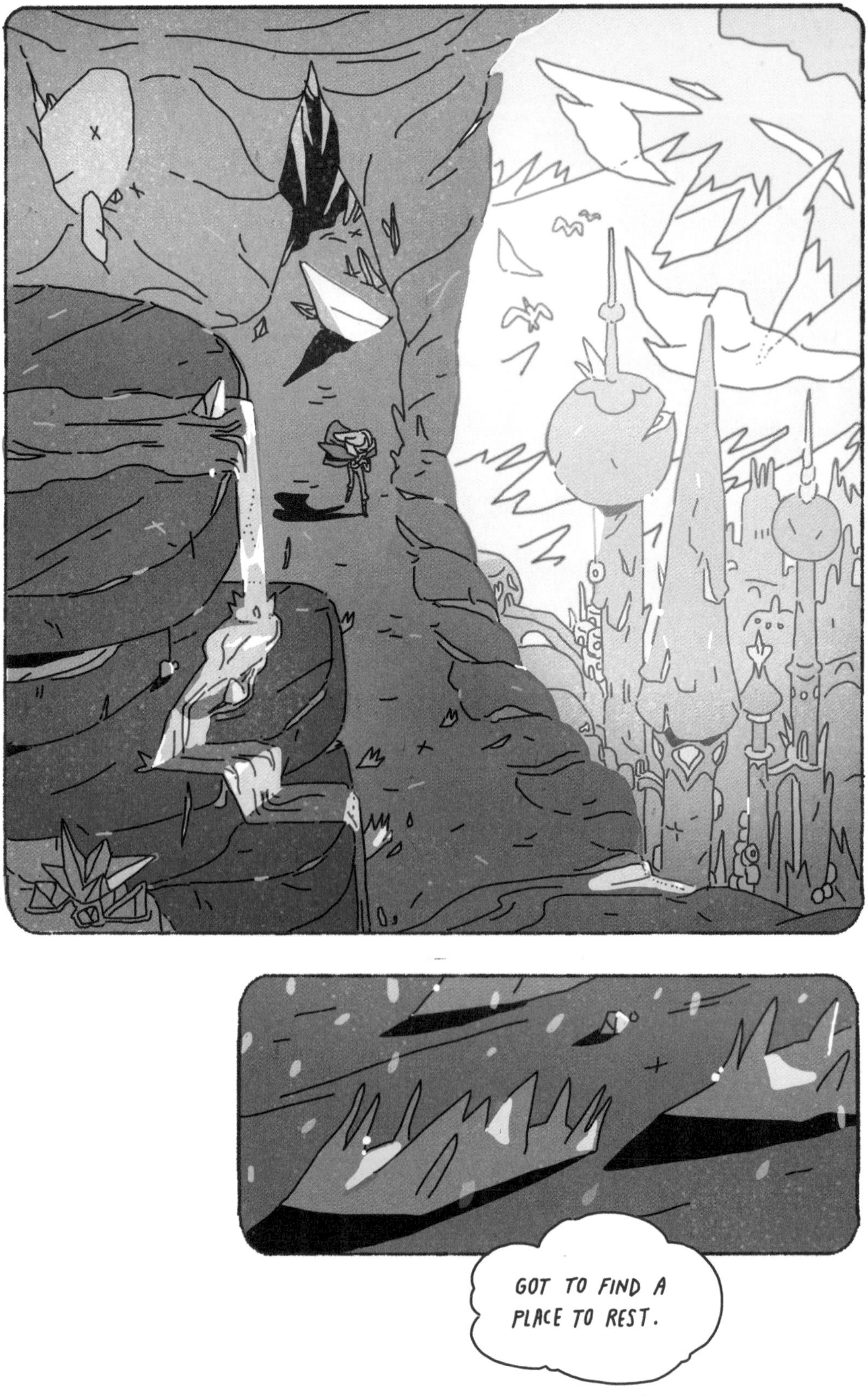
GOT TO FIND A PLACE TO REST.

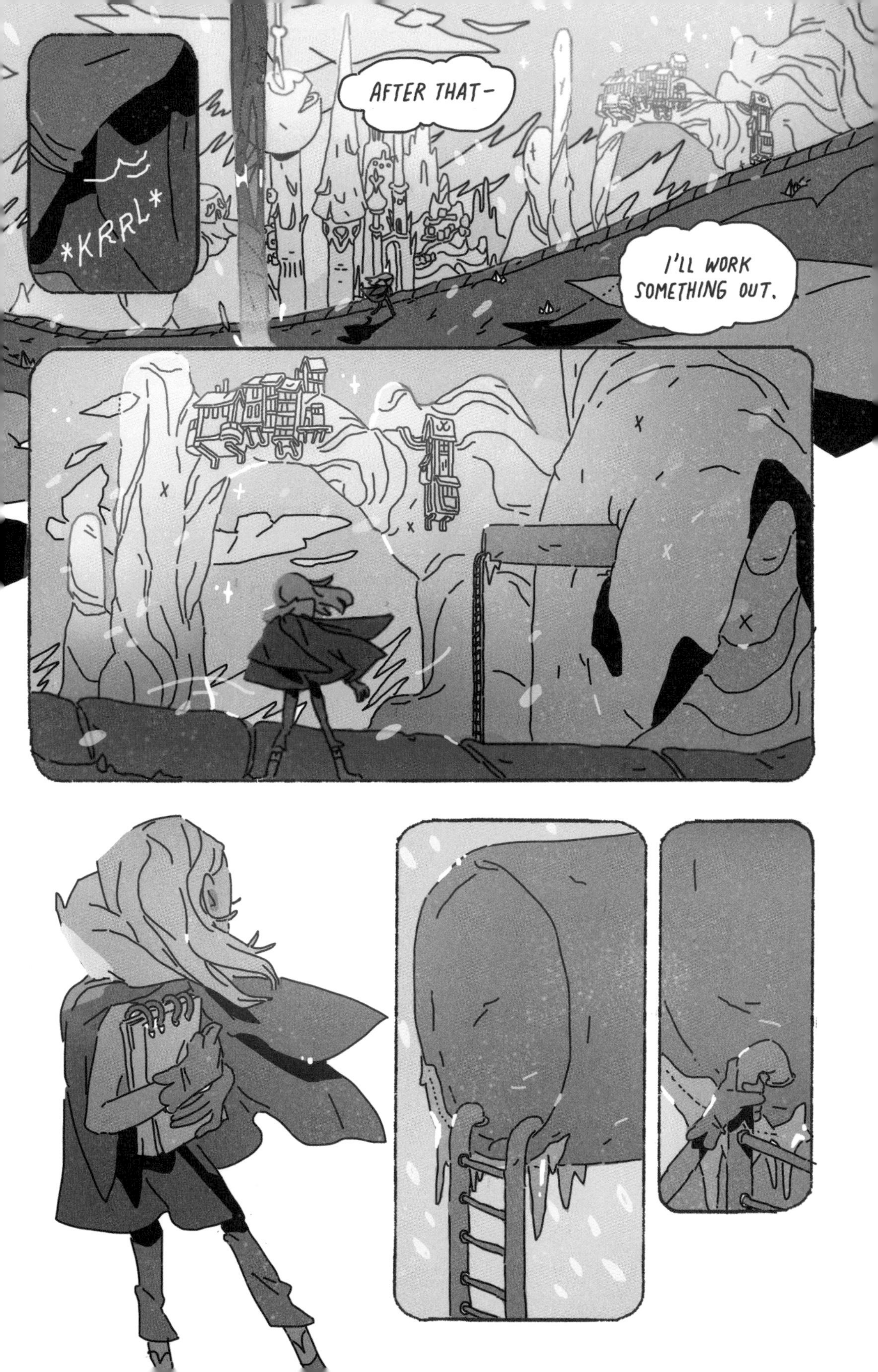
KRRL
AFTER THAT-
I'LL WORK SOMETHING OUT.

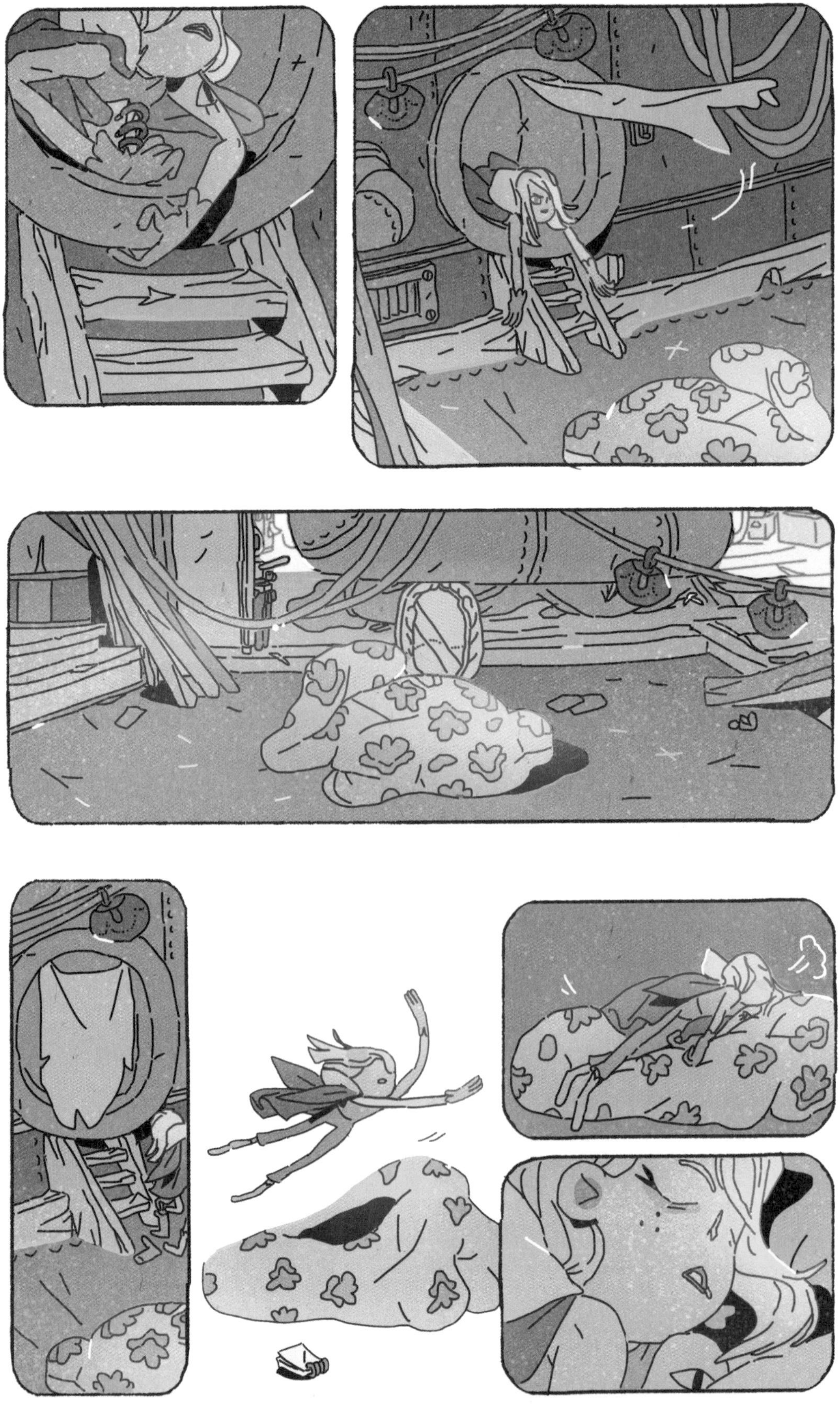

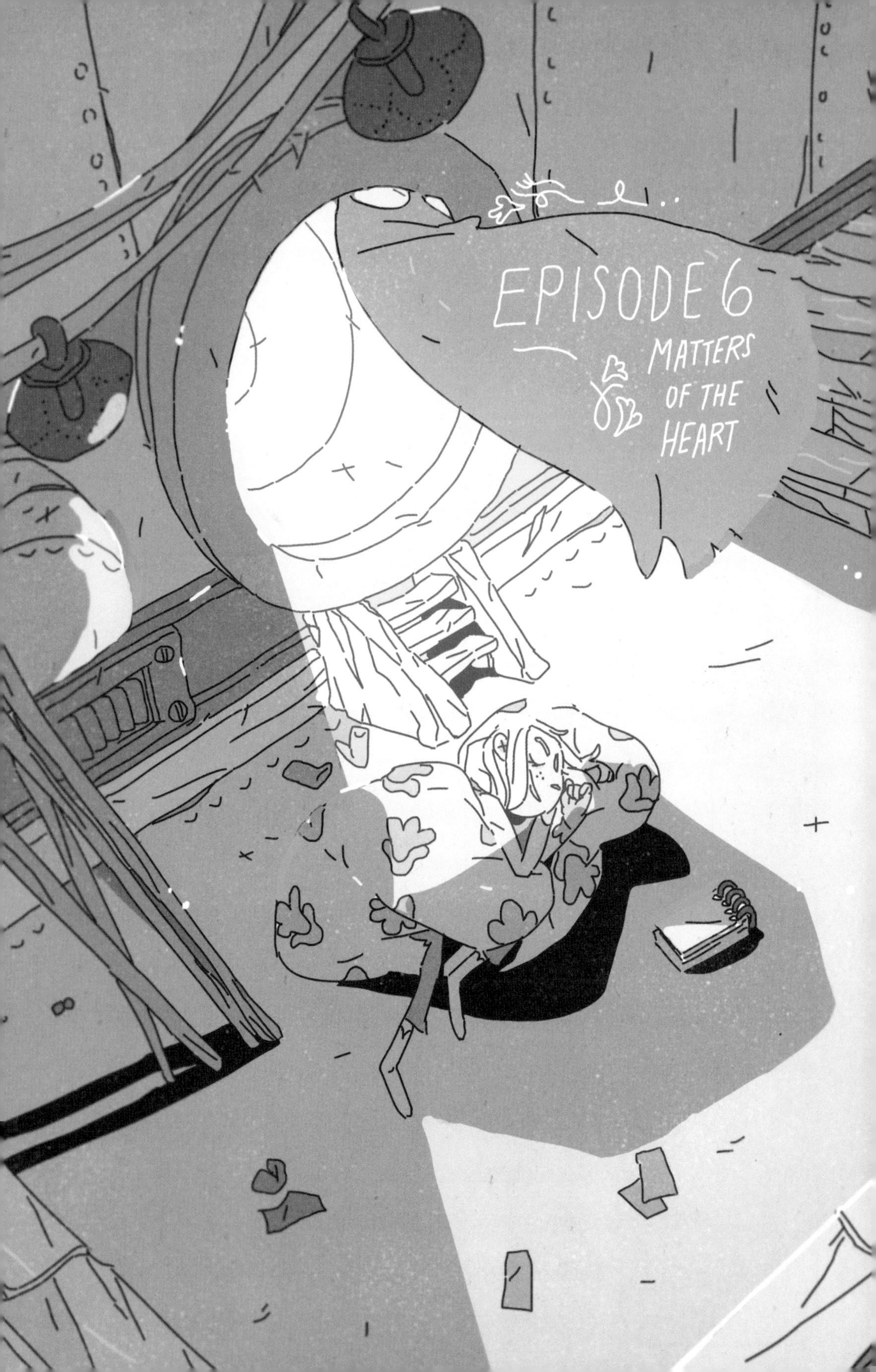
EPISODE 6
MATTERS OF THE HEART

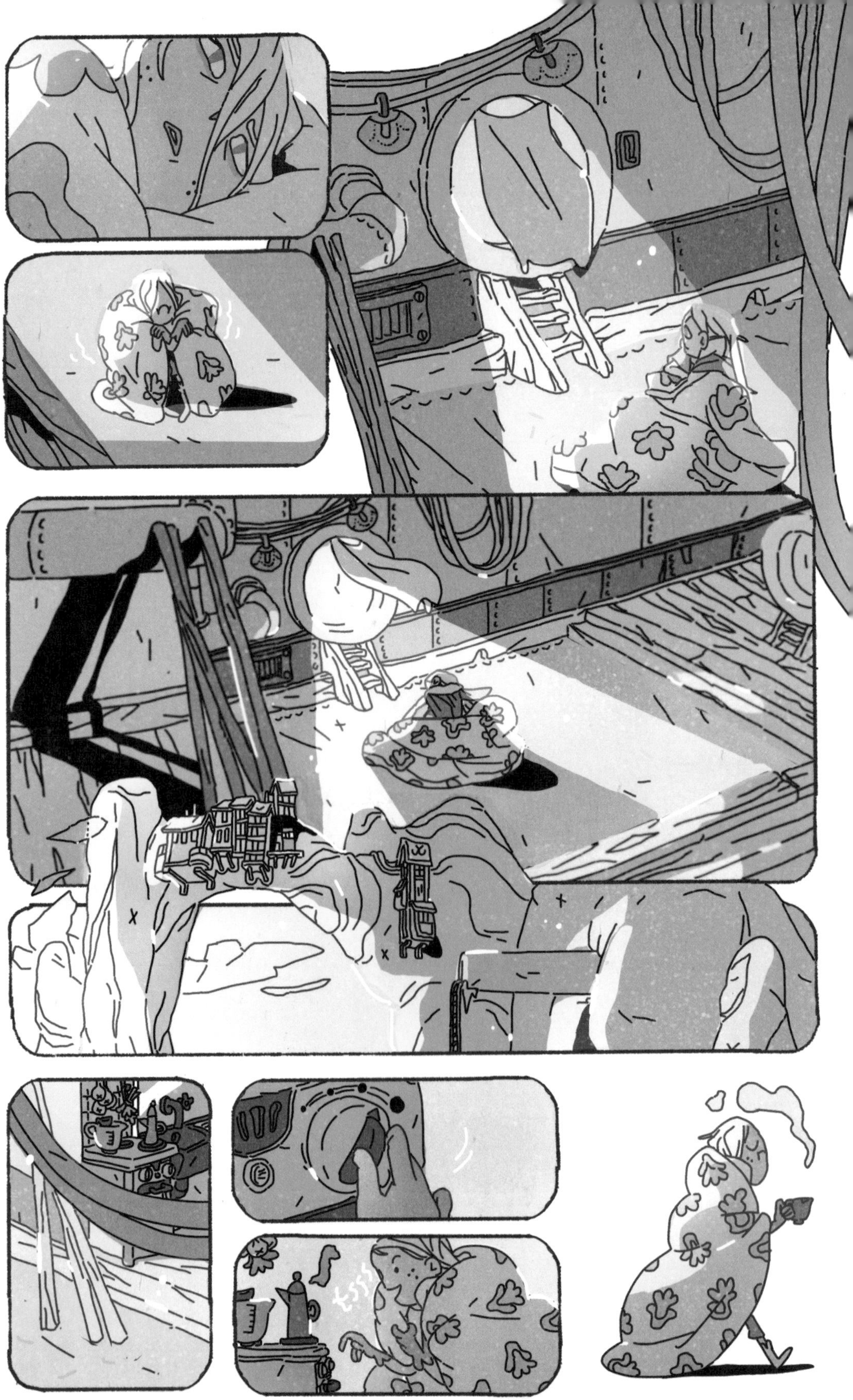
tsss

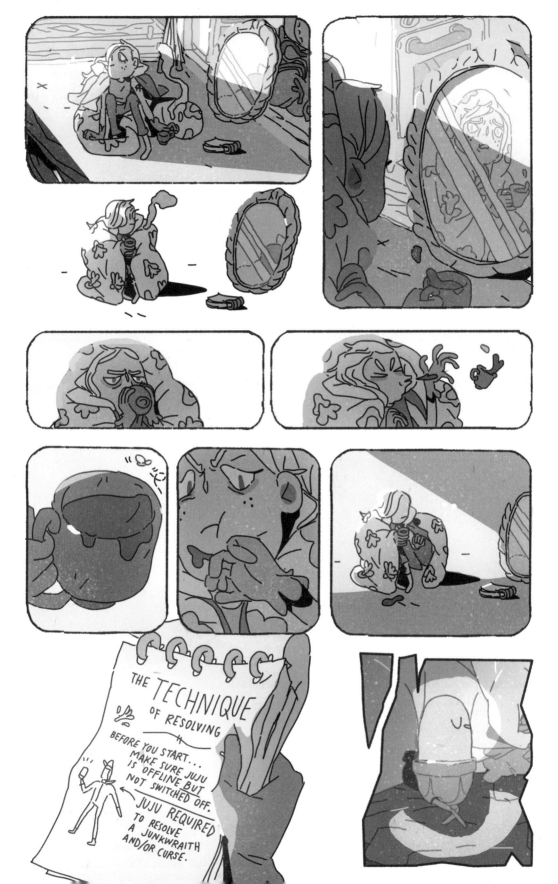

THE TECHNIQUE OF RESOLVING

BEFORE YOU START...
MAKE SURE JUJU
IS OFFLINE BUT
NOT SWITCHED OFF.

JUJU REQUIRED
TO RESOLVE
A JUNKWRAITH
AND/OR CURSE.

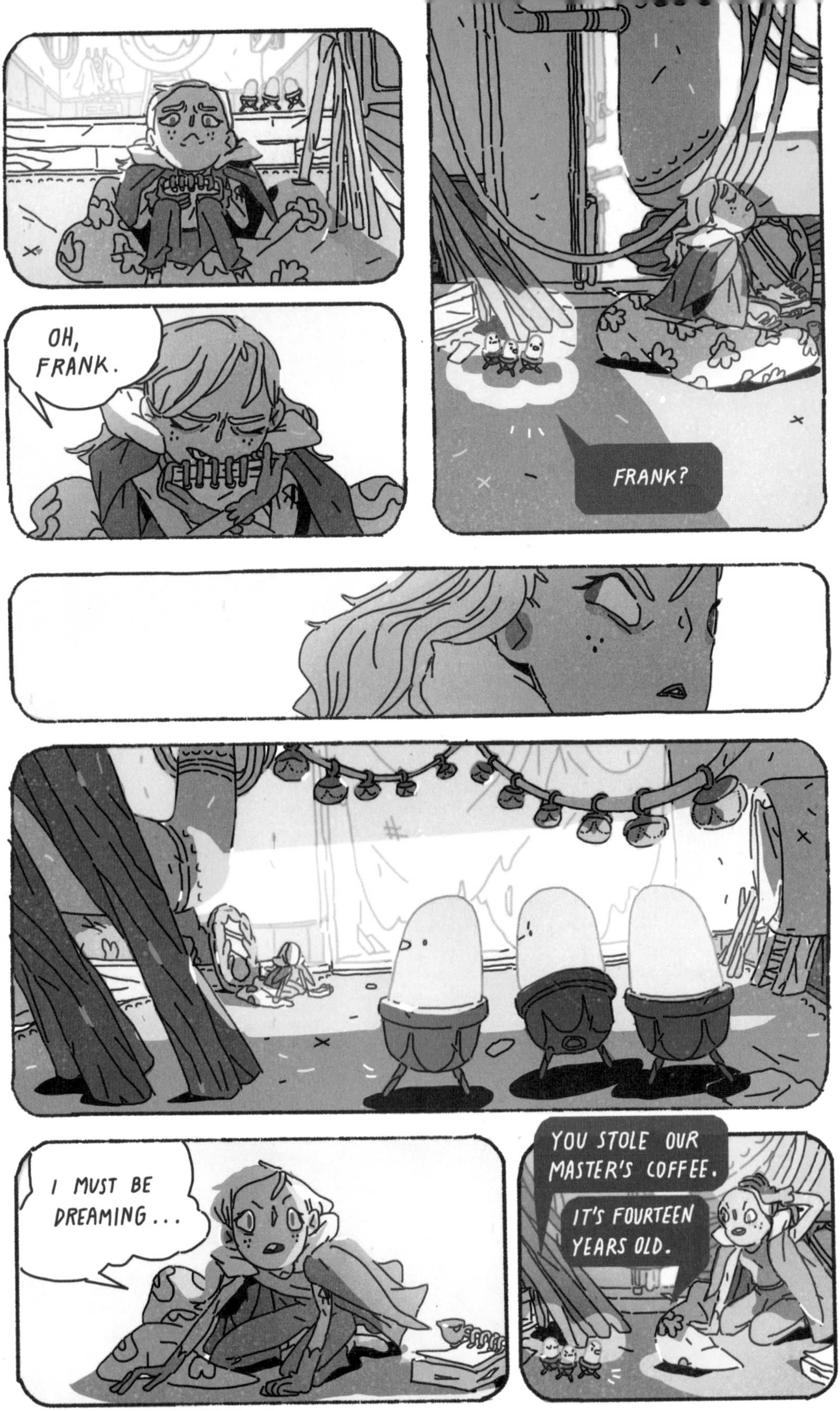
OH, FRANK.
FRANK?
I MUST BE DREAMING...
YOU STOLE OUR MASTER'S COFFEE.
IT'S FOURTEEN YEARS OLD.

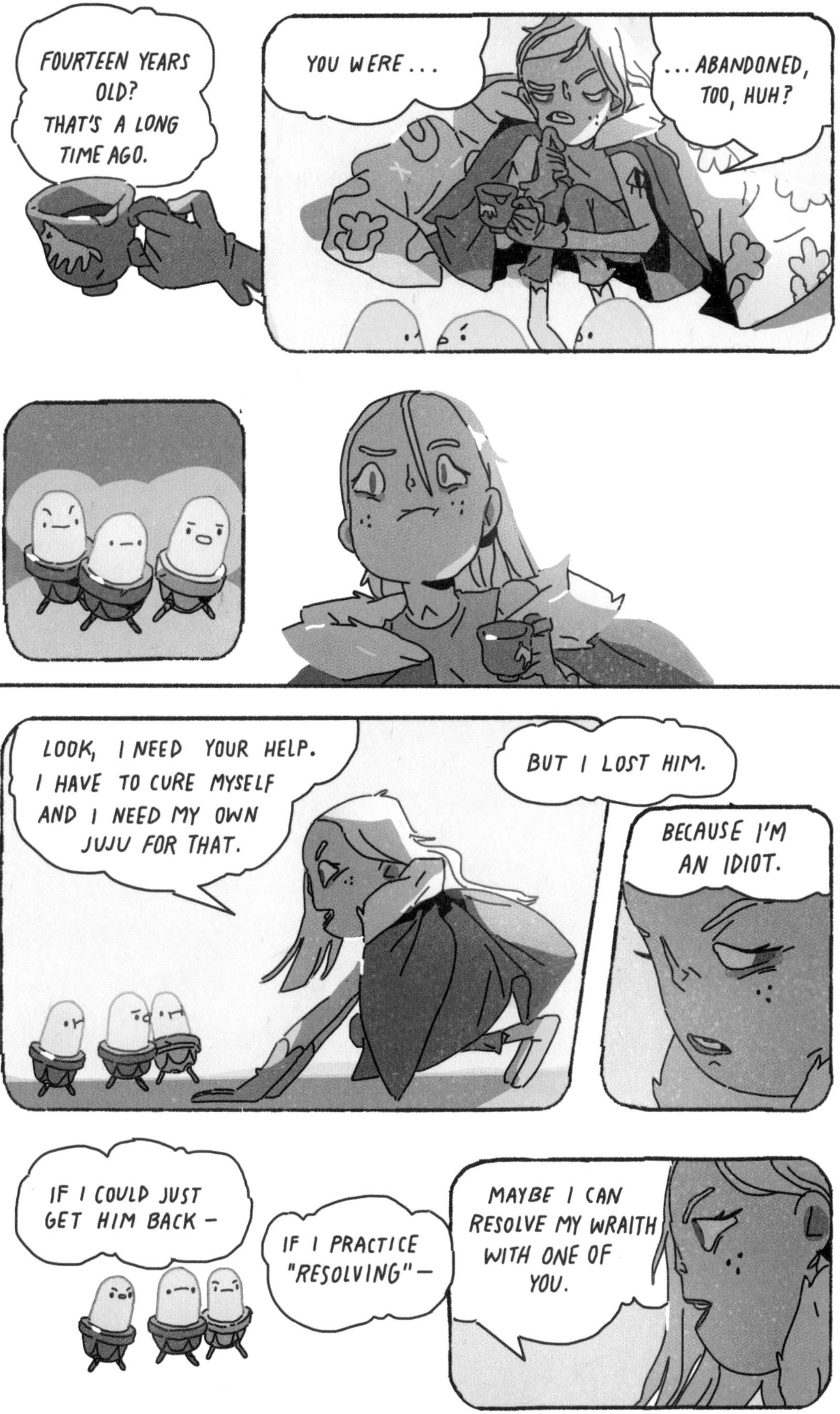
FOURTEEN YEARS OLD? THAT'S A LONG TIME AGO.
YOU WERE...
...ABANDONED, TOO, HUH?
LOOK, I NEED YOUR HELP. I HAVE TO CURE MYSELF AND I NEED MY OWN JUJU FOR THAT.
BUT I LOST HIM.
BECAUSE I'M AN IDIOT.
IF I COULD JUST GET HIM BACK—
IF I PRACTICE "RESOLVING"—
MAYBE I CAN RESOLVE MY WRAITH WITH ONE OF YOU.

ANY VOLUNTEERS?

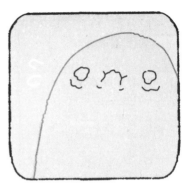

RESOLVING TEST #1

THE RESOLVING PROCEDURE

1. BONDING

DURE

STEP-BY-STEP

1. BONDING

BECOME ONE WITH JUJU TO MANIPULATE HAUNTED JUNK.

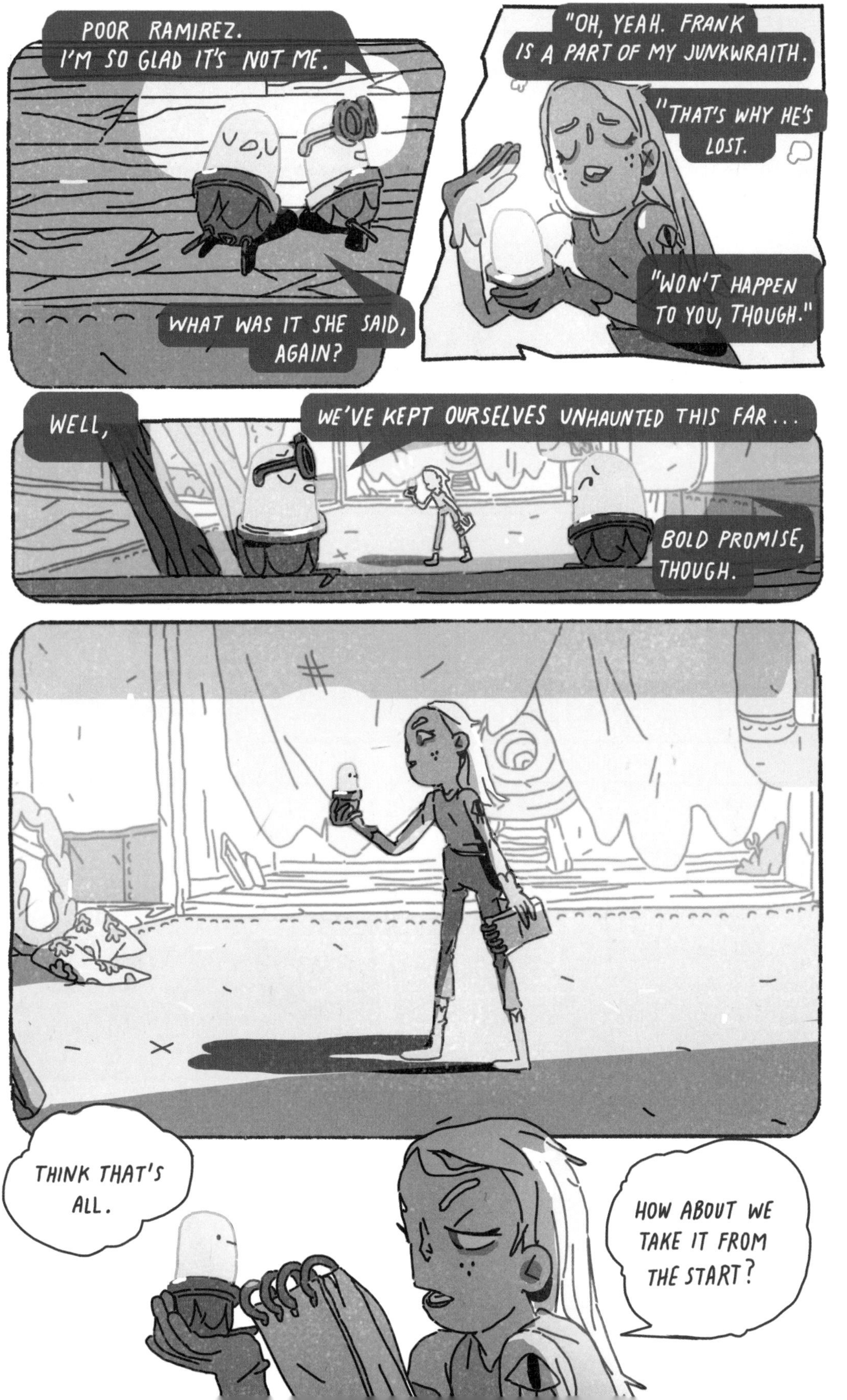
POOR RAMIREZ. I'M SO GLAD IT'S NOT ME.
WHAT WAS IT SHE SAID, AGAIN?
"OH, YEAH. FRANK IS A PART OF MY JUNKWRAITH.
"THAT'S WHY HE'S LOST.
"WON'T HAPPEN TO YOU, THOUGH."
WELL,
WE'VE KEPT OURSELVES UNHAUNTED THIS FAR...
BOLD PROMISE, THOUGH.
THINK THAT'S ALL.
HOW ABOUT WE TAKE IT FROM THE START?

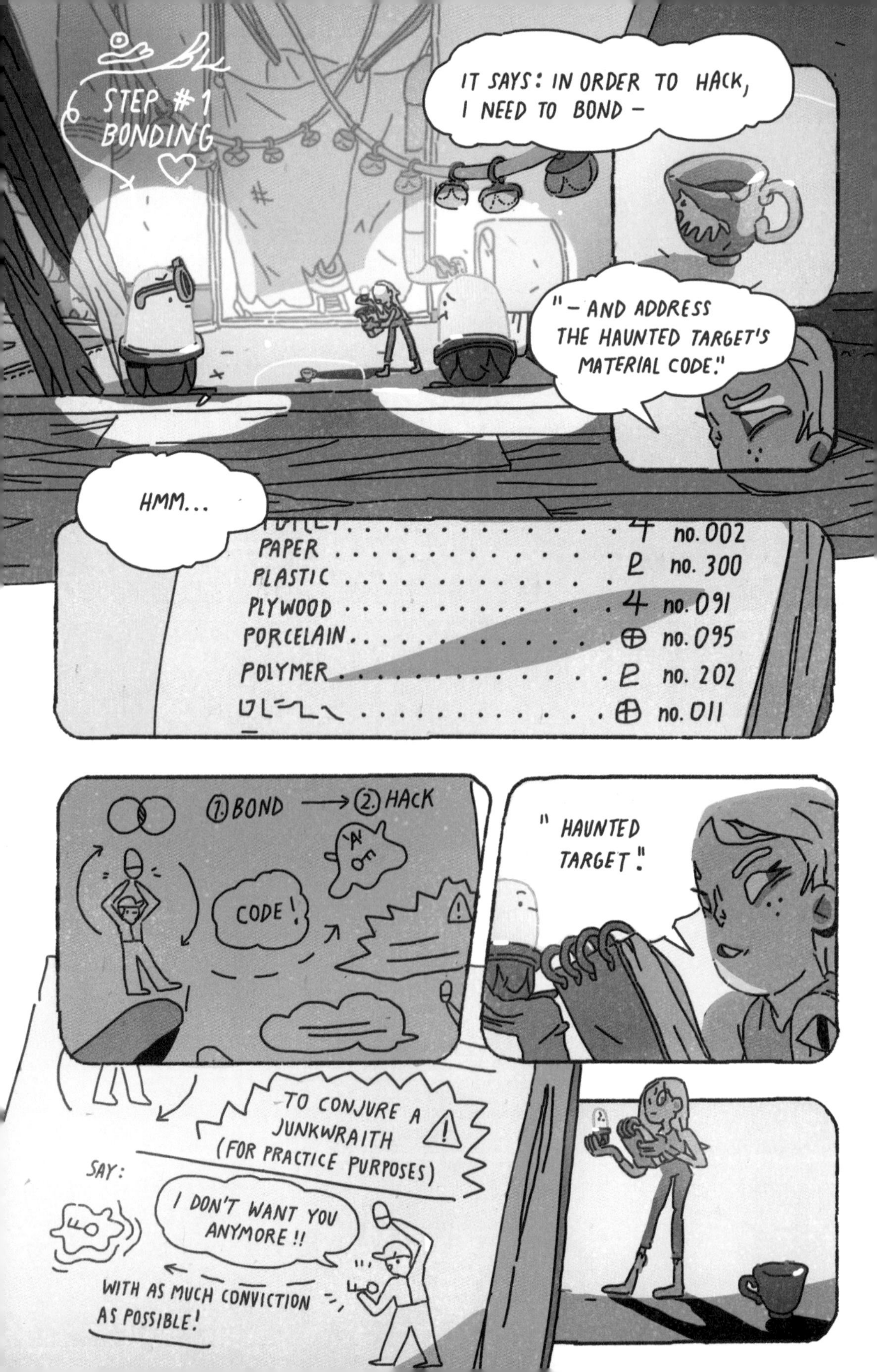
STEP #1
BONDING
IT SAYS: IN ORDER TO HACK, I NEED TO BOND –
"– AND ADDRESS THE HAUNTED TARGET'S MATERIAL CODE."
HMM...
PAPER ... no. 300
PLASTIC ...
PLYWOOD ... no. 091
PORCELAIN ... no. 095
POLYMER ... no. 202
no. 011
no. 002
1. BOND → 2. HACK
CODE!
"HAUNTED TARGET."
TO CONJURE A JUNKWRAITH (FOR PRACTICE PURPOSES)
SAY:
I DON'T WANT YOU ANYMORE!!
WITH AS MUCH CONVICTION AS POSSIBLE!

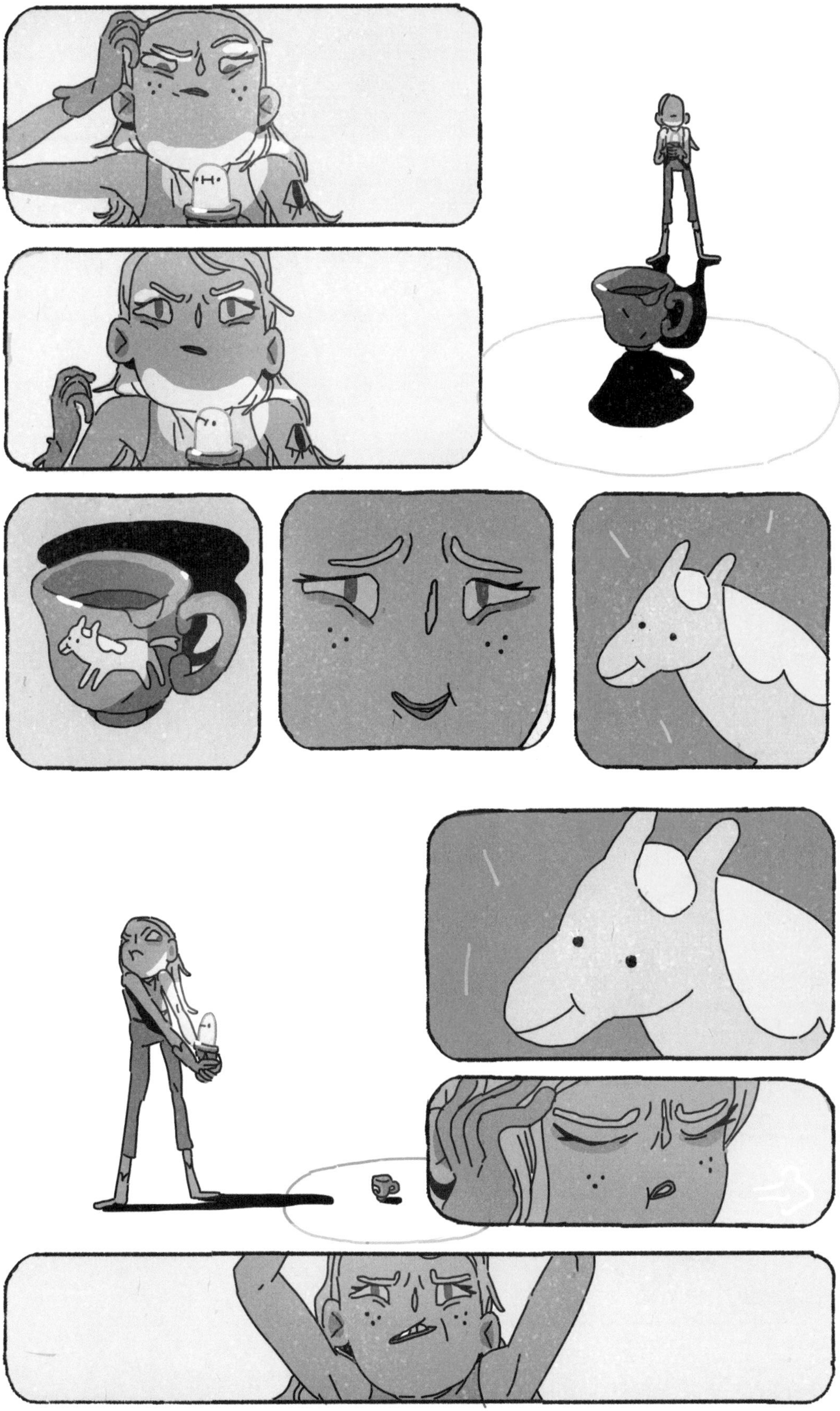

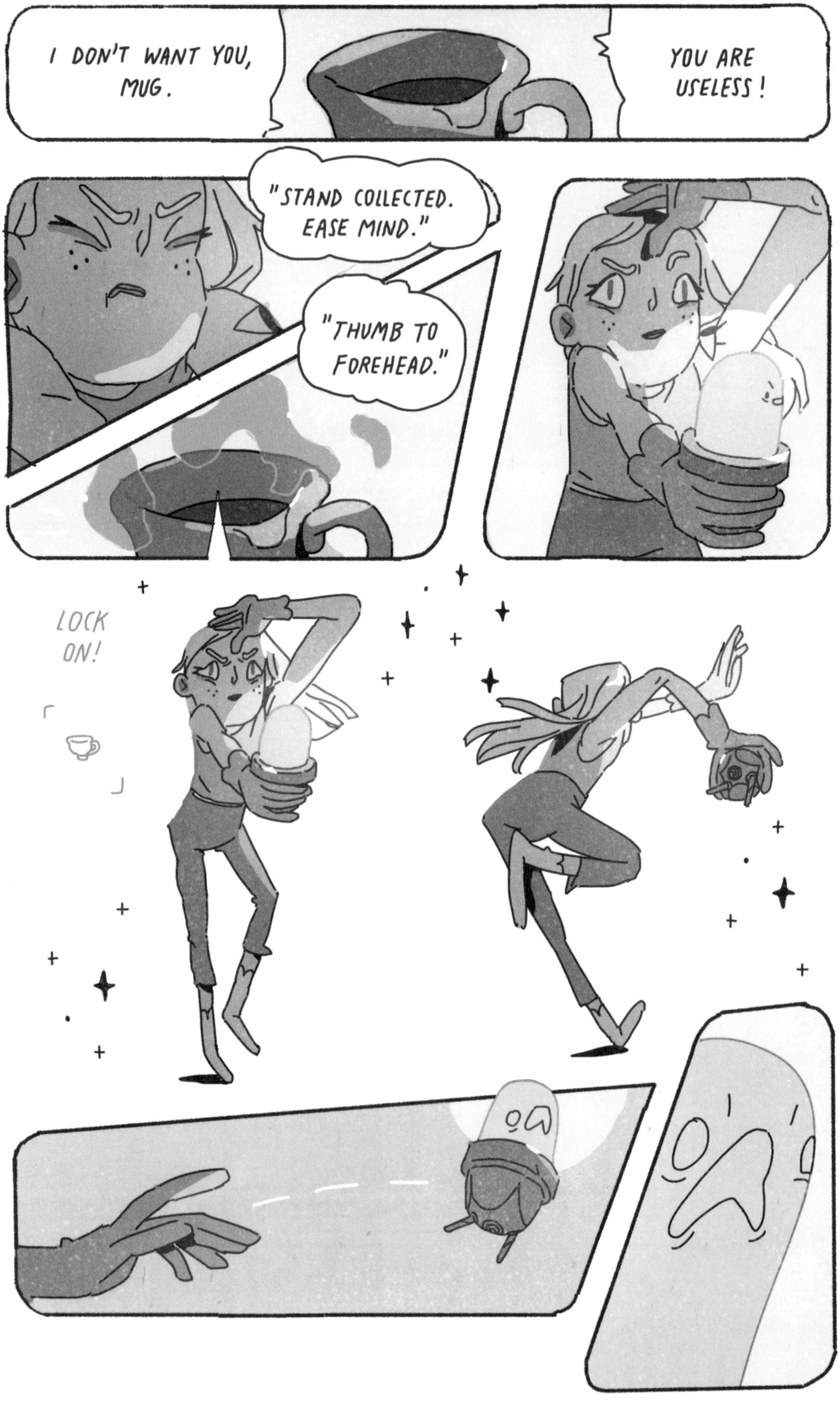
I DON'T WANT YOU, MUG.
YOU ARE USELESS!
"STAND COLLECTED. EASE MIND."
"THUMB TO FOREHEAD."
LOCK ON!

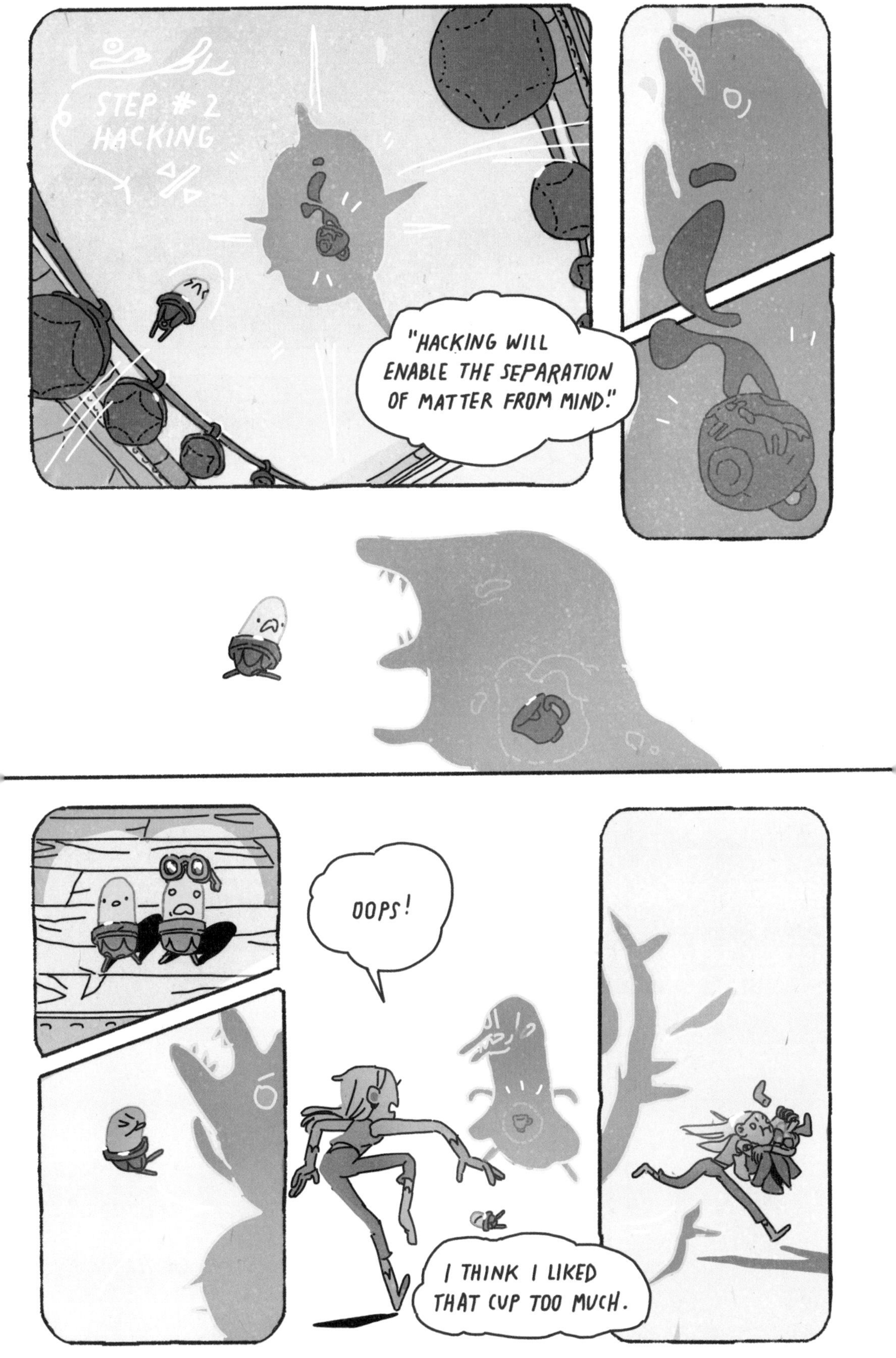
STEP #2
HACKING
"HACKING WILL ENABLE THE SEPARATION OF MATTER FROM MIND."
OOPS!
I THINK I LIKED THAT CUP TOO MUCH.

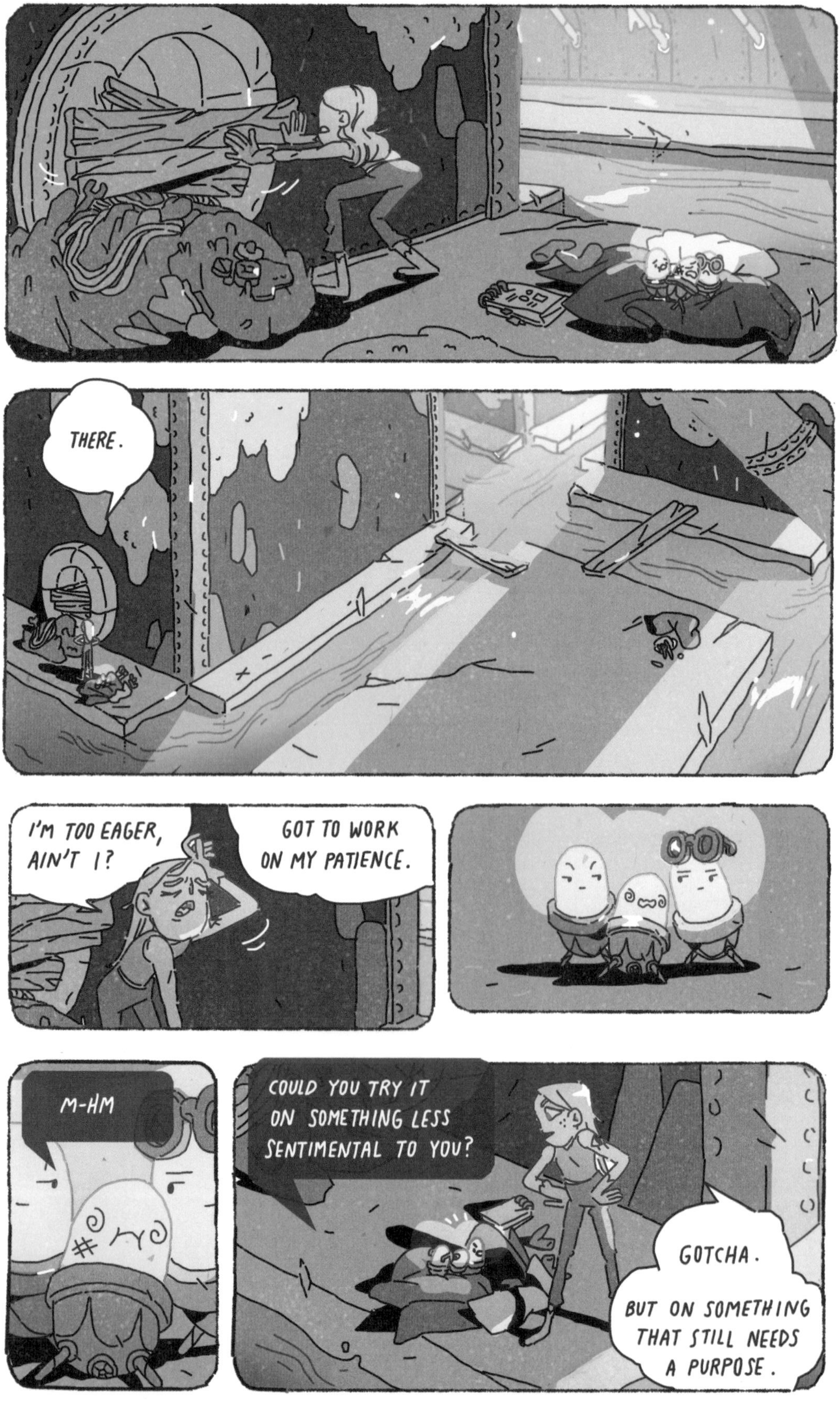
THERE.
I'M TOO EAGER, AIN'T I?
GOT TO WORK ON MY PATIENCE.
M-HM
COULD YOU TRY IT ON SOMETHING LESS SENTIMENTAL TO YOU?
GOTCHA.
BUT ON SOMETHING THAT STILL NEEDS A PURPOSE.

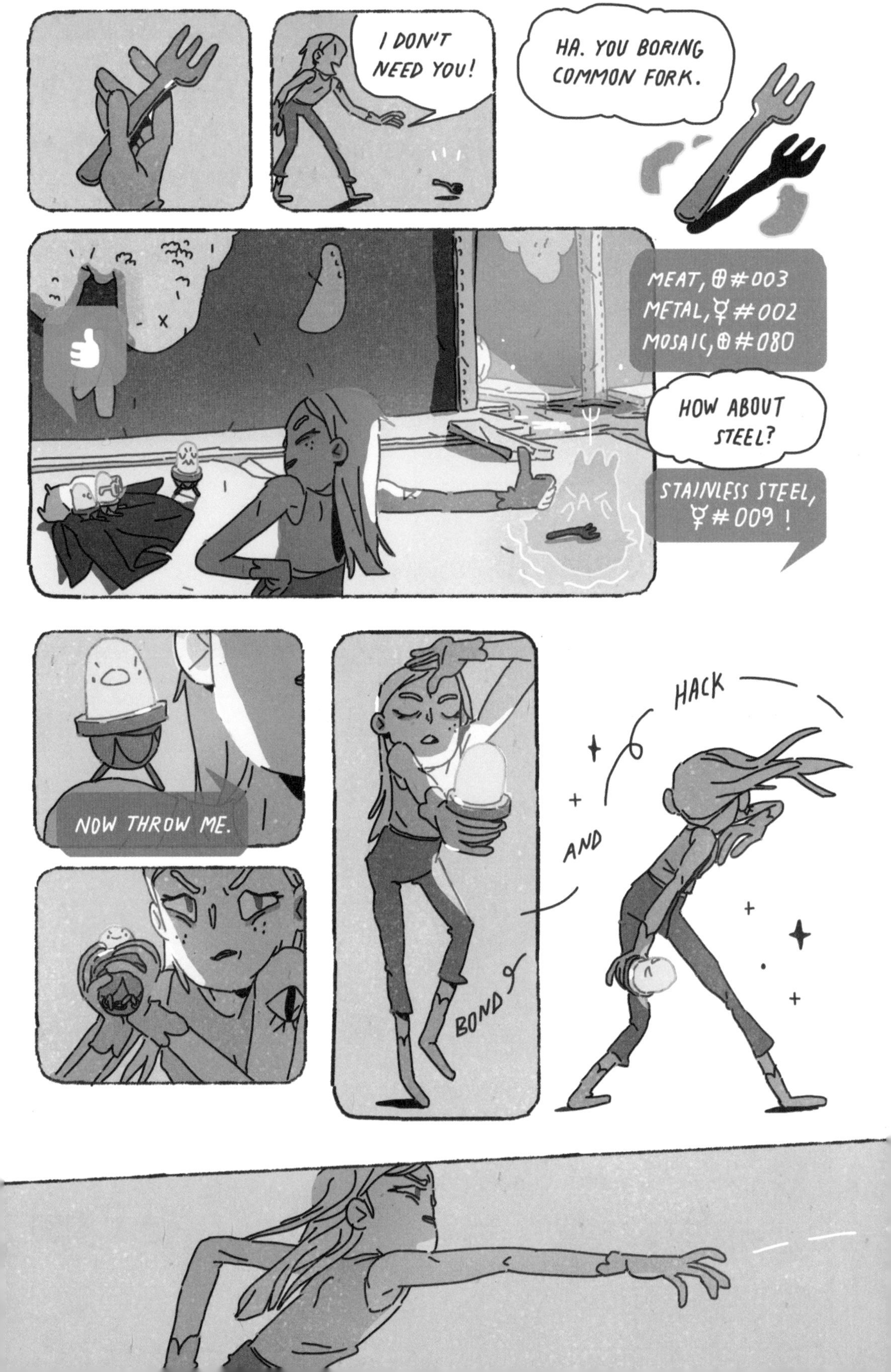
I DON'T NEED YOU!
HA. YOU BORING COMMON FORK.
MEAT, ⊕#003
METAL, ☿#002
MOSAIC, ⊕#080
HOW ABOUT STEEL?
STAINLESS STEEL, ☿#009 !
NOW THROW ME.
BOND
AND
HACK

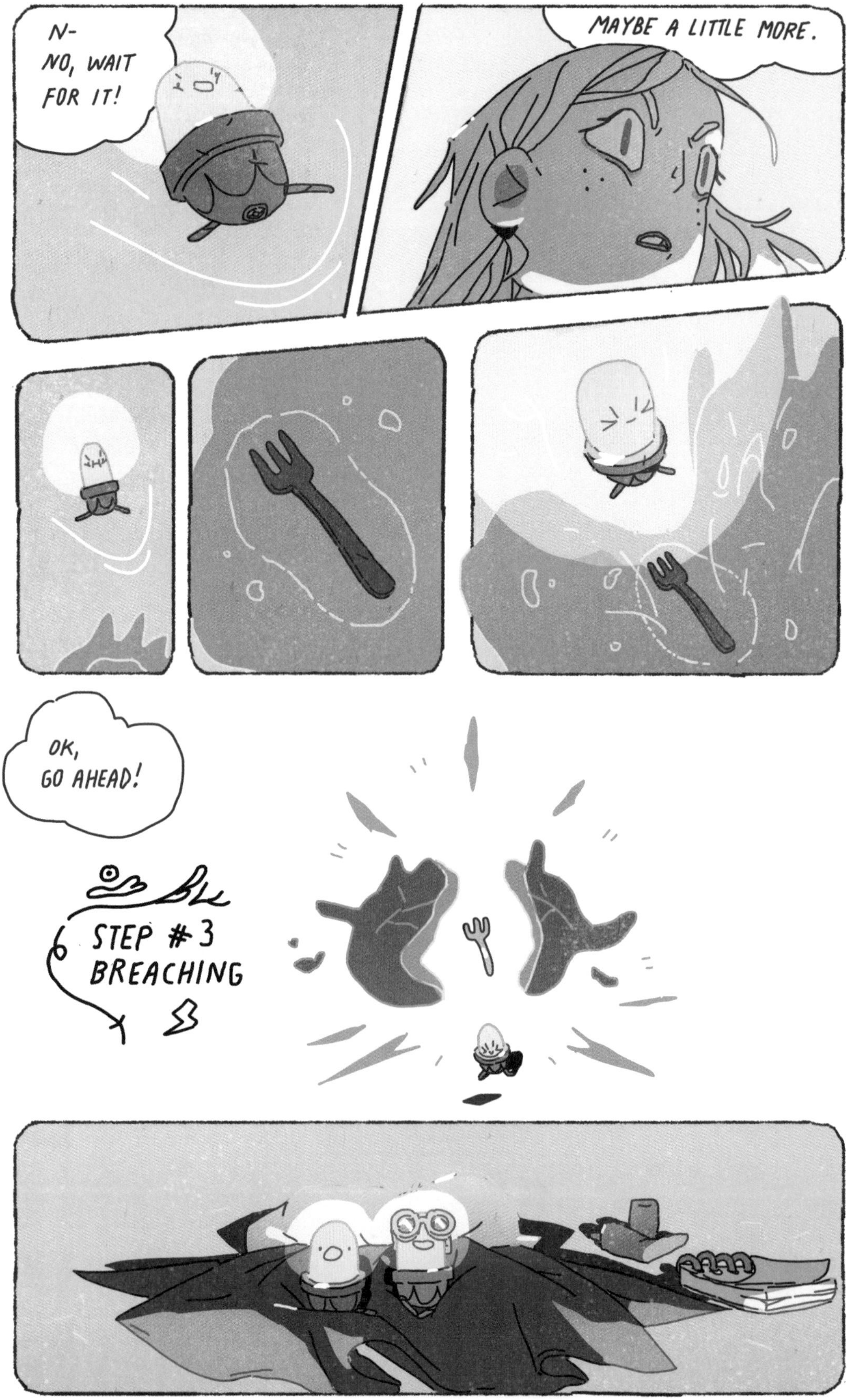
N-
NO, WAIT FOR IT!
MAYBE A LITTLE MORE.
OK, GO AHEAD!
STEP #3 BREACHING

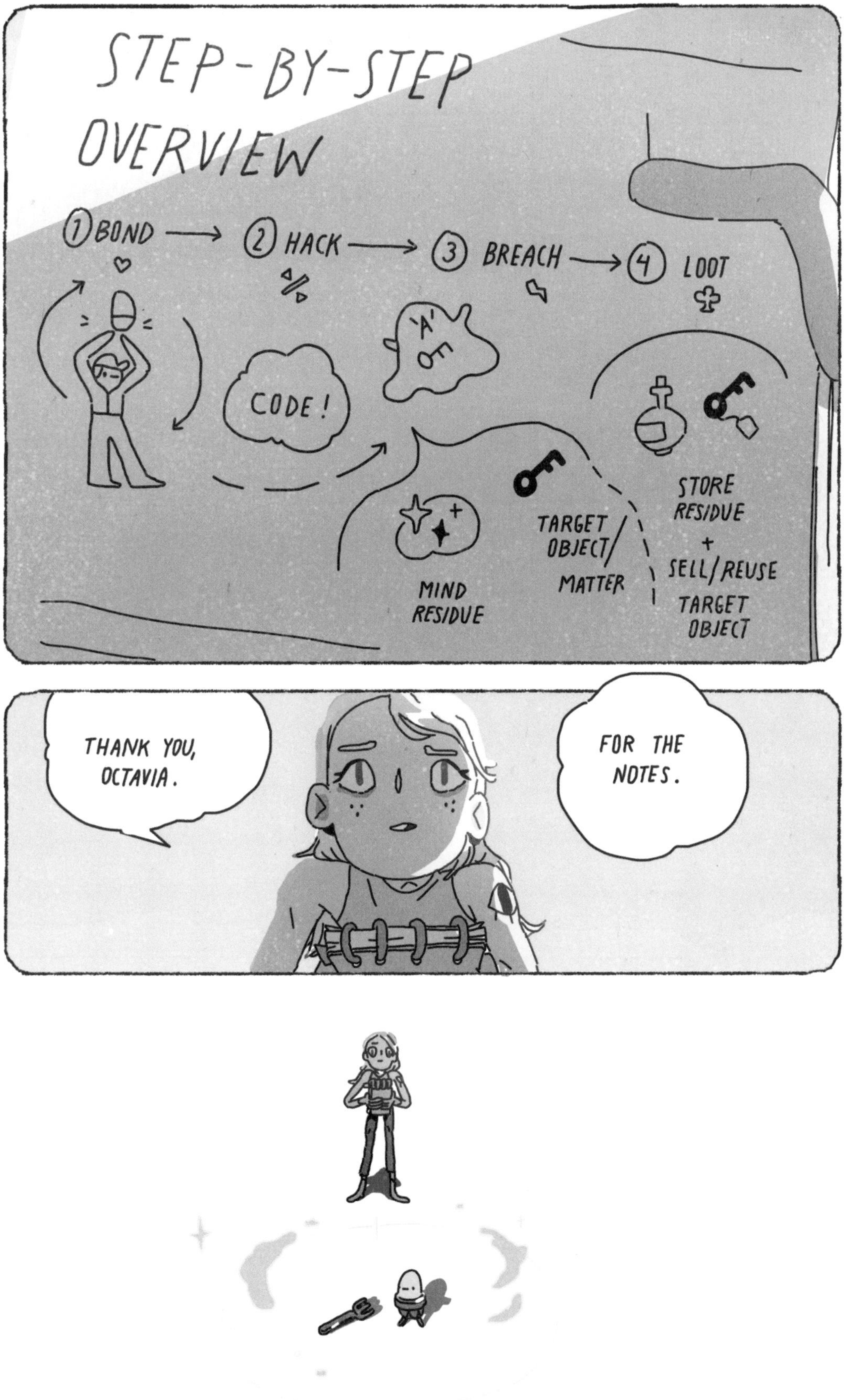
STEP-BY-STEP OVERVIEW
1 BOND → 2 HACK → 3 BREACH → 4 LOOT
CODE!
'A'
MIND RESIDUE
TARGET OBJECT/ MATTER
STORE RESIDUE + SELL/REUSE TARGET OBJECT
THANK YOU, OCTAVIA.
FOR THE NOTES.

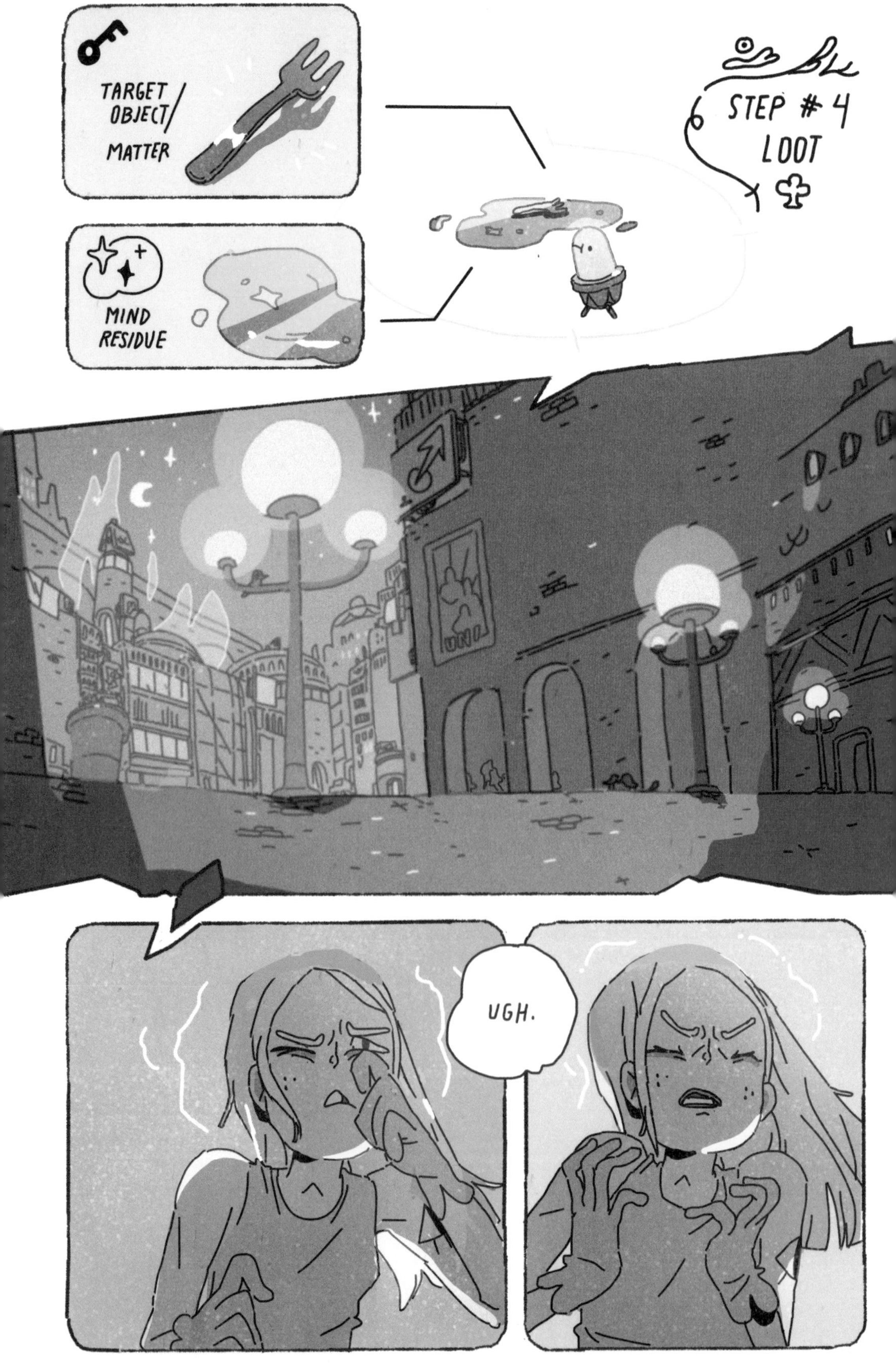
TARGET OBJECT/ MATTER
MIND RESIDUE
STEP #4 LOOT
UGH.

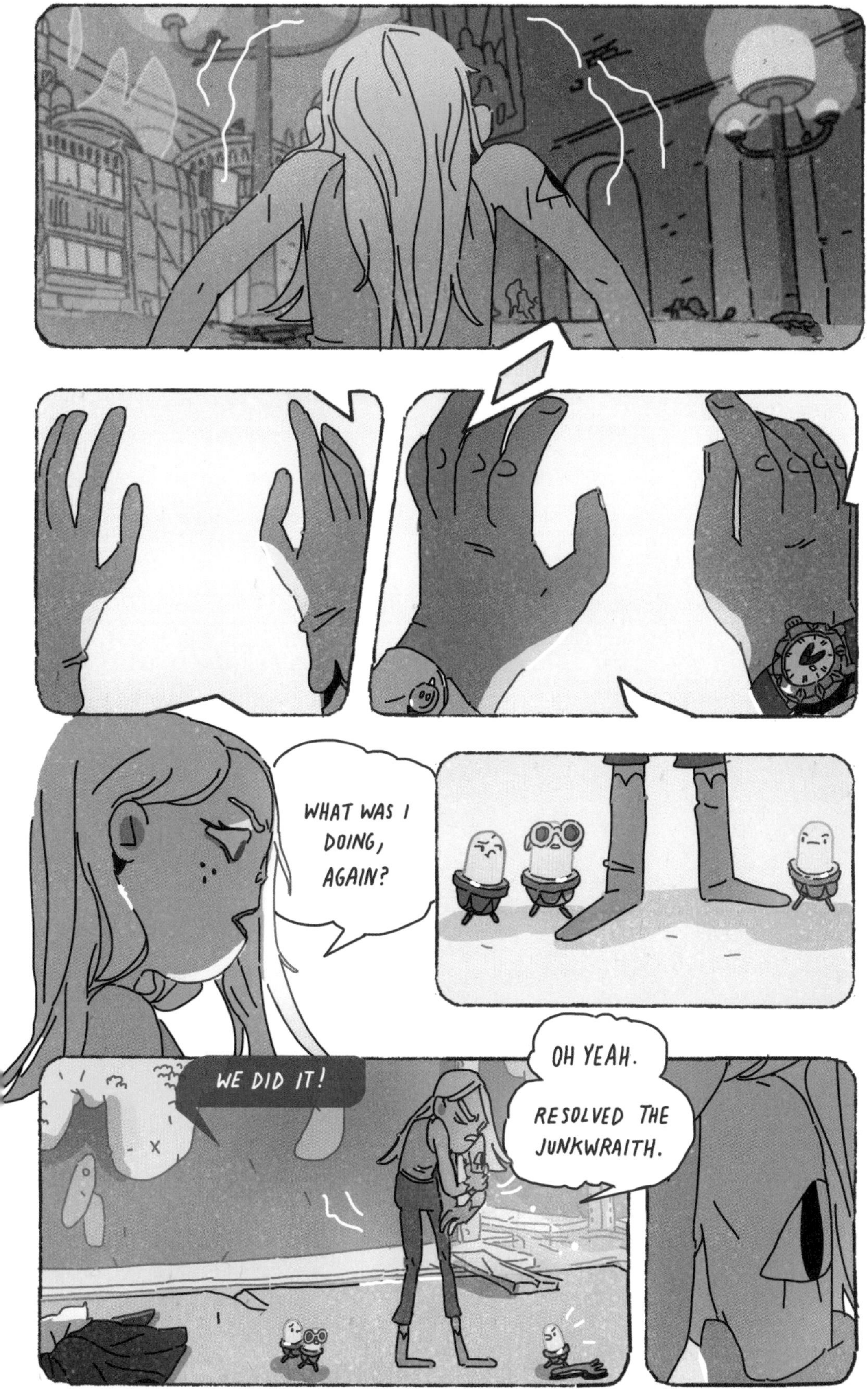
WHAT WAS I DOING, AGAIN?
WE DID IT!
OH YEAH.
RESOLVED THE JUNKWRAITH.

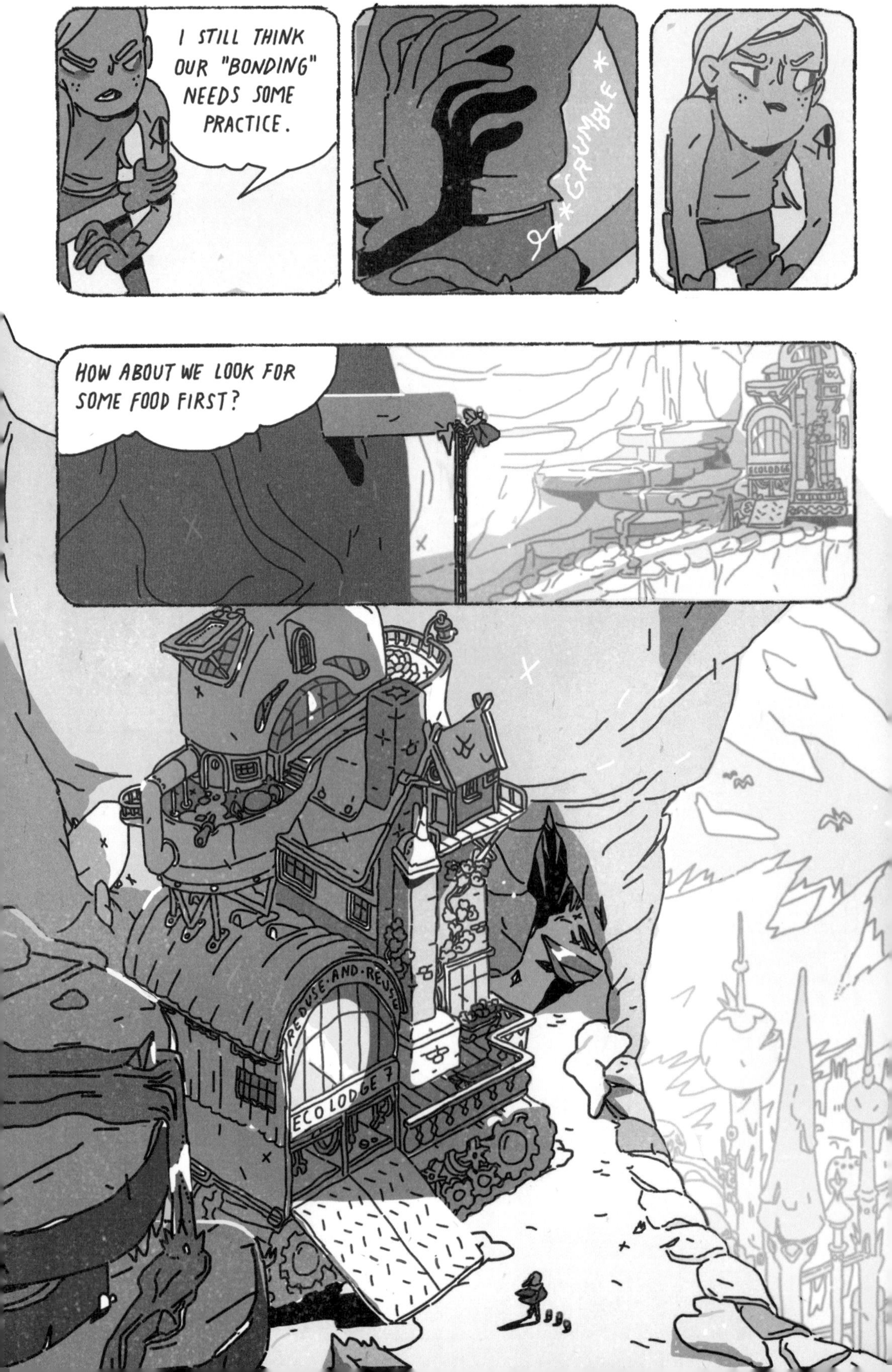
I STILL THINK OUR "BONDING" NEEDS SOME PRACTICE.
GRUMBLE
HOW ABOUT WE LOOK FOR SOME FOOD FIRST?
ECOLODGE
REDUSE·AND·REUSE
ECOLODGE 7

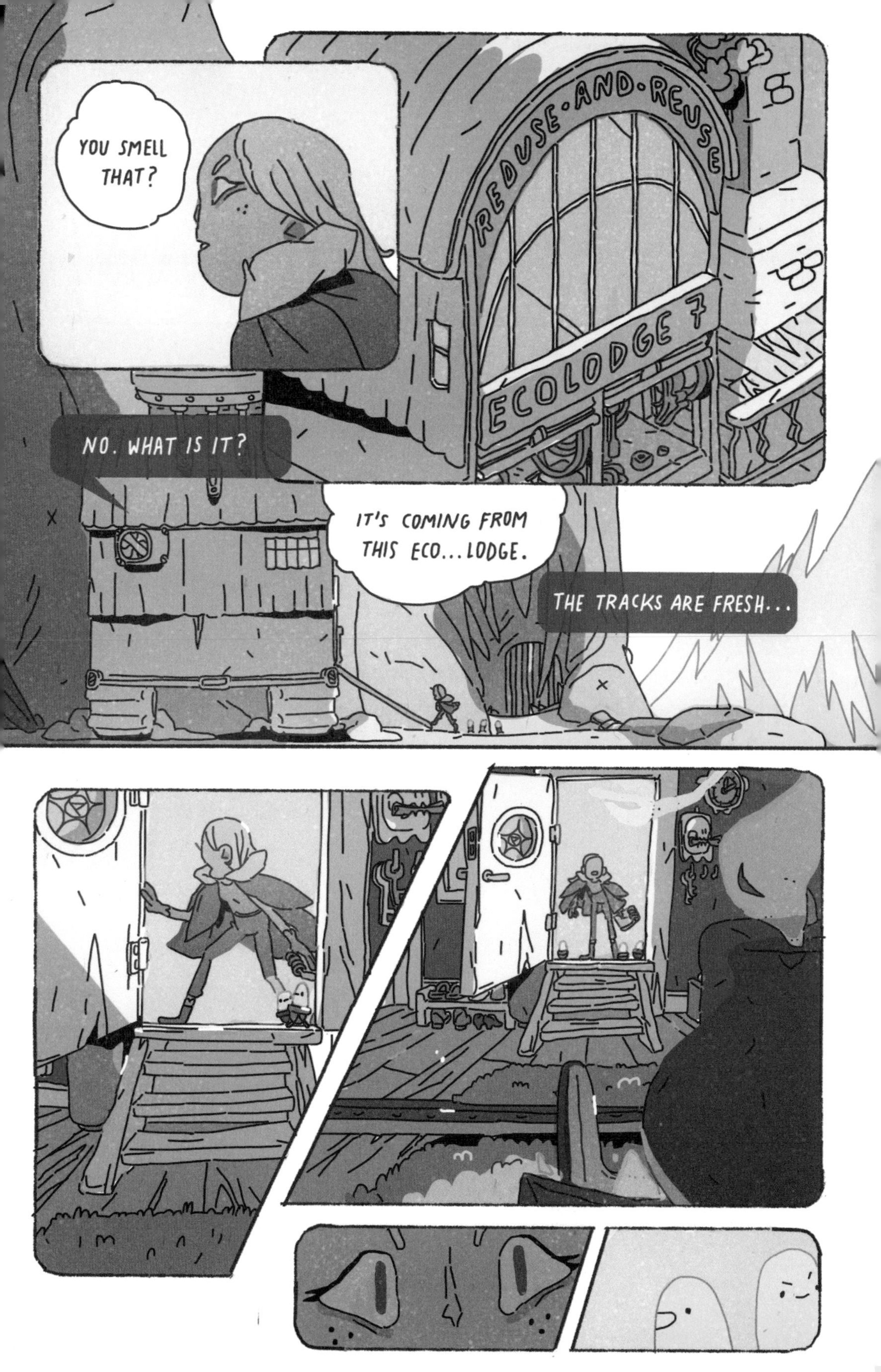
YOU SMELL THAT?
REDUSE·AND·REUSE
ECOLODGE 7
NO. WHAT IS IT?
IT'S COMING FROM THIS ECO...LODGE.
THE TRACKS ARE FRESH...

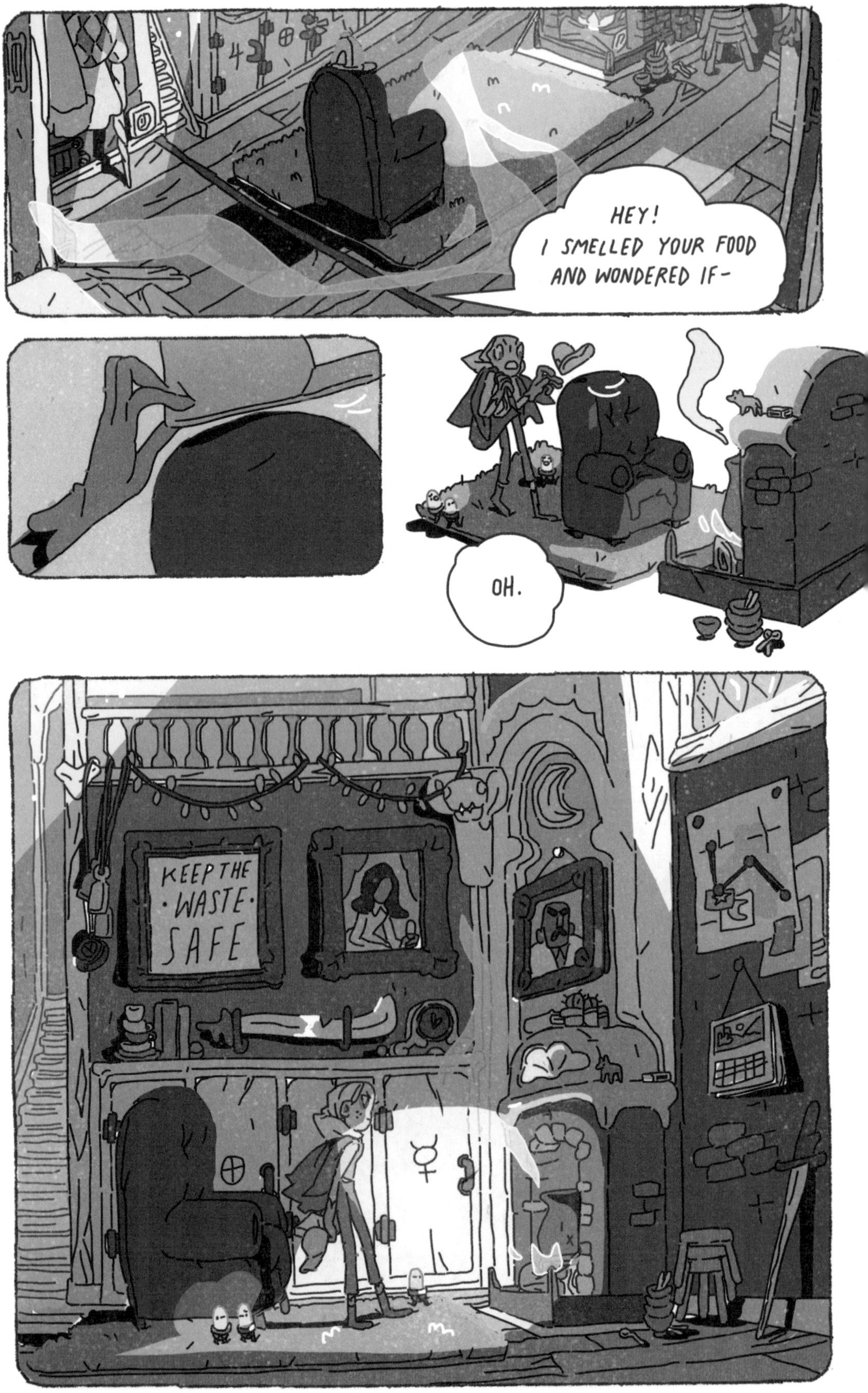
HEY!
I SMELLED YOUR FOOD
AND WONDERED IF-
OH.
KEEP THE
·WASTE·
SAFE

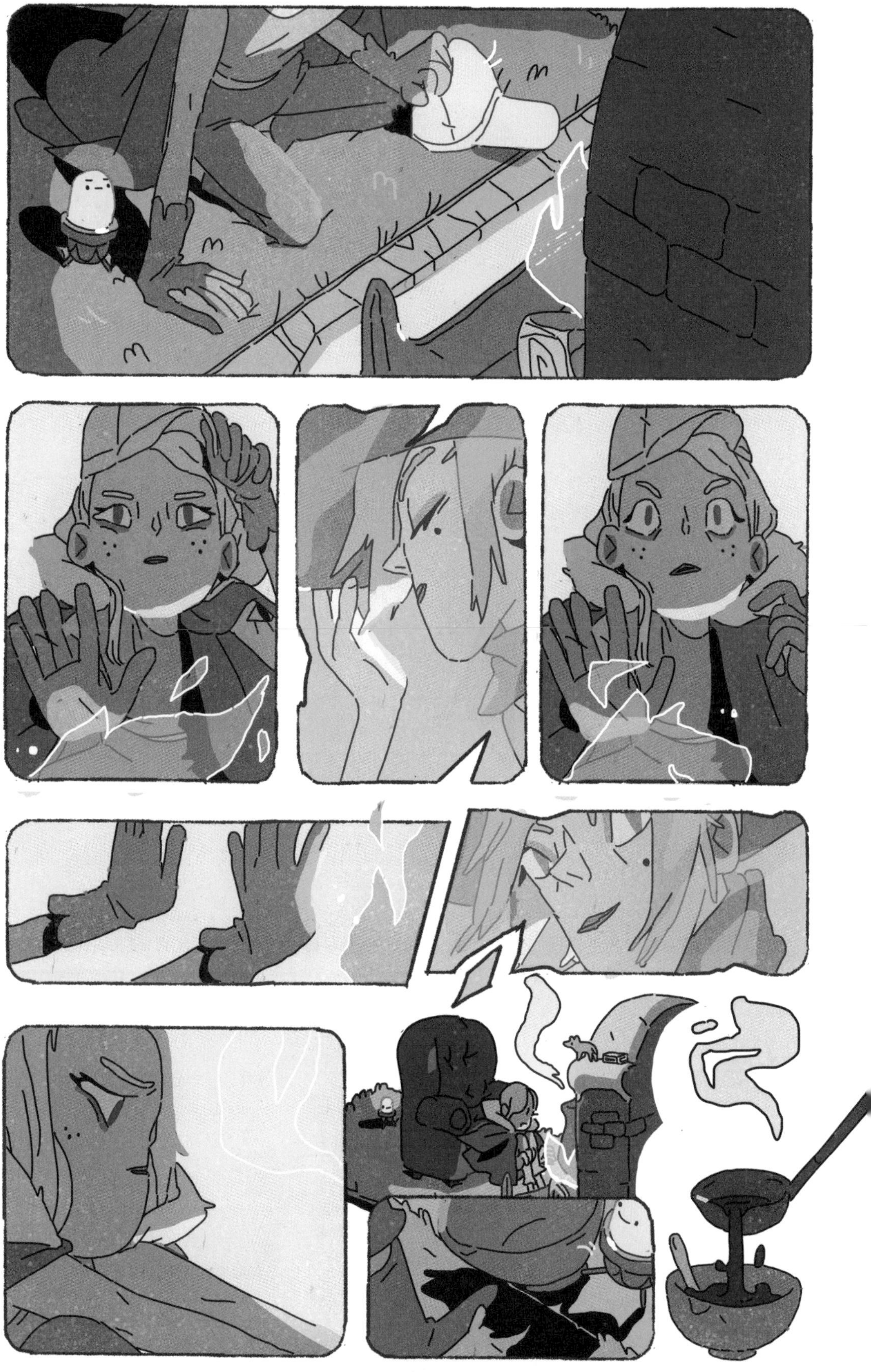

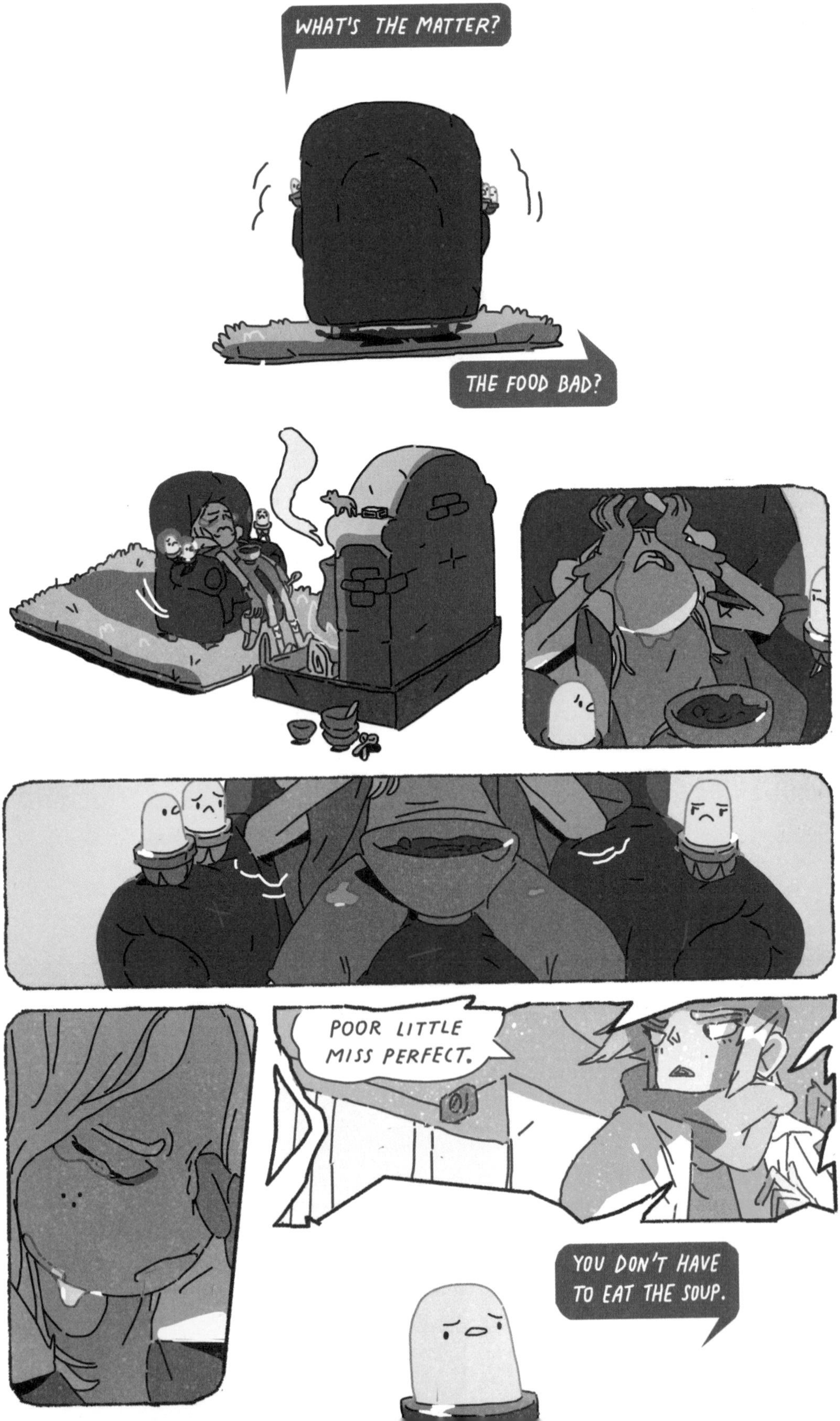
WHAT'S THE MATTER?
THE FOOD BAD?
POOR LITTLE MISS PERFECT.
YOU DON'T HAVE TO EAT THE SOUP.

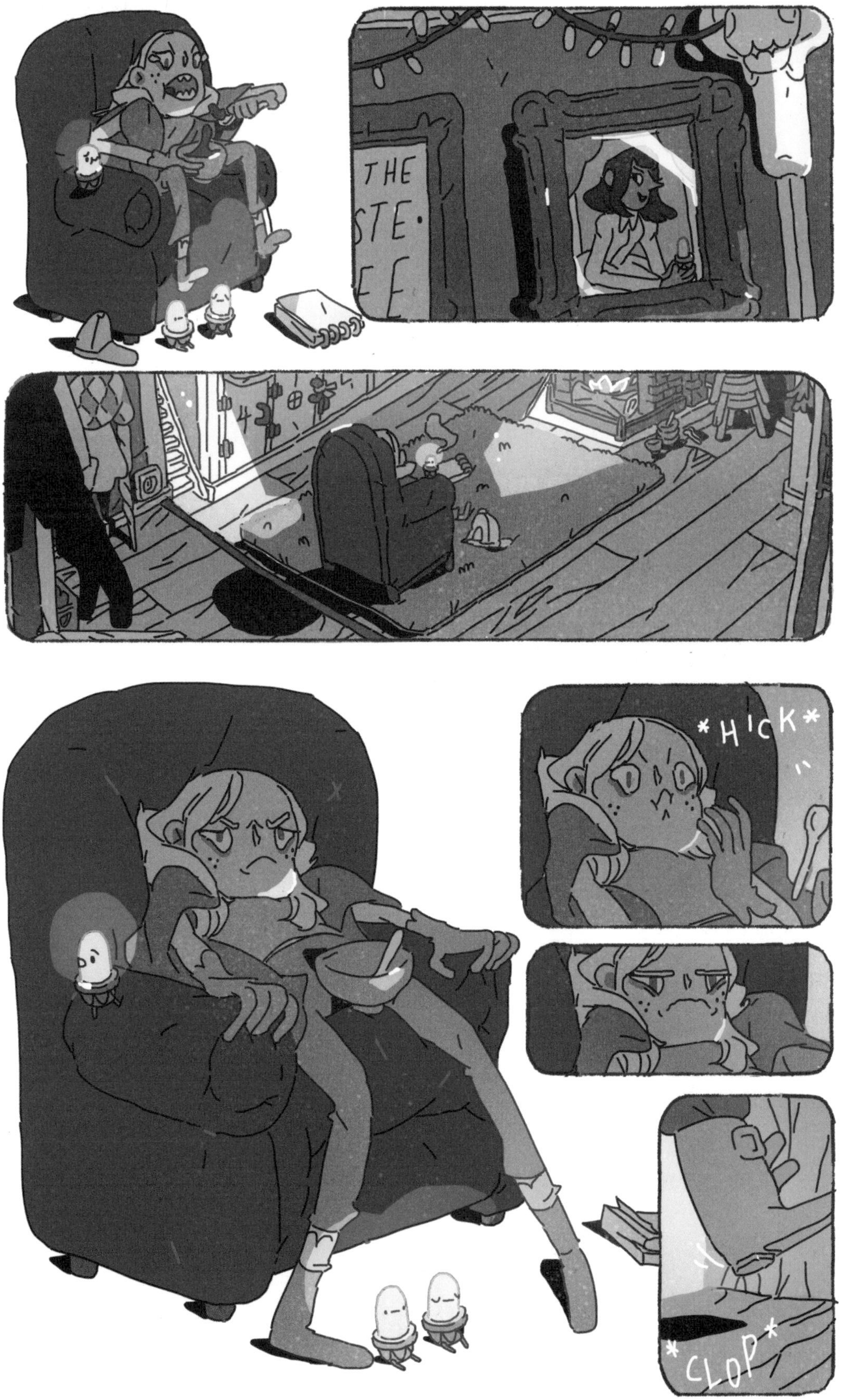
THE
STE·
HICK
CLOP

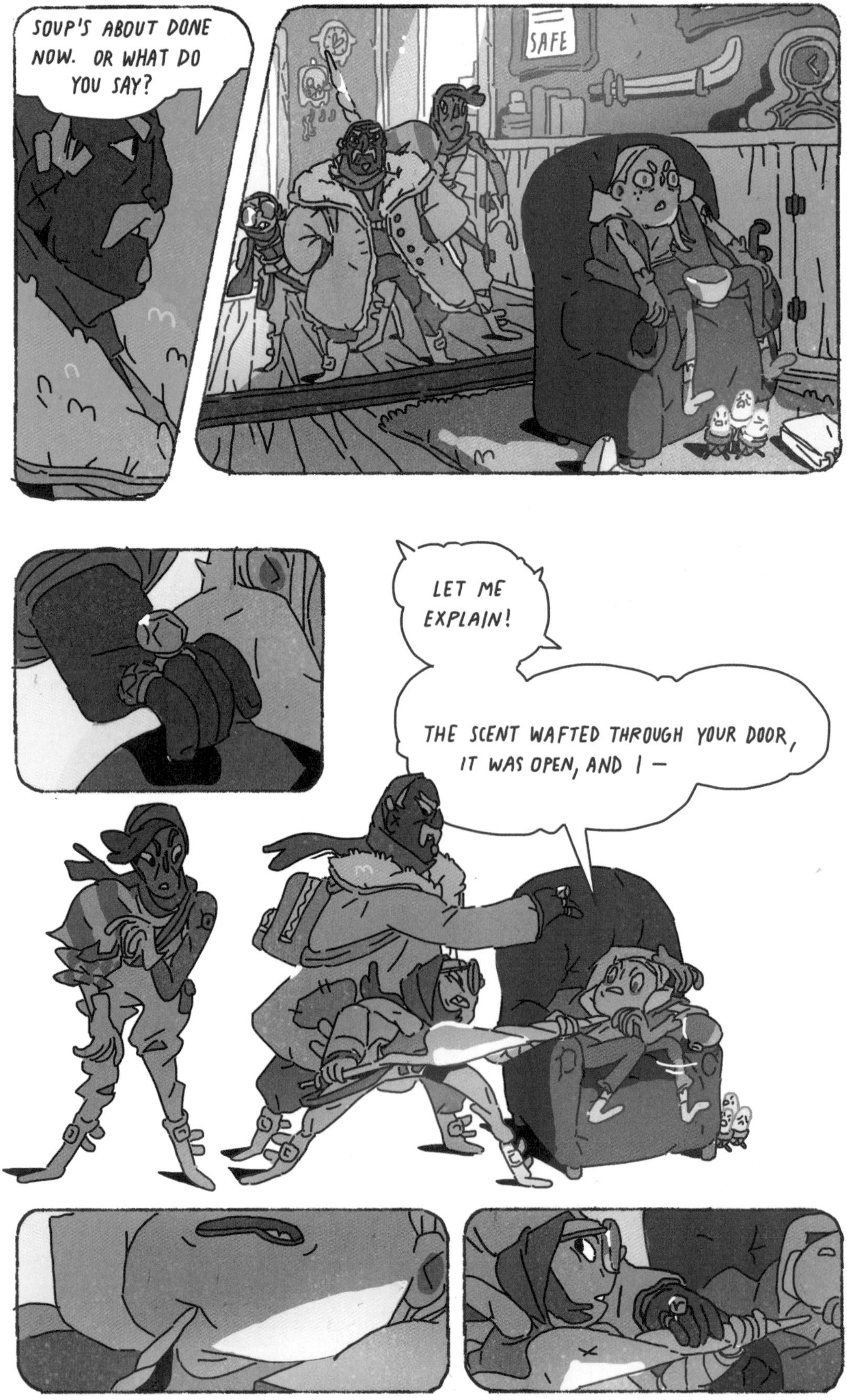
SOUP'S ABOUT DONE NOW. OR WHAT DO YOU SAY?
SAFE
LET ME EXPLAIN!
THE SCENT WAFTED THROUGH YOUR DOOR, IT WAS OPEN, AND I —

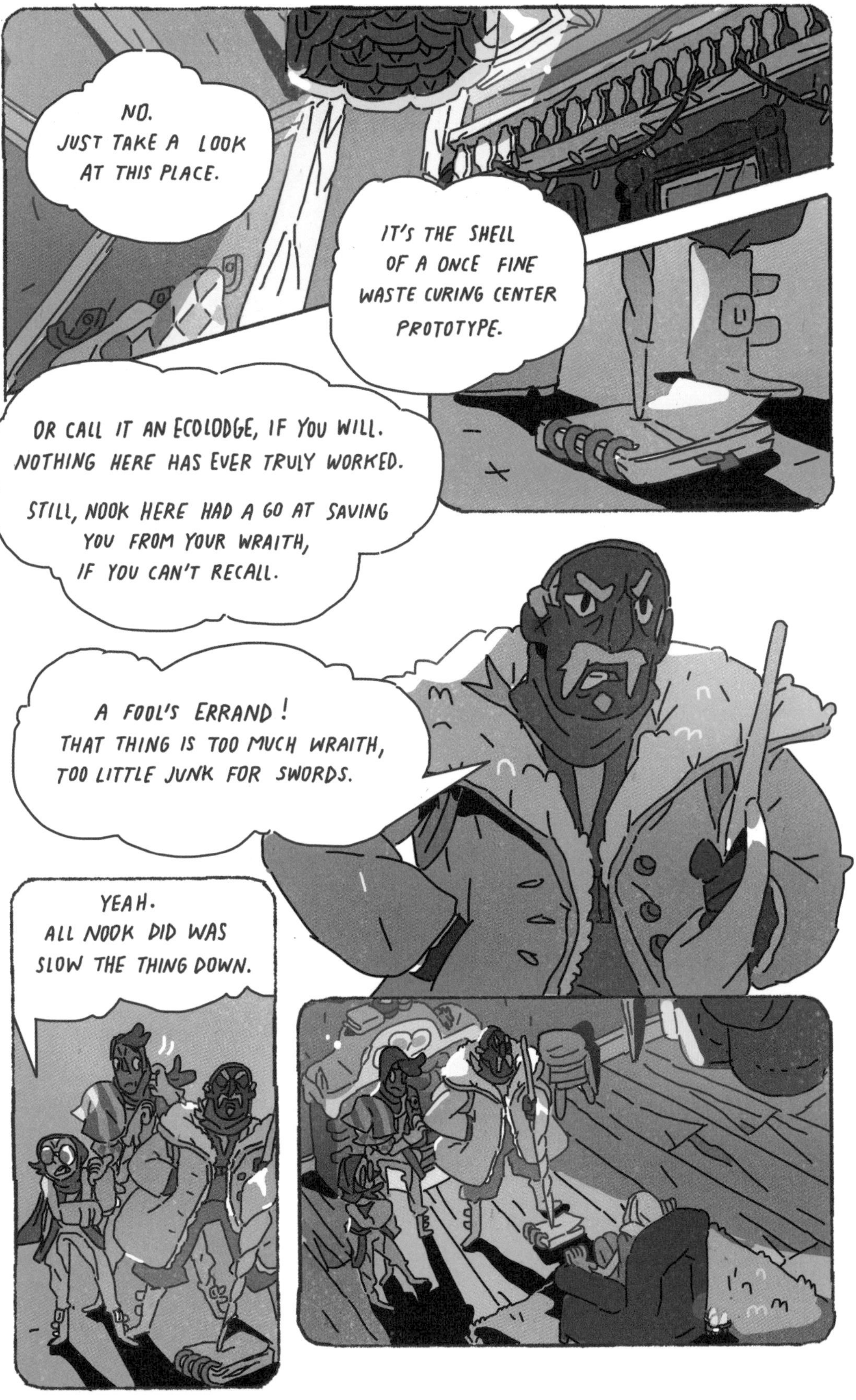
NO.
JUST TAKE A LOOK AT THIS PLACE.
IT'S THE SHELL OF A ONCE FINE WASTE CURING CENTER PROTOTYPE.
OR CALL IT AN ECOLODGE, IF YOU WILL. NOTHING HERE HAS EVER TRULY WORKED.
STILL, NOOK HERE HAD A GO AT SAVING YOU FROM YOUR WRAITH, IF YOU CAN'T RECALL.
A FOOL'S ERRAND! THAT THING IS TOO MUCH WRAITH, TOO LITTLE JUNK FOR SWORDS.
YEAH. ALL NOOK DID WAS SLOW THE THING DOWN.

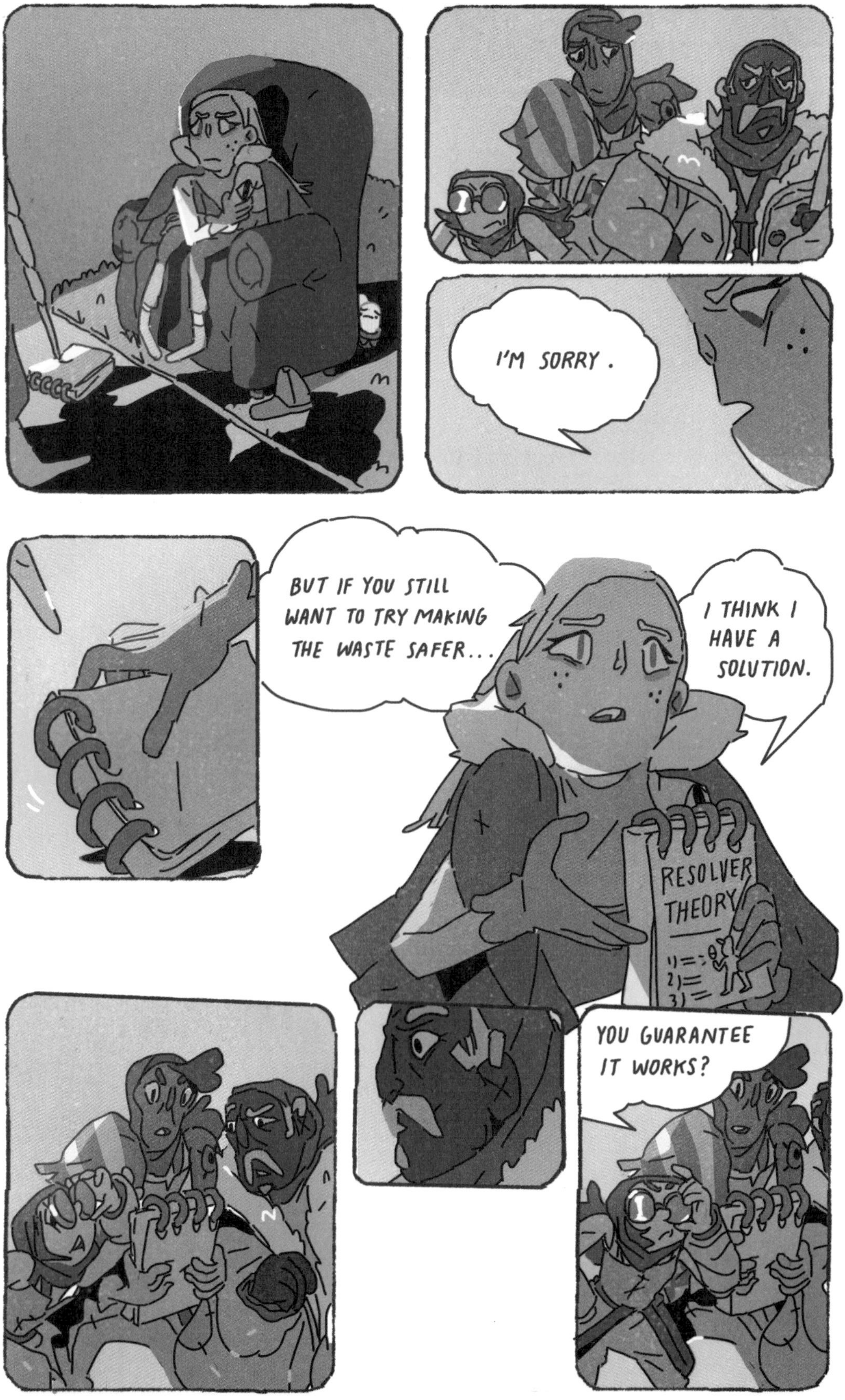
I'M SORRY.
BUT IF YOU STILL WANT TO TRY MAKING THE WASTE SAFER...
I THINK I HAVE A SOLUTION.
RESOLVER THEORY
YOU GUARANTEE IT WORKS?

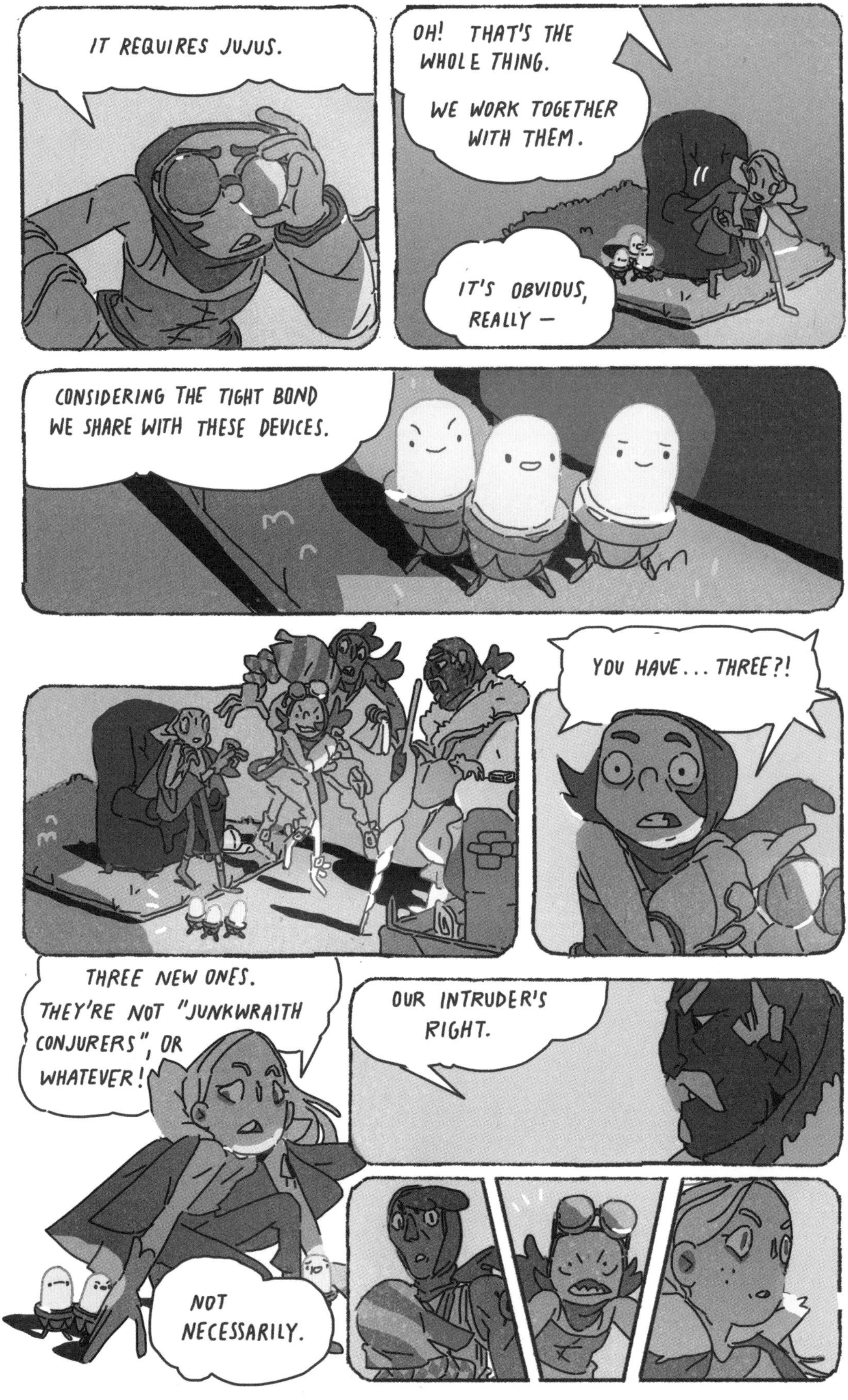
IT REQUIRES JUJUS.
OH! THAT'S THE WHOLE THING.
WE WORK TOGETHER WITH THEM.
IT'S OBVIOUS, REALLY —
CONSIDERING THE TIGHT BOND WE SHARE WITH THESE DEVICES.
YOU HAVE... THREE?!
THREE NEW ONES. THEY'RE NOT "JUNKWRAITH CONJURERS", OR WHATEVER!
OUR INTRUDER'S RIGHT.
NOT NECESSARILY.

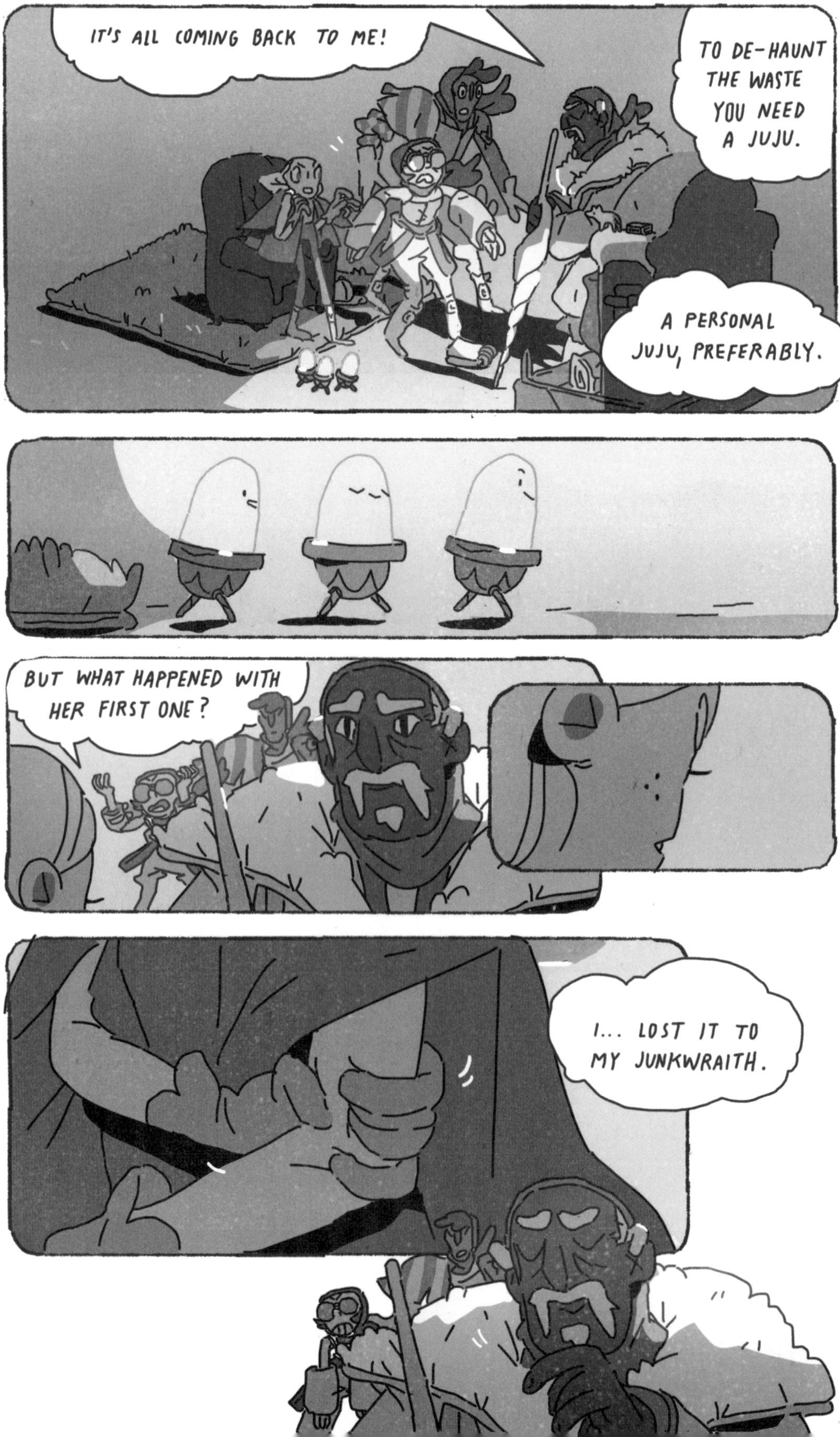
IT'S ALL COMING BACK TO ME!
TO DE-HAUNT THE WASTE YOU NEED A JUJU.
A PERSONAL JUJU, PREFERABLY.
BUT WHAT HAPPENED WITH HER FIRST ONE?
I... LOST IT TO MY JUNKWRAITH.

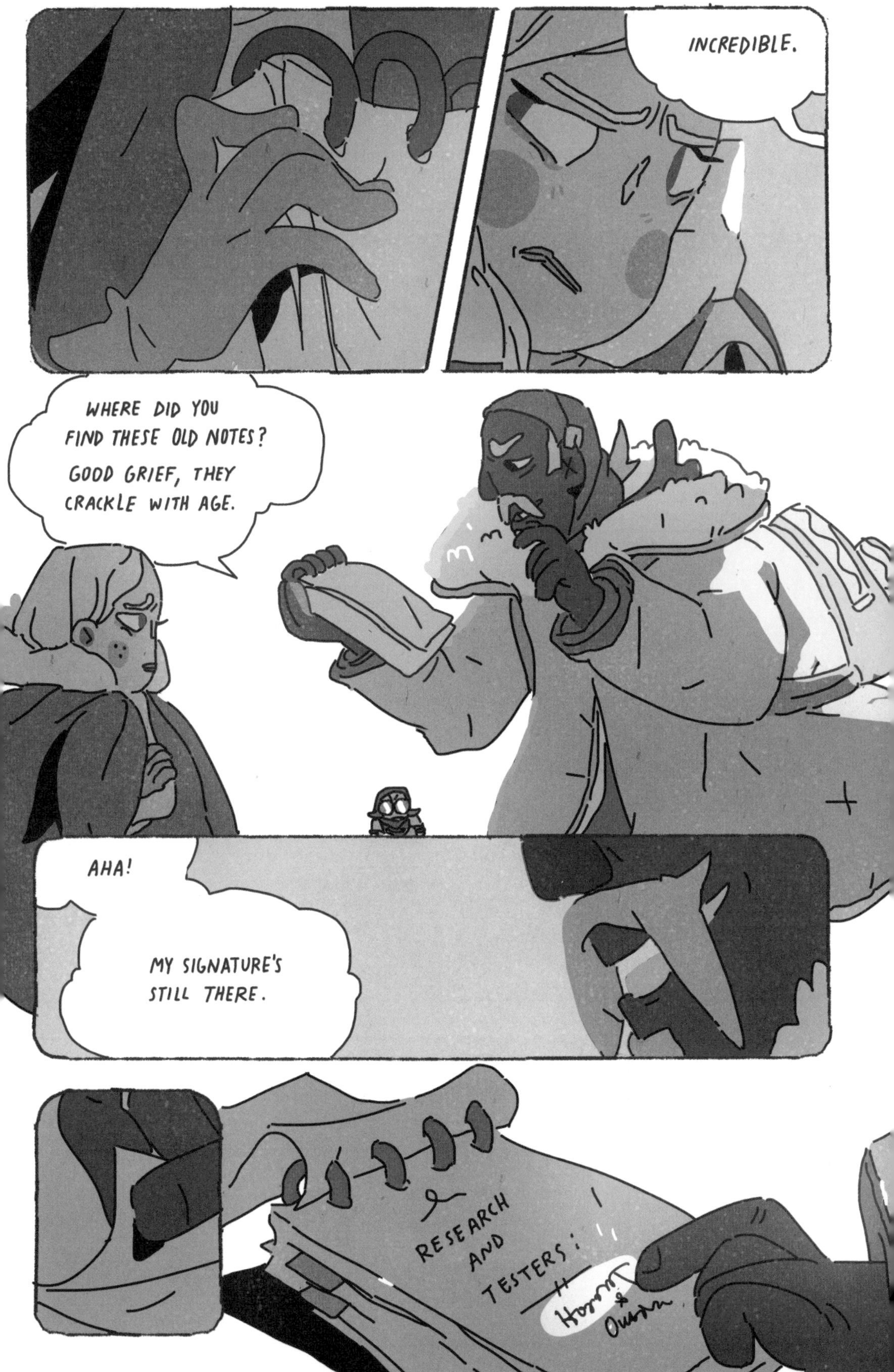
INCREDIBLE.
WHERE DID YOU FIND THESE OLD NOTES? GOOD GRIEF, THEY CRACKLE WITH AGE.
AHA!
MY SIGNATURE'S STILL THERE.
RESEARCH AND TESTERS:

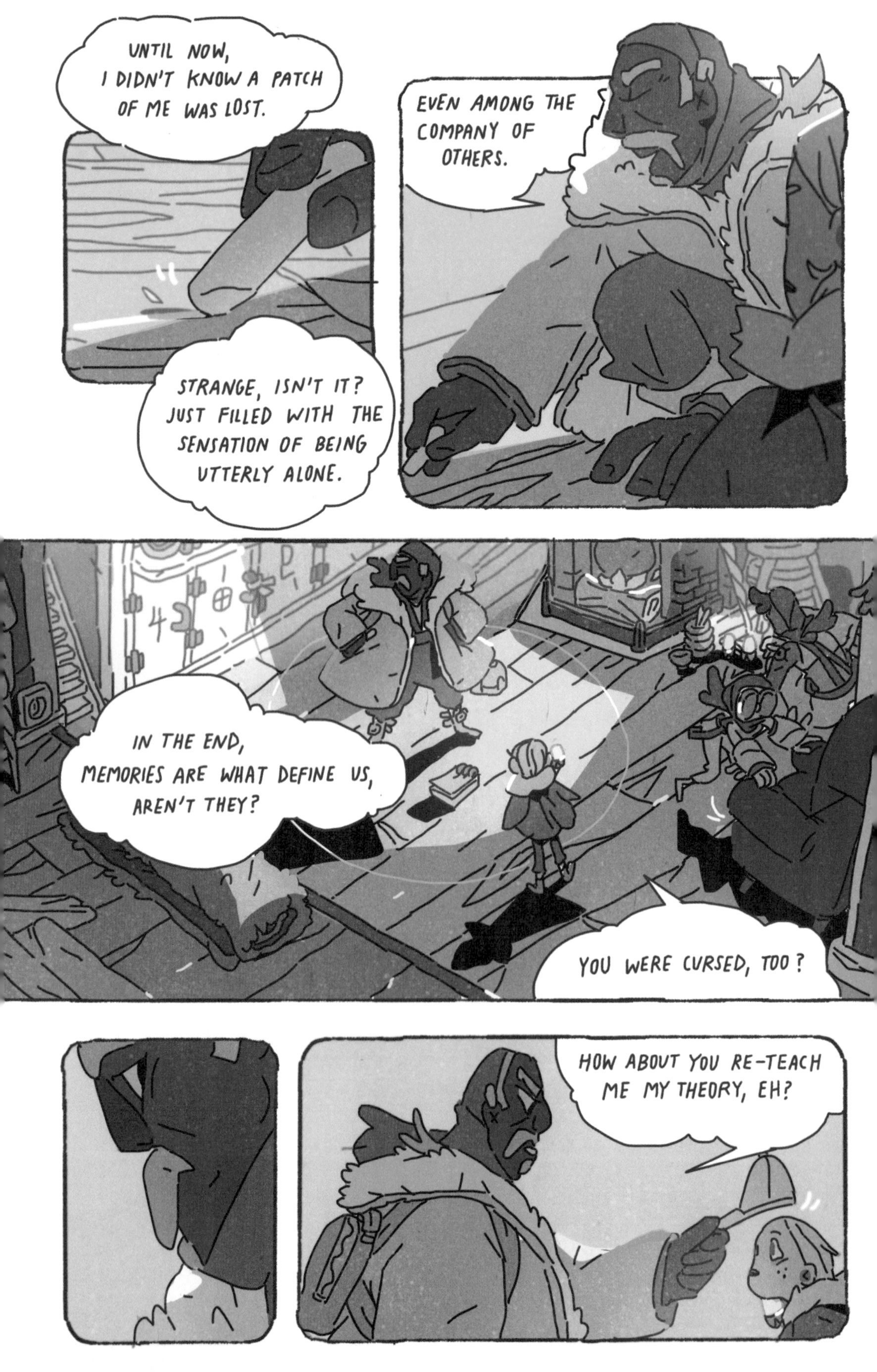
UNTIL NOW, I DIDN'T KNOW A PATCH OF ME WAS LOST.
EVEN AMONG THE COMPANY OF OTHERS.
STRANGE, ISN'T IT? JUST FILLED WITH THE SENSATION OF BEING UTTERLY ALONE.
IN THE END, MEMORIES ARE WHAT DEFINE US, AREN'T THEY?
YOU WERE CURSED, TOO?
HOW ABOUT YOU RE-TEACH ME MY THEORY, EH?

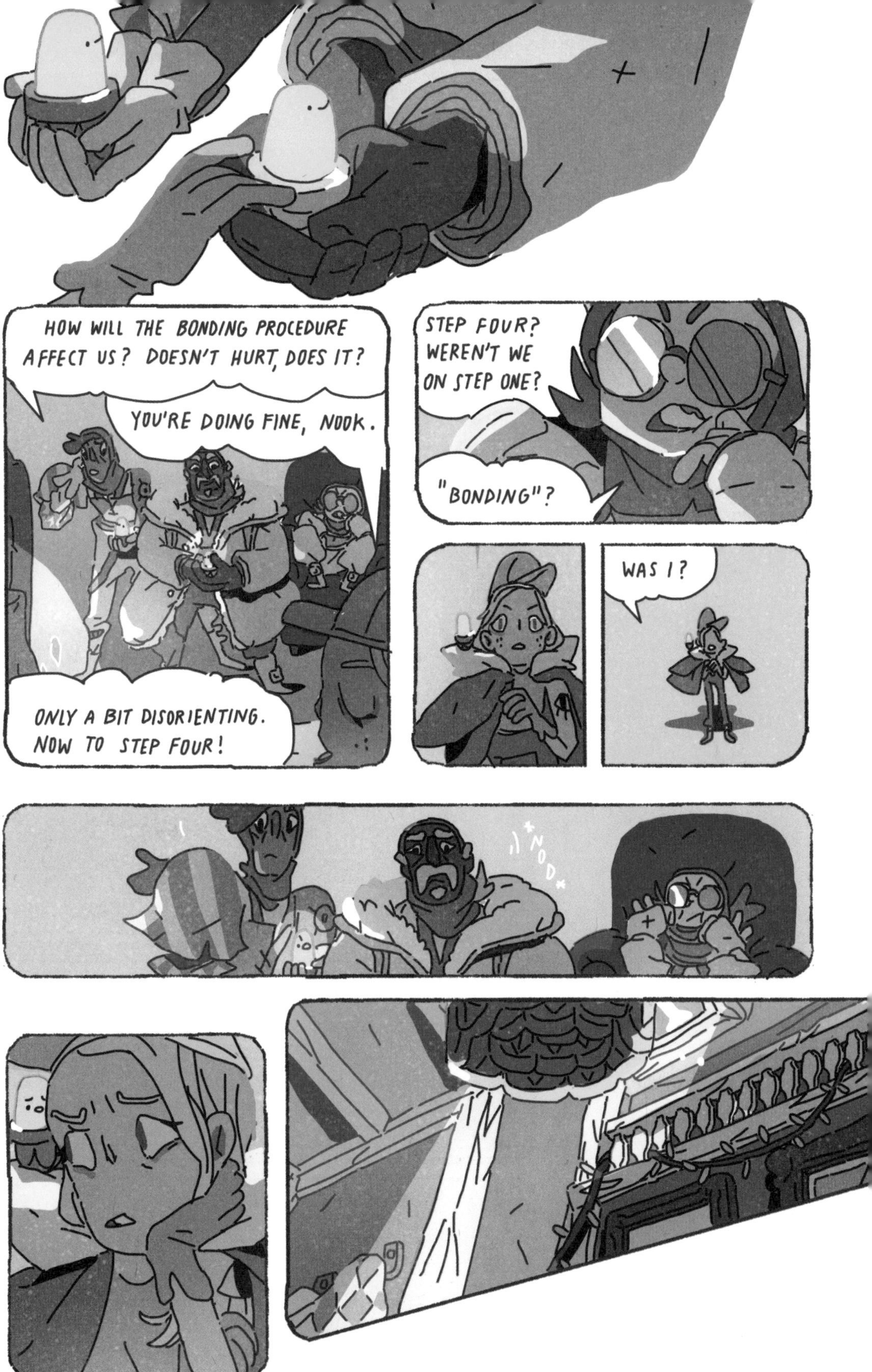
HOW WILL THE BONDING PROCEDURE AFFECT US? DOESN'T HURT, DOES IT?
YOU'RE DOING FINE, NOOK.
ONLY A BIT DISORIENTING. NOW TO STEP FOUR!
STEP FOUR? WEREN'T WE ON STEP ONE?
"BONDING"?
WAS I?
NOD

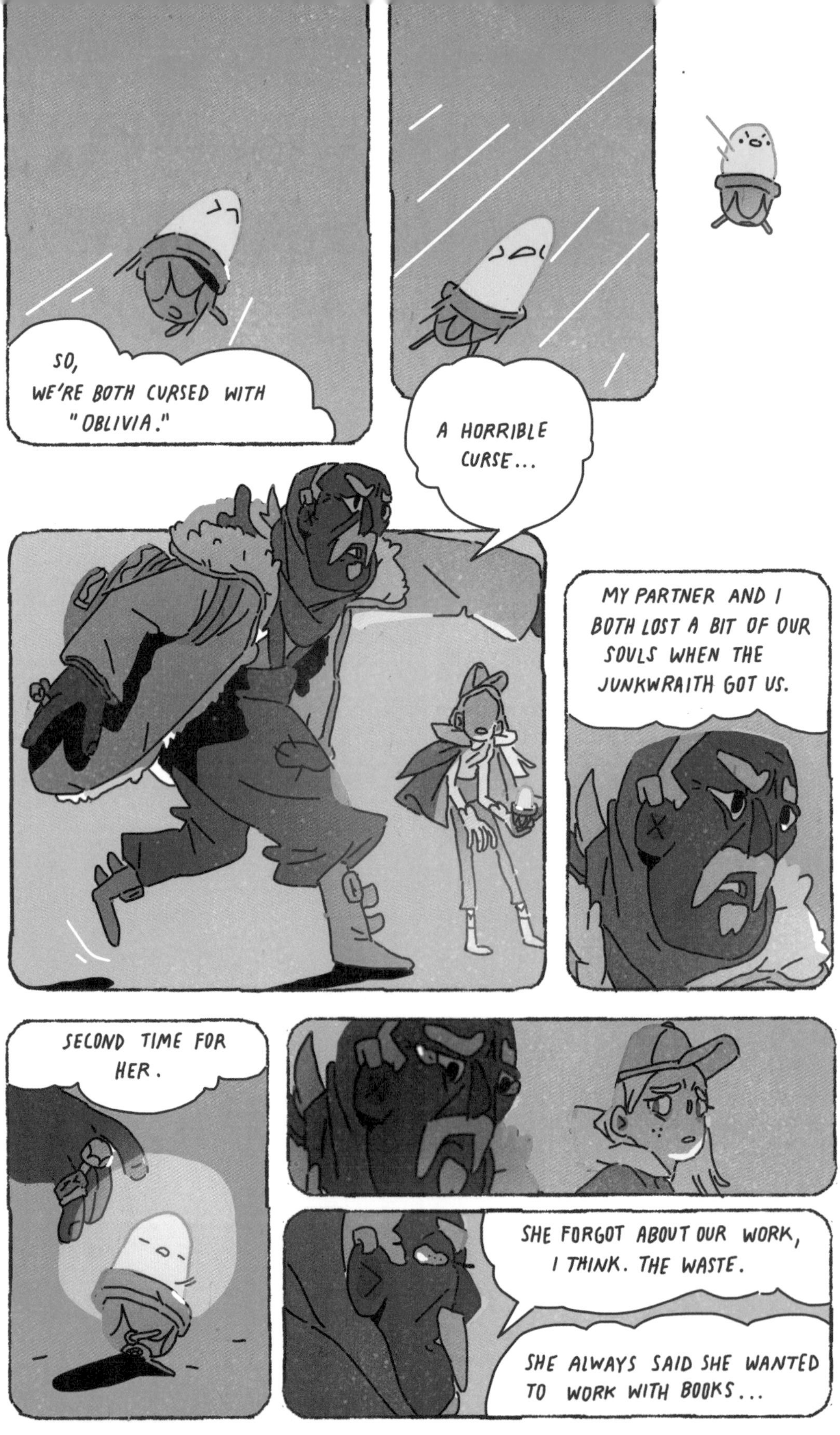
SO,
WE'RE BOTH CURSED WITH
"OBLIVIA."
A HORRIBLE
CURSE...
MY PARTNER AND I
BOTH LOST A BIT OF OUR
SOULS WHEN THE
JUNKWRAITH GOT US.
SECOND TIME FOR
HER.
SHE FORGOT ABOUT OUR WORK,
I THINK. THE WASTE.
SHE ALWAYS SAID SHE WANTED
TO WORK WITH BOOKS...

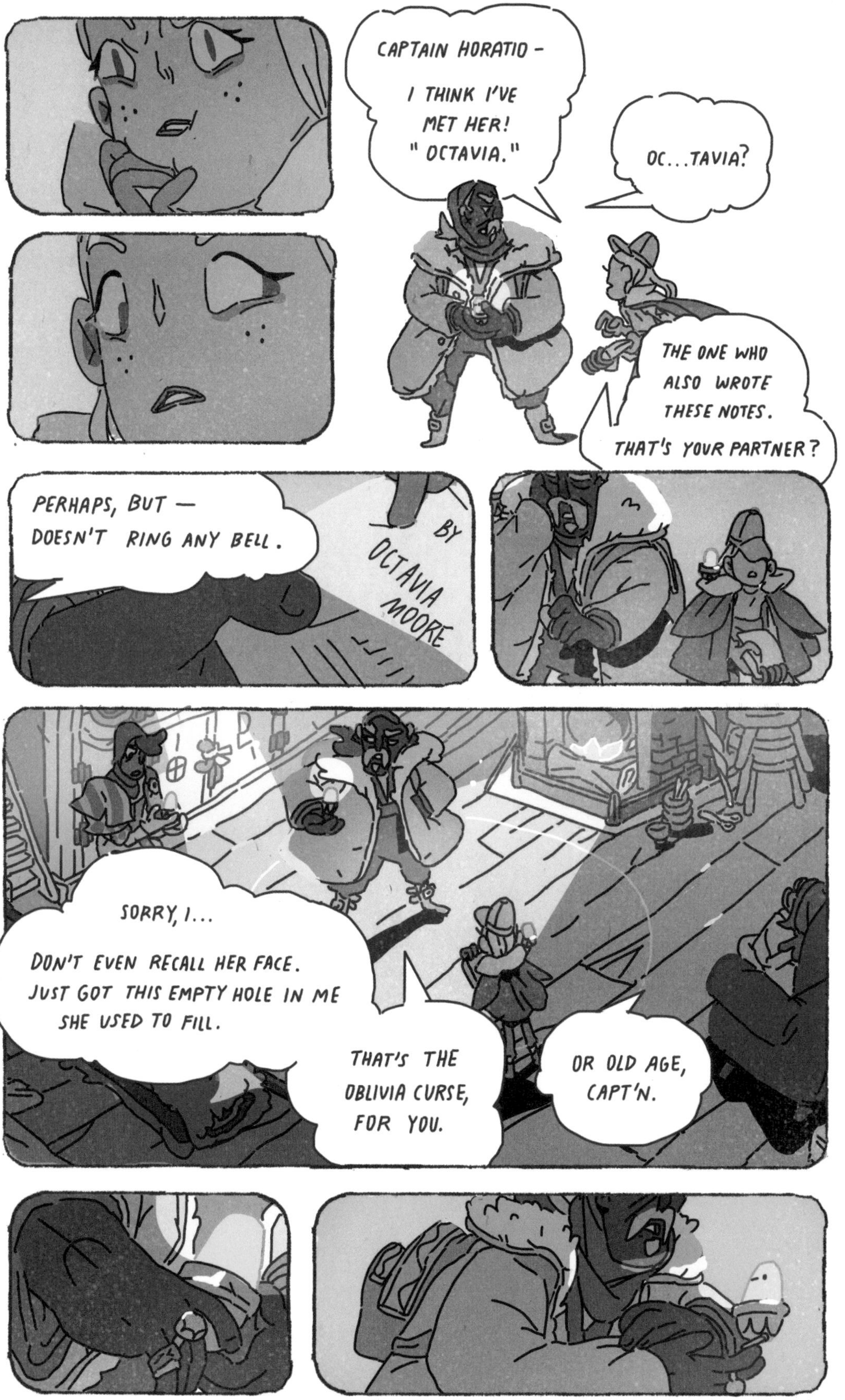
CAPTAIN HORATIO -
I THINK I'VE MET HER! " OCTAVIA."
OC...TAVIA?
THE ONE WHO ALSO WROTE THESE NOTES.
THAT'S YOUR PARTNER?
PERHAPS, BUT — DOESN'T RING ANY BELL.
BY OCTAVIA MOORE
SORRY, I...
DON'T EVEN RECALL HER FACE. JUST GOT THIS EMPTY HOLE IN ME SHE USED TO FILL.
THAT'S THE OBLIVIA CURSE, FOR YOU.
OR OLD AGE, CAPT'N.

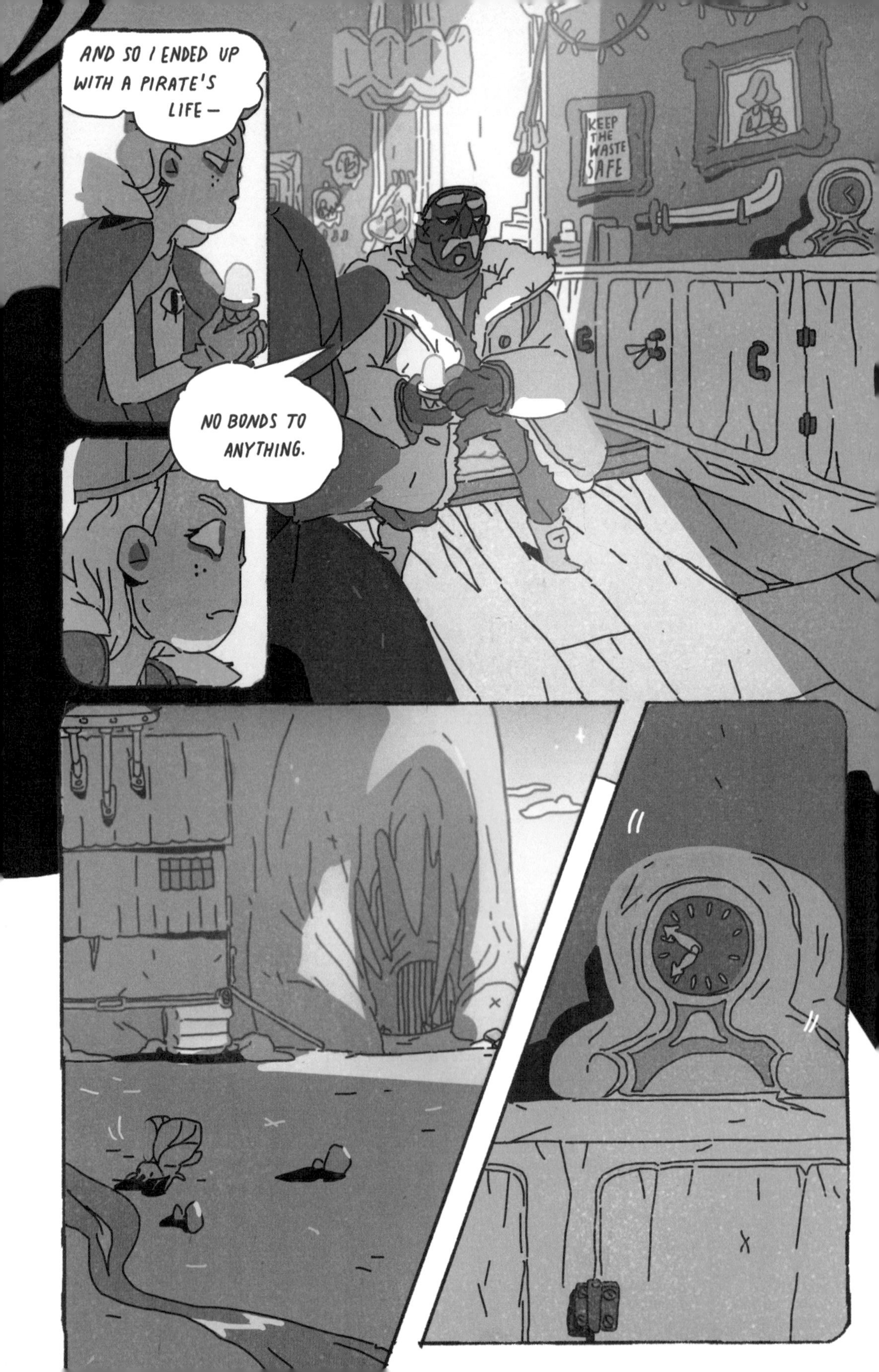
AND SO I ENDED UP WITH A PIRATE'S LIFE—
KEEP THE WASTE SAFE
NO BONDS TO ANYTHING.

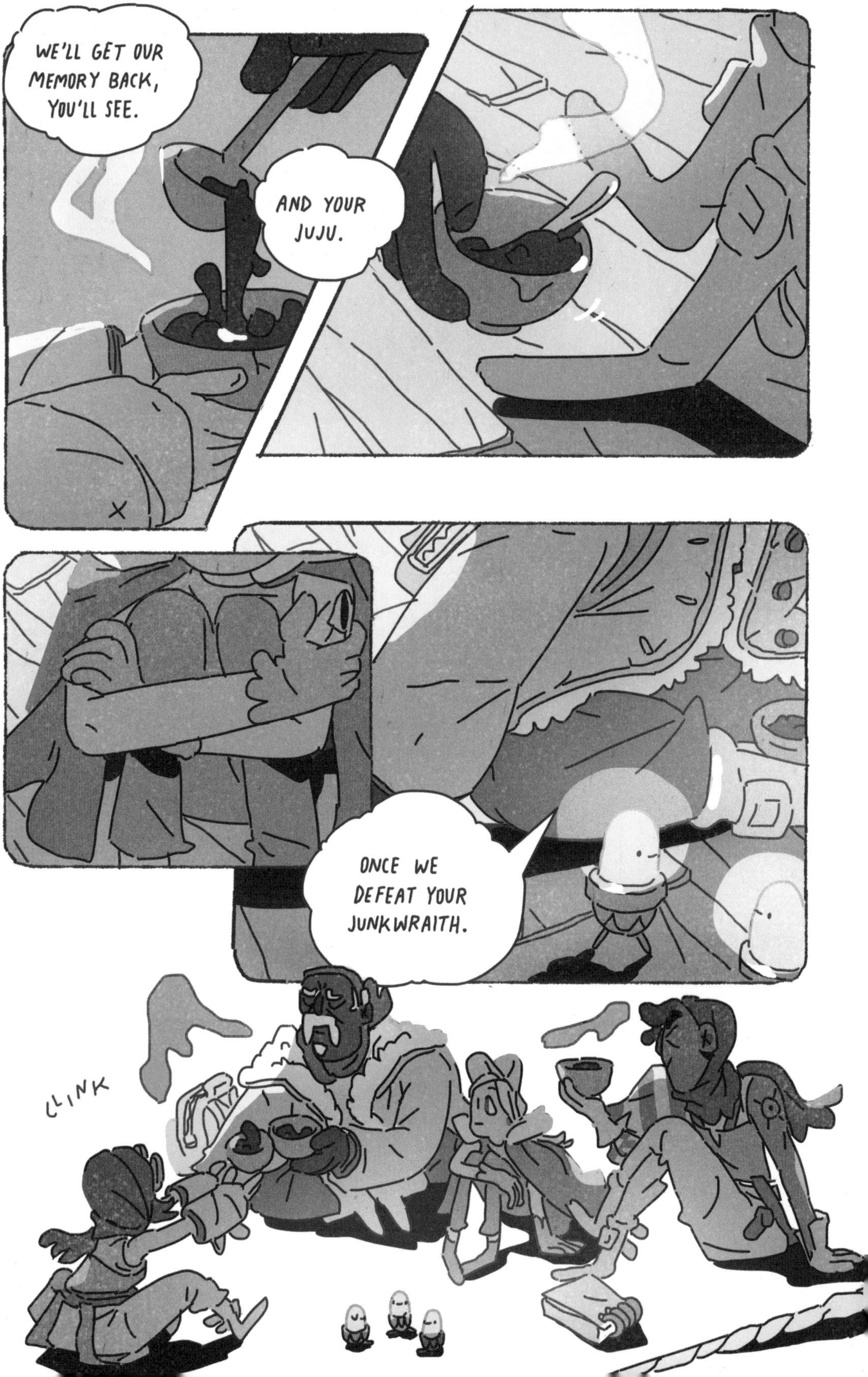
WE'LL GET OUR MEMORY BACK, YOU'LL SEE.
AND YOUR JUJU.
ONCE WE DEFEAT YOUR JUNKWRAITH.
CLINK

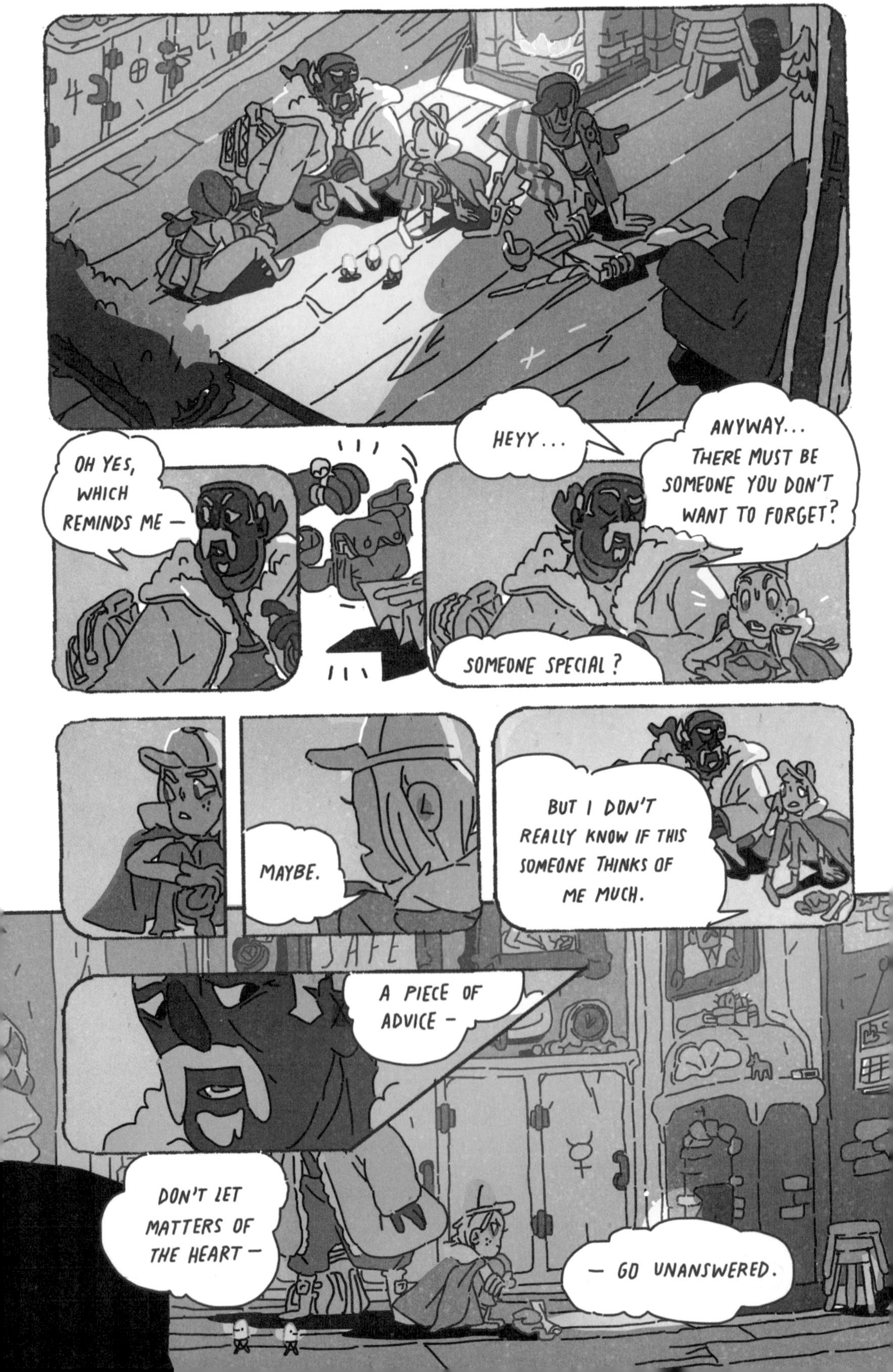
OH YES, WHICH REMINDS ME —
HEYY...
ANYWAY... THERE MUST BE SOMEONE YOU DON'T WANT TO FORGET?
SOMEONE SPECIAL?
MAYBE.
BUT I DON'T REALLY KNOW IF THIS SOMEONE THINKS OF ME MUCH.
SAFE
A PIECE OF ADVICE —
DON'T LET MATTERS OF THE HEART —
— GO UNANSWERED.

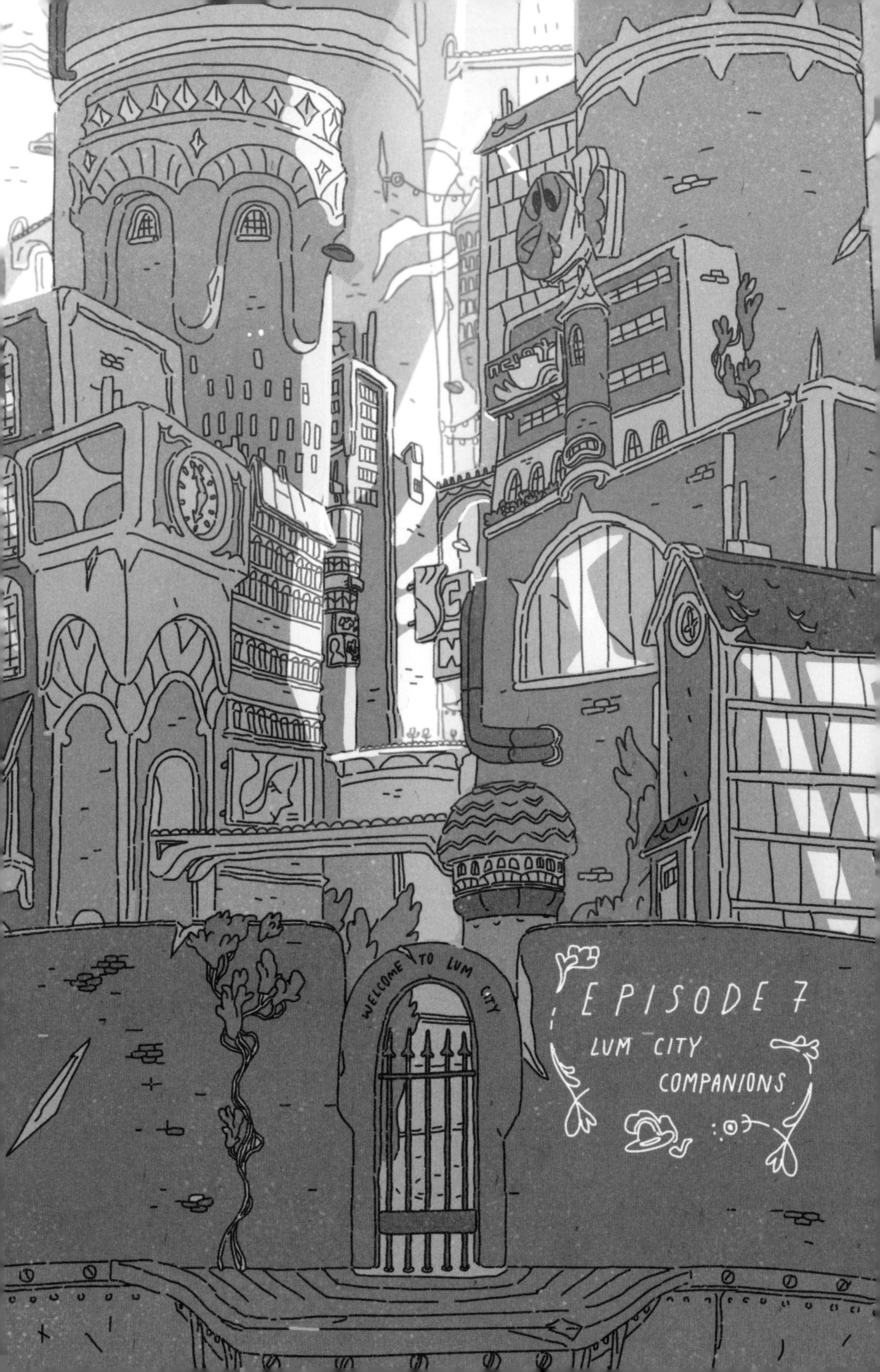
WELCOME TO LUM CITY
EPISODE 7
LUM CITY
COMPANIONS

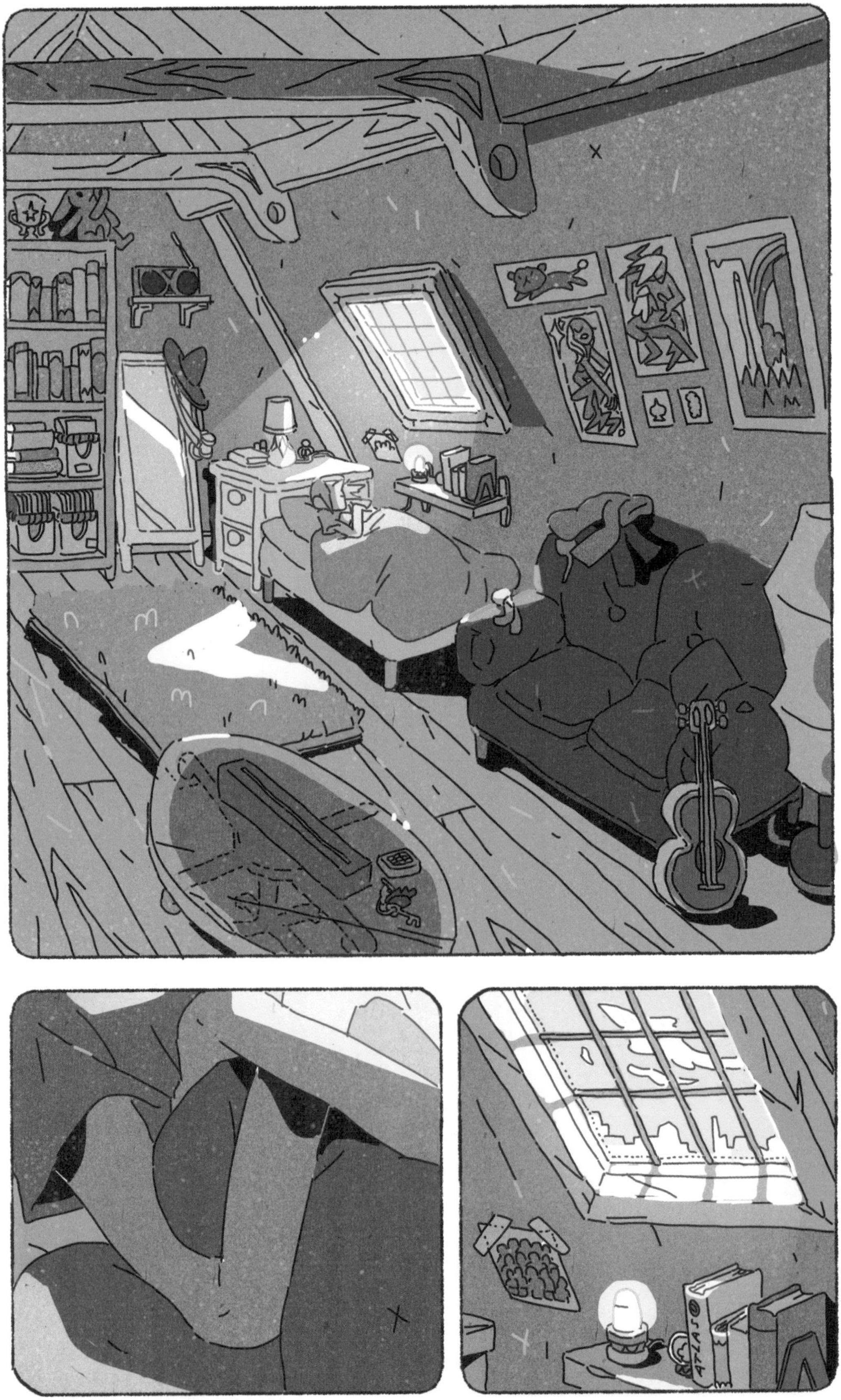
ATLAS

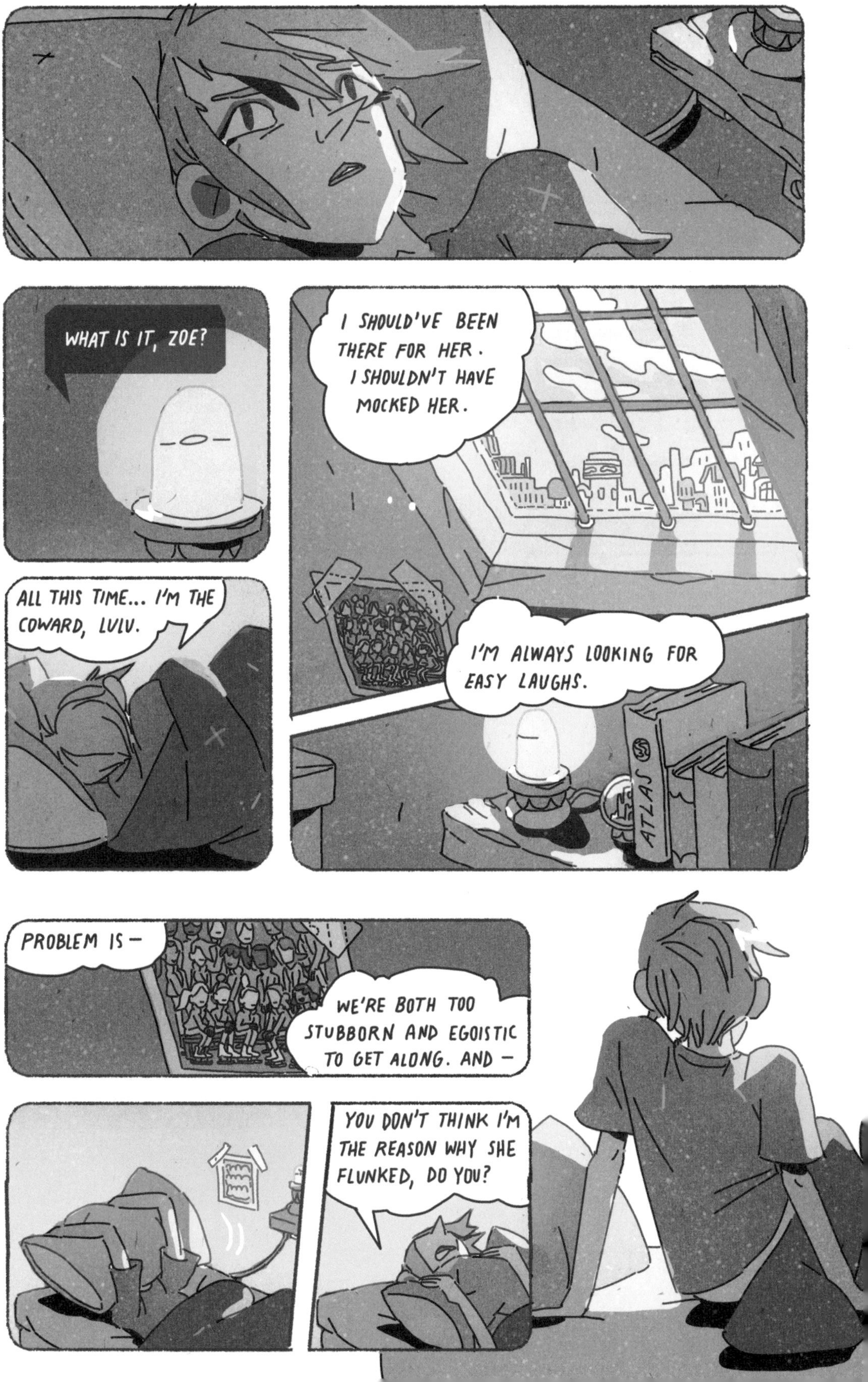
WHAT IS IT, ZOE?
I SHOULD'VE BEEN THERE FOR HER. I SHOULDN'T HAVE MOCKED HER.
ALL THIS TIME... I'M THE COWARD, LULU.
I'M ALWAYS LOOKING FOR EASY LAUGHS.
ATLAS
PROBLEM IS—
WE'RE BOTH TOO STUBBORN AND EGOISTIC TO GET ALONG. AND—
YOU DON'T THINK I'M THE REASON WHY SHE FLUNKED, DO YOU?

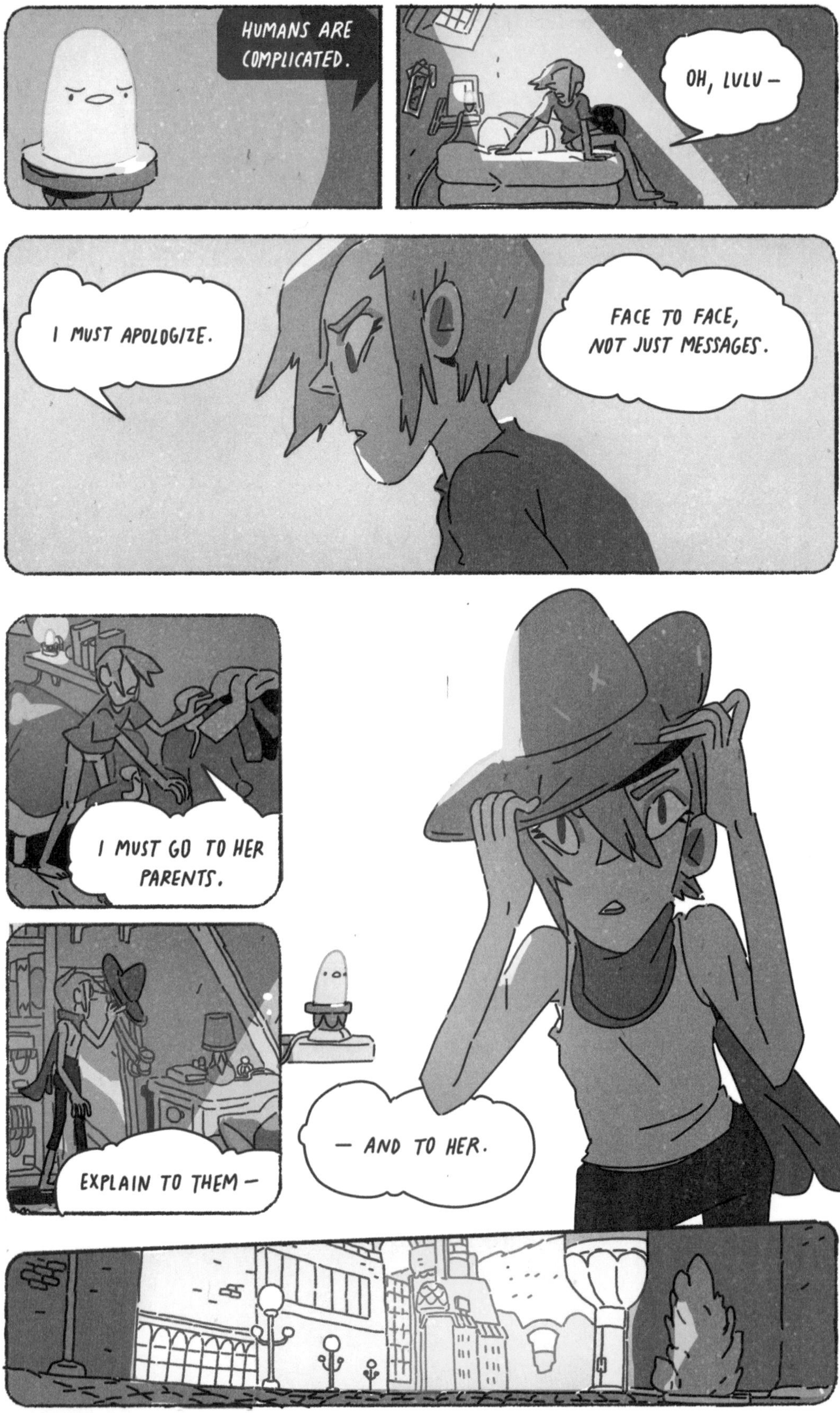
HUMANS ARE COMPLICATED.
OH, LULU—
I MUST APOLOGIZE.
FACE TO FACE, NOT JUST MESSAGES.
I MUST GO TO HER PARENTS.
EXPLAIN TO THEM—
—AND TO HER.

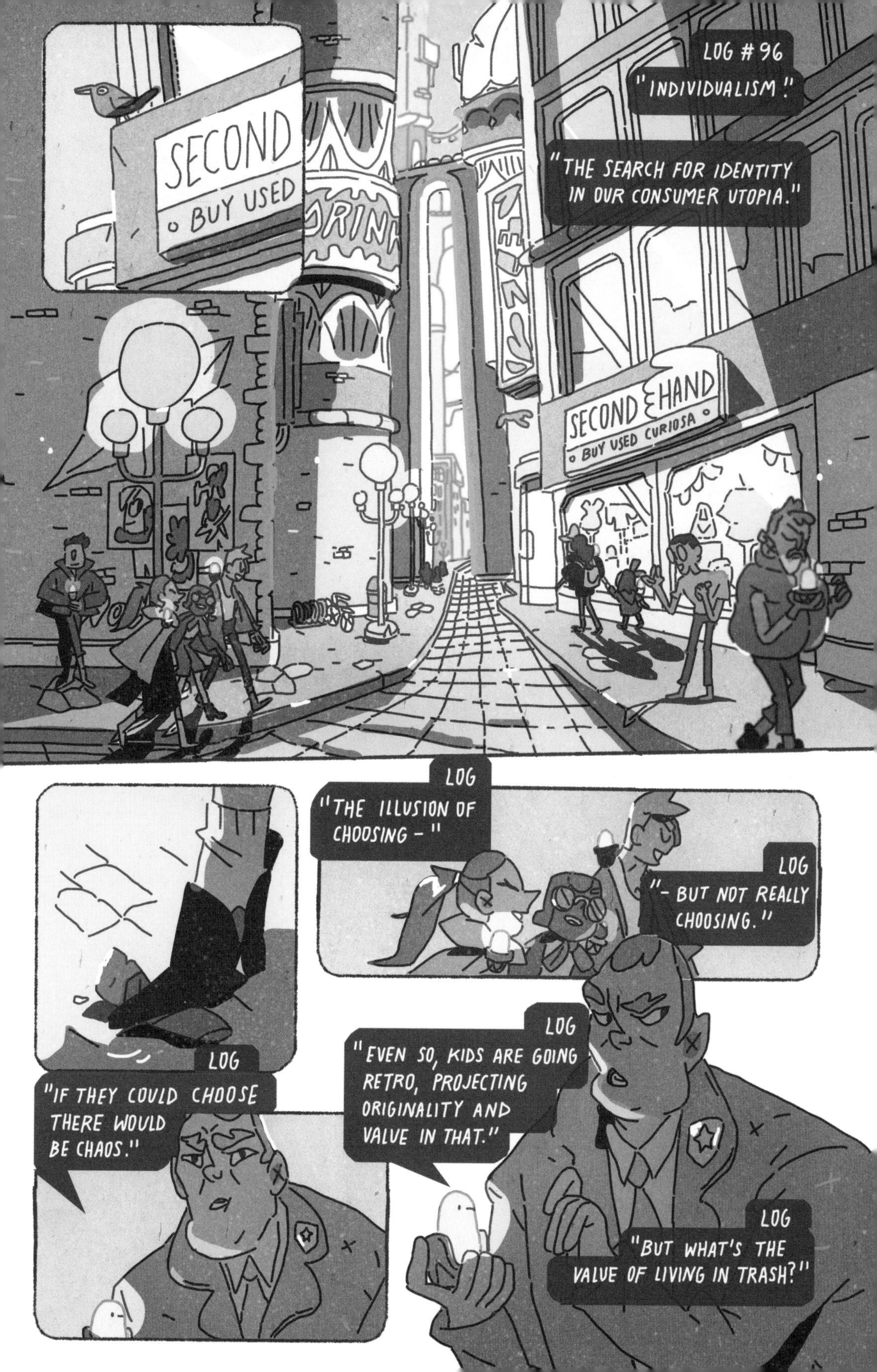
LOG #96
"INDIVIDUALISM."
"THE SEARCH FOR IDENTITY IN OUR CONSUMER UTOPIA."
SECOND
BUY USED
DRINK
SECOND HAND
BUY USED CURIOSA
LOG
"THE ILLUSION OF CHOOSING -"
LOG
"- BUT NOT REALLY CHOOSING."
LOG
"IF THEY COULD CHOOSE THERE WOULD BE CHAOS."
LOG
"EVEN SO, KIDS ARE GOING RETRO, PROJECTING ORIGINALITY AND VALUE IN THAT."
LOG
"BUT WHAT'S THE VALUE OF LIVING IN TRASH?"

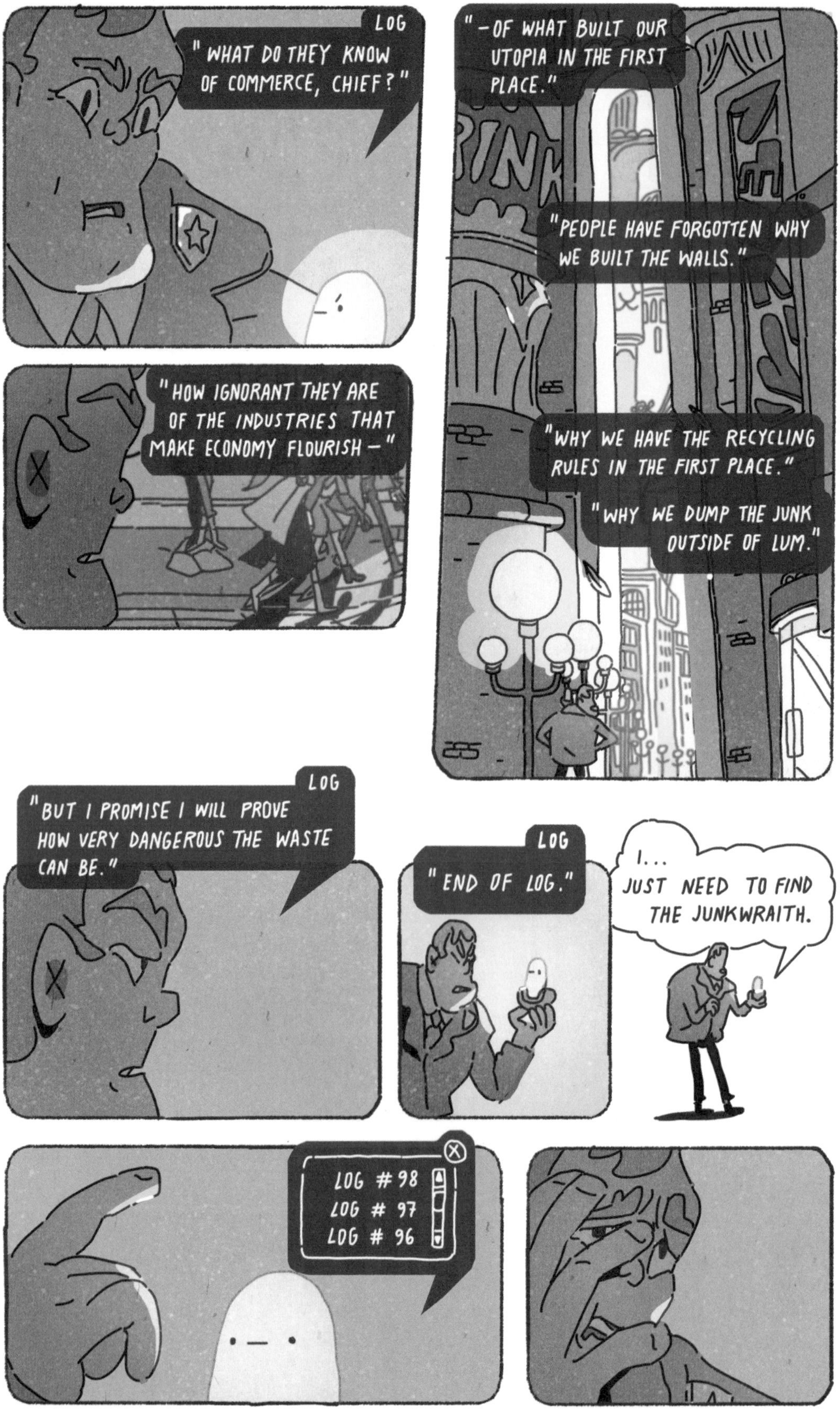
LOG
"WHAT DO THEY KNOW OF COMMERCE, CHIEF?"
"HOW IGNORANT THEY ARE OF THE INDUSTRIES THAT MAKE ECONOMY FLOURISH —"
"—OF WHAT BUILT OUR UTOPIA IN THE FIRST PLACE."
"PEOPLE HAVE FORGOTTEN WHY WE BUILT THE WALLS."
"WHY WE HAVE THE RECYCLING RULES IN THE FIRST PLACE."
"WHY WE DUMP THE JUNK OUTSIDE OF LUM."
LOG
"BUT I PROMISE I WILL PROVE HOW VERY DANGEROUS THE WASTE CAN BE."
LOG
"END OF LOG."
I... JUST NEED TO FIND THE JUNKWRAITH.
LOG #98
LOG #97
LOG #96

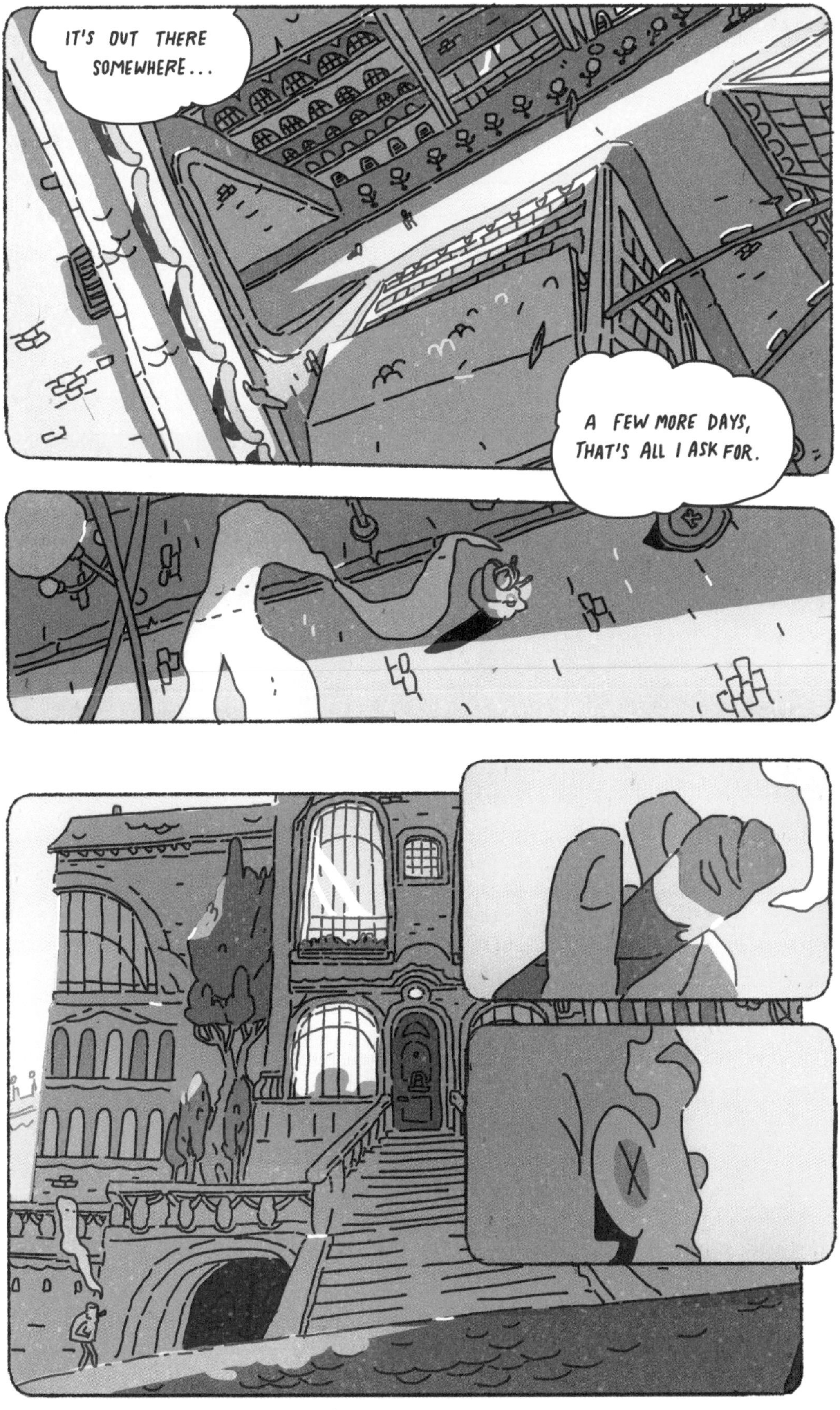
IT'S OUT THERE SOMEWHERE...
A FEW MORE DAYS, THAT'S ALL I ASK FOR.

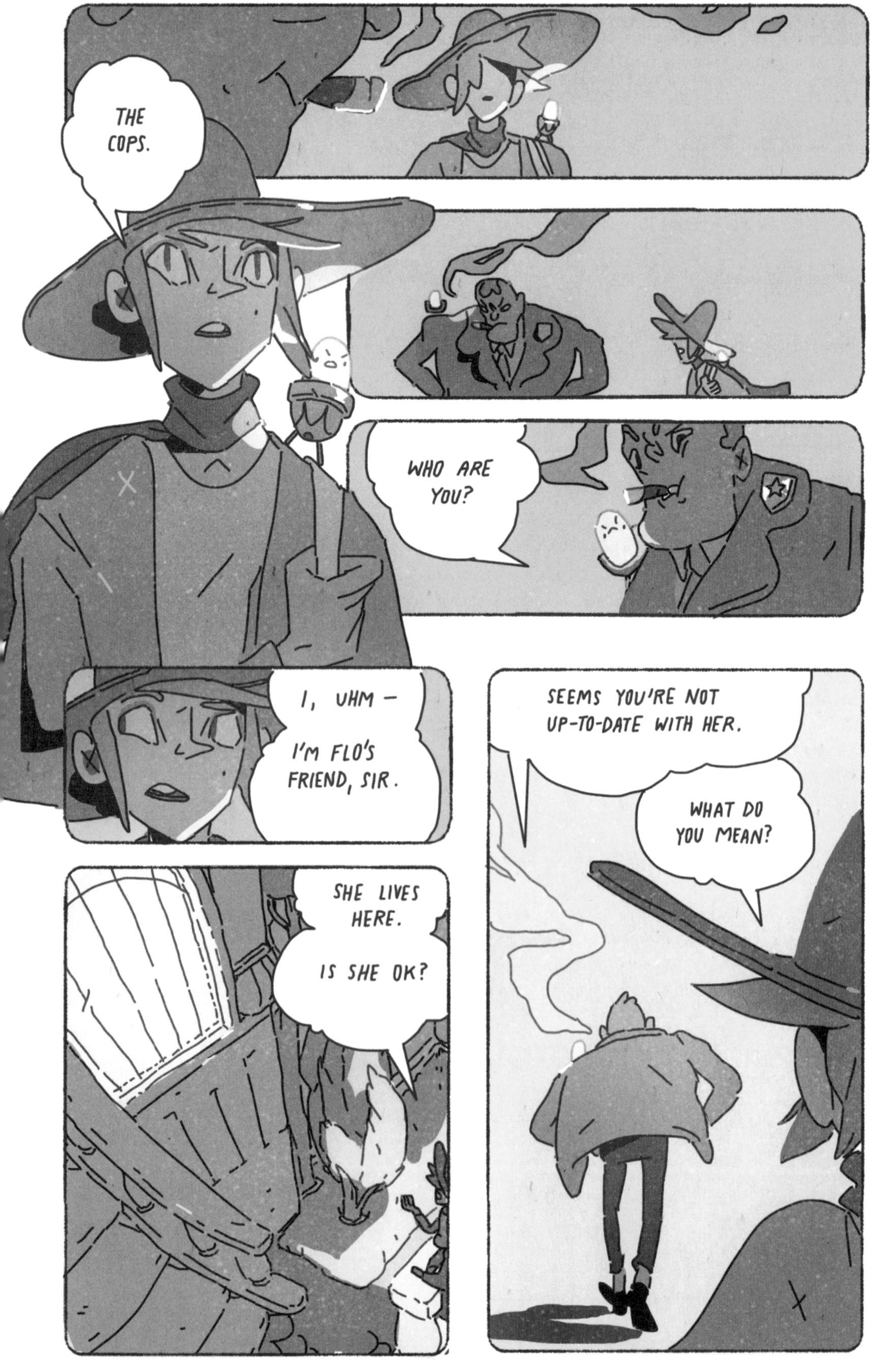
THE COPS.
WHO ARE YOU?
I, UHM —
I'M FLO'S FRIEND, SIR.
SEEMS YOU'RE NOT UP-TO-DATE WITH HER.
WHAT DO YOU MEAN?
SHE LIVES HERE.
IS SHE OK?

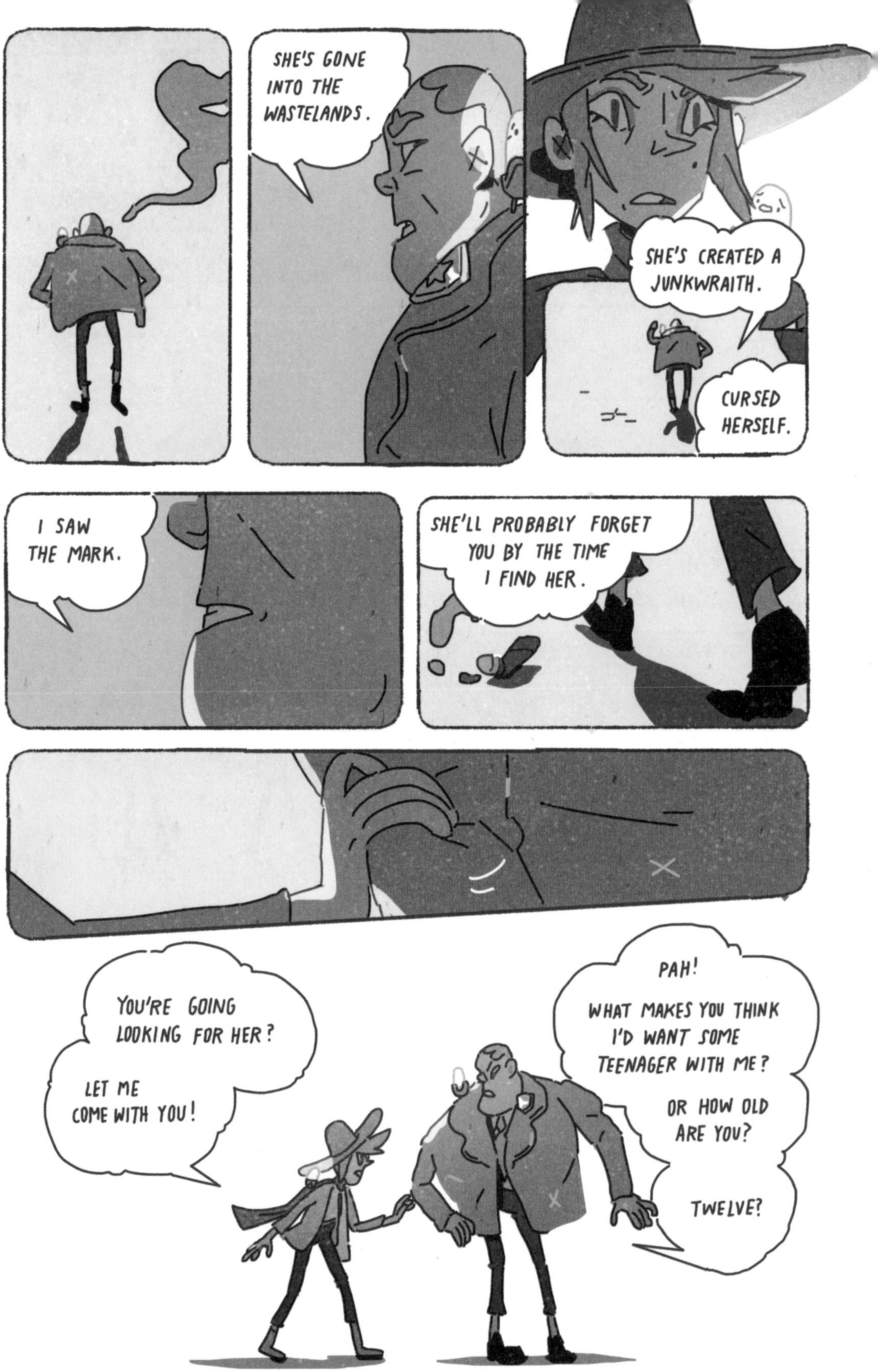
SHE'S GONE INTO THE WASTELANDS.
SHE'S CREATED A JUNKWRAITH.
CURSED HERSELF.
I SAW THE MARK.
SHE'LL PROBABLY FORGET YOU BY THE TIME I FIND HER.
YOU'RE GOING LOOKING FOR HER?
LET ME COME WITH YOU!
PAH!
WHAT MAKES YOU THINK I'D WANT SOME TEENAGER WITH ME?
OR HOW OLD ARE YOU?
TWELVE?

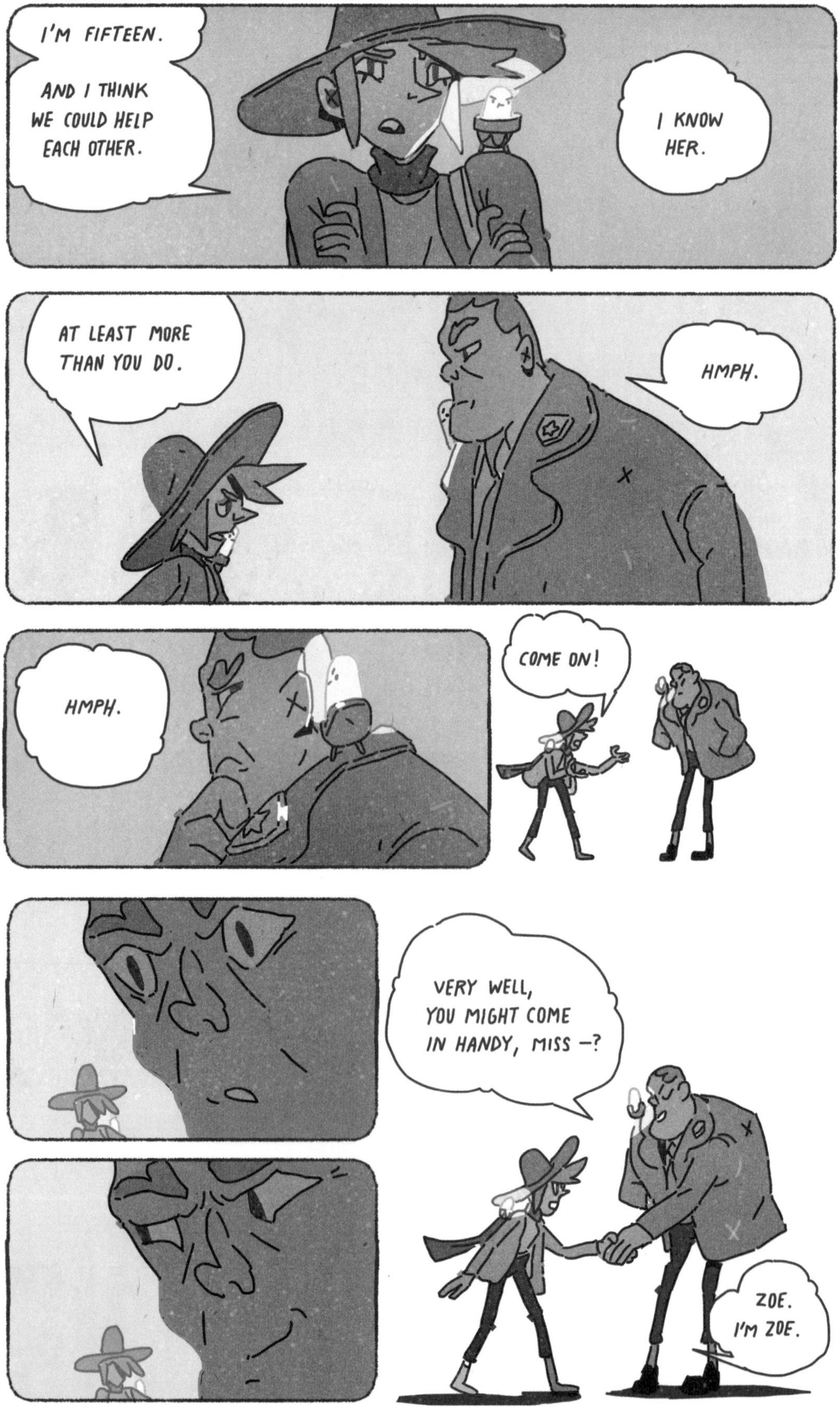
I'M FIFTEEN.
AND I THINK WE COULD HELP EACH OTHER.
I KNOW HER.
AT LEAST MORE THAN YOU DO.
HMPH.
HMPH.
COME ON!
VERY WELL, YOU MIGHT COME IN HANDY, MISS —?
ZOE. I'M ZOE.

EPISODE 8

FAKE FEALTY

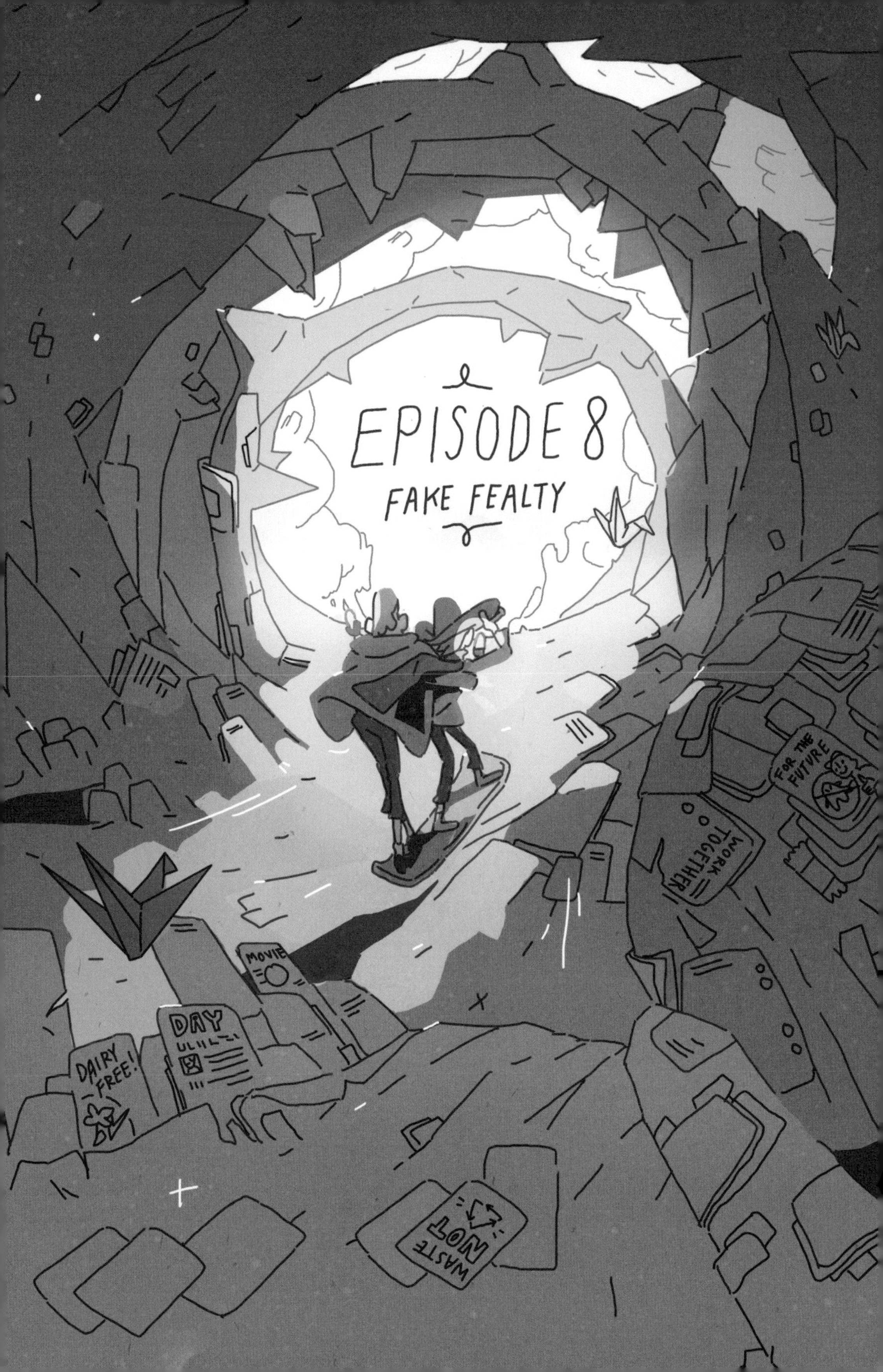

MOVIE
DAY
DAIRY FREE!
WORK TOGETHER
FOR THE FUTURE
WASTE NOT

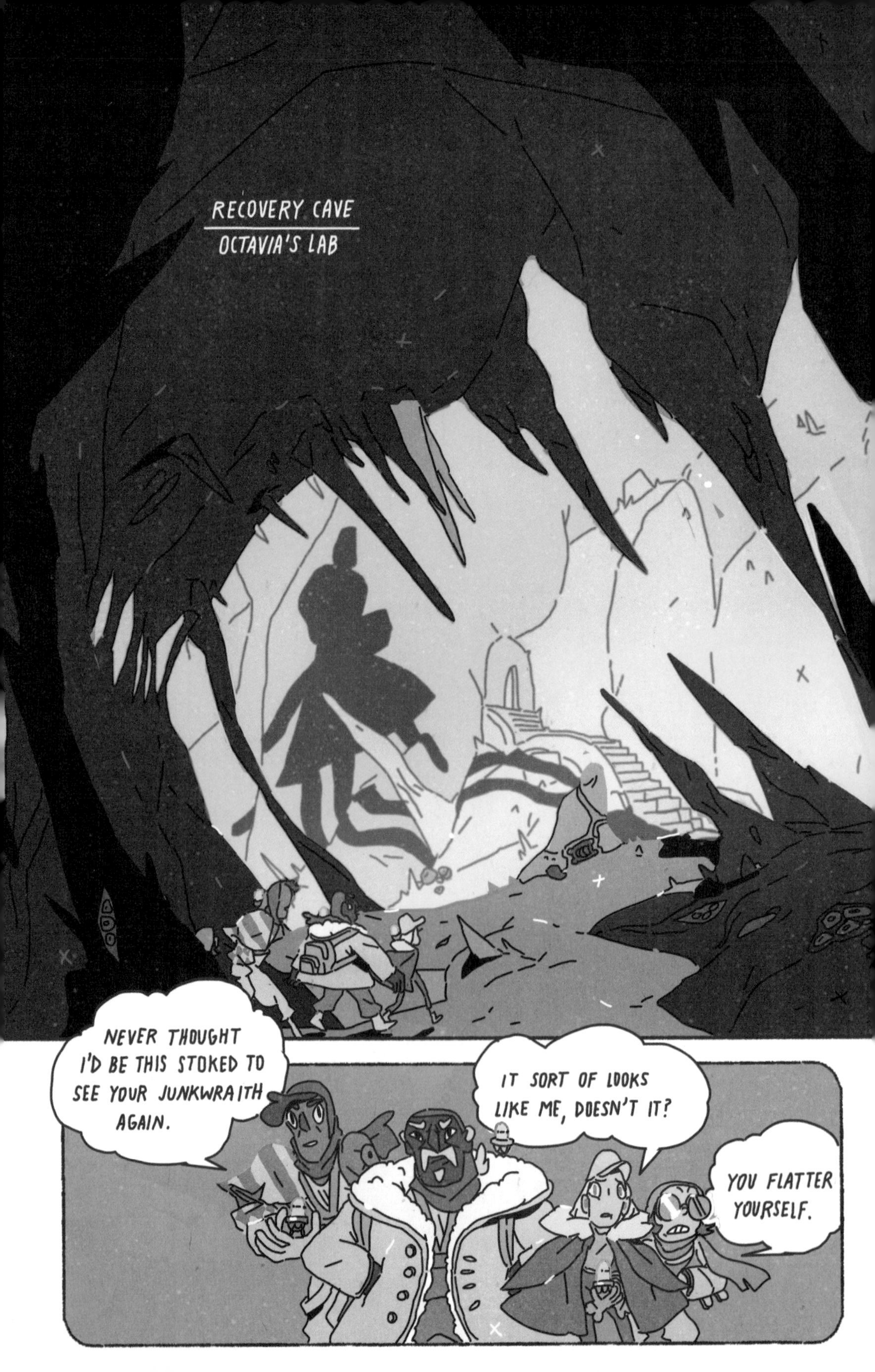
RECOVERY CAVE
OCTAVIA'S LAB
NEVER THOUGHT I'D BE THIS STOKED TO SEE YOUR JUNKWRAITH AGAIN.
IT SORT OF LOOKS LIKE ME, DOESN'T IT?
YOU FLATTER YOURSELF.

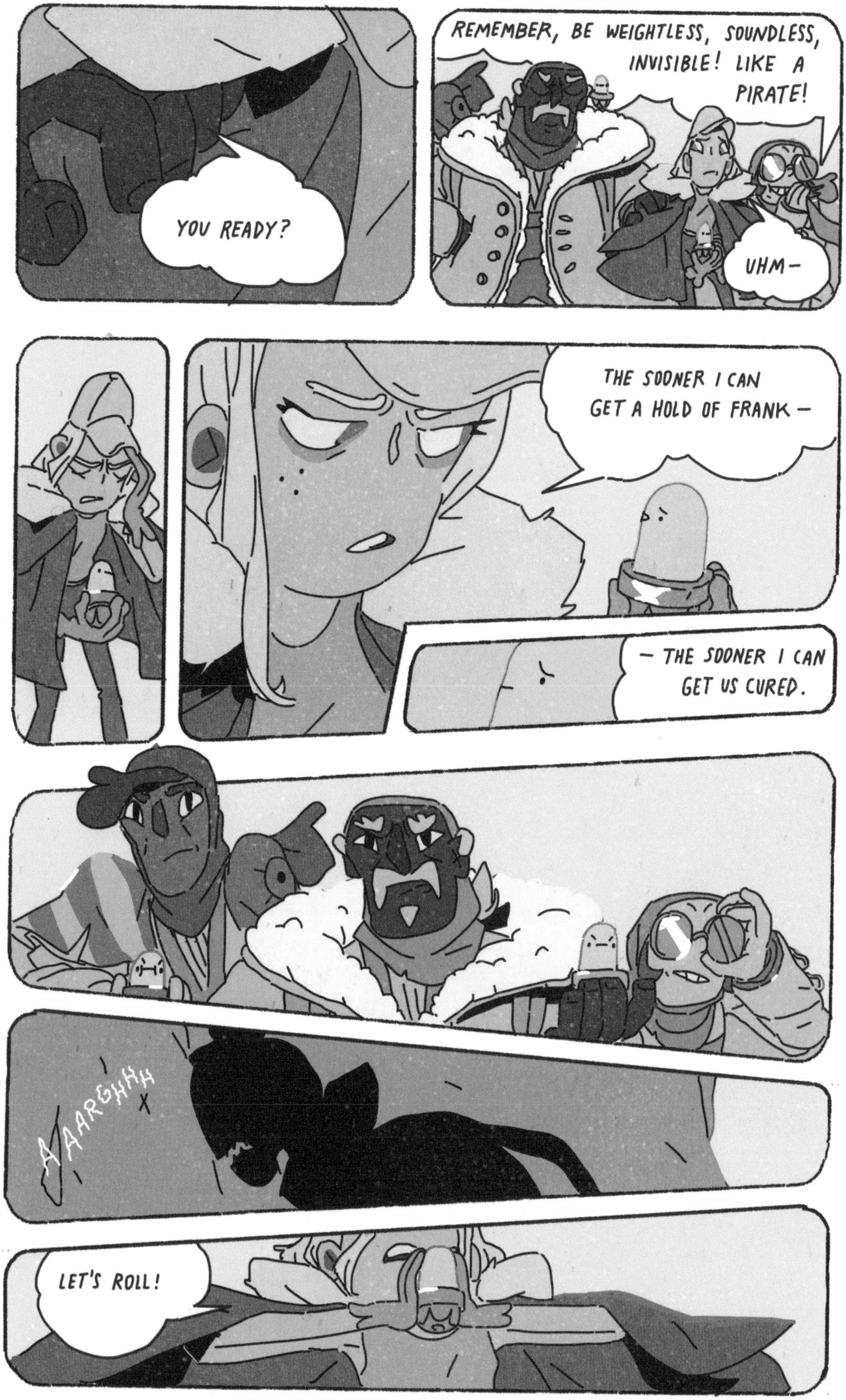
YOU READY?
REMEMBER, BE WEIGHTLESS, SOUNDLESS, INVISIBLE! LIKE A PIRATE!
UHM—
THE SOONER I CAN GET A HOLD OF FRANK—
—THE SOONER I CAN GET US CURED.
AAARGHHH
LET'S ROLL!

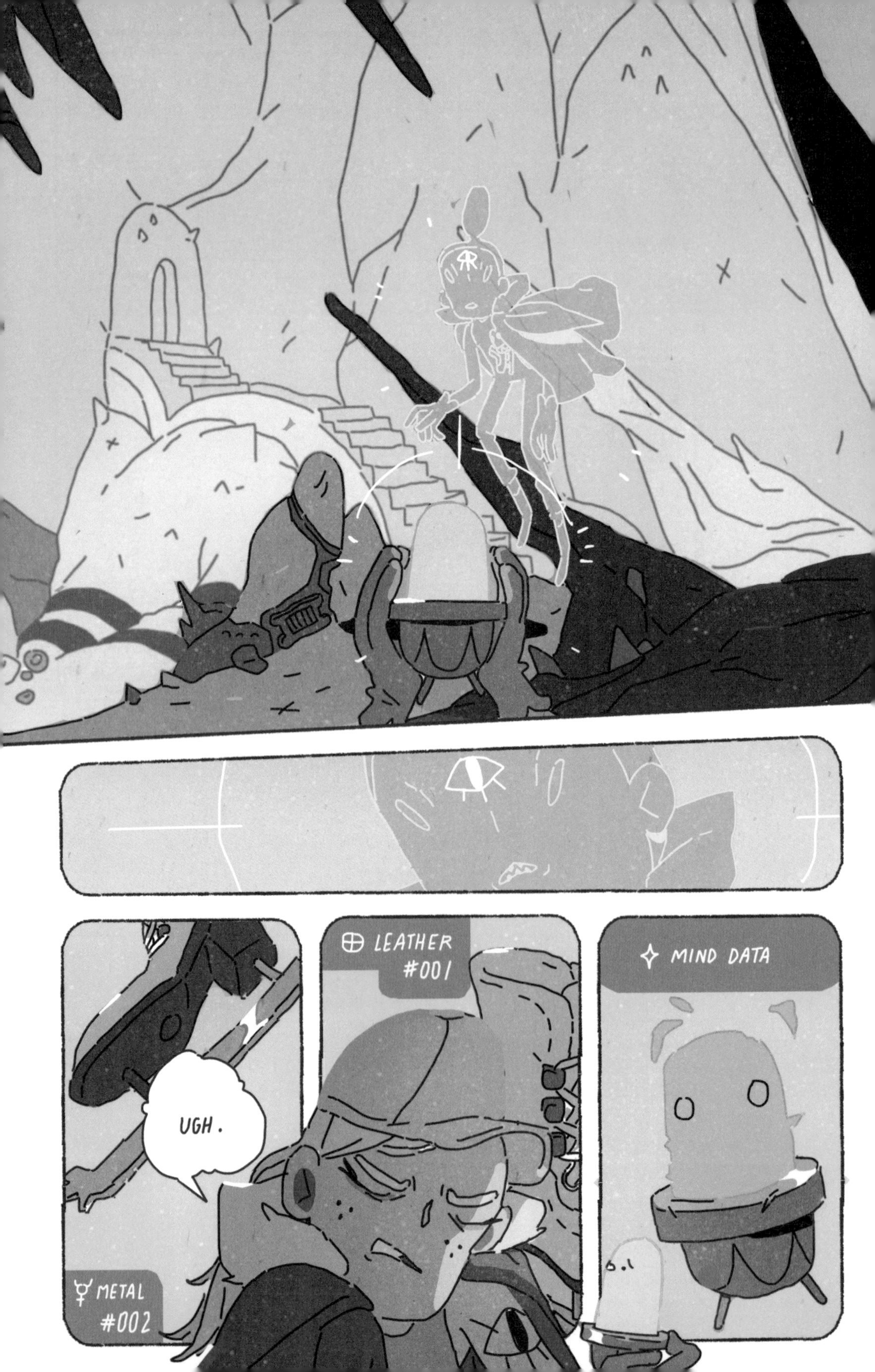
☿ METAL
#002
UGH.
⊕ LEATHER
#001
✧ MIND DATA

EXCUSE MY PREVIOUS USER'S INTERFERENCE...

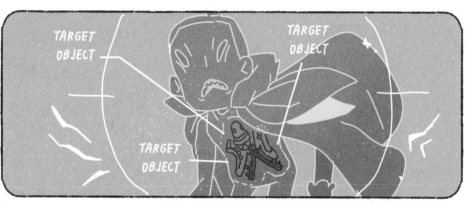

TARGET OBJECT

TARGET OBJECT

TARGET OBJECT

TOGETHER!

TIME TO SURRENDER TO YOUR... JUJU.

THE BOND MUST BE PERFECTLY SOLID.

OK!   BREACH!

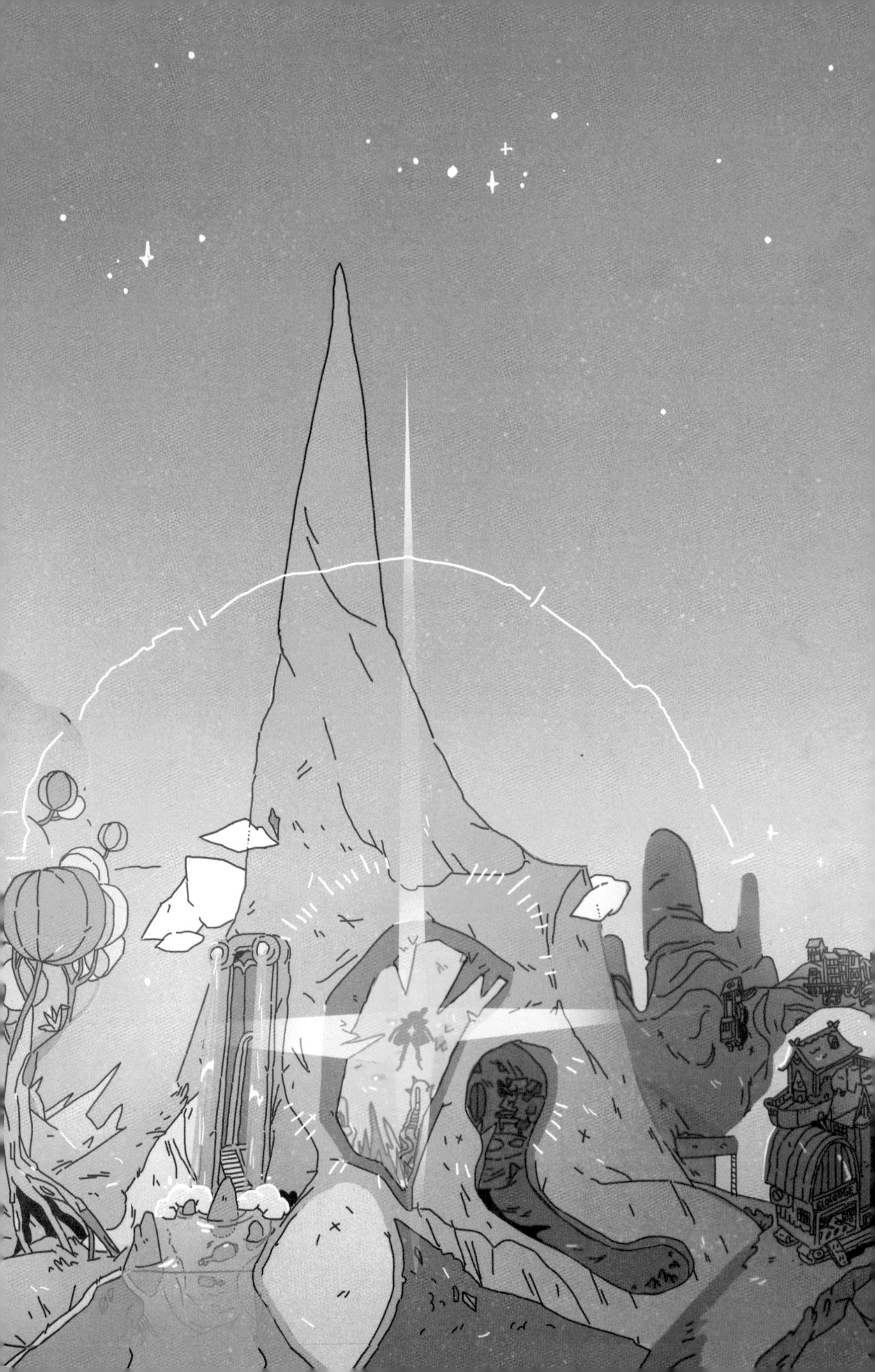

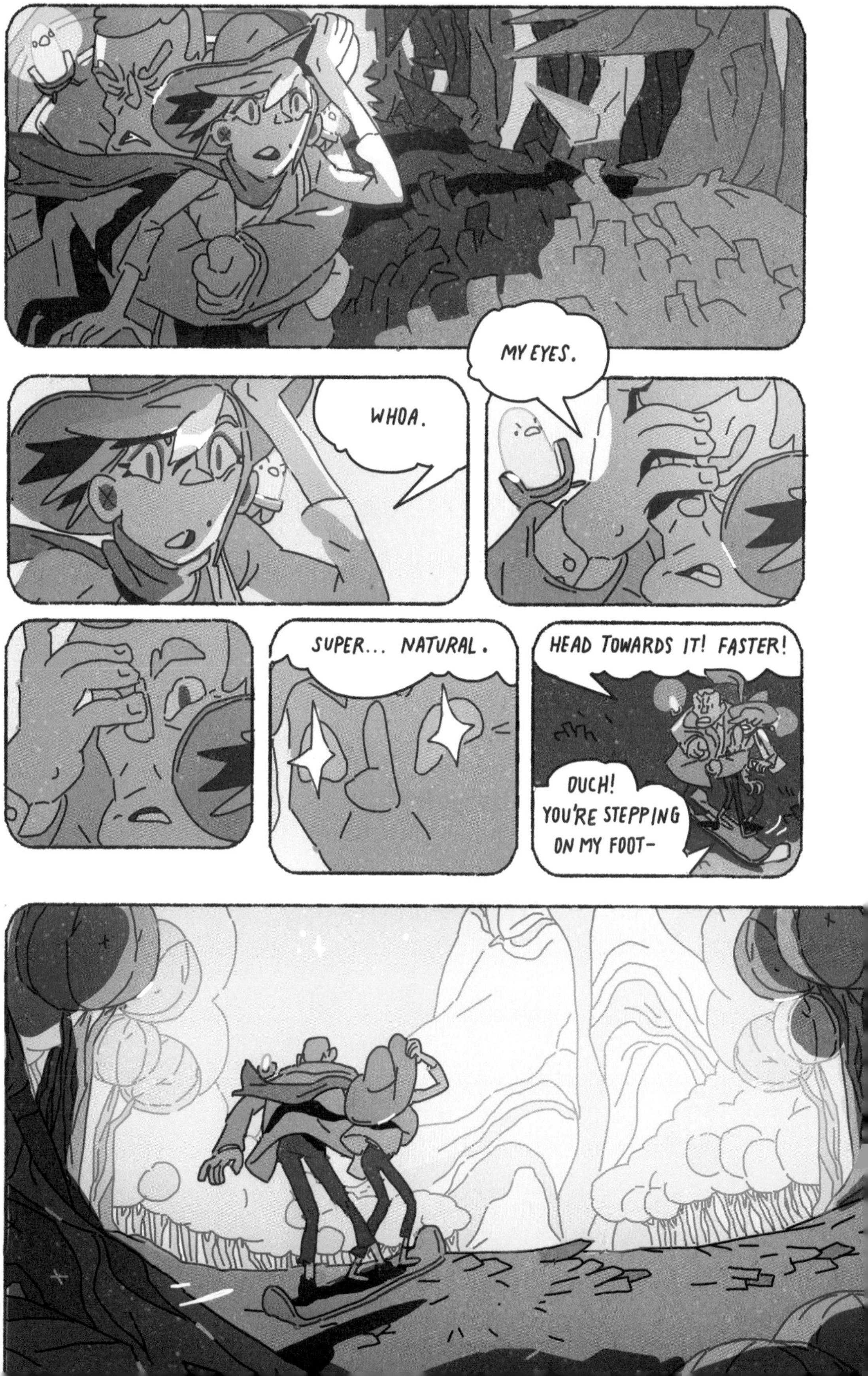
MY EYES.
WHOA.
SUPER... NATURAL.
HEAD TOWARDS IT! FASTER!
OUCH! YOU'RE STEPPING ON MY FOOT-

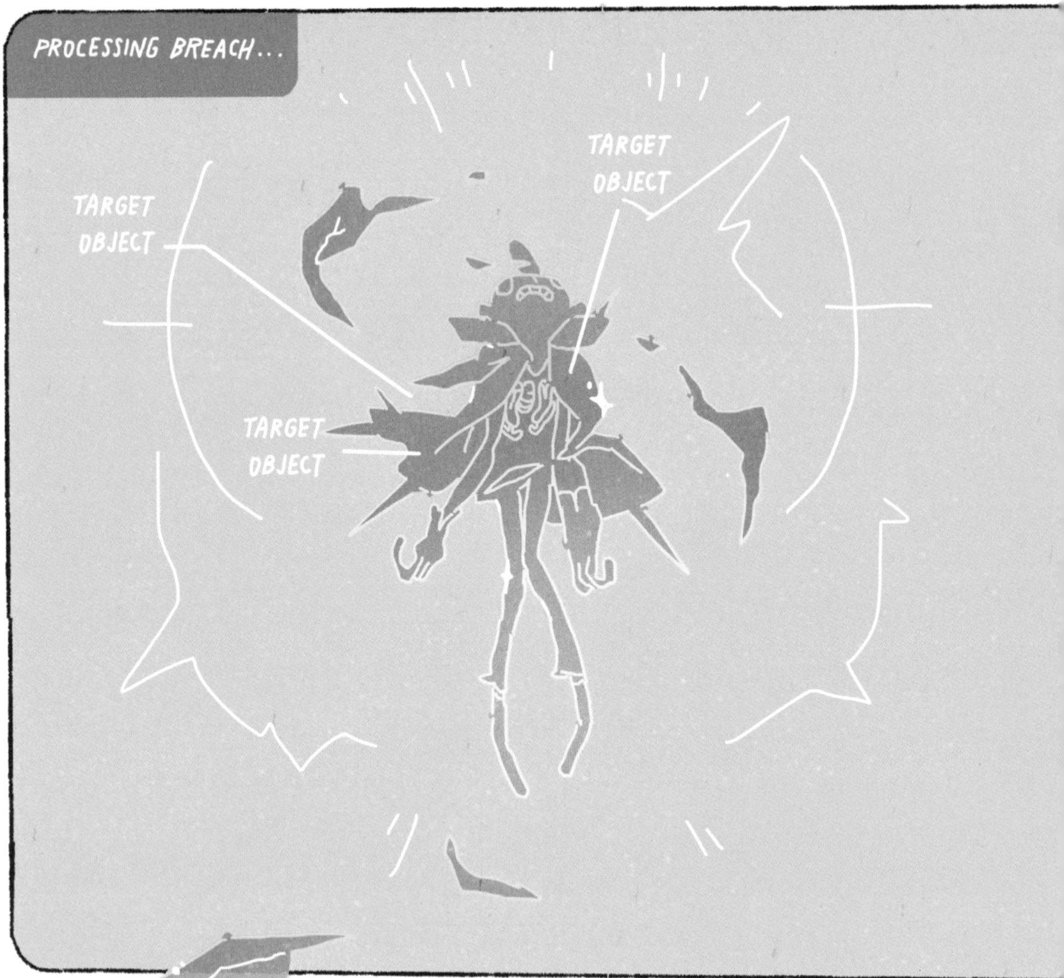
PROCESSING BREACH...
TARGET OBJECT
TARGET OBJECT
TARGET OBJECT

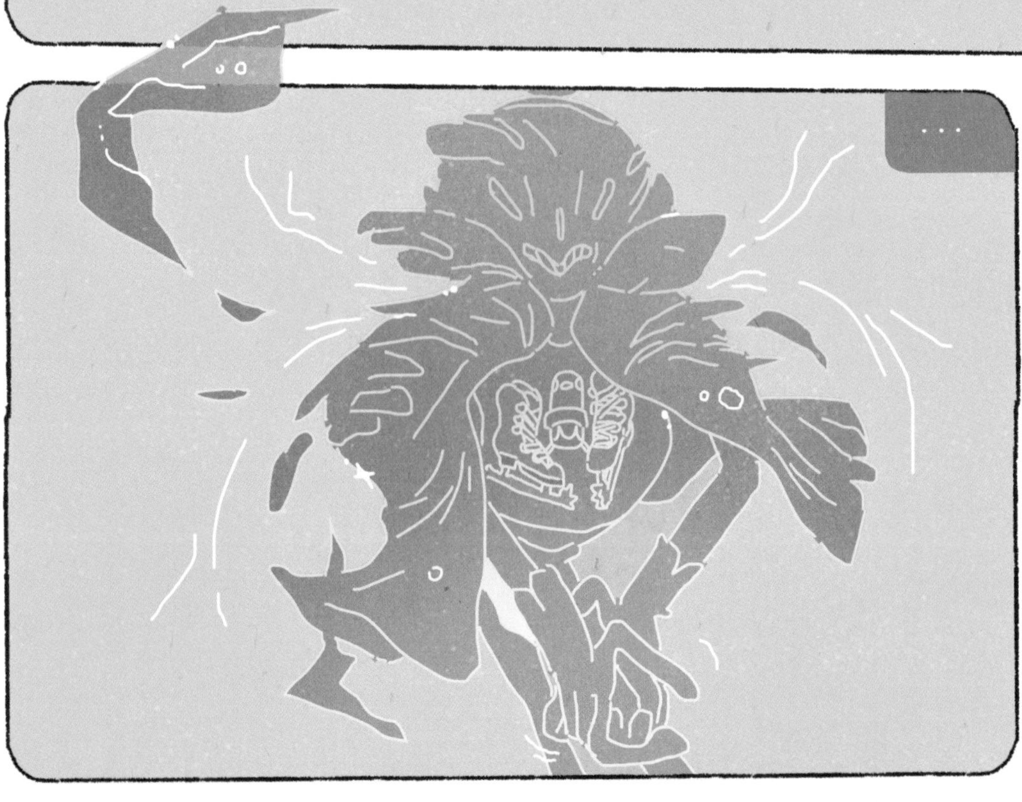
...

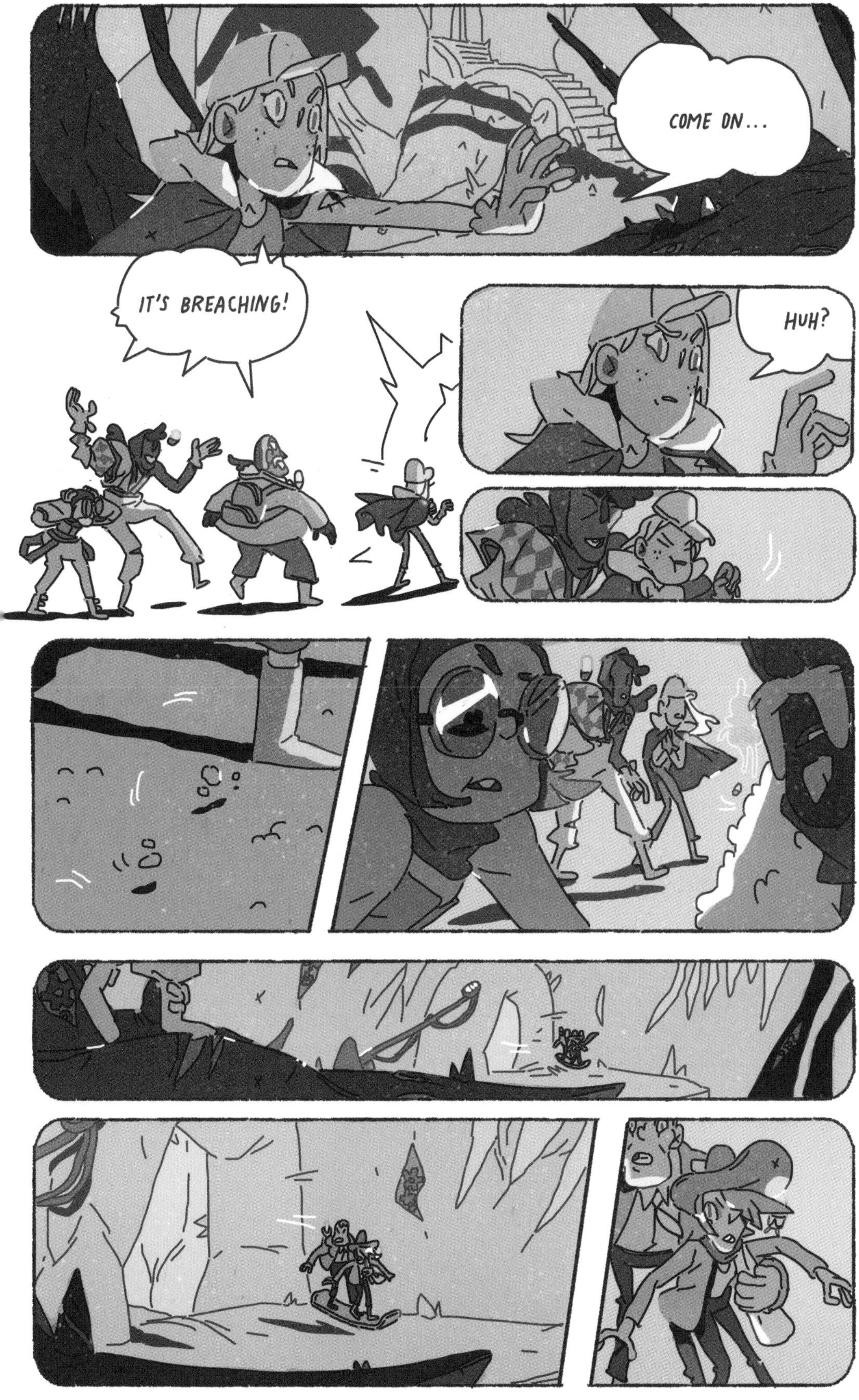
COME ON...
IT'S BREACHING!
HUH?

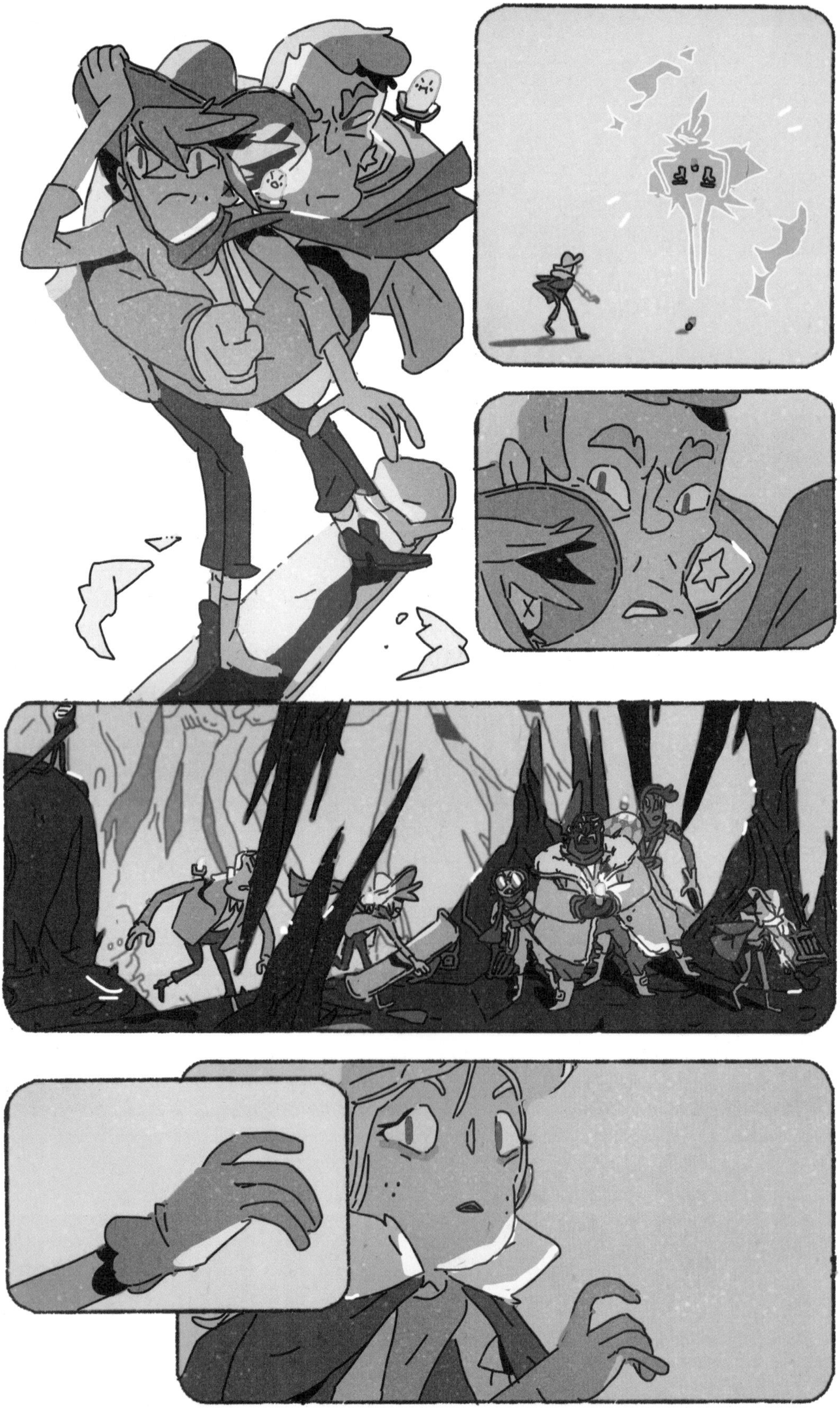

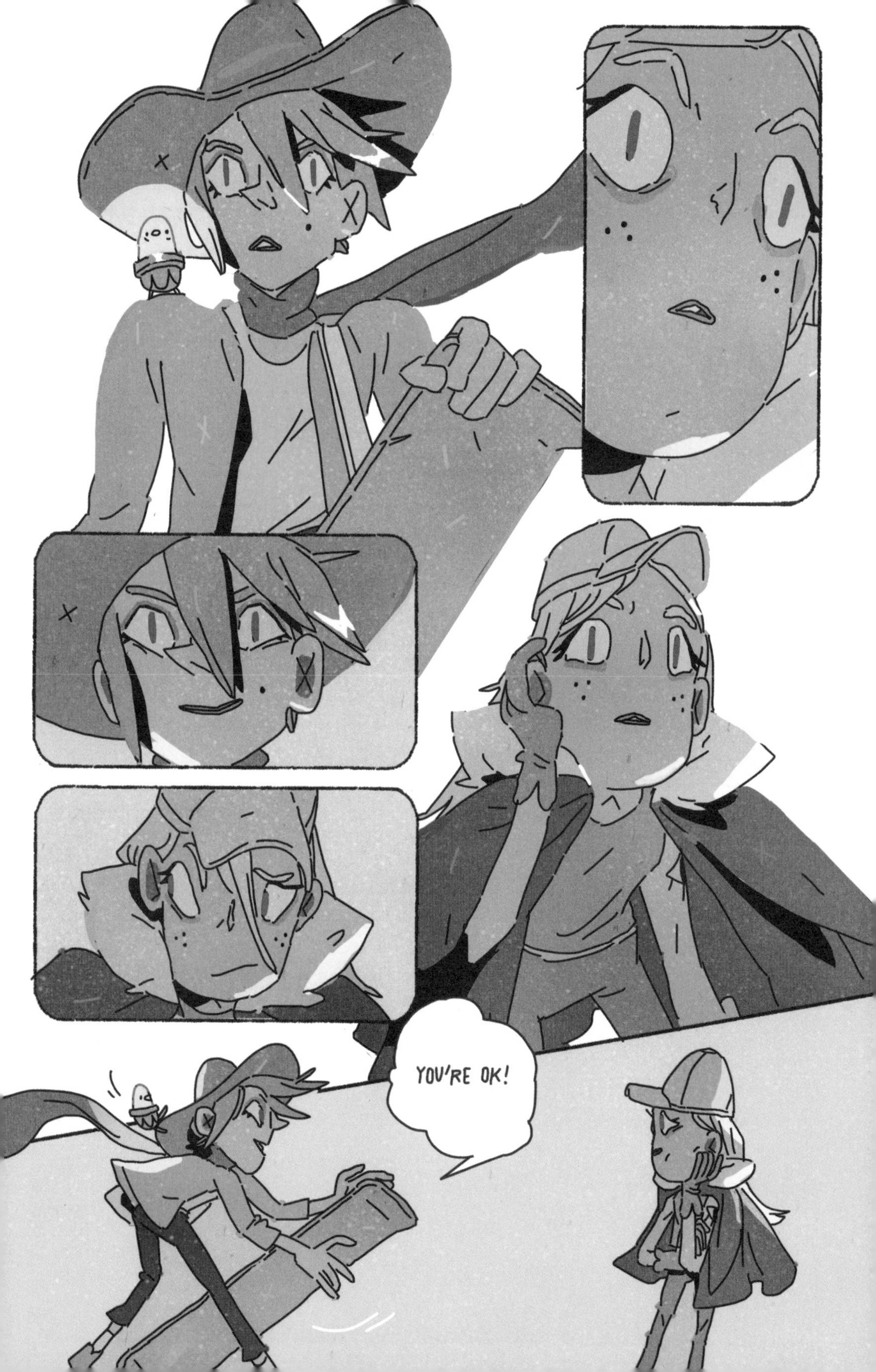
YOU'RE OK!

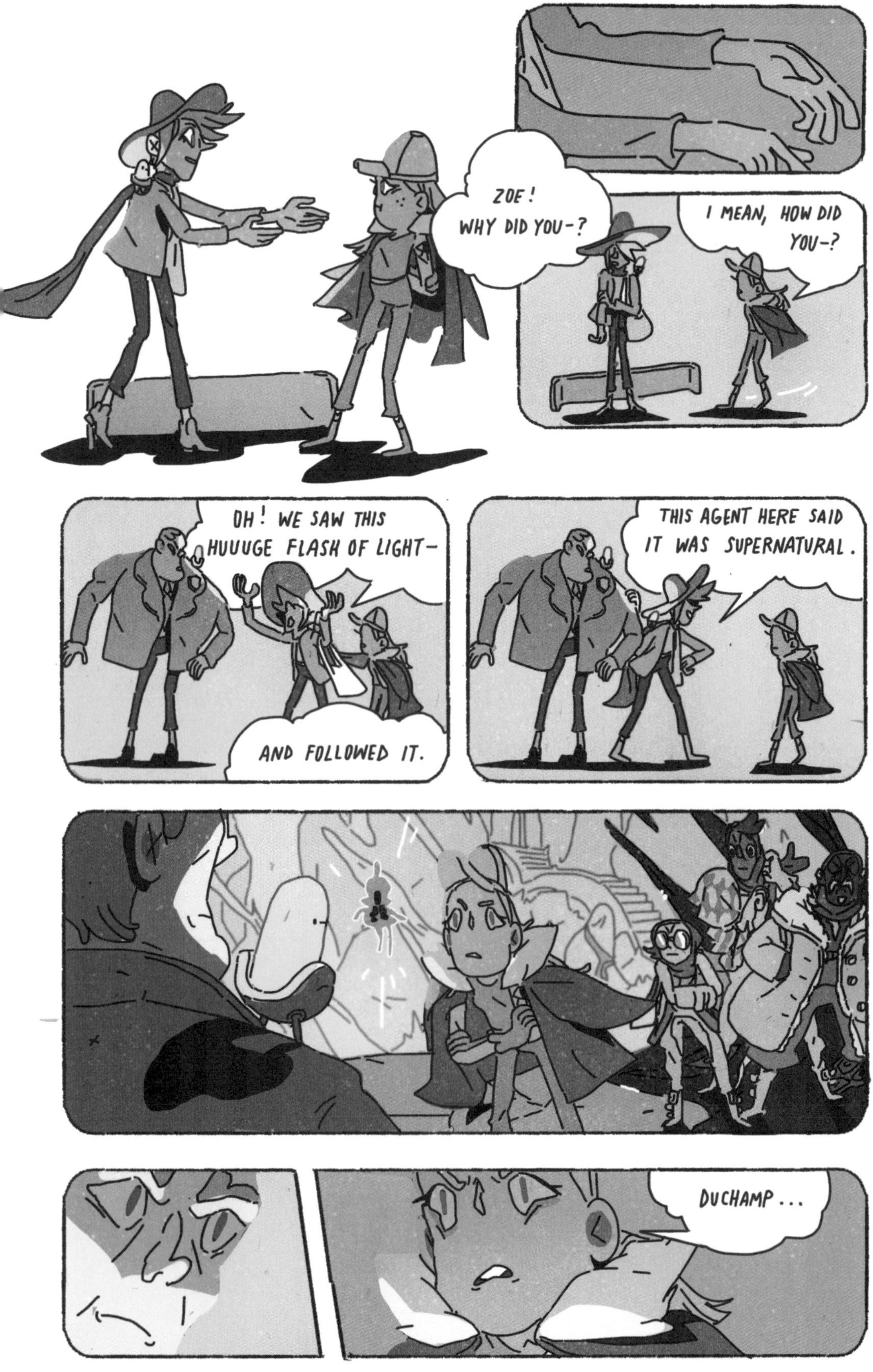
ZOE! WHY DID YOU-?
I MEAN, HOW DID YOU-?
OH! WE SAW THIS HUUUGE FLASH OF LIGHT-
AND FOLLOWED IT.
THIS AGENT HERE SAID IT WAS SUPERNATURAL.
DUCHAMP...

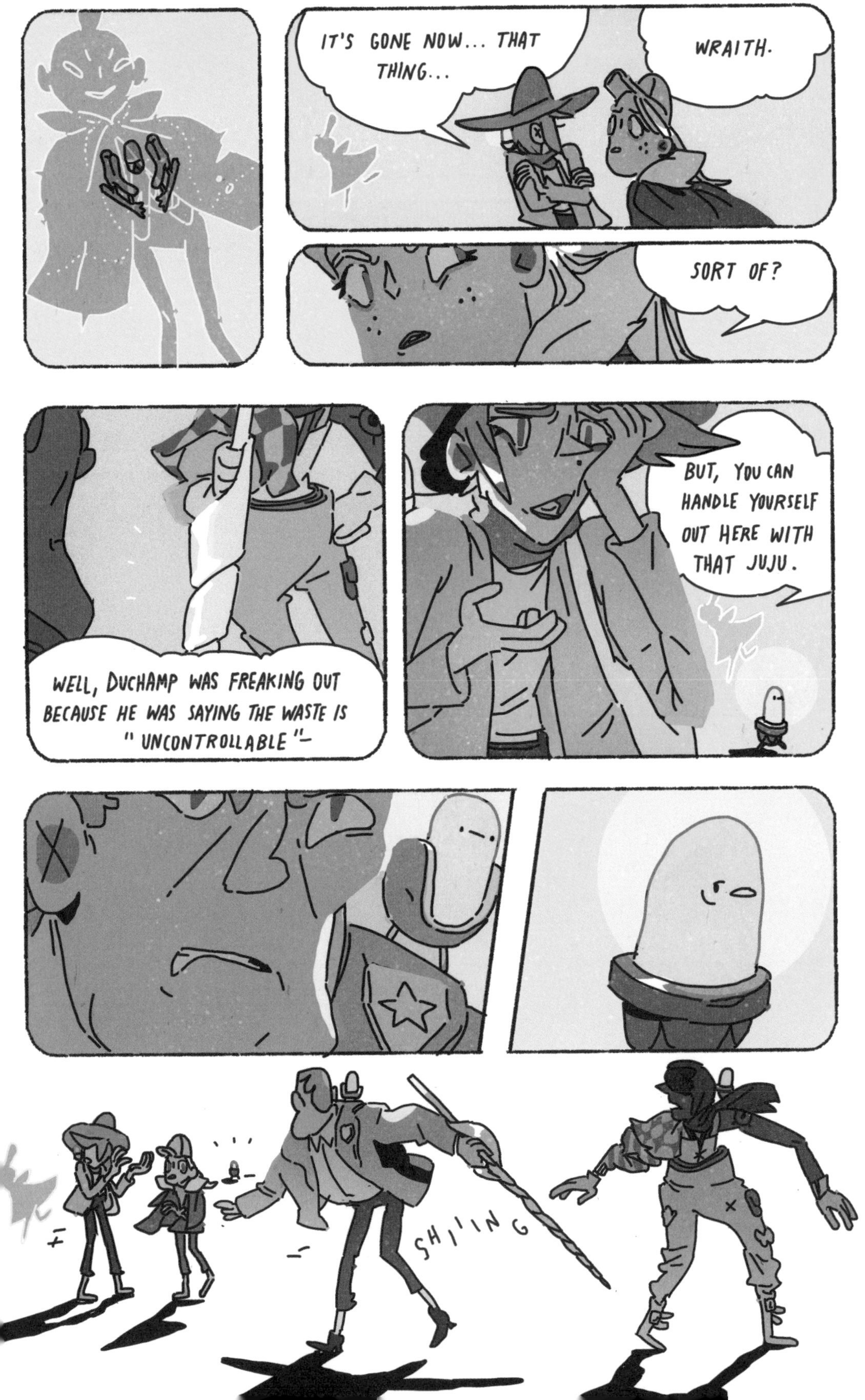
IT'S GONE NOW... THAT THING...
WRAITH.
SORT OF?
WELL, DUCHAMP WAS FREAKING OUT BECAUSE HE WAS SAYING THE WASTE IS "UNCONTROLLABLE"—
BUT, YOU CAN HANDLE YOURSELF OUT HERE WITH THAT JUJU.
SHIIING

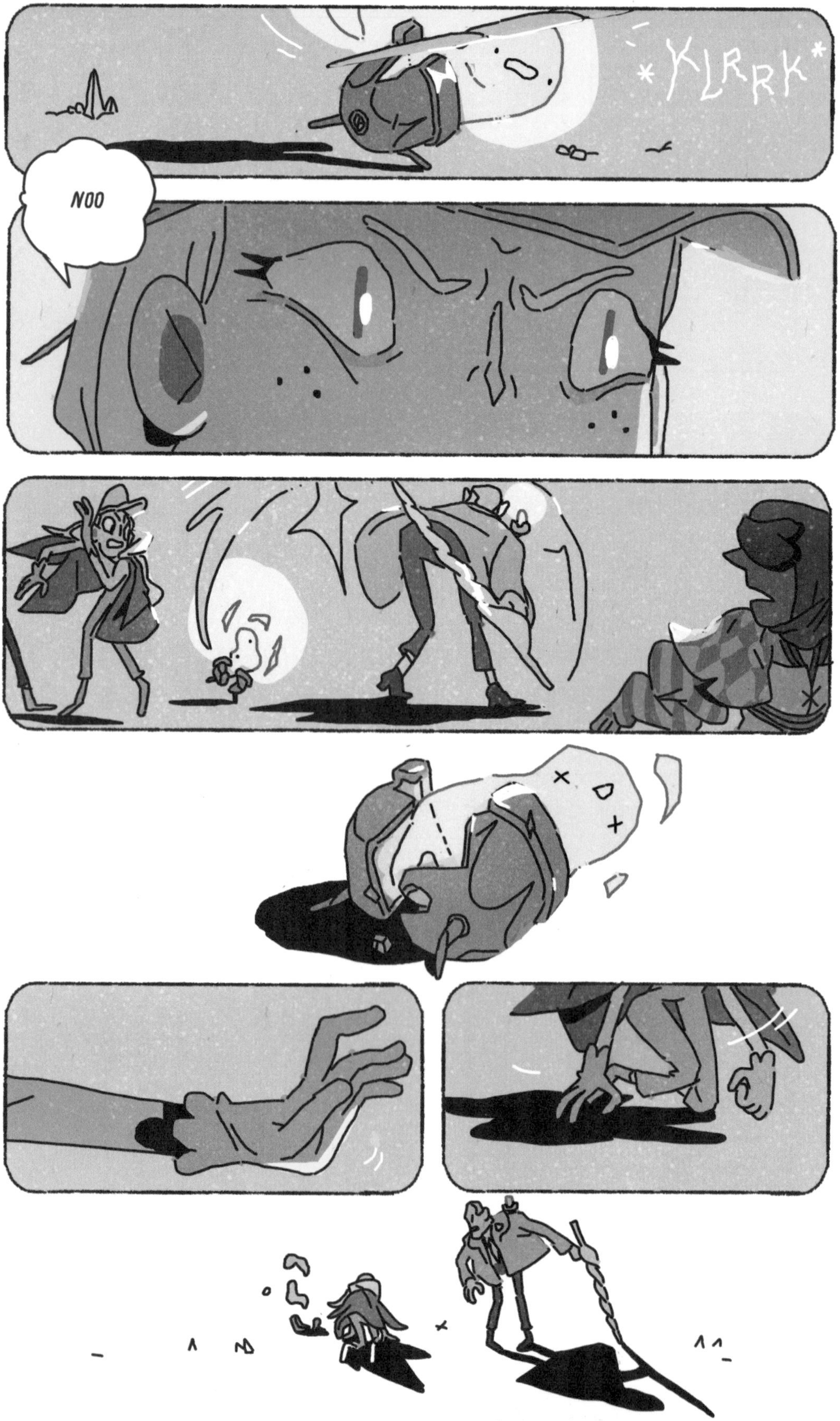
KLRRK
NOO

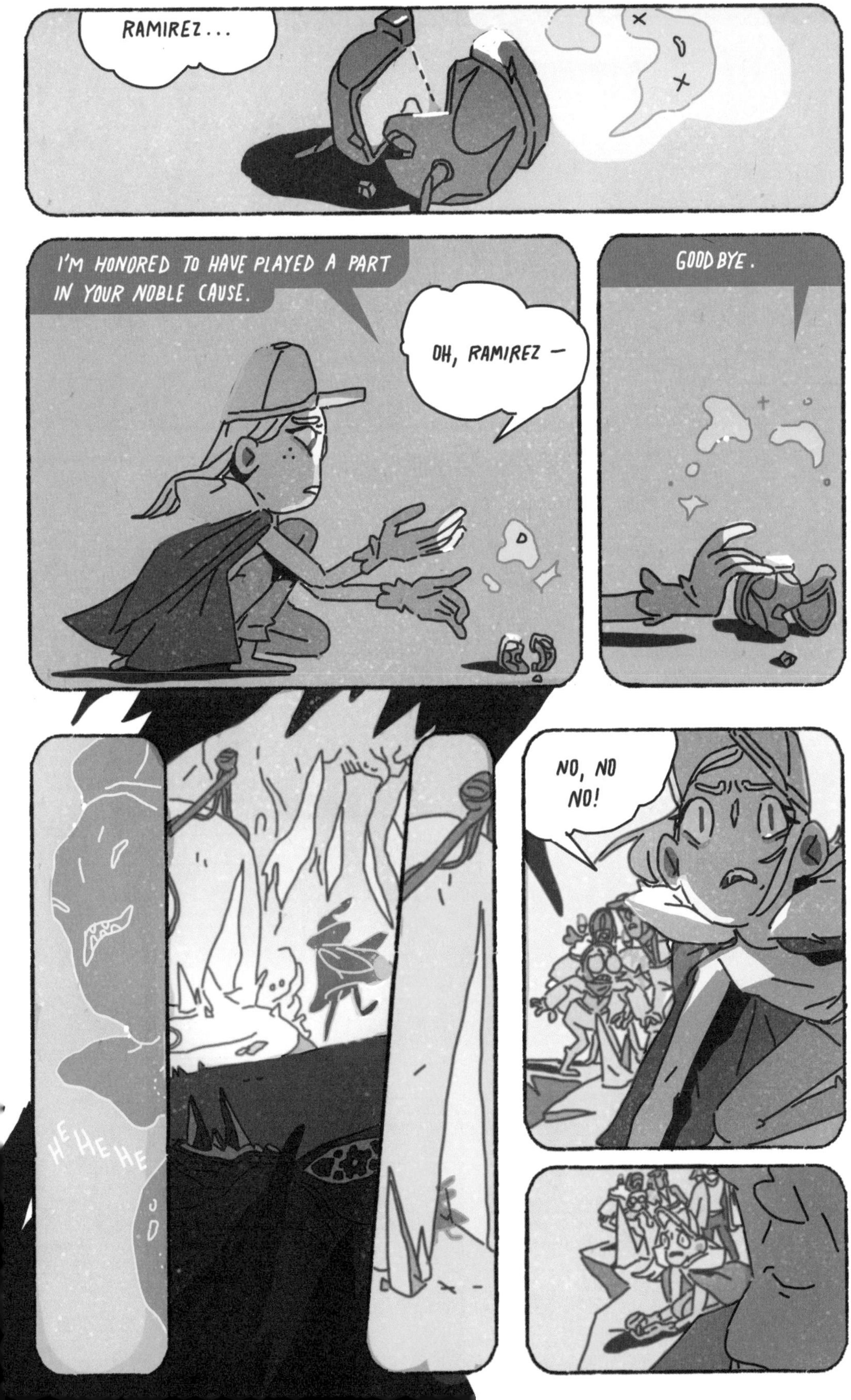
RAMIREZ...
I'M HONORED TO HAVE PLAYED A PART IN YOUR NOBLE CAUSE.
OH, RAMIREZ —
GOODBYE.
HEHEHE
NO, NO NO!

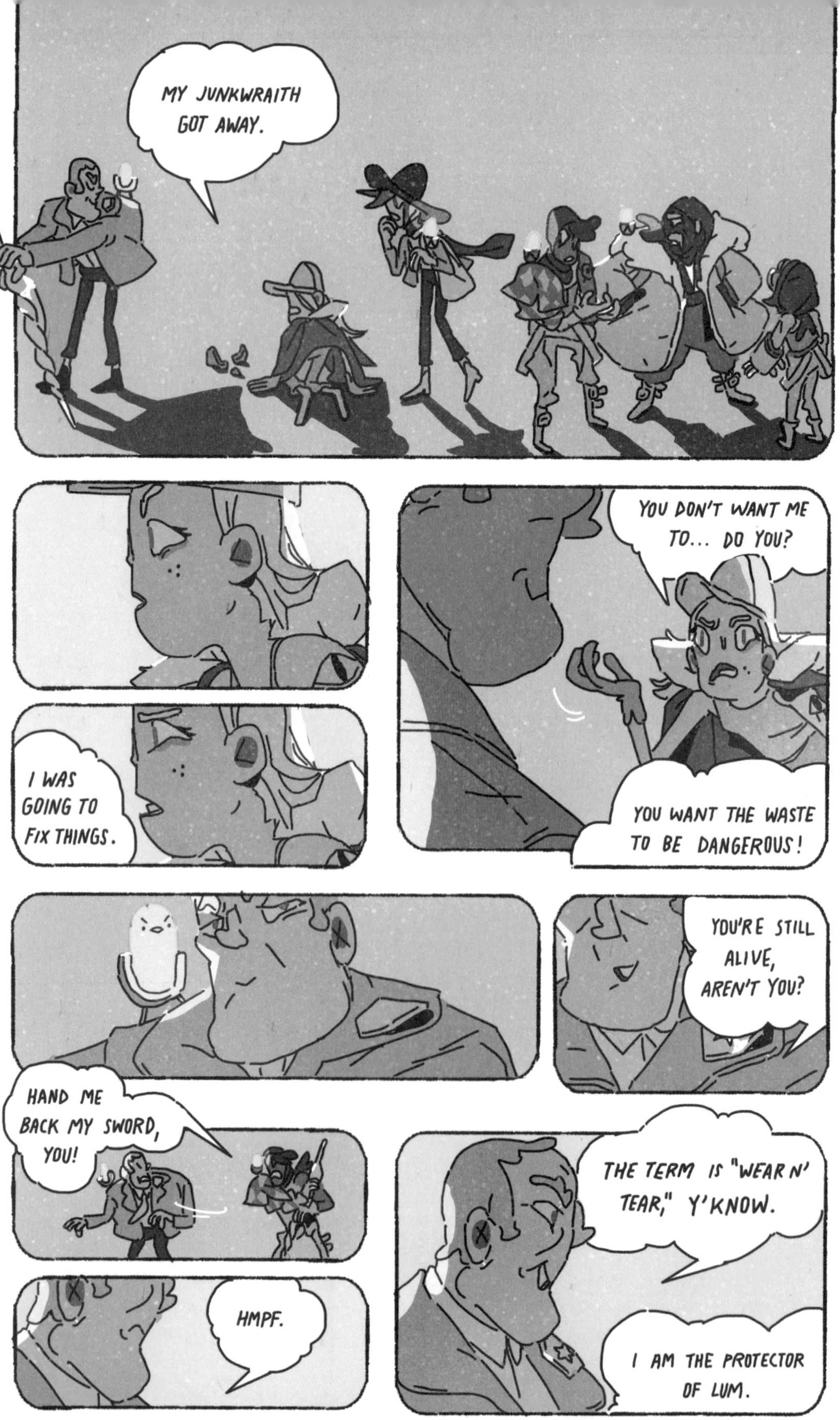
MY JUNKWRAITH GOT AWAY.
YOU DON'T WANT ME TO... DO YOU?
YOU WANT THE WASTE TO BE DANGEROUS!
I WAS GOING TO FIX THINGS.
YOU'RE STILL ALIVE, AREN'T YOU?
HAND ME BACK MY SWORD, YOU!
HMPF.
THE TERM IS "WEAR N' TEAR," Y'KNOW.
I AM THE PROTECTOR OF LUM.

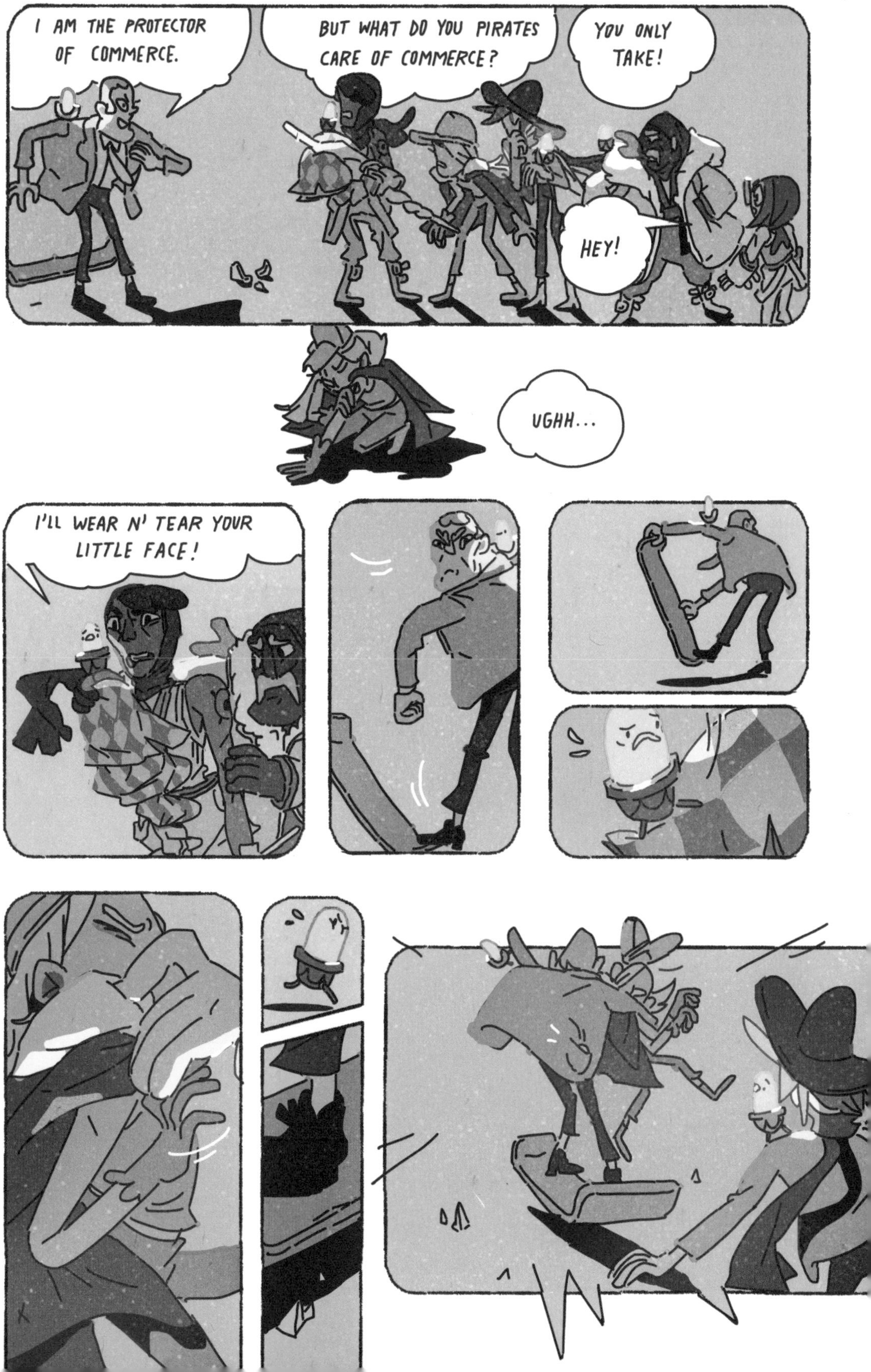
I AM THE PROTECTOR OF COMMERCE.
BUT WHAT DO YOU PIRATES CARE OF COMMERCE?
YOU ONLY TAKE!
HEY!
UGHH...
I'LL WEAR N' TEAR YOUR LITTLE FACE!

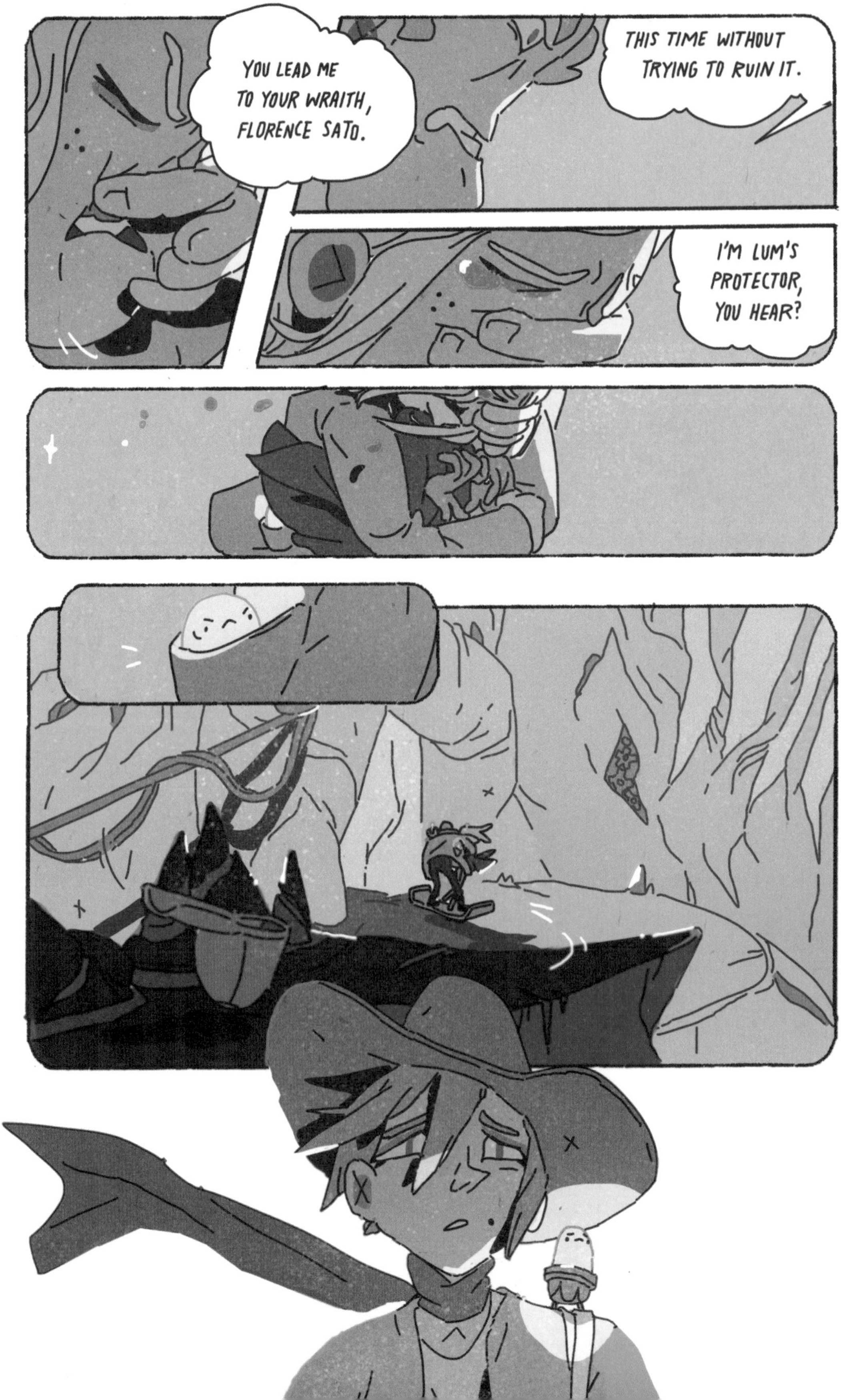
YOU LEAD ME TO YOUR WRAITH, FLORENCE SATO.
THIS TIME WITHOUT TRYING TO RUIN IT.
I'M LUM'S PROTECTOR, YOU HEAR?

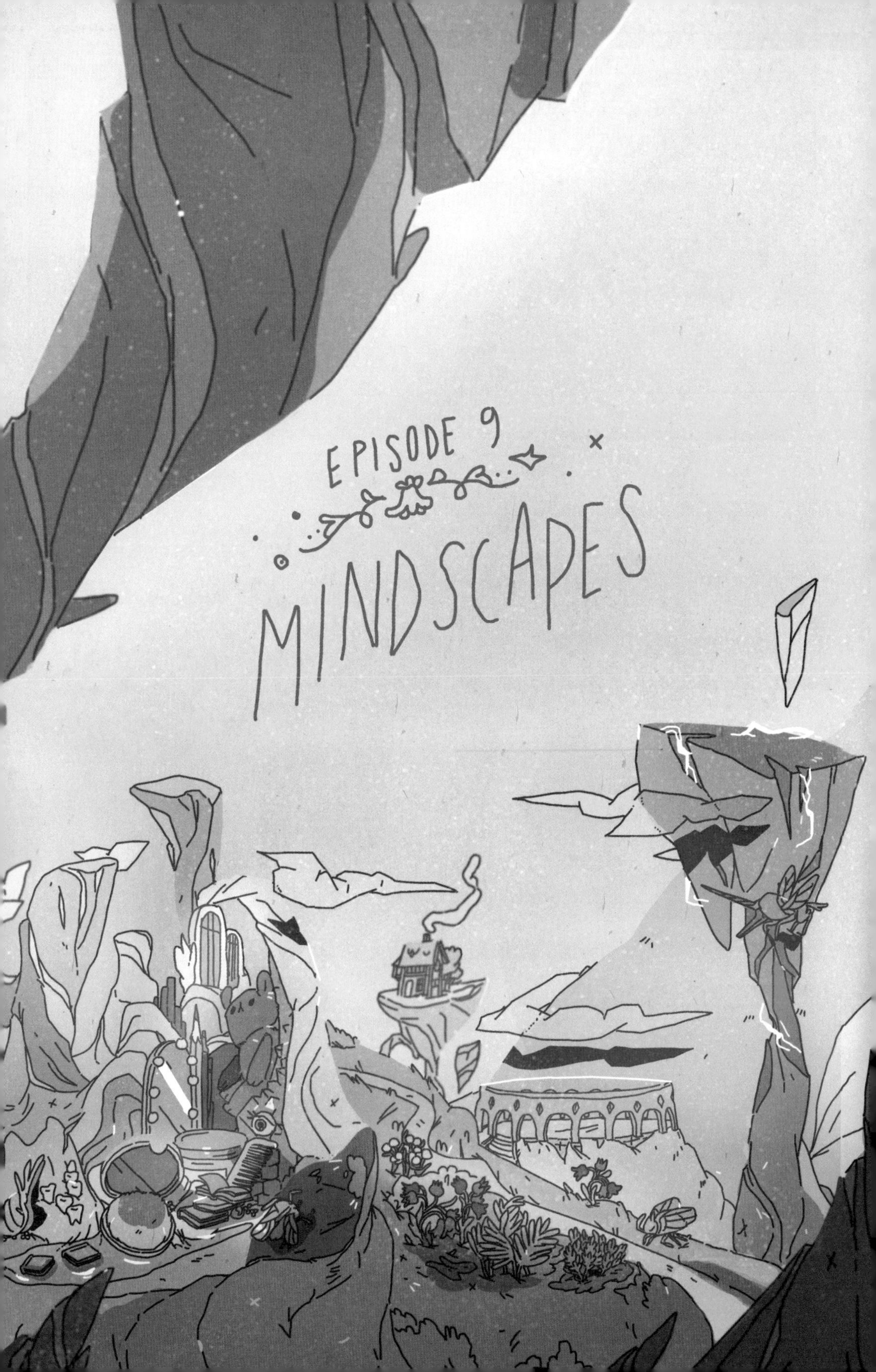
EPISODE 9
MINDSCAPES

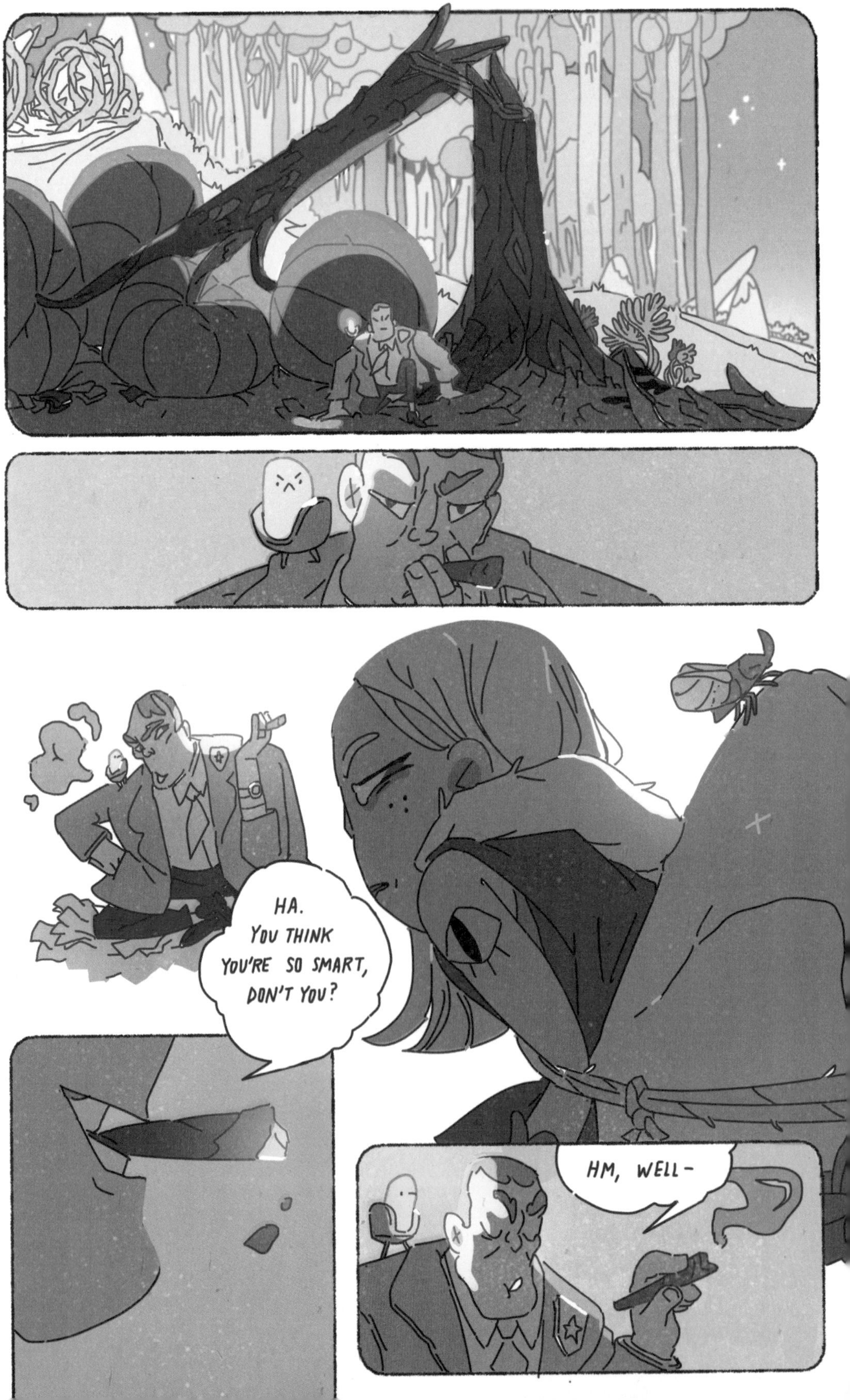
HA.
YOU THINK
YOU'RE SO SMART,
DON'T YOU?
HM, WELL-

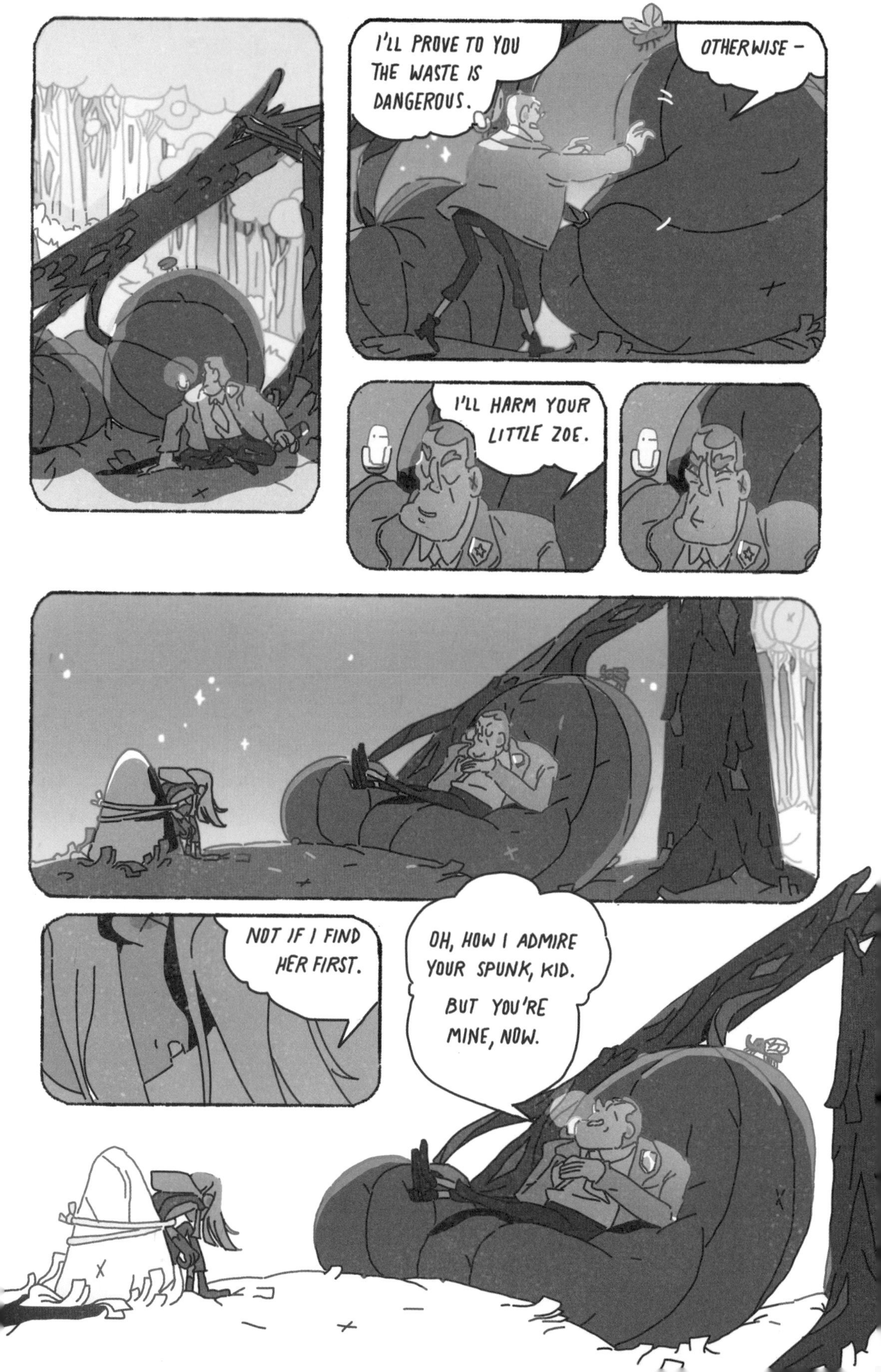

I'LL PROVE TO YOU THE WASTE IS DANGEROUS.
OTHERWISE -
I'LL HARM YOUR LITTLE ZOE.
NOT IF I FIND HER FIRST.
OH, HOW I ADMIRE YOUR SPUNK, KID.
BUT YOU'RE MINE, NOW.

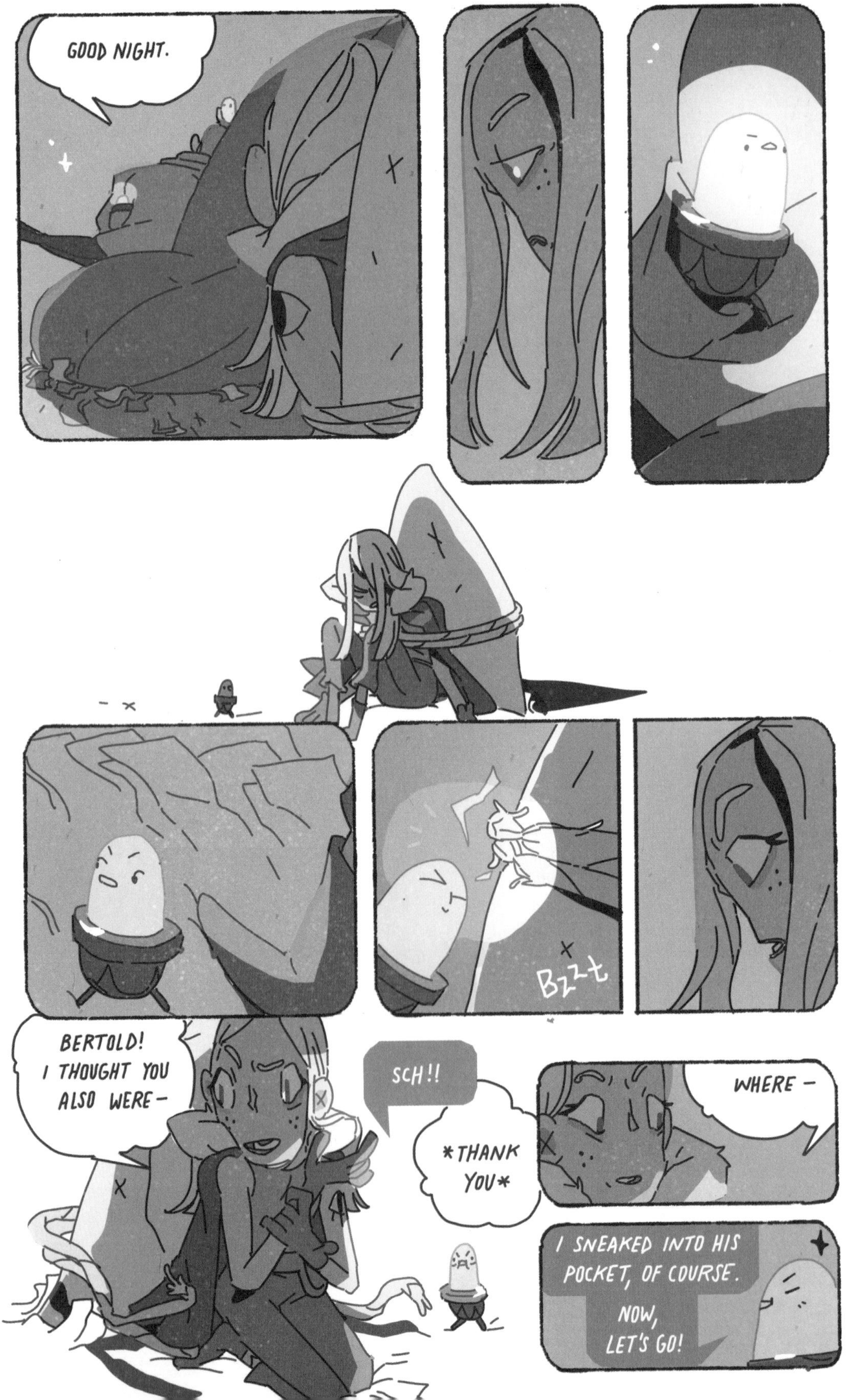
GOOD NIGHT.
Bzzt
BERTOLD! I THOUGHT YOU ALSO WERE-
SCH!!
THANK YOU
WHERE -
I SNEAKED INTO HIS POCKET, OF COURSE.
NOW, LET'S GO!

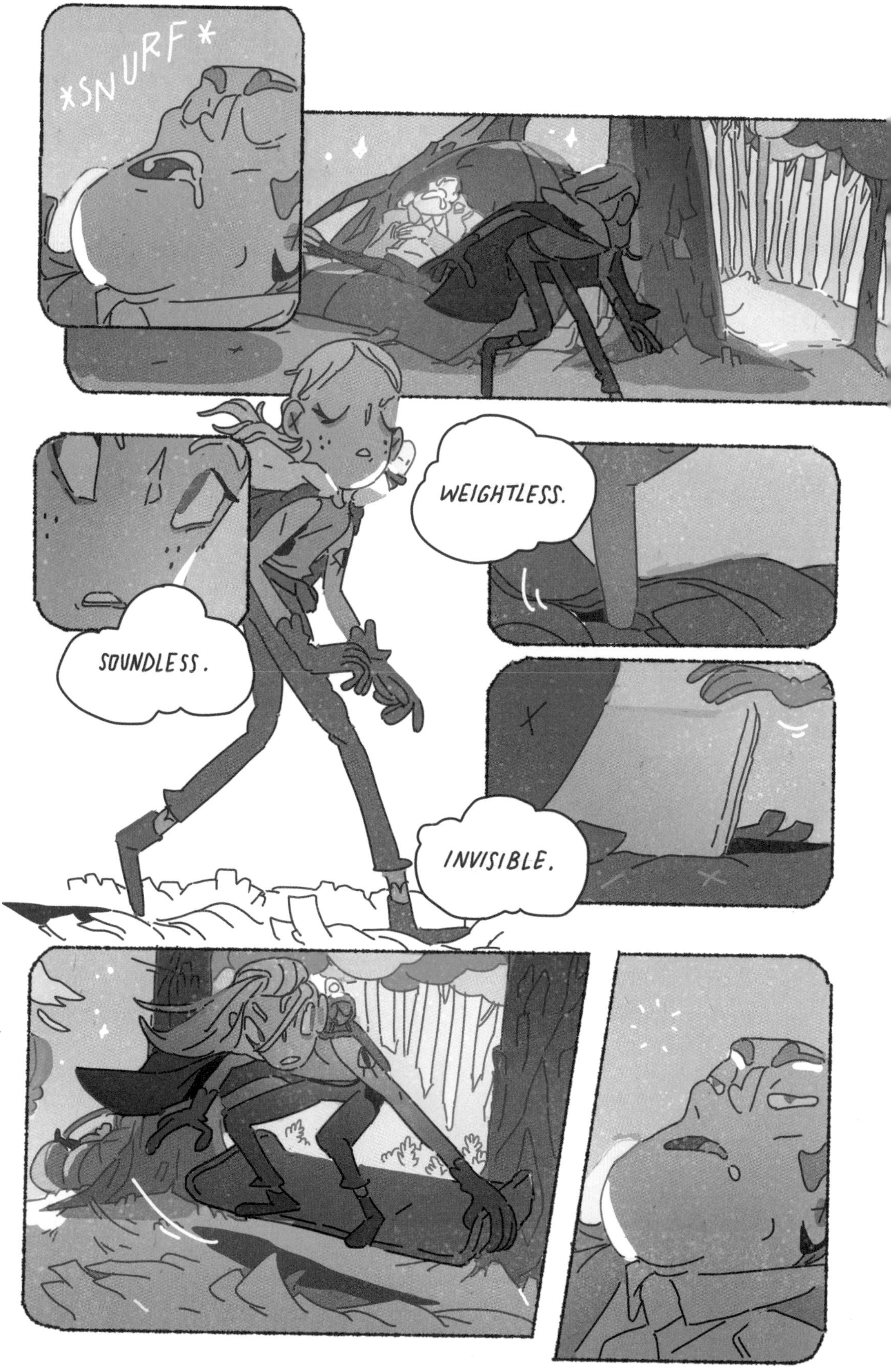
SNURF
WEIGHTLESS.
SOUNDLESS.
INVISIBLE.

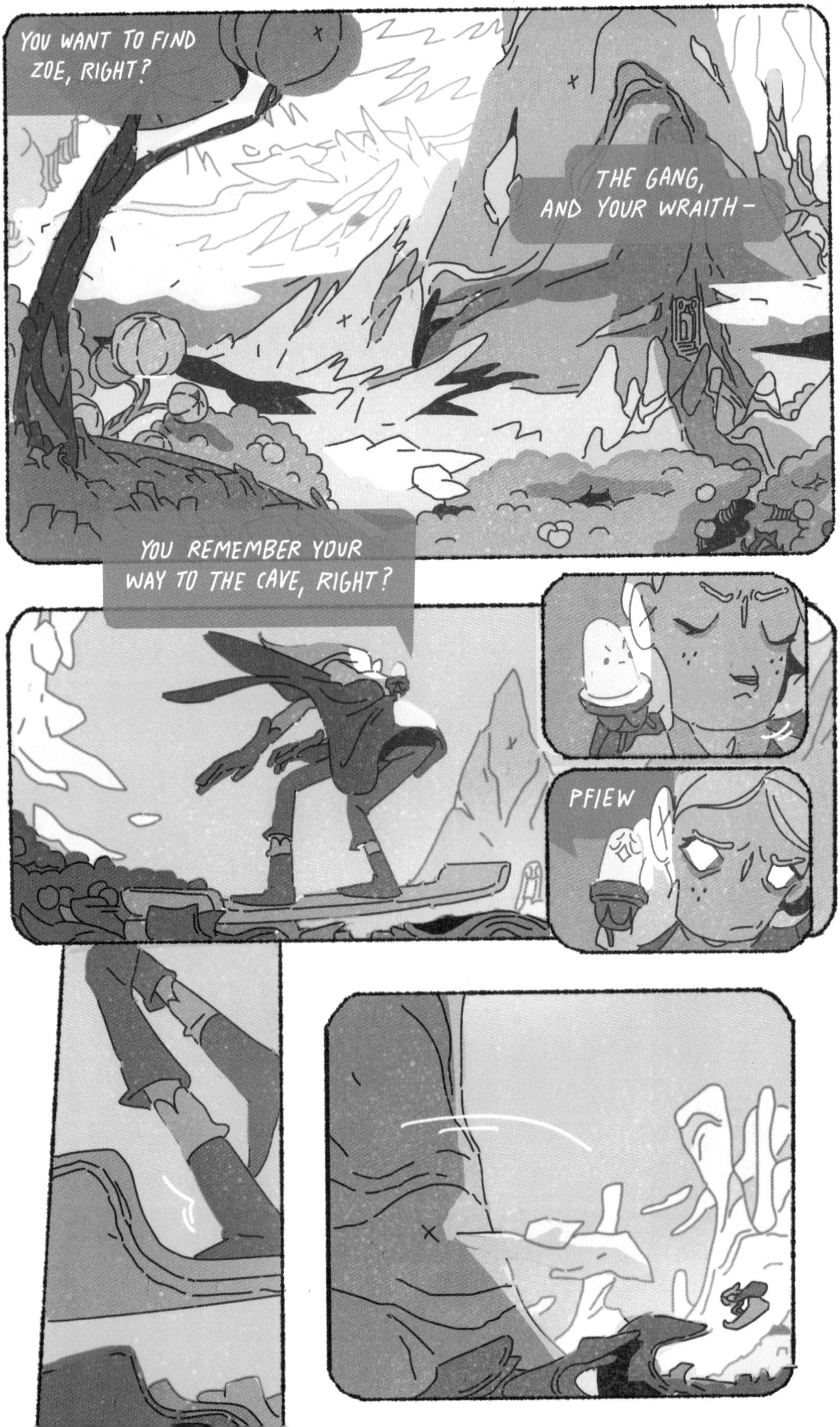
YOU WANT TO FIND ZOE, RIGHT?
THE GANG, AND YOUR WRAITH—
YOU REMEMBER YOUR WAY TO THE CAVE, RIGHT?
PFIEW

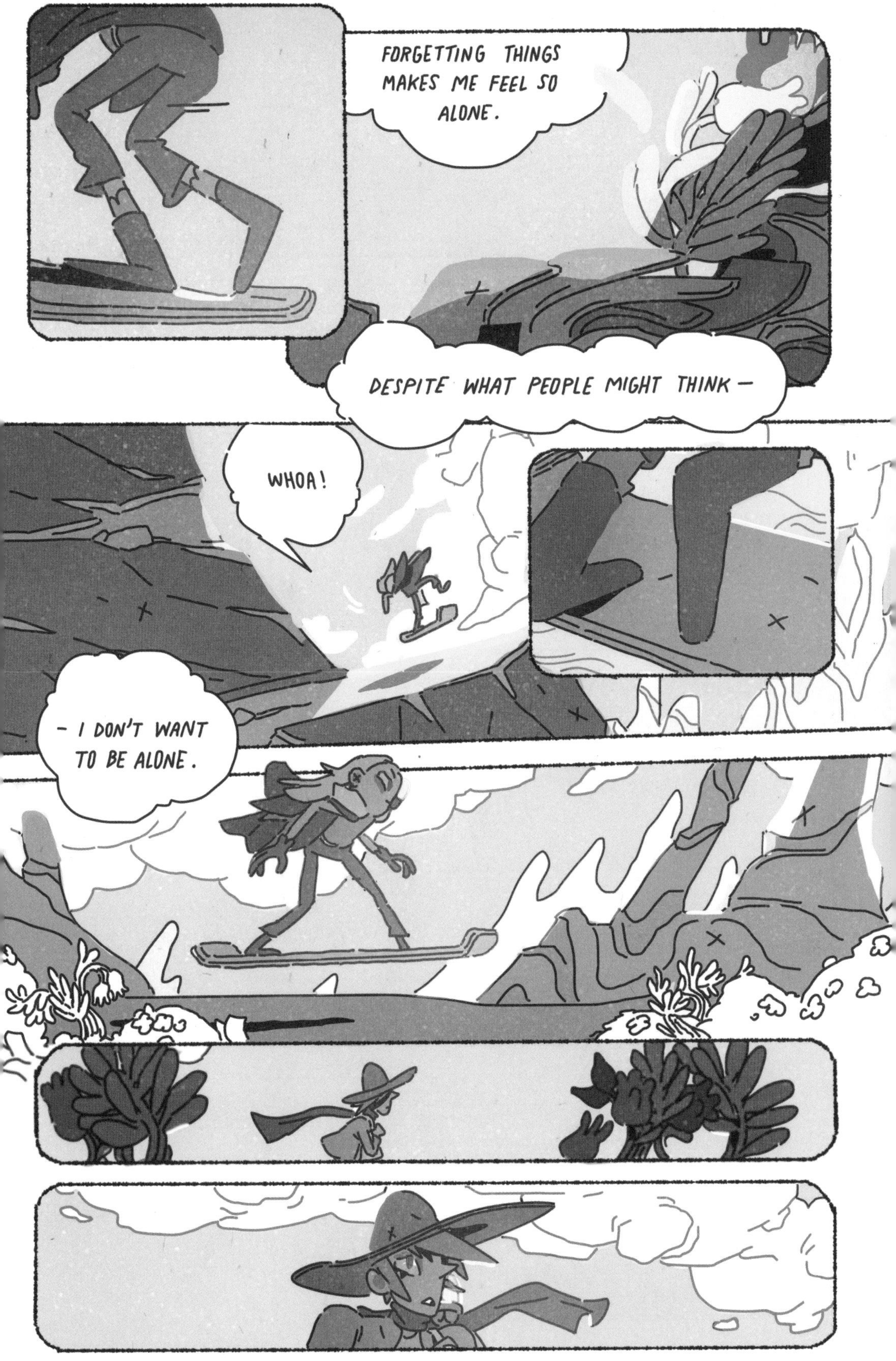
FORGETTING THINGS MAKES ME FEEL SO ALONE.
DESPITE WHAT PEOPLE MIGHT THINK—
WHOA!
—I DON'T WANT TO BE ALONE.

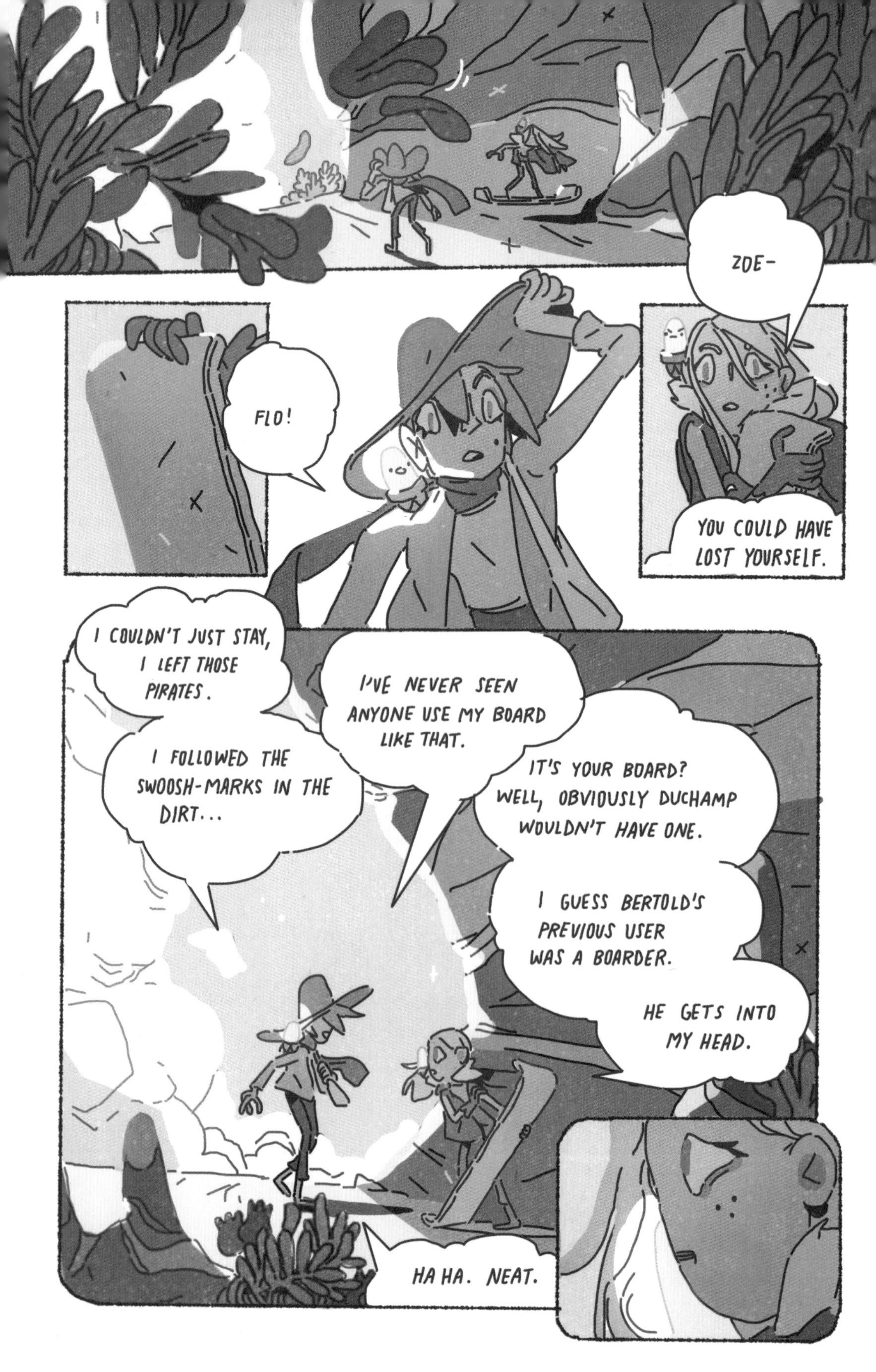
ZOE-
FLO!
YOU COULD HAVE LOST YOURSELF.
I COULDN'T JUST STAY, I LEFT THOSE PIRATES.
I FOLLOWED THE SWOOSH-MARKS IN THE DIRT...
I'VE NEVER SEEN ANYONE USE MY BOARD LIKE THAT.
IT'S YOUR BOARD? WELL, OBVIOUSLY DUCHAMP WOULDN'T HAVE ONE.
I GUESS BERTOLD'S PREVIOUS USER WAS A BOARDER.
HE GETS INTO MY HEAD.
HA HA. NEAT.

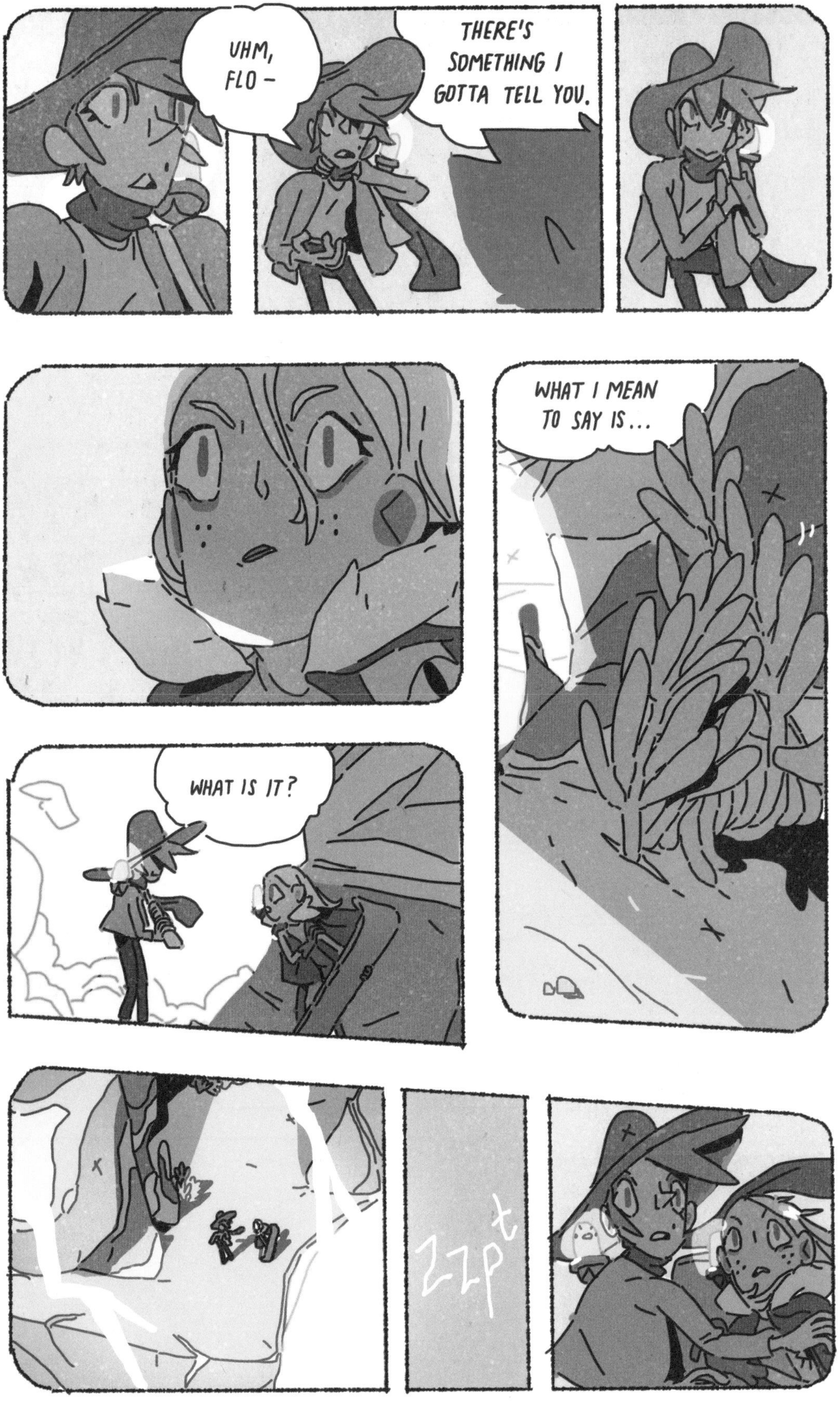
UHM, FLO –
THERE'S SOMETHING I GOTTA TELL YOU.
WHAT I MEAN TO SAY IS...
WHAT IS IT?
ZZPt

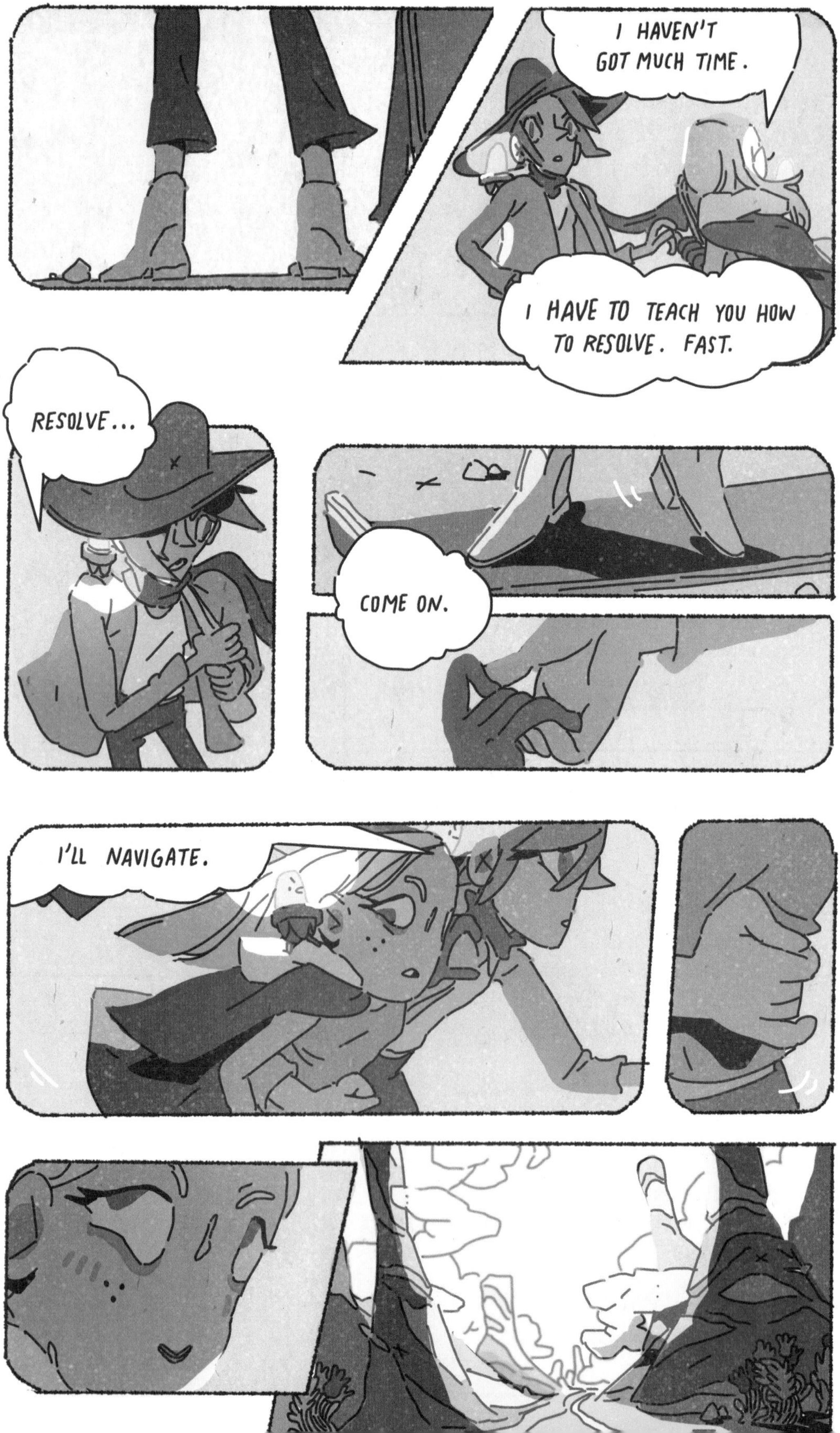
I HAVEN'T GOT MUCH TIME.
I HAVE TO TEACH YOU HOW TO RESOLVE. FAST.
RESOLVE...
COME ON.
I'LL NAVIGATE.

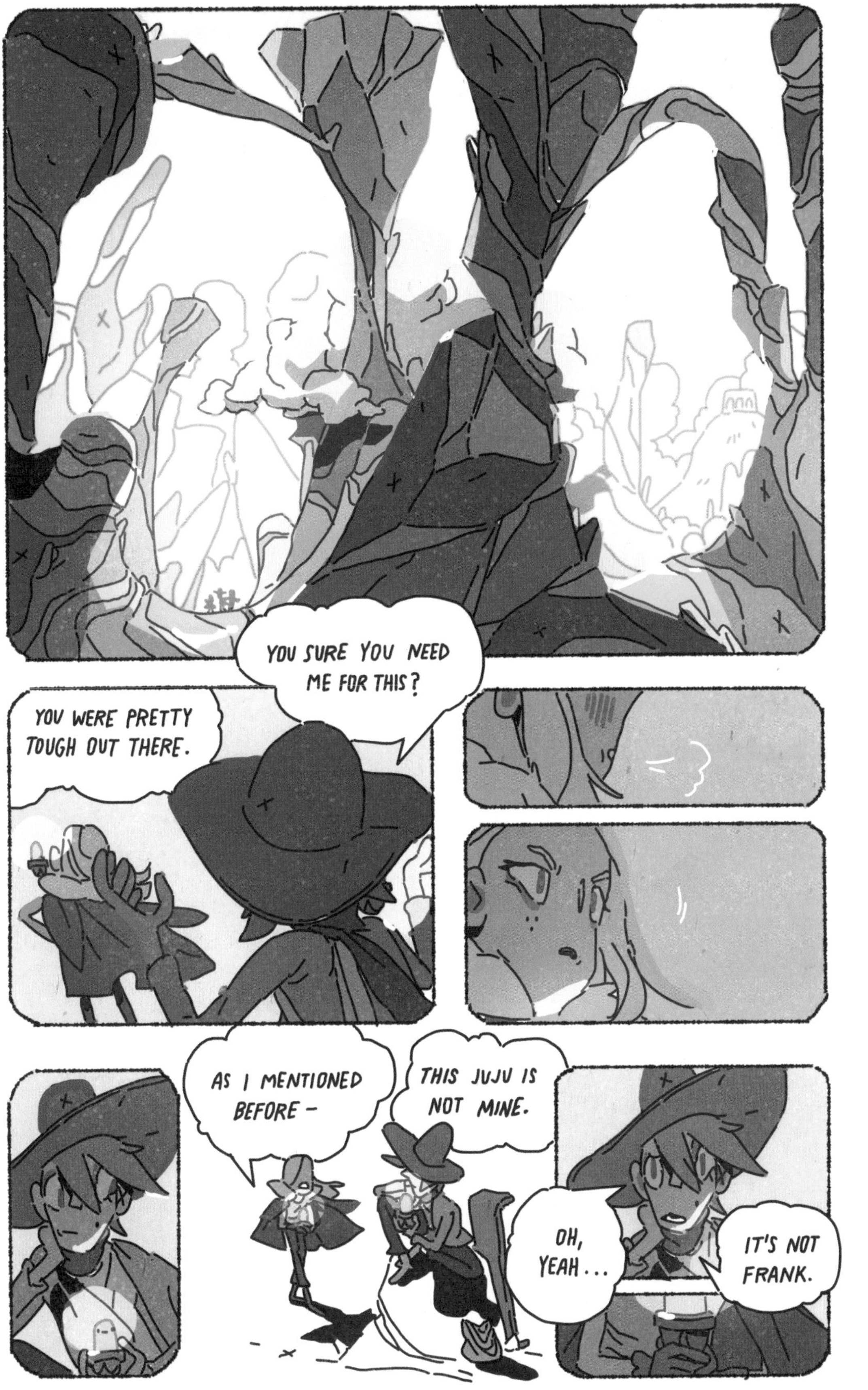

YOU SURE YOU NEED ME FOR THIS?
YOU WERE PRETTY TOUGH OUT THERE.
AS I MENTIONED BEFORE -
THIS JUJU IS NOT MINE.
OH, YEAH...
IT'S NOT FRANK.

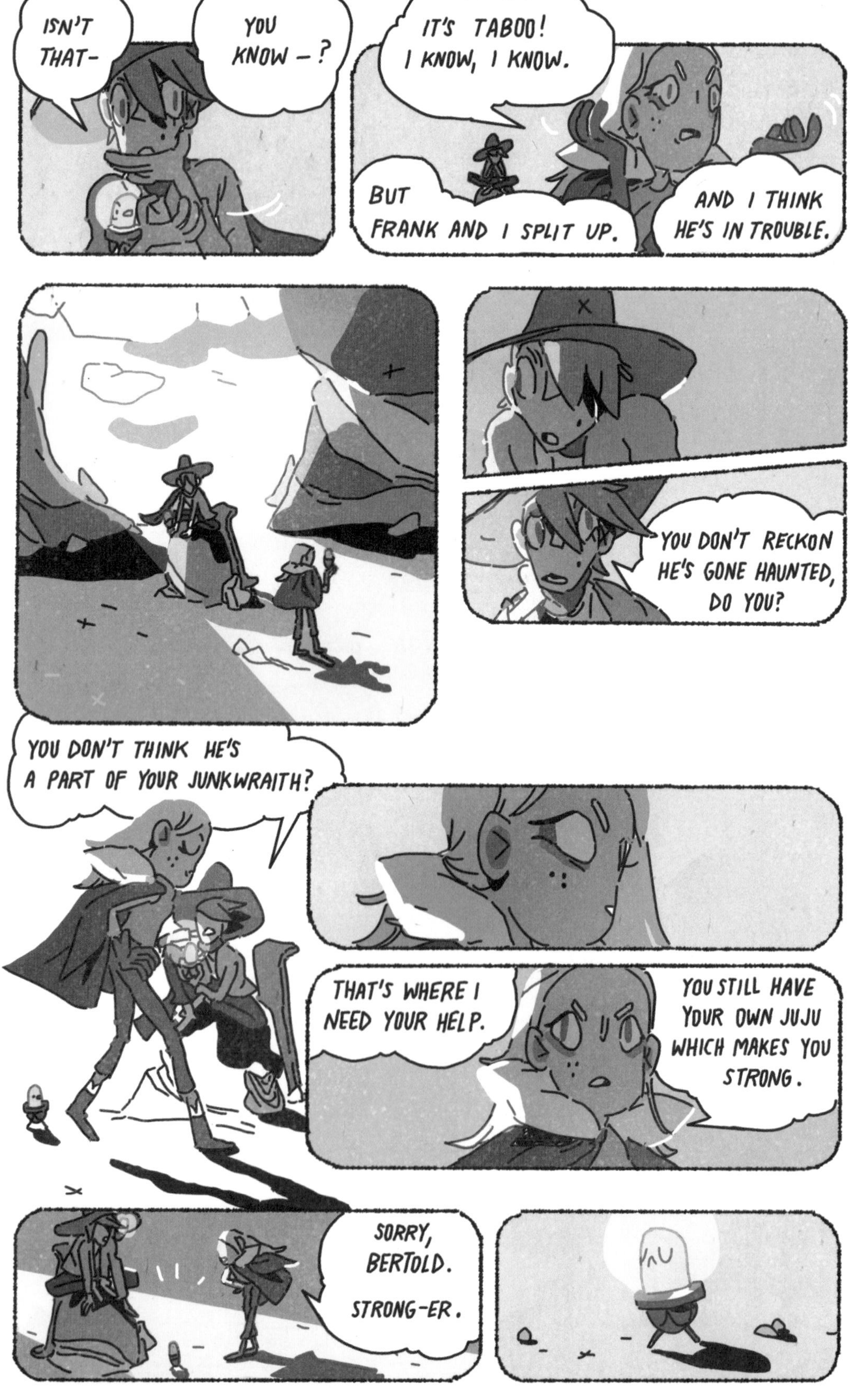
ISN'T THAT-
YOU KNOW -?
IT'S TABOO! I KNOW, I KNOW.
BUT FRANK AND I SPLIT UP.
AND I THINK HE'S IN TROUBLE.
YOU DON'T RECKON HE'S GONE HAUNTED, DO YOU?
YOU DON'T THINK HE'S A PART OF YOUR JUNKWRAITH?
THAT'S WHERE I NEED YOUR HELP.
YOU STILL HAVE YOUR OWN JUJU WHICH MAKES YOU STRONG.
SORRY, BERTOLD.
STRONG-ER.

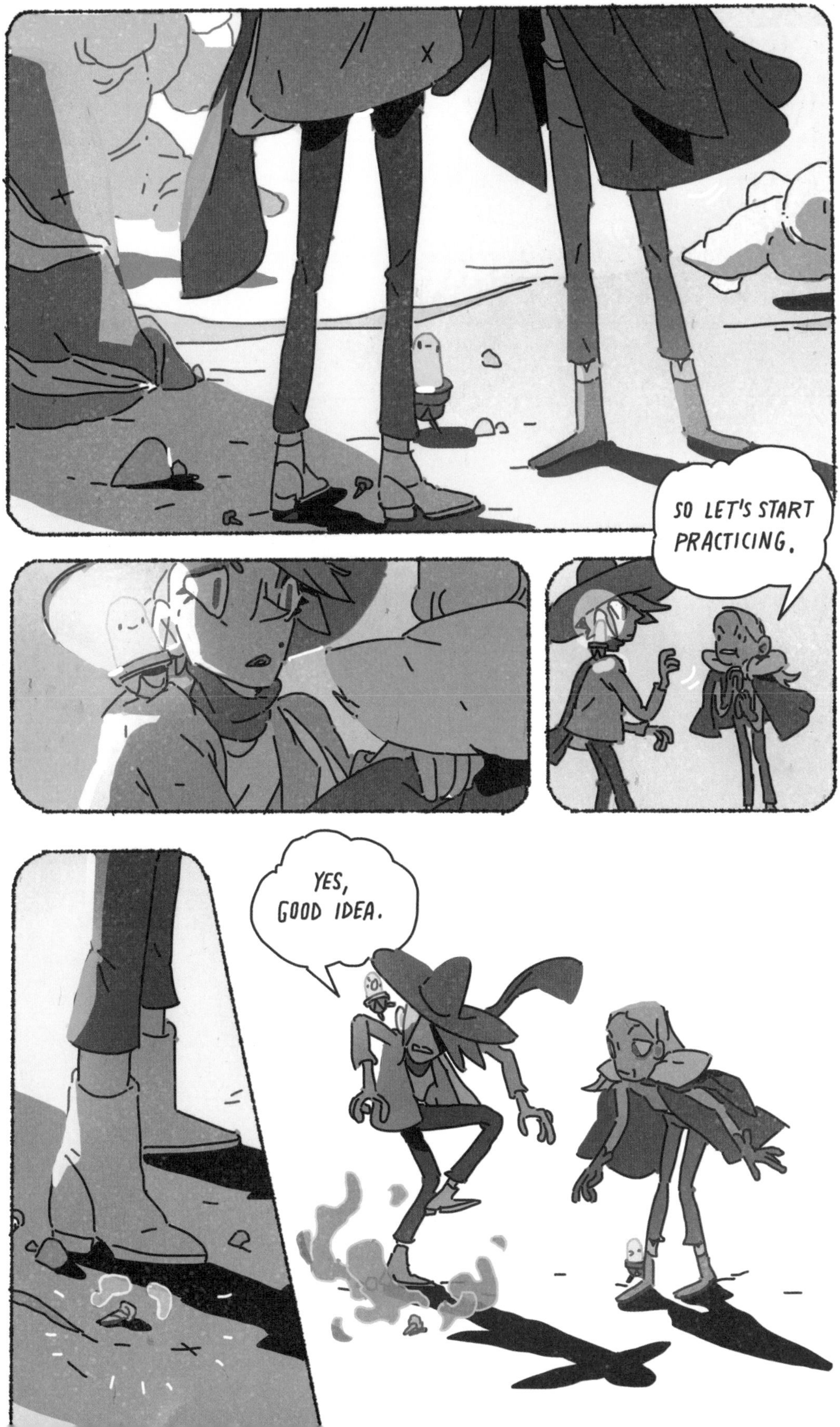
SO LET'S START PRACTICING.
YES, GOOD IDEA.

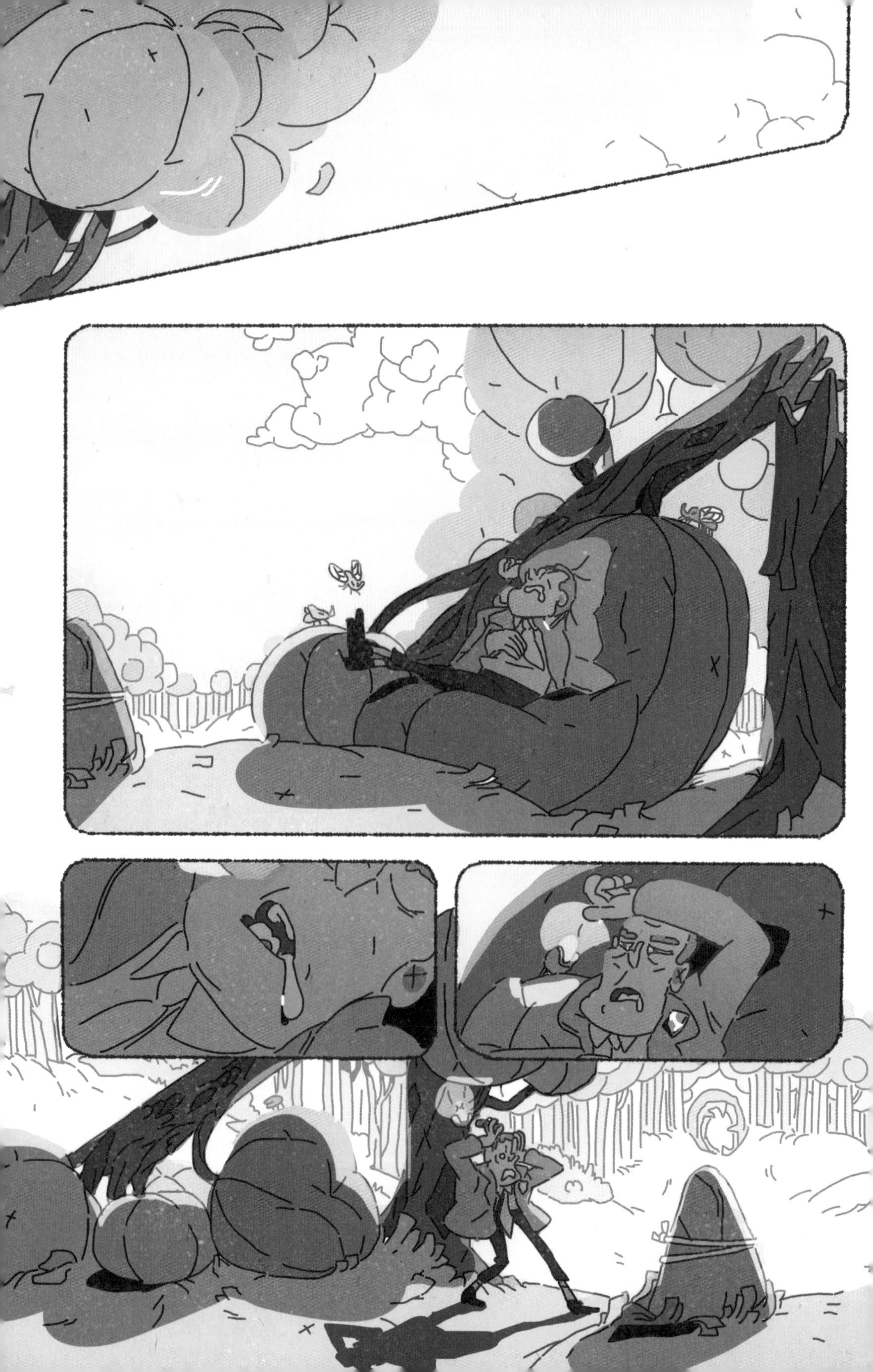

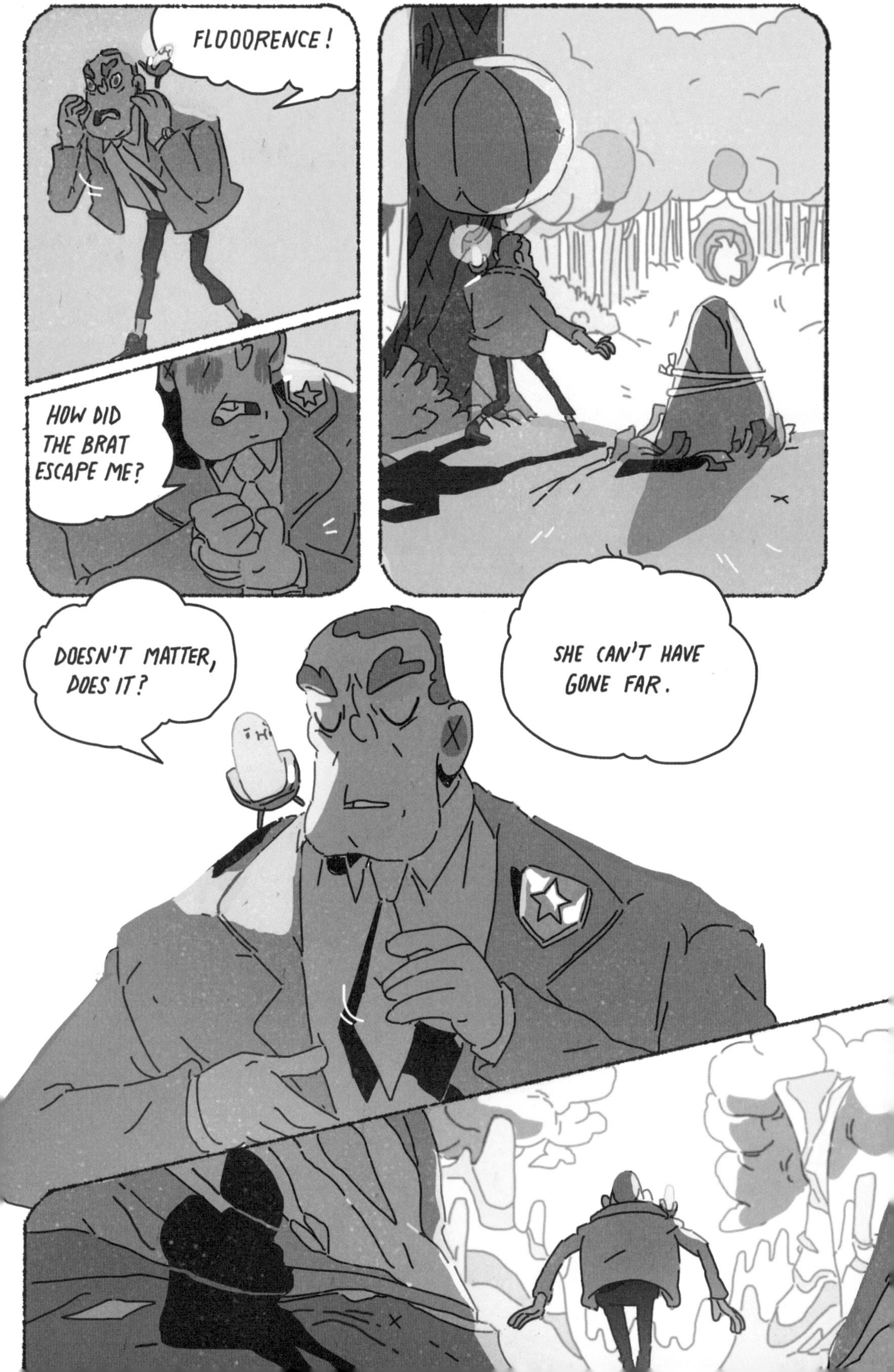
FLOOORENCE!
HOW DID THE BRAT ESCAPE ME?
DOESN'T MATTER, DOES IT?
SHE CAN'T HAVE GONE FAR.

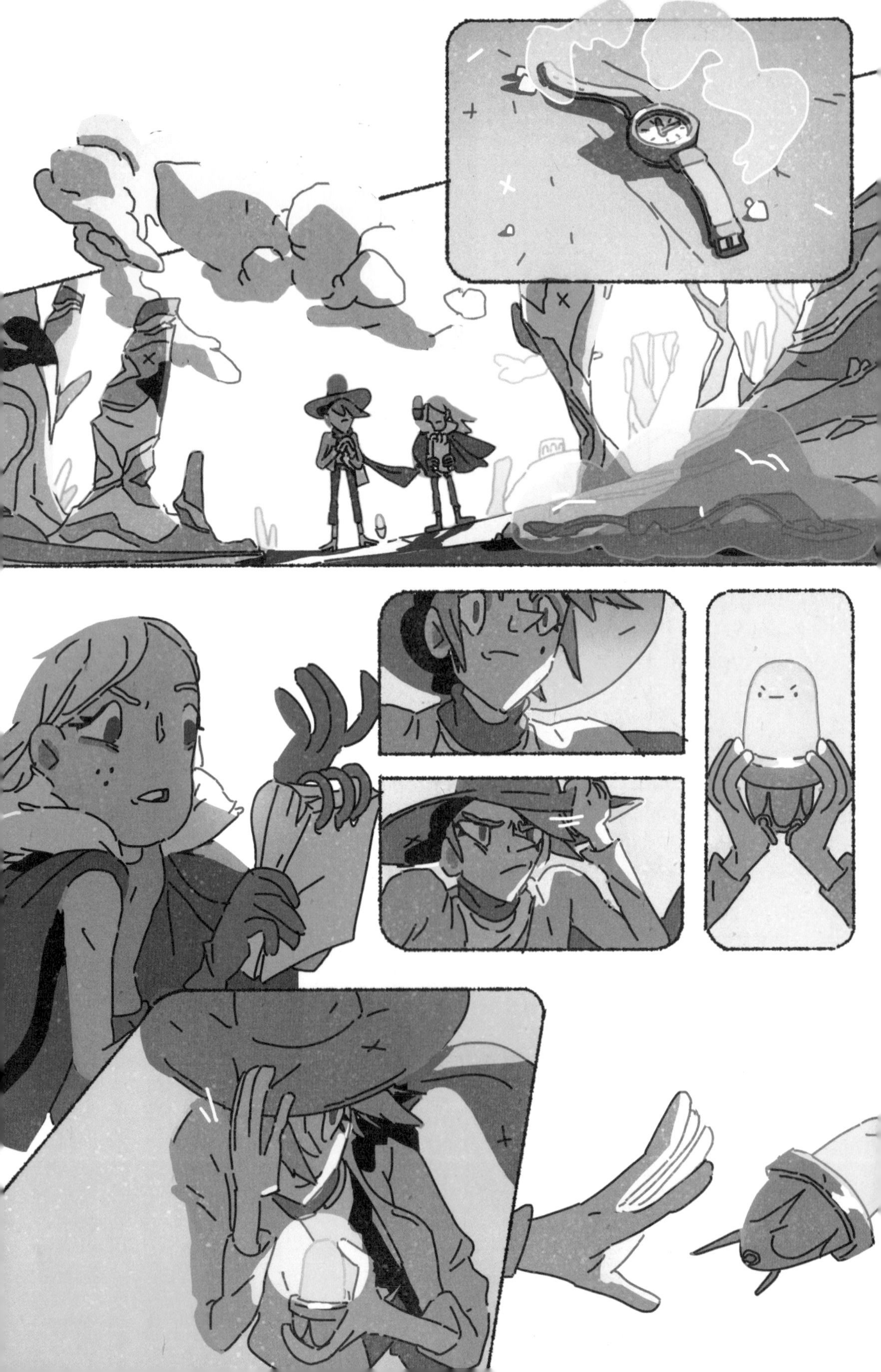

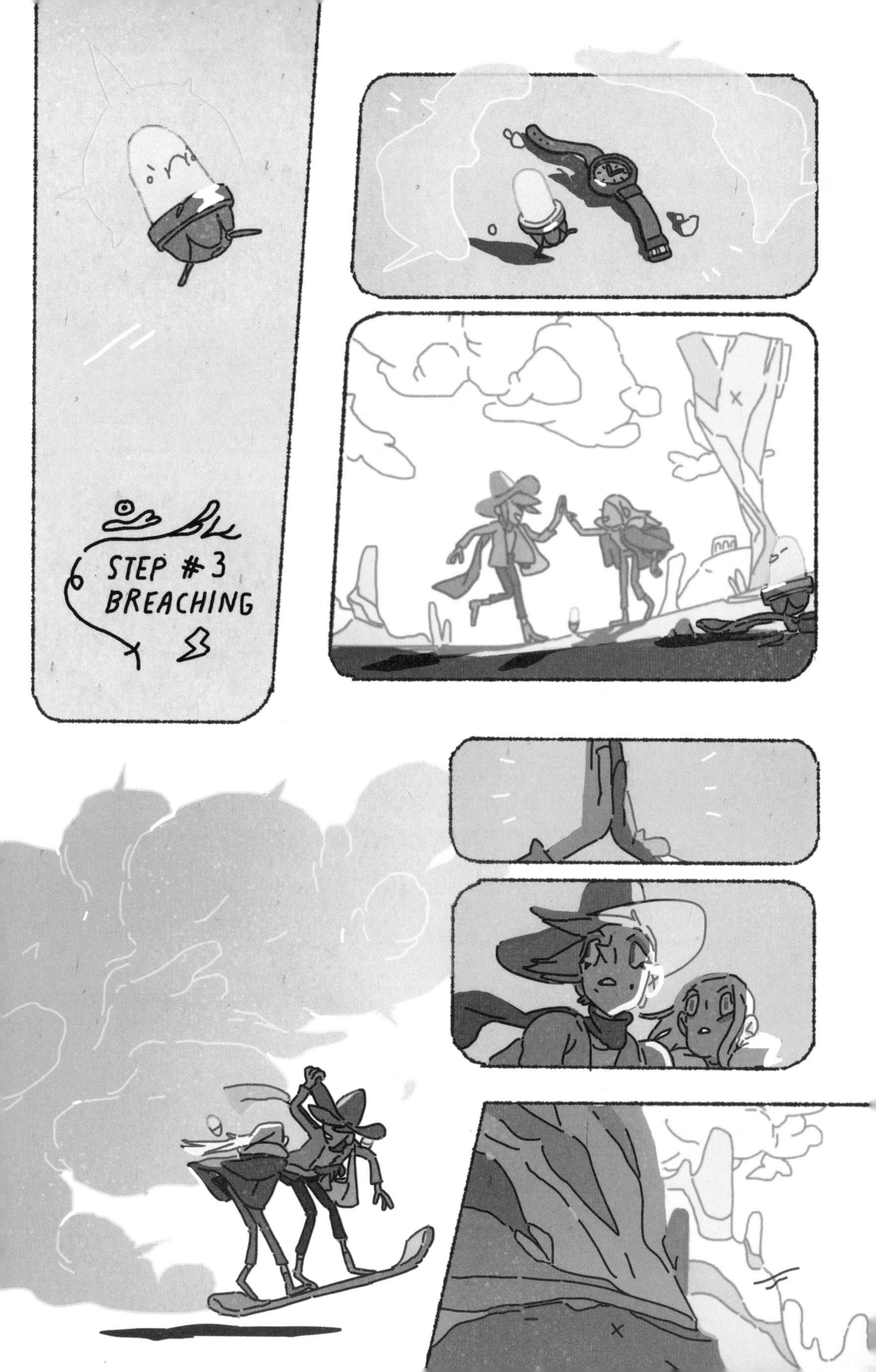
STEP #3
BREACHING

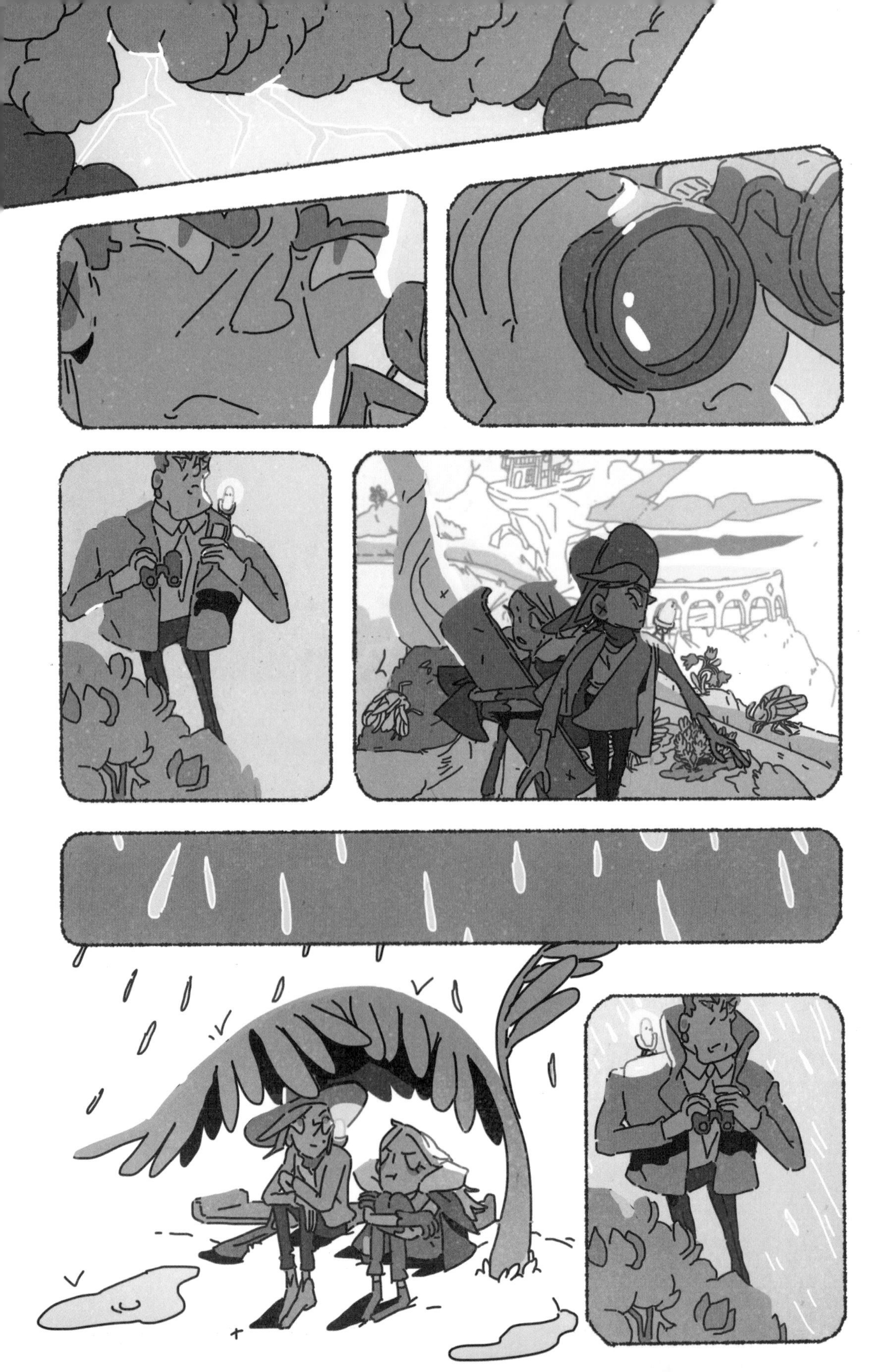

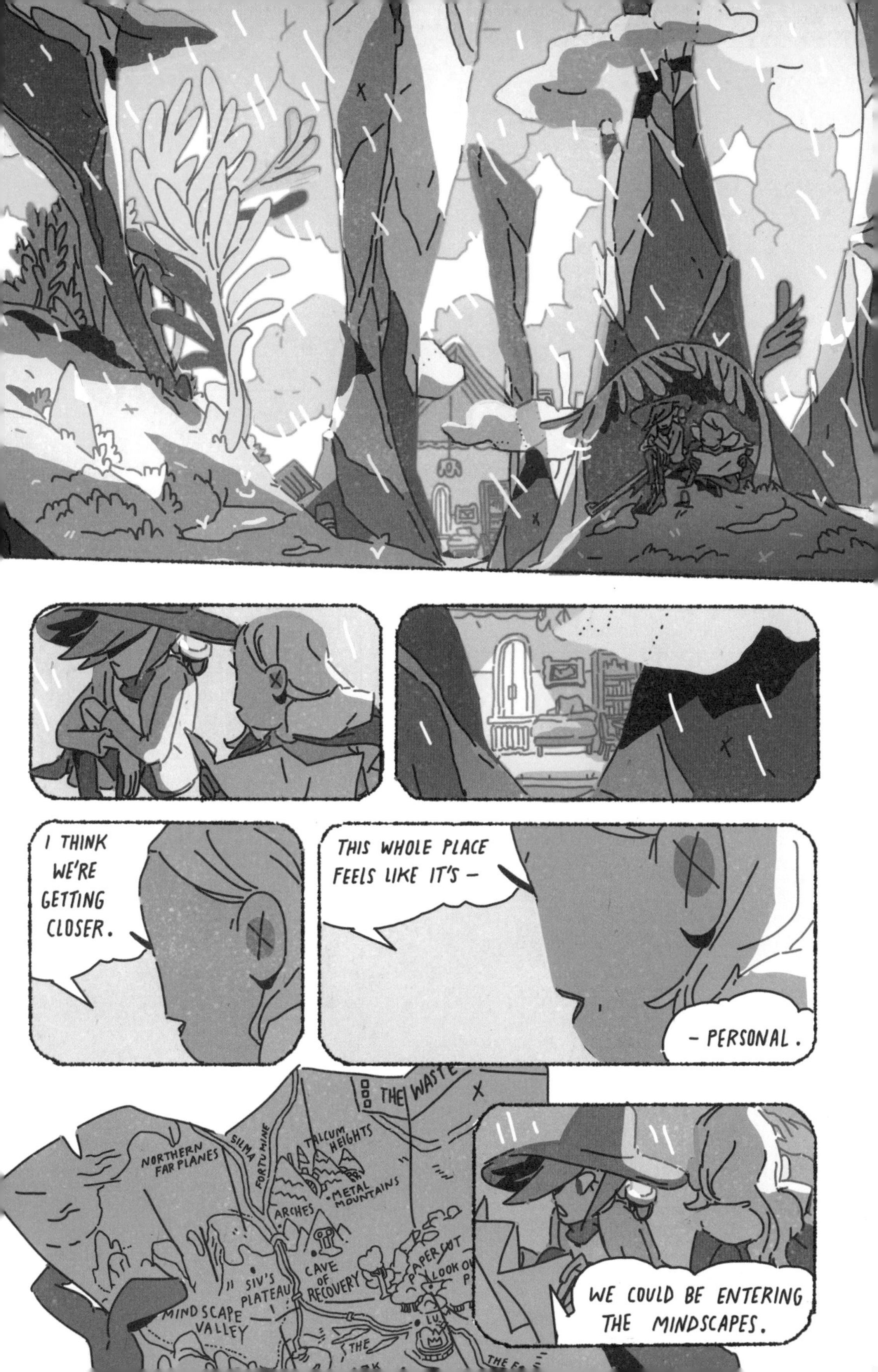
I THINK WE'RE GETTING CLOSER.
THIS WHOLE PLACE FEELS LIKE IT'S –
– PERSONAL.
THE WASTE
NORTHERN FAR PLANES
SILMA
FORTUMINE
TALCUM HEIGHTS
METAL MOUNTAINS
ARCHES
SIV'S PLATEAU
CAVE OF RECOVERY
PAPERCUT
MINDSCAPE VALLEY
WE COULD BE ENTERING THE MINDSCAPES.

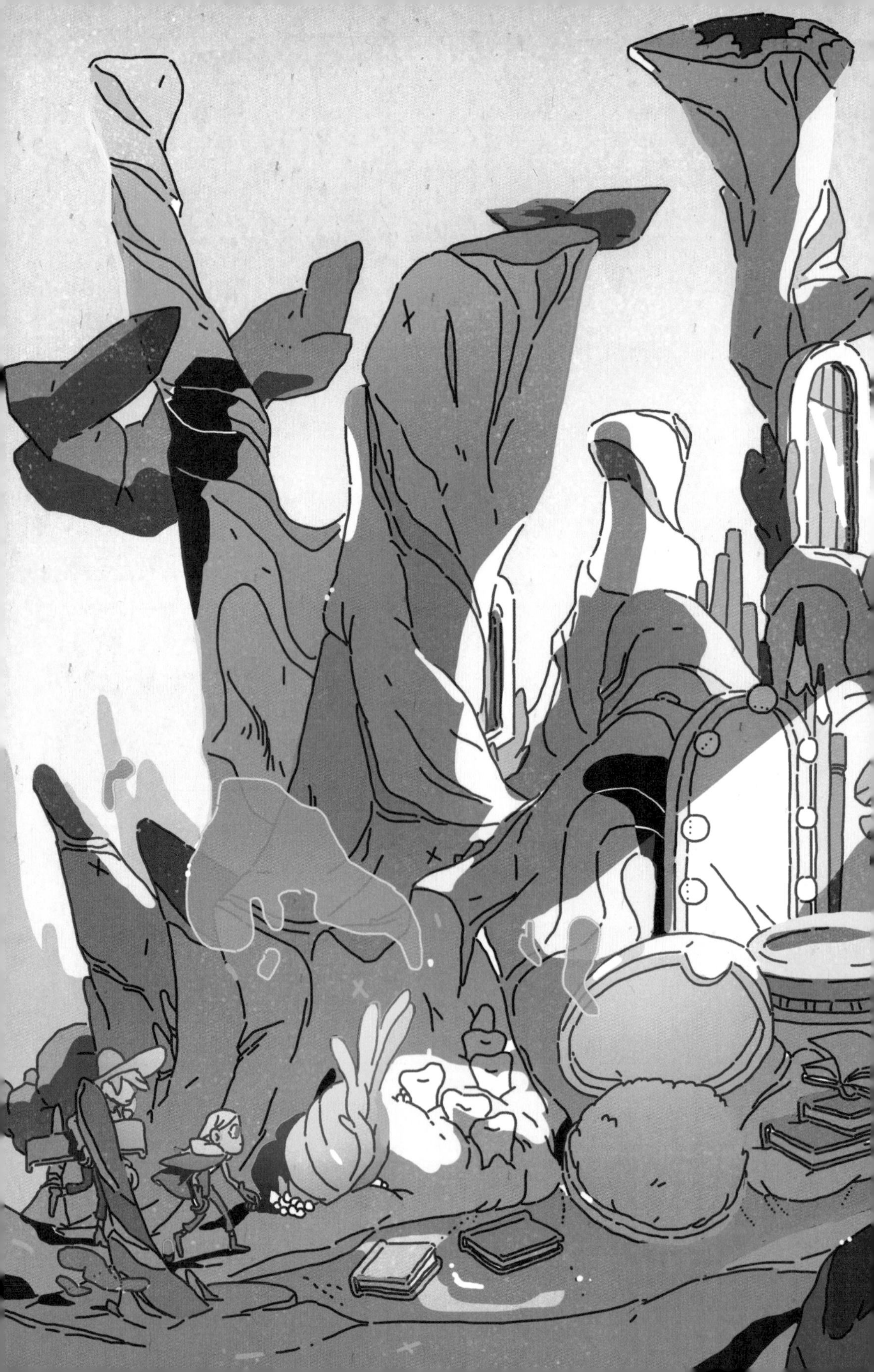

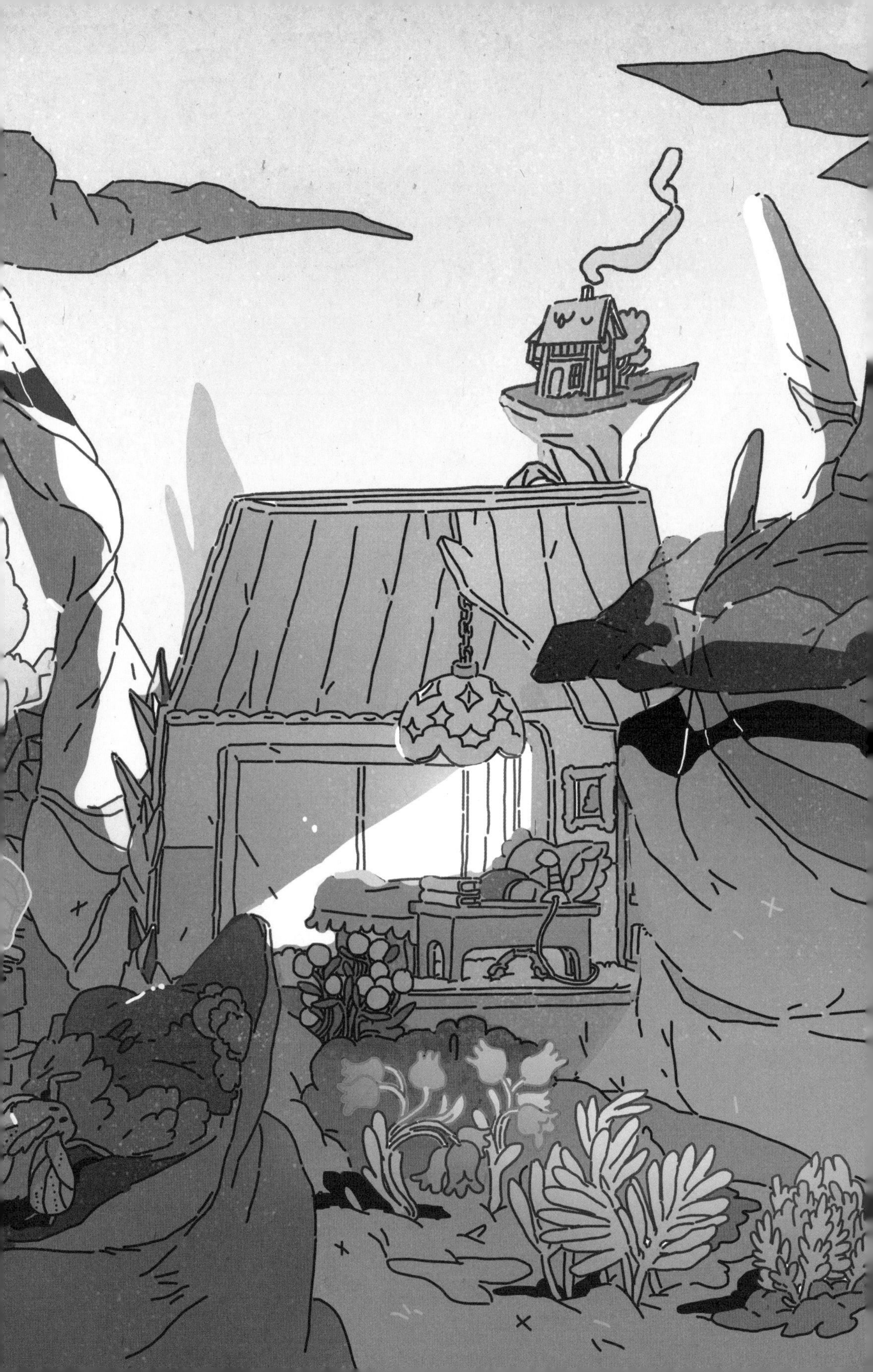

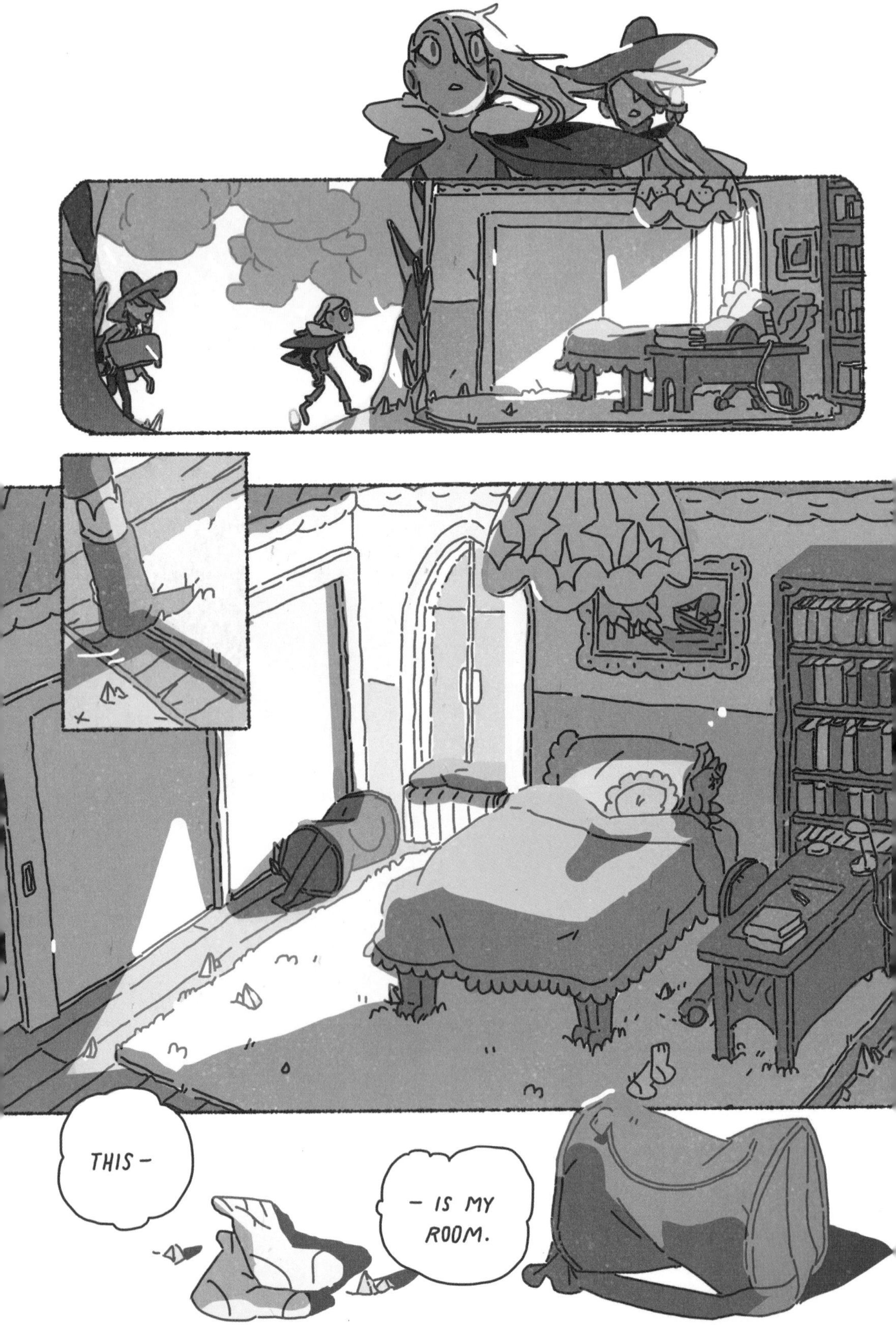
THIS -
- IS MY ROOM.

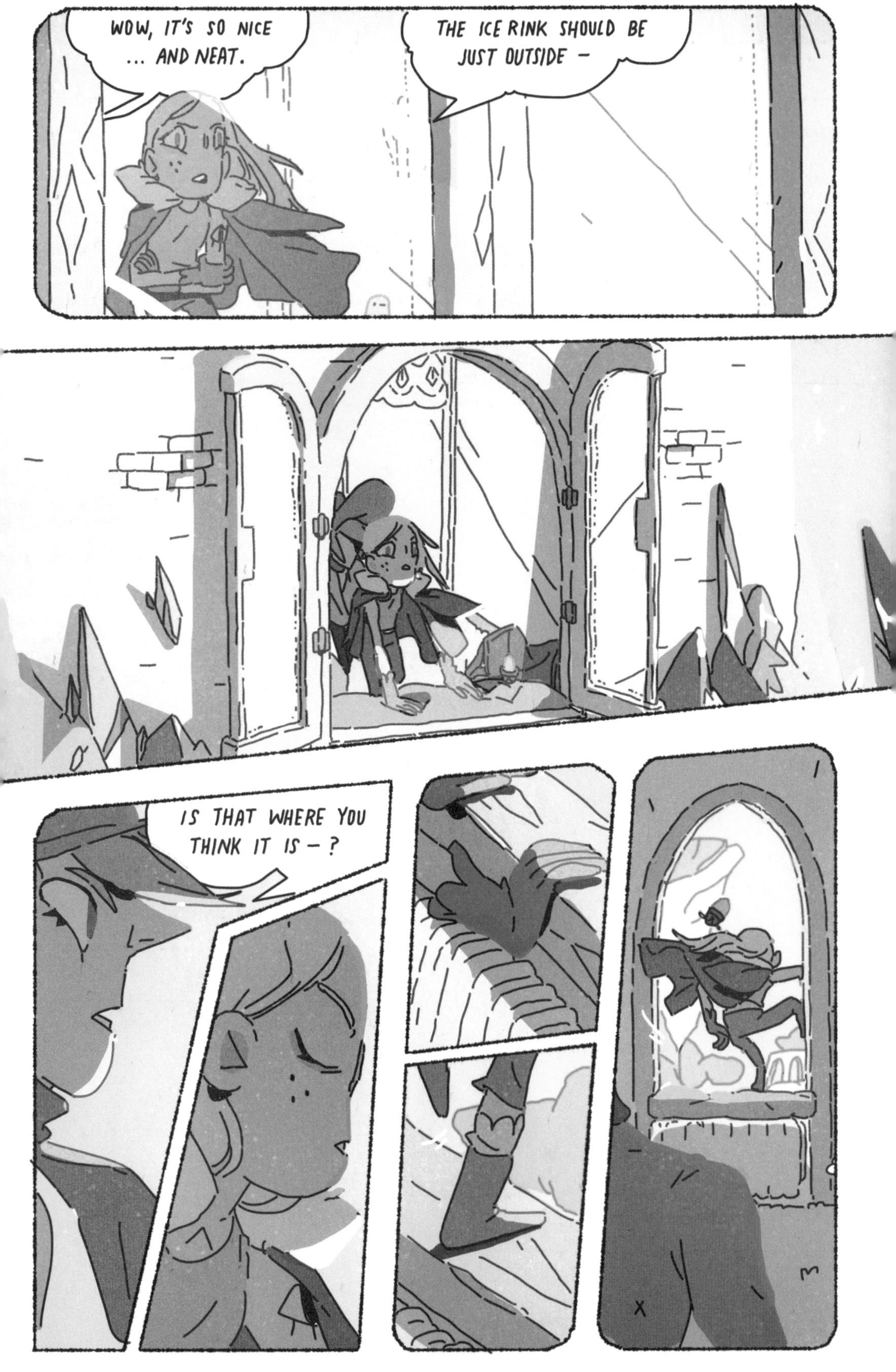
WOW, IT'S SO NICE ... AND NEAT.
THE ICE RINK SHOULD BE JUST OUTSIDE –
IS THAT WHERE YOU THINK IT IS – ?

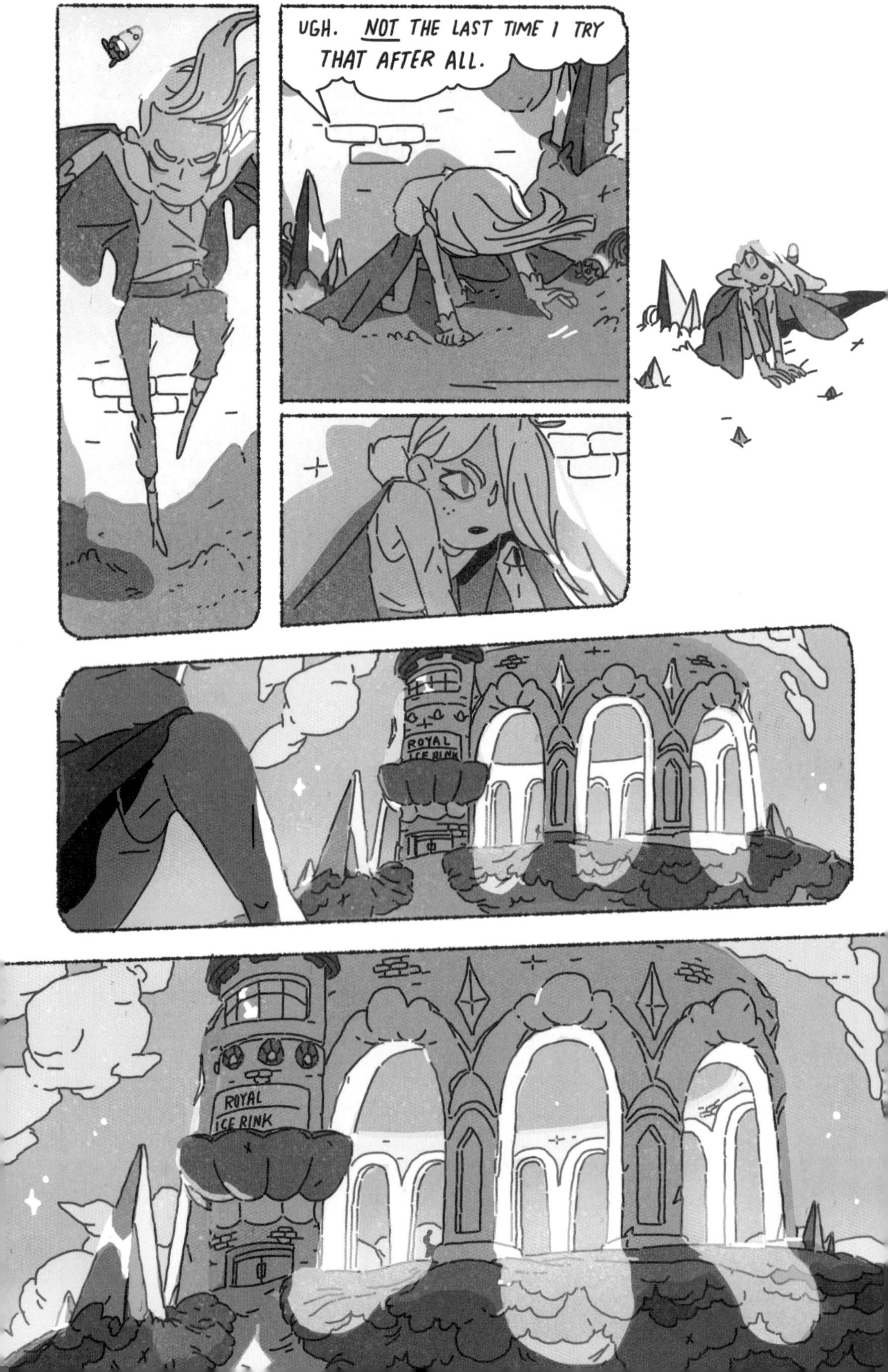
UGH. NOT THE LAST TIME I TRY THAT AFTER ALL.
ROYAL ICE RINK
ROYAL ICE RINK

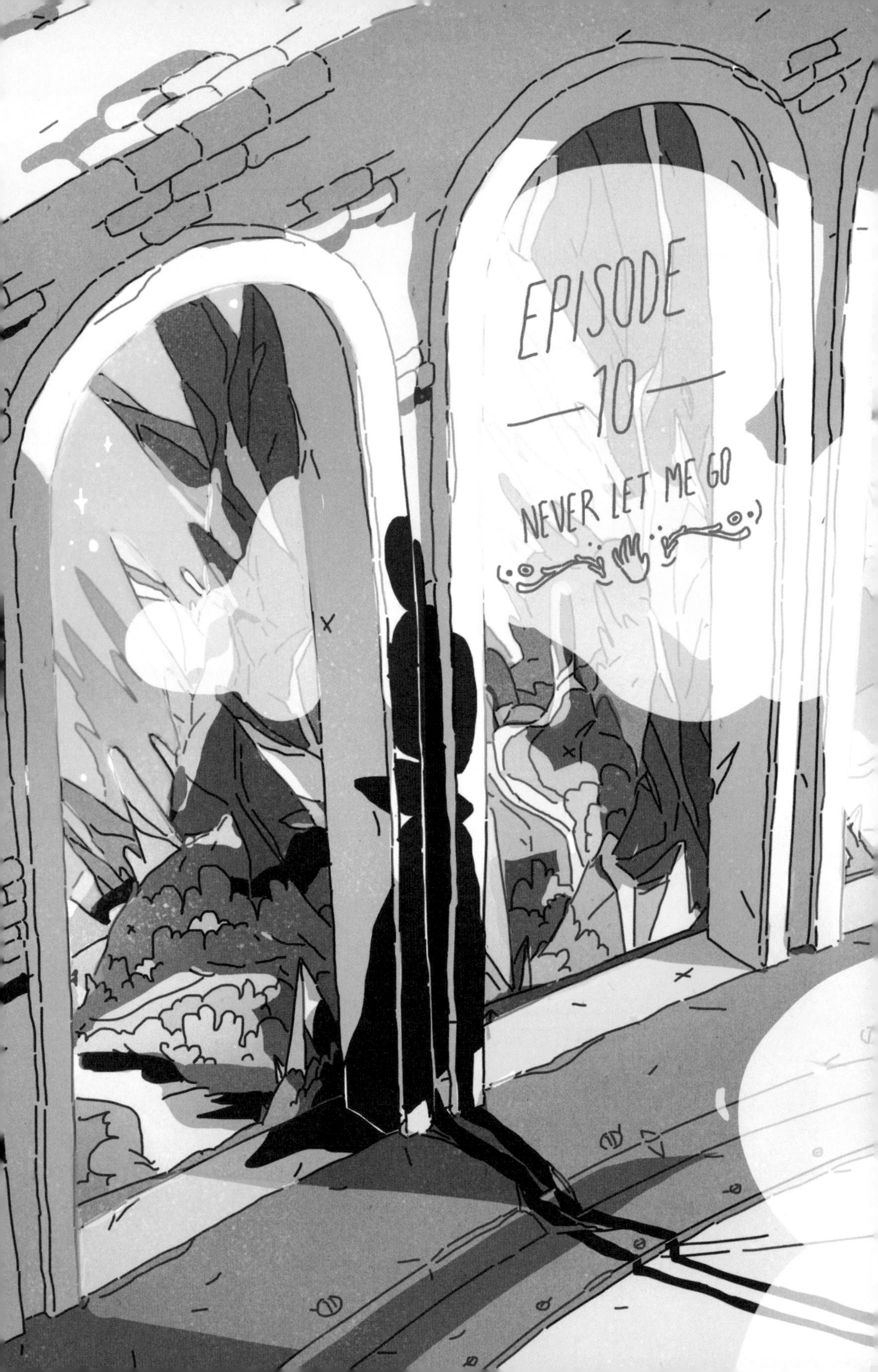
EPISODE
10
NEVER LET ME GO

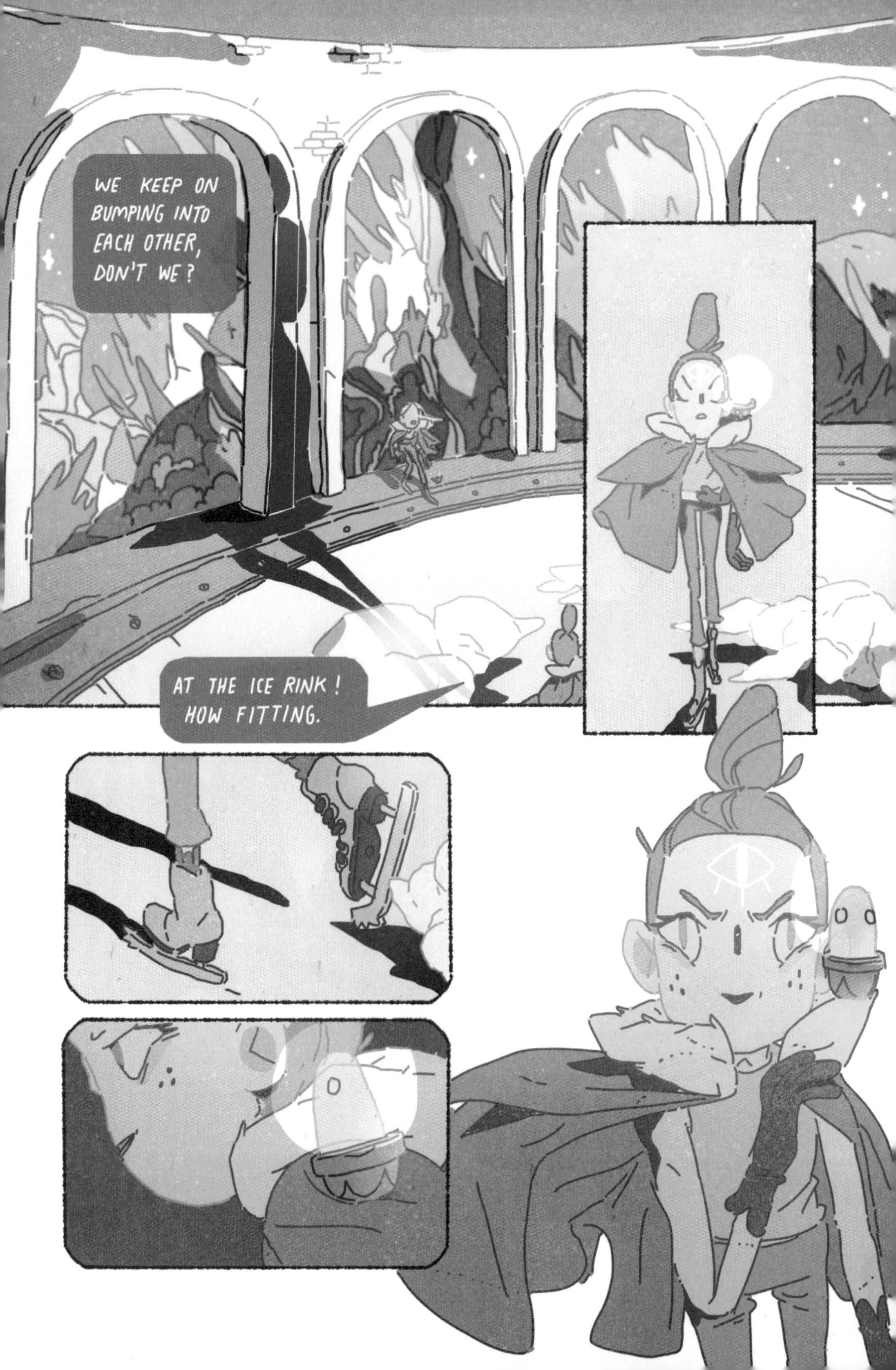
WE KEEP ON BUMPING INTO EACH OTHER, DON'T WE?
AT THE ICE RINK! HOW FITTING.

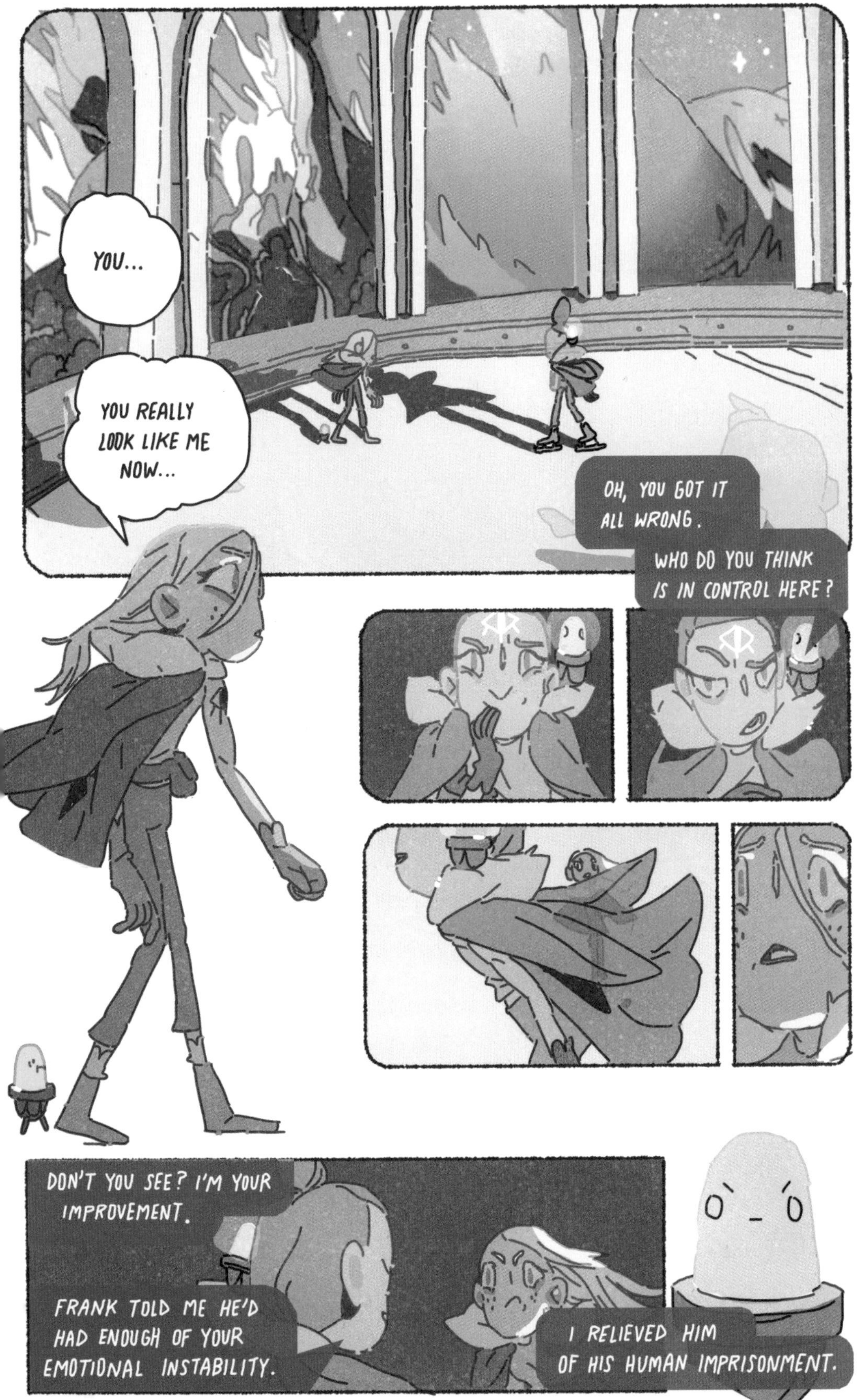
YOU...
YOU REALLY LOOK LIKE ME NOW...
OH, YOU GOT IT ALL WRONG.
WHO DO YOU THINK IS IN CONTROL HERE?
DON'T YOU SEE? I'M YOUR IMPROVEMENT.
FRANK TOLD ME HE'D HAD ENOUGH OF YOUR EMOTIONAL INSTABILITY.
I RELIEVED HIM OF HIS HUMAN IMPRISONMENT.

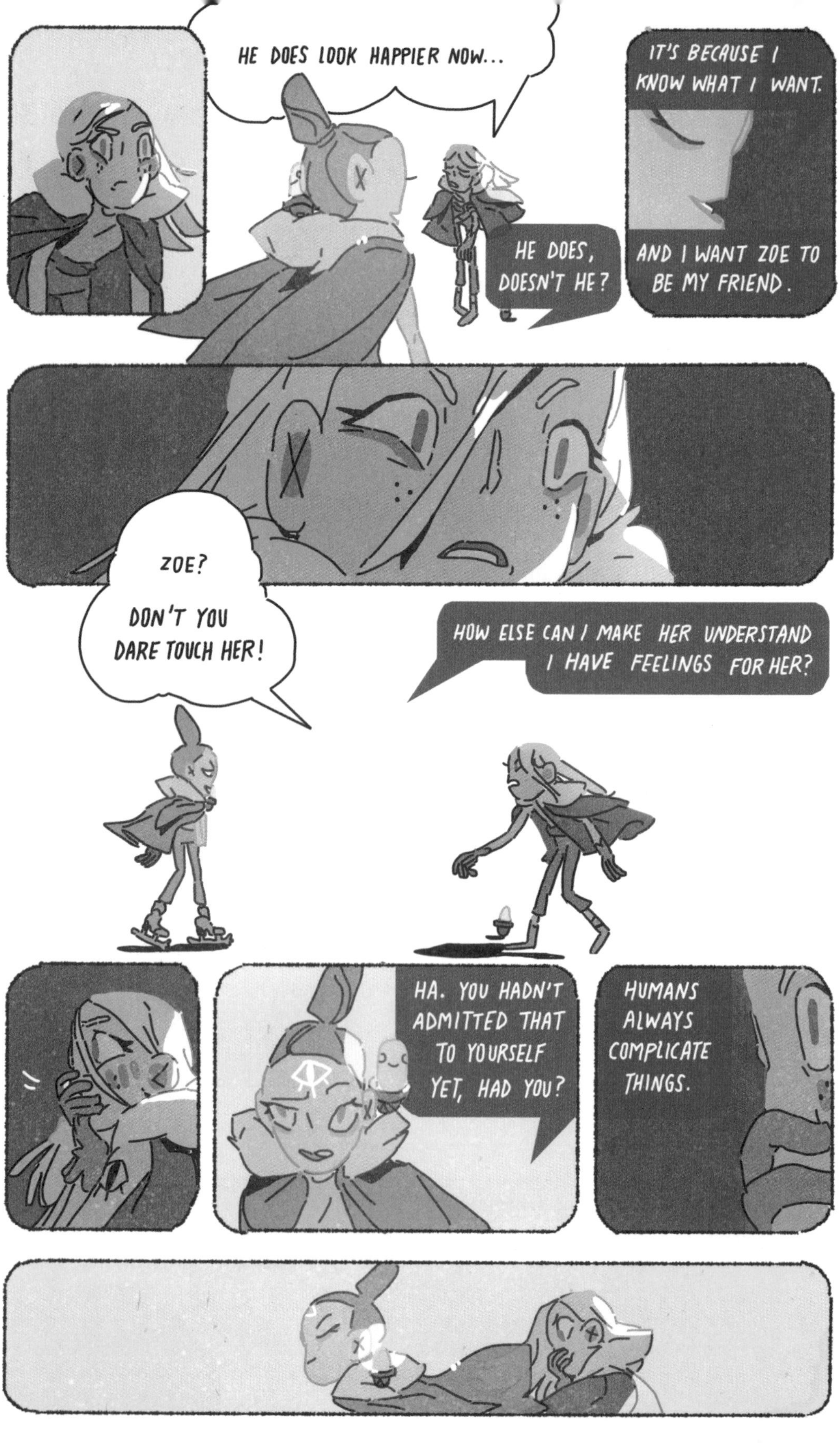
HE DOES LOOK HAPPIER NOW...
HE DOES, DOESN'T HE?
IT'S BECAUSE I KNOW WHAT I WANT.
AND I WANT ZOE TO BE MY FRIEND.
ZOE?
DON'T YOU DARE TOUCH HER!
HOW ELSE CAN I MAKE HER UNDERSTAND I HAVE FEELINGS FOR HER?
HA. YOU HADN'T ADMITTED THAT TO YOURSELF YET, HAD YOU?
HUMANS ALWAYS COMPLICATE THINGS.

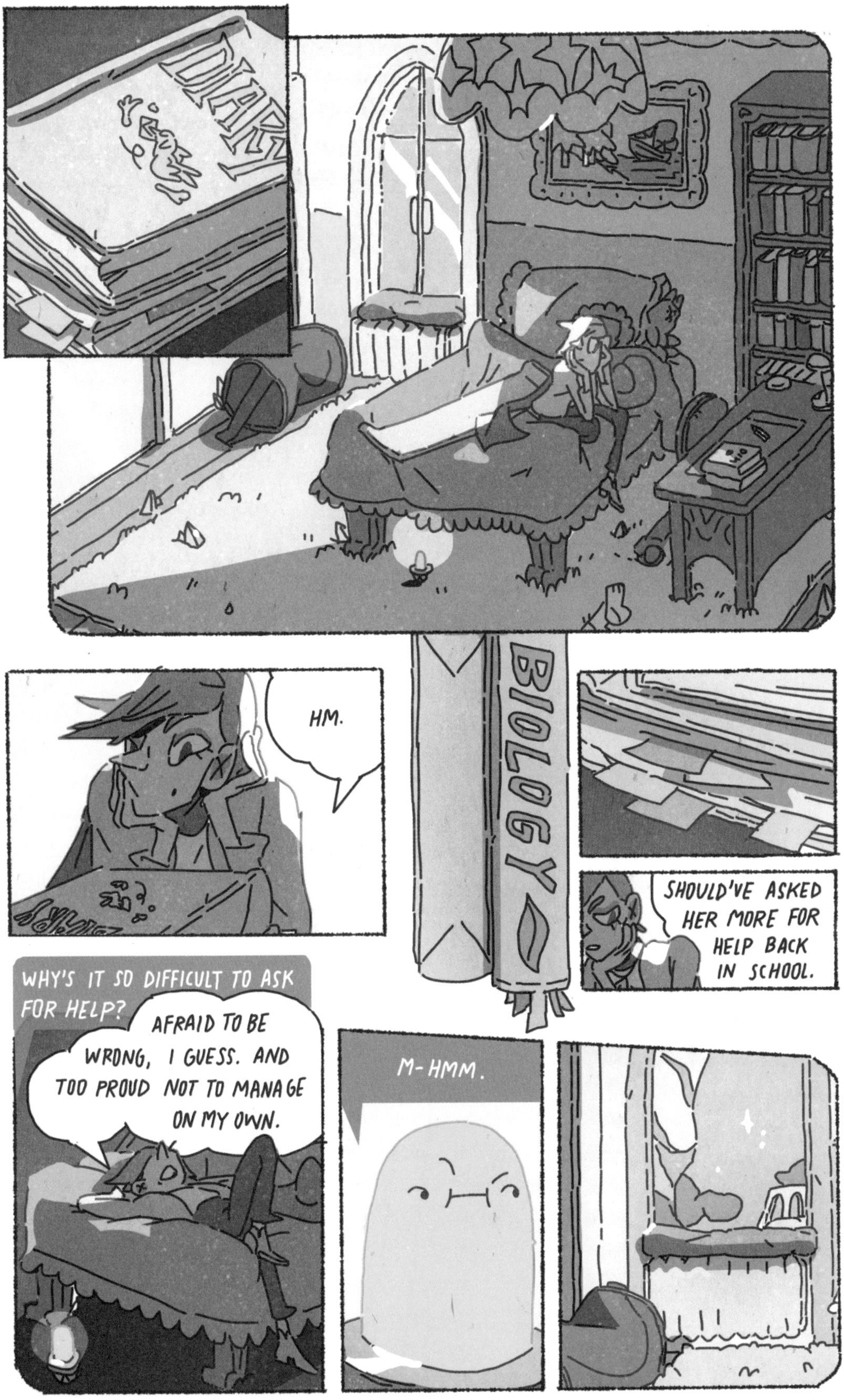
DIARY
BIOLOGY
HM.
SHOULD'VE ASKED HER MORE FOR HELP BACK IN SCHOOL.
WHY'S IT SO DIFFICULT TO ASK FOR HELP?
AFRAID TO BE WRONG, I GUESS. AND TOO PROUD NOT TO MANAGE ON MY OWN.
M-HMM.

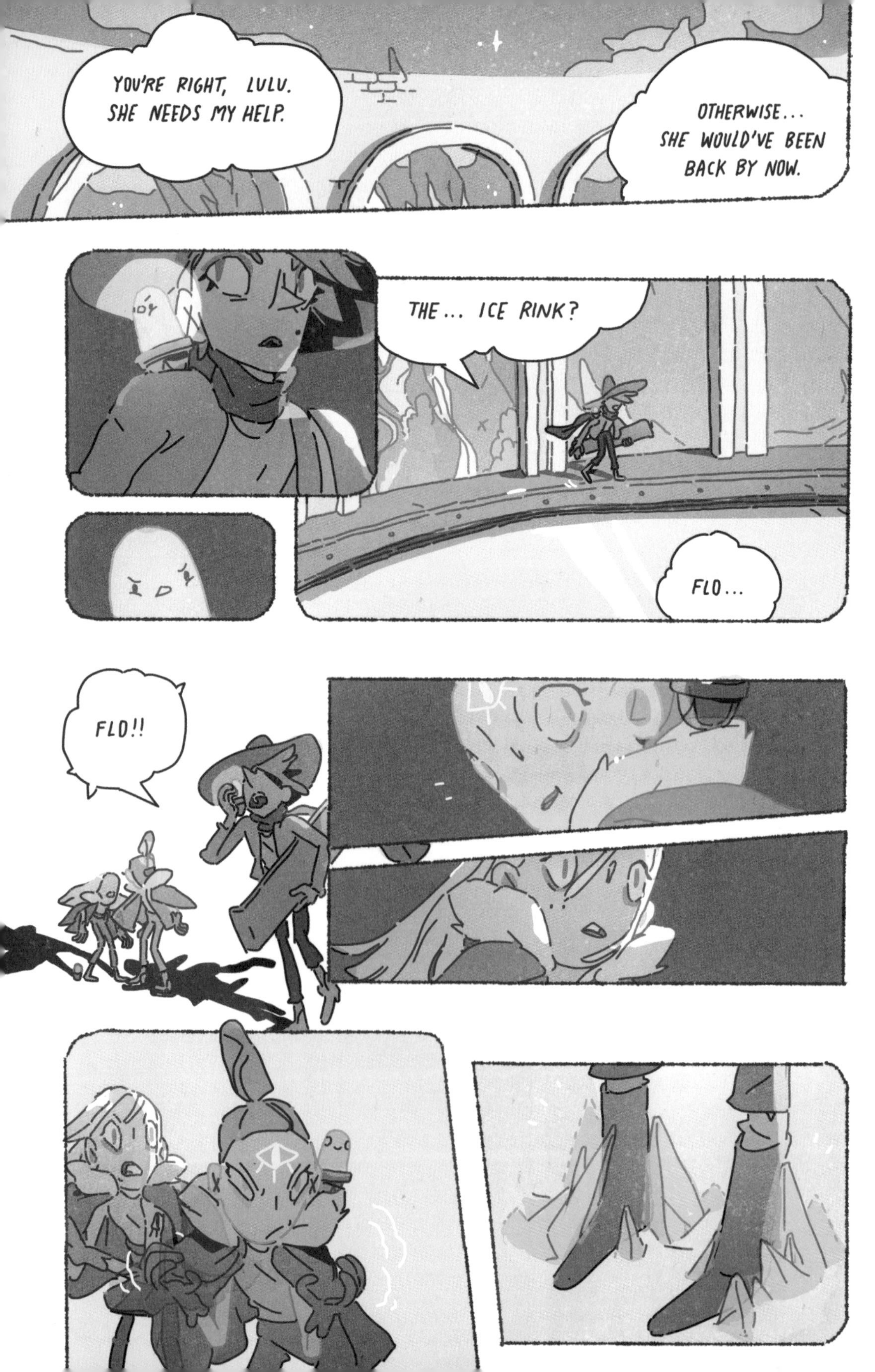
YOU'RE RIGHT, LULU. SHE NEEDS MY HELP.
OTHERWISE... SHE WOULD'VE BEEN BACK BY NOW.
THE... ICE RINK?
FLO...
FLO!!

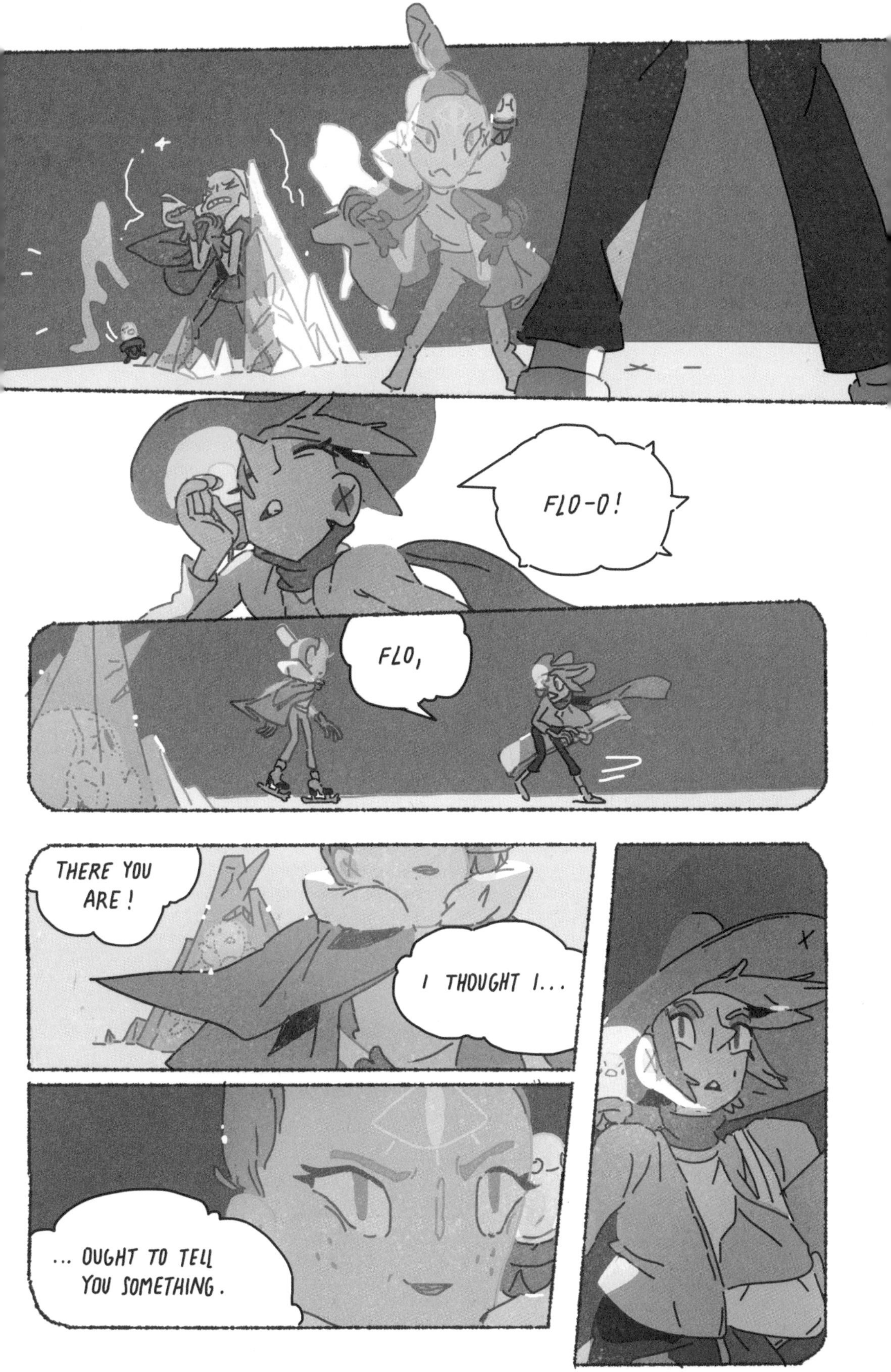
FLO-O!
FLO,
THERE YOU ARE!
I THOUGHT I...
... OUGHT TO TELL YOU SOMETHING.

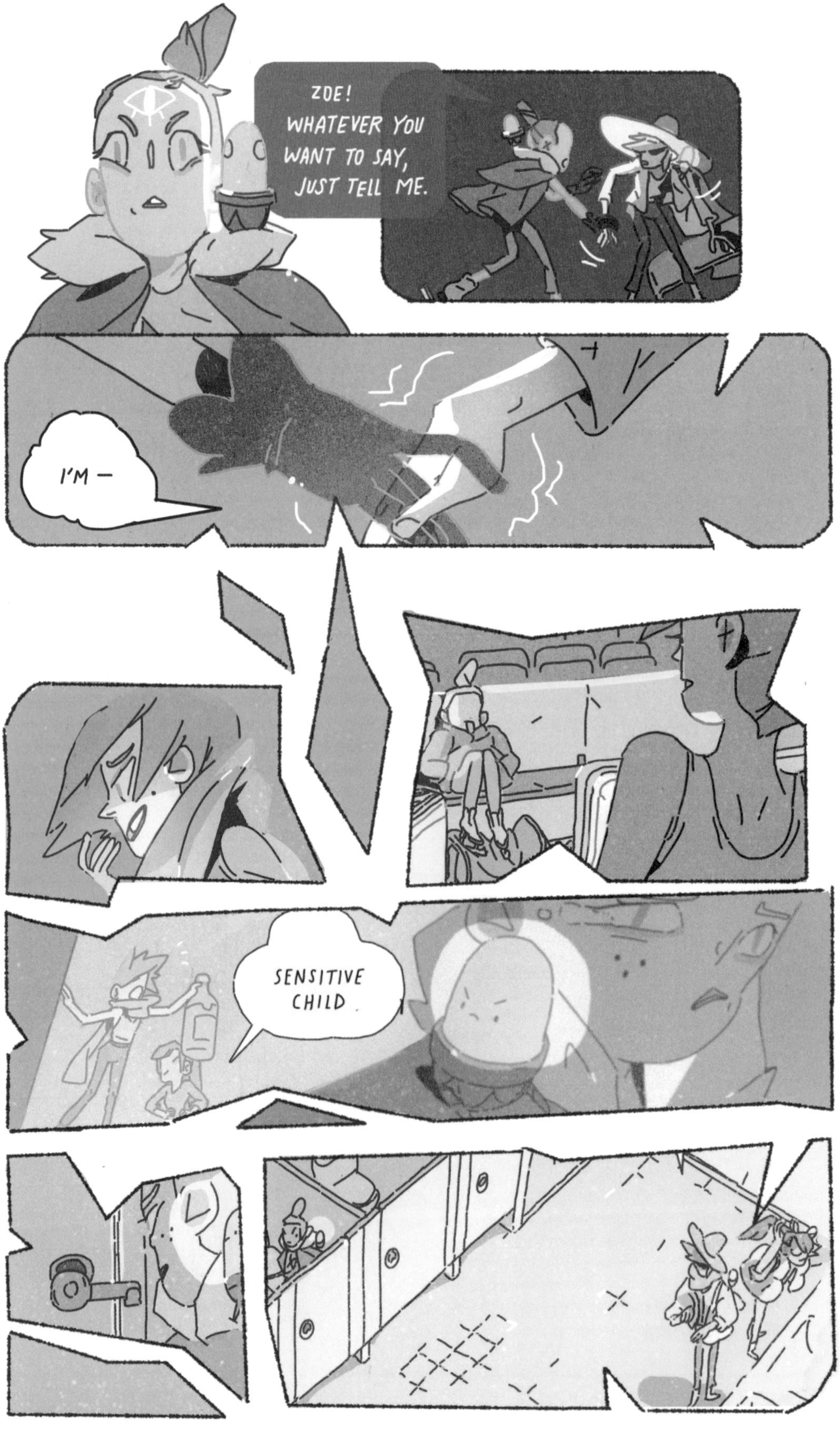
ZOE! WHATEVER YOU WANT TO SAY, JUST TELL ME.
I'M —
SENSITIVE CHILD.

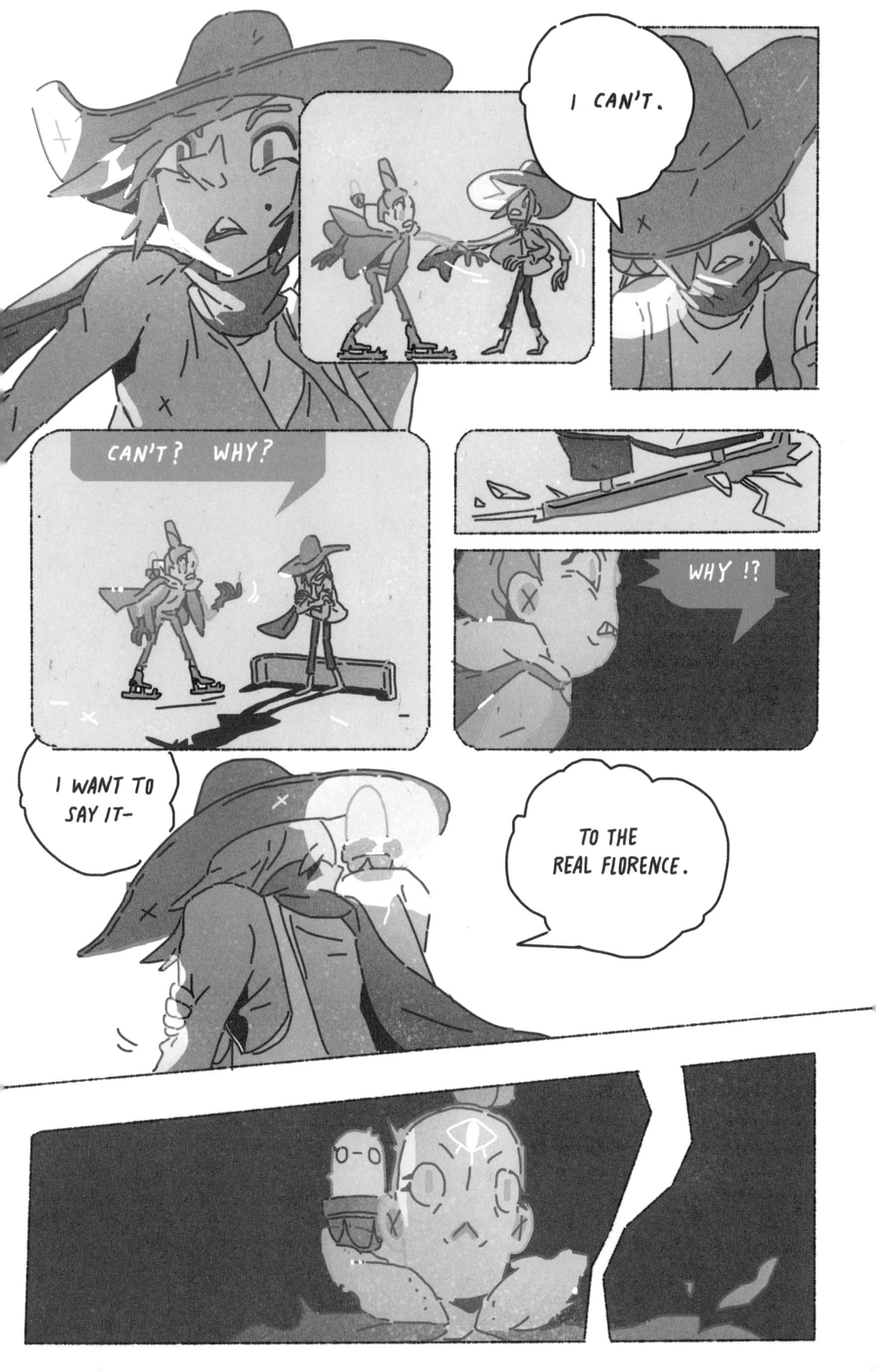
I CAN'T.
CAN'T? WHY?
WHY!?
I WANT TO SAY IT-
TO THE REAL FLORENCE.

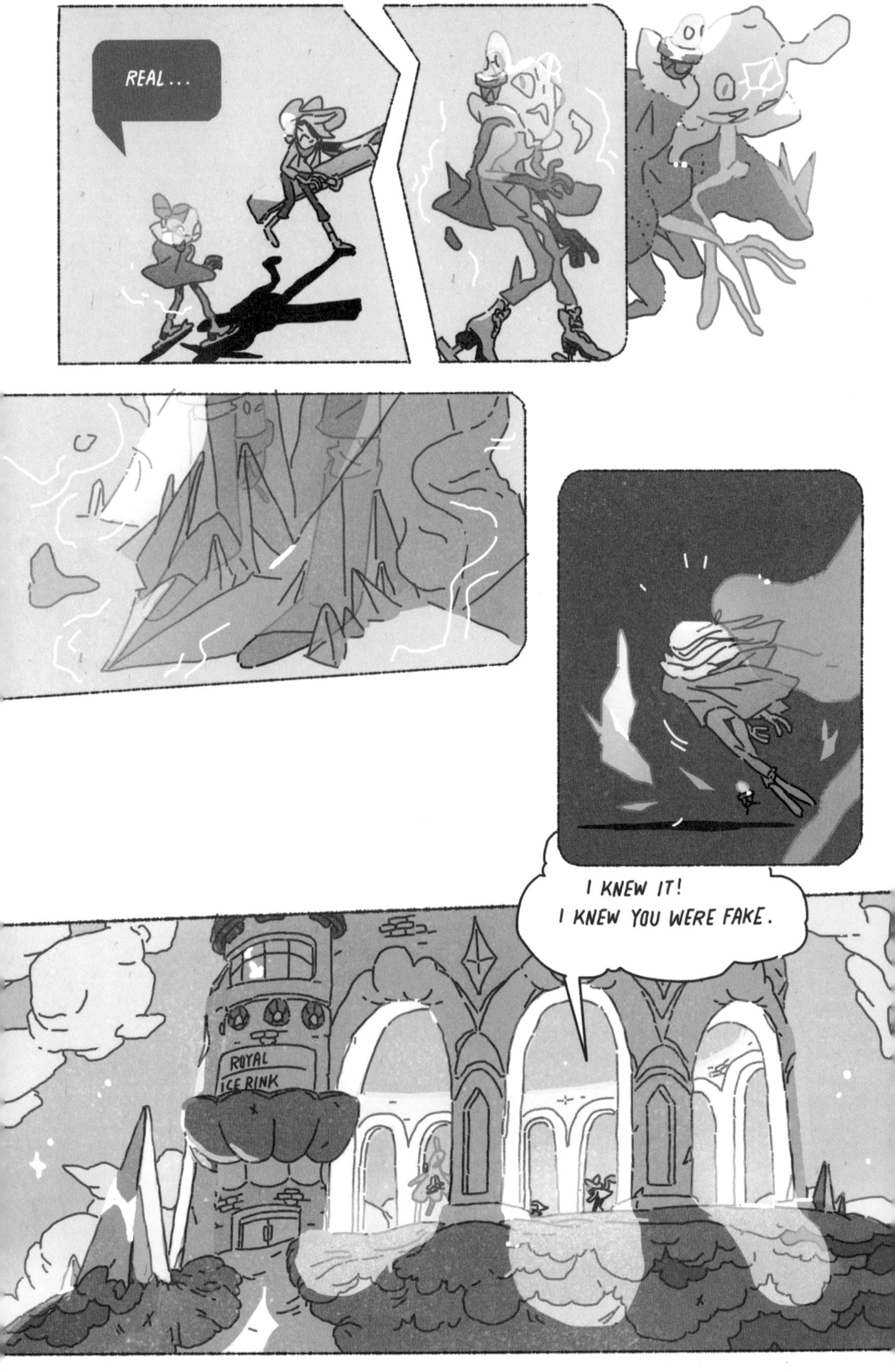
REAL...
I KNEW IT!
I KNEW YOU WERE FAKE.
ROYAL
ICE RINK

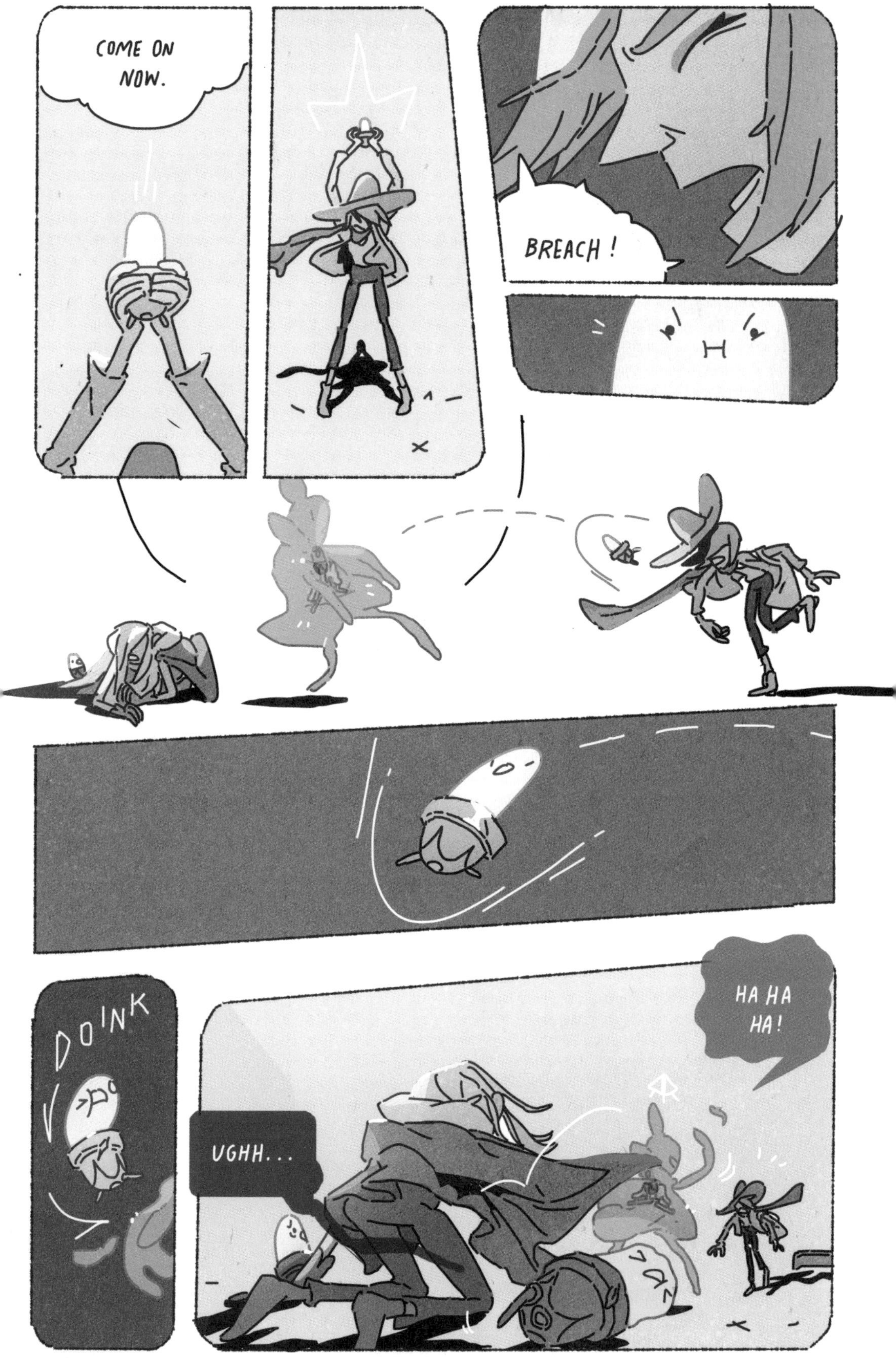
COME ON NOW.
BREACH!
DOINK
UGHH...
HA HA HA!

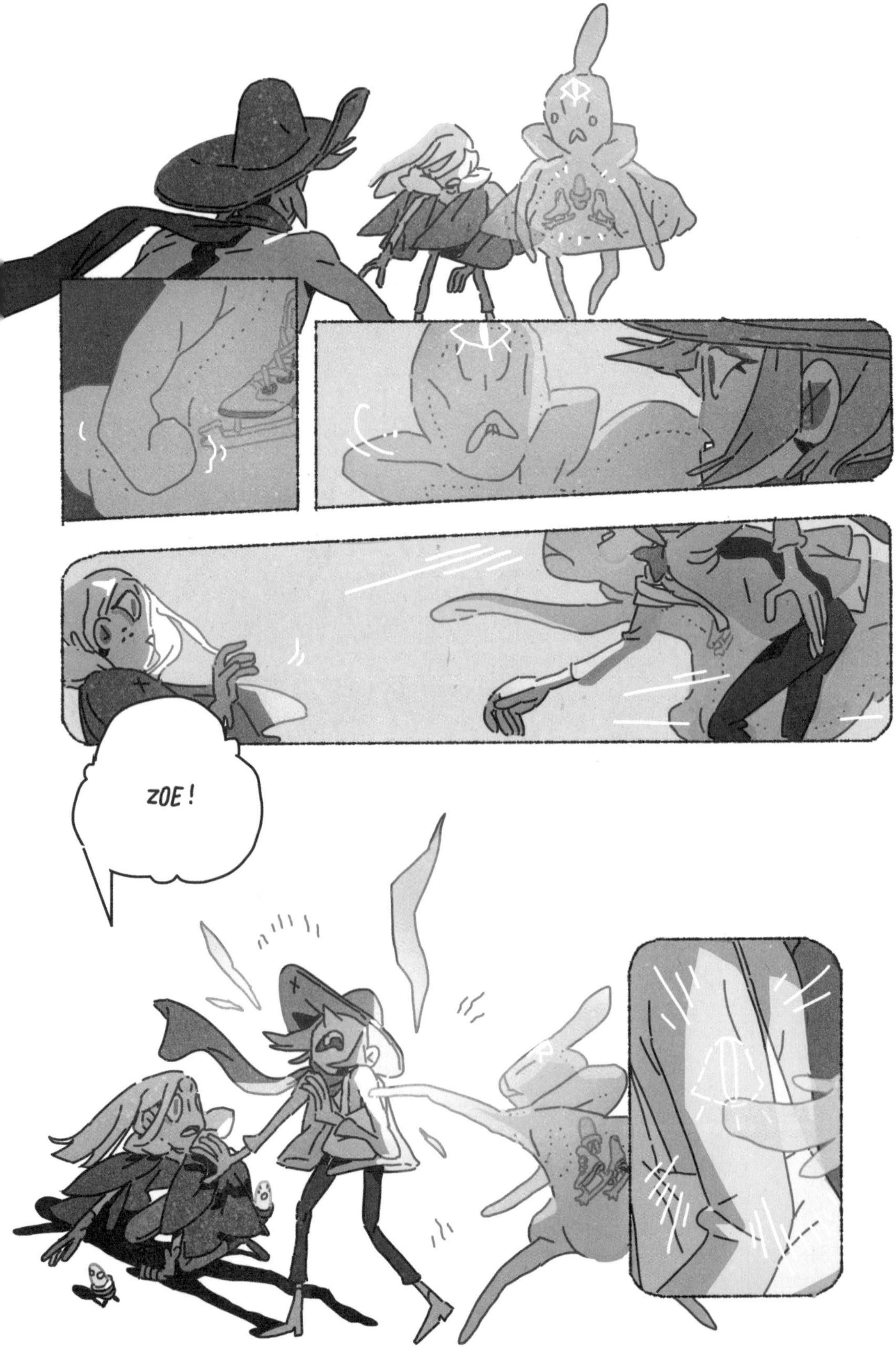
ZOE!

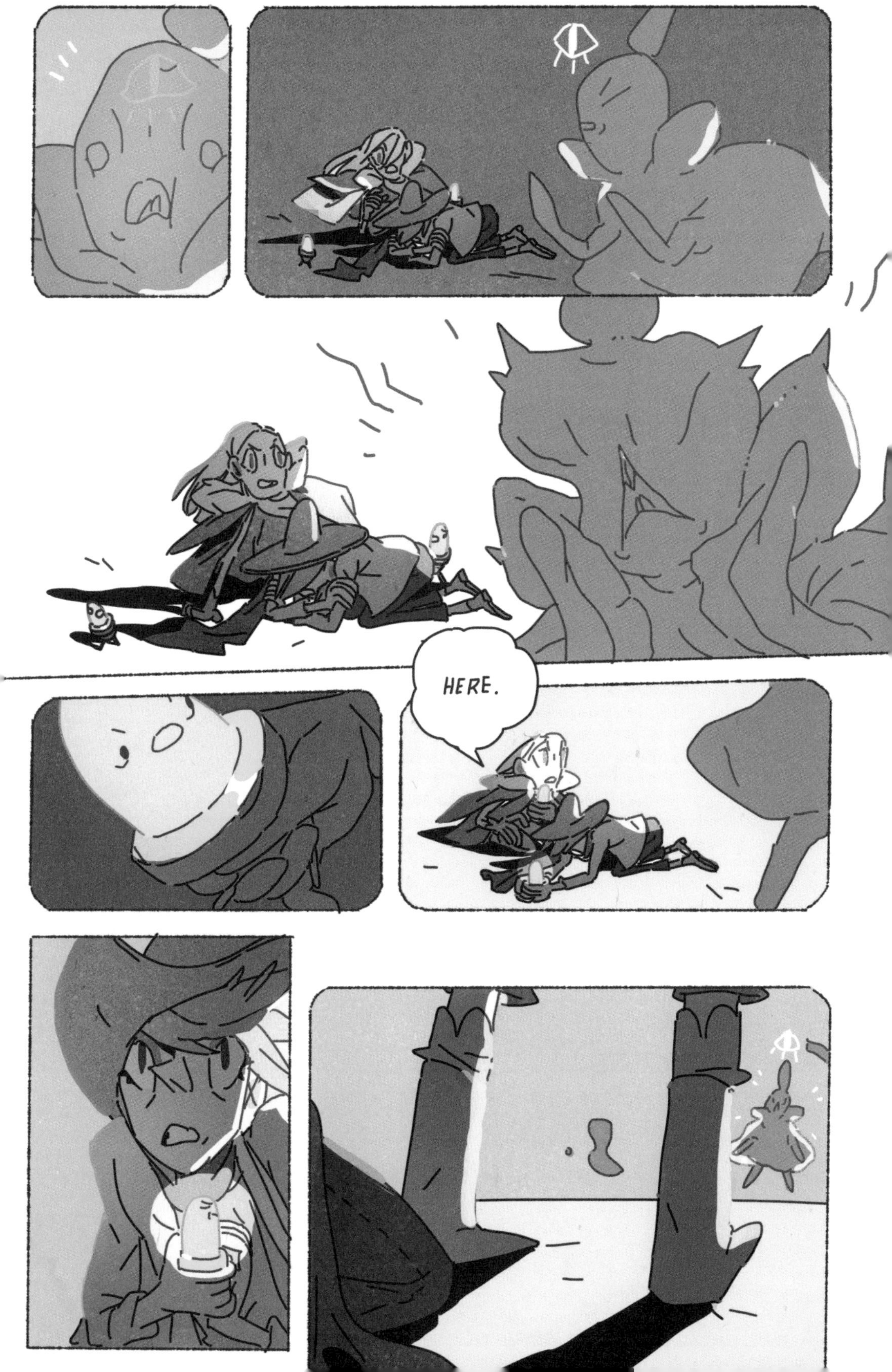
HERE.

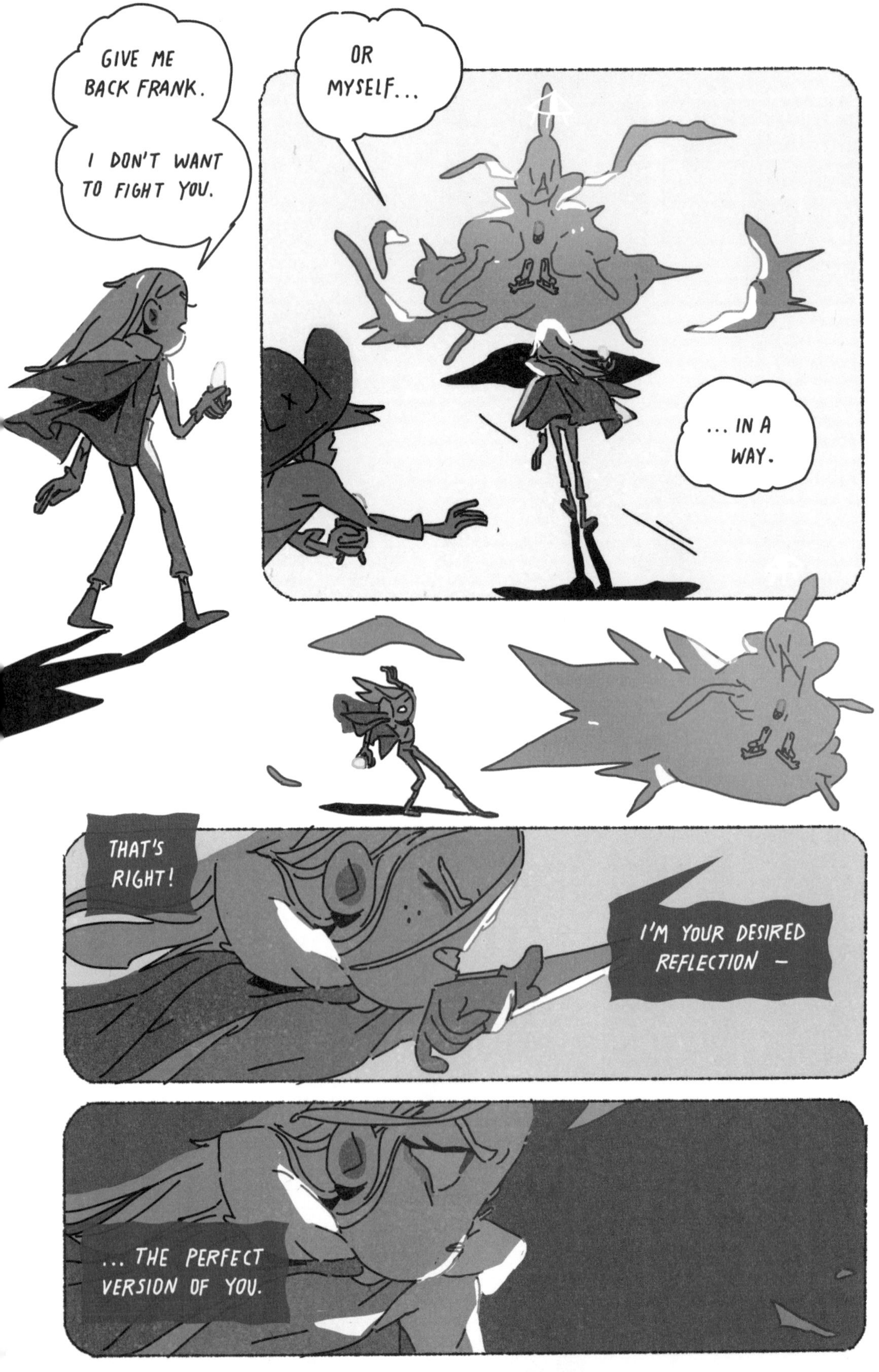
GIVE ME BACK FRANK.
I DON'T WANT TO FIGHT YOU.
OR MYSELF...
... IN A WAY.
THAT'S RIGHT!
I'M YOUR DESIRED REFLECTION –
... THE PERFECT VERSION OF YOU.

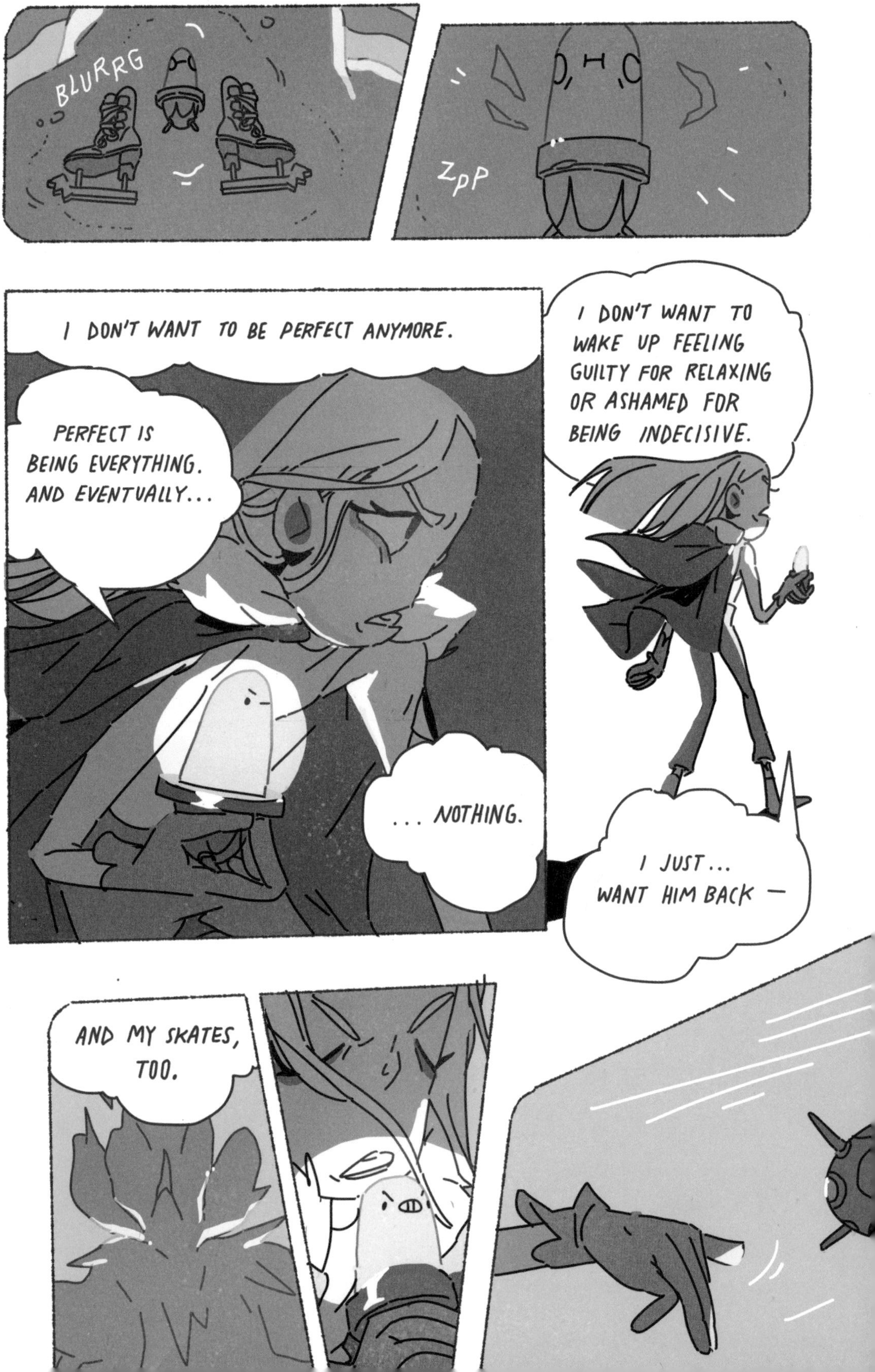
BLURRG
ZPP
I DON'T WANT TO BE PERFECT ANYMORE.
PERFECT IS BEING EVERYTHING. AND EVENTUALLY...
... NOTHING.
I DON'T WANT TO WAKE UP FEELING GUILTY FOR RELAXING OR ASHAMED FOR BEING INDECISIVE.
I JUST... WANT HIM BACK —
AND MY SKATES, TOO.

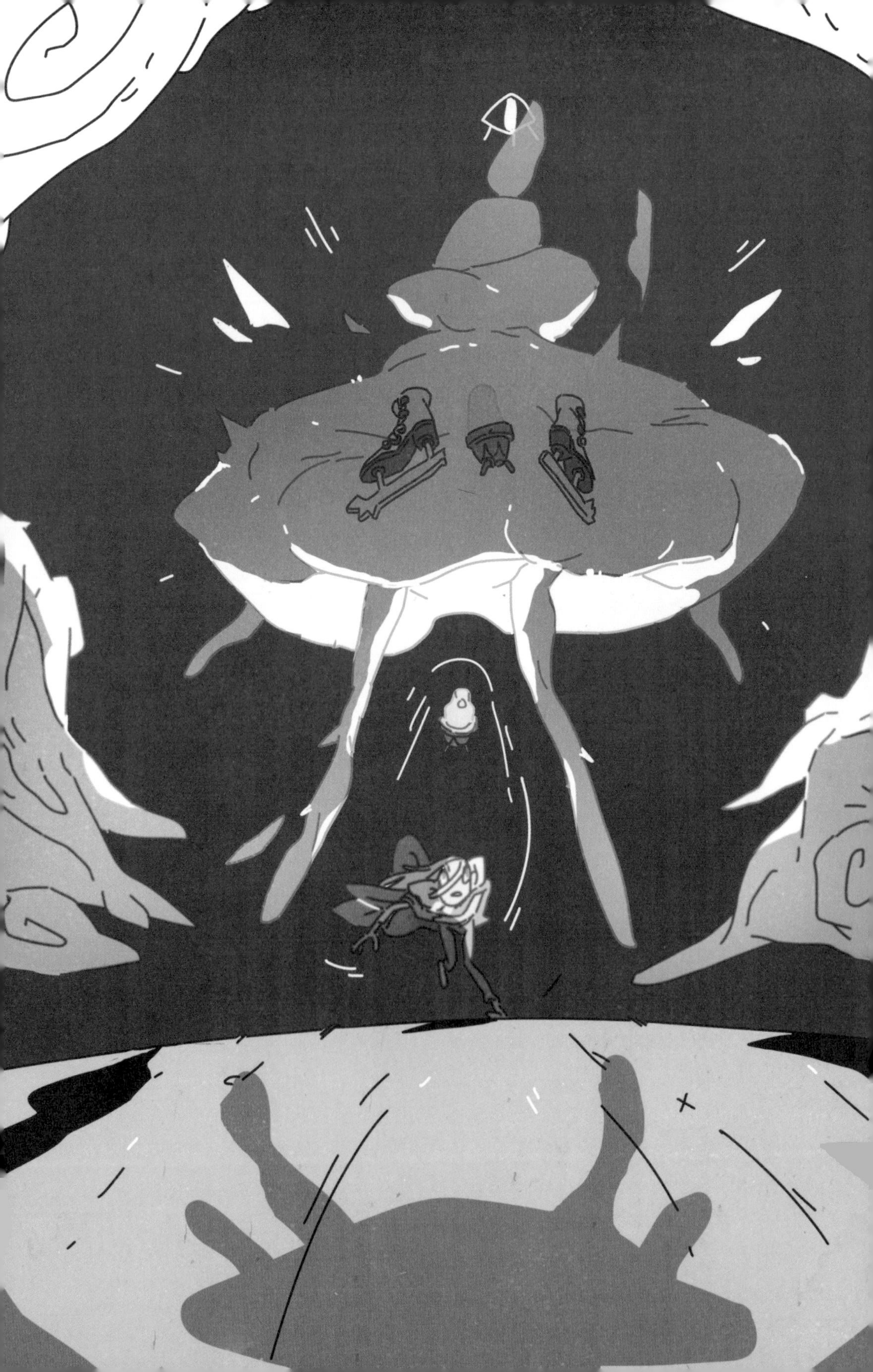

LOCK ON!
HACK!
BREACH.
MIND RESIDUE

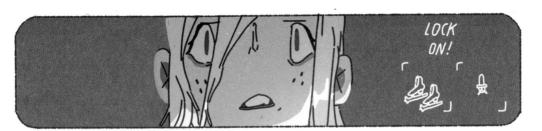

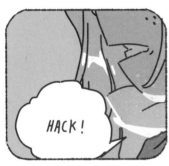

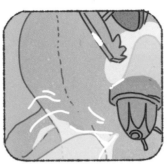

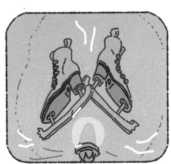

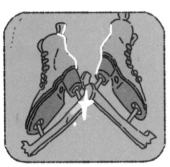

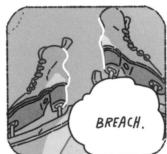

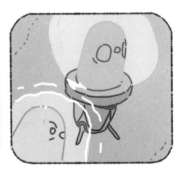

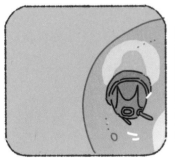

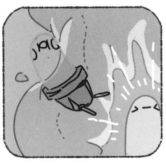

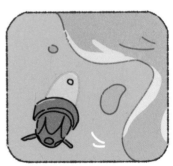

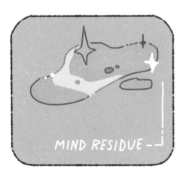

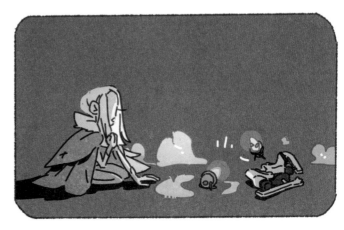

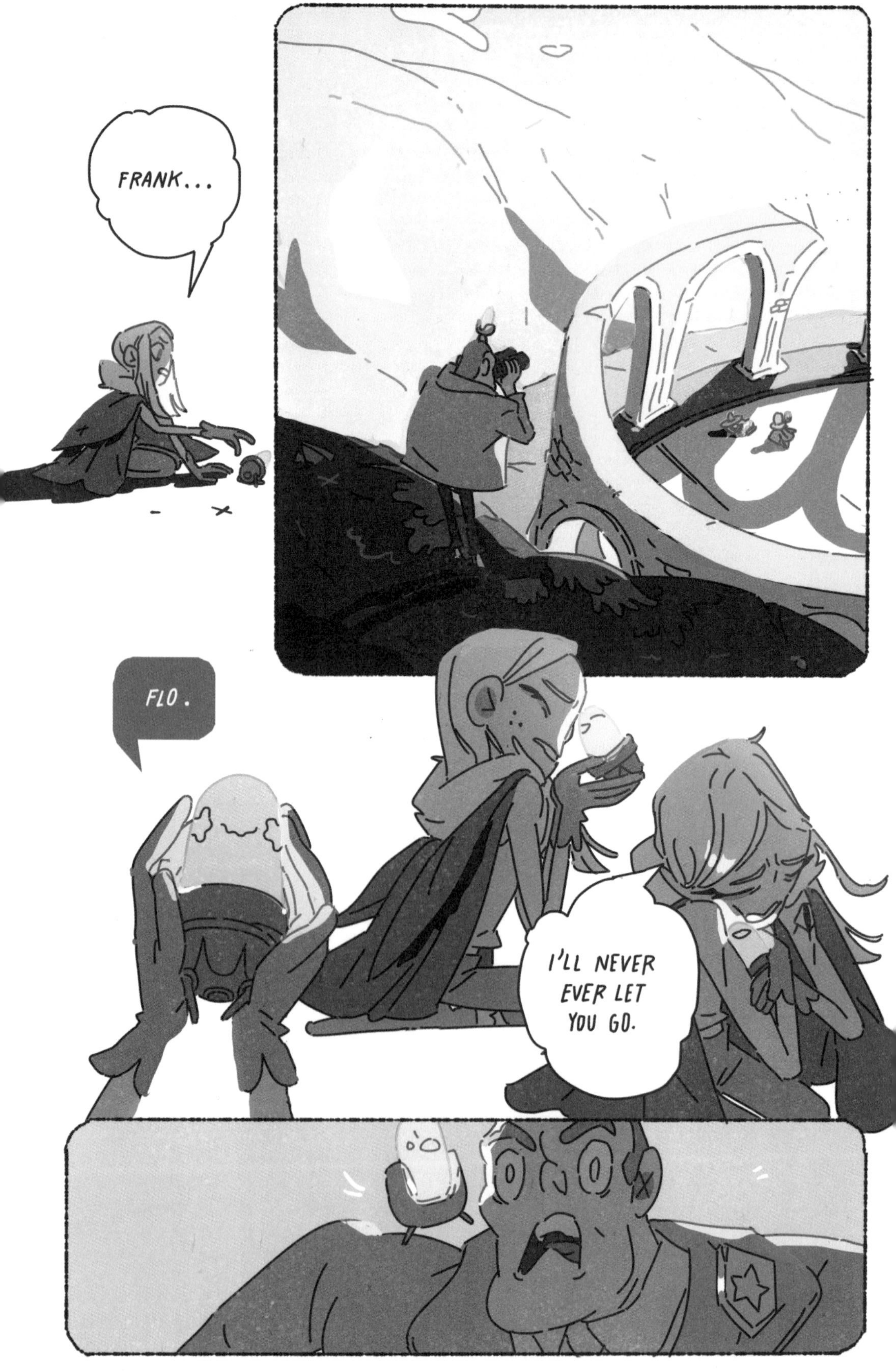
FRANK...
FLO.
I'LL NEVER EVER LET YOU GO.

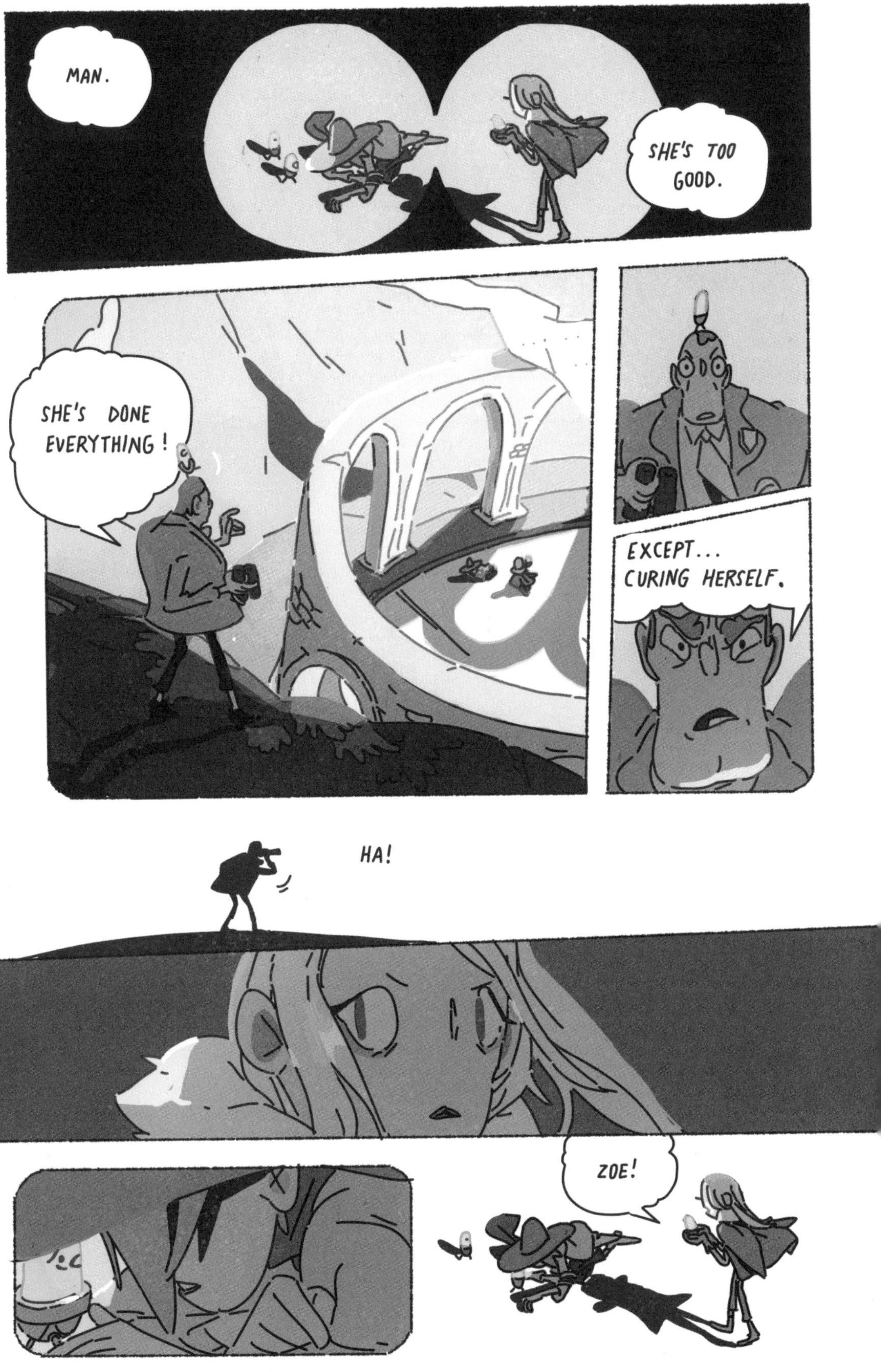
MAN.
SHE'S TOO GOOD.
SHE'S DONE EVERYTHING!
EXCEPT... CURING HERSELF.
HA!
ZOE!

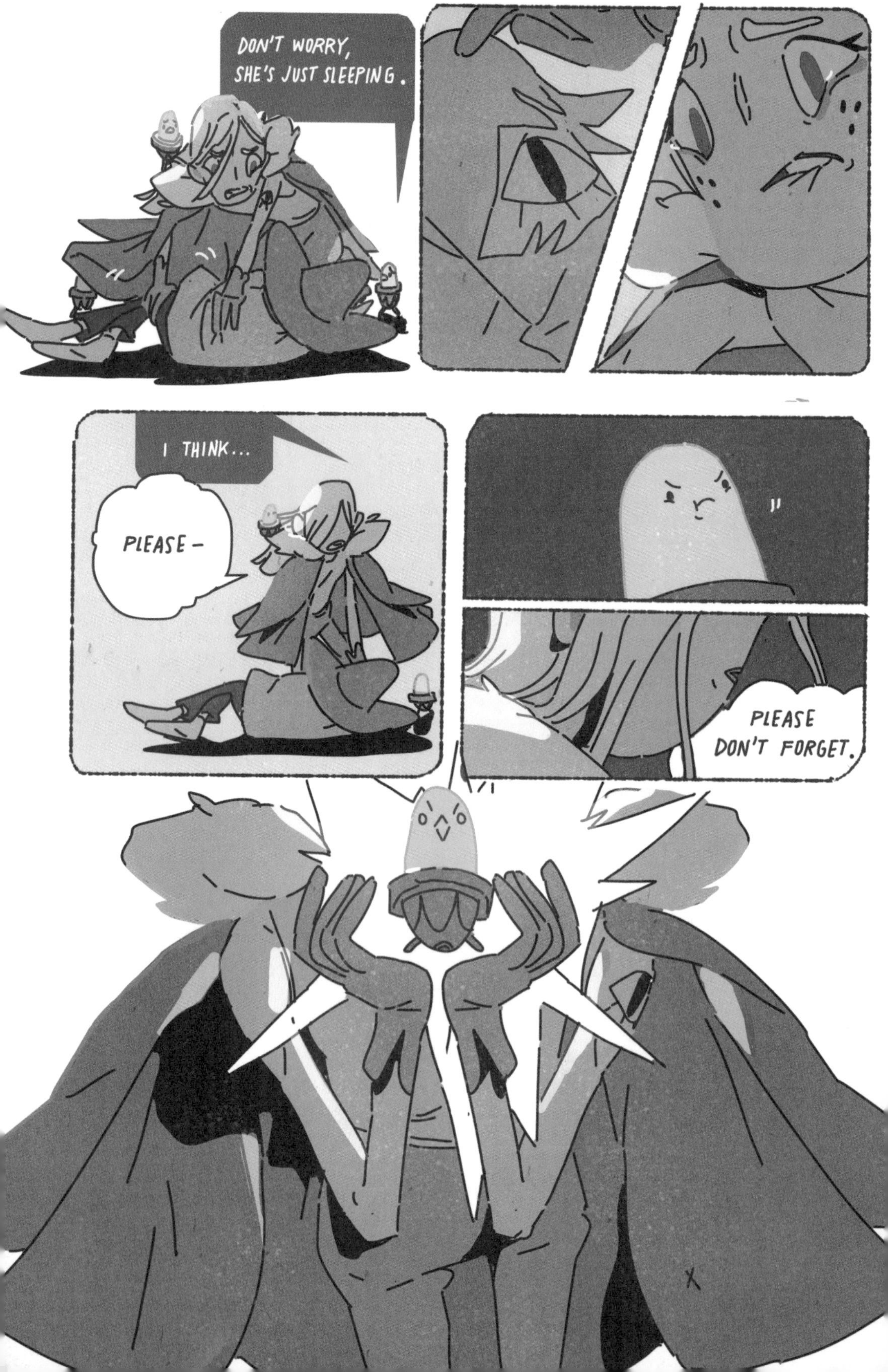
DON'T WORRY, SHE'S JUST SLEEPING.
I THINK...
PLEASE -
PLEASE DON'T FORGET.

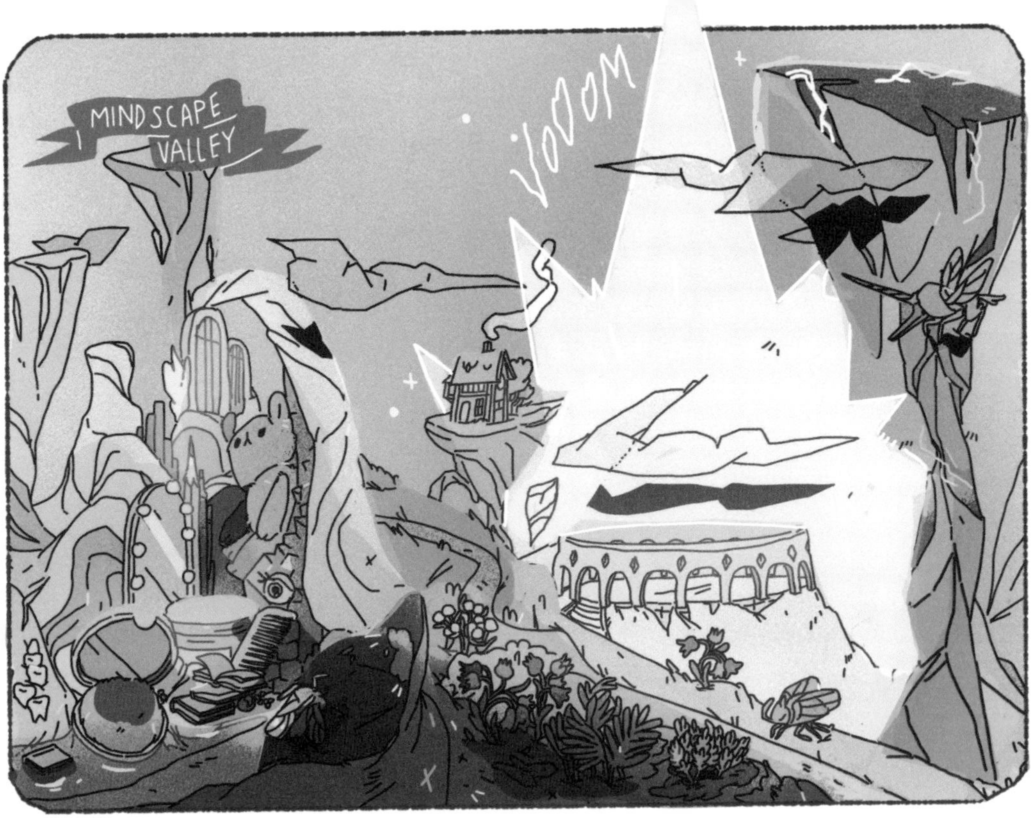
MINDSCAPE VALLEY
VOOOM

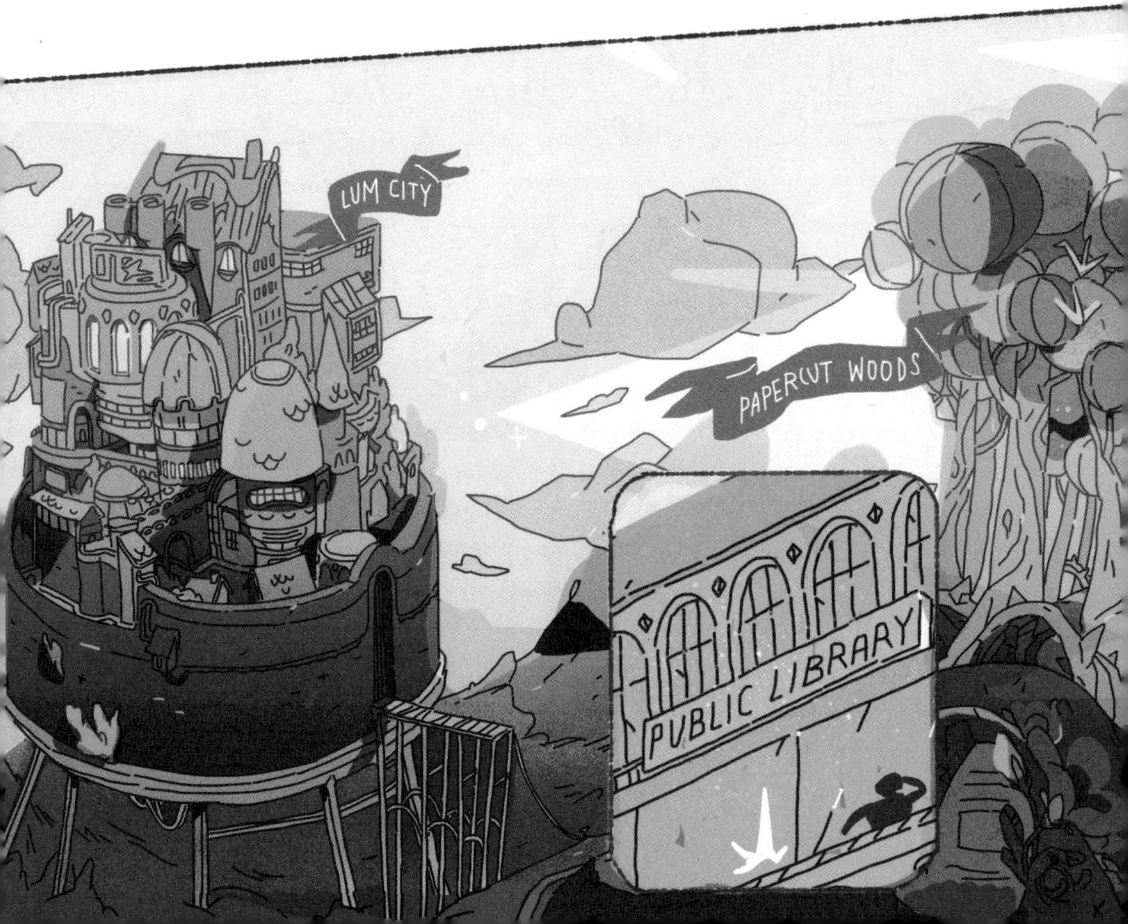
LUM CITY
PAPERCUT WOODS
PUBLIC LIBRARY

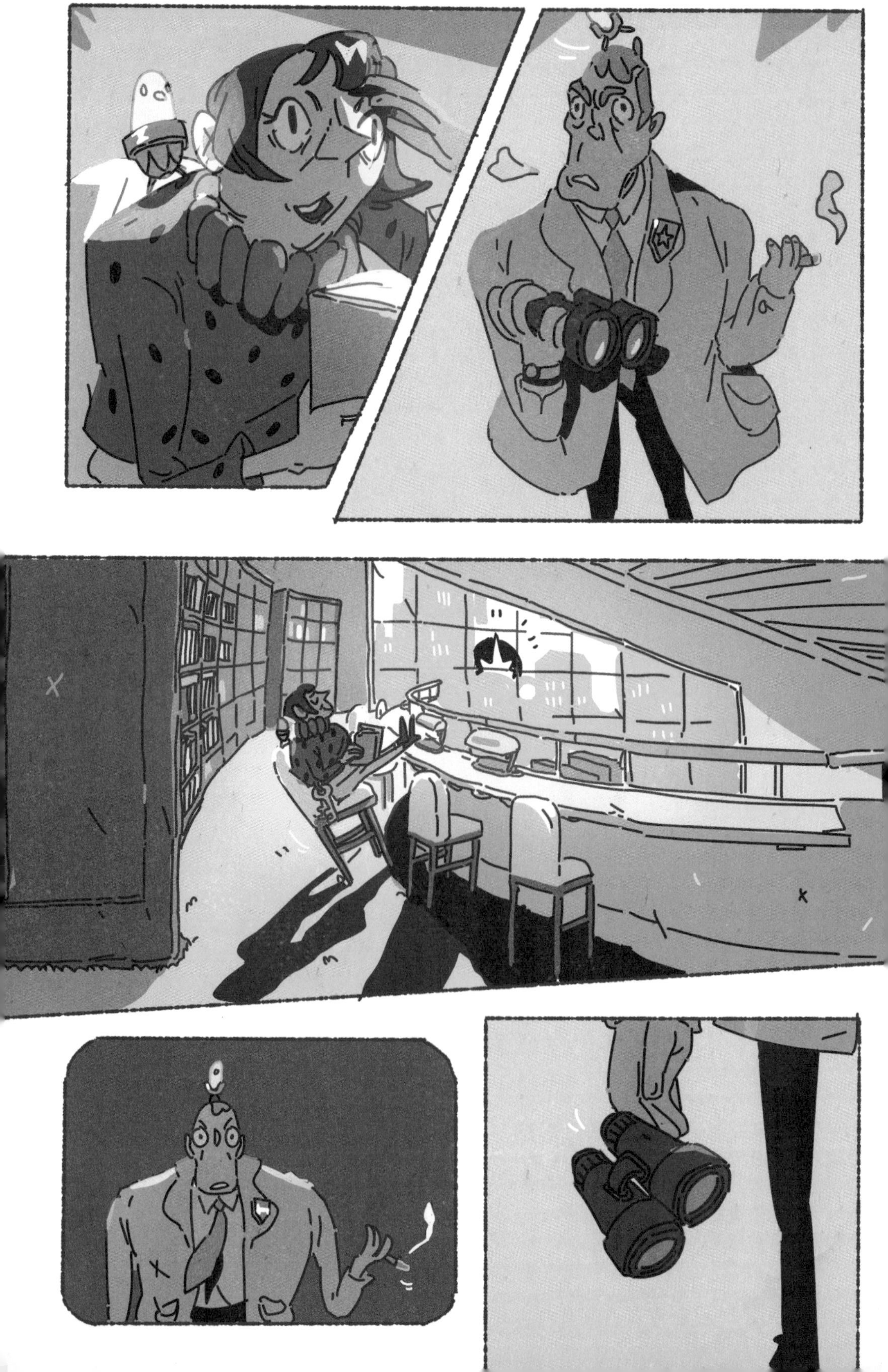

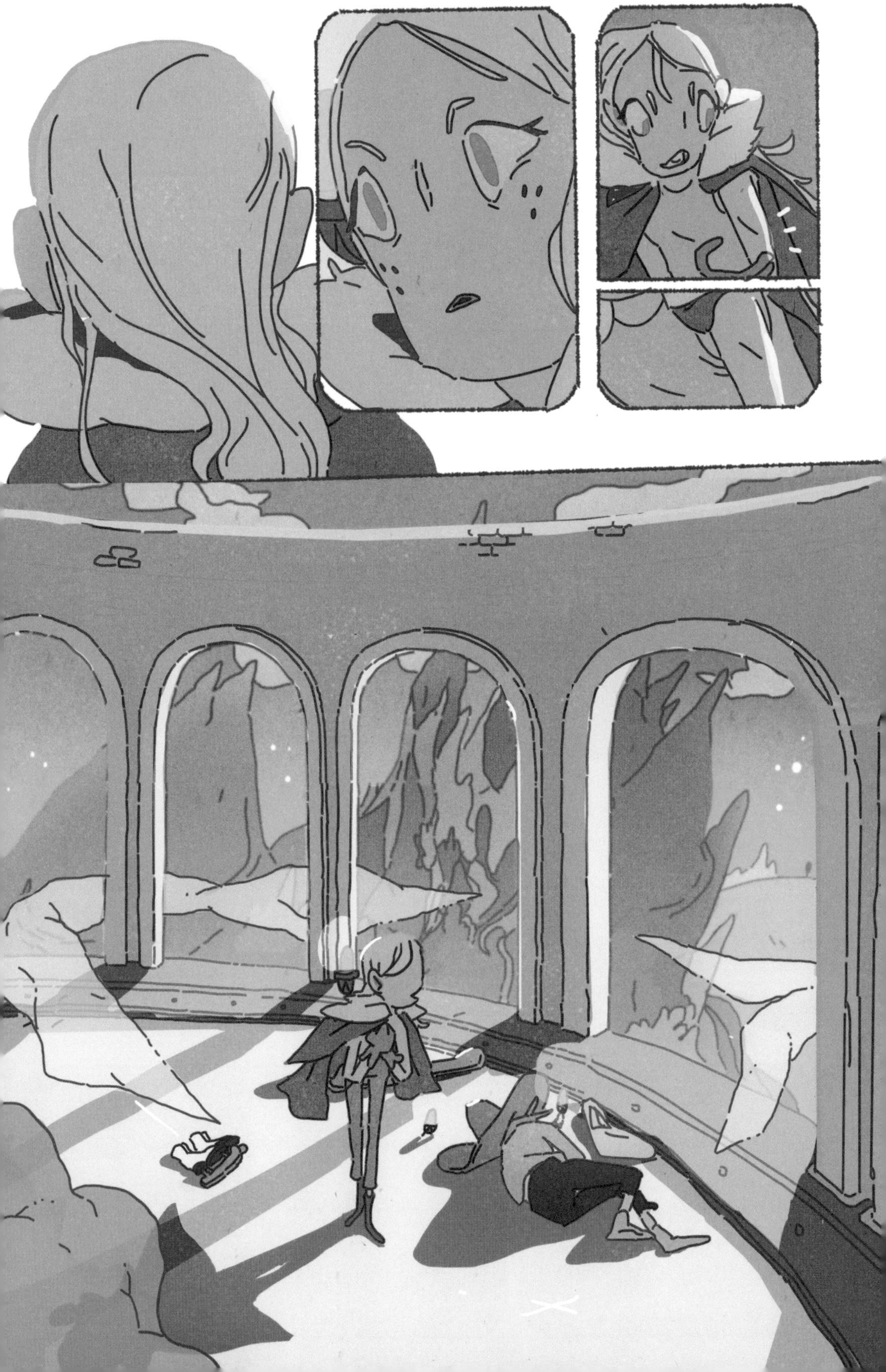

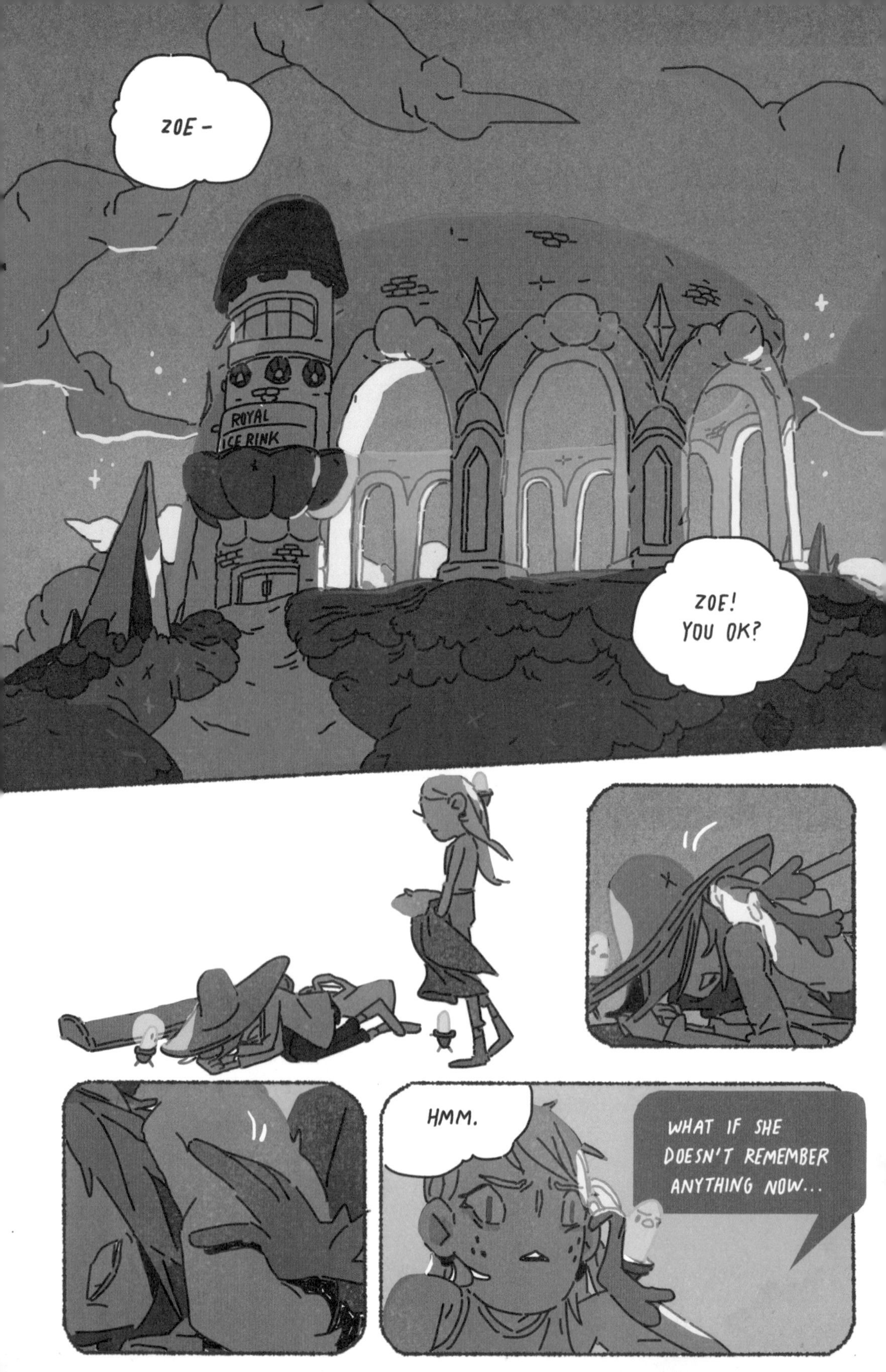
ZOE -
ROYAL
ICE RINK
ZOE!
YOU OK?
HMM.
WHAT IF SHE
DOESN'T REMEMBER
ANYTHING NOW...

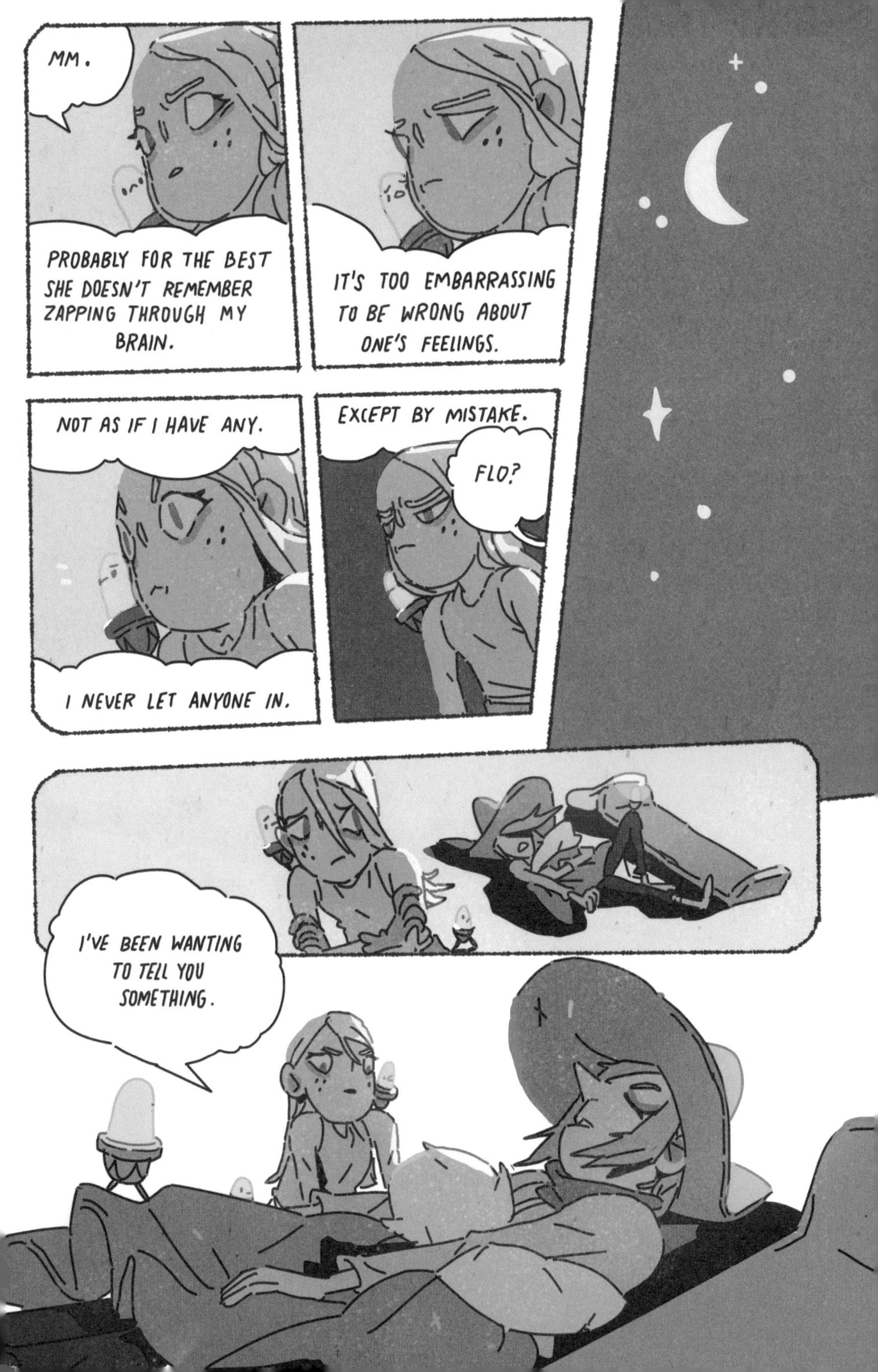
MM.
PROBABLY FOR THE BEST SHE DOESN'T REMEMBER ZAPPING THROUGH MY BRAIN.
IT'S TOO EMBARRASSING TO BE WRONG ABOUT ONE'S FEELINGS.
NOT AS IF I HAVE ANY.
I NEVER LET ANYONE IN.
EXCEPT BY MISTAKE.
FLO?
I'VE BEEN WANTING TO TELL YOU SOMETHING.

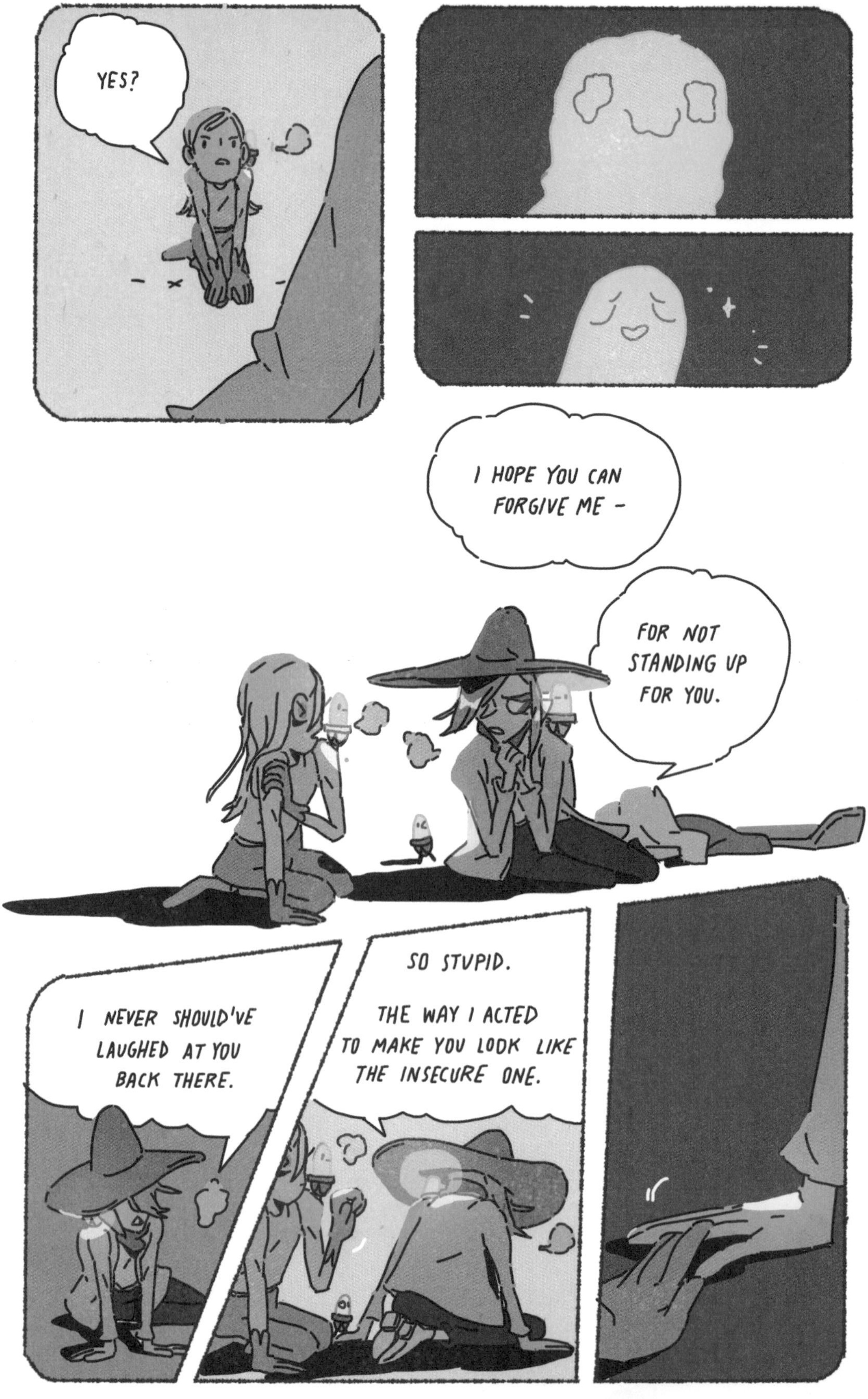
YES?
I HOPE YOU CAN FORGIVE ME -
FOR NOT STANDING UP FOR YOU.
I NEVER SHOULD'VE LAUGHED AT YOU BACK THERE.
SO STUPID.
THE WAY I ACTED TO MAKE YOU LOOK LIKE THE INSECURE ONE.

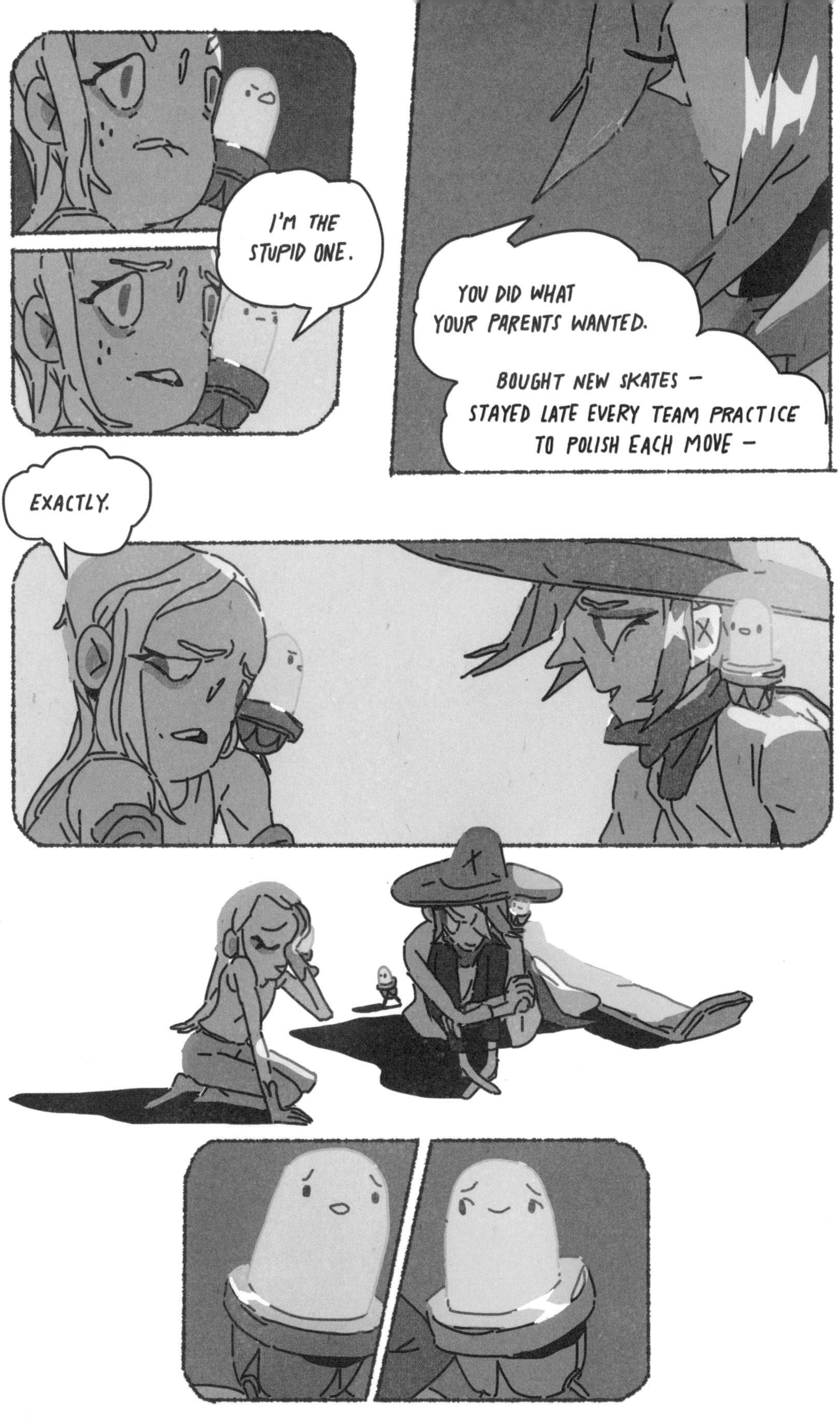
I'M THE STUPID ONE.
YOU DID WHAT YOUR PARENTS WANTED.
BOUGHT NEW SKATES -
STAYED LATE EVERY TEAM PRACTICE TO POLISH EACH MOVE -
EXACTLY.

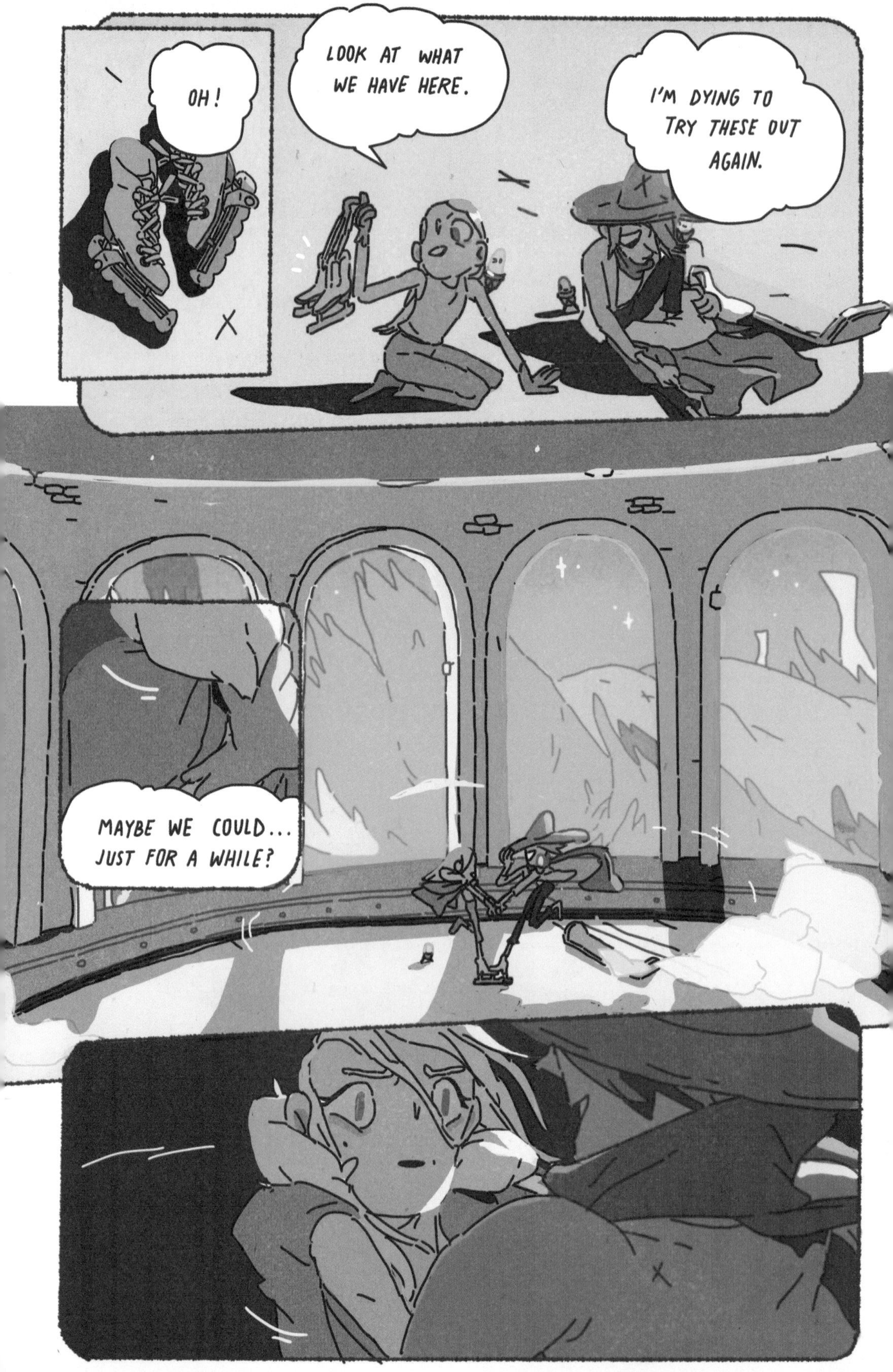
OH!
LOOK AT WHAT WE HAVE HERE.
I'M DYING TO TRY THESE OUT AGAIN.
MAYBE WE COULD... JUST FOR A WHILE?

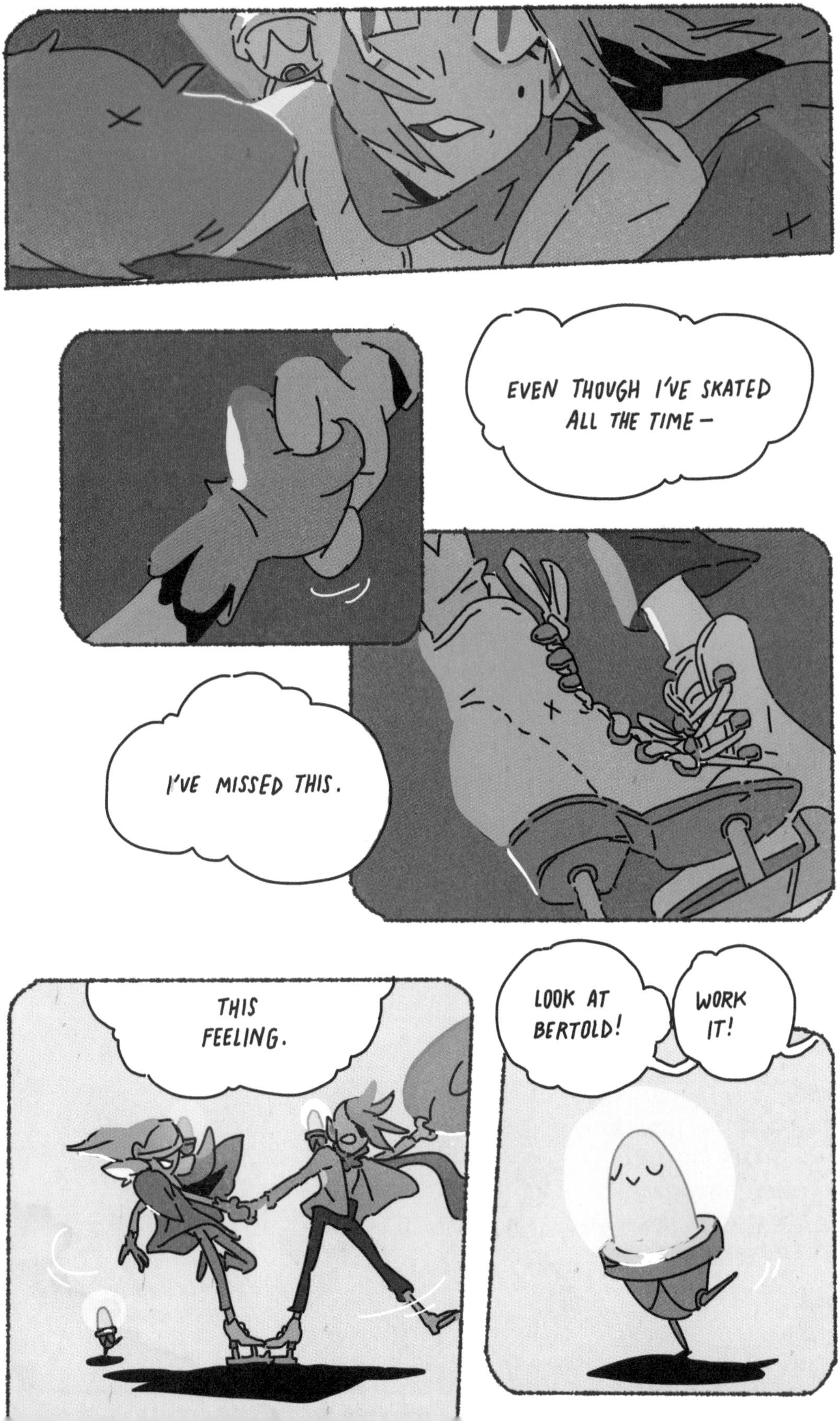
EVEN THOUGH I'VE SKATED ALL THE TIME—
I'VE MISSED THIS.
THIS FEELING.
LOOK AT BERTOLD!
WORK IT!

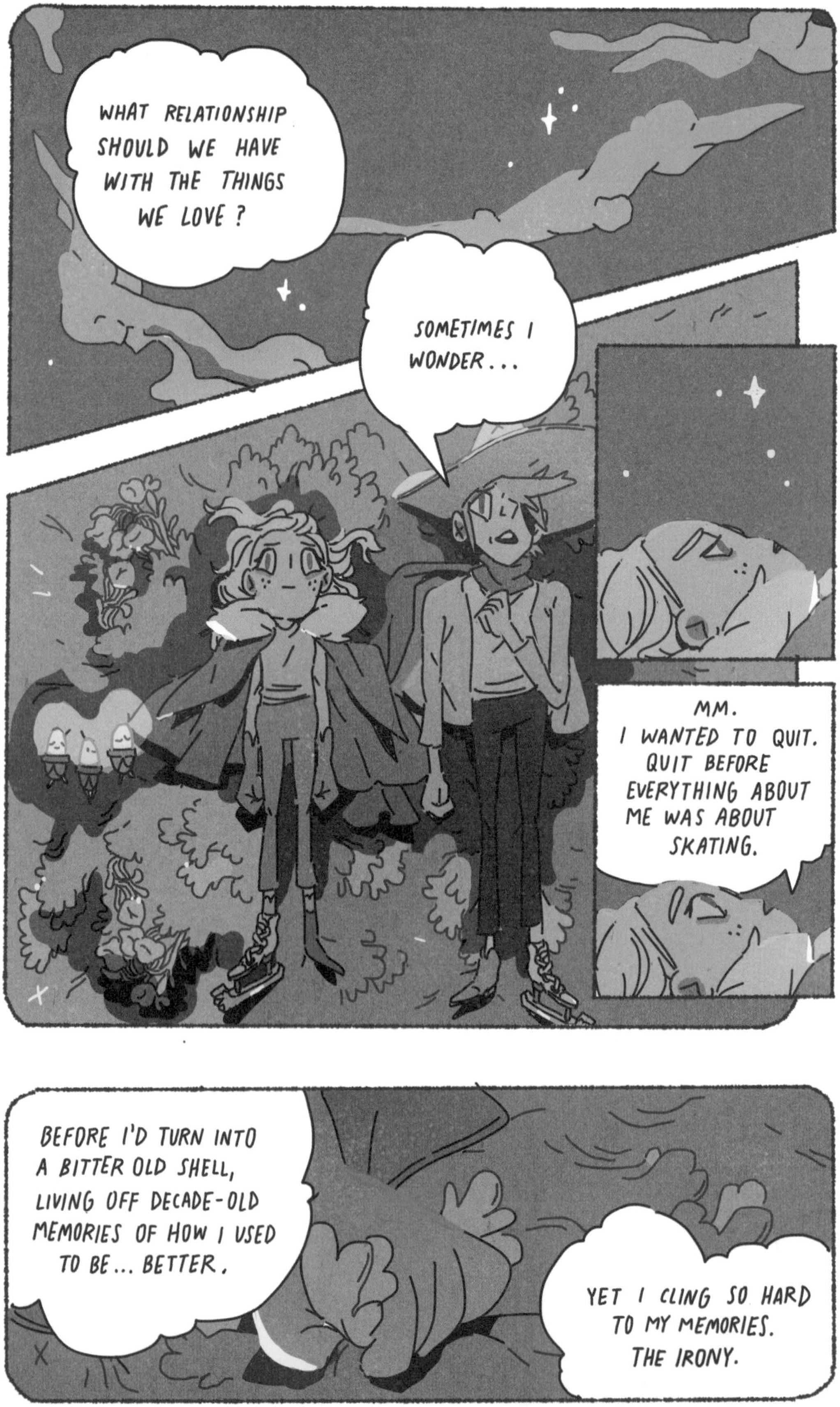
WHAT RELATIONSHIP SHOULD WE HAVE WITH THE THINGS WE LOVE ?
SOMETIMES I WONDER...
MM.
I WANTED TO QUIT. QUIT BEFORE EVERYTHING ABOUT ME WAS ABOUT SKATING.
BEFORE I'D TURN INTO A BITTER OLD SHELL, LIVING OFF DECADE-OLD MEMORIES OF HOW I USED TO BE... BETTER.
YET I CLING SO HARD TO MY MEMORIES. THE IRONY.

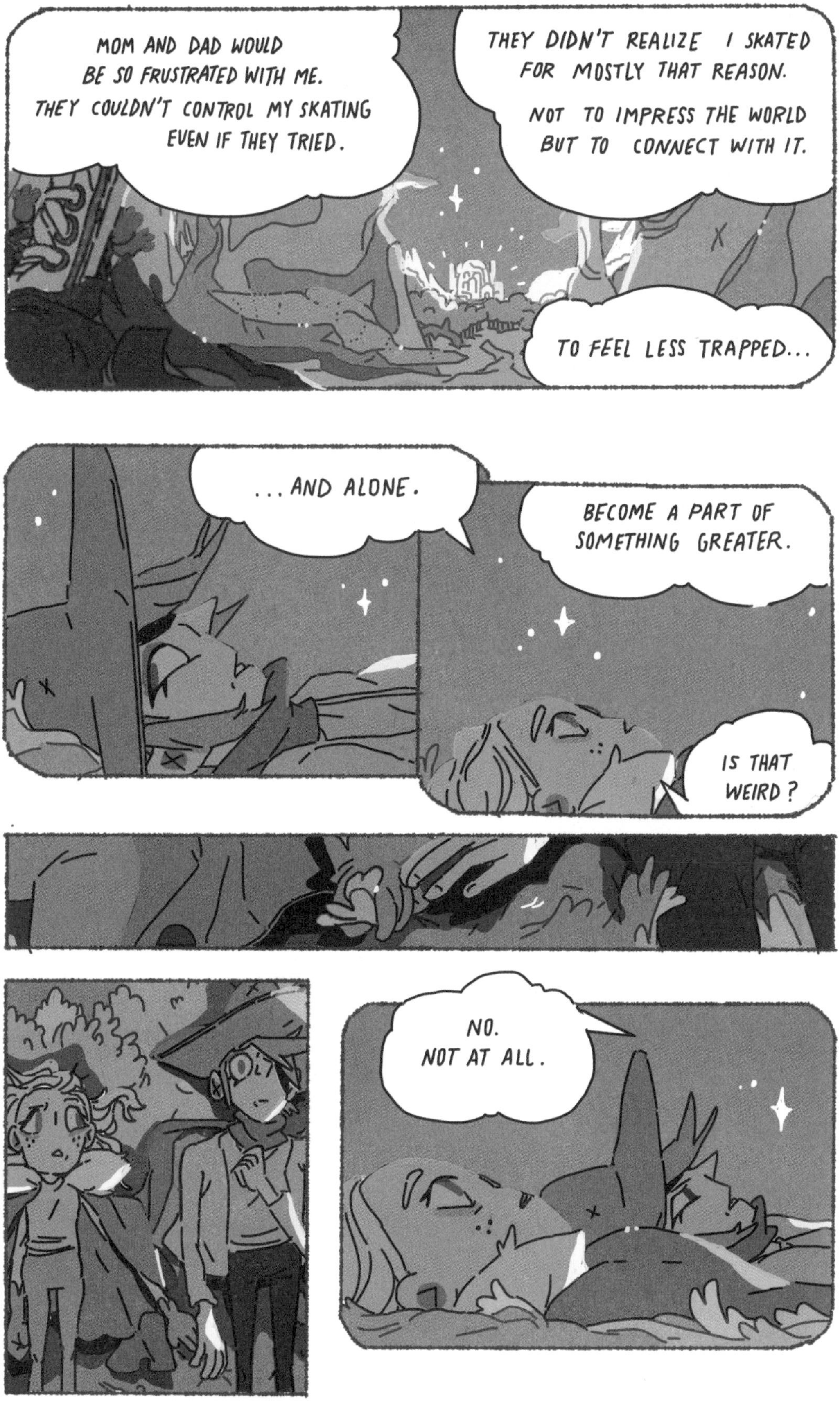
MOM AND DAD WOULD BE SO FRUSTRATED WITH ME. THEY COULDN'T CONTROL MY SKATING EVEN IF THEY TRIED.
THEY DIDN'T REALIZE I SKATED FOR MOSTLY THAT REASON.
NOT TO IMPRESS THE WORLD BUT TO CONNECT WITH IT.
TO FEEL LESS TRAPPED...
...AND ALONE.
BECOME A PART OF SOMETHING GREATER.
IS THAT WEIRD?
NO. NOT AT ALL.

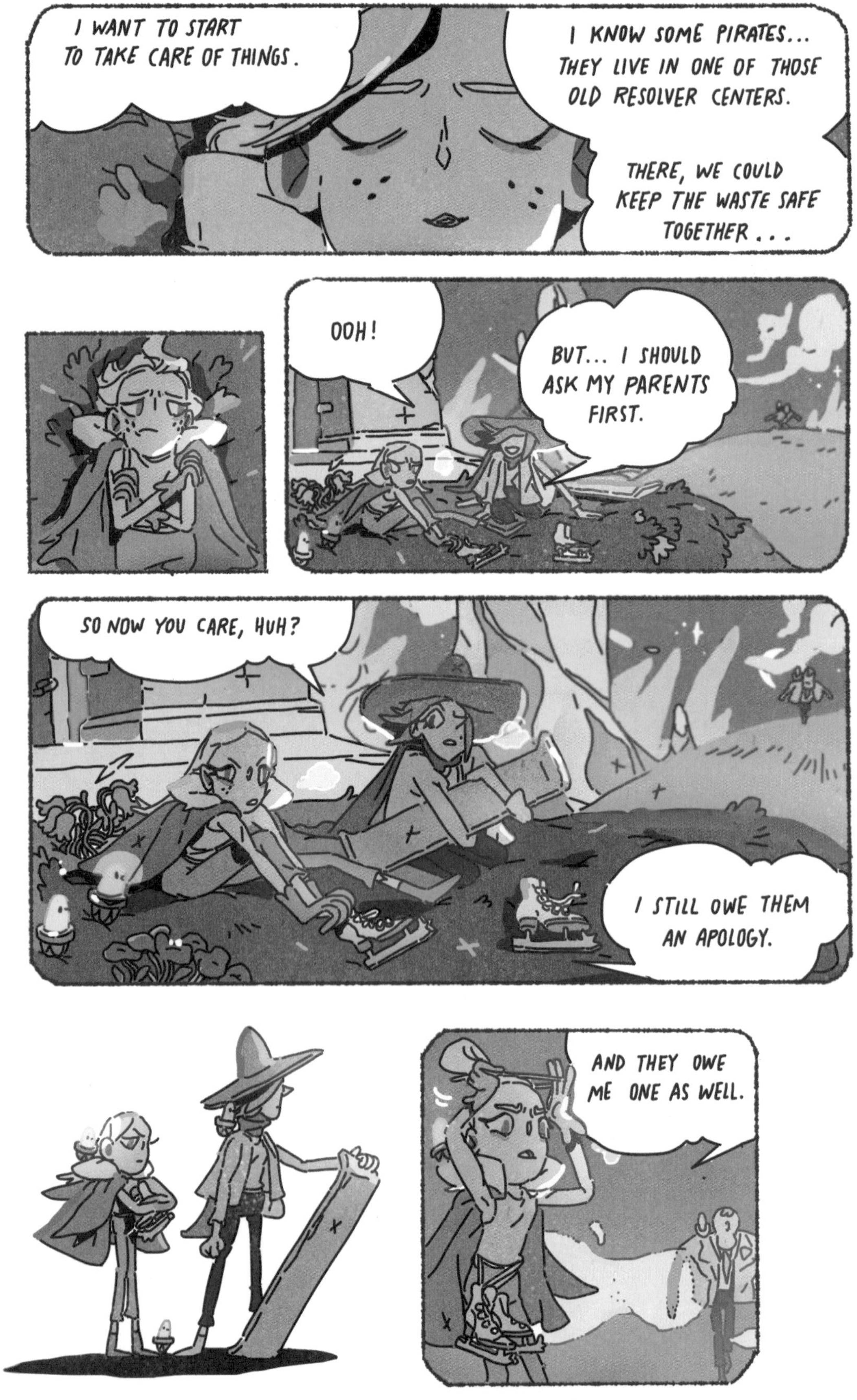
I WANT TO START TO TAKE CARE OF THINGS.
I KNOW SOME PIRATES... THEY LIVE IN ONE OF THOSE OLD RESOLVER CENTERS.
THERE, WE COULD KEEP THE WASTE SAFE TOGETHER...
OOH!
BUT... I SHOULD ASK MY PARENTS FIRST.
SO NOW YOU CARE, HUH?
I STILL OWE THEM AN APOLOGY.
AND THEY OWE ME ONE AS WELL.

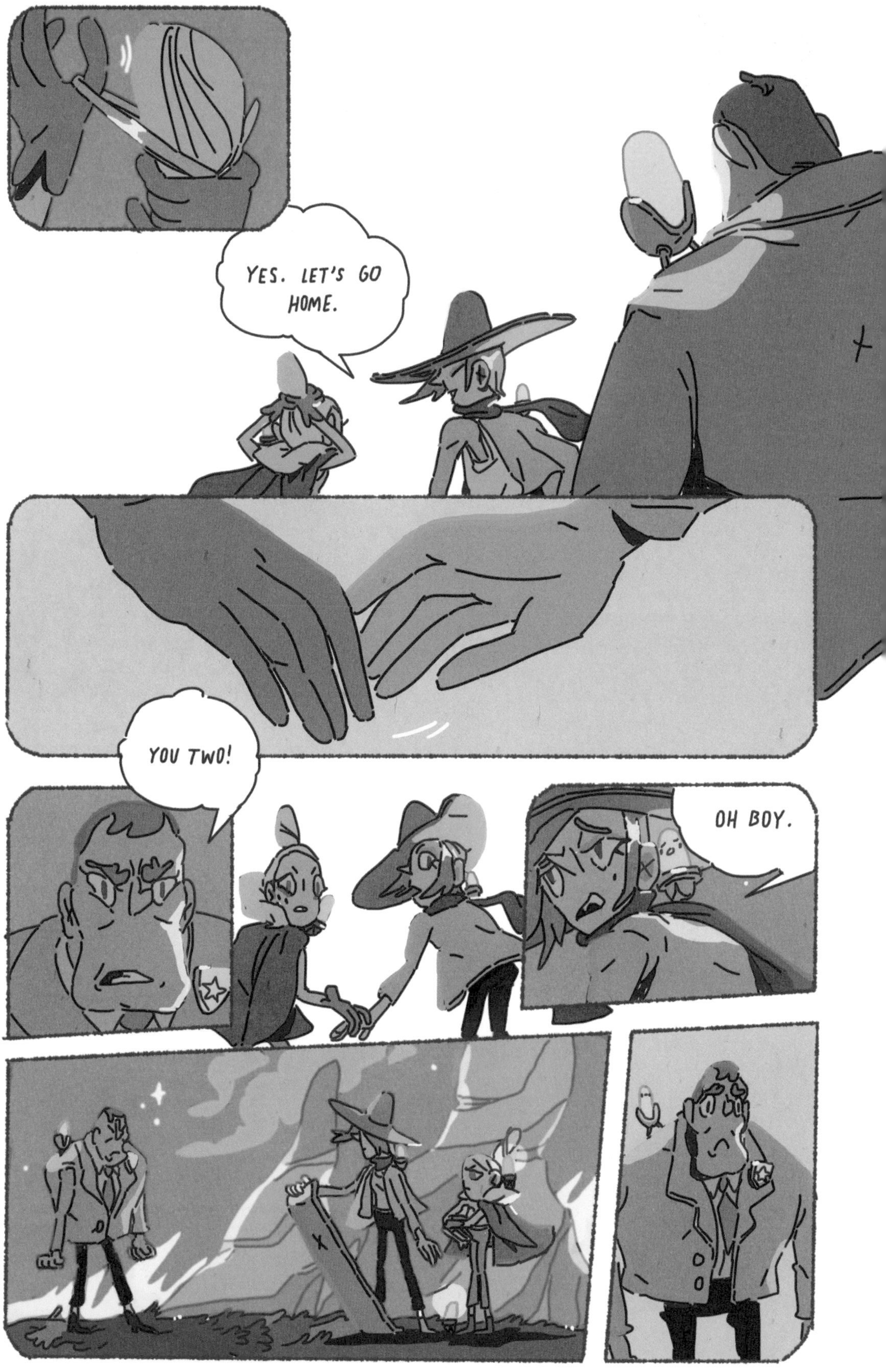
YES. LET'S GO HOME.
YOU TWO!
OH BOY.

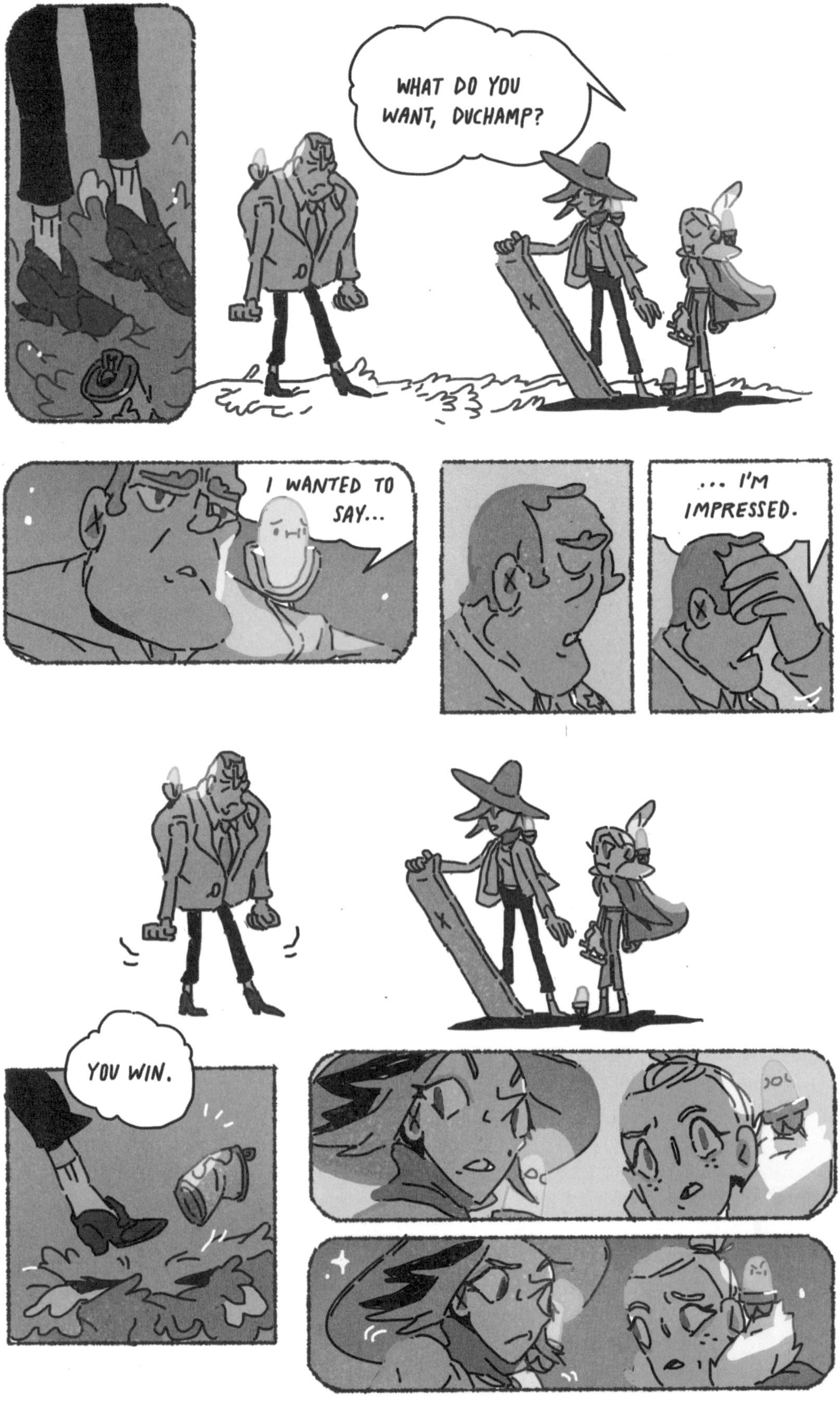
WHAT DO YOU WANT, DUCHAMP?
I WANTED TO SAY...
... I'M IMPRESSED.
YOU WIN.

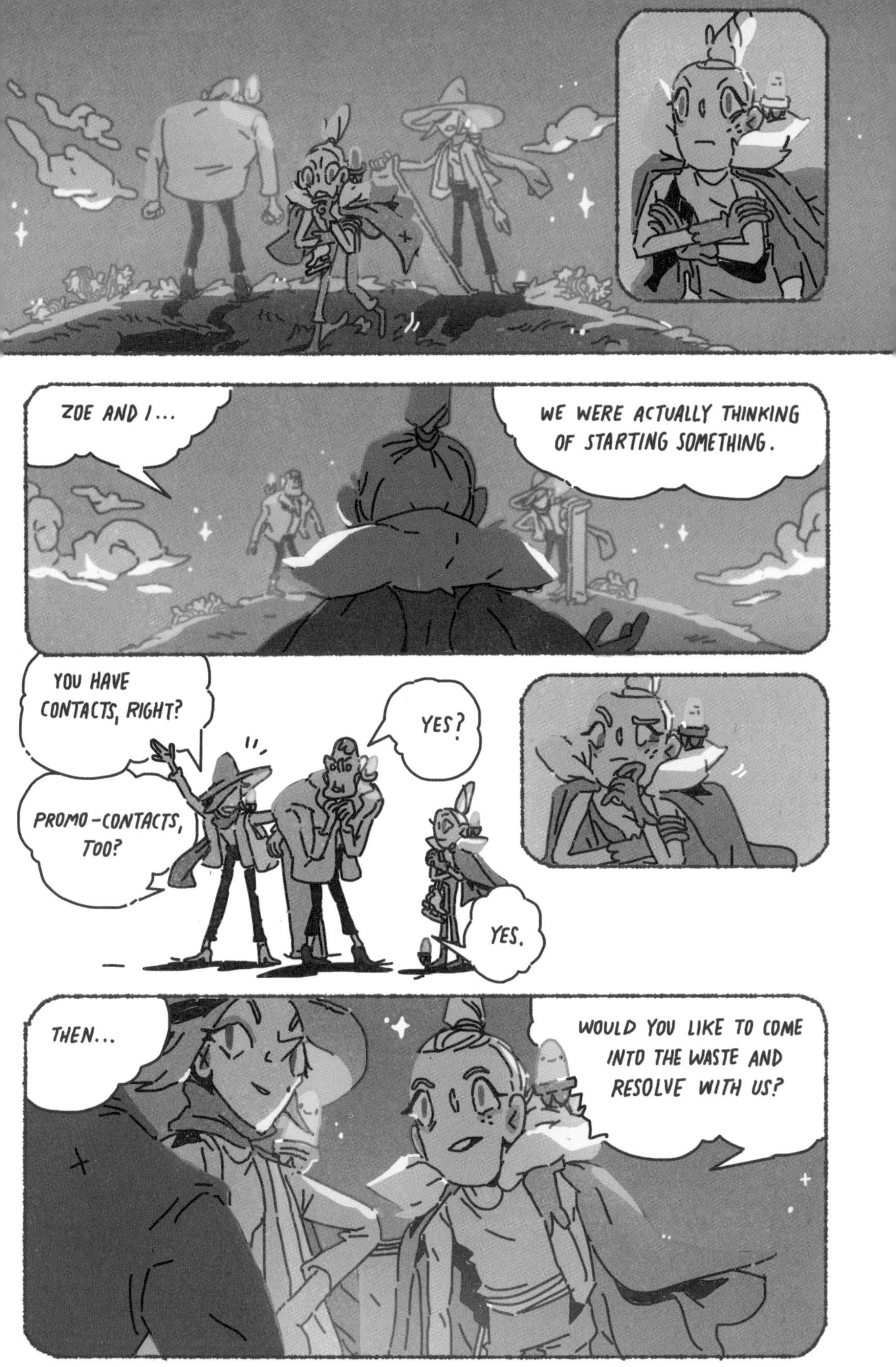
ZOE AND I...
WE WERE ACTUALLY THINKING OF STARTING SOMETHING.
YOU HAVE CONTACTS, RIGHT?
PROMO-CONTACTS, TOO?
YES?
YES.
THEN...
WOULD YOU LIKE TO COME INTO THE WASTE AND RESOLVE WITH US?

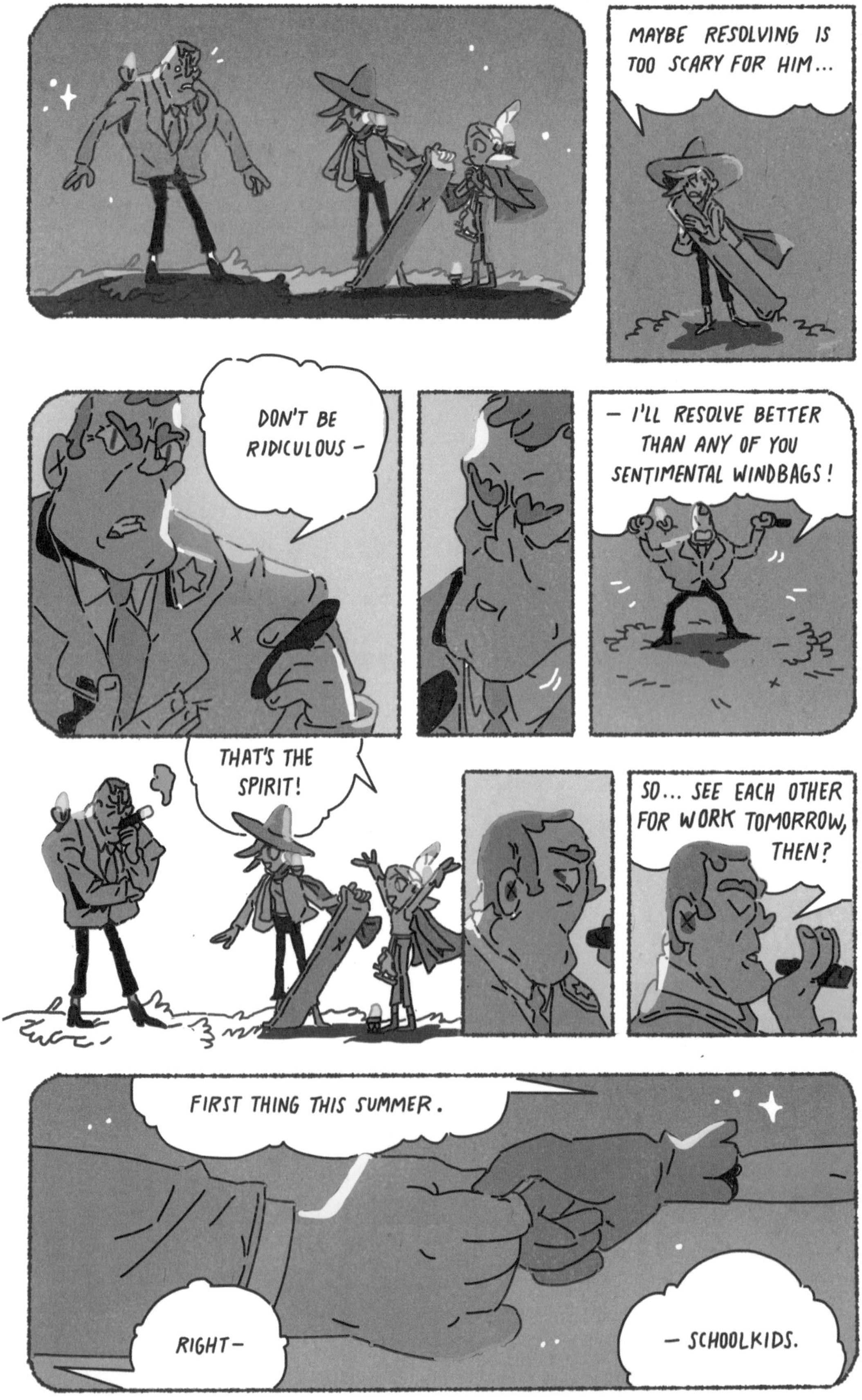
MAYBE RESOLVING IS TOO SCARY FOR HIM...
DON'T BE RIDICULOUS -
- I'LL RESOLVE BETTER THAN ANY OF YOU SENTIMENTAL WINDBAGS!
THAT'S THE SPIRIT!
SO... SEE EACH OTHER FOR WORK TOMORROW, THEN?
FIRST THING THIS SUMMER.
RIGHT-
- SCHOOLKIDS.

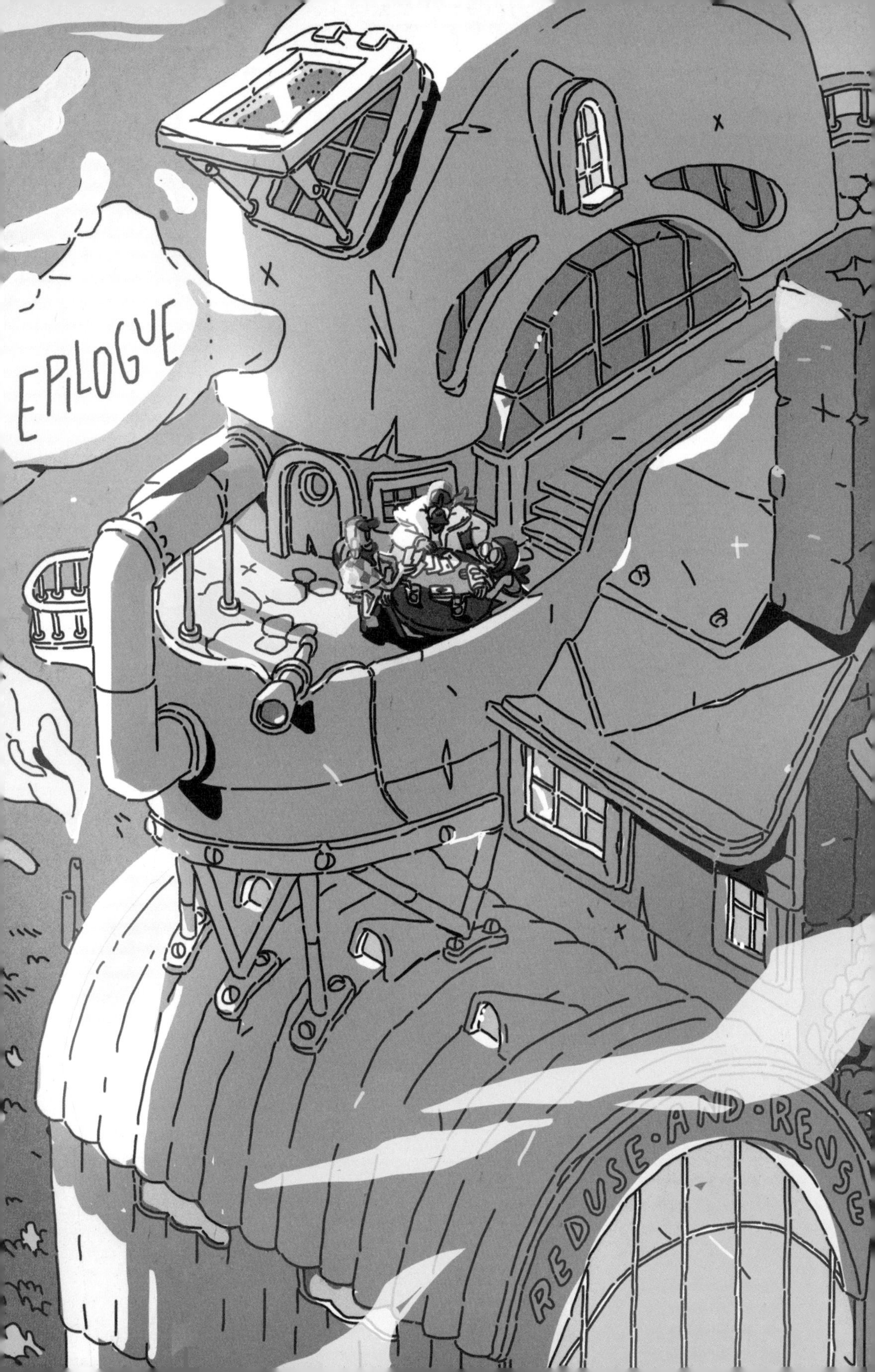
EPILOGUE
REDUSE·AND·REUSE

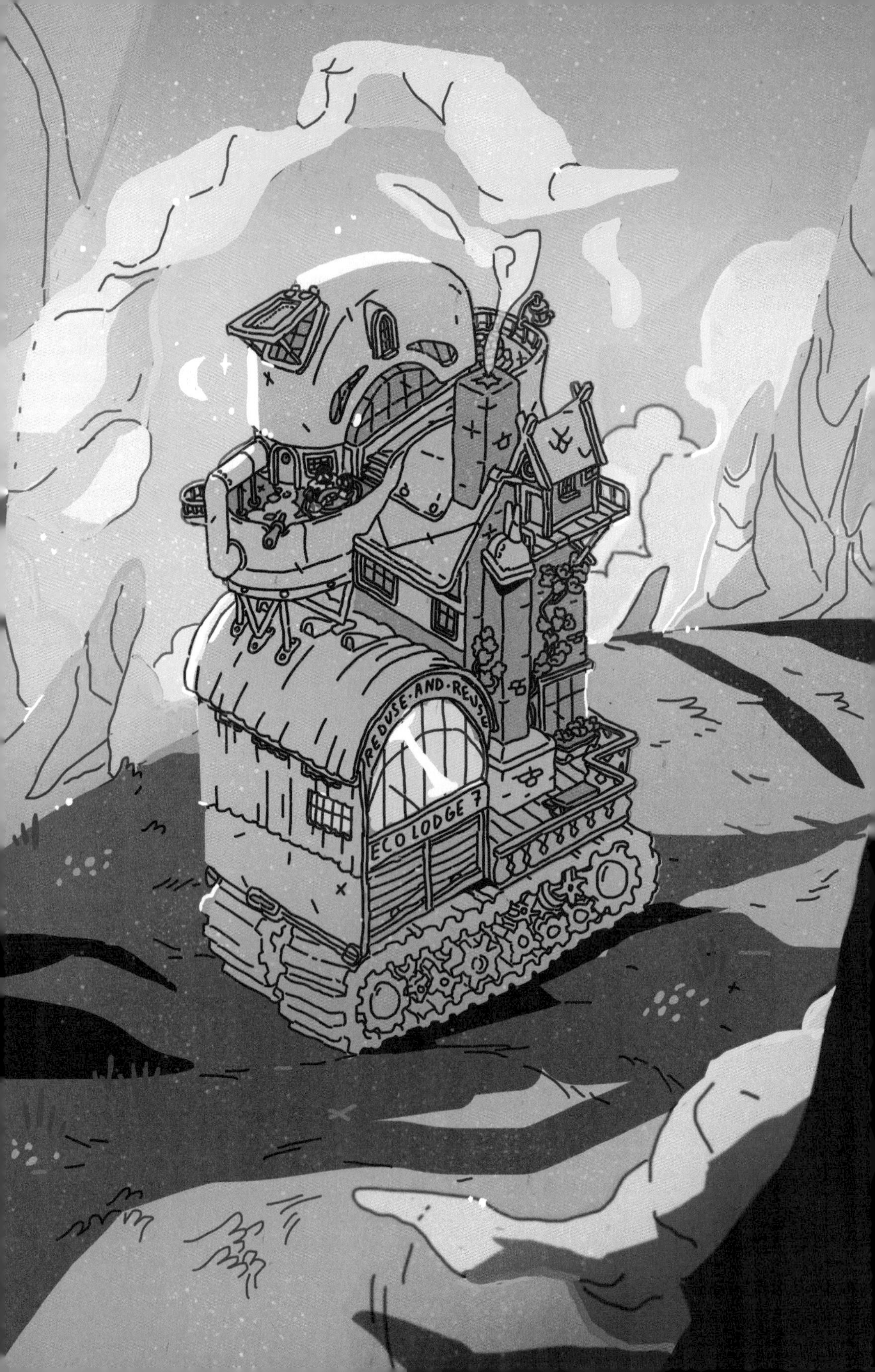
REDUSE·AND·REUSE
ECO LODGE 7

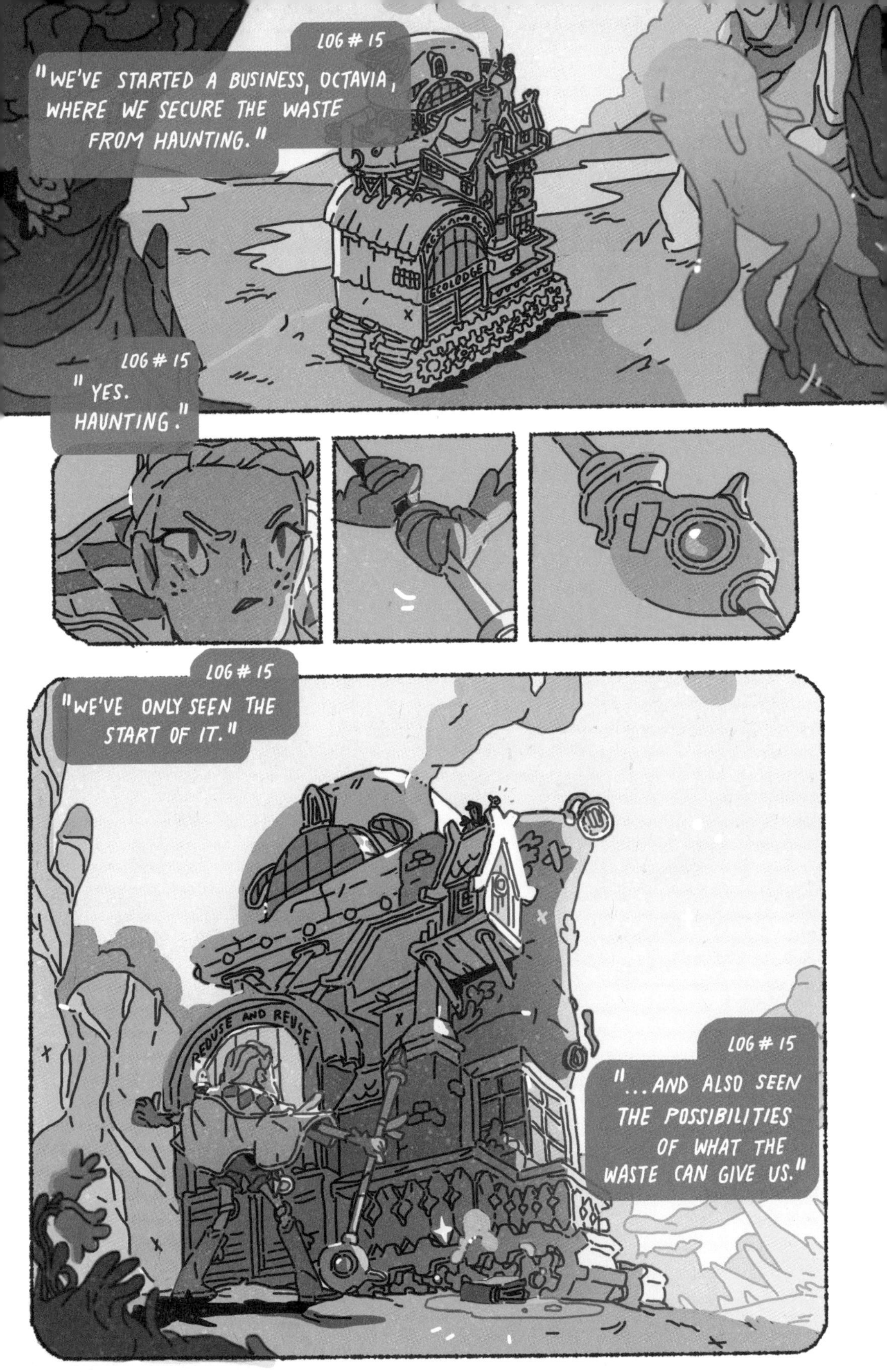
LOG # 15
"WE'VE STARTED A BUSINESS, OCTAVIA, WHERE WE SECURE THE WASTE FROM HAUNTING."
ECOLODGE
LOG # 15
"YES. HAUNTING."
LOG # 15
"WE'VE ONLY SEEN THE START OF IT."
REDUSE AND REUSE
LOG # 15
"...AND ALSO SEEN THE POSSIBILITIES OF WHAT THE WASTE CAN GIVE US."

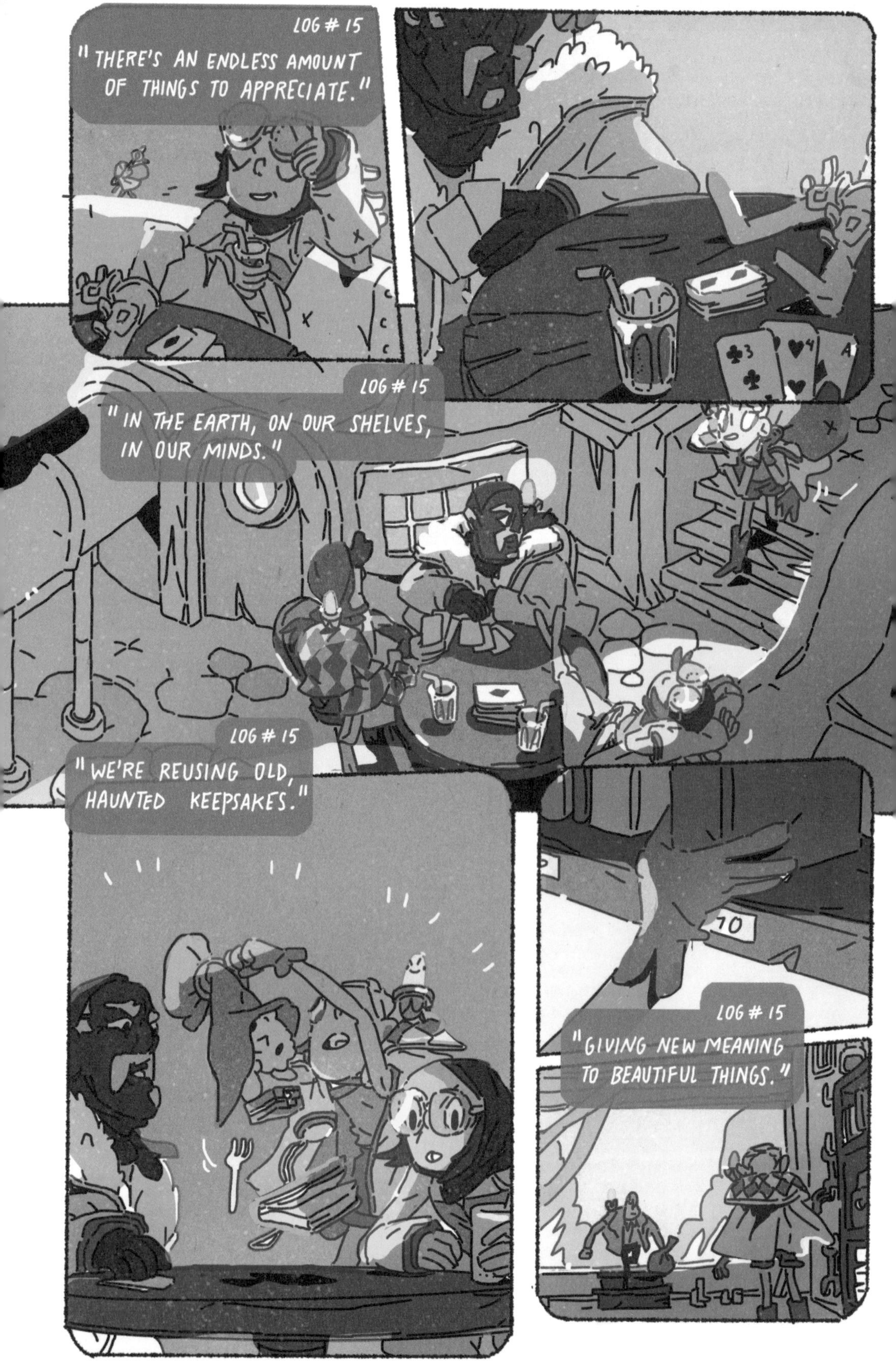
LOG # 15
"THERE'S AN ENDLESS AMOUNT OF THINGS TO APPRECIATE."
LOG # 15
"IN THE EARTH, ON OUR SHELVES, IN OUR MINDS."
LOG # 15
"WE'RE REUSING OLD, HAUNTED KEEPSAKES."
70
LOG # 15
"GIVING NEW MEANING TO BEAUTIFUL THINGS."

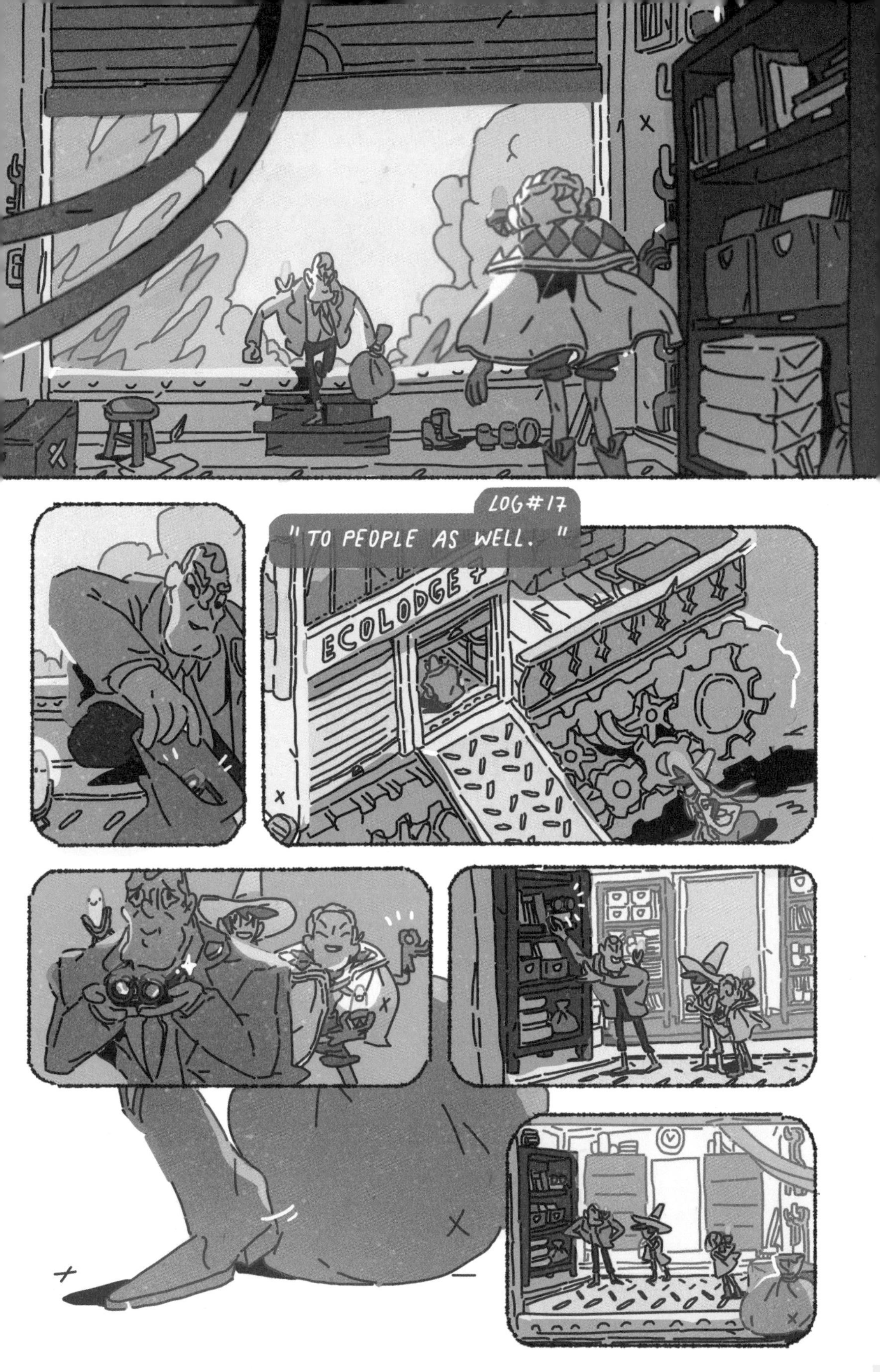
LOG #17
"TO PEOPLE AS WELL."
ECOLODGE

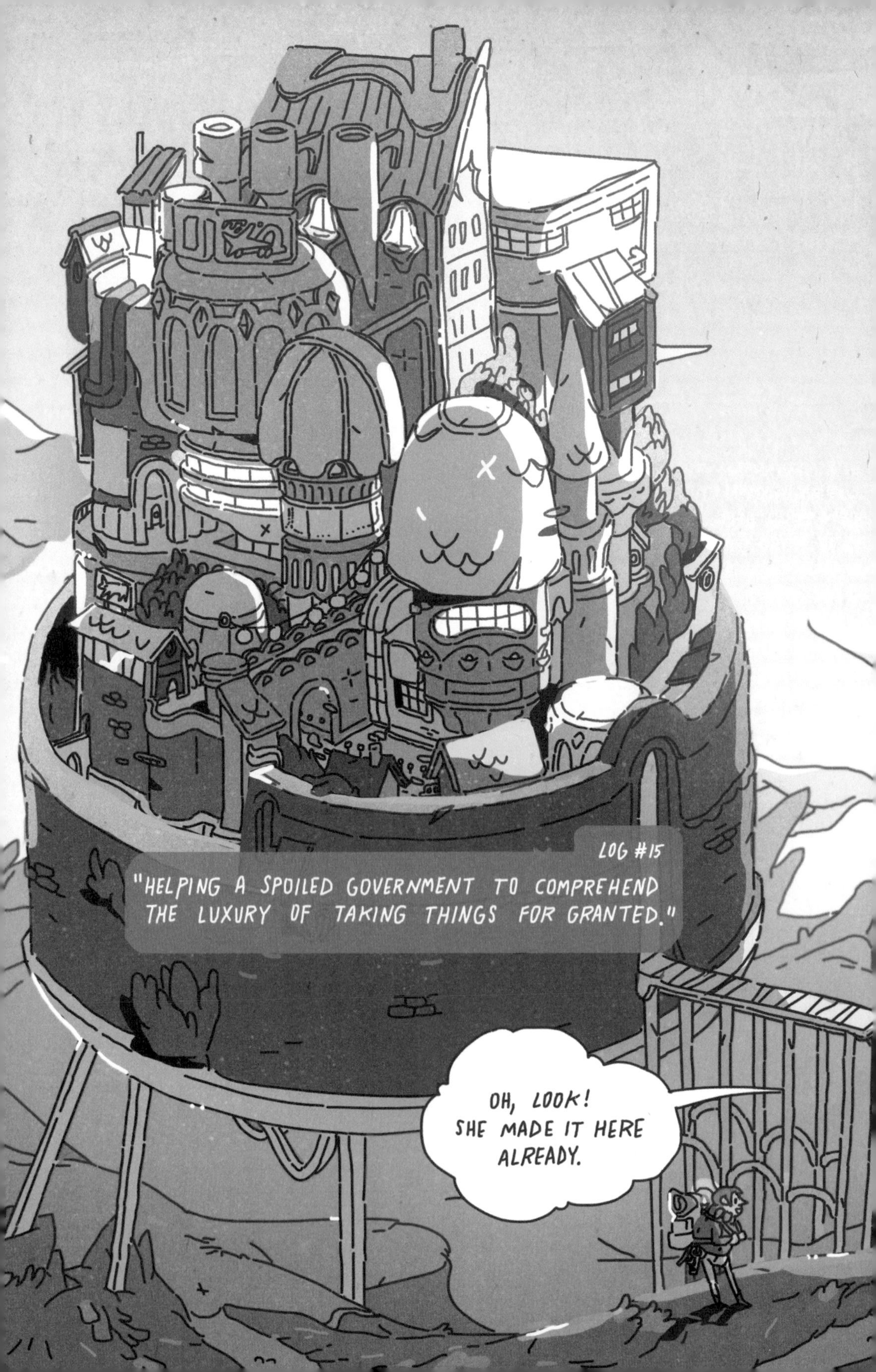
LOG #15
"HELPING A SPOILED GOVERNMENT TO COMPREHEND THE LUXURY OF TAKING THINGS FOR GRANTED."
OH, LOOK! SHE MADE IT HERE ALREADY.

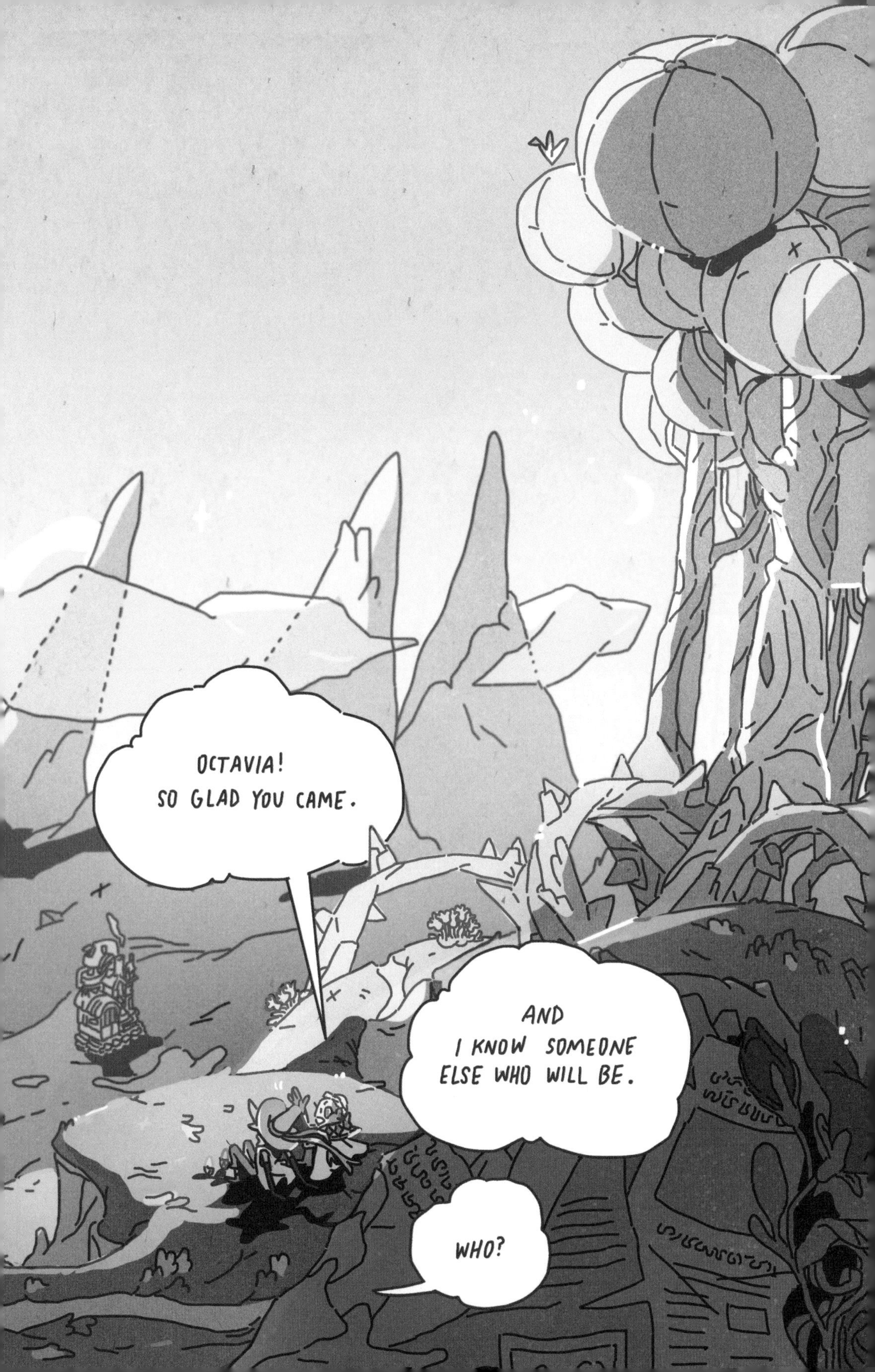
OCTAVIA! SO GLAD YOU CAME.
AND I KNOW SOMEONE ELSE WHO WILL BE.
WHO?

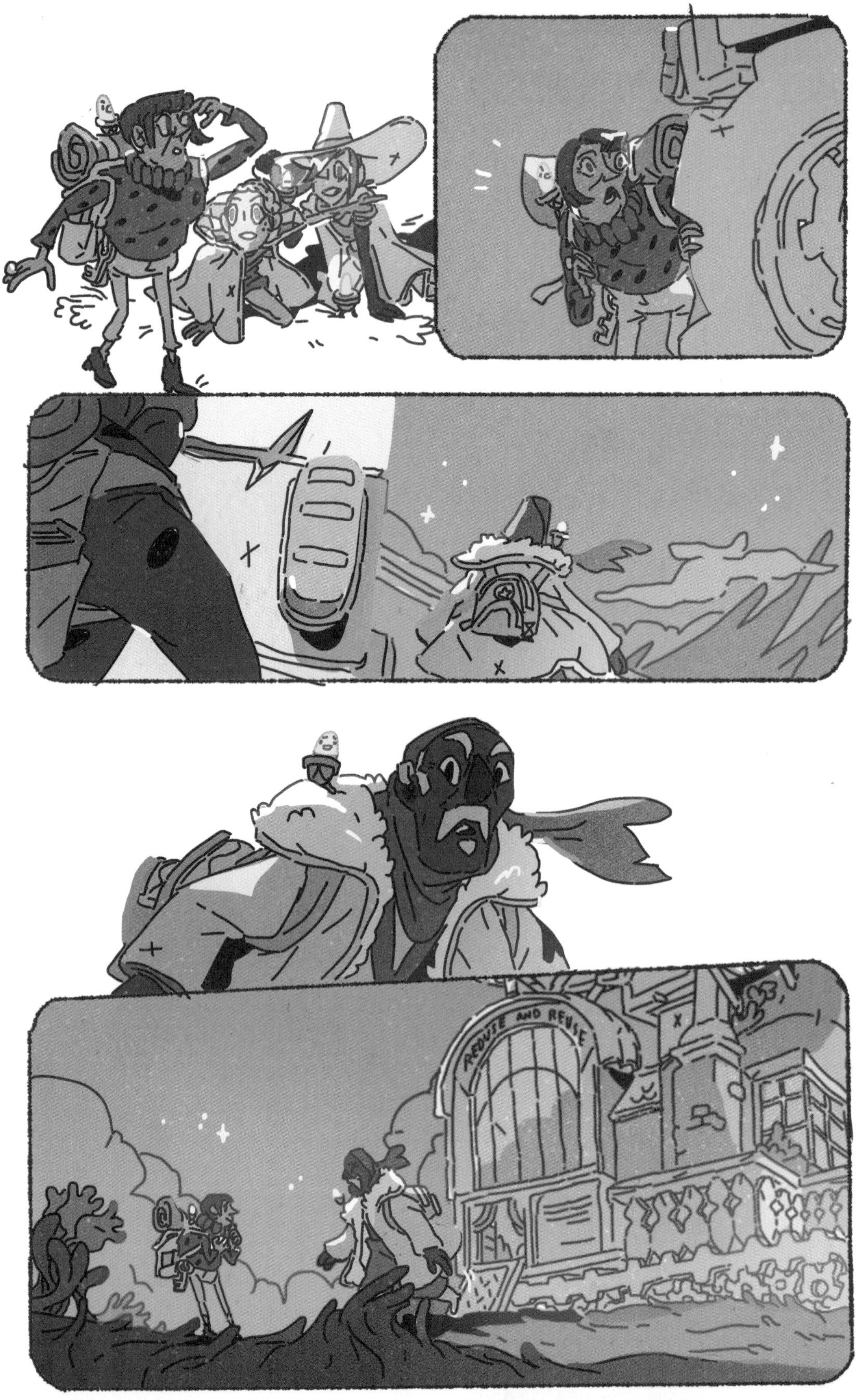
REDUSE AND REUSE

THE END

ACKNOWLEDGEMENTS:

A LOT SURE DID HAPPEN DURING THESE FOUR YEARS THAT I WORKED ON *JUNKWRAITH*.
THERE ARE A FEW PEOPLE WHO I WOULD LOVE TO ACKNOWLEDGE IN THE PASSAGE OF THAT TIME:

MY TWIN SISTER, EMMA, WHO PUT UP WITH ALL THE MESSY SKETCHES. SHE ALWAYS SAW THE THINGS I ALSO WANTED TO POLISH, BUT THAT I WAS TOO LAZY TO CORRECT UNTIL SHE LAID IT BEFORE ME IN NEAT PARAGRAPHS.

MELANIE SASSARINI, WHO TOOK ME TO COSPLAY CONVENTIONS - SHARING THE EXPERIENCE TABLING AT ARTIST ALLEYS WITH ME. HER INCREDIBLE ENERGY KEPT ME AFLOAT WHEN I REALLY NEEDED IT.

EMMA-LISA HENRIKSSON, WHO WAS ALWAYS EAGER TO HEAR NEW IDEAS, AND NATALIA BATISTA, MY MANGA TEACHER AT COMIC SCHOOL, WHO TOLD ME TO DOUBLE THE PAGE COUNT IN ORDER TO PACE MY STORY WITH ROOM TO BREATHE.

TOVE OTTOSSON, WHO WAS MY FELLOW ROBOT-LOVER, AND SAM FRISK, WHO WAS MY ANIME-NIGHT PAL.

EMMA HELLAND, WHO LET ME COMPLETE EPISODE TWO AT HER APARTMENT, SURROUNDED BY PERSIAN CATS.

NATALIA KOZAKOWSKA, WHO LET ME LIVE IN HER APARTMENT AS WELL, AFTER I ALMOST GAVE UP ON THIS STORY BUT ENDED UP PUTTING TOGETHER A PITCH INSTEAD. NATALIA, I'D ALSO LIKE TO ACKNOWLEDGE ALL THOSE TIMES IN THE ICE RINK AS KIDS, BEING JEALOUS AND IN AWE, WATCHING YOU AND YOUR TWIN SISTER, ANNA, PERFORM TEAM FIGURE SKATING - THANK YOU FOR ALL OF THAT. YOU WERE SO DAZZLING AND FIERCE OUT THERE ON THE COLD ICE. (THE MUSIC WAS ALWAYS WAY TOO LOUD. I LOVED THAT I COULD STILL HEAR THE CLACK AND SWOOSH OF YOUR SKATES.)

THANK YOU, ALL THE READERS ON TAPASTIC AND WEBTOON, FOR FOLLOWING *JUNKWRAITH* AS LONG AS IT LASTED AS A WEBCOMIC.

THANK YOU, MY SWEETEST DANIEL, FOR THE TIMES SITTING IN YOUR PONCHO AND DRINKING TEA, LETTING ME DRAW AWAY ON THE FINAL PAGES AS YOU TINKERED WITH OTHER THINGS. IT WAS VERY COZY.

FINALLY, THANK YOU, CHRIS STAROS, FOR BELIEVING IN THIS STORY AND GIVING IT A GO. HAVING YOU AS AN EDITOR HAS BEEN THE BEST. IT IS AN HONOR TO PUBLISH THIS COMIC WITH YOU GUYS AT TOP SHELF!